THE LAST SIESTA

THE LAST SIESTA

J:C:MACK

INGRESSO BOOKS

Copyright © J.C.McAvoy 2014
First Edition 2014

The Last Siesta/J:C:Mack
ISBN-13: 978-1481254946
10: 1481254944

Ingresso Books
J:C:Mack
email: info@ingressobooks.com

The front cover photograph: *Giano Bifronte* (Janus)
Courtesy: *Collezione Privata* GIGLIOLI-BESSI.
Background: Etruscan wall. La Penera, Volterra, Italy.

To my wife:
of whom every thought makes the heart smile.

**All of mankind walks in the shadow of death
But before every end there was once a beginning...**

One warm summer evening, towards the middle of the First Century, in a sumptuous country villa close to the Etruscan city of Sorena, Senator Paetus Cecina picked up the blood stained dagger, placed the sharp tip against his breast, and drove it into his heart. His wife, Arria, already lay dead as he knelt beside her to carry out the death sentence imposed on him by the emperor, Claudius.

In great secrecy their bodies were laid to rest deep inside a vault so cunningly contrived it was expected to remain hidden for the rest of time.

Such was the legend that sprang up round the obscure sepulchre, that kings, nobles and the common 'tombaroli', searched eagerly for the rumoured treasure that lay enclosed. With each failed attempt the legend grew, until the vain and fruitless undertaking exhausted men's ambitions, and their imagination.

Rest in peace.

Chapter 1

The whole building was empty. Not derelict, having only just been built.

Five stories of rectangular slabs as cold and as grey as the sky. Below, the pavements had already cracked, and filled with weeds, the kerbstones fitfully leaning out on even leaner foundations. Prospective flowerbeds lay empty, except for abandoned building rubbish. Desolate. Silently depressing.

In front lay about half a kilometre of empty space, ready for a hundred more rectangular blocks of concrete and glass.

Empty, until interrupted by the railway station.

Major Kopolev changed his point of view to the figure lying in front of the floor level window from which he had carefully removed a pane of glass.

The legs were spread slightly to the left of the body, raised from the shoulders on elbows. The seaman's black woollen cap, tight on their head, had not moved for some time. All the attention beneath it concentrated on the facade of the railway station.

The Major looked at his wristwatch. Only a few more minutes.

The figure on the floor shifted its body slightly, searching for a more relaxed position. Carefully they brought the fibreglass stock of the snipers rifle into their shoulder, made a slight adjustment to the sights and gently loaded a cartridge into the chamber. Silently they slipped off the safety catch, and brought the flash suppressed muzzle into position.

Kopolev glanced over the top of the barrel.

Five hundred metres. The light almost gone, hindered by the first flurry of snow. The rising wind had become agitated, sudden gusts driving white flakes into swirling opaque masses. In this weather, five hundred metres would be very hit and miss. He looked through his binoculars and pursed his lips.

Five hundred metres.

He glanced at his wristwatch again. Mussolini had not been the only dictator obsessed with time. At its first stop the train would be punctual, shuddering to a halt, doors opening.

People came hurrying out of the entrance, blurred figures stooping against the icy wind, tightening scarves, and pulling up coat collars to avoid the freezing air.

Kopolev caught sight of a figure freeing himself from the mass of bodies, and focused the binoculars on him.

Victor Herzen, an engineer at the Yaransk air base. Not hurrying, stopping, clutching a brief case between his legs while he pulled the ear flaps of his cap tighter. He looked as though he was expecting someone to meet him.

An old Gaz Pobeda with split windscreen, and clap-hand wipers passed, stopped, and reversed.

Kopolev smiled humourlessly to himself. A chance encounter. A traitor - about to leave his brief case, forgotten, on the back seat of the car.

Such old tricks always turned out to be fatal.

The driver hurried back, stretching out a hand, embracing excessively, making a show. They turned together, side by side.

In seconds it would be too late.

In seconds they would be out of the line of sight, behind the car.

Kopolev struggling to focus on them through the agitated white flakes, only saw their faces disintegrate, smashed and shredded out of shape by the heavy calibre bullets that passed through their skulls, stopped only by the walls of the railway station.

His breath returned in a noisy exhalation. Five hundred metres. Impossible, you'd imagine. Quite impossible.

He lowered his binoculars from where the falling snow was quickly blushing red round their crumpled bodies.

MOSCOW.

The Russian Attaché closed the door quietly. The room was in darkness except for the pyramid of light that was emanating from a lamp suspended a few feet above a table. A man slid into view, grinding out his cigarette in the metal ashtray. "Well, what did he say?" he asked apprehensively.

2

"Purging the state of its sins is only simple as a concept. Chairman Markov has become irritated by pessimism."

The British FO Secretary lit another cigarette. The tip glowed fiercely as he inhaled deeply. "Am I to believe you've hung up all those bad habits? New directions, with no body bags. Something of an inconvenience you'll tell me."

"It's no longer government policy. But not everyone's in government. Being distracted by dissidents remains an annoyance. In such cases, old habits die hard. But really it's a question of knowing where to pay the monthly cheques. Your cheques as well - old fellow."

The Secretary shrugged, unruffled, leaning back into the darkness behind the table. "Now you're telling me all this international rapprochement's come at a price." He tossed a folder to the side of the table. "I've been through everything. Searching for a raison d'être Whitehall's convinced is here. There's not even a legitimate connexion between Sandquest and Petrov after forty-five, let alone a justifiable reason for its existence."

The Attaché shook his head. "Nothing we can see eye to eye on. Hardly the necessary consensus."

"Exactly. Nothing that's corroborated by Sandquest. When Petrov kissed him goodbye in Berlin, to all intents and purposes, he ceased to be of interest to anyone. Yet, after a ten-year dose of anonymity, he crops up again in your intelligence material along with a highly restricted classification. FCO's decidedly uneasy about 'goings on' behind their back. Sandquest and Petrov, doing the bloody two-step without a company choreographer."

"Does it matter?" the Attaché asked in a tired voice.

"Hell, of course it matters! Sandquest doesn't get invited to Balmoral, but he's no stranger in Whitehall. I need reasons. Reasons, and still more reasons, if he's to be shuffled off this mortal coil. We've got to come up with something."

Sitting down opposite him, the Attaché tapped a cigarette from the crumpled packet on the table. They sat silently watching each other, rolled up sleeves, arms resting on the table, searching for a point of view. How to finally arrive at looking in the same direction. Two men from different worlds with a mutual problem; deciding on the best way to deal with international angst that could lead to a spat, or to a war.

"This is very unfortunate," the Attaché finally concluded. "The collegium Chairman is leaning on the State Minister. He wants the matter dealt with. As soon as possible."

The Secretary pushed the lighter across. "So I've been told. If you're so sure, why didn't you arrange for one of your wet affairs? Or are such methods off side nowadays?

A smoke plume rose until it became trapped in the conical lampshade above their heads, its dim beam gently oscillating, disturbed by the Moscow Metro somewhere beneath the building.

"Fear," the Attaché intoned. "Written all over the fat slug's face. Afraid of any move that doesn't nail this cannon first. Scared stiff he'll end up resembling a nicely done *Kotletki*. So, what's there to go on? Petrov filed everything meticulously, except the assassin's real name. He was a stickler for detail in everything else. Even Sandquest's extraordinary technology is precisely documented. Death, made to measure."

"But, meanwhile," the Secretary reminded him with a touch of sarcasm, "this assassin, Nightingale, remains merely a figment of your imagination."

"No, not just imagination. Their existence is surely demonstrated by the evidence?"

"And orchestrated by Petrov." The Secretary stabbed his finger at the Attaché. "How can he hide a killer employed by the state to do their dirty work, without so much as a clue to their identity? You've actually met this Major General, I suppose?"

"On occasions. Once in Poland."

"Some time ago then?"

"Lot's of time ago. Also in Azerbaijan. April ninety one. Just before independence. Sunni militants were becoming popular. I thought Petrov'd been put on the log pile, but he turned up in Kirovabad. Communists fiddled the polls, and won. Helped by a prominent Lezgian activist dropping dead in a mosque. Petrov's a ruthless man. Organizing death's second nature to him."

"We shall have to give it some very seriɔ
then. Whatever we decide must have no
unravelling. Nothing that might sticł
Government's waistcoat. The timing has to be

The attaché pulled a wry smile. "Chairmɑ
indicated, rather forcibly, the negative aspects ui time."

"We shall also have to be imaginative, even if it's a
shaky foundation for building a consensus. As the whole
team has to be eliminated, including the handler, it's
probably better to keep such things close to our chest."

"You're not trusting anyone?"

The Secretary shook his head. "Nor will this Petrov, I
gather. Not unless there's an element of certitude. That's
exactly what we need. Conviction politics, you know, is
all the vogue just now in dear old Blighty."

The Attaché leant forward, studying the Secretary's
expression to see if he was being serious. It didn't give
anything away. "With respect, one of the aspects of this
affair is that Petrov's clever, canny, and entirely capable
of killing you."

The Secretary shrugged. "Then from what you say,
Chairman Markov should be the author of these
deliberations, not us."

The Attaché sidestepped the acrimony. "There's
nothing further back than Poland."

"Nothing much forward either," the Secretary noted.
"1945. That's where Sandquest and Petrov were in the
same frame. Afterwards, not at all."

"Was Sandquest married?" the Attaché continued,
pouring himself a large Vodka from an almost empty
bottle.

"Twice. One dead. One contemporary."

"Dead before the war, or after?"

"During. Killed in the blitz."

The Attaché, eyes shut, inhaled the ozone in his glass.
"That might fit." He drank deeply, opened his eyes, and
shunted a file across the table. "On loan. Has to go back.
Report by Vice Consul Kruzhkov. Not one of Petrov's
associates, but throws light into some dark corners. And
perhaps - only perhaps - somewhere we can build a
consensus."

"I'm tired of reading bloody reports. Just give me the

om line."

The Attaché took another mouthful of vodka from his glass. "Petrov turned out to be one of our earlier experiments in private enterprise. Came with official permission. He set up a successful business in Ireland as a conduit for KGB activities, most likely to provide access to Sandquest. In the wider regions of the politburo, where policymakers always viewed any sort of success with suspicion, it would be no surprise that Kruzhkov, then at our consular office in Dublin, was asked to prepare a report on him. As a peripheral exercise, Petrov's financial position was also subject to a thorough check." The Attaché gave a big smile. "Actually just to ensure there were no private bank accounts in offshore havens. What they found, instead of illicit millions, was Anna Jehmlich, a Polish farmer's daughter being financially supported by Petrov."

"Petrov hardly seems the supportive type."

"True. He comes across as a man with absolutely no friends. Yet, year after year he provided for this woman we know very little about. Perhaps we're wrong. Even misanthropic generals should be allowed moments of romantic madness. In my opinion though, Petrov had a reason, but benevolence isn't likely to figure anywhere."

"More to the point, does Sandquest figure somewhere?"

"I've no idea. Exactly. But you don't have to be a Descartes to work out when Petrov came across Anna. At that time, Konev's forces were closing in on Berlin. They passed right by Trzcinsko Zdroj where farmer Jehmlich scratched a living, aided by his daughter, Anna. Lieutenant Petrov was on Konev's staff."

The Secretary leant forward. "And so, temporarily, was a Sergeant Sandquest."

"Point. But no point. Petrov had no reason to support Sandquest that we can determine. But something drew them together. So, let's suppose that Petrov's interest in Anna, was actually Sandquest's interest in Anna. As a married man, involved in an illicit affair, Petrov would certainly have seen the possibility of recruiting him. But with the wife deceased..."

"They make an unlikely pair of Lothario's," the

Secretary said dismissively. "More to the point, why did Petrov continue to take this new found responsibility so seriously?"

"The simple answer would be: Anna was behind the Iron Curtain, Sandquest not. But, if you open the folder, towards the back you'll find the psychiatrist's report on Petrov."

The Secretary thumbed through, found the report and skimmed the pages. He looked up. "Why didn't we have this earlier?"

"Not technically a Directorate file."

"What was he doing in a military hospital?"

"Recovering from a nasty aeroplane accident. Ran out of runway on take off, and crashed into a wood. The navigator, and Petrov, were the only survivors."

"Sounds like he'd need a seamstress, not a shrink."

"Oh, he needed a shrink! Hallucinations, impulsive aggression. Something definitely adrift in his neuro circuitry. Not that they were too worried by his behaviour. Any violent traumatic experience has lingering effects. Post traumatic stress disorders they call them. Anyway, a General doesn't come in their direction too often, so they paid particular attention to his ramblings. Report has the Third Directorate stamp on it, and Chairman Shelepin."

"Is that unusual?"

"Your caring FSK? Somewhat unusual. What concerned them was Petrov's relationship with Anna. The researchers interest centred on Petrov's sub-conscious attitude to a person he conscientiously protected. Apparently, in the depths of his being he confronted a problem. Someone had become his bête noire. Unable to resolve it led to him becoming tormented by frustration. In his unconscious state lay failure; a personal humiliation and crushed self-esteem. Not that anyone would have been aware. These were unanalysed motives, suppressed beyond perception. An overwhelming hatred held relentlessly in check."

"I've read his history. He doesn't seem the sort of man to let wounds fester, being an all action hero of the state. He'd have eliminated this 'bête noire', as you call it."

"Not necessarily. As the report explains, it's all a

7

matter of choice. Choice is the conflict. It's not a problem between that which you desire, and that which you don't. You can make a concrete rational decision by choosing the one you desire. However, what happens when you desire both? Psychological frustration. In the end choice is determined by the strongest driving force."

"It would be useful if we could identify these choices."

"Useful, most definitely. But according to the psychoanalysts, the weaker doesn't disappear. It remains a confused, if suppressed, motive."

"What were these - conflicting desires?"

"This you won't like. About to establish the cause of the General's neuroses by getting back to the origins of the trouble, Petrov pulled the plug on them by regaining his wits. Needless to say, he was no longer a compliant patient."

"Oh, shit," the Secretary said softly.

"Quite. But it's the beginning of our enlightenment. I think we know the subject of this conflict. Anna. We also have an idea of the motive, thwarted love. But what was his choice? Between what desires? What rational decision made him suppress his hatred, and suffer this intolerable burden? From our files we know what Sandquest's role was, which doesn't appear to be trading state secrets. He doesn't indicate any desire to aid the Soviets. Perhaps the exclusive relationship between these two men enabled them to create the perfect assassin. Perhaps if we keep our heads together we'll discover the key to cause and effect, which will undoubtably please the Chairman, who has a penchant for separating people from their heads."

"Back to what I said. We'll have to give it some careful consideration."

"And the necessary consensus?"

The Secretary nodded. "All we have to do is find a way to make Petrov unlock the door for us. Now we have the background, I think we should be able to figure out a scenario to suit the purpose."

"The whole proposal will have to be assessed by the Operations and Technology Directorate. Some of their scientists fancy themselves as mind mechanics, so the idea will have certain attractions for them. If it's doable, they'll do it. More to the point, Chairman Markov can have his mandate enabling him to legally pursue the last murky aspect of what is becoming a rapidly outdated security policy."

"Whatever it is, it will have to be absolutely water tight before I can put it forward," the Secretary added.

The Attaché closed the folder. "And with the proviso, of course, that your department approves of the not so small matter of murder."

LONDON

Sitting in a traffic jam under the M4 motorway on the Great West Road, Rex Eldon opened the window a fraction while he listened to the news. The diversion, he felt ashamed to admit, had become a regular habit.

They were making much of another Russian émigré with a clandestine background who had ended up in a suburban park with no physical marks of death - except where someone had shot their spinal chord away. The xenophobic FSK seemed to have as great a fear of its own natives as it did of others.

The broadcaster turned his interview to a director from the British Museum, probing the rise in art frauds, and the momentum given to the looting of treasures by irresponsible curators whose ethical standards, the director believed, had fallen to the level of avaricious antiquaries.

Eldon turned the volume up slightly as the interview now focused on the wholesale plundering of unidentified Etruscan tombs. He possessed a fourth-century vase from Tarquinia, which in all aspects might have been modern. The face within its geometric border reminded him of the poet and critic, Edith Sitwell.

'Too ugly to look at, but, too fascinating to behold,' was how his disapproving father had chosen to describe this acquisition. Eldon's present concern was that the vase might turn out to be 'too hot to hold'.

The taxi driver travelling alongside flicked his cigarette butt out of the cab window on to the bonnet of Eldon's car, where it rolled down leaving a little plume of smoke. He pressed his horn indignantly, but the faster lane had

9

already whisked the taxi away.

However, for Eldon, today was not like yesterday or even the day before yesterday, habitually sitting in a traffic jam on his way to work in the city firm of Weatherfield and Holding.

Temporary was the word that came to mind. It had echoed unpleasantly in his memory, as he'd shut the door of the Chairman's office, giving a rueful smile to the Chairman's thin-lipped secretary on his way out. Eldon's meeting with the company's chairman had resulted in a lecture on the parallel interests of the public and private sectors. He maintained they had an interest in supporting one another, keeping the cogs of commerce turning in an old tradition that stretched back to another century. Then, the Empire had been run by a few dozen men, and huge nations could be held under the thumb of still fewer regiments. Eldon was, the Chairman reminded him, an ex-army man whose commission might yet be extended a little, in the interests of the state. The Government; therefore, didn't want to be seen wasting his experience on financial securities or foreign currency options. If he was needed, then his loan was seen as a good investment. The Chairman considered that Eldon's métier came with compound interest.

There were shadows in the background, of course: faces that had no face, images that were perhaps imaginary, moving pawns made of flesh and blood while knights shuffled back and forth keeping king and queen out of harms way.

Even as the Chairman spoke, Eldon had caught a glimpse that gave form to one such type of face: narcissistic, transcendent, and masked by sophistry.

The permanent under secretary, Sir Edward Kerry, had requested that Eldon place himself at the disposal of the Organised Crime Group. Not directly - coming instead through the mediation of the well disposed influence of the Chairman. Eldon was too shrewd to fall out of favour with the prominent and prestigious company of Weatherfield and Holding, who weren't the only ones to recognize a good investment.

Following this interview he packed his bags at

Southwark Bridge, and headed west of the river Thames to settle down under the temporary aegis of Commander Prinn, Head of the Organised Crime Group.

This time, a ferocious secretary did not guard the outer office, only Maurice Tate, a young policeman who was there on trial. Someone in one of the endless working parties set up to review efficiency proposals had decided that trainee investigators, not yet become detective constables, should have a period of induction that included 'shadowing' their head of department. It was not something benevolently received by those in command, but Tate was a likeable and resourceful young man, with the consequence that Prinn had got over his disapproval sufficiently to now address him by his Christian name.

To everyone's chagrin, Veronica, the secretary with pink nails and 38D-cup bra, had been banished to an adjacent room, while Prinn's staff were directed through Tate's office so that he might acquire a comprehensive insight into the department's workings and machinery. Such musical chairs were a constant source of amusement to the officers involved, who viewed attempts at the administrative running of their departments as mere wish-fulfilment rather than an exercise in management.

The sudden appearance of Eldon was to provide a perfect role model for the impressionable Tate, for the newcomer could be said to posses all the attributes necessary for such veneration. He dressed well, but conservatively, demonstrating that a good tailor was still essential for a particular way of life. His face displayed the sober intensity of someone whose humour had been chastened by the gravity of his past experience: a lean bitterness possessed by men who had no confidence in the world becoming a better place.

Tate held down the switch on his intercom to announce Eldon's arrival, and then stood up. "Try and avoid mentioning money, sir," he advised under his breath, as he opened the door. "The Italian lira's in free fall at the moment."

"Maurice, you remind me of that Doctor in Macbeth," Prinn reproached him from within. "Foul whisperings are abroad."

Tate left swiftly, mumbling an embarrassed apology.

Prinn ran both hands through his hair and sighed. There was a tired handsomeness about him, as though he had reached some critical point in his life where he couldn't quite make up his mind if he needed to bother impressing anyone any more. Did he really need to pay quite so much attention to the cut of his suit, or the length of his hair, which had begun curling over his ears in a way that invited some sartorial concern?

Rising, he shook Eldon's hand, before motioning to a chair positioned in front of his polished rosewood desk.

"Has anyone explained to you why you're here, Eldon?" He pronounced every syllable in a leisurely, deliberate way. He was not intending to be the sort of man you couldn't understand.

Eldon shook his head. "I'm afraid not."

"No, I suppose they wouldn't. It's something of an embarrassment, asking for a favour." Prinn was obviously conversant with the indifferent attitude found among higher civil servants.

"I considered it more of an order than a favour. One of those inconvenient half truths you feel obliged to respond to in an effort to keep your seat warm, if you see what I mean, Commander. However, I was assured this secondment would be of limited duration. I trust you're not now going to disillusion me?" Eldon enquired stiffly.

"An unknown factor, I'm afraid." Prinn interlaced his fingers, sitting back in the chair with a discontented sigh. "I find it disagreeable, having to ask for you. I'm also fully aware of your past controversy with Sir Edward Kerry, and I can't comment on that. I wasn't briefed, so there's no reason for me to consider it. I can only assure you that it has no bearing on this present situation. The list of possible candidates was not long, and you stood out rather like a sore thumb."

"Perhaps you can explain, then, why I'm here?" Eldon was increasingly suspicious. He had learnt to be suspicious; never trusting a man like Sir Edward Kerry, who considered expedience more important than virtue. Commander Prinn was going to have to work very hard to avoid deserving such a comparison.

12

Prinn unlinked his fingers, leaning forward to open a bulky file resting on his desk. "We're at a crossroads, Eldon. Demands are now being placed on the civilian forces that are properly the occupation of the military. Unlike Italy and France, we don't have a tradition of military units policing the nation, and I suspect a government would be short lived that ever entertained any such idea. Nevertheless, society now faces threats of a kind once found only in Northern Ireland. Arguably, some things must change to address them. However, while this touches on one problem, it is not directly responsible for the request that an experienced operative should be attached to my department.

This shift in security operations, as you're probably aware, has been influenced by the collapse of the Soviet political system. The picture is still a little murky, but some features are coming into focus. The fragmentation there has not only encouraged organized crime to actually threaten their state, but appears to have allowed the creation of quasi-autonomous departments that are only loosely tied to an effective ministry. One of these was originally responsible for an undisclosed organization running the most successful assassin it's ever been our misfortune to meet. After such a seismic change in Russia's political and social set-up, we assumed that such an organization would wither away, but apparently, this hasn't been the case. The ensuing disorder has allowed a quite different picture to emerge, affecting the civil authorities and leading to our present situation."

He pulled out a coded document. "Special Branch has sent this over to us. The security services are keeping them informed, never knowing where or when the subject in question might pop up. There's a distinct possibility you'll have to go back into the field. Had enough of that sort of thing in the Pyrenees I suspect, but it's in the nature of the task."

Eldon took the document offered to him, reading through the transcript quickly. It referred to information received from a ciphers clerk who was working as an agent for the Americans in the Eighth Chief Directorate of the FSK, responsible for signals intelligence and communications. The message was short, and by inference, not very informative, indicating that an agent, code-named Nightingale, was about to become active. Whereabouts and details unknown.

"Not exactly a lot to go on?" Eldon remarked as he looked up.

"Absolutely nothing to go on. For the moment, this is just another piece of paper to add to the file. All they ever seem to know is when this agent is due to become active. And the result of their activities, naturally. Always deceased," Prinn added as an afterthought. "They don't even know if it was a Soviet wet squad, or someone working alone. They tell me that only Department 8, in Directorate S, was suspected of carrying out such operations. They're not even sure of that since the KGB was reorganized into the FSK, enabling them to start cleaning up their act."

"Right, familiarization advisable." Eldon held out his hand for the file.

Prinn shook his head. "It's been networked," handing Eldon his security card. "Whoever's running this agent has made life extremely difficult for anyone trying to construct a profile of them." He tapped the top page of the file. "The conclusion is, that once they activate the agent, they short circuit the system in some way. There's no photograph, and no name. As it's landed so heavily on our plate, I'd like you to try and make some sense of their modus operandi, but don't waste too much time on what they've sent us. My opinion is, that carrying so much weight slows us down. Come along," he said, "I'd like you to meet Chief Inspector Gower. He's made room for you in his office."

"I'm not a policeman, sir," Eldon reminded him.

"That's exactly the point. The fact that the problem's now police business, as well as the security services indicates that we'll be immediately right out of our depth. That's something we'll have to address, but for the moment we need someone with your expertise to plug the gap. The Government has agreed a review, but as you'll be aware, God only knows when that will be accomplished."

"I see. How far back does this file go?"

A grimace puckered Prinn's cheek, half wince and half smile. "Oh, I think about twenty years. Thereabouts."

-oOo-

The office Eldon was meant to share with Chief Inspector Sandy Gower was empty. He arrived just as they prepared to leave the room, working up a head of steam about something.

Gower had red hair, with an overlong red moustache, and a penchant for barley-sugar sweets; the paper wrappers conspicuously evident round the office waste-paper basket.

"I'm not late, sir," he defended himself waspishly. "Some of us have to work weekends, so get time off in lieu." His voice had a soft Scottish lilt that had been rudely tampered with by a northern grammar school. "Having to chase a Cambodian diplomat all over the ruddy West End turned out to be completely futile. Obviously the laddie was just out to have a damn good time. If he was meeting anybody at all, it wore lipstick and a seven-o'clock shadow." He meanwhile eyed Eldon with cautious professional interest.

"This is Rex Eldon, Sandy. As we discussed, he'll be lodged with you for a while. If you can provide any help, please do so." Prinn turned back to Eldon. "You'll find the Chief Inspector more amenable after a cup of coffee. Familiarization as you said".

Prinn nodded to them both indicating his departure, while Gower and Eldon shook hands formally.

"I've had a desk and computer set up for you over here," Gower explained. "Your telephone calls are gratis. Clerical stuff, stationary, etc., are in the metal cupboard. Just ask me, if you're uncertain about anything. Commander Prinn will have set you up and running, so I suggest you take a look at wherever you're supposed to be going. Have to say, you're not strictly any business of mine, but don't let that bother you. Just use me as a sounding board, whenever you like."

"Fine. I'll be happier with someone keeping an eye on me."

Gower chose not to hear. "Write up my report, then

I'm off to bed. Coffee?"

He filled two plastic cups from a little machine standing in the corner of the office before slumping into the office chair next to Eldon's computer, holding his own cup between both hands.

It turned out there was nothing wrong with Gower. His father had been a Scottish Labour MP; lost his seat at the last election and now cultivated raspberries on a farm outside Perth. Assisted there by his Finnish wife, he expected his son to eventually join them.

There was always the possibility. Like Eldon, Gower had not seen himself on any particular career path, or as a company man with a pension in mind. Such might be his current lot, but he had contrived to live each day one at a time and, because of that, somewhat more completely than those who manoeuvred their lives in a constant effort to advance themselves.

His choice of career had come as a surprise, not least to himself, when after 'A levels' he decided to enter the Metropolitan Police. Perhaps the lure of a uniform influenced him, though the possibility of squaring up to the vicious underbelly of society provided a more positive reason. After his probationary period, he found himself selected for accelerated promotion and the recipient of a university education resulting in an M.A.

Promoted to inspector led to his posting with a divisional CID, then to the Organised Crime Group as a chief inspector. Finishing his coffee, Gower returned to his own computer, and was soon hard at work in summing up the peccadilloes of his Cambodian diplomat.

Eldon, meanwhile, attempted to achieve the right sense of purpose. If he didn't feel at ease with an unfamiliar computer, he felt even less affinity with the circumstances that had brought him here. The former task he quickly mastered, which at least allowed him a beginning. The rest, he hoped, would catch him up before the consequences of these events themselves materialized. Opening the relevant file, Eldon found his name on the access list, and entered his security number.

Prinn had been right: it described the background of

the victim, possible causes and actual effects. You might look at them - or right through them. Detailed methods and manners, but with not a trace of the perpetrators. No wonder the security services felt this assassin had come to resemble an enigma. What they were considering appeared inextricable: a theoretical concept producing practical results. Dead bodies in all sorts and sizes, all over the place, from Prague to Philadelphia.

Eldon was not a romantic. For him, Nightingale was merely a puzzle on which he would have to test his ingenuity. And probably a lot else besides.

The heavy silence punctuated only by keyboard clatter suddenly paused. "Everything all right?" Gower asked, remembering the new member of staff sharing his office.

"Not sure," Eldon replied. "I feel like a circus trainer with his head in a lion's mouth that could close at any moment."

Gower hit a key to complete his sentence, swivelling round on his office chair to face Eldon.

"What's the problem, or is it classified?"

"An old chestnut I've been given for bedside reading. Case title: 'Nightingale'. Security service work up to now. Have you looked at this case?"

"No. Before my time, I expect. 'E' Squad might give you a line. It's been updated, I suppose?" He swivelled back to his computer, and with a flurry of fingers typed in something that had just occurred to him. He was only mildly interested in Eldon's problem. "Sang in Berkeley Square, didn't they? Well, long before the conglomerates wrecked the neighbourhood, anyway."

Eldon shrugged, returning to the case histories in search of a pattern, which he had quickly come to realize he was unlikely to find.

A shadow fell across his desk as Gower perched himself precariously on the end, looking pointedly at his watch.

"Are you going to be long? Lunch is not a movable feast."

"Time flies when you're enjoying yourself. Weren't you heading off to bed?" Eldon recalled.

"That's a question, not an answer."

"All right, we'll go to lunch. I imagine I shall take a

week reading this anyway. At least, with you away, this afternoon will be quiet."

"Don't count on it. I'm now into my second wind. I'll be past my best around eight-o'clock, when I shall crash out on bonny wee Miss Veronica. Best pair of pillows in the whole of Victoria."

Gower was given to whimsical speculation on the part of Miss Veronica, Prinn's displaced secretary, who neither knew, nor possibly cared, for his passionate designs on her ample and undoubtedly comfortable cleavage. In this he seemed content to be a very disappointed man.

-oOo-

The weather had not improved. An audible patter of rain danced off the stone sills; a duller impact than the metallic ring as it struck the gutters.

Tate arrived, disturbing Eldon's thoughts, and ceremoniously handing over a stiff buff envelope.

"Commander's compliments, sir." He was gone before Eldon could ask any questions.

Gower watched Eldon for a moment. "I suspect that's not going to be two tickets for Twickenham," he finally remarked.

Eldon, giving an incredulous glance, opened the envelope, and withdrew a photograph. He shook his head. "Make any sense to you?" he asked, passing it to Gower. "Because I haven't the slightest idea what they're supposed to represent."

"Always look for the graffiti. I'd recognize Prinn's minuscule scribble anywhere."

Gower skimmed through the information. "Apparently your bird's slipped out of Port Said. The American's intercepted a stray transmission from a Russian Primor'ye-class trawler. Obviously only a confirmation signal in amongst their standard communication traffic, which didn't appear to be repeated. They apparently always use the same numbers group for this message, so ELINT knew its identity immediately. One of their embassy staff asked around until he found a helpful Egyptian policeman who, in exchange for hard cash, told him they'd been guarding a Russian national until they could slip him aboard the trawler. Luckily, the apartment where he was staying had been booked for several weeks, with still some days to run, so they managed to whip inside, and take these photographs before it was turned round."

He handed the photograph back to Eldon, who squinted at the writing.

"Rather a strange administrative system," Eldon queried, taken aback. "Couldn't he send a decent memo?"

"Save the forests, Rex. Admirable concept." Gower rolled back to his desk, continuing his own work.

Propping the print against his computer, Eldon looked closely at the accompanying pictures: an assembly of three uncropped photographs, pasted up and then copied. They were a little underexposed, probably taken without a flash, but with sufficient definition to make out everything in some detail. The prints of the bedroom and bathroom disclosed tidy and orderly rooms. The third, shot through the open-plan sitting room and kitchen, might have been equally tidy, except for a wine bottle standing next to the waste bin.

Eldon rummaged for a magnifying glass he'd already noticed in the desk drawer. He could make out the label, but not the name inscribed on it.

"Do they have a strict approach to alcohol in Egypt?" he asked.

"As a Muslim country, officially they would have, but Mubarak appears a moderate sort of fellow, so they probably turn a blind eye to foreign nationals excesses, giving their own people a hard time instead. Not thinking of going there, are you?"

"No. But I'd like this print enlarged, which is as close as I intend to get to Egypt, for the moment."

Gower took Eldon down to the photographic section where he filled in the form to which a copy would be attached, and a record kept in the photographic archives. The technician was not optimistic.

"Not a spectacularly good print this, because it's come down the wire, but we may be able to enhance it well enough for you to decipher the label." He indicated the area in question with the tip of his ruler. "I shall have to

19

reduce it first, to avoid the bitmap being made up out of false pixels. System can't add what isn't there, so every step will degrade the image. Reducing means the programme will throw some out, but we'll have a little more control. Come back in a couple of hours."

-oOo-

When Eldon returned later he found he had a 70 mm-square transparency to look at. Mounted in an old bellows projector, and focused on the smooth white wall of the laboratory, the bottle was projected life-size, revealing in less than perfect detail the name of the wine: 'Cantina di Verolino.1988'. Something of a long shot, but highly unlikely that such a vintage wine could be purchased over the counter in Port Said. He wrote the name down on a piece of paper, and then signed for a copy of the photograph.

In the office, he found Gower beginning to wilt. Another cup of coffee brought him some way back to attentive.

"How are you on wines?" Eldon asked.

Gower removed himself to the comfortable old wooden office chair, with its bright green cushion and stout arms, which had somehow accompanied the department to these new offices. He popped a barley sugar into his mouth to remove the dry taste of coffee.

"Not a world expert, but I'm all right on Bordeaux and Burgundy until you start talking special crus. First and second growths. That sort of thing. Any help?"

"None whatsoever," Eldon declared "I'm in Italy here. Who do you know that can help me?"

"Someone who pushes plonk, I suppose. There are a lot of wine bars in the King's Road, but you might try Charlie. He's a bit of a lush, but what he doesn't know about the red stuff isn't worth knowing."

"Sounds like the sort of person I need. How do I find this Charlie?" Eldon asked.

"You don't," Gower replied. "That's what I mean about bars. He finds you, but I'll put the word out. Doesn't matter which sort of bar, anywhere from Sloane Square to World's End. He'll connect with you eventually."

"Sounds like a pretty third-rate strategy."

"Possibly," Gower agreed. "But I'm afraid, it just so happens to be the way Charlie likes it."

-oOo-

On the third night, Charlie appeared. Eldon had almost made up his mind that working on the Nightingale file all through the day, then waiting for Charlie during the evening was beyond the call of duty. He'd soon become tired of the scroungers, and of the women who used talcum powder to cover up their way of life.

With a half of IPA and the Evening Standard for company, Eldon sat near the door of the Rose and Crown to get away from the odour of sour beer, and air weighed down by a pall of nicotine.

He spotted Charlie as soon as he came in: a smallish man, emaciated and jaundiced, who approached the bar slowly, taking obvious note of its clients. Buying himself a pint of beer with a handle, he drank deeply, shuffling over to where Eldon sat. His hand had a distinctive uncontrollable tremor. The brown pinstriped suit, stained with dark patches, appeared a number of sizes too large. It had probably fitted him once; sometime before he relinquished the choice between bread and beer. His tie-less white shirt was buttoned up in an effort of neatness, but didn't hide the shabby grubbiness of the collar. Placing himself in the chair opposite, he slowly and carefully lowered his glass on to the table.

"Gower said you had a drink for me?" His voice, thin and indifferent, seemed not to care if Eldon did or didn't, but the fact that he had come meant he lived in some hope.

"Did he also say you had to have something for me in exchange?" Eldon asked.

"Nothing's for nothing - I know the rules. Gower said you were a punter, so you ask the questions and I supply the answers. Quid pro quo. What do you want?"

"I'm interested in wine. Red wine. Italian."

Charlie laughed dryly. "You and half the continent, I suppose."

"I'm only interested in Cantina di Verolino. Doesn't

seem to be listed anywhere."

"Esoteric cove, aren't you? For a punter you know too much already." Charlie lifted his glass carefully in both hands and drank deeply, sucking his lips together noisily so he could savour the bitterness of the malt.

"You know the vineyard, then?" Eldon asked patiently.

"Naturally. Italian wine at that level makes you leery of Bordeaux hype. They only produce 2500 bottles a year, sometimes less, using the Michet sub variety of the Nebbiolo grape barriqued in Slavonian oak barrels. Limousin oak hasn't got the palate. If the grapes aren't perfect, they pulp them for *sfuso*. It's only a small estate near the town of Barolo, in Piedmont; so not just expensive but virtually unobtainable without a special relationship to tap into." The information rolled out as though he still had a professional interest, offering an indication of another, previous life.

"What sort of special relationship?"

"Wouldn't be very special, if I knew that."

"You're right," Eldon said. "Has the importer got a name?"

"The Anglo-Italian Wine Company, in Fulham. They've always specialized in fine Italian wine. Expensive, with a good reputation - bit of a legend in the trade. They've never listed Verolino."

"Thank you, Charlie. You've been very helpful." Eldon finished his pale ale before he picked up his newspaper to leave. He took a five-pound note from his wallet, and tucked it in the top pocket of Charlie's stained suit.

"That'd just about buy the cork from a Verolino," Charlie said sarcastically.

Eldon gave a half smile, took out another five-pound note, pressing it on top of the other. "There, buy yourself two corks!"

-oOo-

The next afternoon, Eldon turned off at Putney Bridge and drove down Fulham Palace Road until he located the wine shop.

Double fronted windows displayed a regional theme, with a wooden *bigoncia*, chestnut staves black with juice

22

stains, and two sizes of hand-blown demijohns. One, minus its protective woven-wicker jacket, disclosed a voluptuous glass form. Obviously, someone had spent time delving into the darker recesses of an Italian cantina. There were no hand-written signs, or whitewashed letters on the plate-glass windows of the kind that indicated one of those burgeoning wine shops touting for business, broadcasting loudly how many wine writers had declared them the biggest and the best. The Anglo-Italian Wine Company was the sort of old-fashioned establishment which never raised its voice, and whose clientele were as faithful as they were fastidious.

Eldon crossed the road to enter the shop.

The young woman standing just inside stepped back, enabling Eldon to open the door for her. She smiled her thanks, displaying perfectly shaped white teeth, tightened the loose belt of a thick camelhair coat, and passed out into the street, leaving a faint trace of expensive perfume in the air. Eldon watched her turn out of sight before he shut the door.

The man behind the counter straightened the pile of blue wrapping paper, expectantly watching Eldon, who was taking in the orderly ranks of bottles arranged in their racks. Charlie would probably have had vintner's notes for them all.

"Can I help you, sir?" the man enquired.

"If you've got a bottle of Cantina di Verolino, I suspect you can."

"Ah, then I can't help you," the man replied sympathetically. "We only have very limited supplies from that particular vineyard. We have a superb range of other Barolos though. Young ones for laying down, or older for immediate drinking. The 1970 Alighieri is just coming round, but has plenty of life, if you fancy some of that for your old age."

"No, just the Verolino. When are you expecting your next delivery?" Eldon asked.

The man behind the counter shook his head. "It's really a question of supplier-led allocation. Two cases are permanently spoken for, and if we're lucky enough to get a third, then first come, first served."

"Well, at least two happy customers, and perhaps someone with a lucky number?" Eldon commented.

A suspicious look crossed the man's face. "We take a pride in having satisfied customers, even if we can't always satisfy a particular need. Mostly, though, we can supply a satisfactory alternative, but if only the Verolino will serve, I'm afraid we're both out of luck."

"That's a pity. The young lady who left when I came in, what did she choose?" Eldon was of a mind to buy something.

A look of satisfaction passed over the proprietors face. "She didn't choose anything, sir. Coincidentally, she came in to verify whether a consignment of Verolino had arrived yet. I was happy to confirm the order. Her employer is an old and distinguished customer of ours."

"That suggests I'll have to wait some time before I can join such illustrious company?"

"I'm afraid, in relation to the Verolino, sir, you probably won't have the benefit of sufficient time to wait."

The red Scimitar GTE turned off the Grosvenor Road and down a side street, passing under the barrier of the Axmar Industries car park, with its large tyres squealing on the smooth concrete surface as the vehicle twisted round the stanchions into a reserved parking space.

Livia Wolfe checked her lipstick in the mirror of the sun-visor, before she swung out her long, shapely legs from inside the car. Pulling her scarf together against the dank atmosphere, she took the staff lift to the international administrative department on the second floor.

At this late hour, the Chairman had remained in his office solely to hear the outcome of Livia's visit to the Anglo-Italian Wine Company.

Discarding her coat, she picked up a spiral notebook, and knocked gently before opening the door.

Arthur Sandquest sat at a small, elegant French writing desk, with his legs and stockinged feet thrust out beyond it. There was a matching chair, angled at the edge of the desk facing him, and, on either side, stood two large mahogany display cabinets housing a minor part of his substantial collection of Etruscan antiquities. He referred to these as his passion, while others called them his obsession.

On the wall behind him a plain torchère carrying a votive bronze head was starkly flanked by a pair of Renaissance cartoons from the hand of Cipriano Vallorsa, an almost unknown Italian from Grosio in the north of Italy, whose valley churches were richly adorned with his paintings. Sandquest liked the idea of this anonymity, knowing things that most others didn't. The characters they depicted aptly reminded Sandquest of his own early life, where hardship was ever present in the grim poverty that touched the dreary streets around him, and opened every door, and sat down at every table. The inter-war depression had provided the opening reference to his life. As one of them, he had seen the faces of the common people who lived there, and because business demanded it, hardened his heart. But it was an image too deeply etched in his memory ever to be forgotten. One lived with the knowledge that if you scratched the surface of society hard enough, you would find the traces of deprivation still festering, like a wound beneath the bandage of prosperity.

"Well, now, what have they to offer?" Sandquest asked, with just a faint trace of a northern accent.

"Mister Copeland phoned Italy this morning to confirm the position," Livia replied. "They have three cases for you, but the third is optional. I'll phone him tomorrow with your instructions."

"Excellent. Let's include the option, shall we?" His mood was now ebullient, more than satisfied with this outcome. Rising from his seat, Sandquest was a tall man, even in stockinged feet. "If you'll call Bob now, he can collect me. I'm just about ready."

Livia telephoned Sandquest's chauffeur, before returning to help him on with his overcoat. He pocketed his cigar case, waved his gloves at her in farewell, and disappeared into the lift.

Crossing to the window Livia looked down upon the curved polished arc of travertine steps descending from the entrance to a wide forecourt preceding iron gates that led out on to the Embankment road, with the oily, motionless Thames just visible through the trees beyond. Sandquest appeared below, descending the steps two at a time, ducking through the wide door his uniformed driver held open for him, into the rear of an elderly Bristol 411.

The vehicle itself was a reflection of those virtues that had made him successful. His companies had a reputation for building longevity into their products by the simple expedient of viewing superlative quality as a component in their manufacture.

Livia watched the vehicle turn out of the gate, the exhaust vapours clearing as it accelerated quickly out into the traffic towards Lambeth Bridge. Returning to her desk, a glance at the appointments diary indicated that the Portland Conference almost coincided with the coming Pakistan Delegation visit arranged last year. Somehow, she had to juggle time between these two events, allowing enough space for Sandquest to fly to

Brussels to meet von Moller, a South African de
antiquities.

Shut away in this executive cocoon, Livia didn't n
the offices fall silent, one by one, until, with a i
flourish, the cleaners arrived with their headscarv
vacuum cleaners and vocal opinions on everything.

When a calm returned after their departure, leavin
behind a smell of furniture polish and window cleaner,
Livia put away her work, listening to a quiet that not
even the incessant roar of the evening traffic outside
could penetrate through the thick secondary glazing of
the office windows. She wasn't interested right now in
this wonder of the glazier's art, only in any sounds that
might emanate from her own immediate environment.

Crossing to the secretaries' office, she looked in and
checked they had gone home, their office equipment
neatly shrouded by covers. There was no sound at all
except the steady, almost inaudible swish of the air-
conditioning. Glancing at her watch, she noted that in
an hour the security guards would begin their rounds.

Livia took a large leather handbag from the office
cupboard. A concealed zip fastener opened the bottom,
revealing a 9.5 mm Minox camera in a black dimpled-
leather case, neatly held in place by elasticated straps.
She withdrew the camera's slim brushed-aluminium
body, rechecked it had fresh film, before slipping it into
her pocket. Entering Sandquest's office, Livia switched
on the table lamp, which cast a low light across the
surface. Swinging one of the Vallorsa cartoons aside
revealed Sandquest's safe. Dialling the required numbers
on the tumbler lock, she opened the door before
withdrawing several files. Taking them over to the desk
she studied their configuration, making sure there
weren't any hidden surprises: telltales that would
indicate illicit handling.

Satisfied that they weren't arranged in any particular
way, Livia laid the first three aside after recognizing the
fourth, entitled 'Acquisitions'. Removing its contents, she
arranged the papers, neatly in a line on the desk. Moving
the lamp a little closer to provide more direct light, she
carefully regulated the shutter speed and aperture on
her camera. Sliding the lid back and extending the

to give the fixed focal length, Livia
'hrough the viewfinder, and pressed
Sliding the lid back again, she
er, replacing each photographed sheet
o the folder in its correct sequence.
of her pulse, and the soft clatter of the
chanism, in the depths of her concentration
sed the sound of the approaching lift until it
to a halt.

sing the few moments delay before the cage door
pened, she swiftly returned the files to the safe, shut
the door, swung the picture back, and quickly switched
off the table lamp.

The sound of voices drifted through to Sandquest's
office, and soon became familiar. One belonged to
Sandquest's wife Rachel, the other to Metropolitan Police
Commander, Nicholas Prinn.

Livia looked round for somewhere she could conceal
herself. To reach Sandquest's bathroom meant passing
the open door lit by the light from her own office outside.
Choosing the only alternative, she slipped in between the
two large cabinets.

"Straight home, then?" Prinn asked.

"My home," Rachel replied seriously. There was a
moment's silence, followed by a slight rustle and
exhalation of breath, before she continued. "Directly
home, Nicholas. Arthur is expecting me. Having
promised to pick up his address book, by no stretch of
the imagination can I take all evening. The Trust meeting
has already been over for an hour. Darling, don't look so
depressed. I'm not some prize in a raffle. Tomorrow or
the day after, I'll phone you, I promise." Rachel entered
Sandquest's office without turning on the light.

With a sinking feeling, Livia realized that in her haste
she had left her camera on one side of the table.

Even in the subdued light, Rachel couldn't fail to
notice it. Rotating the camera in her hand with evident
curiosity she turned to call Prinn into the room. Her
puzzled glance passed over the mirror with its reflection
of Livia huddling between the cabinets. Replacing the
camera on the desk, the smooth metal suddenly
unpleasantly tactile, she took the address book from a

drawer and, without another glance, left the room.

"Rachel, are you all right?" Prinn asked. "You look as white as a ghost."

"Yes. I'm fine," Rachel replied, her voice trembling. "Just a silly touch of the vapours. It will pass."

As Livia heard the lift doors open and close, she continued leaning against the wall. Rachel's response, for the moment, was likely to be muted. At best it gave Livia no more than a breathing space, now that the clock had been set ticking in a count down to the detection of her own betrayal. There was never going to be a perfect time to release herself from this covert gamble, but what she hadn't bargained for was the absence of even an opportunity.

-oOo-

Prinn turned on the air-conditioning as the inside of the car became stuffy. His efforts at conversation hadn't managed to draw Rachel out of her self-imposed isolation.

For Prinn, Rachel had originally become an expedient cover, an accidental and welcome screen, allowing him to observe Sandquest without such attention becoming obvious. Membership of the Sandquest Musical Trust, set up by Rachel's husband, had been the consequence of his late mother's interests, and was genuine enough. Conveniently, it had commenced some time before his department's investigation into Sandquest's criminal interests. As the subject in their covert operation, 'Necropolis', every contact he made, every piece of conversation he shared, and every inference or suggestion, Prinn was able to subject to rigorous consideration. Somewhere along the line he was convinced Sandquest would give himself away.

The department was confident that the antiquarian dealer, Von Moller, was receiving stolen Etruscan works of art from someone: works without a paper trail that silently appeared in Sandquest's possession. These were not the mere dross of plundered tombs, but exquisite pieces wrought in precious metals, or of significant, sometimes unique, historical importance. Sandquest was quietly assembling a collection that rivalled those of prestigious national museums.

How a private collector could thus compete in a market strongly contested and oversubscribed by public institutions was a mystery that, as yet, seemed beyond Prinn's resources to resolve.

In the pursuit of this inquiry into Sandquest, he was beginning to realize he'd become too single-minded; using the investigation merely as an excuse to escape the consequences of the growing attraction of Rachel.

Reaching Maidenhead in silence, they drove alongside the river to reach a mock-timbered lodge. Turning through heavy iron gates and across a cattle grid, the gravel drive curved gently ahead past well-maintained lawns; a greensward lapping against well established oak and beech trees edging the lushly planted Jekyll-inspired gardens. He drew up in front of a long sprawling brick and timber mansion with tall whimsical chimneys, mullioned windows, and a robust doorway of quarter-sawn oak. At night, as now, there was a distinct air of the theatrical about such architecture. 'Hollywood spook' was how Rachel described it. This evening it seemed an almost ridiculous pastiche, with a solitary ground-floor window glowing with a distinctive yellow in the blackness of its overall silhouette.

-oOo-

Sandquest inside heard the car approach. Lowering the book he was reading on to his lap, he listened to the unwelcome crunch of tires on the gravel outside. With a frown, he glanced irritably at his watch. Both car doors shut with a thud, one echoing the other, which suggested that Prinn was intending to come in. Sandquest hoped that Rachel would not, by way of thanks, invite him to stay for supper.

He strode out into the large entrance hall to greet them. Rachel kissed him lightly, while handing him his address book. Taking her coat, he enquired if Prinn would like a drink, and was relieved to see him decline, with a shake of his head.

"I won't this evening, Arthur, thank you all the same

Still things to do back at the office. A desk as large as mine is designed to accommodate a lot of work, for which I can only blame myself, having changed the regulation one for something on which you could probably play table tennis."

"Hence a policeman's duty is never done," Sandquest remarked. "And Rachel dragging you all the way out here can't have helped."

Rachel hastened to apologize. "Yes, I'm sorry if I delayed you. I've taken you well out of your way. I hope it wasn't too much trouble?" They shook hands. "Now, if you'll excuse me, I must do something about supper. Thank you so much for your help, Nicholas. Don't forget, the next meeting is on the last Friday of the month. A date for your diary?"

"I understand this is the first time Rachel's had any trouble with the Bentley?" Prinn enquired from Sandquest, as he turned to leave.

"Yes, apparently it needs a new part the agency doesn't hold in their stores. It's a slow moving item. They tell me it'll be 'expressed'. At Rachel's expense no doubt, but at least repaired and ready by tomorrow evening. Thank you for bringing Rachel home." Sandquest stepped over and opened the front door.

After they shook hands, Prinn was surprised to find that Sandquest had shut the door almost on his heels.

-oOo-

Sandquest closed the door of his study just as firmly. From the crowded bookshelves he hastily picked out a small green volume of The Odes of Pindar which had been pushed in among a varied collection of poetry and other classical works. He had not read any of them, being also quite sure he never would read any of them. They were there solely to disguise the uniqueness of this one volume of Pindar's obsequious lyrics to long-dead sporting heroes.

Of all the printed editions available, in translation, of this eminent Greek poet, only one would do. No other had its exact pagination or textual layout; nor was it in print, the publisher having long ago ceased to exist

31

operating at their offices in the Strand. In this, he considered the book he held, a most admirable volume.

Yet even that was not what made it unique. Its uniqueness lay in the fact that there were precisely 366 pages of text. Of the millions of people inhabiting the planet, only one other person shared his particular enthusiasm for the foot races, the wrestling, the discus throwing and the chariot races that were extolled within.

Checking the date on his watch, he noted the number of days away from the vernal equinox, did a quick calculation on the number of elapsed days since the beginning of the winter solstice, before turning to the page in the book corresponding to that number. This wouldn't be significant to anyone unless they happened to draw a parallel between the number of seasons and the complicated order of Greek festivals in the Olympian period. On a piece of paper Sandquest wrote down his message, turning it into a numerical code from the chosen page.

Occupying no more than ten minutes of his time to encode the message, he knew that for the uninitiated to decipher it would be beyond the measure of a lifetime.

From the back of a cupboard he next withdrew a metal attaché case converted to contain a Morse transmitter and receiver, with an external antenna allowing a range of three thousand miles in ideal conditions. Having constructed two of them a decade or more before, discarding transistors for more reliable valves running well below their maximum capability, he hadn't been concerned how they looked, or any tolerable disadvantages, only how they performed.

Placing it on a small table, Sandquest made the connexions and adjusted the frequency. At precisely 21.35, propping the piece of paper in front of him, in the top of the case, he tapped out his coded message. At 21.40 he received confirmation.

Consigning the piece of notepaper to the shredder, Sandquest disconnected the transmitter, closed the case securely, and returned it to the cupboard.

He turned and reflected on the purpose of his communication.

Italy was becoming more of a problem now that his

expectations were so high. He should have become more actively involved, not leaving it all to Petrov, who wouldn't know the difference between a crater and a carrot. He laughed quietly to himself. There was something amusing about a purveyor of death taking such an interest in Etruscan tombs.

But it was his show, and for the moment Petrov was the only one who had the contacts to see it through.

Technical difficulties, he had said, with the digging, and being mostly in sand, Sandquest could see that it would be.

Or perhaps it was with Brizzi, the agitated little Italian senator he said he was dealing with.

Slipping the Pindar back into the bookshelf, he picked up the decanter so that by the time Rachel phoned through to inform him that supper was ready, he was back in his armchair with a whisky and soda.

Chapter 3

Finetti was just closing the door of his car when he looked up to see Senator Brizzi waving to him from across the wide thoroughfare of Milan's Corso Venezia. He made a gesture of greeting in return.

Brizzi had a short tidy figure, made somewhat taller by old-fashioned Cuban-heeled boots. His wiry, grey salt-and-pepper hair, he'd combed into as quiet a style as possible. Despite the boots, he was long past making fashion statements.

They walked together into the vast Piazzale Loreto where in 1945 jubilant partisans, mere hounds among the hunters, hauled up the lifeless bodies of Mussolini and his mistress, to dangle by their ankles outside a petrol station. At least, Finetti recalled, amidst the braying mob, someone had felt sensitive enough to tuck Clara Petacci's skirt between her legs.

The windy concrete waste of the Piazzale wasn't so crowded now, and the little restaurant to which he led Brizzi made no reference to its shared history, being too new for any association.

Their orders taken, Finetti leant closer across the small table, smiling uneasily at the senator. "Well, Roberto, it makes a change for you to be chasing me. I hope you're not here to discuss worker's councils or co-operative partnerships. You should have lunched with Agnelli."

"No, Massimo," Brizzi said in a low voice, "I want to talk about us."

Finetti leant back, wary. "Us?"

"You're a rich man, Massimo, and I've heard you're interested in sound investments. Perhaps you could consider investing in a project of mine?"

Finetti replied carefully. "Roberto, socio-commercial enterprises are passé. Just lame ducks."

"No," Brizzi lowered his voice, "this isn't that sort of offer. It's one, though, where I can guarantee that the total revenues will far exceed the total costs."

A look of doubt crossed Finetti's face. "That sounds like a lot of money for a socialist to be throwing about;

therefore, I have to ask you bluntly, what sort of percentage yield are you forecasting on this investment?"

"Return of investment, with thirty percent after all costs have been met."

"That's thirty per cent of zero," Finetti countered sceptically.

"It's also thirty per cent of one hundred per cent. You have to be either an optimist or a pessimist," his companion said peevishly.

Finetti looked at the optimist opposite him. "Don't bother me with statistical possibilities, Roberto. Just give me the bottom line; remembering I'm not in the venture-capital business."

"Perhaps fifty million pounds, gross."

"That's a great deal of money," Finetti said, taken aback. He was silent for a moment. "If you're working in sterling, you must have a UK associate."

"One I'd like to trade," Brizzi answered irritably.

"Tell me about him?"

"English entrepreneurs are opportunists. Whatever serves them best is all that matters. I've hardly met him, but straight away he's laying down rules that suited him. Arrogant bastard. We'd be better off without him. Are you interested?" Brizzi asked impatiently.

Studying the senator closely, Finetti toyed with the idea of giving it a miss. Serious money like that meant serious criminals, with accountants and law practices of their own. It meant family brokers who could afford to move anything from cigarettes to people, to anywhere in the world. He decided otherwise; however, for Brizzi was a serious man, not given to wild speculative proposals. "In for how much?" Finetti asked finally.

"Three million."

"Three million?" Finetti echoed, looking up sharply from the menu he was studying.

"Sterling," the senator qualified.

Finetti shook his head. "I don't have that kind of money, Roberto."

"But you could get it?" The senator pressed.

"Not that much liquidity. I might raise the amount by converting one or two of my holdings, but these companies are integral to maintaining a varied portfolio of financial securities. I have some debentures where the fixed interest is beginning to look negative. Those I might be inclined to off load, but they won't realize the sort of money you're asking. So, sorry, my answer is no."

They ate their antipasti in silence. When the waiter took their plates away, Finetti dabbed his mouth with his napkin and returned to the subject. "I've been thinking, perhaps someone else?"

"I don't know anyone else." Brizzi remained bad-tempered.

"Union funds? That's a place to start."

"No, I'm looking for a discreet person; private money. Not needing to answer to a board of directors, or some nit-picking committee. Your sort of person, Massimo."

"I'm not your sort of person," Finetti said firmly.

Brizzi took the rebuke with a weak smile, gambling on Finetti being interested; knowing he wasn't averse to bending the rules. Whether he would break them as well, was not so certain.

"Capitalism is about risks and rewards, isn't it?" he went on. "In the modern world, profit margins are squeezed by fiscal policies. Therefore, you increase profits by innovation and getting rid of employees; or increase productivity by making them work harder and longer for little extra remuneration, and, if you're feeling bullish, through increasing your market share by buying up your competitors. But something for almost nothing - that should be attractive to a clever entrepreneur like yourself?"

"I wonder. It sounds remarkably like robbery."

They smiled together, a little more easily now, allowing their second course to be laid on the table before continuing the discussion.

Finetti nodded thoughtfully. "I might know someone who'd be interested. He's the only person I can think of who's rich enough to risk that amount of capital, and," - he paused to emphasize the inference, - "who'll know if the gamble's worth taking or not. The problem is, he's also English."

Brizzi thought about it. "Only one person?"

Finetti nodded again. "So, how would he make this profit? I might just mention, that he won't take kindly to romantic possibilities, and neither will I. You'll need to provide a cast iron case that can fool his accountants who have very sharp eyes. If it's good, he'll probably agree to give them a miss."

"Antiquities, Massimo. Etrusco-Romano," the senator said eagerly.

"Really?"

"An untouched tomb complex, almost a mini-necropolis. Specimens as perfect as though they were crafted only yesterday."

Finetti paused with the butter-laden *pansoti* halfway to his mouth. He returned it to the plate, cutting it in half with his fork, inspecting the borage and chard within. Adding some Parmesan, he swivelled one piece in the walnut sauce, then popped it into his mouth, savouring the flavour.

Those family brokers would be just as happy with antiquities, he realized. It was all the same to them. He sipped some wine.

"The milk is a little too curdled, Roberto," he said. "With pasta, the sauce is everything."

Brizzi refused to be distracted. "Think about it, Massimo: an untouched tomb complex."

"If that's the case, perhaps you should stick to your UK associate?"

"As I said, avarice feeds on itself. Enough is never enough; like giving aid to the starving masses in Africa." Brizzi became testy again. "He's started private negotiations with a South African dealer who can pass the finds through his international auction houses. Who did he consult? Well, it wasn't me. Anyway, that should suggest that the projects viable for someone with the sense to grasp it."

"Profit's always the motive, Roberto, even among the proletariat with their addiction to lotteries and the shaky ethics of the get-rich-quick school of revolutionaries. They endlessly complain about the cost of their health, or the paucity of their pensions, while they spend billions on smoking and gambling. Now your old friends, the Soviets, have joined the club. Plenty of big investors there, flinging around public money they've made private."

"That I wouldn't know about." Brizzi sat back in his chair, his pasta still untouched. "So, would your man be interested?"

"Depends on the return. Such investments are difficult. Add in the insurance, the security, the routine maintenance to make sure the pieces aren't rotting away behind your back, the environmental costs, the demon inflation, and you'll be long dead before it realizes a worthwhile gain." A thought struck Finetti. "Who is this English associate of yours?"

"Sandquest...a man named Sandquest."

Finetti relaxed. "Where did you meet him?"

"He came through my partner. He'll only be interested in showing himself after all the hard work's done."

"When it's done, Roberto, you move on. That's the first rule of the entrepreneur." He waved at Brizzi's untouched plate. "Don't let your pasta go cold. I'll put in a word for you, as my contact might be interested in such a deal. Who knows?"

-oOo-

"Sandquest!" The man in the spotless linen suit rammed his walking stick down hard on to Finetti's polished oak floor. "What do you mean do I know him? There's only one Sandquest interested in Etruscan pots, rich enough to buy the bloody things, and bent enough to turn a blind eye to where they came from. The tosspot!" He spat the words out.

Sir Maxwell Blain was not a man to mince his words. He retained the vigorous aggressiveness of a self-made man who still saw himself occupied 'in trade' long after his mercantile career had brought him success in the business world. Chairman of the Lister Group, he'd risen from being a lowly sole proprietor to become chairman of numerous public companies through rude bloody-mindedness and skilful business expertise. He was a disagreeable, dishonest and ruthless predator; an asset stripper long before the dozing imperial world of ancient family businesses woke up to the realization that their brand names were almost worthless, while their physical assets, represented sizeable fortunes.

Finetti had been Blain's protégé in his post-war expansion overseas. A devastated Europe had proved fertile ground for those with enough money, and a sound method for increasing it. It was Blain who had taught Finetti the first rule of the entrepreneur. Blain was the perfect exemplar for the pirates of the commercial and industrial world, disliked and feared in crusty boardrooms where the balance sheets were undervalued, or the share prices were plummeting. No one liked to have Blain peering too closely into their company books.

Finetti drew himself closer to the Regency table that served as his desk. "Then Brizzi may well have a secret hoard of these things, Max?"

"If Sandquest's in for three millions, the man will have a warehouse full of the stuff, maybe two."

Sandquest had come to be a thorn in Blain's side, a piece of history that he'd never been able to shake off. In the beginning, Blain had shown, through his own innate ability, how to create and accumulate wealth. His slow, anxious partner, Sandquest, had tagged along after him as they struggled out of grinding, northern, inter-war poverty. But Blain had left to escape the dreary backdrop of his youth, leaving his partner out in the cold. Even Sandquest's wife found it warmer elsewhere. In the years that followed, their paths had crossed several times. Sandquest had since cost him a lot of money. But, far worse, when they did, he'd been made to look an amateur, a bungler out of his depth in the main stream of corporate management. No one would say so, of course, but everyone knew it. Sandquest, who would lose a sale rather than sacrifice his profit margins in the dank, dismal northern markets where they first traded, had come from nowhere, even from certain failure, to show him - Sir Maxwell Blain - how it was done. That stuck in his throat.

"Still, not something to tempt you with, though?" Finetti broke into his thoughts.

"Why not?" Blain asked sharply.

Finetti was taken aback. "Well, antiquities."

"Can I make a profit?"

"Possibly," Finetti shrugged. "You'd be in only for the residual return after all expenses have been met. You'd need to know more about how the profits are being allocated."

"There's always a profit if you squeeze hard enough," Blain said absently, his thoughts still on Sandquest.

"This is a criminal enterprise, Max. Being paid in cash can cause problems, even for you."

"I'll put the money under my bed, Massimo, so don't start fretting. You're always worrying about consequences. Since when has an Italian worried about consequences? Tell me some more about this tomb? Grave-robbing's a tad unseemly for Sandquest to be dabbling in."

"I know nothing of the tomb. Didn't you say he was in the market for Etruscan antiquities?"

"He's a collector. Has been one for years. That's common enough knowledge. But he buys privately, and at auction. Damn it, he's rich enough to get what he wants without risking his neck. Why would he get mixed up in this?"

"Why would you?"

"Because he is. That's good enough reason."

"I see. How much of a collector is Sandquest?" Finetti asked.

"Don't ask me. I'm not exactly welcome in his bloody company. Etruscan's all I know. He's a big-time punter with deep pockets, and a fixation. What's the beef?"

"As you said - why should someone so rich risk their neck? Brizzi said the tomb was untouched, and that the specimens would be perfect. 'As though they were made yesterday' were his exact words."

"What are you driving at?" Blain said impatiently. "Repro stuff?

"No, I was considering what such a possibility would mean to an obsessive collector. If the grave goods were perfect, Max, someone obsessed by a single idea of quality and perfection might stoop to anything to obtain them. Perhaps even murder. You've known this Sandquest for a long time. How does he strike you? What sort of man is he?"

Blain looked hard at Finetti. "Are you trying to wind me up? If you are, you can stuff it. If Sandquest's in, then there's a lot of mileage in getting him out. I want him out. I want that son of a bitch so far out, I can't even see the smudge of his smoke on the horizon."

-oOo-

Having left Milan and reached Rome before the ten o'clock Italian breakfast, Finetti passed by the tons of travertine and marble, with a central obelisk that made up Bernini's Fountain of the Four Rivers, with hardly a glance. He crossed quickly out of the Piazza Navona and proceeded into the Corso del Rinascimento.

Opposite lay the massive baroque Palazzo Madama, named after Margaret of Parma, natural daughter of Emperor Charles V, and, since 1871, the seat of the Italian Senate.

Senator Brizzi was waiting nervously for him in front of the right wing of the great building. Under his arm he held a small brown-paper parcel, neatly tied with string. Finetti was almost alongside him before Brizzi noticed his arrival.

"Ah, Massimo," he sighed, taking his arm and walking with him out of sight of the entrance, away from the prying eyes of loafing police officers. They went a little way down the Piazza Sant' Eustachio before he slowed down.

"Keep walking." He still had his arm tucked under Finetti's. "You say your man is interested?"

"Apparently."

Brizzi held his arm more tightly. "You don't sound very enthusiastic?"

"I'm not."

"Well, you hardly matter, do you? What about him?"

"He's interested in your project, but you can't expect him to lay out three million pounds without knowing who you are, or what it's all about."

"Show him what's in here." Brizzi thrust the parcel into Finetti's hand. "In the middle of this book you'll find a photograph. It shows the sort of item that'll more than help to pay off his investment. A whole tomb full of such things. You be sure to tell him?"

"I'll tell him, Roberto."

"On the inside of the wrapper I've written the name of

41

a man, with his telephone number in Milan. He can provide the item itself for you to look at. If you like what you see, tell him to show you some more. He'll then give you further instructions."

Brizzi squeezed Finetti's arm, and turned back the way he had come, heading towards the Palazzo del Senato.

-oOo-

Finetti stood in the shop doorway as the rain penetrated the stone-columned arcade, splashing his polished brogues. Opposite, the white marble mass of Milan cathedral had become tinged and mottled with yellow. He was, at that moment, on the wrong side of the Piazza del Duomo, trapped in a sheltering crowd by the deluge of water. This temporary inconvenience, he knew from experience, would stop as quickly as it had started.

A large, robust woman, smelling of mothballs, and too infrequent laundering, elbowed her way out of a doorway into the arcade. Raising her umbrella with a flourish, and little concern for the huddled ranks around her, she marched out into the already faltering shower. By the time she had reached the side of the cathedral the rain had stopped. Finetti crossed the piazza in the wake of her majestic floating figure, skirting the puddles round the transept and making his way to the west front, embellished with Pogliaghi's bronze central door. There he entered, using one of the small flanking doors.

Inside, he stood for a long moment, letting his eyes adjust to the heavy gloom. At first there appeared only a vast void of a dimly lit mystery stretching out before him: an overwhelming emptiness that reached into infinity beyond the cluster of gigantic pillars springing from the marble-paved floor. The atmosphere was still heavy with incense from a recent mass. He carefully dipped his thumb in the stoup, making the sign of the cross on his forehead. He then turned right; crossing into the deepest recesses of the south aisle, where shafts of stone helped support, somewhere above his head, the unimaginable weight of the vault, thus casting an even deeper mantle of shadow amid the weak light. Heading along

42

the aisle, he came to a small door hidden in the transept.

Across his shoulder, Finetti had slung an empty photographer's bag made of a soft material, and an equally empty camera. Ignoring the lift, he climbed the one hundred and fifty-eight steps, as he had been instructed. Exiting from the lantern at the top, he paused to readjust his sight to the brightness reflected off the white marble, exploding in a glare that hurt his eyes. Finding his sunglasses in one of his windcheater's pockets, he put them on. Stepping closer to the ridge, formed into a flat parallel pavement, he felt safer. Everything felt safer than the shallow pitch of overlapping plates that formed the roof and terminated at a pinnacled edge festooned with statuary, once described as a 'marble army', perilously hanging some sixty metres above the earth.

Walking carefully along to the western perimeter, high above the doors where he had entered, Finetti saw no one waiting. He swung round at the stone-tracery screen, making his way back over the still steaming flagstones. There was no actual hurry, except that he wanted to get this meeting over with. Once having decided to proceed, Blain was inclined to become impatient.

Suddenly a figure stepped out from the lantern's door. Just another photographer. As he approached, the man turned away, as if busily arranging a shot. On the slab next to him lay a bag that, Finetti could see, bore more than a passing resemblance to his own.

"A dome over a dome," Finetti offered by way of introduction, coming up behind the photographer.

The man raised his eye from the finder to observe him.

Those eyes Finetti would remember, eyes that would haunt him, even during his last few hours on earth. They were indolent almond-shaped Etruscan eyes, with the palest blue pupils under transparent eyelashes. Even the blink had a lazy motion about it; like a gentle nod of the eyelid. His receding pale-red hair, trimmed short, outlined an upper cranium burnt to a brown eggshell tinge, except for pink, peeling skin on the forehead.

"What is?" he asked in a flat, colourless tone.

"The lantern," Finetti replied. "It sits above

43

Brunelleschi's conical vault at the point where the nave forms the transept crossing below. As lanterns go, it's extremely large, don't you think? The interior dome doesn't actually protrude much above the roof, so there's another one, about the same size sitting behind this octagonal facade."

The pale-blue eyes didn't blink. Unimpressed, they returned to the view- finder. "Doubling up on things like that seems a waste of time," the man said.

"Not for Janus?" Finetti enquiringly suggested.

"Depends," the man countered, adjusting the stop to reduce the aperture of the lens, before winding on the film. He returned to the eyepiece, and pressed the shutter release.

"*Certo*," Finetti conceded, feeling the unease of a gambler.

"Which Janus are you referring to?" the man enquired, adding a lens hood.

"Either of them. Doesn't matter which." Finetti shifted his position a little nervously.

The sleepy eyes blinked; the head nodded. "One must be persistent in these things, getting everything properly in focus. My name's Saxe. You must be Finetti, right?"

"Right," Finetti replied, placing his bag next to the one already resting on the marble slab.

"I suggest you take some shots while you're waiting. But be careful, stepping back too far up here could lead to a little overexposure," Saxe added. Finetti took some imaginary shots. When he looked up again, Saxe had gone.

The weight of the camera bag told him that the arranged switch had taken place. Brizzi's three-million-pound gamble was in the bag.

Hanging it over his shoulder, he looked at the horizon of neon signs, a roof-scape that was a jumbled mass of receiving aerials and transmitting antennae. He felt suddenly quite alone. What was there to be afraid of, he asked himself. He was only acting as a go-between, and could deny knowing what was in the bag. But that was the problem. Someone might not even bother to ask because they had a greater claim to them than Saxe. Especially if they'd been stolen. But from whose ownership? Finetti was well aware that sometimes it turned out to be not what you stole, but from whom, that posed the greatest threat of all.

-oOo-

"So what did this archaeologist, Ferrari, say?" Blain enquired, pouring himself a glass of dry spumante and adding a generous amount of Campari. He stirred vigorously, stopping to admire the swirling colours for a moment before turning back to Finetti. "What do I actually get for all this money I'm to shell out?"

"An opinion Max." Finetti lifted two identical double-faced bronze statues on to the table. "These items are, according to Ferrari, extremely valuable."

Blain leant forward a little. "Because there are two of them?"

"Identical. 'Four faces each had, like a double Janus'. Milton, 'Paradise Lost'. Everything has a value, Max, depending on how desperate the owner is. There are a lot of asset-rich people out there, but with not a lot of ready cash."

Taking a pair of gold-rimmed spectacles from his top pocket, Blain perched them on the end of his nose and studied the statues with a heightened curiosity.

"Valuable, eh! Who is this Janus you're rabbiting on about?"

"An Italian divinity featuring in Roman mythology. When the Romans living on the Palatine, and the Sabines on the Quirinal were united, they built a gateway between them. The bronze doors were thrown open in times of war, when they marched out, to be closed again behind them when they returned in peace. Hence, Janus was always facing the army as it marched through the gate in either direction. Legend says they were only closed three times in the whole of Rome's imperial history. Professor Ferrari tells me the earliest known representations of Janus were found at the old Etruscan cities of Volterra and Sorena."

"What's he saying? Does he suspects they're stolen from one of them?"

"Who knows? Janus was an important deity, guarding

45

gates and doors, so they might have been used in a private house. Or even a castle."

Blain looked suspicious. "What sort of castle?"

"The one I understand Brizzi bought, where they're supposed to be finding items like this."

Blain smiled. "As long as they're valuable, they'll be enormously expensive bait. That's the important thing, since Sandquest just won't be able to resist them. What do you know about this Brizzi?"

"He knows a lot of people, but uses none of them to his advantage. For a senator, he's not exactly well off; therefore, I've no idea how he got mixed up in this, but he seems to have partners. A Fausto Paba is one, spent time in the Fortezza di Portolongone on Elba for murder. Seems to have been beneficial though, as he now heads a successful company called Caparra. Anyway, it's why you'll be in for thirty per cent. The other ten per cent goes to Brizzi's brother-in-law."

Blain gave a dry laugh. "Caparra, is it? That's a rum crew, even without Sandquest."

"So it may be, Max, but greasing a few wheels doesn't make us all racketeers. We don't have to mix with those sort of people. We've still time to pull out."

Blain rose from his chair impatiently. "I'm not interested in pulling out. I just need something to get my teeth into quickly. 'Subito,' don't they say in Italy?"

Finetti waved Blain back into his chair. "No doubt you'd like me to gloss over the fact that one Janus is 0.003 grams lighter than the other?"

"Jesus!" Blain protested. "Is that what I've paid all the money for? Just get to the point."

"The point is this, Max." Finetti's voice had grown both tired and serious, as if now carrying some unwelcome message he would have preferred to avoid. "Because of their rarity, if you chose to make an offer for them, they'd absorb a fair slice of your investment."

"That's what I wanted to know," Blain acknowledged cheerfully. "The real thing."

"That much we do know, along with two pages of quantitative data. For the inscription, you'd need to be a palaeographer - one specializing in the Etruscan language - to decipher it. Ferrari doesn't know of one

46

that wouldn't rush straight off to report to the academic journals."

"There you are, then," Blain said dismissively, rising to pace the floor again. "It's a runner. I'm relying on you to push this through with Brizzi, Massimo."

"You should meet him, Max."

"Where have I time to meet him?" Blain flattened a horizontal hand in front of his eyes. "Tomorrow I leave for Frankfurt. After that I'm back in London. I'm up to here with meeting people."

"No, Max, you must make time. You must weigh up the whole proposal for yourself. I won't be responsible. It involves three million pounds!"

"That makes sense." Blain stopped pacing. "I need to know exactly what Sandquest's up to. Not a regular business deal, is it? Not likely to see a balance sheet either, are we? Plus, you aren't going to have your eye on the ball so there's a chance of it getting clean away from you." He raised his hand, as Finetti seemed about to protest. "No good beating about the bush: this is something I can't afford to leave to chance. I'll have the funds moved into my Italian bank as soon as I get back to Town. We may have to move quickly when the time comes. After London, I'll be going immediately to Spain, staying with friends near the French border, so I'll still be close at hand. I've got some meetings laid on over there, but I can slot him in for preliminary talks. After that, perhaps, we'll go and see his ruddy castle. Yes, you're absolutely right, Massimo. Brizzi and I should have a talk."

Chapter 4

Margaret Morning was up early, partly motivated by the necessity of assisting her daughter Melissa's education, which started early, and finished in the same vein. But it was not the only reason. Her late husband, a doctor, had philosophically reasoned that as a human life span was not exceptionally long, time spent sleeping unnecessarily shortened one's enjoyment of it. The brevity of his life had underlined this point. Feeling lost without him, and suffocated by the close, well-meaning attention of family and friends, she'd sat down with Melissa, and decided to put a gap between their solicitous presence and what remained of her nuclear family. France was only a few hours drive away, parts of it being rather closer than the North of England, while Italy restrained them from visiting without stopping them completely. It had thus proved the perfect solution.

Margaret juggled the boiled eggs with a serving spoon into the two eggcups with as much dexterity as she could muster at six-thirty in the morning. She looked at her watch and groaned. Going to the kitchen door, she called up to her daughter.

Melissa finally appeared, fixing her long blonde hair back with a band. There never seemed to be any sense of urgency in the abstracted inertia of youth. They sat together, side by side, at the ancient wooden table, its dark polished surface originally hewn flat by adzes. They didn't converse, concentrating on their breakfast instead.

Melissa took another piece of toast, buttered it lavishly, spreading honey in a generous stroke, before giving half of it to Bastion, the golden Labrador.

By the time they had finished breakfast and washed up, Margaret was getting agitated again, which had the desired effect of encouraging her daughter's progress towards the front door.

Backing the Volvo out on to the track, she waited while Melissa closed the gate, suspiciously eyeing a white Mercedes Benz parked on the flat grass verge a little way ahead. The two men inside it, who were closely studying a map, gave that up in response to her unguarded curiosity, and the car pulled away.

In her side mirror, Margaret continued to watch the receding car heading on its way up to the ruined Castello di Pietra. It seemed rather early in the morning for tourists.

"Mummy," Melissa complained, too suddenly aware of the time, "I'm going to be late again."

Margaret released the handbrake. "Not if I drive like an Italian, you won't. All the bother I've been having. I've just realized they drive like the English - on the left hand side of the road!"

She slipped the car into gear, taking a last glance in her driving mirror towards the castle on the hill, where the two men were now walking towards the entrance. They looked as though they needed more than a boiled egg to start off their day.

-oOo-

Having dropped her daughter off at the school, and parked the car, Margaret found the climb up into the town an exertion. She consoled herself with the thought that the physical effort was dealing with that extra slice of toast. Like her contemporaries, she obviously put too much store on the dictates of fashion magazines, as the occasional passing of one of Sorena's sub-forties, flabby joggers, now demonstrated.

Catching sight of her reflection in a shop window, she felt disappointed in what she saw. A masculine arbiter might likely be enamoured of such a full figure, with curves where it mattered, but full undeniably it was, and to a woman regaining a consciousness of her femininity that was not something to be contemplated with any satisfaction.

Later, standing in Lucia Iannello's store amongst assertive odours of roasted coffee, salami, prosciutto and Parmesan, the reproachful image slipped out of her mind, distracted, as she was, by the range of culinary temptation. Margaret plaintively surveyed the damage already done to her shopping basket, then, looking anxiously at her watch, she gathered the purchases about her and went clattering down the steep, flagstoned streets towards the bar Amadeus.

The bar was already full, but no one was seated except Pamela Jordan who, with a long slim cigarette in one hand, and coffee in the other, intently studied the local newspaper spread before her.

Margaret pushed her way through to greet her friend, ducking under the hovering bird-like gesticulations of stuffed *panini* and cups of *cappuccini*, calling for her own coffee as she passed.

Margaret apologized for her lateness, before sitting down untidily, legs and bags uncertain of their best position.

Pamela waited silently for her to sort herself out. "Are you comfortable now?"

"No!"

"Why is that?" Pamela enquired, folding up her newspaper, sensing that Margaret was still flustered.

"How do you manage to stay so slim?" Margaret inquired peevishly.

"After two failed love affairs I have no responsibilities, therefore, I only eat when I can be bothered, not when I should, or even when I'm hungry. I am a wreck, as you can see, not to be pitied and certainly not to be admired." Pamela stubbed out her cigarette, fanning away the acrid smell.

"You know that the Castello di Pietra's just been sold", she commented.

Margaret sighed. "That's a great pity. Well, it couldn't last for ever, I suppose." She brightened up. "Looking on the credit side, it might mean new friends for Melissa, who I'm sure is getting very bored with her old mum's company. She's the wrong sort of age for bedtime stories now." She moved her handbag so that one of the bar staff could find room for her coffee on the small table.

Pamela eyed her friend sternly. "Monte Petrolla is virtually a nature reserve. The new owners might be absolute philistines."

"That's true," Margaret conceded.

"Have you seen anyone yet?"

"I've noticed some workmen, but I assumed they were carrying out work for the local bank. Then there were two gentlemen there this morning, very early - city types driving a nice car."

"Could be architects or engineers," Pamela noted. "Too early for public servants. Given the lack of political transparency in Sorena you never know exactly what's going on. Having been lumbered with that property as a bad debt some years ago, the bank has to spend a fortune trying to keep what remains of it from falling over. Probably all pie in the sky, this purchase"

"Don't you think that would be a pity, Pamela? It could mean work for some of the people here in the town."

Pamela frowned. "I doubt it. A castle isn't exactly a farmhouse. It would probably be a large construction company from Livorno or Pisa. If it's big money, German or Swiss employing their own architect, they might only use a local *geometra* to push the paperwork about. That won't add up to much." She considered the issue for a moment.

"Right," Pamela urged suddenly and decisively. "Come on, finish your coffee. We'll go and visit Paolo at the museum. He's bound to know for sure."

-oOo-

The curator, Dr. Paolo Guelfa, was an old friend of Pamela's. A dignified, reassuring man, with frame-less spectacles worn on the end of his nose, he stepped out to show them into his office.

When they were all seated round his desk, Guelfa remonstrated with Pamela for not coming to see him more often. "I know. I know," he said, "pressure of business. Anyway, now you're here, how can I help?"

"Margaret lives at Petrolla, just below the Castello di Pietra. We've been hearing rumours."

"Have you now? In the local paper, no doubt. That's usually where they start." Guelfa looked at Margaret steadily over the top rim of his glasses. "The Castello di Pietra, that's a beautiful area in which to live. The winters are cold of course; nevertheless most attractive. How long have you been living there?"

"Three years in June."

"Then you bought it from Gamba, I think. That was

51

about the time the Castello fell into the hands of the Banca Popolare di Sorena. Gamba acquired the land that immediately fronted the castle, selling off the abandoned houses: yours, and the one at the end of the track."

"That's still only three walls and a heap of stones," Margaret remarked. "Nothing's been done yet."

"Eventually it will. The Sorenese are a speculative bunch. They all need a place in the country when they retire, twenty years from whenever. Children to pamper perhaps. Quite normal to have to wait some time for a neighbour round here. Perhaps not so long now, in your case."

"That's exactly what we wanted to know", Pamela explained. "We heard that someone had bought the castle?"

"True enough. I think the bank was glad of the opportunity to dispose of that white elephant. Such is in the nature of things; large ruins tend to stay large ruins. This might be the exception, however. The new owners seem very accommodating. Firstly, the project's for a private residence, which means that the strain on the environment due to infrastructural changes will be minimal. Secondly, they want to do the right thing for an historic monument, incorporating any changes Belle Arti feel necessary. Madonna, they're saints! Seven hundred years after devils pulled it down, angels want to put it up again."

"A foreign buyer, I suppose?" Pamela suggested.

Guelfa laughed. "The senior partner's a businessman from Naples. Don't ask me about that, though. One should never enquire too deeply about a person's wealth. The bank seems satisfied with his funds, which is all that matters. Two other partners are local."

"So there really is a good chance of the project proceeding?" Margaret inquired.

"Hopeful, yes. The *comune's* given permission for site clearance in preparation; so it's probably only a matter of legal loose ends to clear up. All they'll need is a signature on the paperwork. Good luck to them, as long as nothing Etruscan turns up."

"In a mediaeval castle, Paolo?" Pamela queried.

"This is what used to be Etruria, Pamela. Everywhere

is a potential depository of the past. You move a stone you find a stone, one on top of the other. Building blocks of history. The Lombards and Carolingians were economical builders, inclined to carry away, for their own use, the exertions of others. The Castello di Pietra lies on an ancient trading route long since vanished from the maps, but the evidence of a necropolis on the site existing back into pre-Roman times means even earlier civilizations." Guelfa leaned forward conspiratorially. "And then there's the legend."

"What legend?" Pamela challenged. "I've never heard of one."

"Why would you? The Sorenese are a people as close with their legends as they are with their money. You're a foreigner, after all. Who would be inclined to tell you?"

"Then why are you about to tell us?"

Guelfa leant back again in his chair, an amused smile brightening his face. "Because I'm not a Sorenese. My father was from Pisa, where I was born and brought up. Only my mother came from this town. From her I inherited a home, which is convenient. I hear things because I'm family, but my mother used to say that they would only ever tell me half the story, because I'm only half family. She was probably right. I don't like secrecy that tends to keep people ignorant."

"Please go on," Margaret pressed. "Aren't legends often the basis of historical truth?"

Guelfa nodded in confirmation. "That's often so. However, this one suggests something of the fabulous, though I cannot deny certain aspects ring true enough. You've heard of the Cecina family? Well, for us the stuff of legend lies with Paetus Cecina, sentenced to death in 42 AD for conspiring against the Emperor Claudius, and author of a number of historical works, sadly none of which survived. They would have been of far greater worth than all this mumbo jumbo about lost treasures. Anyway, the death of Paetus alone has the making of a legend, for when he hesitated to take his life, in accordance with the sentence, his wife Arria took up the dagger, plunging it into her own heart, declaring, 'See, Paetus, it does not hurt'. But I can see that you are wondering what all this has to do with the Castello di

Pietra? We don't know. The legend only says that Paetus Cecina was buried in the family tomb that occupied a site identified as lying on the hill known as Monte Petrolla. Hmm! Now I see you take notice. Sadly nothing's been found, despite there being enough clues to pinpoint its whereabouts with a fair degree of accuracy."

"I'm sorry, Paolo," Pamela queried. "I know Paetus belonged to an important local family, which suggests he's buried somewhere near here, but so were a lot of others. Why a legend?"

"Many people have lived in hope. Emperors, popes, grand dukes, petty barons and *tombaroli* - the tomb robbers - all have searched in vain. Fortunes to be found you see, Pamela. There has been a considerable amount of conjecture that Paetus was buried alongside his massively accumulated wealth. One has to be sceptical over that; given the nature of man, it would - like the soul - have soon departed from the body. But objects have appeared occasionally. Some are housed here in the museum, helping to keep the legend alive, if nothing else. No one bothers to look any more, but the locals used to gossip to amuse the credulous. I trust we won't see Margaret here combing the hill with a metal detector?"

"I think I agree with you," Margaret assented. "I suspect that whatever remains will be nothing other than mortal!"

Pamela stood up. "Thank you, Paolo. At least Margaret now has a clearer picture regarding what's happening to the castle. We've taken too much of your time. I'm sorry."

"How can that be?" he protested kindly. "It's always a pleasure to see you. Of course, you must bring Margaret again, when you have more time. Perhaps we'll have more to talk about with reference to the castle. They're bound to unearth some new and fascinating material. Let's hope the *soprintendente* has his eye on them."

He accompanied them to the main entrance, where they shook hands, and with a wave they turned away down the street.

Chapter 5

Massimo Finetti had driven south, under the Milan *tangenziale*, into the Place Alfonsin, a zone that the cartographers had included by name but neglected in detail.

Standing by the litter-strewn kerb, he viewed the miserable conformity of the towering tenements, the identical decay that made one building merge into the characterless image of another with a sense of alienation.

Following his instructions, he entered the block nearest to him, looking round for some indication that Block C, apartment number six, was actually in this building. The cold stairwell smelt of sewage, merging with the acrid, sweet caustic mixture of Italian domestic chemicals and human detritus. All he could detect was where an information board had been ripped from the cold cement facings, leaving just a faint impression of its passing.

The weight of the bag in his right hand, holding two extremely valuable Etruscan bronze statues, reminded him of why he was there. However, he would have felt anxious wandering into the antique shops on the Via Monte Napoleone, where, in all probability he would have been no safer. For if these abject slums did not conform readily to a nation's laws, it did not follow that laws were non-existent. Here, they were entirely dependent on the whims of transient autarchs.

From somewhere above his head a sound broke the silence. A sharp metallic click without any resonance, ceasing abruptly, as though a door had swung shut. Finetti glanced up the spiralling stairwell, but could see nothing. He walked up on to the first landing, and was faced with two numberless doors. If he knocked, no one would answer. Behind every paint-chipped, finger-stained entrance, he imagined someone would be eavesdropping. In the silence he could almost hear them listening.

He decided apartment six must be on the third floor, but at a glance the floor seemed very little different, except the bolt of the tumbler lock on the further door rested against its metal catch. He assumed Saxe would be waiting there. Pushing the door open gently with his bag, he stepped closer, blocking it with his foot.

The entrance disclosed a short hall with blank, white walls, recently painted. At the opposite end, a translucent glass-panelled door provided weak internal illumination to this windowless space. From where he stood, the closed door appeared freckled with spots of paint. Courtesy, perhaps, of careless workmen subcontracted at half the price of regular painters. An open door on his left led to the kitchen.

"Saxe," Finetti called out urgently, only half expecting a reply in the affirmative. After a moment's hesitation he stepped inside.

The front door bumped against its metal catch with a click. Finetti spun round, annoyed by his own nervousness.

He turned back to the kitchen. Besides a metal-tubed table with a pale-green Formica top, and a single matching chair under the window, the room was empty. On his right, an open archway allowed access into another room that Finetti presumed could also be reached by the door leading into the hall.

"Saxe," he called out again, a little more loudly now that he was further away from the stairwell, aware of the smell of paint - and something else. Stronger than a cigarette and weaker than a cigar, familiar, yet at the same time elusive. An in-between essence still hanging in the air. Tobacco, yes; and something else that burnt with a pungent odour.

He was halfway into the room now, lowering his bag to the floor, looking round more urgently; filling in the little details, sparse as they were, that explained his situation.

The apartment was clearly unoccupied. Where, then, was Saxe? Where was he supposed to be if he wasn't there to meet him? He considered another apartment, but realized that was idle speculation. This was the apartment. All Finetti wanted to do was to hand over the contents of the bag, as instructed.

Stepping through the arch he instinctively looked to his right. The body had been thrown up against the wall, like a discarded marionette sprawling in the angle beside the door leading into the entrance hall.

He knew it was Saxe. In the distorted manner of his death he might have been unrecognizable, but some little resemblance still remained that, even in their brief acquaintance, leant a glimpse of familiarity on which to hang a name.

Close up, Finetti could now see that the glass was not splashed with paint, but dark spots of congealing blood.

He shut his eyes, opening them again with terrifying suddenness. Saxe's gouged-out eyes hung by their retinal arteries in smears of blood just above the cheekbones. Pale Etruscan eyes; sole witnesses to an incomprehensible savagery.

Finetti gulped back the vomit in his throat, unable to look away from the gaping sockets in that face; or overlook the manner of Saxe's final moments.

He didn't know how much pain a person could suffer before the mind bent itself to its own destruction? His death had been a slow process, exacted with an inhuman attention to the morbid delight of inflicting pain. Saxe had suffered not in a form of retribution, but for some unwholesomely diseased pleasure; a systematic torment continuing long after his persecutors had extracted whatever they had wanted to know.

Each of Saxe's limbs had been torn from its socket; his feet flopped inwards, perfectly flat on the floor; the hands, freed at the upper extremity of each arm from the collarbone, were turned upwards, with the elbows facing outwards.

The victim would have screamed, but nobody would have heard. Any noise would have carried no further than the agony in his mind; his mouth stuffed full of rag that was bound tightly in place with parcel tape. His muffled cries and groans wouldn't even have been heard in the next room. The pungent smell that had struck Finetti as familiar was the scorched, rank aroma of burning flesh. An accident with a soldering iron or a cigarette would produce it just as well. Someone had applied one or other to Saxe's face. It had not been done randomly, in an insane act of violence, but with a measured barbaric severity that had changed the

57

smouldering contours of his face to a bloated cinder, pockmarked with the bubbling, boiling eruptions of ashen weals. One would have been hard stretched to recognize Saxe in that incinerated countenance, if it had not been for the eyes.

Then they had broken his neck.

Finetti at length turned away, suppressing the resurgent nausea. He leant against the wall of the arch for a moment, legs shaking, sucking in deep gasps of air to settle the convulsions in his stomach. His hand moved towards the wall to lever himself upright, only to be jerked away, his brain working on a different level than his consciousness.

Had he touched anything? No, that was something he had to avoid, like a criminal protecting their identity. The police would look for fingerprints, as one of the few clues they were likely to find. Witnesses they would not have, and had learnt not to expect. Not here in the Place Alfonsin.

Escape became a fear in itself. A fear that had never become dormant since Senator Brizzi had arranged their meeting; constantly travelling with him even as he searched for an impossible exit. The consequences of his actions had become inevitable. There was no way out. He understood now that there never had been.

Pulling the front door open awkwardly with his foot, he'd descended to the second floor when he heard the door above bounce against its catch.

A sharp metallic click, without any resonance.

Finetti shuddered. Whoever killed Saxe had been waiting on the landing above. Why hadn't they come for him? He had the statues. Gradually he stopped shaking and took some more deep breaths in repeated efforts to calm himself. He had to make some sense of this confusion. Starting from the beginning. Add it all up so he could see where he was going?

Chapter 6

In Finetti's apartment, the telephone's insistent jangling woke him from a fitful sleep seated in an armchair. He smelt of whisky, with the empty bottle lying on the floor by his foot. At least it had served its purpose, blotting out the panic-stricken images he had failed to shut out by any other means. The camera bag lay unopened, a few metres further away under a table.

He ignored the telephone. After a long while it stopped ringing.

Finetti thought about going to the police, but what implications would there have been in this for Blain, or for those friends of Brizzi to whom silence was the gospel? He'd spent the night wrestling with such questions. Probabilities? Possibilities? Only, the answers continued to elude him.

Raising himself from the chair, he walked unsteadily over to one of the windows hidden by heavy ruby silk-damask curtains. He gripped the thick tasselled cords, and pulled them back.

Outside was an overcast morning, dull with inner-city pollution that settled soon after daybreak into a thick sludgy membrane, drifting in from the encircling motorways. Finetti pinched his eyes in an effort to focus on some sharp contrast that eluded him. He needed to think clearly, and organize himself so that nothing would come as a surprise.

He might not have killed Saxe, but the police were hardly so obtuse as not to realize the possibility that you didn't end up discovering a dead body in an out-of-the-way place without some positive connexion to its fate.

Why had Saxe been murdered? The obvious answer lay under the table. Someone wanted them back, and didn't seem to care how they managed it.

Perhaps Brizzi's changing of partners had been a bad decision. That was something he'd tried to impress on Blain, with little success.

He ought to phone Brizzi. Instead, someone phoned him.

He let it continue ringing for some time before

answering, whereupon he recognized Professor Ferrari's plump, melon-round, Florentine accent.

"Where have you been, Massimo? Where *have* you been?" Ferrari demanded, in an exasperated-sounding rush of words. "Yesterday evening I tried you every hour, right through until eleven o'clock. Then I gave up. Not even an answer phone for company. The police have been to see me. Quite a shock, I can tell you."

"The police?" Finetti enquired anxiously.

"Yes, during the afternoon," Ferrari confirmed. "They brought me a photograph of something you'll be familiar with. A pair of Etruscan votive statues."

Finetti's eyes glanced towards the bag lying under the table. "It can't have been the same statues. Not the very same."

"The very same," Ferrari insisted. "Flown over from the United States by the FBI. Rome has asked for an evaluation, considering they're stolen treasure-trove. The description matches your pair exactly. You should have warned me, prepared me, Massimo. I can give them a verbatim report, right off the shelf. If they knew, they'd lock me up."

"They're not the same statues," Finetti insisted, "I can assure you." He saw the chasm widening. Brizzi had not mentioned that he was trawling for other interested partners. Interested, and perhaps with a grudge.

"What's going on, Massimo?" Ferrari's voice was beginning to carry an uneasy edge.

"That I don't know. The information came in from the United States, you said. Did they tell you in what circumstances?"

"Not in any detail, and I couldn't show any sign of interest, could I?" Ferrari emphasized. "Apparently, a passenger suffered a fatal heart attack on an outbound Alitalia flight to New York. The photograph was found inside a book in his possession. Complicity is a serious matter."

"Nothing can be done about those statues that won't get you into deeper trouble. Just put in your report. That's all they've asked you for, isn't it?"

"But what about the statues? I've had them in my possession. That means finger-prints, Massimo. They'll tie me into this case for sure, I can tell you."

He needed to allay Ferrari's fears. "The police didn't mention any statues, only the photograph. Just be quiet, and listen. I have the statues, so no one will find them, or dust them for fingerprints. This is something you should put right out of your mind. Believe me, saying nothing and being sealed up in gaol is a better alternative than squeaking and being sealed up in the foundations of a motorway flyover. No one knows about the statues except us, so keep it that way."

Finetti was interrupted by the house phone's high-pitched buzz.

"Someone's at the door. I must go. Stay quiet and make your report, *capito*? Good. I'll phone you later."

He replaced the receiver gently, as though someone might be listening.

The metallic buzz came again, more forcibly. He walked over to the intercom by the door, and pressed the microphone button. "*Chi è?*" he asked.

"Captain Pascale of the State police. Signor Finetti?"

Finetti cursed under his breath. How could they have made the connexion between Ferrari and himself?

"Signor Finetti," the intercom squawked more insistently.

"Yes," he answered.

"May we come up?" the captain asked politely.

Finetti released the catch on the front door below, trying to formulate some sort of tactic while they ascended the wide marble stairs to the first floor. Tactic. For what? There could be many reasons for the police wanting to see him.

The doorbell rang, and Finetti let his visitor in.

There was not one, but two. An inspector in uniform carrying a thin briefcase under his arm accompanied Captain Pascale. They shook hands before he showed them into his study.

Pascale was holding a trilby, carefully placed on his knee as he sat down. He had a pallid, lined face, with that polite, ingratiating manner policemen regularly affected, and which fooled no one.

The inspector, who was not in any way memorable, had little to say, but spent his time looking around the room with a practised eye. Finetti saw him notice the bag under the table, then let his gaze pass on.

Captain Pascale was short on preliminary exchanges. "I understand you're a friend of Senator Brizzi?" he enquired.

Finetti had to be careful, not denying it, but distancing himself from Brizzi. "A friend? That's probably a little too generous. A business acquaintance, yes. We have some mutual interests."

The captain exchanged glances with the inspector, who pursed his lips thoughtfully as though these mutual interests might have some significance.

"Mutual interests. Might I ask about those?"

"Of course," Finetti consented. "I have six hundred full-time employees. They all belong to a *sindicato*, mostly the Unione Agricoltori. Senator Brizzi has a strong interest in labour markets and their organization. So do I. Bad labour relations lead to poor productivity. Senator Brizzi is very influential in this field. Quite simply, if I have a problem, he's the person to sort it out."

"Reliable then, you'd say?" The captain, anticipating the answer, rotated the hat on his knee, silently phrasing his next question.

"In the context of my limited experience, yes."

"Of course. Your business takes you away from Milan a lot, I suppose?"

"Yes, I travel a lot."

"Sometimes to Rome?"

"Very often to Rome."

"And when was the last time?"

"Hmm! Two weeks ago. Thursday I believe."

"You met Senator Brizzi?"

"I did. Just for a few minutes. He had something for me, which I collected."

"No time to relax, then?" the captain said, fixing his eyes firmly on Finetti's. "Work managing to overlap with leisure. Golf perhaps?"

These questions were leading somewhere, in incremental steps. The unravelling of something Finetti couldn't yet understand. He had little idea of what Brizzi did in his spare time, only that it would hardly be a middle class-diversion like golf.

"No, we don't share similar leisure interests. The occasional dinner together, perhaps. More of a convenience after a meeting. Not always official, but always related to business."

"I see. You're not married are you, Signor Finetti?"

"No." Finetti was guarded now.

"Did you ever meet the senator's wife?"

"No, I never had the pleasure."

"Never mix business with pleasure, they say." The captain smiled softly. "These dinners, you mention - restaurant and a club afterwards?"

"*Caffè* afterwards. Sometimes a *gelato*."

The captain gave a second smile. Just a hint to show that he was reading Finetti perfectly, just as Finetti was reading him.

"Coffee and an ice cream. Just the two of you?"

Finetti shook his head slowly, almost derisively at the inference. "Our meetings are always a time for delicate negotiations. Witnesses are unwelcome for a number of reasons. I think you'll understand what I mean."

The captain pressed on, ignoring this negative answer. "Not a ladies' man, by all accounts, the senator?"

"I don't think I follow."

"If there were only the two of you, I mean. He never brought along a companion? No, I suppose not, being a married man. You might have, though."

"As a sweetener, you mean? It's done - but not a facility I've ever had cause to provide. Entertainment of that nature suggests a less than professional approach to the health of ones business. May I ask you a question, Captain?"

Pascale nodded.

"Can you explain the purpose of this enquiry?"

The captain looked at him intently, letting the pause work on Finetti's inner concerns. "Yes," he replied finally. "We're investigating the murder of Senator Brizzi, which occurred in - how can I put it - somewhat unusual circumstances."

-oOo-

Finetti rolled and unrolled distractedly the piece of paper

he held between his fingers. He sat at his desk trying to reorganize the sequence of recent events, in much the same manner he had done so for the last twenty-four hours. The death of Brizzi only added another dimension, and he was aware that the answer to part of it rested only a few metres from where he sat.

After Captain Pascale and the inspector had left, he had tried to make contact with Blain. A fruitless hour on the telephone produced no information as to his whereabouts. For over forty years he had discussed his problems with Blain. Now he had an even greater need to discuss his fears.

Finetti's own position had become vulnerable, since everything was being channelled through him. After all, he had possession of the statues that weren't going to be quietly forgotten. Even if Brizzi hadn't talked, he might have still left some clue. If he had, someone would likely find it.

Opening the drawer of his desk, Finetti removed a sheet of notepaper placing it carefully on his blotter. Picking up his fountain pen he began to write a letter to Blain, in a neat, but hurried hand.

When he had finished, he tucked the letter into an envelope, slipped on his jacket and descended into the Corso Magenta, heading past the terracotta-and-brick Santa Maria dell Grazie, and then the adjoining Dominican convent refectory where Leonardo's obliterated and ruined quasi-tempera painting of the Last Supper demonstrated the price of invention. From there he crossed into the Via Cardoso towards the railway station. He posted his letter first class, returning slowly against the hungry crowds proceeding on their way to lunch.

The aroma of fresh coffee drifting out of the open doors of a bar made Finetti stop. First purchasing the conservative 'Il Giornale', and a day old 'Telegraph' from the newspaper shop next door, he entered the bar ordering an *espresso* with a glass of iced water. Sitting down at one of the small tables, he distracted himself by leafing through the pages, checking for things he shouldn't miss: reminding himself to study them later when he had more time. But miss something he nearly did.

An item, obviously scraped in before the editor had put the newspaper to bed. A footnote at the bottom of the page. Too late to become a news story of its own, it reported the unexpected death of Sir Maxwell Blain in a car accident close to the Spanish border.

-oOo-

No matter how many times Finetti mulled over these events, one thing always stood out. Brizzi's partner, Paba, must know that he was the temporary custodian of the statues. There would have been no need to search indiscriminately for them. He would have known exactly where to come.

More than ever Finetti wanted to be rid of these statues that now appeared more Jonah than Janus. But not actually having the figures had made no difference to the survival of anyone. As he couldn't now return them to Brizzi, he must return them to Paba instead.

Finding Paba's number through the telephone enquiry service only led to continual fencing with receptionists and secretaries, who eventually wore him out. Growing tired of their unnecessary evasiveness that represented the habitual practice of public organizations or criminal associations, Finetti finally asked the most sympathetic-sounding ear to deliver an urgent message.

Thirty minutes later his telephone rang.

"Finetti?" The voice on the other end of the telephone was coldly impassive.

"Paba?" Finetti asked, his voice a hoarse whisper.

"You phoned about Janus. What about Janus?"

"I have them both. I need to know what to do with them."

"What would you like to do with them?" The voice spoke carefully, giving nothing away.

"What do you mean?" Finetti's voice rose. "They're yours. I don't want them. I don't want to end up like Brizzi and Saxe, or..." Finetti's voice trailed away. Paba might not know about Blain.

"Or?" the voice asked.

Paba didn't miss anything, clearly questioned everything. To Finetti, he sounded like the sort of man who would trap you with words - even kill you with them.

"The investor Brizzi was angling for," Finetti continued, in an unsteady voice. "Something's happened to him as well. I read it in the newspaper. A vehicle accident. I can't believe it. It seems that leaves only the two of us."

There was a distinct pause before Paba spoke again. "In that case we must consider ourselves lucky. However, I understand your concern. You must try not to let the coincidental develop into the intentional."

"Coincidental!" Finetti caught his breath.

"Such things are unfortunate," Paba said. "Nevertheless, try to be rational instead of hysterical. You are sounding overwrought, liable to make mistakes - thus making life difficult for all of us."

Finetti fell silent for a moment, before further voicing his fears. "I don't want anything to do with you. Nor anyone else, either. I never wanted to be mixed up in this in the first place. All it's done is brought me trouble and now I just want to be rid of it. Can you understand? I want nothing to do with you," and, in a final whisper added, "nothing at all."

Paba's reply was sharp. "A little late to change your mind." Then his tone moderated: "But I do understand. You would be better absolved of all your responsibilities."

"What do you mean?" Finetti asked, feeling the panic rising again.

"The Janus pair, they serve no purpose to you except to excite a dangerous anxiety. You must return them."

"Yes. You'll collect them?" Finetti enquired eagerly

"Well, now," Paba considered. "I'll have them collected, but not from your apartment. Nevertheless, you'll be happier with somewhere familiar. Brizzi was telling me you have a bottling factory at Lodi. Is that correct?"

"Yes."

"Perfect," Paba said. "I suggest you go there this afternoon. Take the statues with you and leave them on the back seat of your car. Whether it's locked or not makes little difference. I'll have them collected, and then you'll be free of further responsibility. We're agreed?"

"I can do that." Finetti mumbled. "But at what time

should I be there? And what about the book? Tell me. What am I supposed to do with the book?"

There was only the dialling tone. They were agreed.

-oOo-

Finetti headed south through the suburbs of Milan on the old via Emilia, towards Melegnano to Tavazzano, where he turned off for Lodi. Finetti preferred this quieter route.

However, he didn't feel at ease.

The camera bag holding the statues, along with Brizzi's book and the photograph, had been placed on the back seat, and thus out of his line of vision. It still managed to remain a constant distraction.

There were no reserved places or executive parking lots at the factory, everyone being obliged to find the most convenient available space. Swinging in between two other vehicles, Finetti applied the handbrake, released the seat belt and leant back to shut his eyes.

Just for a moment.

Finetti hadn't realized how tired he'd become, just sitting there, letting the sun's warmth press heavily on his closed eyelids. The comfort drew him in, spreading a delicious sense of buoyancy through his tired limbs. In the distance he heard the familiar rattle of empty bottles loaded on a forklift truck, and the hiss of compressed air as the factory's rubber doors opened and closed.

A few minutes waiting here in the sun would make all the difference, before he climbed out and made his way to the office. He only barely sensed the worries of his last few days soothingly slipping into emptiness, just pleased to relax and let them go.

As he drifted deeper, he remained unaware of the back door being eased open, a slight motion inside the car, before the door gently closed again.

Chapter 7

Gower's mood remained gloomy. His request for the installation of a probe microphone and a telephone tap on the Cambodian diplomat's Kensington apartment had not been smiled upon by the Home Secretary.

Eldon looked up from the Nightingale file, trying to divert the other man's low spirits. "Your man Charlie seemed a mine of information?"

Leaning against the radiator, Gower grumbled. "He may be, but he's a warning to every second generation business man."

"He gave the impression of sounding successful, once." Eldon commented.

"Sad story." Gower explained. "Charlie's father founded the Western Wine Emporium. Since it was a boom time for plonk, Charlie went all over the world buying up a whole vintage, until his father had a stroke. Charlie wasn't a maverick or anything like that, but he was a bit of an expert on the seamier side of the trade: what went in and what stayed out. Unhappily, his management style let him down. With outlet sales at saturation point, the only way to keep moving was by expansion. The banks persuaded him to invest in more branches, knowing well that when the downturn came they could bleed him to death. Some people manage to pick themselves up, and make a new life. Not Charlie, though. He had access to a lot of bottles somewhere: hidden cellars the bailiffs had never found. After that, it was downhill all the way into tippling anything that kept him senseless. His sister looks after him, but she's married to a circuit judge, so understandably it's at arms length. Nobody wants a soak hanging around the house, getting argumentative with their friends. But, as the saying goes, one man's meat is another man's poison. A good pair of ears, no matter who they're attached to, can often be put to good use. Charlie gets to know all sorts of things. Useful things, overheard in bars where no one takes much notice of a drunk."

Gower pushed himself off the radiator, and returned to his desk, followed by a faint odour of hot flannels. He picked up the phone, almost intuitively.

"Ah, Maurice," he said, slumping into his chair, "how is Miss Veronica this morning? ... Blossoming. First sign of spring. What did you want anyway? ... Eldon, hmm! Flavour of the month, you say? ... You didn't say. ... Oh, best behaviour for once. I'll tell him."

Gower gestured with his thumb to his office companion. "On your way. Man upstairs is asking for you."

-oOo-

Tate, looking busy, with a ballpoint pen clamped between his teeth, inclined his head towards the door apologetically. Eldon knocked, and then peered round the edge of the door to see if he was to go in.

Prinn nodded assent. "Shut the door, Rex," he said, scribbling a few final notes with his fountain pen in the wide column of a document, before closing its cover.

If the serious note in his voice was anything to go by, then Eldon foresaw a crisis looming.

"Two things, Rex. Firstly, I'm shortly going to be absent from the department for a little while, and probably out of touch. It's somewhat premature, leaving you without proper support, but one of our operations, Necropolis, seems to be coming to the boil. I've briefed Chief Superintendent Hart to liaise with you temporarily. I think you'll get on very well. Secondly, there's this."

Prinn handed Eldon a late edition of a daily newspaper. The pink-highlighted article seemed to be of no immediate interest, reporting the death of Sir Maxwell Blain, killed in a car crash near Solsona in the Sierra Del Cadi Mountains. It was a common enough tragedy in mountainous country of a car driving into a lorry on a narrow road.

Eldon looked quizzically down at Prinn.

"The F.O. has just sent this report." Prinn shuffled through some papers on his desk. "The Spanish police have managed to establish that the brakes on Blain's car failed after the master cylinder was ruptured by a small remotely activated explosion. It happened conveniently on a blind corner, where a Scania truck pushed him over the edge into oblivion. Whoever had their finger on the button must have been sitting watching on another mountain. The Spanish police aren't releasing any information prior to discussions with Special Branch. By the by. One of Blain's American associates, Kirby Rich, was extradited last year from Grenada to the United States on corruption charges, and sentenced to five years imprisonment. Within two months he was dead. US sources indicated that he was into plea-bargaining on appeal by implicating Blain, and identifying his shady investments in Eastern Europe, and North America. At the time it was considered that Blain had contracted Rich out. Now, Blain is dead, so did somebody have a contract on him as well? Time, I think, to reassess everything we have."

"Do we, by any chance, know if Blain had any business links with the Soviets where he might have upset someone?"

"None established. Russia is a farrago at the moment and there's no telling what angle anyone's coming from. If Nightingale's slipped out into the private sector we'll have a lot of trouble on our hands. I suggest you run through the Blain documents, but start afresh, as though there's no history. Forget the Nightingale file. History's about the past, Rex. Even Blain is a step in the wrong direction."

-oOo-

Eldon ran Blain through the computer: corporate movements, mergers and overseas acquisitions, financial trading, any economic links with suspicious groups he might have engineered over that particular period.

A personal file indicated that Blain had been subject to a formal investigation procedure, meaning someone, somewhere, had suspected him of doing something questionable. The three subject headings didn't disclose the manner of these deceptions. Special clearance was required to open the file, recording the reader's name, so no one could peek at it out of curiosity.

Eldon typed in his identity number and day code, tapping the mouse impatiently until the 'read only' file opened, listing his name and number along with three others.

Two involved routine enquiries, cross-referencing material, the other referred to an Irish/Italian joint stock company through which, allegedly, money was transferred to Blain's European interests before being finally deposited in Swiss and English bank accounts. At this point the Serious Fraud Squad seemed to have run into the sand. They could only be pro-active up to a point.

Eldon clicked on to information outlining Blain's company structure. There was a tortuous network of interlocking arrangements with the usual hidden partners: acquisitions and mergers, buy-backs and bankruptcies, providing a long list of places to look. He obviously had a firm grasp on statistical probabilities. Blain had developed risk management into something of an art. Eldon continued to scroll through until his eye caught the name, Italvini.

He recalled that a delivery vehicle was off-loading cases stamped 'Italvini', in large black letters blazoned across the Italian flag, outside the Anglo Italian Wine Company as he'd left. When Gower returned to their office, Eldon asked him to put the word out for another meeting with Charlie. He needed a little more than the information held in the Trade and Industry files.

-oOo-

Whether Charlie was hard up, or by mere coincidence, Eldon didn't ask, but he made an appearance on the very first evening.

Charlie ordered his pint, took a first long mouthful, paused, then finished off the rest in a matter of seconds. Belching indiscriminately, he was pushed aside by some aggressive new customers with crew cuts and head tattoos, then walked shakily to the door, and out into the night.

Eldon didn't follow. For some reason, this moment couldn't be right. He looked at the customers round him, mostly young and foreign: Near East, Far East, places in Africa that most people wouldn't have heard of unless they were philatelists or social scientists. Too many persecuted, too many persecutors, either sharing a tip on the dogs or plotting to blow up a government - all on the run and washed up in the King's Road.

Eldon finished his beer. Gower was right: if there was something to know, Charlie was bound to have come across it.

Out on the street, traffic swished by on the wet roadway, illuminated by shop windows and car headlights. On the pavement few dawdled, hurrying by with collars turned up.

Eldon stood in a darkened doorway of an empty shop, watching their progress, or perhaps for a face he might recognize in a crowd. He finally turned left towards the sports centre, and headed into the next public house along his route.

Buying his routine half pint of pale ale, Eldon found a seat by the door. A pretty young thing, with too bright a lipstick, shifted along a bench invitingly. He smiled politely and sat down on the chair opposite. From somewhere, Charlie turned up with his half empty glass and the shakes. He sat down, rather in the manner that he would fall down if he didn't. The pretty young thing now decided she had better things to do.

"Gower said you were out punting again?" There was an additionally hoarse quality to Charlie's voice, his watery eyes mere slits in a blue-mottled face. "Still chasing phantom crus are you?"

Eldon nodded. "I'm still interested in wine, Charlie. Probably red herrings, too. I need some information on another imported Italian wine. What do you know about Italvini?"

Charlie downed his glass. "You're a joker, you are." His eyes opened fractionally wider. "Why are you messing me about?"

Eldon shook his head. "Wrong, Charlie, I never mess anyone about."

The razor in the edge of Eldon's voice might have made Charlie reconsider, or more likely that he'd already forgotten the source of his outrage - until he remembered Italvini.

"Crap!" he spat out, a dribble of saliva running from

the corner of his mouth.

"As in dice, or in crapulence due to intemperance?" Eldon asked drily.

"As in Italvini," Charlie replied. "Didn't you ask me previously about Verolino?"

"A long time ago. Let's stick to Italvini." Eldon didn't want him to be sidetracked.

Charlie looked doubtful for a moment, searching his memory. "Mass-produced bilge for the plonkers market, where they don't know the difference between a grape and a gooseberry. You can sell them anything, even fermented vomit."

Eldon raised an eyebrow, but didn't interrupt.

"They're the sort of company who'd buy anything. Any grape from anywhere; in any quantity; labelling it with what you fancy. Chianti, Barbaresco, Merlot; whatever you want from wherever you want. A nice Bordeaux or Burgundy? No trouble. Popular among *trattorie* needing a cheap house wine." After this extra verbal exertion, Charlie ground to a halt.

"Anywhere else besides restaurants?" Eldon prompted.

Charlie's head had slumped on to his chest, his bottom lip jutting out, and his glass was empty.

Eldon went to the bar, and reluctantly ordered another pint.

The barman pulled his tap in a disapproving manner, not for any moral reason, but for the anticipated complication at closing time when getting Charlie out would be a job for the devil. There was nothing more discordant in a publican's life than an irritable drunk.

Eldon set the pint down in front of Charlie, urging him to continue. "Who else beside these bargain-basement *trattorie*?"

There was a long silence before Charlie answered. "God, I need this drink." He drank deeply, collecting his thoughts again. "Dodgy supermarkets - to them reliability means availability. Continuity is more important than quality. You can't sell quality if it's out of stock. Suits their customers, too. Any one with half a wit knows you can't produce a decent wine for no money, meaning you have to tie up a lot of capital. The whole cost of production for two, three or more years. Do you know how much an oak barrique barrel costs? Four hundred pounds. Speeds things up, but expensive when they only last a couple of years. Managers kid themselves they can make a bundle by bulk buying liquid, special price for the lot. They could always see you coming, ordering up another tanker from Apulia. That's the name of the game: marketing. Just convince the punters you've found the Promised Land. New Zealand today, Bulgaria tomorrow, Chile the day after. As good as Bordeaux, at Bolivian prices. The trick is knowing the difference between honest wine and a *pasticcio* squirted full of acorn juice, or laced with Ada."

"Ada?" Eldon enquired.

"Aliphatic dihydric alcohol. Glycol."

Eldon noted Charlie didn't even stumble over the words.

"Ah, yes," Eldon said. "But Italvini just sells vinegar, you say? Not even good vinegar, perhaps, but unlikely to stay liquid in the deep freeze. What makes an old established business like the Anglo Italian Wine Company stock vinegar, when supposedly dealing exclusively in fine wines?"

Charlie grunted irritably. "The Anglo Italian Wine Company just pass it through their books as a favour for one of their important customers who has a need for both ends of the market. They won't even look at the paperwork, only the bottom line. The bilge goes in at one door and out of another. Have you finished?"

"I suppose I have. Bit of a dull lead that." Eldon rose and opened his newspaper. Slipping two ten-pound notes inside, he pushed it across to Charlie. "There you go. Double your money."

Charlie looked up at him, and for the first time Eldon thought he saw just a hint of a smile on that liverish face.

"Always saves the best bit for last, does Charlie." He raised his glass, drinking deeply while Eldon waited. for him to finish.

"They own Cantina di Verolino, don't you know - the one you were inquiring about before. That crap owns the best Barolo estate in Piedmont." He shook his head

74

sadly, as though the thought was enough to drive a man to drink.

-oOo-

"Run me through that again," Prinn said.

"Only a tentative idea sir. Let's say Nightingale left Port Said for the proposed target, leaving behind a very tidy apartment. Tidy except for an empty Italian wine bottle from an estate linked to Sir Maxwell Blain through a stake in the holding company, Italvini. Subsequently, Sir Maxwell is pushed off a mountain in Spain. Confirmation from Naval Intelligence of a Primore'ye-class trawler passing through the Straits of Gibraltar suggest that Nightingale might have gone ashore earlier, somewhere along the Spanish coast."

"And there's some significance about this wine bottle?"

"Yes. To me it appears a sort of gesture. Here is a space professionally wiped clean, then, someone adds a smudge. A fingerprint. Almost arranged so that you can't miss it. Only about two and a half thousand bottles of Cantina di Verolino are produced. It's a connoisseur's wine, normally bought by the case, which means about two hundred distinguished clients - probably less. Are we looking at an oversight, or a suggestion? If someone's genuinely pointing a finger, they must know the chances of us getting a client list are high."

Prinn agreed. "As a non-betting man I generally need a lot of convincing, but I have to admit this aspect does have a genuine feel about it. It's worth pursuing. This agent Nightingale exists, but does not exist. That has always been our problem. There has never been a positive trace, or even an indication of a trace. Now, you're suggesting we have a reliable piece of evidence that can be linked to a proven source that we almost fall over. Presented to us on a plate? That strikes me as a funny thing. And a dangerous one if Nightingale does turn out to have been the occupant of that apartment. We shall need to be careful, finding out why someone wanted us to know, because in this case, with someone 'pointing a finger', it's very likely to be round a trigger."

Chapter 8

Prinn sat finishing his coffee, looking out of the bay window of his apartment on to the bay windows of similar Kensington apartments

Later, he carried his two suitcases out of the bedroom, and deposited them by the door. He checked his travel documents and money; wandered through his apartment on a last inspection, tapping the old Fortin barometer in the hall that, as far as he knew, had not risen or fallen in his lifetime.

On answering the house phone, the sound of Rachel's voice restored the humour that had earlier deserted him. Releasing the catch of the main entrance, Prinn left the apartment door open while he fetched his hat from the bedroom, returning to find her standing in the doorway.

"Are you ready," she enquired, "because I'm double-parked?"

Prinn kissed her on the cheek, and then pulled her gently into the hall to kiss her on the lips.

Lips were so erotic, Prinn mused. Soft and full of sensations, like a fragrance drawing you towards the inevitable desire. Full of suggestions.

"I suppose you've got to go straight home?" he asked, in a veiled reference to their last meeting.

Rachel shook her head. "No, but you, sir, have a plane to catch."

"I'm almost ready." Prinn reluctantly acquiesced, looking at his watch. "I just need to make a telephone call to Morefield's in Oxford. Redfern should be there by now. Shouldn't take a minute." He quickly dialled the number, and sat tapping the table while it connected.

"Good morning. Is Mister Redfern available? - He isn't. - No. No matter. Could you ask him to forward the two volumes of the 1820 Petrarch to me in Tuscany? - Yes, that's right. By Luigi Vannini of Prato. Commander Prinn. You have my address on file. Many thanks."

Prinn replaced the handset. "Where was I? Ah, yes. Now about a later flight?"

Rachel shook her head again. "Sorry, chum I've checked. Not even steerage. Everyone's going your way except me. Later, means tomorrow."

"Oh, well," Prinn sighed, "I must pin my hopes on the Petrarch. Libraries are congenial to celibates." He stood up, straightened his tie in the mirror, and placed the trilby firmly on his head.

-oOo-

BA Flight 2601 from Gatwick to Pisa landed on time. Collecting his cases from the carousel, Prinn passed through the customs and made for the airport concourse.

The face Prinn searched for sat directly opposite the arrivals entrance, reading the L'Unita newspaper and smoking a crooked Tuscan cigar in a stubby black holder. The hands holding the newspaper were large, of a coarseness possessed by a builder or a farmer used to the roughness of stones or vines. He was not so tall as he was round, wearing an old but not neglected suit, with a white shirt open at the neck. His sturdy black boots were tightly laced and well polished

Seeing Prinn, a smile creased his spherical brown face, rippling across the top of his baldhead. He folded the newspaper untidily, half stuffing it into his jacket pocket before shaking Prinn's hand firmly.

He took one of the cases from Prinn, and they walked out into the frail sunshine, under a sky in tints of chalky blue, the air agitated by only the slightest trace of a breeze.

Scillone drove the short wheel-based Land Rover out on to the *superstrada* heading for Florence. Both sat in silence for a few kilometres before Prinn turned to the driver. "Did you get my message, Ettore?"

The man nodded, took the cigar holder from his mouth as though he was going to say something, and then replaced it firmly between his teeth before nodding once more. He would never be able to say anything again after his larynx had been burnt away by oil of vitriol: an alternative form of justice inflicted on a prosecution witness providing evidence in a Mafia trial twenty years before. The men of honour, a Carabinieri officer pointed out, had chosen to be lenient with him.

Prinn was not inclined to raise his voice above the drumming of the vehicle, abandoning their one-sided conversation while acquiring as comfortable and restful a position as possible on the firm squabs.

Prinn had known Ettore Scillone for a long time. He had hardly left his prep school for Winchester when his father had bought the Villa Lazzi. His Italian mother, the Marchesa Abbate D'Aberrello, had declared it providential that the large villa was situated next to the farm of the Scillone family, since so large a property needed willing hands to tend it.

Scillone was the youngest son, entitled to a hereditary share in a farm that was not, in a modernizing economy, large enough to support more than one family, so he'd packed his bags and left home to make his own way in the world.

He had worked in a bar in Rome, before moving south to Bari as gardener for a southern businessman. The job proved to have little future, his employer dying shortly afterwards from a shotgun blast. Scillone had identified the killer as Fausto Paba, subsequently sentenced to thirty years imprisonment, while Scillone himself was sentenced to silence.

Coming back to Sorena, now a brooding, embittered man, he'd found employment with Prinn's parents, keeping the gardens of the Villa Lazzi somewhere near the standards of the utopian ideal they'd achieved.

Scillone eventually left the superstrada, passing through a clutter of small towns before escaping on to the state highway that followed a flat, river-less depression running between steep valleys. Prinn had closed his eyes against the sun, opening them only as the vehicle swung sharply right to begin its climb up a twisty metalled road through a low forest of holm oaks. They continued climbing for eight kilometres, into the long line of hills that swept south down into the Maremma. Occasionally they broke out on to a plateau, with the road skirting perilously round it, giving a view of folded misty valleys surrounding protruding hills, resembling islands tinged with mauve from the sinking sun.

At the top of a small rise, Scillone turned the vehicle

into a private road next to a crumbling stuccoed barn.

Stopping at a pair of iron gates set in algae-covered walls almost disappearing under the weight of smothering vegetation, Scillone pulled on the handbrake. Prinn touched his arm to restrain him, indicating that he'd walk the rest of the way up to the house.

Stepping down stiffly from the vehicle, Prinn opened the gates, waving Scillone through and along the dark line of cypress trees, parted by a narrow strip of blue sky, running up to the Villa Lazzi itself.

The gates had a rusty, damascene-weathered surface that only time and the elements can create; they sighed open on ancient hinges before bumping softly against the moss-padded walls, evoking an unfathomable wealth of history.

Prinn had swung on them as a boy; ridden his bicycle into them once and broken an arm; pressed Tiziana Garipoli's young body against them with the weight of his own, holding on to their strong bars in case his trembling legs gave way.

He recalled the departure of the former owners, the Adami family, whose predecessors had lived there from the seventeenth century, only to relinquish the estate when, without any land, it served little purpose to their own needs, and its upkeep was only a drain on their dwindling fortunes.

His father had made his last journey through these gates in a black-lacquered catafalque suspended comfortably on leaf springs, drawn by two black horses with restless black plumes. A sombre spectacle; yet as exquisitely dramatic as his father had been. Under a pedimented canopy lay an Empire-style faux chest shrouding his coffin, ornamented with gold-leafed olive branches, and illuminated by the fluttering flames of tapers held in iron brackets, their heavy kerosene fumes lingering in the cool evening air.

Prinn tapped a heavy stone to one side of the drive. While at Oxford, he'd hitchhiked one spring all the way through Italy to the Villa Lazzi with Curly Zilliacus. The young American had stopped - Prinn paused for a second to look round, sensing he stood roughly at the same spot - covered his eyes with both hands, and when asked what he was doing, Curly said he was fixing the view in his memory so that he would never forget it.

Prinn felt a sudden bitterness surface, its pointless rancour defeated by his inability to alter anything; to metamorphize history from the thread of life to which Curly presently hung.

He continued towards the villa, wondering if, beneath his friend's mute emptiness, somewhere trapped in the unconscious part of his mind, Curly might still hold an image of this view that had remained unchanged through the intervening years. Some small thing left to him by Nightingale within the empty, traumatized shell he inhabited.

That was all in the past now, leaving Prinn to make what he could of the present.

The tall slender trees channelled a view of the house, an ochre-stuccoed Renaissance villa waiting quietly for the spring jasmine that would threaten electricity and telephone cables alike, filling the air with a heady perfume long before the building itself emerged from the avenue. The villa took the southern sun, so that visitors came in from the side that had retained a small portion of a frescoed facade: faint brown depictions of pillars and panels juxtaposed between the faded blue shuttered windows under their moulded drip stones. The terracotta of the roof, and the huge vases on the terrace, had faded to a pale biscuit, and in places almost to the colour of cream. The largest vase, standing by the arched portico, he had helped old grandfather Scillone stitch back together again with wire after his mother had reversed her already battered Lancia saloon into it. The little roofed chimneys bristled like so many pagodas at every angle; though only one retained a black, sooty appearance, leaving the others, through lack of use, to be scoured clean by the wind and rain.

The villa was mellow, even a little sad, as though still waiting for a sight of the long-lost Adami brothers who had gone with Garibaldi to Sicily and never returned. Their joint portrait still hung in the hall: both of them slim bodied and effete, but strong in spirit, filled with the romantic notion of a united Italy.

Prinn reached the terrace, to find Scillone waiting

patiently, with the two cases resting on the gravel drive. He now picked them up with his big hands, preceding Prinn into the house.

The large hall was dark, lit by a feeble bulb inside an octagonal iron-and-glass shade adorned with griffins that made it seem disproportionately large for its purpose.

Signora Scillone stood waiting for them in front of a chestnut coffer that rose as high as her waist. She was a small beetle-brown woman with black hair shining as lustrously as burnished ebony, neatly complimenting the crisply pressed black cotton of her attire. Prinn bent down to kiss her cheeks, and was regaled by the odour of rosemary oil and wild oregano, after which she fussed around him as though he was one of her own - which in a way, he was. Satisfied that his needs were met, she took herself upstairs to make sure his bed was properly aired.

Followed by Scillone, Prinn entered the library, a long room holding his father's extensive collection of books, documents and maps covering the region's history. The tall shuttered French windows allowed access on to the south-facing terrace.

Prinn dropped into a chair that seemed to absorb his body readily into its softness, the cushions giving way gently under his weight with an almost inaudible sigh.

"If the Castello di Pietra's been sold, who are the new owners?" Prinn asked. "Who's rich enough in Sorena to underwrite a venture of that sort?"

Scillone jammed his cigar holder between his teeth, his round tanned ball of a head nodding fiercely at the question.

"No one round here except the bank, and they've just disposed of the ruin." Prinn rubbed the stubble on his chin thoughtfully. "I know this is the worst possible moment, with a great deal for you to do in the garden but, if it's possible, I'd appreciate some help, Ettore. What do you say?"

Scillone knew it would be difficult to find the time, given the essential preparations for the summer, but he would not allow that to stand in his way. Prinn was, after all, the only man who had learnt to share his thoughts.

81

The fact that he continued to be a loyal and committed communist did not clash with this deep affection for a man whom he knew to be rich and successful. He also had enough sense to know they were equals only in those rights that the legal definition of their citizenship enshrined in the laws regulating their liberties. Therefore, there was little use wasting his time in regretting this social discrimination. He was a man of the soil, and if in the past that had meant you were low enough to feel the foot on your neck, now you were tall enough to feel that they were only standing on your toes. You might need to grit your teeth to do so, but you could look them straight in the eye.

Scillone removed the stub of his long-extinguished cigar, placed the remains carefully in a matchbox, pushed the holder into his top pocket, and pulled himself up a chair.

Chapter 9

Eldon sat in Gower's office searching for leads that would enable him to open a line of inquiry into Sir Maxwell Blain's recent movements. He felt he was getting nowhere.

Blain was known to have been en route for the Ligurian coast. This, in itself, didn't suggest a great deal - possibly a preferred route to Savona before joining the fast *autostrada* to Turin, which passed close to the Cantina di Verolino estate at Barolo, or further on to Milan.

The transfer of a large sum of money to an Italian transport company, Traslochi Ital, provided rather more interest. Ostensibly, it appeared as a loan through a bank in Nassau, identified as a branch of Blain's clearing bank, Societa Credita Vernier in Switzerland. Credita Vernier was responsible for transferring money in the form of fiduciary deposits, to be eventually recycled by Blain in his international business interests. The transport company was a subsidiary of Italvini, in which he had significant holdings.

He had a small foothold in another Italian company, Caparra, whose expanding commitments might need financing. A large Calabrian construction company with strong underworld connexions, Caparra had undertaken a legitimate joint venture with F.I.Electronics, an English company based in Yeovil, part of the giant Axmar group made up of high-technology industries.

The Italian authorities had a keen interest in Caparra, who appeared to have been active in 'fixing' a large development in Tropea, now under investigation. Despite Blain's reputation, it was hardly likely that he would commit funds there.

Eldon fretted at getting bogged down in the minutiae. With Prinn out of the country he sensed the return of an old uncertainty. His employment called for a type of specialism that the police didn't have - and by reading Nightingale's case file, he understood why.

Time then, Eldon decided, to start from scratch. Put it to Chief Superintendent Hart, and see how Prinn's contingency plan would work out.

-oOo-

Hart proved to be an elastic man, accommodating due to his flexibility, representing the ideal person to form a buffer between his chief and the frustrated agitation of staff grown too wise to push the bounds of personal initiative beyond that of the official line.

As an experienced policeman, he couldn't remember an outsider who'd ever proved a reliable insider, so Eldon's arrival he; therefore, viewed with a great deal of suspicion. Eldon had been drafted in from the enemy, as far as he could judge, and Prinn's instructions to handle this interloper with circumspection hadn't improved his insight into the basis of Eldon's terms of reference. Which camp was the man supposed to be in? Assassins, he would assume, were used to getting involved in something more lethal than works of art. With Operation Necropolis long past its eleventh-hour, the prospect of a distracting diversion would call for all of his unquestionable tact. Eldon might seem to be just the sort of specialist to glue shady government scoundrels to the post, but the effort might still forfeit responsible detective work. As such it worried him almost as much as where the noble knight and criminal Sir Maxwell Blain fitted in. That was, for the moment, anyone's guess.

"We need a change of direction," Eldon indicated.

"Persuade me," Hart said in a clearly dissenting voice.

"Blain, not to put too fine a point on it, is a dead end. All we'd be doing is chasing shadows. Along the way he wandered off course, meeting people who had nothing to do with the Office of Fair Trading. We need to discover why someone saw fit to push him off a mountain - for which any suspects would all have cast iron alibis. So why waste time asking them?"

"Granted", Hart agreed. "He seems to have had some funny pals, but, from what I read, Blain obviously had underworld business. If he was dabbling in Mafia waters, perhaps positioning himself for some sort of a takeover of this firm, Caparra, then it could add up to an

84

assassination profile."

"It could," Eldon acknowledged.

"What's that supposed to mean?"

"A coincidence," Eldon explained. "Blain's murdered in Spain, but hardly because of a takeover. Caparra's stock value is disproportionately large against the amount of money Blain was moving into Italy. Hardly a target firm ripe for acquisition, either. Anyway, Caparra's voting shares are tightly controlled by a financial consortium, therefore not accessible to Blain."

"Well, I'm given to understand you're the analyst," Hart conceded grudgingly.

"Blain, by all accounts, was a ruthless business man," Eldon continued. "He must have made many enemies. If Caparra's nothing more than a blind alley, we'll waste too much time investigating it. Italvini's arguably more interesting, since that's where the money is - for the moment. Perhaps young Tate could conjure up some figures on Italvini, along with a profile on its MD, Finetti. Starting with their assets."

"And what will you be doing?" Hart asked suspiciously.

"I'll go back to the beginning."

"Port Said?" Hart queried, somewhat taken aback by the thought.

Eldon shook his head. "No, sir, Cheadle."

"Manchester. What on earth's up there, beside scuttles full of soot and rain?"

"A beginning," Eldon replied. "Commander Prinn told me to start afresh. All right, that's what we'll do. We'll go back to the very beginning. Back to where Sir Maxwell Blain was born."

-oOo-

Violet Penny was ninety-two years old, and easy to trace. She had lived in Foundry Street for all of her life. What there was to know about the area lay deposited in her capacious memory. People often marvelled at the changes she'd experienced, while Violet herself remained dismissive of their interest. Why, she wanted to know, did they only emphasize the positive when they'd endured two world wars, and too many Tory governments? It was a wonder they were still here at all!

No one, in the event, was better qualified to discuss the early life of Maxwell George Blain.

Eldon found her by visiting the corner shop that sold everything from newspapers to cornflakes. He asked the jovial West Indian owner if he knew of the Blain family. The man shook his head, calling out to an elderly customer rummaging in the cool chest, who didn't either, but who pointed Eldon in the direction of Violet Penny.

Violet had become reconciled to the disadvantages of age, and philosophical about the outcome. Tonight, tomorrow or the next day, she would be dead, and she knew beyond a doubt that she was quietly waiting in the departure lounge for her turn. The delay merely suggested a lot of rude people had been pushing in ahead of her.

The motor itself appeared to be all right, according to her doctor, if not the ancillaries. She had a penchant for saying a lot of her parts were made in Japan. No one had the heart to remind her they were made in Manchester.

The room she occupied held a musty smell of ancient lavender mixed with old age. Violet's sixty-year-old daughter cautioned Eldon not to tire her mother out.

Violet had been a schoolteacher all her working life, and a little after that as well. One of eight children she had managed to bring up six of her own, none of which had stopped her pursuing her vocation in life for long. Children were God's gift, but they didn't come with any money.

Violet chuckled a great deal at her past indiscretions, saying she didn't laugh too much these days in case her two remaining teeth fell out.

Eldon listened to her, fascinated, but was forced eventually to bring the conversation round to Blain. He didn't lie to her. He could have pretended to be writing a book, or more probably an obituary, but he wasn't, and within a matter of minutes she would have detected the pretence. He played it straight; therefore, telling her exactly why he'd come; explaining how they weren't happy about the nature of Blain's death.

"I'm not surprised," Violet said calmly. "Not a great

deal mentioned in the papers, so I guessed there was more to it than was being said. I imagine you'll want to ask me about his early life."

"Yes. I don't have anything in mind, and if you think that's a good place to start?"

"Probably the only part you won't see documented. You'd hardly come all this way to discuss matters you could research in the local library."

So they talked about the young Blain, with inevitable reference to the poverty of the Thirties, which helped shape his character, besides covertly determining the direction of his life.

"He was a bright boy," Violet remembered, "but always in trouble. It stuck to him like a magnet because young Maxwell always had a rather casual attitude to other people's property. I think I could even have got him into Manchester Grammar School, if the poverty round here hadn't been so great. He would dodge school regularly at thirteen to help out in the markets. Quite a few started missing school at eleven, and the truancy officers couldn't keep up with them all. Eventually he got his own stall, afterwards a shop, before moving out of the area entirely. Some say he made a fortune during the war itself, others after the war by dealing in army surplus. He certainly had a way with money." Violet laughed softly. "Very often other peoples. He never came back here, hating his past I imagine. In a way, I think Maxwell hated us as well, because we came to represent a life he didn't want to remember. People can be funny that way, when all the time they're still carrying their past with them, unseen like a mole on their back. So, Maxwell fancied he was lucky getting out - something most locals would have liked to do. But he didn't escape, his past went with him all right."

Violet had shut her eyes, and they remained closed until, eventually, Eldon thought she had silently dropped asleep.

Rising quietly, he went towards the door. He had half opened it when Violet spoke again.

"Not like Arthur," Violet continued.

Eldon turned to look back at her, saw her eyes fixed on him, as if waiting for a response.

"Arthur?" he queried, returning to his chair.

"Arthur Sandquest was Maxwell's best friend, but as different as chalk from cheese. Friend, as well as enemy. I taught them both. Later they became partners, working on the market. Arthur stayed on here long after Maxwell had left. He married a local girl called Joyce in 1940, nice looking, just a little flighty. She liked Jazz and black music, which was thought a little risqué round here at the time. Nowadays there's more rap than tap. Joyce would have been right at home. Arthur wasn't a great patriot or anything, but seeing his friends joining up, he followed suit by enlisting in the army. The war made him as well - both him and Maxwell. In quite different ways, of course. Arthur had always been interested in electrical stuff, like making a crystal radio out of the odds and ends he'd scrounged when he was still at school. The army found a good use for him. There was a rumour of being dropped inside France and Holland, but Arthur never enlightened anyone - though he did receive a lot of medals. Joyce was killed in a bombing raid, so when the war was over he didn't really need to stay. Unlike Maxwell, who couldn't wait to get away, it was Arthur's business needs that eventually compelled him to leave, coming back only from time to time. 'Weed his roots', he used to say. He became a great benefactor of our local hospital. Something to be said for competition I suppose. At least, between those two."

The next chuckle was extensive. "Didn't convince them to become Tories, even so. They named a whole hospital wing after Arthur. Not a ward, mark you, but a whole wing crammed full of electronic thingamies. Cost two million pounds, they say. Two million! When he worked the markets that would have bought the whole of Cheadle. Good on him, he wasn't a man who forgot, like Maxwell Blain. Arthur was an only child who never knew his father. Deserted them both when he was still a baby, so his mother brought him up alone. She wasn't married either, and being an unmarried woman was a great stigma back then. But his mother worked hard, always managing to keep a shirt on his back. Luckily, no one held that against them round here. Too many worries of their own. The hospital wing was a way of repaying their kindness, I suppose. You'll see it as you drive out on the London road: the Arthur Sandquest wing. Very grand."

When they shook hands, Violet didn't get up, but held on to his hand for a long moment before letting go, as though all the memories would leave with him.

As he opened the door, he paused to repeat his good-bye.

"I'm so glad he used his mother's name," Violet said. "Much nicer than Berkeley."

Chapter 10

Little daylight remained as Margaret pulled up at her gateway, opened it, and drove up to the house.

The ruins of the castle beyond appeared as a mass of deep shadows with only the tower faintly highlighted, as though the setting sun had caught it in a final brief pale spark of daylight.

She reached down, ruffling the Labrador's ears, preoccupied with another distraction. The intrusion of a sound, though almost inaudible, had become instantly noticeable. Soft and rhythmical, neither increasing nor decreasing, its pulsation could have been coming from beneath her feet.

Margaret slipped a lead on the Labrador. She heard a car turn in at the bottom of the track. A dark Mercedes Benz sped by, weaving slightly, wheels tracking alongside the overgrown grass verge.

As the tail lights turned out of sight into the bailey, Margaret followed until the castle walls began to rear abruptly out of the ground in front of her. Seeking a position where she could get a better view of the inner courtyard, Margaret scrambled up the escarpment, over the fallen masonry and crumbling mortar, with the Labrador padding closely behind.

In a relatively narrow space between the existing inner and outer defences, a large canvas awning had been erected over an area abutting the base of the tower. A half-raised flap on the side exposed a small angle of the interior, lit by lamps powered by a small, rhythmically pulsing generator.

Due to the collapse of the severely truncated tower, the surface level, combined with the ruinous state of the walls, had created a deep infill. The close proximity of the two had allowed it to be swiftly covered by wind-born debris, levelling further the irregular surface. As a result a great door, for all of its massive proportions, had been buried from sight. Its arched entrance, supported by heavy stone voussoirs, had now been unearthed, to expose an opening that had been hastily filled in with rough layers of brick and stone several centuries earlier.

Workmen were in the process of cutting a trench no wider than the entrance itself, with little intention of clearing the site of other debris that would enable them to access the foundations forming the most critical part of the original construction. Two men, with high velocity rifles slung over their shoulders, stood idly watching.

As she stretched to get a better view, perished mortar crumbled under Margaret's hand, dislodging a loose stone that rattled down the inside of the castle wall.

Faces turned immediately, seeking the cause of this disturbance, while from below, heavy footsteps approached, followed by a torchlight beam playing over the surrounding walls. Drawing the dog closer to her, Margaret placed a hand gently on his muzzle.

In a matter of minutes the interest below had subsided. The workmen drifted back inside the awning, leaving the guards, after further suspicious glances along the walls, to continue their regular routine round of the bailey.

Looking for a line of escape, the sombre mass of the woods following the downward slope of the valley appeared to Margaret her only choice.

Edging along the narrow grass ledge to the furthest corner of the castle, she moved off across the adjoining field without attracting any immediate attention, covering half the distance to the safety of the trees before she heard a shout pierce the air.

Like a disturbed hare, unsure of the focus of the alarm, Margaret broke into a run, the descending slope adding impetus to her speed. Having let go of Bastion's lead, within a matter of moments they both crashed wildly into the woods. A shot rang out, its ruffled crack echoing back from the castle walls, followed by distant curses and orders not to shoot.

Margaret struggled through thickets and sprawling brambles in her panic-stricken haste, aware that any pursuers would be as much at home in this environment as the animals they more usually hunted.

A branch lashed her face with stinging force making her swerve, before she swung back again, trying to keep as close to the forest edge as possible, in case among the dense cover of trees, she lost her bearings. Stumbling blindly against a trunk, she grasped at ivy creepers to pull herself upright. A hand grasped her shoulder roughly, nails digging into her flesh before, just as suddenly, with a groan, it released its grip

Between her painful gasps for air, she heard a voice commanding her to be silent.

-oOo-

Prinn sucked in his breath painfully, fearing he might have cracked a bone in his hand. He hadn't come prepared for quite so active an evening.

When the sound of Margaret's pursuers began to drift away, Prinn considered it prudent to leave her unconscious attacker where he was, and get them back immediately to his parked Land Rover.

"*Mi segua,*" he urged Margaret softly.

As he moved off, a muffled expletive made him turn back to find her kneeling on the ground.

He crouched down beside her. "Well, well, you're English."

"Of course I'm bloody English," Margaret hissed through clenched teeth.

"Can you manage to stand up?"

Margaret eased herself upright, with Prinn's help, but couldn't put any weight on her right foot without considerable pain. "I think I've sprained my ankle. I don't think I'm able to walk."

"I'm afraid, if you can't, I'll have to carry you. Not very far, but definitely uncomfortable - fireman's lift. Give me your right hand and lean across my shoulder."

Margaret did as she was bid, feeling Prinn's shoulder hard against her stomach, his arm clasped round her legs. Terrified by the harrowing expectation that her assailants might still overtake them, Margaret closed her eyes to this discomfort, and to the throbbing in her ankle.

Reaching the metalled road, Prinn paused to regain his breath before crossing over to the Land Rover. Opening the door, he carefully eased her on to the seat.

Margaret protested. "I can't go without Bastion."

"Who's Bastion?"

92

"My Labrador. He was with me when we entered the wood." Margaret attempted to step out of the vehicle.

Prinn gently restrained her. "There's no need to worry about Bastion; he'll find his own way home. I'm shutting the door now." He closed the door off the catch, easing it into position.

Climbing into the driving seat, Prinn released the handbrake, letting the vehicle roll down towards the main track, bump-starting the engine once they reached the bottom. "Keep as low as possible, as they're bound to hear us," he ordered.

Prinn accelerated smoothly on a light throttle, urging the vehicle along quietly in a high gear for four hundred metres before abruptly sliding to a stop on some loose gravel. The back door opened, and Margaret looked back apprehensively as the rounded bulk of Scillone scrambled in, grasping at the back door, swinging wildly as Prinn took off again.

"Bit of a party going on," Prinn called over his shoulder. "I imagine you heard the shot?"

Scillone mumbled something questioningly from behind.

"Ah, yes," Prinn acknowledged. "Our passenger, here, was out walking her dog when some hunters thought they'd spotted a deer. In this poor light one thing looks very like another."

Margaret eased her leg to one side in an effort to find a more comfortable position for her throbbing ankle.

"I can see you've rather frightened Mrs Morning, Ettore."

"How do you know my name?" Margaret muttered through clenched teeth that threatened to emit a curse at every new bump.

"You're a resident in the *comune* of Sorena and as such, you're a matter of public record. Anyone who wishes to know, can know."

Margaret considered this for a moment. "That's true. However, it doesn't tell me how you would know I'm the Mrs Morning you're referring to? Why did *you* come to know?" she demanded indignantly.

"It's rather an old-fashioned concept, anonymity," Prinn remarked. "The only way to hide your identity is by staying out of the system: the tax system, the medical system, the banking system, - owning a car, owning a home, having a child at school, even going to work. On and on, one system after another. To avoid anything requiring documentation, you have to be always on the move. Then you aren't on a public record. No one needs to know who you are... until you get a toothache."

He turned the vehicle to the right, driving more cautiously, and Margaret realized they were heading up the track towards her house. A fear launched itself into the pit of her stomach. Or towards the castle!

Prinn continued, "Neither do personal rights have much relevance. Someone knowing your name doesn't take it away from you. Living in society gives you an identity, but not immunity. As for the reason why I acquainted myself with your circumstances, I have to plead that was quite accidental. My interests necessitated becoming familiar with this area, whereupon the information relating to your property came to my notice. A natural curiosity at seeing an English name where I didn't expect to find one. At first I considered that it commanded a little more of my attention than was perhaps justified. Now I'm not so sure."

Switching off the lights before they rounded the corner visible from the castle, Prinn drew up at the entrance to her house. Scillone got out quietly, opening the gate to let the Land Rover through.

A little more confidently, Margaret put her arm round Scillone's shoulder as he helped her down from the vehicle. Supported by his strong arm, she hopped on one leg towards the porch.

In the darkness of the doorway Margaret made out the even darker shape of the Labrador. Giving a sigh of relief that Bastion had found his way home; she bent down to pat his smooth fur, before she quickly drew her hand away, uncertain of its sticky feel.

Switching on the porch light Margaret saw immediately that her palm was covered in blood. Bending down again, she prodded the recumbent Labrador gently at first, then a little more firmly, willing him to respond.

94

Prinn crouched down alongside her, examining Bastion carefully. He straightened up, sitting lightly on his haunches, and shook his head at Margaret's pleading eyes already filling with tears.

-oOo-

Placing the coffee pot on the hob, Prinn glanced back at her. Margaret sat motionless, dazed and empty, staring at the kitchen table, or occasionally lifting her eyes to look fleetingly at Bastion's basket, with its untidy bean-bag, squashed into the angle between the old terracotta Felici stove, and the wall.

Scillone came in, and stood awkwardly by the kitchen door, his tanned face wearing a troubled frown.

"You've put Bastion in the cantina for the moment?" Prinn asked, lighting a gas ring. "And left the lights on outside?"

Scillone nodded, but the frown remained.

"Why did you do that?" Margaret suddenly asked.

Prinn turned towards her, motioning for Scillone to take over making the coffee. Drawing up a chair he sat opposite Margaret so that she could look straight into his eyes, ready to channel her anger when it came, offering a conduit to empty itself through.

"I don't believe the people who shot your dog knew that they'd hit him. What I do know is that if they start looking for a person with a dog, they'll come and look here. You can count on that. If your luck holds, they won't have realized the intruder was a woman, but you can guarantee they'll know the intruder has a dog. Everything depends on how closely they've already been watching you, and whether they're capable of putting two and two together."

Prinn eyed Margaret reassuringly, trying to reinforce his next words. "I don't expect they'll come too close, only near enough to establish if your situation appears normal. Ettore, we might try turning on the radio, but not too loud. Mrs Morning mustn't seem to be in any way concerned. Can you manage that?" he asked her.

Margaret didn't answer him, lines of anxiety creasing the edges of her eyes and lips, while her look held his firmly even though she wasn't seeing him, her hands placed flat on the table, her fingers drumming the wood.

"Can you manage that?" Prinn repeated softly.

"We must phone the police," Margaret burst out, her whole body suddenly agitated.

"That's not to be recommended, not just yet." Prinn tried to calm her.

"Recommended!" Margaret stood up, her knuckles turning white as she pressed her clenched hands on the table, only to sink back down again with a grimace of pain. "Damn this ankle," she moaned, adjusting the plastic bag full of crushed ice, strapped in place with an elastic bandage, which Prinn had prepared for her. "Someone's just shot my dog and you recommend I don't report the incident. Well, someone's committed a wanton criminal act. I intend phoning the police, at once."

Prinn withdrew a wallet from the inside pocket of his jacket, before quietly handing her his warrant card. "Put your leg back up on the stool," he ordered firmly.

She looked at the card, then back at Prinn. "The Metropolitan Police?" She gave a small nervous laugh. "But this is Italy?"

"Indeed it is. Not exactly my patch."

Margaret tried to ease herself into a more comfortable position, with her foot back on the stool. Her ankle was still painful. "Commander Prinn," she looked at the identity card again. "This is very confusing. What's it all supposed to mean? I don't understand."

Prinn nodded. "For the moment you must realize that Italy has become two different countries, the one you lived in until about an hour ago, and the one you inhabit now. As I said, the men in the forest probably have no idea who they were chasing. As for the local police here, they may not necessarily be what they seem. There's no way of telling. If you make a fuss, then your pursuers will instantly know the intruder was you."

"I don't understand," Margaret emphasized. "Who are they? People can't go around shooting anyone they like."

"Which people do you have in mind?" Prinn asked, taking one of the cups of coffee Scillone had placed between them.

"The people from the castle. You saw them?"

Prinn shook his head. "I saw someone, yes. I heard people in the woods. I couldn't tell for sure who they were. The hunting season may be over, but not for poachers. It's illegal, but only amounts to a fine. A dog, or a person might as easily be a wild boar in the dark. Then apologies all round. Another tragic hunting accident. Who shot Bastion? Can you identify them?"

"No," Margaret replied weakly.

"No, and no one will," Prinn affirmed. "Sometimes, not even when it's people that are dead."

"What am I supposed to do? I can't just pretend it never happened, and do nothing."

"For the moment, nothing is exactly what you must do."

"But why?" Margaret demanded.

"Unhappily, I can't give you a direct answer," Prinn hedged.

"Well, I must have an answer, Commander Prinn. I'm just not prepared to turn the other cheek. I have a daughter to think about, and Italy has a modern police force, with a democratic judicial system. Their job's to protect the innocent, and apply the law, as in any other Western country. I have to have a reason from you, or I'm going to the police."

"Mrs Morning, knowing too much can be a dangerous thing. My being here would be embarrassing to certain people, if it became public knowledge. This is extremely awkward, but I can see you won't be satisfied with less than the truth. So, to put it simply, the interests of the Italian authorities and the United Kingdom have for some time run a parallel course. There has been a serious flow of art treasures from churches, palaces, public buildings and archaeological sites in Italy. And no wonder, since no other country in the world possesses so much treasure, with such minimal security. Lesser items from this wholesale ransacking filter through to the dealers and auction houses. You've probably read about some sensational cases that attracted headlines? The public, by considering any antiquity fair game, hasn't helped. Finder's keepers. Once an artefact becomes a legitimate possession, purchased through a bona-fide source, things become difficult. Statute of Limitation laws protects the criminal so long as they can remain undetected for a number of years. Very valuable items may go into hibernation for up to thirty years, reappearing with a total loss of original ownership."

"But who would wait so long to dispose of them?" Margaret remained puzzled.

"They're considered investments, not for individuals, but for criminal organizations that function like regular businesses. While spectacular thefts are often carried out by amateur individuals, systematic robberies on the scale demonstrated in Italy, and elsewhere, suggest a level of expertise well beyond the means of a lucky, but inexperienced thief. Indeed, such is the level of criminal sophistication, that they now have experts of their own, mainly to pre-empt any adverse publicity, and to provide smokescreens to cover the true purpose of their activities. Specialists, for example, will 'grid' a large canvas, turning it into five or more individual pictures, seemingly bearing no relationship to the original. One of the most successful enterprises in our modern world is crime. It is a growth industry like no other. Illegal money creates a sellers market, so competition is fierce among both buyers and sellers for different, but compatible, reasons. A few dead bodies are of little moment. Business is business, and being natural exponents of free market economics - with special emphasis on the free - they tend not to be concerned with the niceties of business ethics."

"But governments can do something about it surely?"

Prinn gave a disapproving laugh. "I'm afraid the Italian political system does not allow for consistency in the policy of governments. Criminal tampering with legislation, either to pervert or annul it, has become a regular element in the running of the state. Those tentacles are long, spreading through all the organs of authority and constantly changing, infesting even ministerial departments, the judiciary, and all the forces they command. No one can be confident that their legitimate investigation will not be tainted by the corruption of those in whom they must confide. It filters its way down, in the sweat of a hundred Judases, to reach the smallest corner of the smallest *comune*. Any public servants who seek to minimize this corruption in national life are severely disadvantaged. I'm afraid any modern society is incapable of dealing with organized crime. Human rights, open borders, legal restraints, bureaucracy, international diplomatic agreements, and all the essential elements of a civilized community are the very components of its ultimate failure. The sad fact is, that governments can only apply the rules to a civilized people, not to criminal syndicates."

"But how can these things effect me?" Margaret asked. "I don't know anything."

"I'm afraid you do, Mrs Morning. The circumstances are that you know too much already. By being too inquisitive, I believe you've observed what's going on inside the castle?"

Margaret shook her head. "I've seen them at work, but I've no idea what they're doing."

"As the Castello di Pietra is pivotal to this investigation, I'd like to know exactly what you've seen. I expect you know the castle's recently been sold? A tentative link has been established between the new owners and a British connexion currently under surveillance. We decided to have a closer look, and you seem to have stolen a march on us."

Margaret looked doubtful. "You're saying an organized crime ring from Britain has been operating here as well? That you've identified a collaboration between a British suspect and the Italian owners of the castle?"

"Simply put, but yes. In addition, I have a personal reason for being here, since I too have a home in this *comune*. The Villa Lazzi, bought by my parents from the Adami family whose ancestors purchased it from Pope Urban VIII, along with a redundant Medici estate, including the Castello di Pietra. I apologize if I sound like a pedant, but these details are of some importance. My father, amassed a large collection of documents relating to local history and; therefore, the subject of my current investigation has become linked with my own property's history."

"But what could be worth stealing from an empty and desolate ruin?" Margaret interjected. "I know the castle well. I've been over nearly the whole structure from top to bottom. There isn't anything to steal there, except the stones themselves. Unless these people are silly enough to believe they've located the legendary treasure of Paetus Cecina."

"Proclaimed with all the conviction of the apostle Thomas," Prinn remarked with a smile.

"The treasure's just a tall story."

"That may turn out to be so, but the fact that someone's willing to invest a great deal of money in purchasing the castle, hiring thugs to protect it, possibly to kill if necessary, persuasively suggests an alternative opinion," Prinn admonished her.

"Perhaps it would be better if Melissa and I went back to England?" Margaret suggested negatively.

"I'm afraid that would be unwise, as you'd hardly be any further away from them than you are now. No, I regret to say you would be better advised to stay here. You must thus convince them that you aren't a threat, by seemingly being unaware that they are."

"What about poor Bastion?" Margaret complained. "My daughter's not going to understand."

"That's unfortunate. Bastion will simply have to go missing. Tonight, I'm going to stay here just in case. I'll sleep on the sofa," he gestured. "Where is your daughter at the moment?"

"She'll be back about one o'clock in the morning when friends bring her home from a concert in Pisa. She's not normally out this late."

"Excellent," Prinn concluded. "That will explain why you're up so late. Introduce me to her as an old friend from England. I'll get Ettore to take Bastion away with him when he leaves. He can leave the body in another part of the forest some miles away, where he'll be found quickly. Tomorrow you must report to the police that Bastion went missing. Can you do that?" Prinn inquired.

"Yes, ... but I've never lied to Melissa before."

"You've probably never had to protect her life before," Prinn replied seriously. "One more very important thing. You can't totally rely on friends in Italy. Don't discuss this with anyone."

Margaret protested. "Commander Prinn, I'm not made of wood."

"Tell no one," Prinn reiterated. " Silence is your only safety. Sometimes, in these places, you're dealing with a quasi-mediaeval people long conditioned by a tradition of fear and servitude. They trust nothing, except the hair on their own head. Not their government, the police, or anyone official and, above all, not the stranger next door. You'll ultimately mean nothing to them; so don't be fooled by the trappings of a modern society. It's only a facade. Their culture is one of suspicion, of having constantly to prevaricate, equivocate and deceive in order to protect themselves. You, when all is said and done, are not really one of them. Your expectations of them, and theirs of you, are not the same. They will let you down when you need them most. You can't afford such a foolish mistake."

"Who can I trust then?" Margaret demanded.

"Start with no one: not Ettore, not even me. Treat us all with a great deal of caution, for scant allowance will be made for your mistakes." Prinn turned, and spoke to Scillone. "Now Ettore, I'm staying here tonight, but I still have to go to Rome in the morning, and I don't want to be late for the train. So collect me nice and early, if you please."

Scillone grunted his assent, shook Margaret's hand, squeezed Prinn's arm, and let himself out.

They sat in silence until the sound of the Land Rover died away.

"To me this seemed just the sort of place where you could regain your sanity after too much of the big city tempo," Margaret lamented. "I had such high hopes. The quiet seems to wrap itself around you - my friend Pamela says it's like playing a violin without strings. To hear it, you have to listen to your own imagination."

"You're quite close to this Pamela?" Prinn asked.

"Yes," Margaret replied, seeing through his ambiguity. "Close enough for her to be a confidante, if that's what you mean?"

"Mrs Morning," Prinn insisted forcefully, "you really will be in grave danger if you can't manage to keep your own counsel. Both you, and Melissa. Your daughter is young, and I wouldn't doubt she is very pretty. These people have a way of making beautiful things ugly."

Margaret said nothing for a while; her eyes cast back towards Bastion's basket by the stove. Then hesitantly, she nodded. "I suppose you really can't know anyone that well. Pamela must surely have a past I'm not a party to, involving people she doesn't need, and perhaps doesn't care, to share with me."

Chapter 11

In the post-war climate of push-and-shove, Blain had developed the artifice necessary to broker the complex deals that formed the foundation of his expertise. Companies supplying the domestic market were starved of materials, while export-led industries wallowed in glut. Blain was exactly the talent for those times. Robbing Peter to pay Paul. Yet these were no longer those times. Times had changed.

Eldon noted that Blain's fund-management group worked offshore, setting up new funds based on already existing products that had proved profitable in the past, a sound business policy for which he had ample resources. Most of these deals were based on low capital gearing, relying on shareholders rather than banks, suggesting a careful approach to acquisitions that they might not have intended keeping for long. Blain was obviously not a man to saddle himself with debt.

The worrying question at the back of Eldon's mind was that this didn't seem to fit Violet Penny's image of Blain. He was intrinsically a commercial bruiser; therefore, such sophisticated market manipulation that may well have suited his business team, would lack the immediacy and aggression suited to such a temperament. Yet Eldon realized there was no real reason why such qualities might not have been complimentary - as long as they didn't lose sight that the department was dealing with the private Blain, not the public one.

In which case, Blain's private life might throw up some answers. The local CID would have done a thorough search, uncovering everything possible, but there was still the off chance they'd managed to miss something.

Picking up the telephone, he dialled Hart's number to obtain clearance.

-oOo-

"One thing before you go, Rex," Hart added. "Special

103

Branch has mentioned that the French have a counter-intelligence agent attached to the squad investigating Blain's death. I'll need to keep you up to date on that one, as the risk of political fall-out will need watching. Anyway, Blain has a house in Chertsey, an estate near Nailsworth, and another at Macroom near the Boggeragh Mountains in Southern Ireland. Apparently, he lived out of a suitcase everywhere else. Veronica has all the details. I understand C11 haven't come up with anything, which means it's going to be given a lower priority shortly. Do you know what you're looking for yet?"

"Not exactly," Eldon said. "What I need to come across is baggage."

"Baggage?" Hart echoed, a note of scepticism creeping into his voice. He preferred 'plain speak', rather than Eldon's figurative descriptions.

"Blain seems to have tried to erase everything from his early life," Eldon explained. "People, places, events. But of course you can't. According to Violet Penny, something always remains of the past. My father thought much the same, believing that in every garden you'll find a marble - something left behind. Blain will have left something, somewhere."

"Well, let's hope you find these marbles in Chertsey," Hart grumbled.

-oOo-

They were all high-profile residences, the traditional trappings of a wealthy man, yet nowhere for a past to sit around in. Even the Nailsworth estate was something of a deceit, given a top chef from Monaco's Hotel Palm, an eighteen-hole golf course for paying guests; with Blain himself crammed into a pied-à-terre under the roof. Nothing startling would be discovered there. The Irish estate appeared to have possibilities, but, with a peripatetic owner, probably not. That left Chertsey, with its easy access to the City and Heathrow.

Discovering that the house lay nearer to Virginia Water than Chertsey, Eldon came down the Great West Road, out of a nostalgic preference for the fleeting holiday memories of his youth.

Beacher's Hill was a mid-nineteenth-century red brick house set in a small wooded park, with a steep slate roof and stone bays that supported balconies for the main bedrooms. It was a masculine house that might have been an independent school dormitory wing, reflecting his aspirations at the time, before his wealth had grown so enormous that only faraway Ireland, with hundreds of acres between himself and the *hoi polloi* provided sufficient protection from their existence.

A truculent housekeeper, now squatting on borrowed time, let him in, her agreeable appointment there shattered by a threatening notice to quit from the estate solicitors.

Blain had never married, a state affected by his penchant for constant travel in search of wealth; therefore the house displayed an eclectic taste that suggested he had little interest in creating a home. The sensitive world of polished mahogany and fine porcelain seemed extraneous possessions to a man of Blain's temperament. He probably was happier living out of a suitcase.

"The police have gone over everything thoroughly," the housekeeper commented disagreeably. A bitter, middle-aged woman, her long-term avarice had taken on a kind of physical presence: a forceful, pugnacious insinuation that was as repugnant as it was insistent. The constant absence of Blain had developed in her a discourteous and indifferent attitude to any visitors.

"They were in searching; turned the place upside down. Looking for money, I expect. Not that I'll see any of it. Worked for him for twenty years, I did, but he won't have left me a farthing. You got a warrant?" she finally asked.

Eldon shook his head, handing her his identity card. "Inspector Winter should have phoned this morning."

"Oh, that one. Yes, he called. Came in with Sir Maxwell's solicitor, making a big fuss about a missing inventory. Rich always get made a fuss of, even when they're dead. What will he ever know of it, blown to kingdom come?"

"Why do you say that?" Eldon asked curiously.

"Overheard one of them coppers talking. IRA, they said, given he's got a place in Ireland, like. What you here for, then? Thorough they was. Can't be much left for you to look at."

Eldon agreed that they would have been thorough. As thorough as anyone who didn't have the slightest idea what they were looking for.

"Oh, I'm sure they've done a good job, but I've been asked to have another look."

The woman eyed him nervously. "Anywhere special you want to see?"

"Yes," Eldon replied, eyeing her directly. "I'd like to see the study."

"Oh, they went through there, all right." She pinched her nose, sniffing heavily. "Took me a day to tidy the mess up. This way. You're not going to pull the place to pieces again, are you?"

Eldon shook his head, following her through a door on the left side of the hall. It was a small room full of leather, and the smell of books. Rather a lot of books, neatly arranged in oak bookcases. They felt right there, so probably most of them came with the house.

"Thank you." He waited for her to leave.

There were a lot of volumes on biography and travel, a few on aspects of business and economics. Eldon took down part one of a familiar volume. 'A Treatise on Money', by Maynard Keynes. He looked for its companion volume before finding it on another shelf. The housekeeper might be tidy, but one couldn't expect her to be methodical. The tightness of its spine told him the book had probably never been read. Blain was obviously not a man to be lectured on money. Not by Keynes, anyway.

Eldon ran his hand along the surface of the oak partners' desk, not stopping to open the drawers, only looking for inspiration.

On the bottom shelf of a bookcase he noticed a series of photograph albums. He would never have imagined Blain to be a man with the time to indulge in happy snaps, or even with the inclination to own a camera. But photographs there were, mostly official or with a business context, supplied by a photographer or studio.

Some were obviously missing, taken away by the CID.

A small, battered cloth album looked different. Untidily kept, it contained black and white prints in a variety of obsolete formats, providing what Violet Penny had claimed you could never quite escape. People, places, a whole history - a history; however, from which Cheadle was conspicuously absent.

Eldon leafed through them until he found tucked in the back an old postcard carrying a faded George V stamp almost obliterated by the postmark, and addressed to plain Master Maxwell Blain. Miss Penny, describing briefly her holiday, had sent him a thoroughly uncharming view of the pier at Bournemouth.

Beneath the postcard he found a smaller photograph, somewhat creased, as though it had spent a considerable time in someone's wallet. A young woman stood by the door of a thatched cottage, her arms round a boy leaning back against her. Eldon turned the crumpled photograph over to read the inscription. In childish writing, it disclosed they were: 'Mrs Penny and me. 1932. Moreton'.

-oOo-

Returning to the office, Eldon phoned Violet Penny.

"Well, now, you certainly are good at your job," Violet affirmed. "Ignore the obvious; as nothing interesting ever happens there. That's why I haven't seen the local police yet, and I can't say I expect to. They'll be chasing phantoms of their own, filling in lots of paperwork to show they've done their job properly. You, on the other hand, will want to know about Moreton in Dorset, which is the only connexion between Maxwell and me, and a holiday."

"Any specific reason for not mentioning it before?" Eldon enquired.

"Mister Eldon," a slight note of exasperation slipping into her voice. "I knew Maxwell Blain for twenty years. I know everything you could ever want to know during that same period, right down to the fact that he was circumcised, and once stole the communion money from a local Catholic church. We might sit chatting about him for weeks, so it's up to you to be more specific."

"Point taken," Eldon acknowledged. "Tell me about Moreton, then."

"Well, now, let me see. What a jumble of memories. My elder sister Louise married a gamekeeper from Bere Regis. Left the grime of Cheadle for a tied cottage just outside Moreton village. Once a year I visited them. I couldn't afford to take my whole family, so they used to pack me off in the train for two weeks during the summer to stay with Louise. God bless her, she was homesick for her family, though I could never understand why she missed Cheadle. The owner of the estate was a grand gentleman who used to send his chauffeur with a Rolls Royce to collect us from the station at Wool. It's from hearing about him that Maxwell probably got the idea that 'rich' was the way to be. Louise's husband, Harry, died early, but she managed to stay on in the cottage, working as a cook in the manor house. From hearing my accounts, Maxwell came to take an interest in Dorset. He drew maps from my descriptions, indicating all the places where I'd visited with big red circles. It was as if he'd entered another world - one in which he could escape from Cheadle.

In the summer of 1932 his mother had to go into hospital for a spell, so I offered to take him with me to Moreton. The headmaster actually paid for him, believing, as I did, that Maxwell had something special needing to be channelled in the right direction. 'Realizing his potential,' they say these days. He came with me every year after that, until he was fourteen when he developed ideas of his own, and started putting into practice his new view of life. He knew by then that Cheadle most certainly wasn't for him. One time, during his second visit, he asked how much the cottage was worth. I said something like ninety pounds, but I didn't really know. That was probably about right for the early Thirties. He whistled on hearing that, saying one day he'd buy the cottage. I don't think I believed him. 'Moreton', he once said to me after the war, just before he left Cheadle for good, 'I've closed the door on that one, Mrs Penny. No money to be made getting your feet muddy'. I don't suppose there was, but I wish he'd got his feet muddy instead of his fingers sticky."

She laughed again, this time with a touch of sadness. "Strawberry Cottage ... they were times full of happy memories. Somehow, I think Maxwell felt that as well. I hope so. Something that brought back the smiles every now and again."

Eldon thanked her, replacing the receiver thoughtfully.

Moreton wasn't a big village. Eldon remembered cycling there once, from his uncle's house at Winterborne Kingston, to look at Whistler's engraved-glass windows in the church. T.E.Lawrence was buried in a new cemetery close by: a small, tidy grave for so great a legend. The cottage might still exist - only a hunch. But Violet Penny had said, Blain lived behind a mask: that of an important man, a public man with a knighthood and country estates, a million miles and a million pounds away from his past. Behind the mask may still have been a boy, dreaming of a Dorset world he'd once created for himself.

-oOo-

Eldon drove down to Moreton. He could have looked in at Wareham police station to find out what he wanted, but that would have soon found its way on to a crime-squad desk, and sending them scurrying down after him in case they missed out on something. By going straight to the local public house in the village, he assumed he would find residents who would know if Strawberry Cottage still existed.

The Harvester was almost empty. Eldon bought himself a pint of Bass.

"Come far?" the barman asked, taking up a cloth to polish a glass.

"Popped down from Town," Eldon replied. "Friend of mine's in the property business - gave me a bell, about a cottage that might be for sale. I'm in the market if the price is right. Have to watch the pennies these days."

"Don't I know it," the barman nodded effusively. "I've been in this trade for twenty years, and the bottoms been knocked out of it by the breathalyser. Inner-

109

city pubs can make a bob or two - with fancy lunches and the like. Then in the evening they'll still have walk-in social customers, but it's all tub-thumping, and kids being sick all over the place. Not my sort of pub. The only walk-in trade I get, is on a Sunday: hikers on half a shandy an hour. No one's any trouble, though. Even the army lads are polite hereabouts. Professional soldiers they are. The summer gives me a boost, otherwise I'd go under. What's your line of work?"

"Graphic design," Eldon replied. "That's why I can look out for a place in the country. I work from home mostly, just needing to shoot up to Town to confer with clients a couple of times a week. As I said, heard of this place, Strawberry Cottage. No one else seems to know it."

The barman shook his head. "Can't say I've come across that name, but then, I've only been here two years. Bit too much of a new boy yet to share in the local gossip. Got to prove my worth. Allow a bit on the slate, a bit of after hours drinking, support local events a bit. By the time all the 'bits' have been added together, I'll be more than a bit older. Bert in the corner over there might know. He's been a farm worker, man and boy, round here for fifty years."

Eldon nodded and the barman called out to a tweedy, ruddy-faced drinker in the corner, currently absorbed in the racing pages.

"Hey, Albert, we need a piece of local knowledge over here."

Bert brought his drink over to the bar. "Bit of poaching, is it?" he asked.

The barman and Eldon smiled together.

"Bit of something called Strawberry Cottage," the barman continued. "Up for sale, this gentleman reckons. Can't say I've ever heard of it."

"Strawberry Cottage," Bert mused. "No, you wouldn't. It went years ago, when they sold Bridge Farm for redevelopment. Private housing estate, market garden and the new school's located there now."

Eldon felt disappointed to have his theory fall at the first hurdle.

"No," Bert corrected himself. "I tell a lie. That was Strawberry Farm Cottage. Always caused a lot of confusion, did that. Lived in by the herdsman. Strawberry Cottage proper was a lot older, and up in Hanger Woods. Always served to house the gamekeeper until Harry Adams popped his clogs. Wife stayed on as cook for Major Lewes. She was a nice old biddy but still just a lass when Harry went. Never married again. Saw the light, I reckon. Company that bought the home farm didn't get around to developing the woods. Planning problems, I dare say. About a hundred acres of mixed hard wood, worth a bob or two in timber, but the bird spotters now hog the lot. R.S.P.B have the lease, I'm told, but I reckon the developers offloaded the place before they got stymied."

"The wood?" Eldon enquired.

"No, just the cottage. Hung on to the woods. Long time back, mind you."

"Who lives in Strawberry Cottage now?"

"Same chap what bought it. Blimey - let me see - some thirty years past, I reckon. Bought the cottage direct from the company who developed the farm. Course he's not there full time; in and out, sort of thing. Weekend home, I s'pose. Nothing regular, mind. Down in January last. Not wed, as far as I know. Folks reckon he's something in the city. Always on his own. Quiet like. You know him, Reg?" Bert insisted. "Always smartly dressed, sometimes in a blazer and cravat."

The barman nodded in recognition. "I know the one you mean. What's his name? On the tip of my tongue. Pearson, Perkins?"

"Parsons," Bert corrected him. "Had him play darts here once, couple of years ago when we was short of a hand against the Tank Regiment lads. I think the holes are still in the wall. Rita reckoned he threw them with his eyes shut. He only ever hit the board with one dart out of the three."

"I remember." The barman roared with laughter. "Second week I was here. Absolute magic."

"Blimey, was it," Bert agreed. "Tied at the last game, you see. Our Mr. Parsons against their captain, that big sergeant from Sunderland," he reminded the barman. "Real nice fellow. Here we go, everyone said, beer's on us. Parsons played six hands, with only six flights hitting the board, and another, which went AWOL. You remember, Reg, it bounced back out and stuck in a squaddies boot. He soon shifted."

They both laughed.

"So you lost?" Eldon commiserated with Bert.

That's the magic, we didn't. We were playing two hundred and one, being big teams. He ran two fifties, the bouncer, ran a seventeen, another fifty, then wiped the sergeant out with a double seventeen, all with his eyes shut. Gawd, was he bad. We never asked 'im again, but what a great night."

"So the cottage isn't for sale?" Eldon brought them back to earth, nodding at their now empty glasses.

The barman pulled a pint of bitter for Bert, taking the top off another bottle of Bass for Eldon.

Bert raised his glass in appreciation. "Haven't heard a rumble about him selling. Can see why if he is - place's pretty well buried up there. No road to speak of, only a track. Get there in a Land Rover, maybe. You into Land Rovers?"

"Can't say I am," Eldon replied. "But I'm into walking."

"Wellington boots, then," Bert said before giving Eldon instructions on how to get there.

In the car park, Eldon took his laptop from the boot, sitting in the passengers seat while he opened the already extracted information supplied from public records regarding Blain's business enterprises and equities. He typed in Phoenix Estates, locating them in a pair of folders. "Well, well," he mused, "in every garden you'll find a marble. Sometimes even two."

-oOo-

The main road ran through the centre of the wood. Eldon found the lay-by with the five-bar gate Bert had indicated, along with the track leading into that section of the wood where Strawberry Cottage was located.

He climbed over the gate with its long galvanized hinges, and locked with a stout padlocked chain. The track went straight ahead, before entering a clearing and emerging as two diverging paths. Bert had seemed unsure which direction would now lead to the cottage.

Eldon studied the wheel tracks on them: heavily ribbed Land Rover tyres were common to both. But only one had the large diagonally splayed impressions of a tractor tyre and, as Mr. Parsons was unlikely to use an old Massey Harris for popping about in, the other path appeared more likely.

A little further on, Eldon glimpsed the cottage itself through the trees. Robustly thatched across a neatly netted roof and dormers, with walls long faded into a weather-scrubbed, patchy pink. It might have appealed to anyone for whom privacy was at a premium. Surrounded by a tight beech hedge, the garden appeared rather jaded, probably unattended through the long winter months, or the absence of the mysterious Mr. Parsons. The open-sided log shed, was full and clearly unused. He recognized the porch and front door from Blain's photograph.

Eldon stood by the gates for some moments. A bird flew out from under the porch; another disappeared into the holly tree at one end of the wall facing him. He decided no one was there.

Pushing on the gate, allowed him access down the path to a stout oak front door. Getting in might not have been an easy thing for a novice, but it was all routine to a professional. Eldon wasn't taking any bets that the forest workers weren't also on to a nice retainer for minding these premises. There were no telephone lines; therefore, no alarm system that would have the boys in blue rushing over at a moment's notice.

A cigarette carton lay carelessly discarded on the path. Blain didn't smoke, and no one had said if Parsons did. Looking inside he found half a dozen remained. Not discarded, but accidentally dropped, and probably not by some forestry worker. Unless one of them had developed an unlikely penchant for Turkish cigarettes.

Eldon pocketed the packet. Walking round the cottage, he looked for any sign of forced entry. A Yale lock secured the back door, which he opened easily. On the back of it, two hefty bolts were left drawn. People were careless, which was something burglars had come to rely on. Eldon smiled to himself - and others too.

A whitewashed corridor ran the full length of the

building, with two rooms leading off on either side. At the top of a steep staircase, another long corridor ran the length of the cottage, but with the rooms all on one side, providing a quaint disparity in configuration. The resulting eight rooms more than adequate for a gamekeeper. Apparently also for a well heeled nabob. Eldon looked into each room in turn, disturbing nothing.

The two front rooms downstairs were lined with oak panels. The larger was used as a formal reception room, the smaller as a 'snug', fitted with comfortable furniture, carpets, bookshelves crammed with contemporary novels, a table with a large television set. Perhaps this could indicate the Maxwell no one saw: the ordinary face behind a complicated mask.

Eldon noticed two indentations in the carpet made by moving the armchair. They were still fresh and deep. Directly behind the chair, a set of three oak panels almost reached the ceiling, each panel abutting another, and tidied by a strip of half-round moulding. One of the mouldings wasn't quite flush, and he pulled gently at it. The panel moved smoothly on hinges, revealing a small enclosure behind. Stepping inside, he slid open a drawer in one of the filing cabinets, shuffling through the folders. Some legal documents addressed to Blain, gave the game away. He closed the panel again. Further investigation was a job for experts.

Considering the ambience of the room, Eldon tried to discern the character of Mr. Parsons. All he could ultimately decide was that he had a very strange taste in aftershave.

-oOo-

Eldon made it back to London in a little over two hours, with his car smelling faintly of overheating. Going straight up to see Hart, he found him about to leave for a meeting with the Assistant Commissioner.

"It won't take long, but you're going to need a head start over the crime squad," Eldon advised him. "I'm afraid you'll need to bend the rules a bit."

"That usually implies interfering with the course of justice," Hart cautioned. "Can't say I'm happy with that."

"You remember the baggage I was talking about?" Eldon reminded him.

Hart leant forward. "Marbles, I remember."

"All right, marbles then. I think that Sir Maxwell had one tucked away in Dorset, where he lived under an alias: name of Parsons."

"What do you mean he had one tucked away in Dorset? A woman?"

"No," Eldon shook his head, "a place of his own. One with an interesting line in movable oak panelling. It's called Strawberry Cottage, near the village of Moreton."

"You have been busy. We'll need a team to go over that at once. Discreetly. Copies only. I'll get E3 down there, but we hand what we find over to our colleagues, 'untouched' as they say."

"Ah! I broke the rules there, I'm afraid. Someone's a step ahead of us."

"Now you're spoiling my day."

Eldon dropped the packet of cigarettes on to the desk. "Well, whoever they are, they wear Jean Patou's Joy perfume, and smoke Turkish cigarettes."

Hart picked up the packet, and passed it under his nose a few times, with something resembling pleasure. "Turkish you say? Opulent sort of type."

"No doubt." Eldon opened the door. "Perhaps someone from Special Branch."

Chapter 12

Waking with a start, Prinn recognized the approach of Scillone's less than sensitive driving. He pulled on his shoes, and stroked his unshaven chin ruefully.

In the hall, Margaret fully dressed, instructed Scillone to clean his boots before entering the house. He obeyed reluctantly, his face a petulant frown. She next turned to Prinn, shaking her head disapprovingly at his amusement. "Signor Scillone has brought your shaving equipment. Manifestly, not before time. You do look awful."

Despite a cautious limp, she swept past him into the kitchen. "First door on the left upstairs, and don't wake Melissa. Not that anything will. Breakfast in ten minutes."

The door clicked shut behind her.

A heavy silence succeeded her passing. There was an attractive air of bravado about her manner, which both men considered cautiously. Something positive, in the manner of her carefully applied make-up; the confidence of her precise instructions.

During breakfast, Prinn decided to let Margaret talk.

"Commander Prinn," she commenced firmly. "With regard to your advice, I've decided to stay. Firstly, I don't wish to leave, and if I do as you say - acting as though nothing has happened - perhaps I won't need to."

"For the moment that seems the sensible option," Prinn agreed. "And secondly?"

Margaret took a deep breath. "Secondly, it's quite apparent that my position here is strategic."

Prinn raised an eyebrow. "Strategic?"

"Yes," Margaret affirmed. "From my terrace the castle is partially visible. But, more importantly, to get there you go up, and as Newton says, what goes up must also come down. Everything passes my front door," - inclining her head in one direction, then the other - "*Su e giù.*"

"I see." Prinn gave a nervous cough. "What exactly are you suggesting?"

"As I'm here, and meant to be here, I can take note of everything without arousing suspicions."

Prinn studied her earnest face. "I don't think that's such a good idea. Rushing to the gate every time a vehicle passes, will hardly do."

The stern lines at the corner of Margaret's mouth thickened. "I have enough wit not to do any such thing. I'm quite prepared to follow your instructions, precisely."

"You can't have considered anything I said last night," Prinn said severely. "What you're suggesting is extremely dangerous."

"On the contrary, I've given it a great deal of thought, and you've certainly made me fully aware of the danger. Having decided to stay, it's pretty obvious that any lack of commitment on my part will demonstrate that I know something. At the same time, for safety's sake, I can't be seen to be in a funk."

"I must object," Prinn said impatiently. "There is the small matter of my responsibility." He paused to consider his weak position. Legally, he realized he was outside his remit. When he spoke again, the reluctance was obvious. "I'm thoroughly against this. In fact it's incredibly foolish, but I understand your reluctance to stand around doing nothing, and I realize I'm in no position to demand otherwise."

"Quite so," Margaret pronounced, in a markedly citrus tone. "We must avoid Satan finding mischief for idle hands."

Prinn pointedly ignored the jibe. "As far as this practical assistance goes, I cannot give you any instructions. Much will depend on your own judgement. The difficulty for you will be the lack of training; finding it awkward to remember things without writing them down - car number plates, for example." He made one last attempt at discouraging her. "Small details can be most important, but the most difficult to retain. Really - perhaps the demands will be too difficult for you?"

"Why? What I say to you will be like any other evidence from a member of the public. You must make of it what you will."

"Nevertheless, such activity is the task of a trained person, quite beyond your experience."

"Hardly," Margaret retorted. "Before I married I was an actress. LAMDA, and straight into rep. You'll have no worries on that score, I'll be quite capable of remembering my lines."

"An actress!" Prinn looked a little surprised. "I don't think I'd have guessed. Clearly, in that case, I must take back what I said."

Defeated, he gave the corners of his mouth a final dab with the napkin, pushed his chair back, and rose a little stiffly.

"Well, I must go. Now remember, Margaret, a look is not always a glance and will signal quite a different message to those who may be watching you. Someone, or something new can, naturally, be stared at, after which they should hardly be noticed. Good. *Saluti a* Melissa, I'm sorry to have missed her before I leave. This hour is not conducive to the life of a night owl."

-oOo-

Scillone dropped Prinn off at the entrance to the railway station booking office, where he collected his ticket, and a newspaper from the news-stand, passed through the jostle round the bar, fed his ticket in the yellow franking machine, and negotiated the tracks through an underpass on to the platform.

He moved away from the crowded entrance with its milling distractions. Here the platform was quieter except for a blustery wind driving loose paper bags along the cold, polished-steel of the tracks that arrived and departed in chilled-silence.

On the furthest concrete bench, he sat idly on the end, with his own uncertainty. Prinn had broken the rules; the ethical guidelines that regarded the protection of the public as a prime responsibility. Running through all the reasons that mitigated this course of action, he found they were all based on extrajudicial practical considerations; none addressed the principal argument of the safety of Margaret Morning, and her daughter. Such matters would override all others if they came to any harm. The train arrived on time and departed as promptly. Prinn found himself a place by the window on the upper level of the compartment, where, between brief periods of reading his newspaper, he returned to the troublesome theme of Mrs Morning that had no solution. Having used up the margin of energy depleted by a short and disturbed night, somewhere overlooking the lagoons of Orbetello where the train had rejoined its flat coastal route after swinging inland to Grosseto, he fell asleep, his head rocking gently against the window.

-oOo-

With a jarring crash of carriages the locomotive came to a rest at the Stazione Termini in Rome. It was an ill-mannered station, full of idle groups of men and indolent policemen in cars, indicating that Rome, in harmony with all modern cities, was an extraordinary layer of civilization and depravation.

Prinn walked past their interested and calculating stares, into the piazza where he queued patiently behind the tubular barrier of the taxi rank along with other more exasperated clients who could do nothing to accelerate the arrival and departure of the cabs.

Across the Piazza dei Cinquecento, he could almost discern the outline of the National Museum built into the giant Baths of Diocletian. Given that Emperor's proclivity for the massacre of Christians and undesirables, the terminus behind him would have been remarkably empty.

-oOo-

Questore Tomaso Vignozzi was a large man with quick, darting eyes. He wore a baggy blazer over a pale blue shirt, with a diagonally striped silk tie much favoured by career officers, and seen as the nearest thing to a uniform. His grey hair was cut short - a little too short for his over large ears.

Vignozzi had already arranged lunch, but it was unlikely to be a restaurant he had visited recently, despite the unlikely intention of underworld threats and promises. He was too astute to ignore fate entirely. For the moment he sat at his desk, out of the morning sun that streamed through the large window of his office, hands crossed comfortably over his stomach.

"Nicholas, I've made the enquiries you requested. The new owner of the Castello di Pietra is a company called Bimax, fronting the operation for another registered company, Caparra: construction interests, cement and gravel works, building materials and vendors. The castle has been legitimately bought for 1.4 *miliardi*, about seven hundred thousand pounds, sterling. Interestingly, the chief executive of the company is launching out in a different, but not illogical, direction. Property. They've bought the castle out of existing facilities - this, on top of the fact that the group has also negotiated a further loan debt of up to twenty *miliardi* to fund their purchase of the small hotel group, Adripui. That amount of leverage indicates their borrowing requirement is going to be adrift of their market capitalization. Someone has confidence in them."

"Well, we know it won't be a Chinese laundry," Prinn humorously speculated. "Who's the chief executive?"

"Now there's a thing." Vignozzi's eyes narrowed. "One Fausto Paba."

Prinn was silent for a moment, considering its significance. "I presume you're referring to the Mafioso hitman, who gunned down Sergio Birelli in Bari?"

"I am," Vignozzi continued. "And I have in mind, that an employee of yours, is a not disinterested party in the matter. An older, wiser man perhaps?"

"Older and wiser, certainly, and like all wise men, he has an exceedingly long memory. He will not have forgotten Paba. But I thought Paba received a sentence of thirty years in gaol?" Prinn queried.

Vignozzi nodded. "Paba was released in 1985, after serving six years. He was too important a player to leave languishing in a cell. Information discreetly surfaced implicating a senior government official in the judicial findings, enabling his lawyer to orchestrate an early release. Cheaper than a retrial, they say. From that point on, his rise appears to have been swift - with a little help from his friends. The death of Birelli allowed a massive expansion in the south-eastern ports by underworld interests, waiting to fill the vacuum. Paba found himself rewarded by being levered into the driving seat as chief executive of Caparra. A clean start, in a legitimate enterprise. A new type of criminal, *il mio amico*. Rich, successful, with friends in high places. Eventually they'll run the country, you wait and see."

"If they already don't," Prinn considered thoughtfully. "So Paba is back, then?"

"He is. Ruthless, clever, with enough collateral to buy a lot of favours - and moved in next door to you and Scillone," Vignozzi said pointedly.

"That's something of a bother, Tomaso."

"Yes, well one thing we can be sure of, if these barons have got hooligans on the payroll they're not there for altruistic reasons. However," Vignozzi brightened, "there is some better news. Everyone has to have a piece of luck. Luck is like money, it has to go round, and eventually round to us. One of Paba's senior managers - no criminal record - had a heart attack on a flight to New York, carrying a photograph, hidden in a book, of what appears to be a recently stolen work of art. The dead man was on a two weeks holiday to visit his sister, so implicating Paba doesn't have a lot of traction. What the man did in his own time is no affair of Caparra's. Enquiries don't indicate he was working as a broker or anything like that. He didn't even have friends who collected antiques. Not an easy fix, but he must have got the photograph from somewhere, and his association with Paba gives us a strong lead we can follow up. We sent copies to London, so one should reach you eventually."

Vignozzi opened a folder on his desk, pushing a photograph over to Prinn of an elderly, well-groomed man.

"Is this your New York man, that had a heart attack?" Prinn asked.

"No, that's Massimo Finetti. Found dead in his company car park, with a bullet through the roof of his car. Unfortunately, it passed through the back of his head, first. We're not sure yet if he was arriving at, or departing from, the works."

"Very obviously departing. What's his connexion with our investigation into Sandquest?"

Vignozzi smiled at Prinn's levity. "Finetti was the managing director of a company you may have heard of.

I say that because just recently his financial associate decided to take up flying. Now a Rolls Royce has strong links to aviation, but I don't believe a Silver Cloud comes with wings - not even as an extra."

"Now that *is* interesting," Prinn agreed. "Blain has recently come into the picture, but not in relationship to Sandquest. That would be an entirely new lead."

"I think it might be. The company, Italvini, is a wine producing and export business, which may be where your Sandquest fits into the picture. Blain, was a close friend and associate of Finetti. Italvini is one of the biggest such companies in Italy. We know Blain put a lot of capital into the company. On the face of it, nothing to do with Paba and Caparra. Except, we found an identical photograph to that carried by the dead man on the New York flight, in the back of Finetti's car. These things are appearing like handbills, Nicholas, but how do we tell if he's a seller, or a buyer? Finetti was certainly comfortably off. More importantly, if he'd run foul of some mob, why didn't they remove the photograph there and then? Nothing seems to have been stolen during, or as a result, of the murder. Finetti it appears, led an unblemished and uneventful life."

"Not so uneventful," Prinn said absently. "Leaving yet another untidy set of clues."

"*Credo di si.* For the moment, everything's going to go back on hold," Vignozzi continued. "If this organization's using Italvini to ship stolen antiquities out of Italy, for example, with Finetti dead, the operation will be shut down for the time being. Italvini exports worldwide. From their records we can see that the United States is one of their biggest markets, but the hot money for this illicit trade is on the London brokers who've got the perfect infrastructure. That market may dry up temporarily, until they find another carrier."

Prinn looked apprehensive. "That's one thing to keep an eye on, but Italvini also crops up in a roundabout way with the Russian lead Eldon has unearthed on Nightingale. Are we to assume that this new connexion with operation 'Necropolis', might be less than coincidental?"

The Questore nodded in agreement. "My friend we sit

122

on a hornets nest. If what we suspect is true, we're going to be in for a very uncomfortable ride."

"I suspected that the moment Sir Edward Kerry insisted Rex Eldon join us. You don't send someone with his CV on a picnic. Kerry's reasons might be becoming clearer by the day, but I'm damned if I can see the consequences."

"I'm not happy with all this ministerial interference, Nicholas. They tell us to do this, only to castigate us because we shouldn't have done that. Governments, everywhere, merely react to scandal by passing ambiguous legislation designed to make litigation a most useful tool in the promulgation of its failure. Now, with this more sinister thread being woven into an ostensibly conventional criminal case, we shall be for ever looking over our shoulder, and thus miss what's going on in front of our noses."

"I have to admit, Tomaso, I've had no experience of parallel cases - one where a suspect has a foot in both camps. There's an obvious danger in treating them as one, and confusing the two."

"You're right, which is why I've made a move to bring us into line with these developments, at the same time as taking a leaf from Sir Edward Kerry's book. The agent I've managed to place on the case is not strictly legitimate, but one who's familiar with the ropes, having stayed on for a period after his mandatory military service. For security reasons, I had to find someone who was squeaky-clean. He has a personal interest in Nightingale. His father was a Sicilian judge, and a very good friend of mine - until someone murdered him. For this reason, both young Vergellesi and I have a personal interest in the matter. Naturally, we won't let that interfere with judicial procedures. The young man has developed some significant circumstantial clues that need solid evidence attached to them. I'm considering letting Vergellesi and Eldon loose to flush out anything that can confirm these ideas, if that's all right by you?"

"I see." Prinn wasn't overenthusiastic. "All right, for a limited period we can try, but until these two operations do physically overlap, Tomaso, let's keep our sights on Operation Necropolis. At least with that, we have some idea of where we are, and I have a feeling it will very quickly expose the point of convergence with Nightingale."

"Let us hope so. Tell me, what makes you so convinced Paba will find anything in this *castello*?" Vignozzi asked, shifting to a seat in the sun. "After all, it has stood the test of time, has it not?"

"Time may be continuous but it has dimension," Prinn explained. "Castles can have a lot of history. My father, because of his unrequited passion for Sorena, has provided us with a great deal of circumstantial evidence on which to reflect."

"You can't build much of a case out of possibilities, Nicholas."

"Indeed not," Prinn assented, " but good police work has always centred on gathering evidence - much of it quite useless - some of it very profitable."

"So what do we know, then," Vignozzi inquired, "that will be beneficial to this investigation? Put me in the picture."

"First of all, we needed to know why this castle is of interest to the likes of Paba. Besides hearsay, we actually have a rather good idea of the events leading up to the making of a legend. The earliest records my father collected suggest that Paetus Cecina actually was a native of the area, and after being found complicit in the failed attempt of the republican Scribonianus to usurp Claudius, committed suicide, and was buried in the family vault. One document even manages to identify a locality, apparently erroneously. Thereafter, there is nothing of any substance until 1535, when Alessandro de Medici, Duke of Florence, appointed an early lithologist, Count Lutz, to excavate the site in a methodical and scientific manner."

"The Duke was an astute business man, and like most of the Medici's, avaricious. You can see by their profiles that they had a nose for booty," Vignozzi grumbled.

"Apparently so. By then the legend of the tombs wealth, and the possibilities of finding it, had become a characteristic of the Renaissance period. Allessandro was assassinated in 1537, but his successor, Cosimo, thought enough of the enterprise for Lutz to continue.

Which was just as well for us, because though Lutz didn't find the tomb, like a good scientist, he documented everything he did find, until he died in one of those periodical European epidemics. Copies of the documents remained in the Medici family for a few generations, though they've never been published. Until recent times they were, as our American friends say, gobbledygook. They consisted of a minute and detailed study of the rocks and stones discovered during the excavation under his stewardship. This, in itself, seemed to tell the world absolutely nothing about the tomb of Paetus."

"Meaning you consider it did?" Vignozzi speculated.

"Yes, I do. For this reason. During the nineteenth century, a much more scientific approach to archaeology took place. Reliable information, and descriptions, were accurately recorded, allowing a body of knowledge to become available for the analysis and construction of independent theories. This represented a great improvement on the old find-and-plunder methods, so beloved of archaeological despots."

"Not that it led to anyone giving up the old practices," Vignozzi pointed out.

"*Lo so*, but an improvement in printing at least allowed a freer circulation of knowledge among international experts. This spawned a rash of obscure books that by the paucity of their editions - some were by subscription, others out of the author's pocket - make them rare in modern times. Their penchant for annotation and footnotes provides a hard read, but the qualification of their sources is invaluable to those searching for something in particular. Which brings us to another of your pieces of luck. The envelope I passed on to you last month."

"We couldn't make much of that, I'm afraid," Vignozzi said apologetically. "Postmarked Rome, and type written, probably on a Remington. Inside was the plain card, instructing you to take special note of Hellbom and Simpson. That was all. No identifiable signature."

Prinn gave a frown. "Pity. The instructions were spot on, anyway. Simpson, I guessed, was Leonard Simpson the historian, whom I'd come across before, as he'd written a meticulously researched book on the Risorgimento, which featured an interesting section on the Adami twins. Nothing untoward there, except whoever it was, knew I'd be familiar with Simpson. Hellbom was another matter, and took some tracking down. If Simpson remains notable into our own times, Hellbom sank as rapidly into obscurity. Doctor Otto Hellbom was a German anthropologist whose interest lay in folklore and superstition. A most fastidious man where details were concerned, in the summer of 1820 he came to stay at a village, La Colle, lying a kilometre and a half to the west of the Castello di Pietra. Now ruinous, at that time it was occupied by a lively peasant community - always a fertile ground for the anthropologist. In the event, he was told of a fabulous labyrinth lying in the vicinity of the castle, littered with carvings, broken ceramic pots and artefacts everywhere. Few visited, as rather too many who were bold enough, disappeared. However, after persuading an old man to accompany him, he readily saw why people were frightened away. The labyrinth was found to be a highly complicated series of hazardous tunnels, where even Hellbom managed to get lost for some hours. In the process, he discovered that the roof and walls, carved out of the sand, were in an unstable and treacherous condition. He imagined that the lost souls had probably been buried alive, as many of these tunnels were blocked by falls. Only three hundred copies of his anthropological discourse were ever circulated."

"This is the necropolis, directly behind the castle?" Vignozzi queried.

"Yes, and well excavated. By 1904, when the historian Leonard Simpson wrote his definitive work on the mediaeval castles of Tuscany, the Castello di Pietra had long ceased to be of interest. Simpson includes drawings of the castle, managing a brief discourse on the legend of Paetus. In the text he doesn't mention Hellbom, but there's a footnote - Dr Otto Hellbom's reference to the peasants of La Colle, including the mysterious labyrinth."

Vignozzi gave a dubious look. "Modern historians would need more than speculative opinions, surely?"

"Very probably. Anyway, I managed to find a copy of Hellbom's little book, in Oxford. Our mysterious benefactor appears to have pointed me in two directions. The one that ties Simpson and Hellbom together, and, thereafter, to footnotes in Hellbom's book that refer to Count Lutz, and his deliberations on the geological strata of Colline Petrolla. The Count was stating that, in his view, the likelihood of the tomb being situated in accordance with historical opinion was improbable. He based this on his study of the cuts they had made into the hill, which demonstrated the presence of massive intrusions in its formation: pockets of a harder rock, which in a molten state, had been pushed through other rocks during volcanic activity. In his opinion, tomb excavators would have found the labour too problematical, forcing them to seek more conducive conditions in which to dig. That footnote was as much as Hellbom was prepared to trespass on another discipline. I was deeply intrigued to know what, if anything, Lutz might say about these more 'conducive conditions'."

"Didn't you say the papers were never published?"

"True. However, the originals do still exist. The Lutz family died out in 1787, resulting in the estate being broken up, except for the library, which eventually passed through the female line into the Bankes family. Sir Thomas Bankes assembled an important collection of early Italian manuscripts, which on his death were transferred to the crown, and eventually the British Library. The Lutz documents describe him making several other cuts into the hill at the cardinal points, both latitudinal and longitudinal, coming to the conclusion that the most likely area for such a tomb would be on the western slope of Colline Petrolla not, as had always been believed, on the south-western slope. End of story, end of Count Lutz, who died in a delirium, probably typhus."

"*Incidente!* So this error might explain why no one ever found the tomb of Paetus. So where are we now, in modern times, Nicholas? Historical matters aside."

"Beside the Castello di Pietra being built on the same western slope, as Lutz described, Simpson's sketch was of the tower, including a detail not apparent until today.

Mrs Morning, an English woman living locally, has just confirmed that a doorway, long hidden from view, has been brought to light. Its significance remains to be seen, but what she saw suggests that the doorway is of prime, if not exclusive, interest to the excavators."

"And naturally, not reported. You mentioned a man, Capagli. Nothing on record," Vignozzi added.

"Well, there certainly should be," Prinn objected. "He's a local excavator, who's in the habit of sourcing material illegally from the castle. Now, we find he's a minor partner with Paba, and can dig at the castle legally."

"And you remarked that Sandquest stands to gain a great deal, if all this is true?"

"Very definitely. Should the tomb of Paetus be found, and the legend even partially confirmed, he probably stands to acquire a collection of Etruscan works unrivalled anywhere in the world."

"From a Roman tomb?" Vignozzi queried.

"If the available contemporary records are correct, the whole of the empire might be Roman, but only by legal writ. Cecina was Roman by birth, but a hereditary Etruscan. We're told he amassed a collection of the finest items representing their culture to substantiate that fact. It might just be there, somewhere."

Vignozzi rose, crossing to the window, where he stood with his hands behind his back. "True. Dig a hole out there, anywhere, and you'd probably uncover a fortune. Difficult, of course, with six million people milling about." He turned. "Not even six, on this hill called Petrolla."

He looked at his watch. "*Andiamo.* We'll go to lunch. I want to know more about Mrs Morning, who appears to be sitting in the eye of a storm."

Chapter 13

The driver of the hired limousine picked Sandquest up from his New York penthouse suite, driving him to an international auction house on East 74th Street. Sandquest had decided to bid on an Etruscan bronze, which represented part of the Merle Cookson collection of votive objects. The little twenty centimetre high statue, in mint condition, was expected to fetch a high price.

Picking up the Herald Tribune, brought with him from the hotel, he turned to the financial pages, interested to see what knowledgeable outsiders made of the markets.

It represented a good coverage of Axmar's latest acquisition, coinciding with the death of Blain. Some mild corporate raider criticism: share price volatility, previous bullish trading forcing prices up before the bid, and a forecast on expected future earnings growth. The editor had provided analysis of those companies with similar competitive segments, along with a bland and guarded article on Blain's illustrious career. Even without him, the ever-present sting of legal writs for the unwary, lingered on.

One of these potential competitors caught Sandquest's eye. An Italian company, Sirena Systems (1988), employed two hundred and thirty people, with post-tax profits of seven point three million dollars, on sales of eighty million dollars. With offices in Milan and Dallas, the company traded mostly in the Asia-Pacific region, supplying innovative communication systems to hospitals and banks. A well-coordinated and successful business, that the newspaper's analyst doubted, was financially strong enough to fend off a hostile bid from a company such as Axmar. The suggestion; however, that they could be an attractive acquisition was dangerously untimely to Sandquest. It wouldn't be long, before some eagle-eyed financial journalist noticed that Blain's associate, the chief executive, Massimo Finetti, was also newly, and violently, deceased.

Sandquest let himself out of the limousine in front of the auction house in a distracted frame of mind. He could do nothing, except shrug it off irritably.

The sales room, reached through a richly upholstered entrance, deteriorated into a large paint chipped auditorium, with stiff, uncomfortable plastic seats, facing the auctioneer's stand. Behind this elevated redoubt, aproned porters hovered among the assembled lots like vendors at a horticultural show.

Sitting discreetly at the back, Sandquest politely acknowledged a few dealers, without engaging them in conversation. He wasn't in a conversational mood; thoughts being constantly distracted by the outcome of his American subsidiaries recent bid for part of Blain's empire. Successful as it had been, and bending to the arguments of his company executives who had engineered the take over, he couldn't explain in terms of company policy why he would have preferred the deal to fail. They wouldn't have understood his purely personal considerations.

With Blain dead his empire would slip away, absorbed into the league of minnows snapping at the carcass as its complicated financial structure unwound. No one shared his intrigues, or remained to steer the ship. Blain had taken the tiller with him to the grave.

Sandquest didn't want to own anything that retained the odour of Blain, and this latest acquisition was not blessed with a commendable fragrance. Tainted with an executive whose philosophy would be more destructive than constructive, the weeding out would be a bloody and acrimonious business.

The auctioneer, a plump, overindulged factotum, in a carelessly worn polka-dot bow tie, knowing a small amount about everything, appeared a most illuminating savant. He passed humorously through the first forty lots, regaling old cronies and novices alike in an effort to break the chill of reluctance that permeated the early bidders call. Timid and apprehensive, they would be struggling to find the courage of their convictions - saving their powder for a bigger moment, or hoping for a sudden death in the bidding that would let them in.

Reaching the more important lots, he became more intent on working up the bids, his eyes studying every movement in the rows of faces. There were no favourites today, or the usual odd missed calls, with the chief auctioneer demanding positive results, and everything related to a percentage. To this end he kept a wary eye on the taciturn man at the back who waited patiently for Cookson's votive bronze - good practice for the moment when a nod meant another five hundred dollars.

The auctioneer rapped his gavel, and called up lot seventy.

The competition was lethargic, intimidated by the presence of an acne furrowed face buried under a large black Homburg who'd let it be known he'd reserved a special interest in lot seventy. Unfortunately for him, his homicidal uncle Leo owed Sandquest a bigger favour than lot seventy.

The auctioneer, frustrated by this lethargy, racked the price up too high, bouncing a false bid off the wall. Backtracking on the bidding with considerable fuss over spurious calls, the auctioneer bowed to the inevitable, knocking the bronze down to a satisfied Sandquest below the catalogued estimate.

Recollecting that the Cookson collection had also contained a fine bucchero pitcher that hadn't been entered in the published catalogue, Sandquest decided to stay on in case any supplementary lots should conveniently appear by special arrangement with the auctioneer.

Somewhere, towards the end of the sale, a man slid into the vacant chair next to him.

"Hello, Willie," Sandquest said, without looking away from the auctioneer.

"Hello, Mr Sandquest. Nice purchase, lot seventy. Not a lot of bother there. Punters seem rather reticent today."

"Uncle Leo's dull-witted, infantile nephew, Willie. They'll bury him, or lock him up before long."

"Didn't know he was a collector of antiquities, Mr Sandquest," Willie commented dryly. "Parking tickets perhaps."

"Takes all sorts, Willie."

"All sorts," Willie repeated. "Thought you'd bought a similar lot in Milan, though?"

"I did indeed, but I consider this a finer specimen. Crisper, not bumped about so much. Fresh from the grave, wouldn't you say?"

Willie was noncommittal. "One careful lady owner. They don't come with a better provenance than that."

"I dare say. I heard friend Brizzi was just beginning to find your services most useful. What have you in mind, now he's inconveniently gone?"

"Business as usual. Remain open to any new opportunities that come my way." He lowered his voice, and leant closer. "For example, Von Moler tells me he's lining up a major deal that's likely to stretch his resources."

"Yes, I heard that somewhere. But we must keep that to ourselves, Willie."

"Absolutely, Mr Sandquest. Mum's the word. Von Moler was saying he'd need to offload the lesser items on to the market. Something I can arrange for him. Discreetly. Goes without saying. London, Paris, New York, everywhere - except Rome, where they might have a vested interest."

"No one has a more profound knowledge of the trade than you, Willie."

"One must be professional," Willie sighed. "Auctions are so predictable. There's always a deceased collector, like Mrs Cookson, whose collection can be augmented by a piece or two." Willie tapped the side of his nose, knowingly. "This will need a deal more savvy than that. Did you know I once arranged a complete sale of a collection for someone who never owned anything more valuable than a Wedgwood earthenware ashtray?"

"I've heard it said Willie, that it was the only thing he did own."

"True. Turned out to be the most expensive ashtray ever to go under the hammer!" Willie laughed, tickled by the thought of it. "While you're in town Mr Sandquest, I know of someone who might have a piece or two that would interest you."

"You should come back to England, Willie," Sandquest advised. "Market's boomed in your absence. Have to tighten up your act a little, no shady items with unknown provenances."

"Not so. Not so. These have pukka bills of sale." Willie protested. "I don't do forgeries any more."

"Then I suppose I'd better see them. Collect me

tomorrow evening, at seven thirty. And Willie, make sure this 'someone-you-know', realizes I won't accept goods that have doubtful histories. No Jewish canoes with bent mileage."

Willie laughed gently again, recalling a past embarrassment. "Mannie's sticking to Cadillacs now, I hear. But you have to agree, it was a very nice piece?"

"Yes, very nice, and belonging to someone else!"

"How could anyone know, Mr Sandquest?"

"The Museo Nazionale di Cosa knew, Willie," Sandquest remarked. "Very embarrassing. Such a disappointment too."

"For all of us, Mr Sandquest. For all of us."

"I suppose so. You'll make sure that I won't be disappointed?"

"I will, Mr Sandquest." He lowered his voice. "Might I just say, that there's a very nice gold tazza among the pieces. Gold's so risky these days. Appears to have been born out of wedlock. Dodgy birth certificate, I wouldn't be surprised - If you take my point?"

"Point taken, Willie," Sandquest acknowledged.

"Just so, Mr Sandquest," Willie said, slipping out of his seat. "Your apartment at seven thirty tomorrow. I must say, things have moved on a long way since we traded out of the back seat of a Mark X, Jaguar."

Chapter 14

The vacillations of a watery midday sun had given way to drizzle, with the weather station forecasting worse. Hart had found himself in a mood to match the weather. With all the extra responsibilities, he could do without the constant surprises his secretary firmly rescued from her in tray, and deposited on his desk.

Pulling out a yellow African meerschaum, Hart stuffed the bowl full of tobacco from a leather pouch. The perished rubber lining, mixing freely with the tobacco, inevitably found its way into the bowl where it emitted a fearsome smell of latex that hung around his office for days. Oblivious to the smell, he lit the offending instrument. The pipe gurgled aqueously, rendered silent by stuffing the tobacco deeper into the bowl with the end of a pencil.

Hart took up the file Commander Prinn had unceremoniously given him to digest. It was something Prinn had brought with him from his time with Special Branch. Not important enough to sit on a desk, merely remaining a memory on a bottom shelf of a dusty place.

When the file had become active again, Sir Edward Kerry had sprung the ex-special forces officer, Eldon on them, shortly followed by the unearthing of a Blain-Sandquest connexion. Hart immediately recognized the hidden currents in the waters that ran surreptitiously through Whitehall. He was decidedly uneasy about them being diverted through the Metropolitan Police, but like any civil servant, he had early learnt to 'mind his P's and Q's'. Waves in the water were a destabilizing influence.

Nightingale was an isolated phenomenon that Hart had come to realize provided a bridge between two quite dissimilar investigations. Such an inexplicable chance relationship had doubled their complexity. The departments own operation 'Necropolis', was so convoluted and involved, that any auxiliary elements could easily turn the whole thing into an impossible nightmare. Hart was determined to keep abreast of proceedings. Opening the bulging file, he found the Baker Street omnibus ticket that served as a marker.

Nightingale was an old, and a bad memory, a hang over from the cold war that should have quietly slipped away. Once loose strings were history, they hardly served any purpose. MI5 had never identified the British members of the Rote Kapelle, putting the file gently to bed, too old to pursue any longer. The historians could beaver away at their identity for as long as they liked. Nightingale, by contrast, seemed to be a phoenix rising from the funeral pyre of Soviet communism, reborn, ready to pass through another cycle.

Recently, a Questore from Rome Prinn was acquainted with through European Interpol conferences and intelligence committee meetings, had flown over especially to brief Specialist Operations. Subsequently, Eldon had been seconded to the O.C.G.

His placement wasn't standard practice, but then, from what Hart could see, neither was anything in the least bit standard about Nightingale.

The Soviets were known to have employed an assassin since the mid seventies, accompanying the Marxist MPLA in Angola under the guise of a Soviet military adviser. The CIA had given the assassin a retrospective code name of Nightingale in 1978, after a Palestinian organization's Berlin representative was murdered as he arrived for a meeting with a United States congressman; the marksman vanishing into the darkness without trace. According to the congressman, the only sound had been a nightingale's harsh 'kerr' of alarm a moment or two before he heard the shot.

Thereafter, the name had stuck. Among others cases, there had been a Bulgarian defector who reached Istanbul before meeting a similar fate; then a Soviet double agent blown to pieces along with his American courier as they switched trainers in a gym. Later, the methods of execution had become more ingenious. Sometimes it was difficult to obtain any evidence of the crime, illustrating Nightingale's contemporary methods. In all these long years of murder only one, small and indecisive verification had surfaced of Nightingale's existence. During 1984, Nikolai Sapunov was enrolled into the KGB's Seventh Directorate, responsible for external surveillance. After four years the directorate

135

transferred him to Vilnias in Lithuania, a move providing the catalyst that would shortly turn him into a traitor.

Sapunov was an analyst, responsible for overseeing the reports sent in by a team of agents. This low-grade occupation he found singularly tedious in a Soviet republic not previously noted for anything in particular, least of all as a hot bed of subversion and insurrection.

In the autumn of 1988 he received orders to concentrate his team of agents on John Duncan, a Canadian businessman with engineering interests who, under Mikhail Gorbachev's perestroika reforms, had used the opportunity to open talks with a Lithuanian State Company specializing in mining tools. Ivan Favorsky, known to be a leading member of the Council of Sajudis, a political party deeply committed to Lithuanian independence, was the director. At that time, a journalist and unknown KGB agent, Yaroslav Proskurov was the executive secretary of the council. It became obvious to Proskurov that Duncan and Levchenko were negotiating more than the export of machine tools for North American mining interests.

Moscow in turn handed Sapunov his brief. The hotel room where Duncan was staying was already fitted with concealed transmitters. Similar devices were installed in Levchenko's office. Subsequently, Levchenko was flown to Moscow to be accompanied through the door of Lubyanka prison. He was never seen again.

Duncan had been allowed to slip out of Lithuania, returning to Canada, where six months later he was found floating, face down, in Lake Huron. Weights had been tied to his body; a miscalculation permitting the natural body gases to overcome the weight of the scuba belts, allowing Duncan to float to the surface.

Hart took another match to his pipe. Nightingale until then had been a theory, a convenient idea held to explain a number of insuperable facts, until an event took place that allowed the security services to form an outline of the assassin. Thanks to Nikolai Sapunov.

In the February of 1989 Sapunov jumped ship. Having been sent to Klaipeda on the Baltic Sea to supervise agents aboard a ferry bound for Rostock, he stayed with them until they landed at the German port and calmly followed them ashore. Finding his way to Denmark he turned himself in, explained who he was, and requested political asylum in England. The Danes had obliged, sending Sapunov to London. Believed to be a plant, the Foreign Office didn't insist on protocol, considering Sapunov would soon be on his way back to Russia. They were wrong. Sapunov wanted to stay, with no one to change his mind. No weeping wife on the end of a telephone; no frightened parents; no family, with the prospects of a new address in Siberia. Nothing to encourage Sapunov to change his mind.

MI5 had taken their time with Sapunov. As an agent he would be of limited use, but he was not an empty vessel. There were matters of organization, of names, of policy. Innocuous pieces that might provide important evidence when added to the broader portrait of enemy espionage. Unlike a defector-in-place, remaining in their original occupation or, even better, being promoted to ever more sensitive, and useful employment, Sapunov had only the one story to tell. Over some months they cross-examined him, until feeling the first signs of déjà vu, they decided to give the interview a rest. Start again afresh. MI5 circulated his dossier to those departments with a reason to know.

Thus Prinn's department, investigating the mysterious death of an Armenian dissident on the London underground, came across the first positive evidence that the enigma, code named Nightingale, might actually exist; was flesh and blood, not the figment of some CIA operations officer's imagination in Langley, Virginia. There, in the frozen words of the transcript, a brief but significant event took place in Sapunov's lacklustre story.

During that autumn of 1988, when John Duncan had come under suspicion, and Sapunov's team were collecting material on his activities, Sapunov received a telephone call from his Moscow departmental chief, Lieutenant Colonel Sergeyevich of the Seventh Directorate. Sapunov was to expect some visitors who had an interest in studying the subjects under investigation.

Two officers arrived. One, Colonel Tazov, older and

very serious, as career officers in the Soviet forces tended to be; the other, a Lieutenant Colonel called Kalugin, obviously well connected, fresh faced, looking no more than an attractive youth. Though they were both staff officers, it became apparent that Colonel Tazov was extremely deferential to his subordinate, opening doors and standing back to let him pass through. Unusual conduct, Sapunov related, in a stiff hierarchical organization like the KGB.

Kalugin was demonstrably important, seemingly the only officer interested in the subjects, especially the Canadian, making notes in a small but expensive leather bound book of a quality that probably didn't even come with special privileges.

On one occasion, while they were shadowing an agent, Kalugin dropped his book. Sapunov retrieved it, noticing that it was written in an extremely small and neat Slavonic script, possibly Polish or Czech. Certainly not Russian. Kalugin had taken it, turning away without a word. Indeed, one of the significant facts about the lieutenant colonel was that he said very little. Looking back, Sapunov couldn't recall Kalugin taking part in a conversation during the whole time he was there.

One evening Sapunov received a coded message that had to be delivered at once. Taking it up to Kalugin's hotel room, he knocked heavily, but could receive no answer due to loud classical music coming from within. The music took him back to his youth, reminding him of a visit he'd made to Ljubljana, a town in Slovenia. They'd picnicked by the River Sava, with the radio on the coach providing background entertainment, an opera by Stravinsky, *'Le Rossignol'* - 'The Nightingale'. The message had eventually to be delivered by Colonel Tazov.

Prinn had formally requested an interview with Sapunov. The meeting proved to be as disappointing as the possibilities had been auspicious, and desperately far-fetched. Prinn felt that his department was being driven to chase even the most superficial of clues.

Given Sapunov's acquaintance with Kalugin, his description of the officer was not very informative. The disclosures seemed of insignificant interest. The lieutenant colonel had a penchant for fine Italian wine, obviously liked classical music, and smelt of soap. Prinn, querying the reason for this last remark, had drawn a laugh from Sapunov. In Russia, soap was soap; sodium salts of fatty acids, with the only aroma best described as carbolic sweat. In his opinion Kalugin had either very useful connexions, or he travelled abroad where access to these forbidden fruits was possible.

The information had taken Prinn so far, but not very far.

After that everything had fallen flat. Prinn had been promoted and his career took a new path. Old cases just went to ground, wrapped up, or put on hold. Sapunov had been lost to sight until Prinn had decided to conjure him up again for Gower. The Commander obviously wasn't leaving anything to chance.

Hart sucked furiously on the dying embers of his pipe to no avail. He drew his ashtray across the desk; placing his pipe there, bowl up, to cool down.

Nightingale, for all practical purposes, had remained invisible. No identity, no warnings, and no mistakes. The security services seemed to be forever opening the front door while Nightingale was closing the back one.

Now, according to Vignozzi, Nightingale was very definitely a killer with a musical streak, and out and about on Civvy Street. He could see the connexion Prinn was making, but you needed a quantum leap in imagination to see one between an opera-loving soldier and the assassin Nightingale.

As the most recent manifestation came in the form of the Blain-Parson documents, safely deposited with the Support Branch, Hart decided he needed to keep up to date with all these divergent elements and considered it might be tactful to pay them a visit and see what progress was being made.

-oOo-

Hart opened the door of Gower's office, temporarily parking his umbrella in the paper bin.

"That was a job well done, Rex."

"They've finished the preliminary work, then?" Eldon enquired.

"Yes. One or two interesting items have come to light already, but we'll have a better idea of the contents in a few days time. C11 telephoned this morning demanding to know how Strawberry Cottage appeared on our books, and whether, or not, we had any other little surprises up our sleeve. Told them we haven't." Hart cautiously added, "I don't suppose we have, have we?"

"Not at this very moment, no. You mentioned to them that Blain might have had an alias, in the name of Parsons?"

"They're looking into that. Just a credibility name, I imagine. Speak to Sergeant Douglas of the Support Branch to find out the latest results."

Hart turned to Gower, who was engrossed in compiling a graph on his computer. "Sandy, how many days can you give me, without upsetting your schedule?"

Gower rotated his chair to face Hart. "Let me see. Our Mr. Nol is flying back to Phnom-Penh tomorrow, for a week. I could spare a few days. Something up?"

"In a manner of speaking. I want you to fly to Sundsvall in Sweden, then take the ferry to Vaasa."

"I can fly straight into Vaasa, sir?"

"I know, Sandy, but then you'll miss the man Commander Prinn wants you to meet. He'll be travelling on the same boat, having developed something of an affinity with ferries. Nikolai Sapunov. Russian national living under an alias in Finland."

"Right. How will I know this chappie?" Gower inquired

"I'm told, by his socks. The Macpherson tartan."

"Is that all, sir?"

"Well, it's a detail a Caledonian will recognise better than I. Miss Veronica will make your travel arrangements. Four days. No more," Hart added seriously. "I'm not forgetting the last time we sent you abroad. Mislaid your ticket, and found a blonde. Commander might have smiled at your nonsense, but I won't."

"Fly back out of Sundsvall then, do I, sir?"

"Yes. Keep you out of mischief." Hart paused by the door. "In between, you won't even need to get off the ferry."

"Spoilsport," Gower muttered to Hart's retreating

back. "Well, I wonder what all this is about. Nothing to do with you I suppose?"

Eldon smiled. "Cross my heart."

-oOo-

At certain times of the day, Fulham had the manner and nature of a provincial town. Eldon, having turned into a cul-de-sac off the Lillie Road, parked in front of a square brick building that might have been a cash and carry warehouse, rather than the offices of the Intelligence Support Branch, engaged in sifting and filtering information for Specialist Operations.

Eldon stood in the entrance porch, out of the rain, and pressed the buzzer. He gave his name and number, waiting a few moments before he gained admittance to the austere and colourless reception area. The police-woman, over transparent behind a glass desk, asked how she could help?

"Sergeant Douglas is expecting me," Eldon replied.

The constable gave a short flickering smile, dialled a number, and then tapped her fingers in a drum roll on the glass top.

Relaying his request, she smiled again in confirmation. "He'll be with you straight away, sir."

Sergeant Douglas was a dapper man with dark brilliantined hair, and a fresh, clean-shaven appearance. His little outpost of the Intelligence Department was not long for Lillie Road, now that everything was being centralized and air-conditioned elsewhere.

"Hello, sir. Chief Superintendent Hart said you'd be along." They shook hands. "Come through here. We're making progress, but I'm not exactly sure what you're looking for."

"Ditto!" Eldon confirmed.

Passing down a corridor, through electronic doors opened by digitally coded locks, they reached an artificially lit area divided into a dozen large sections, each containing a research unit handling the material and documentation for an individual case.

"Here's Strawberry Cottage, Mr. Eldon." He stopped where three officers were diligently sorting their way through cardboard boxes.

"Looks a bit of a handful," Eldon commented.

"We took down a pair of portable Photostat cameras, plus some photocopiers. Mostly hard graft feeding everything through. Finished the business orientated sections this morning. We've just made a start on the personal documentation."

"How far back does it go?" Eldon inquired.

"1944, I believe."

"1943, Sergeant," one of the research officers corrected him, holding up a photocopy of a letter and envelope. "Earliest so far. A billet-doux from Joyce."

Douglas took it. "Postmarked Wolverhampton, May 1943. Not a pleasant time." He read the letter before passing it to Eldon. "Just Joyce. No surname, and no address. Anything of interest to you?"

The letter was brief, but Blain had obviously made an impression on Joyce, who expected their illicit liaison to continue.

"Possibly. Are there any similar letters from women, other than Joyce?" Eldon asked.

The research officer nodded. " Half a dozen or so from a Mrs Violet Penny."

"Make any sense?" Douglas asked.

"That depends on Joyce."

"You think she's still alive?"

"If she's the same Joyce who was married to Sir Maxwell Blain's early partner, Arthur Sandquest, then no," Eldon affirmed. "She was killed during a bombing raid, in December 1943."

Sergeant Douglas huffed. "I hope we're not beavering away here on a domestic matter, Mr Eldon. Did Sandquest know of this paramour in his bed?"

"That we don't know," Eldon confessed. "All we know, is there's a connexion between Blain and Sandquest. How do we find out if Joyce is the glue?"

"Circa fifty years ago, Mr Eldon?" And then as an afterthought, "But perhaps not."

"Perhaps not?"

"Depends if your mysterious visitor to Strawberry Cottage, was Sandquest." Douglas turned to another of the assistants. "Chris, you dealt with something to do with that, didn't you?"

"Don't think Sandquest's the right track, Sergeant." Chris turned to face Eldon. "The cigarette packet you found at the cottage, sir, was a Sullivan Powell Turkish No 1. Roger, over there, fancies himself as a bit of an amateur psychologist, reckoning that people who smoke are often stress related victims. If so, the person who dropped the packet most likely needed a confidence booster somewhere, and the most likely place for that would be at the entrance to a stress related environment."

"The gate in the lay-by?" Eldon suggested.

"Exactly, sir. The entrance to the wood. One of the seven cigarette butts we recovered, was a Sullivan Powell. But the smoker wasn't a man. Whoever worked through Blain's personal files, was a female. Forensic established that, by the traces of lipstick on the cigarette butt found in the lay-by. They were from the same packet you brought in."

"Time scale?" Eldon enquired.

"Lab' say's, between fourteen to twenty days."

"Let's say, two to three weeks to organize the parting of Sir Maxwell," Douglas contemplated thoughtfully. "Bit tight for a precisely executed plot. Not a plan that saw a lot of rush. Weeks of surveillance, inside knowledge of his movements, tactical procedures. A lot of weeks, even for a professional."

Indicating that this letter wasn't a motivating factor in his death." Eldon handed back the photocopy.

"Anything we should be looking for in a hurry," Sergeant Douglas inquired. " So we can brief you?"

"Whatever comes up on Italy, I think. That's where Blain seems to have been heading, before he fell off a mountain."

-oOo-

Eldon sat in his car staring at the rain running in sluggish rivulets down the screen, the telltale sweep of the wipers having left an iridescent sheen on the glass. He was frustrated. A case this old wasn't going to suddenly unravel. A lot of space existed to hide things in, needing a considerable amount of time to seek them out.

A knock on the window startled him.

The traffic warden peering through the car window looked morose in her black raincoat, and sodden cap. Eldon lowered the window.

"Yes, I'm just going," he said, starting the engine, and releasing the handbrake.

"You can take this with you, then, sir," she replied, passing him a ticket in a polythene bag. "You've been parked on this yellow line for forty minutes."

-oOo-

Eldon looked up from his computer as Hart placed a neat pile of papers on his desk.

"Sergeant Douglas has sent these along. Bit of a jumble," Hart said disapprovingly. "Dossier of letters from a man called Massimo Finetti. Have you come across him yet?"

"Not personally, no." Eldon said. "Though a new face is always interesting. Especially one that has a touch of contemporary Italy about it."

Hart tapped the top of the bundle. "Latest was picked up from the Post Office, day before yesterday. Must have got lost in the Dolomites. Talk about that later."

Watching the departing figure, Eldon considered whether the talk had to do with the Post Office or the Dolomites? He eased the first sheet from under its paper clip: a photocopy of the original envelope - Italian stamp, neat handwriting - and the letter.

Caro Max
You wouldn't listen to me, would you? Now we're in serious trouble. Brizzi and Saxe are dead. I still have the statues. I intend to get rid of them immediately, to the man Paba we talked about. That's all we can do. You must be careful. Forget your vendetta with Sandquest. Phone me the minute you get this letter. I'll keep trying, in the mean time. Don't come back to Italy until I can talk to you. Keep out of the way.
Massimo.

Eldon smoothed out the folded photocopy on his desk. Progress of a sort. The letter proved that Blain and Sandquest had remained current enemies until very recently. What form the animosity had taken, was not clear. Statues might represent antiques - or might not.

He wondered how Sandquest would react to knowing about Joyce and Blain?

Chapter 15

Threading his way up the steep metal steps, Gower passed through the car decks with their dense smell of diesel into the fresh air.

Slipping on a pair of sunglasses against the dazzle of freshly painted sides and rails, he found himself a seat that looked out over the stern. Drawing up the collar of his 'British warm' against an icy wind, he pushed his hands deep into the pockets. No point wandering about looking at other people's ankles, he thought, pulling his legs under the seat.

One or two passengers joined him in the stern, their breaths rising in silent plumes into the cold air as, almost imperceptibly, the ferry pulled gently away from the landing, sliding quietly sideways from the quay, before reversing out into the channel followed by the gyrations of chattering gulls.

He knew he would see little of his cabin bunk in deference to Nicolai Sapunov.

Having located Gower, Sapunov would spend time studying his contact, making sure that Gower was not under covert surveillance. Sapunov would have learnt to appraise every move, every person, and every condition, with an intense prejudice. His very life depended on it. Even with an alias, and a new home in a secret location, he still remained in danger from a chance Soviet mole buried deep within the British security system, who would instantly divulge his whereabouts to Moscow. How long he took was as long as it took to feel safe.

Therefore, Gower appreciated the care that Sapunov must take, despite the fact that it wouldn't cease to be tiresome. Remaining hunched against the cold, he sat stoically until the coastline merged into the anthracite coloured sea. Returning to the musty inner warmth of the saloon, Gower leant against the bar.

"Something more than a wee sensation. No soda, no lemon, no ice. Leave plenty of room for the Scotch."

The steward raised his eyebrows. "Canada Dry, sir?"

"No. If it looks a wee bit mean, add more Scotch."

Gower took his drink to the comfortable bulkhead seat

146

that curved in a serpentine swathe of blue velour, with a commanding view of the sparsely occupied saloon. At this time of the year, the ferry was used almost exclusively by truck drivers, saving the long haul to the north round the tip of the Baltic. Not the sort of place where you could blend easily into the crowd. One or two representatives on their way to Helsinki via a major town or two perhaps, but that was all. Sapunov was going to have to be good.

Feeling a little flushed in the airless warmth, Gower folded his coat neatly next to him. Extracting a book from the inner pocket, it looked unlikely to delay the gathering onset of ennui.

Gower had hardly commenced reading, when he became aware of three men, studying him solicitously from the central island: truck drivers in overalls, wearing thick, heavy woollen jackets. Gower of a mind for a diversion returned their interest. Eventually, they came across.

From their accents he recognized two of the men came from the far north of Finland, on the Norwegian border. The third, having an accent that was movable, falling on different syllables during the inflexion of a word, he failed to place.

They liked to play bridge, only for small stakes, but as their usual fourth hand was on holiday, they wondered if he might like to sit through a rubber or two.

Gower agreed - as long as they kept the stakes within bounds. He was also conscious that the party would provide a modicum of cover, though Sapunov would have no difficulty recognizing him. The man with the movable accent chose to partner him, sitting down on the bulkhead seat. The others drew up chairs, to sit opposite.

Gower's partner didn't hurry, making his bids with monotonous success. He was a man who read the cards surprisingly well, but unlike his friends, drank very little.

"Plenty of time to sleep off the effects," Gower commented, when their opponents left to replenish their drinks.

The man nodded his head. "No good drowning your sorrows on a boat, in case they drown you."

Gower heeded the melancholy in his voice. "I hope you're not going to get maudlin?"

The man smiled, looking deep into his glass, but didn't pursue the line of conversation. "We don't get too many British up here. Not at any time of the year. Are you on business?"

Gower gave his prepared answer to the question. "In a manner of speaking. Firm's sent me to Gävle. Ball bearings. I've a couple of days off, so I thought I'd have a trip to Finland. Regular run for you?"

The man looked at him silently for a moment. "No. Nothing's ever regular. I work for a haulage company. Whatever needs carrying, we'll oblige. Goes with the job. As I don't have a family to worry about, I handle all the long haul work." The melancholy had returned, but his friends came back with their oversize glasses, and the general conversation took another turn.

Gower cut the cards, as his partner dealt for another rubber, taking in the room for one more of an endless number of times. Sapunov must be out there; any one of a dozen or so people he'd idly noted as possibilities, watching him win a few stakes, and lose a few more.

A sonorous voice announced over the PA system that the restaurant was now open. The bridge club drew a line under the last rubber. Gower declined their invitation to join them for a meal, explaining he'd settle for a sandwich, expecting to have a decent dinner in Vaasa. They slapped him on the back, taking off with practised sea legs, in the direction of the restaurant.

Gower counted his small change, finding he'd made a small profit, enough for another Scotch. Perhaps not. Drinking on duty was a bad habit, and Sapunov would be waiting by now to make contact with him.

Instead, he shut his eyes to conjure up the image of Miss Veronica. If ever there was a lass who could turn a laddie's fancy, Miss Veronica more than qualified. Perhaps he'd ask her out when he got back. A swish restaurant in the West End, and coffee back at his apartment afterwards. A double bed could be a very lonely place on a Saturday evening. He opened his eyes with a start, laughing at being fanciful.

Gower picked up the book he'd left on top of his coat

Shuffled through the pages, stopping mystified by a bookmarker he hadn't placed there.

A souvenir from a trip to Scotland in the form of a highlander's stocking. Gower picked it up and noted it was complete with dirk and pumps and in, what was most definitely, the Macpherson tartan.

Chapter 16

Hart's thoughtful face was pulled into an uncharacteristic frown. He needed to consider carefully Eldon's proposal - neither did he exactly have time to sleep on it. He found it troublesome, and though he had half expected it, Eldon's investigation was beginning to impinge on Operation Necropolis's territory at an alarming rate.

"Something we should try and avoid just at this moment, Rex," he advised. "Speaking to Sandquest."

"I don't think we're at liberty to create our own plot, sir."

"You're not being very helpful." Hart returned to his chair.

"Is that what I have to be, helpful?"

"Sounds better than being awkward," Hart said roundly.

"The truth's always unpredictable."

"I'm well aware of that. Makes me uncomfortable, that's all. But don't take that as an indication I let sleeping dogs lie. Because I don't. I'll wake them up when necessary." Hart tutted, and looked bad tempered, but Eldon remained insistent.

"We have to know about Joyce? We have to know why Sandquest and Blain still seemed to be at each other's throats, fifty years later? Was Joyce the reason? Where else do you suggest we find out? Joyce and Blain are dead. At the moment I haven't even a trace of Nightingale, except in the shadow of these two men - and I don't even really know if they're significant. But, I have not the slightest doubt, that a great deal might hinge on it."

"I know, I know." Hart resigned himself to the candour in Eldon's argument. "Sandquest just happens to be something of a legend, Rex. A big man: in size, in wealth, in influence. Digging over his coals is going to cause a lot of smoke."

"We're hardly going to get warm without a little fire."

"I think we'll have more chance of being burnt," Hart countered. "The information you've dug up on Sandquest commenced before his official history begins. No one's ever had a reason to go there. All I can do is fill you in on what has emerged since anyone bothered to take notice. What's written in the book," Hart emphasized. "Nothing about juveniles?"

"All right. Let's settle for that then."

Hart considered the proposal, and then nodded. "I haven't got all day, so just the basic facts - for what it's worth. Without the misfortune of war I doubt if anyone would have heard of Sandquest. He was hauled out of a signals unit into the Code and Cipher School - a square peg in a round hole, among all those middle-class highbrows. Given the dubious relationships that were supposed to have developed down there, his difficult personality might well have ended up being a liability. He would have thought the precious inmates of the place were looking down their noses at him, feeling like the first black boy in an all white school. A problem, when no one was ever allowed to walk away from the place. Apparently something of a genius, he was able to break down and factorize electronic apparatus at a fair old rate. Rather than lose these talents altogether, they had him recruited into the Special Operations Executive. While his colleagues on the operation were causing mayhem, he was gathering intelligence useful to Bletchley Park. Tricky business, identifying components and systems, while people are trying to blow your head off. Getting out again was equally difficult. How he managed to get back from some of the places they parachuted him into - sometimes he was the only one to get back - is part of the history. In 1945 the RAF dropped him east of Berlin, to arrange the retrieval of valuable electronic experiments being carried out by German scientists willing to flee to the West in the face of the Russian advance. They were due to be flown out under cover of darkness, but because there were more than expected rushing to the lifeboat, the aircraft couldn't lift off on the short runway. Sandquest volunteered to stay behind, with anything the aircrew could jettison. Nothing was heard of him for six months. S.O.E. assumed he'd been killed when the Russians overran the area only hours later in their advance on

151

Berlin. Instead, Marshall Konev's 1st Ukrainian Front had picked him up near Baruth, eventually sending him back. He was decorated for his efforts. Military Medal."

"And that was all they managed to write up on him?" Eldon reflected. "Nothing that's likely to switch on a light somewhere."

Hart shrugged. "There is a little more. You have to remember, that everything was very confused at that time, not only in continental Europe. All I can tell you is, he appears to have been extensively de-briefed on his arrival in the UK. Anyone who had contact with the Russians, received a pretty severe interrogation, especially someone involved in a high-level operation like Sandquest. Nothing suggested he'd been turned. In any case, he was soon to be demobbed. If he'd applied to stay on, I suspect he'd have become the subject of long-term assessment. His strong entrepreneurial streak allowed him to get started in the electrical business. Later, he progressed from manufacturing light bulbs to making valves, rectifiers and receivers - that sort of thing. Government contracts followed, along with stricter security checks. Today, his electronics empire covers top-secret development work, not only for our own forces, but NATO as well. To get to my point, Rex, if he was instrumental in the killing of Sir Maxwell Blain, a known, or at least suspected criminal, no one would want to hear about it."

Eldon had listened intently. "I do take your point, sir. However, in my opinion, Sandquest appears pivotal at this moment. What do you want me to do?"

Hart shrugged. "Nightingale's your case. Commander Prinn asked me to advise you on operational issues, that's all. I only wish he'd been able to indicate some less flexible parameters to your activities. Not your fault, but I can't give the Commander a bell every time things don't add up. You just have to be aware of the politics. Sandquest has friends that whisper all the way to Downing Street, and the Oval Office. You'd better not make too many waves."

-oOo-

Eldon travelled in the lift up to the second floor, to be directed into the executive corridor. A door opened at the end, where one of Sandquest's secretaries met him.

He sat in the outer office studying the modern prints on the walls, until he realized they weren't prints, and the telephone rang.

"This way, sir," the secretary said, opening another door.

Eldon's gaze never left Livia's face as they shook hands. He'd taken in the well-proportioned shape of her ankles, the elegant shoes, the impeccably tailored suit, and the long pale hand, perfectly manicured. For the moment he let himself concentrate on the blueness of her eyes. The one thing he confirmed, from their brief meeting in the doorway of the Anglo Italian Wine Company, was that the meeting with Sandquest would be an anticlimax.

"Mr Eldon. Mr Sandquest sends his apologies. He'll be with you in a little while, if you'll forgive him. I'm his personal assistant, Livia Wolfe. I've taken the liberty to order coffee. If you'd prefer tea?"

Eldon shook his head. "No. Coffee's fine. Thank you."

She put her hand out towards some armchairs.

In the soft movement of her blonde hair, he caught the passing fragrance of her perfume. He was reminded that certain things refer themselves to the senses in particular situations. Jean Patou's Joy was one of them. His mother, and Her Majesty, would certainly have approved. Perhaps the elusive Mr. Parsons wouldn't.

They sat down together. A low glass coffee table between them. He liked the way she placed her legs, elegantly symmetrical, to one side. Everything about her had a natural symmetry.

"I also have to apologize," Livia said, "for the fact that Mr. Sandquest can only spare you thirty minutes, but he has a late ten o'clock flight to Vancouver tonight. We have a tight schedule. If you could confine yourself to that amount of time, I would be grateful."

Eldon nodded.

The door opened. One of the secretaries brought in a tray, bearing their coffee.

"Mr. Sandquest said you were from the Metropolitan

Police?" Livia continued.

"I expect they requested the interview."

Livia thought he was being rather non-committal, but didn't press the point. "Mr. Sandquest hasn't given me any instructions, so I'm afraid I haven't prepared anything. Cream?"

"Thank you. No sugar." Eldon took the cup and saucer. "It's unlikely the answers I'm looking for will be found in any files, so I think we can say it's not that important."

A spent cigarette in the ashtray at the end of the table, where it had been placed to accommodate the tray, caught his attention. He saw she'd noticed, and grasped the opportunity.

"They say that smoking can damage your health," he said, smiling at the same time, in case it sounded too aggressive. He couldn't help it sounding stuffy.

"Can I speak with my lawyer before I answer that question?" Livia laughed easily. Even that was attractive.

"If they're an antidote for habits, why not?" Eldon added, a touch too seriously. He hated sounding like an evangelist.

"Well, it's certainly an antidote for stress," she replied, with a flash of perfect teeth. "On that we can agree."

"Why not? Turkish cigarettes might suggest a lot of stress."

Livia gave a surprised glance back at the ashtray. "You must definitely be a policeman."

"Oh, something like that," Eldon agreed.

"Exactly like that," a firm voice spoke from the side.

They both rose, turning towards Sandquest who had quietly joined them.

"Mr Eldon, Mr Sandquest." Livia introduced them. "Apparently the Metropolitan Police did request this interview." She shot a half curious glance at Eldon.

Sandquest had an excessively firm grip. "Doesn't matter who, they're all busy-bodies of one sort or another. Come on in Eldon."

Sandquest shut the door behind them, indicating the seat in front of his desk.

"I understand you wish to discuss Maxwell Blain? Bad business, Eldon. I'm told the brakes failed. Not possible

154

on a Silver Cloud as well maintained as his would have been. Something for you to ponder on."

"Yes, sir. His death was unusual." Eldon took note that Sandquest was very well informed.

"Everything about Blain was unusual. A type of entrepreneur that's going out of fashion. No frontiers, no rules, no walking away from the business. Can't say he was the sort of man to trade with. However, when you shook hands, you had a deal. That was his style."

"You went back a long way, I believe?"

"No. We were intimates before the war, and nothing afterwards. We both dug up our roots to go our separate ways."

"No business associations?" Eldon enquired.

"Absolutely not. We didn't have the same interests, or the same company ethics. Mine has always been to build up a strong, effective international company. One I could be proud of: technically comprehensive, in line with my aim to diversify within the disciplines of the industry. Please the shareholders, please the employees, and please the government. My company ethics. Blain's was merely to make money. A great deal of money. He didn't have to have any particular reason. Nothing wrong in making money, of course. I've made a lot myself, but too many people start in business just to get rich. Their company is a means to an end, not an end in itself. Most of them sell out, or get thrown out. Modern way of doing business."

"Obsessive, would you say?"

"You could say that. Sometimes such men don't know how to stop, even when the water's murky, not knowing what they're dealing in, or who they're dealing with."

"These murky waters," Eldon asked. "From your experience, would you say he made enemies? The sort who might kill him?"

"Very probably. He had the reputation for being something of a sharp operator with big feet."

Eldon looked uncertain of his meaning.

"He was always stepping on people's toes, Eldon. Seemed to make a habit of it."

"But loose ends there were not?"

"Exactly." Sandquest looked at his watch.

Eldon continued. "He appears to have been engaged in some business deal in Italy when the accident happened?"

"Was he?"

Eldon's tone became judicial. "One that might have been linked to a subsidiary company of yours, based in Yeovil."

Sandquest frowned. "FI Electronics? I don't see why. I'm not aware of any such dealings with Blain in this respect. He never had any parallel business interests, though of course, he might buy shares, but unless he'd acquired them under another title it was never apparent. Not that it would have done him any good. All my companies are heavily invested in each other. No bidder could ever accumulate enough voting shares."

"No, I don't think he had any interest in buying into FI Electronics itself. Have you heard of a company called Caparra?"

"Yes, We have limited dealings with them." Sandquest shook his head emphatically. "Not one Blain would have been interested in, I'd have thought. He liked sailing close to the wind, not bringing attention to himself. Wait a moment." He clicked the intercom button on the small chrome console on his desk. "Livia, what have we on Caparra, in Italy?"

Livia's voice returned immediately. "Caparra is one of the partners in Bimax, a company set up with FI Electronics. You gave the Chief Executive, David Temple, the go ahead last year. Caparra is a construction company, contracted to build a new prison near Foggia. FI Electronics is involved in security and surveillance systems, on the same project. Neither of the parent companies had enough spare staff to organize a proper audit of the work, being stretched in other directions. Would you like me to elaborate on that, sir?"

"Why not? Eldon will want the whole story."

"Bimax started from scratch with two executives from each parent company, and contracting a new labour force. David Temple insisted we weren't tied directly in to Caparra, having been advised underworld interests controlled them. He believed the arrangement would limit any collateral damage should the enterprise go

156

sour. I also have the figures on this development, sir?"

"No, Livia. Thank you. I just wanted their background. Does Sir Maxwell Blain - did Sir Maxwell Blain, have any interest in Caparra? I know he didn't have any in FI Electronics."

"Yes, he did. Not representative really. Possibly no more than one percent. Something that came with the Neapolitan, Emertan deal, local cement manufacturers bought by Caparra in 1989. He retained the shares. David Temple mentioned the fact in his report when they were proposing to set up Bimax."

"Right, Livia. Thank you." Sandquest released the switch. "Well," he said thoughtfully. "He'd have needed a lot more than one percent to be a player there. Perhaps it was coincidental. What sort of deal were you alluding to anyway?"

"Sir Maxwell was transferring a large sum of money to Italy. We thought it might be for Bimax. Perhaps Caparra?"

"Bimax isn't possible. Bimax, as a joint venture, was expected to have limited potential. We were asked specifically to tender for the project by the Interior Ministry, and I remember Temple wasn't all that happy, but cognizant of other defence contracts in the pipeline. Bimax would have been wound up after the contract expired. But Bimax isn't a listed company. There was no share issue."

"Could he have been buying into Caparra, do you suppose? If they eventually had to realign their strategic position back to their core business, it might be useful to have Blain's financial injection to secure control of Bimax assets, even though not actively trading." Eldon suggested.

"Hardly possible. Such an arrangement would have to be discussed with FI Electronics. But, as I said, Blain was a man who dealt in murky waters. One where Caparra would have been quite at home. But why?"

Caparra might have many reasons to maintain a company that could obtain a stock exchange listing relatively easily."

"Perhaps. But that's really of no interest to me."

"I see. Not worth pursuing then," Eldon reflected. "To

recap, Sir Maxwell had no business contacts with you, ceasing to be a friend or colleague many years ago?"

Sandquest nodded. "Correct. We had no business or social connexions."

"Not a very productive line of inquiry?"

"Nothing will be very productive in respect of Maxwell Blain, Eldon."

"So it would seem. May I pursue your earlier relationship with Sir Maxwell further? That might be useful."

"To whom?"

"To my investigation, Mr Sandquest. In the strictest confidence."

Sandquest gave him an incredulous look. "Why are you all such maggots Eldon? The state is a rust bucket, full of holes, more interested in calumny than in protecting the interests of the nation. Confidences filter out in such a garbled manner, that a confession today becomes a calamity tomorrow. Tell me about confidence?"

Eldon chose not to argue. "In the strictest confidence."

A look of exasperation crossed Sandquest's face, along with another glance at his watch. "If you must."

"You were married during the war I understand?"

"I was."

"Was this at a time when you were still friendly with Sir Maxwell?"

Sandquest looked puzzled. "I don't think so. Perhaps. I can't recall, precisely."

"You were called up in 1941 I believe?"

"I volunteered, Eldon," Sandquest snapped at him.

"Volunteered. My apologies. Blain of course didn't, being exempt due to a perforated eardrum. He remained in the Midlands until 1944. You didn't see much of him during that period?"

"Eldon, there was a war going on. I was on active service. We were too busy dodging bombs to worry about our social lives."

"In between the bombs?" Eldon persisted.

"Not that I recall."

"Would your wife have seen anything of him?"

"My wife? Why should she see him?"

158

"If you were friends at the time?" Eldon offered.

"Eldon, my first wife's been dead for nearly fifty years. I cannot follow your intimation, or reasoning. We all grew up together, so of course she knew Blain. We were married in 1943, when I can remember all sorts of relationships changing. People are part of a formula. Blain would have drifted away about then. He'd started developing business ideas way ahead of my capabilities at that time, having the right management dynamics to balance capital to labour, which I didn't. Then, of course, the war started in earnest, and the formula changed again. I wasn't given much chance to make anything of my marriage. Over before it began. Happened to many people, Eldon. I'm damned if I can see the reason for all these questions. There is a reason, I suppose?"

"Yes, unfortunately there is. Did you know your wife, at that time, was having an affair with Blain?"

The surprised look on Sandquest's face was a mixture of disbelief and then pain. His eyes didn't seem to focus anywhere. Mouth opening and closing, but saying nothing, sparring with a private torment. He'd been punched a long way below the belt.

Sandquest was a proud man, experienced, successful, confident - used to fighting wars, political, economic, whatever came his way. Now, he could only back into a corner and try to fend off the blows: face retaining a far away vacant look, shutting out all ideas and emotions, leaving only a puzzled response to his thoughts. "I never knew. How could such a thing happen, that I never knew?"

Eldon offered an explanation. "The war. Active duty. You weren't there to know,"

"I wasn't there to know," Sandquest repeated. His voice sounded far away, saying the words but not hearing. For some moments more he wrestled with his pain, before punching his way back into the present.

"How could I know?" His angry eyes settled on Eldon. "More to the point. How could you bloody well know?"

"We found a letter in Sir Maxwell's effects. The writing matches another letter in the possession of a Mrs Penny of Cheadle. You'll remember her."

"Yes. Violet. You've been back a long way. Still, best to

make sure of such things." Sandquest had recovered his composure to the extent that he began to rationalize Eldon's train of thoughts. "You suspect me of killing Blain?"

"That's not my job. I don't have to draw such conclusions."

"For God's sake, Eldon, I never knew. Over fifty years ago. I had no idea. Use your brain man. Who waits fifty years to settle a score like this? Fifty years!"

"Perhaps not a question of fifty years. It might only have been a few weeks."

Sandquest fixed a steady eye on Eldon. "What exactly are you implying?"

"Someone recently broke into one of Sir Maxwell's properties, searching through his personal files where we were to find the letter from your wife. If you, or an agent of yours was responsible, then such a discovery may have triggered a whole series of events that culminated in Sir Maxwell's death."

"You're very brazen with this line of inquiry, Eldon." Sandquest gave him a calculating look. "Though I can see it's not an unreasonable assumption, I think you're only clutching at straws. I was not aware of this letter from Joyce. That you'll have to accept, because I don't believe anyone is going to ask you to prove otherwise."

"As I said. That's not my job."

"You compile reports, without giving opinions. I know." There was a hard aggressive tone in Sandquest's voice. "In any case, your opinions don't matter. Being a party to so many sensitive assets, I've made myself quite indispensable. Can we say that of you?"

Eldon wasn't going to be drawn into a useless argument. "We've cleared up a number of loose ends: fragments of Sir Maxwell's past. I appreciate that you've given me the time."

Sandquest looked at him dismissively.

The intercom clicked on his desk. Livia reminded him of his schedule. They rose together and shook hands.

Eldon knew that an avenue had been closed that was unlikely to be opened again. But nothing had been wasted. He was now at least sure that Sandquest had been genuinely unaware of his wife's infidelity, though

160

not so sure, that Livia had.

-oOo-

When the door shut behind Eldon, Sandquest turned back in on himself, twirling between his fingers a silver paper knife.

Fifty-year-old muck. What was the point of digging that up? Joyce. He might have known. But he didn't. What were they driving at? Blain, on the make, coming unstuck when the cuckolded husband found out. Routine inquiry. Prima facie evidence. Not where they were coming from. Run of the mill CID work. A bit late for them to consider him a risk. There was another agenda. There had to be another agenda. He stabbed the paper knife hard into the desk.

"You bastard Blain. You'll have the last laugh, even from the grave."

His face knotted in anger, he hurled the paper knife across the desk, rising to his feet about to send the desk after it. Stopping on the edge of his violence, he lowered the table down, his whole body trembling at last into a fitful, nervous laugh.

"You bastard Blain. What the hell. No one will hear you from there."

Chapter 17

"Latest report confirms Blain was staying with friends in Spain before starting for Italy." Hart picked up a sheet of paper and passed it to Eldon.

"Routine service on his Rolls Royce was due, and though fussy about maintenance, Blain seems to have considered the local Citroen dealership up to the job. Two nights before the car was due for collection, someone stuffed the security system in the garage. Absolutely nothing was missing, though something nasty had been added. A clever little implant secreted away inside the master cylinders. The inventor was way ahead of conventional, Rex. No backstreet boffin either, as the electronic miniaturization must have been extraordinary. A bomb the shape of a ten pence piece, crammed with electronics, and the punch of a hand grenade. Evidently, only this Nightingale person has that sort of technical support. Also explains why DST are shadowing the case for the French. Someone walked off with a small quantity of explosive they're developing. Looks like plasticine, waterproof, but reacts rather badly to hydrocarbon chemicals. Apparently, they didn't steal much. About the size of a ten pence piece."

"No wonder progress on this case has been slow." Eldon remarked. "Besides knowing everything about Blain's movements, they're flexible enough to seize on random opportunities."

"Tell me another. Sounds something of an inside job to me."

"Ah, yes. You were planning to tell me something yesterday."

"Right. Coming to that. Commander Prinn has decided you're to move on."

"Move on," Eldon queried suspiciously. "Now that might be a pleasant surprise. Or not. Back to where the money is, or to where, exactly?"

"Out of my hair, is exactly where. You're to report to an old friend of the Commander, Tomaso Vignozzi. He's a Questore in Rome, responsible for the Investigation Division overseeing the case relating to the death of a

162

Senator Brizzi. Like everything else, these ideas pop up like worms after a spot of rain. I understand you speak the language?"

"Hmm! Product of a misspent year before the university took me in. Rome? Looks like someone's changing the goal-posts again," Eldon mused, with a touch of irony, minus the smile.

"Stick to the official line, Rex, instead of following your nose. Bloodhounds went out with bicycles. You just present yourself to this Vignozzi."

"And drop the investigation on Sandquest?" Eldon enquired.

"You want an opinion?"

"It might help."

"Look Rex, I can sit here all day lecturing you about Blain's affair with Sandquest's wife; about his motive and the repressed violence that grows in a man's soul. But your assessment concluded that he was unaware of any infidelity, until you told him. Caparra is much the same. Hardly under Sandquest's control, and you say he'll ultimately wind up Bimax, given that Caparra has a shaky board of directors. Verolino and Italvini, where you came in, suggests Sandquest buys the wine of the former, not knowing it's a subsidiary of Italvini. Why should he? They don't advertise the fact. In the UK, only the Anglo Italian Wine Company are the official distributors. Even I can smell something cooking in the kitchen, Rex, but when you open the door there's no one there. Where's the chef? That's our problem, Rex. Where's the chef? Besides, I've got enough feet trampling all over this case as it is."

Eldon let Hart's lack of imagination ride. Experienced policemen fought shy of creative detective work. But he didn't mind throwing a punch in that direction, just to shake things up a little.

"And what about Miss Wolfe? I could put money on her being the person one step ahead of us at Strawberry Cottage."

Hart's eyes grew evasive. "Now that is something else," he emphasized. "Something of a coincidence. No need to add anything to the pot, just because there's a touch of cordon bleu about it. No good chasing shadows. What you need is evidence that stands out like a carbuncle on Michelle Pfeiffer's bum. A building block to fit in somewhere. Something this department can go along with."

-oOo-

The quaint analogy of building blocks and beautiful bums, Eldon decided, meant a lot of office work. Gower, having departed for Sweden and a chilly sea voyage across the Gulf of Bothnia, had left him with no one to bounce ideas off.

Eldon balanced the keyboard on his knees. Running a search on Livia Wolfe, produced more than he expected, if less than he wished. The disclosed file was brief and truncated.

'Livia Vanessa Wolfe, born 1958, Wakefield, Yorkshire, to Baron and Lady Wolfe. Educated Bedales, Sciences at Oxford, Harvard Business School, British Telecom, IBM Headquarters, Axmar Group. Registered voting address, 125 Wilton Street.'

A very neat resume of a young lady heading for the top - in the fast lane. Neat, with all further information classified! What was that supposed to mean?

Telephoning the archive registrar, Eldon enquired if he could obtain clearance, only to be told that there was no access without the AC's permission, being covered by a Code 2 security screen. The AC was away until Wednesday.

Axmar Industries were involved in a lot of sensitive Government work, but a Code 2 screen on his PA, was curiously excessive.

Eldon looked for Livia in the telephone directory. She wasn't listed. The ex-directory list drew the same result. Post Office engineers finally came up with a telephone number for a Wilton Street address, so he rang the number.

A man's voice answered: the sort of voice that didn't waste time answering telephones. Eldon asked for Miss Wolfe. The man remained expeditious. A Miss Wolfe didn't live there. Perhaps a previous owner.

Eldon obtained the estate agent's name, found the

telephone number, and was passed to several employees before making an appointment with the agent who'd handled the property; a loquacious, pompous sounding young man, grown used to being deferential in chasing elusive company sales targets.

-oOo-

Catching a taxi on the Albert Embankment, Eldon crossed the river to the estate agent's Sloane Street offices.

The agent in an off-the-peg dark suit shook hands limply, settling himself back into a chrome and black leather chair, erratically swivelling from side to side, conscious he was not dealing with a potential client.

"Wilton Street. Bit of a plum that. Belgravia's an area where we can always sell properties. Sole agency would be nice. Still quite a few established families maintaining the right life style. House in town, something in the country. Just the reverse of a century ago. This is where the business is now. Belgravia's a decent base for the top end of all those success stories: millionaires on the move, or someone going international from across the pond. From anywhere really. Number one-two-five's a bit of a roller coaster at the moment. Sometimes happens when a long established family sells up. Two or three new owners in quick succession. Aspirants who find the going too expensive, or those on a whim who don't like the area after all, having hoped for something more St.James's. Takes all sorts, for all sorts of reasons. Number one-two-five's a case in question. We've just sold it for a Mr. Singh who wasn't anything in shipping, but everything in the Indian cinema. The latest owner, conversely, isn't in anything, having sold his chain of restaurants to do absolutely nothing. Working sixteen-hour days has burnt him out, so he said, but how long do you keep a workaholic down? He'll be back in the market doing something, and number one-two-five will be too. Collateral for some new venture."

"The house," Eldon inquired, "was owned by a long established family, you say?"

The agent gave an amused laugh. "Since 1948, until

165

sold to Mr. Singh. Before that, we weren't in business."

"Not an old established company, then?" Eldon noted, moving on before the agent could voice a reply. "Baron Wolfe owned the property before Mr. Singh?"

"Lady Wolfe," the agent corrected him smugly. "Baron Wolfe is a respected academic, but comes from more humble surroundings. An extremely clever man, but grammar school. Lady Wolfe is titled in her own right, you know. Through the Wroxley line. No son, I understand. When their daughter was killed in a motor accident, the property became superfluous."

Eldon stopped him. "Killed in an accident. When?"

The agent looked taken aback. "I'm not a policeman. That's your job. You asked me about Wilton Street. I've added some passing conversation. They didn't elaborate, you know."

"No matter. It might be possible to dig the facts out. Traffic will hold records."

"I gathered the accident was on the A303; somewhere in Wiltshire. That's all I know."

Eldon thanked him.

Walking back to Sloane Square to find a taxi, he considered an important, and about to be neglected, line of enquiry.

Livia Wolfe was alive and well, and working for Sandquest. Eldon realized there was little chance finding out why someone wanted you to think otherwise. Sandquest would have done somebody a favour. Everybody a favour. He would have more outstanding IOU's to call in than William Hill. All of them would have a reason, many reasons, for keeping him pointed in the direction he wanted to go. As Hart had said, a little matter of murder didn't carry much weight in the scale of things. Sandquest's intrigues would be classified as a matter of national security. As there wasn't anything higher than that, Livia Wolfe was as good as a closed book.

Nevertheless it was a queer pitch, and Italy was way down the field at long-off. Eldon wondered how much Prinn thought he would see of the game from there.

He nodded to the first taxi in the rank.

Chapter 18

On the outskirts of Sorena a policeman stepped into the road, raising his white disc with a red centre, beckoning Margaret to pull in.

Pulling the car over, Margaret lowered the window. The policeman adjusted his dark glasses slightly as he took her proffered documents, scrutinizing them with slow deliberation.

The action was methodical, a matter of routine, checking the boxes one by one. He returned her identity card, taking the licence and insurance over to his colleague who inspected them just as carefully. Together they came back.

The first policeman leant forward so she could hear him, speaking slowly and firmly in fluent English.

"This is a United Kingdom licence, *Signora?*"

Margaret nodded. "Yes. They're valid until some indeterminate age when I have to convince my doctor I'm not a geriatric." She laughed half-heartedly. The policeman didn't.

"How long have you been in Italy, *Signora?*" the policeman asked.

Her heart sank. "Some months."

"I see. Some months. This is an English registered vehicle," pausing for her nod of assent, "and the road fund licence has run out." He tapped the screen. "Over twelve months ago."

"I'm sorry. I didn't notice. Living in two countries is so confusing."

"You cannot live in two countries, *Signora*. You either live in one or the other, for the purposes of Italian and English vehicle licensing laws." The policeman handed back her documents. "If you are resident in Italy, and are intending to drive an imported vehicle for longer than six months, then the vehicle must be re-registered and licensed. You will also need to apply for an Italian driving licence. It is not an option. It is obligatory. I strongly advise you to take account of this matter."

"No one's mentioned this before," Margaret replied.

"It is entirely your responsibility, *Signora*.

Take heed of what I say. You're committing an offence that won't be taken lightly. *Buongiorno.*" He stepped back, waving her away impatiently with his disc.

-oOo-

Margaret brought Prinn tea on the terrace in deference to Scillone's smouldering root where, in response to Margaret's distressed telephone call, he could tell her what he had discovered about the circumstances of her encounter with the police.

"You seem to have made an enemy," Prinn said, stirring his tea rhythmically.

"Enemy? I never see anyone up here to disagree with," Margaret rebutted his suggestion, passing Scillone a large compensatory mug of coffee with a fading transfer of the Science Museum on its side.

"Nevertheless, you have," Prinn continued. "Do you know a local farmer, called Franchi?"

"No".

Prinn laughed. "You probably wouldn't want to. He apparently lives over the hill at the *podere* Olezzante, which means sweet smelling on account of the Mimosa that grows particularly well there. The word also, colloquially, means 'smelly', alluding to old Franchi's aversion to water."

Scillone grunted in agreement, warming his large fists on the mug.

"But why?" Margaret persisted. "I don't think I've ever seen him."

"He seems to have implicated you because he's managed to get himself into hot water over his road tax, lashing out at foreigners who get away with this sort of thing, citing you as an example. He hasn't denounced you by making the digression official, but the police took the opportunity to guard their backs in case his whistle-blowing develops into anything, by giving you a warning."

Scillone nodded sagely. Perhaps from experience.

"The mean little peasant!" Margaret expressed loudly.

"Well, I don't know about that, but his action is certainly an Italian characteristic," Prinn explained.

"You'll find nothing's exactly to the point when Italians want to make one. Ettore believes one of his nephews works for Capagli, which might provide a reason for his vindictiveness. Getting you spooked so you don't cause them any trouble. It's all bluster, but in the circumstances, do as the police officer indicated."

As for poor Bastion, Ettore decided to place him close to the crossroads of Fornello, just a track crossing in the woods above Piaggia. The area's thick with Ilex up there, and a favourite with truffle hunters, besides being in the opposite direction to the castle. As he expected, Bastion was found the next day. When they receive the report I'm sure the Vigili will be in touch. I'm sorry this is such an unhappy experience. If you prefer, Ettore will reclaim him for you?"

Margaret nodded. "Perhaps the farmers and hoteliers who work and build on Mount Vesuvius are right. Living for tomorrow always spoils the wonderful hours of today."

"Living for today hardly takes care of tomorrow," Prinn corrected her.

"True, but I came here to live on the margins of society, without the distractions of the old world that hadn't served me very well. A clean page if you like, where my past only exists in a form I choose. Whoever I say I am - I am. Whatever I have done - was done. Accepted without question. Why would I lie? You don't have to in a land where you can so conveniently forget, what's inconvenient to recall."

Prinn shook his head. "Unfortunately, we must look elsewhere for our salvation. As you seem to have been successful in your deception, continue your credible performance of a nice English lady. That's important. After all, as the Italians are, on the whole, a sympathetic and generous people and not all like this Franchi, I think we can rely on them being extraordinarily partial to the romantic in our race."

-oOo-

After they'd left, Margaret began preparing the evening meal. The kitchen window overlooking the track, gave an uninterrupted view of the area beyond her front gate. Removing the strings from the celery, she looked up to see a white Mercedes Benz turn the corner and stop. Opening the window slightly, she listened to hear if the engine had been switched off. Efforts to restart the vehicle were being made without success. Margaret recognized the same large occupants she'd noticed a week before, who hadn't been seen since.

Finally the car started, clearing the injection system sufficiently for the vehicle to limp erratically up to the gate before spluttering to a halt. Subsequent efforts merely exhausted the battery.

The driver stepped out, intently observing the house, scrutinizing the whole façade carefully.

Margaret drew back from the window. Close up the man portrayed a physically intimidating bulk, his head resting on wide, muscular shoulders with little to see of his neck. It was a face that neither loved nor hated, but remained expressionless, completely indifferent to the feelings and fate of human existence. Only the eyes moved in a blank, impassive survey of her property.

Another man got out, arranging his navy cashmere coat over his shoulders. Walking towards the house, he waved the driver back as he moved to fall in behind the man's slim stature, a vast border of suppressed violence.

Pausing at the gate: dark, clean shaven, neatly dressed in a bespoke suit, he was not a man to be seen very often on dusty Tuscan roads, exhibiting the groomed perfection of one long used to the manicured world of a metropolitan city. In his left hand he held a pair of black kid gloves, lifting the latch with the other, closing the gate tidily behind him.

Removing her apron, Margaret went into the hall to open the door. No one knocked. He seemed to know she'd be there. Slipping the catch, the door swung back.

Close up he had a firm, lightly tanned skin, with a clean bluish haze where he'd been shaved. His slim angular nose parted pale azure coloured eyes that signalled their own withering animosity in a disarmingly handsome face.

Margaret felt a shiver run involuntarily through her body. She forced herself to smile politely. It was returned with a movement at the sides of his mouth, an automatic reaction lacking any interest.

He spoke in English, perhaps because of the GB plate on her car which he could have noticed, or equally, because he already knew who she was. A soft voice, practised and polite, never betraying the nature of the speaker.

"Good afternoon," he half turned towards the car, then back again. "I'm afraid we have trouble with our car, which I don't think can be resolved by my driver getting his hands dirty. Would it be possible to use your phone? Perhaps the local break-down service."

"Of course," Margaret consented, standing aside. "Please, come in."

He passed her with the lotioned smell of the city following him, and waited by the hall telephone.

"Perhaps we have some grit in the injection system. I'm not an expert," he explained, by way of conversation.

Margaret rang the number found in her telephone book, letting him explain the problem to the mechanic, who would know where to come.

"He says he can come immediately." Paba replaced the receiver. "My name is Fausto Paba."

"Margaret Morning," she replied, shaking hands politely. His grip was firm, holding her hand a little over long.

Paba looked at her with an absence of any pleasurable interest, before his eyes travelled round the hall, taking in the domestic ambience, and the lack of a masculine presence.

"You live alone?" he asked directly.

"With my daughter." Margaret realized there was no point in being vague. Evasion would be a contradiction of what he might already know.

"And you are not afraid?"

"Is there a reason to be afraid?"

He smiled again, the same cold fluttering at the corner of his mouth. "Probably not. This is Tuscany, after all. Here they retain a respect for people. It's important that people should have respect for each other, especially in matters of privacy."

Margaret nodded in agreement. "As you have to wait,

would you like some coffee, or a drink perhaps?"

"That's very kind of you," Paba accepted for himself. "But my associates will not. Not because they wouldn't, but because I'd rather they didn't. Neapolitans tend to work hard all day, and because of their addiction to coffee, remain awake all night. An unfortunate habit. Perhaps we fear going to sleep."

"Don't the Sicilians have the same passion for coffee?" Margaret remarked, in an effort to make conversation.

"Ah, the two Sicily's. An idea that comes and goes. From the Rhodian navigators to the petty Bourbons, we have never had a moment to ourselves." He turned his attention back to the coffee. "It's an Arabic custom you'll find, and as their influence is everywhere in the south we tend to drink coffee in the manner of the Semite shepherds, who because of the presence of wolves didn't dare fall asleep."

Slipping off his coat, he placed it on a chair, before following Margaret, who was still considering the equivocal nature of his statement, into the kitchen.

"You have been to Naples?" Paba asked.

"No. One day," Margaret affirmed. "The Amalfi coast has an enviable reputation. Perhaps in the autumn, when it's not so hot. To meet the Duchess, do you think?"

"The unfortunate Joanna of Aragon. Who knows? A woman of secrets. Not too well kept, which proved her undoing. But you should go to Amalfi, before it's too late."

"Too late?" Margaret paused, with the coffee pot in her hand.

"Yes. The whole of the Costiera Amalfitana is threatened with that deformity found along the Costa del Sol. Ribbon development is a contagion of contact. A disease. One following the other, until the blight is universal. You have something similar in England too."

"We do?"

"Yes. I visit Somerset every once in a while. On business. Sometimes I get the chance to visit Devon, and the coast. They're not building like Malaga or Rimini, but still not appreciating that an empty space has as much value to society as one covered in concrete and glass."

"I do agree. Somerset. That's why your English is so good."

He bowed slightly at her compliment. "The practice has certainly helped, but my English is really not so good."

Margaret disagreed. "But why are you visiting here? I don't think you can visit the castle any longer. I understand it's been sold."

He looked at her steadily, gauging the quality of the remark. His hand, with the perfectly clipped nails, traversed the view outside the window. "I have to confess, I've bought the castle. A building too beautiful to have people trampling over everything for no more reason, than curiosity. Tourism will destroy the nature of the place. Don't you agree?"

"I'm biased because I live here." Margaret removed the coffee pot from the stove, turning it over to let the water filter through. "Are you intending to live in the castle?"

"Yes. I hope we shall become real neighbours."

Finding a seat in the old yew Windsor chair she'd brought from England, he provided an unlikely contrast to the rusticity of her farmhouse kitchen - and to an isolated medieval ruin

"You've seen the inside of the castle?" Paba inquired.

"I'm embarrassed now to say I have. Such a temptation proved too much of a playground for my imagination."

"Are you concerned I might spoil such a thing?"

"You said not," handing him his coffee.

"True. You go there often?" Paba inquired.

"I did when I first bought this house. Now I have little time."

He gave a real smile, at last. "You must come again. I must show you what I'm proposing before they start building, then the site will be too dusty and dangerous for a casual visit."

"You've plenty of ideas?" Margaret enquired.

"Some. The decision is between things as they were, or how we would like them to be." Placing his empty cup on the worktop, Paba sought her opinion. "Tell me Margaret, how would you like things to be?"

"I'm not sure I understand you? If you're referring to

the castle, I'm sure you must have given it a great deal of thought"

"Of course. But how would you restore the castle? I'd welcome another opinion. An intelligent opinion. I can't reconstruct the castle as original, so I must keep all the architectural elements I can, while creating a sensible alternative."

The sound of the garage mechanic arriving turned their attention back to the problem outside. Paba collected his coat, thanking her for the coffee and the conversation. "I'm pleased we've met. Change can be such a worrying thing, unless you also have ownership of it. Let me call on you when I'm next in the area? If you give me your number, I'll remember it."

Margaret nodded, feeling she was standing on the edge of a precipice. She gave him the number, knowing he might as easily find her name in the directory.

They shook hands on the doorstep. Margaret tried to keep an open countenance, one with which Paba could be satisfied.

Giving a faint pull of the lips, that might have been a smile, he departed for his car where an overalled figure already leant inside the open bonnet.

Margaret closed the door behind him and leant against it. Her legs felt weak. Working without a script was going to be the devil. Words, she felt, had never held such meaning, or their intention been so dangerous.

Realizing Paba had probably found their meeting opportune, as much as by design, she calmed herself. The very proximity of her house to the castle meant she couldn't help but be inquisitive. In such an event, not to be could have implied an alternative motive, and one that Paba would have sensed at once.

Chapter 19

The white Mercedes Benz had travelled down the A1 from Florence, past the neat, empty vineyards of Umbria in their chocolate coloured soil, and round the Rome *tangenziale* before finally leaving the Tuscolana exit for Frascati, with the huge crater of the Alban Hills behind.

The silence that surrounded Paba created a distraction he felt a necessity to fill. His two colleagues in the front took no interest in the landscape or each other. Their instructions had been given, and on that they had nothing to say.

There was his preoccupation with time. Time to Paba was money, and he was accountable to 'friends' who would take exception to that money not being well cared for. Convincing Mario Giuliani that the enterprise had more than just merit, had not been easy.

-oOo-

Giuliano and his '*Concilio*' had approved of the Castello di Pietra - converting illegal funds into legitimate money by eventually selling the property. Persuading them that the castle provided an investment of a quite different kind had appeared nothing more than an insane gamble.

His mentor's first reaction was one of polite indifference. Paba was a man of the future, being groomed for higher things: in business, perhaps in politics. He would always be afforded a hearing, even when the argument lacked credibility. But risk was something left to amateurs; petty gangsters pretending to be more than they were.

Knowing this, Paba had done his homework well. Initially selling the idea to Vincent Bersagliera, the seventy year old don whose banking interests made him a powerful voice in Giuliani's inner circle. Paba also counted on the fact that Giuliani, though a sober man, admired grand gestures in others that carried something more than mere effect.

When Paba had finally been asked to make his presentation in person, he placed on the table an

Etruscan gold cup with handles in the shape of frogs, confronting the doubters with a tender for whoever had the most small change in their pockets. They had all dug deep. He promised the losers more for less.

From his position at the head of the table, Giuliani had laughed at the scramble, thanking Paba for his dissemination of the proposal, dismissing him while the ageing elite argued over the wisdom of financing a fantasy.

Two hours passed before Paba was summoned back into the room, and Giuliani expressed their agreement. Bersagliera would make the financial arrangements. Giuliani shook his hand, remarking as he walked to the door, arm through Paba's, that he should remember unpaid debts were like a bad odour - not becoming of a gentleman.

-oOo-

On the outskirts of Frascati the Mercedes Benz turned off the busy main road into a quiet, prestigious domestic estate. The park consisted of tall blocks of apartments occupied by residents mostly employed in professional occupations in Rome. It provided a litter-less, well-watered environment, tended in accordance with the expected standards of the fashion conscious clones that lived there.

Leaving the driver in the car, his partner accompanied Paba to the twelfth and final floor. Reaching the end of a travertine paved corridor, Paba pressed the bell.

The stout mahogany door opened on atmosphere charged with unctuous decadence, heavy with maroon brocades, and dark nineteenth century walnut furniture. There was a smell of dust, a sickly, over-sweet odour of furniture polish. Paba did not take his coat off, shaking hands curtly with the man who greeted them.

Of medium build, he wore heavily framed spectacles that didn't suit him. His hair rode well clear of his shirt collar exposing a thin neck and sharp Adam's apple. A nervous, breathy disposition came courtesy of the cigarette between his pale fingers that fanned out from one of his thin hands, wired by blue veins to his wrists

Paba did not admit to many that this opportunist and mercenary antiquary, Alberto Gerosa, was his cousin, preferring to have quietly forgotten him. In the scheme of things he had a use that Paba regretted every time they met, and hoped might have been concluded sooner than had been the case.

"Well, Alberto, what can you tell me?" Paba asked.

The answering voice was shrill, an octave lower than painful. "I can tell you something Fausto, they're impressive pieces."

Gerosa opened a cupboard door, withdrawing a shoebox, and placing it on the table between them. "The Museo dell'Accademia Etrusca in Cortona have such a double headed divinity of the second century BC, though these are somewhat later - say the first century AD." He set the two nude male statues on the table. "But two Fausto, in perfect condition, is unheard of. The inscription on the leg of this one is interesting. The beginning reads: 'O celebrated fathers...', but the other lines are too obscure for me. Never mind, any sort of scribble makes them very valuable. The second statue has no inscription, but all the measurements indicate they were cast from similar moulds. I made silicone casts of them to check. You know they are unique?"

Paba picked one up from the table. "And yet there are two?"

His cousin shrugged. "Where did you say you acquired them?"

"I didn't say. They've led a charmed life, considering they've been bartered about like second hand motor cars." Paba could hardly conceal his irritation. "All I needed to know was whether we'd been sold a dummy or not. If I'm to lay out a small fortune, I need to know if it's in safe hands. One can never be sure of these things. At least you've verified they're genuine."

"I know a little more than that," Gerosa retorted. "We can form a fairly accurate opinion on these objects. For a start, we can tell they came from Etruria, because they can be subject to scientific analysis. Technicians at the University carry this out for a small charge. Off the books. An extra income, every now and again, is welcome."

177

"You gave them to someone else?" A disagreeable tone entered Paba's voice. "You were told not to let them out of your sight."

"Of course I didn't let them out of my sight. What do you think I am? Stupid! I stayed with them the whole time the process was being carried out in the laboratory."

Gerosa was not going to admit the few minutes when he'd gone to the washroom. They were insignificant minutes. Nothing would be served by invoking Paba's wrath.

"Go on." The displeasure remained in Paba's voice.

"All that was necessary were two small scrapings from underneath. Almost invisible to the naked eye. Ours was the second such scraping. A previous expert, no doubt?" Gerosa said pointedly.

"Well?" Paba said, ignoring the comment.

"Assay tests established they were, most probably, cast in Populonia."

"Populonia. Is that nearer than nowhere?"

Gerosa became impatient "As close as anyone can get. Analysis of the copper and tin that make up the bronze of the statues match the specification of ore mined on the island of Elba, lying off the promontory on which Populonia was built. As the only major Etruscan city to be built by the sea, with foundries that supported the iron industry right up to later Roman times, we can make a reasonable deduction that they were manufactured there."

"Why did they make them?"

"The Etruscans were good at divination, I am not," Gerosa snapped irritably. "They might have been part of a batch produced for shipment throughout Etruria, which doesn't explain why only one was inscribed, though why they should be together would tax a mind rich in imagination. Such objects might have many uses, perhaps as offerings in exchange for some benefit. They would be purchased, and offered to the particular deity, especially if a son was involved in a dangerous diplomatic undertaking away from home, or in times of unrest to ensure his house and family remained safe."

"Yes, yes," Paba said irritably. "How far would they

transport these objects?"

"To where you didn't say you found them." Gerosa's piercing laugh grated on Paba's nerves. "Rather a large area to cover. The Etruscan influence was felt as far south as Pompeii; to the north beyond Bologna. This inscription indicates they probably didn't travel outside Etruria, though Populonia traded with Greece and Asia Minor since early times. Given their present undisclosed history, you now know a great deal more than I do."

"Let's hope so, Alberto." Paba picked up the statues, carefully wrapping each in the tissue paper, returning them to the box.

"Useful having a specialist in the family, eh?" Gerosa's shrill laugh jarred again on Paba

"You were paid handsomely to become one," Paba forced a smile, "so you could be useful."

"Useful in making you rich," Gerosa said, heatedly.

"Is that what you imagine?"

"You can't fool me Fausto. They're too unbelievable to have been turned up by a tractor, or a plumber putting in a drain. The majority of such objects are mere fragments, pieces that have been knocked about by centuries. These come from an untouched tomb; a family tomb. Where are the rest of the furnishings for the sepulchre? If those appeared on the market they'd start an art war."

Paba smiled thinly. Almost as thinly as his patience. "Then you are right. In a war one can always get rich."

"It's a question of worth, Fausto," his cousin insisted.

"Worth?" Paba said softly.

"I have proved my worth. Merit has a value."

"You are valued," Paba continued quietly.

Gerosa was insistent. "I mean a monetary value. Stop being obtuse. I'm worth money. A lot of money. The information I've given you couldn't be obtained safely from anywhere else."

"You've been gambling again?"

"So what? My private life is my own. Yes, I need cash to service a debt. This work comes with a fat fee which you must pay me."

Paba's face became almost expressionless. "Just like that?"

"Just like nothing. A percentage of the expected value. *Capito?*"

"Well, Alberto, you are mistaken if you are expecting a percentage in something that doesn't exist."

"Doesn't exist!" Gerosa exclaimed. "You wouldn't go to all this trouble if you hadn't uncovered a tomb. Certain people would pay big money to know about such a find. I don't mind who pays me," he threatened rashly.

Paba's eyes narrowed, forming a frown across his forehead. "Certain people, Alberto? Big money?" He shook his head. "You should have learnt to live within your means. Money will be the death of you."

Gerosa, recognizing the chilling change of tone, back-pedalled.

"I'm sorry, Fausto. I didn't mean to sound off like that. You know me. Look, you're staying in Rome tonight. We'll have dinner. You remember the Café d'Este near the old Quirinale hotel? The new management has made the wine list even better. Food, good as ever. Of course expensive, but where isn't these days?"

Paba, picking up the shoebox, leant across and squeezed Gerosa's arm gently. "The problem with having expensive tastes Alberto is that sometimes they cost more than you can afford."

"Have dinner with me Fausto? Promise me? I can afford it." Gerosa's shrill voice pleaded desperately for Paba to listen.

Paba stopped on his way to the door. "Oh be assured Alberto, I will be there. The Café d'Este. And don't worry, I'll take care of the bill."

Gerosa couldn't be sure if there was a special emphasis on what Paba had said. A trick of his imagination. "Eight o'clock," he called out urgently after Paba, who didn't look back.

With a start Gerosa realized he hadn't been left alone.

-oOo-

Cradling the box in one arm, Paba passed along the travertine corridor to the lift, and waited patiently for it to arrive

He entered the cubicle that smelt of disinfectant,

180

reminding him of the sterile, purging atmosphere of a hospital. Or perhaps of a morgue.

He walked out to the front of the building, sliding into the back seat of the car. Placing the box in the opposite foot well, he tapped the back of the driver's seat impatiently, instructing him to drive on and wait round the corner.

As the car turned into the main road still thick with traffic, Paba caught sight, out of the corner of his eye people gathering round a distorted, broken form in the piazza. Their white faces were turned upwards, to the dizzying heights of the top-most balcony.

Chapter 20

From the cabin window Eldon recognized the sprawling, flat Agro Pontino stretching from Anzio to Terracina, a neat geometrical entity protected by the ribbon of its Lido and linked to the architectural modernity of Mussolini's new towns. Banking sharply over Latina, the aircraft began its descent towards Ciampino, the vague outlines suddenly taking on material shapes whose gentle, sliding images turned gradually into a blurred rush.

A plain-clothes policeman in an unmarked car drove Eldon quickly down the new Via Appia into the city centre.

"London!" He threw up his hands at forty miles an hour in the thick of the traffic. "*Una bella città*. I've been a few times. They say it's forty kilometres across. *Giusto?*"

"Probably nearer fifty between the extremes of the M25," Eldon confirmed.

"*Mamma mia!* Rome's about twenty." He shook his hand, as though flicking something unpleasant away, at the same time as weaving round a coach full of Japanese tourists, and a white taxi full of gesticulations and expletives. "You're from London?"

"No. From Beaminster, Dorset," Eldon replied.

The policeman shook his head, not knowing Dorset.

Vignozzi had given instructions for Eldon to be booked in at the Olympic hotel close to the British Institute, a short five-minute walk from the offices of the Questura.

"We have plenty of time." The driver's tone was nonchalant. "Enough for you to freshen up and catch the news."

After a shower Eldon listened to the policeman complaining about his lot, something in the manner of a piano tuner listening for the dull notes.

"What sort of man is Vignozzi?" Eldon asked.

"He's fifty-three, dislikes the left and Inter Milan, and every day's a headache."

"Tell me about the headache?" Eldon prompted.

"Well, I'm not passing on any secrets that haven't been in the news. All the media does is worry over rumours, or promote disasters. They all make better stories than the facts. However, one story they're playing straight. The government wants to know who killed Senator Brizzi. You know about Brizzi?"

Eldon shook his head. "Not really."

"A thing like this throws them into a panic. Was his murder political, or domestic? Shades of Aldo Moro. Are they on somebody's list?" The policeman laughed, and added, "They're on everybody's list."

Eldon slipped into a clean shirt, adding a tie. Holding up his trousers, he checked the state of the creases before pulling them on. "Are Italian policemen always so cynical?"

"It's the way you are. You investigate, you apprehend, you deliver the evidence to the court for judgment. You don't always agree with the result, but everything is transparent and above board. In theory, everyone is accountable."

"That's the sort of enviable situation which more than half the world wishes was their lot," Eldon commented, lacing his belt through the trouser loops.

"Oh, sure. It would be fine, except in Italy every case ends up on appeal, or under the table until the statute of limitation has elapsed. There may even be another layer where it just disappears from the books. Whichever way, it just passes into the shredder. Yes. I'm cynical."

"Politics was ever so." Eldon having let his hair get too dry fought some stray strands into place.

"No doubt, but where's the justice?" the policeman asked. "Collect your pay cheque without concerning yourself over equity or constitutional probity. That's not a well fitting cap for an honest man."

Eldon put on his socks and shoes. "Perhaps not. But at least it keeps your head dry."

"That I cannot argue with. You've developed an interest in this Brizzi, all the same?"

"That I don't know. I'm here to find out. Whoever killed Senator Brizzi may also have been responsible for the death of a British citizen." Eldon finished dressing. "So, where shall we make a start?"

The policeman looked at his watch. "The trouble with this country is that nothing's a matter of urgency.

Perhaps the Questore will be back. Perhaps not. *Speriamo.*"

He drove Eldon round to the Questura, organized the security formalities, and then took him upstairs to Vignozzi's office. Not being in, he sat Eldon down in the corridor outside, giving him a magazine.

"You can mark the days off on the wall. If he hasn't arrived in an hour, I'm the fourth door down here on the left." He departed, leaving Eldon to flick open the first page of the magazine.

-oOo-

Ten minutes later, as Eldon concerned himself with a spider patiently spinning a web above the office door, Vignozzi arrived in a rush accompanied by another man. Stopping, he looked Eldon up and down, decided who he was without asking, and waved for him to follow them into the room.

Vignozzi entered his office and appeared to tidy up a blitz from the morning's turmoil, pushing papers into files, gathering up others from his desk, sorting them into one pile or another. Suddenly he stopped, looked round, and with a final flourish, stuffed some into his brief case. Sitting down heavily, he fixed an eye on his guest.

"So you're Rex Eldon?" he said, matching the picture of him he had in his mind with the reality. His own face wore a worried frown, as though he alone bore the weight of the world on his shoulders. "This is Piero Vergellesi. I'm Vignozzi." Eldon shook hands with them both. "Pull yourself up a seat. You too, Piero." Vignozzi spoke in a rush, one word sprinting ahead of the next. "I expected you this morning, but no matter. I haven't much time, so Vergellesi can fill in the details and outline the strategic objectives for you. The pair of you have arrived at an opportune moment, as I'm up to my eyes in a South Korean delegation concluding a trade agreement. That's all the world seems to do these days, conclude trade agreements. Apparently someone wants to rock their boat, which wouldn't go down so well if one or more of the passengers fell out. Not your problem.

Domestically, the death of Brizzi came as a shock. Commander Prinn has known him for a long time. Then this man Finetti, following hard on his heels."

"We're particularly interested in Finetti," Eldon acknowledged. "Being Blain's partner could mean he's significantly involved. Include Brizzi, and you create an interesting triangle."

"Hmm!" Vignozzi agreed. "You're probably right. I also knew Brizzi slightly, in the way of duty. Receptions, symposiums, anywhere we could get a free lunch. Always had the feeling he was a moderate man, admired as a tireless supporter of causes that benefited the underdog. Made himself a nuisance, but not enough for anyone to kill him. I'm not aware of this connexion with Blain."

"Just a notion," Eldon admitted. "But the evidence, admittedly not very strong at the moment, suggests the two were working in concert towards some deal with Brizzi. Blain was certainly not a quintessential saint. Just the opposite. If Brizzi was something of a paragon, at least two of the trio made strange bed fellows."

"We're not always lucky in choosing our friends, Rex. Sometimes they're chosen for us. Brizzi didn't have any business experience. He steered well clear of such entanglements, being almost impossible to lobby. How he came to cosy up to these two business associates may not be so straightforward. I've given Vergellesi an office down the corridor. Fit in with him. Cramped, which means you'll keep your heads together."

The telephone rang, jarring them into sudden silence. Vignozzi picked up the receiver, grunting tersely, "I'm on my way."

He clutched his brief case under his arm. "I'm leaving the rest to you two. Dig deep, and don't look in too many mirrors."

The door slammed behind him.

-oOo-

Vergellesi was a compact man with quiet, thoughtful eyes and a Roman nose; a face distinctly out of place on top of a tweed jacket, and twill trousers. A large red silk handkerchief, stuffed into his top pocket, contrasted badly with a thick woollen tie. Eldon looked down at his hands. They were tidy and sensitive, crossed as though in prayer. If he was not every one's idea of a farmer, then he was no one's idea of a policeman.

When Vergellesi spoke, it was slowly, choosing his words with care. "Have you ever had the feeling that the situation you're in resembles stepping out of a car into a puddle?"

"You mean we're parked in the wrong place?" Eldon enquired

"Yes, and no. Yes, we have stepped into a puddle. No, we didn't park the car."

"Then from here, I believe, we have to walk."

"I'll show you the office," Vergellesi said.

They walked to the end of the corridor, stopping at a door with a frosted glass panel.

Small, as Vignozzi had intimated, and equally sparse, with two desks, a telephone and a computer on one, nothing on the other. A filing cabinet with an empty open drawer stood in one corner.

Eldon shut it. "What's next?" he asked.

His new colleague dumped a brief case on the empty table, pushed the chair aside and sat on the desk. Opening the flap on the case he took out some compact discs, shuffled through them, and handed one to Eldon.

"People," Vergellesi said. "For the moment, just look up Brizzi."

Eldon connected the plug, settling himself into the chair, hard like the one in the corridor. He couldn't see himself spending long hours there. Perhaps that was the idea. Pushing the disc home he opened Brizzi's file.

His history was meticulously recorded, from the very beginning to the very end, until punctuated finally with a death certificate. An accumulation of data on an important, but essentially modest man. Eldon had a feeling there would be a gap somewhere.

He scrolled through, leaving out the pimply period of his youth: university, geology, volcanology, communist affiliations, pedagogic aspirations, and later political ambitions until he reached something a little more contemporary. Brizzi appeared to lead a hard working existence, sitting on various committees, though never

186

chairman of any. All sound, socially motivated groups, tending to address the problems of unemployment, trade union affairs and housing for the poor. Not the sort of places you were apt to make many enemies. Not the sort, anyway, where you ended up a corpse.

Everything about the man was seen in low profile. Someone who didn't stand out from the crowd; a blending in man, submerged in his surroundings so that he was indistinct from all the other commonality. Something he might have trained himself to do, out of necessity.

Eldon pushed his chair back. "Well, chronologically tidy. But where's the real Brizzi?"

"Yes," Vergellesi agreed. "The one nobody seems to have mentioned." He tapped the top of the computer.

"Deliberately, do you think?"

"No. I suspect this is as much as they've been able to compile. Part of a charade where no one has yet solved the riddle of who was Senator Brizzi?"

"Still, this is a very comprehensive file," Eldon argued. "Not a great deal left out."

"Something's left out. That's the problem. This is what Vignozzi had in mind when he told us to avoid images in mirrors. The substance is standing somewhere else. Here is Brizzi, a respected politician, happily married with two children, a family man leading an exemplary life from university to teacher, to mayor, to senator. A steady progressive life respected and trusted. And how do we get to know him? A man with a broken neck consorting with a suspected transvestite in an airport hotel." Vergellesi shook his head. "He was a man with many sides. We shall have to look for them. Tomorrow we can make a start."

"Where will we start?" Eldon asked, closing down the computer.

Vergellesi took the compact disc. "In a small provincial Tuscan town, called Sorena."

Chapter 21

The room was in darkness when Prinn opened his eyes. He shut them, ignoring the perfectly round, orange circle, that seemed to be cut into the wall of his bedroom. When he opened them again it hadn't remained motionless; being a moving, solitary transcendental disc amongst the self imposed darkness. It moved as mysteriously as the summer solstice rose over the heel stone at Stonehenge.

Prinn's feet found his slippers. Traversing the dark space, guided by the ray of light cast by a hole in one of the shutters where a knot had fallen out, he unhooked the panel and swung it back allowing the sun to flood into the room.

Showering quickly, he dressed and hurried downstairs. Scillone's mother had laid out his mail carefully on the hall table. Sweeping up the letters, together with a small parcel, he continued on to the kitchen where he could hear her preparing lunch.

Standing by the kitchen door, he watched for a moment the small woman stuffing pasta sheets with cooked spinach rolled up into tiny balls.

"*Buongiorno Signora,*" he said finally.

The little figure in black never stopped her work, but tossed a head sideways in reproof. "The day is done. The English have no respect for time. Nothing is therefore ever in the right place. Breakfast can be anywhere between five o'clock or twelve o'clock. You should be consistent like the Italians, eating breakfast on your feet at ten o'clock."

Prinn gave a good natured laugh, "Coffee and toast *Signora.*"

A small flour dusted hand waved him in the direction of the dining room, unimpressed. He did as he was bid.

Prinn placed the parcel on the table, thumbing through the envelopes, mostly with little cellophane windows. These were set aside. Turning to the parcel, he carefully undid the tape. Inside were two volumes on Petrarch by Luigi Vannini.

A compliment slip fluttered to the table. Prinn studied

the telephone numbers at the bottom, noting '2' and '160' were double imaged.

Taking up volume two, he turned to the uncut pages preceded by 160. Tapping the crease, Prinn shook the book gently. A small cellophane packet, of the type used for postage stamps, slid out. Pressing the edges of the packet lightly he could see inside four 16 mm microfilm negatives. He would look at them later.

The toast and coffee arrived on a tray so large that it seemed *Signora* Scillone would topple over. Prinn didn't make a fuss, chastened by countless reprimands over his concern that she required something a little more manageable; even the unthinkable, that he could have his breakfast in the kitchen.

Pouring a coffee he added hot milk, buttered a slice of toast, spread a thick layer of marmalade, and proceeded with his hands full to the study.

Crossing the hall, *Signora* Scillone looked sternly at him. Prinn gestured with the toast. "Eating breakfast on my feet *Signora*, like the Italians do," passing out of sight before she could lecture him.

Finishing the toast, Prinn washed his hands in a small closet adjacent to the study. Taking out the negatives, he placed them carefully in a microfilm reader to enlarge the image.

The pieces of microfilm showed two identical double-headed bronze statues standing side by side, with what looked like an inscription on one. A final piece of microfilm contained a short note from the Met's antiquities expert, Professor Gledhall:

'Nicholas. Info' update. You were right. Finally something has surfaced. Enquiry on Janus items made by a professional antiquary in Rome prior to purchasing the statues, and authentication due to the high price being asked. Such *'divinità bifronta'* pieces are not unknown on the market, but extremely rare. The photograph was taken by a laboratory scientist in Rome working undercover, and in his opinion was almost certainly cast in Populonia. Nothing else is known about the statues except they do not appear in any archival material. Therefore, must assume they have been recently unearthed, or released from a private collection not previously documented. The photograph from Questore Vignozzi is included. It appears the same as that found among the personal effects of the Italian citizen who suffered a heart attack on his way to the United States. No more information relating to their source is available. Of course, we cannot say if the Milan and New York statues are the same as the Rome example as they are at a slightly different angle, but such a coincidence would be stretching the bounds of possibility, I think. Have a nice holiday. Gledhall.'

Putting the equipment away, Prinn locked the microfilm in a drawer. He walked out on to the terrace. There was a wind amongst the sunlight, bending the tops of the tapering cypress trees.

Round the house the terracotta urns had been tidied, the soil freshened, the gravel weeded and raked, and the first batch of pruning had left shrubs and trees leaner and tidier. Scillone had been tending the box hedges, the odour of weak liquid manure gusting up on the wind.

Prinn turned down the terrace past the library, the stones still dark and damp beneath his step. The villa, brooding over the traumas of winter, remained scaffolded by the empty wisteria vines, knotted and dense round the shuttered windows.

Reaching the corner, Prinn caught sight of Scillone in his faded brown overall in the lean-to next to the barn. His attention appeared fully concentrated on directing the contents of a large oil can down the small oiling tube that led into the engine of a wide and very low OM caterpillar tractor. The machine was almost as old as Prinn, standing no higher than Scilone's waist, its orange bonnet faded to a murky pink. Scrupulously maintained, Scillone claimed it knew the land better than he.

Scillone looked up as Prinn crossed the compacted gravel road that ran along the front of the villa. Seeing that Prinn had something on his mind, he put down the can and wiped his hands on a rag he drew from his pocket.

Dusting off the abandoned tubular steel chair with its

peeling plywood seat, Scillone propped it up against a wooden roof post.

Acknowledging the gesture, Prinn sat down. "I've been intending to have a talk with you, Ettore."

The gardener grunted, working at a stubborn oil streak on his thumb with the rag.

"I wish I knew how to put this simply, Ettore." Prinn stood up, pacing along an imaginary line in front of Scillone, absorbed in how to word his next sentence. He came to the conclusion that nothing would soften the impact. "Someone saw fit to release Fausto Paba from prison eight years ago, Ettore."

Scillone's face hardened.

"Justice sometimes seems to play strange tricks on us, my old friend," Prinn continued.

Scillone wasn't listening, only remembering the faces of the men who forced his mouth open and poured silence down his throat, clamping his head tightly back as he tried to spit out the searing bitter liquid. Scillone closed his eyes, remembering the screams that gurgled into nothing; sounds that drummed inside his head, echoed still inside his head, and had no voice. Pieces of Prinn's conversation forced him back into the present.

"It's an odd set of circumstances that seem to have led Paba to cross your path again."

Scillone opened his eyes, his attention fixed on Prinn's lips.

"Paba is the major partner in the Castello di Pietra, Ettore. I know how you're going to feel. Society will seem to have turned against you. That's a big problem for me, because I need to know that I can still rely on you." Prinn raised his arm dejectedly for a moment, letting it fall to his side.

There was nothing to read in Scillone's face as he walked out of the lean-to, crossing the road to stop by the box hedges, staring out over the soft hills to the bright sky. A cypress tree dotting the horizon of his vision stood solitary and lonely in the expanse of emptiness that surrounded its existence. It might have been Scillone's soul.

Prinn drew alongside, putting an arm round his broad shoulder. "Be patient, Ettore. Do what good gardeners

191

know how to do best. Wait, and be patient."

Pulling at the oily rag he still held in his hand, Scillone mumbled some indecipherable sounds.

Prinn squeezed his shoulder. "A good gardener also knows when it's time to prune. Is that what you said, Ettore?"

A long moment passed before Scillone wiped his eyes with the back of his hands, and nodded.

Chapter 22

Having taken his coffee and custard doughnut at a small bar squeezed in between the travel agency and the Leopold restaurant where they had eaten late and regretted the experience, Eldon, stood on the pavement with his back to the wind, waiting for Vergellesi.

Glancing at his watch he saw it was exactly seven o'clock, and at precisely that time Vergellesi turned into the Via Garibaldi in a red Alfa Romeo sports car.

Eldon opened the door of the GTA using the slim rod that passed for a door handle, and dropped into the black bucket seat. He groaned inwardly. You were either an aficionado, or you were not.

"Why spoil a nice day hemmed in by lorries and diesel fumes?" Vergellesi asked, putting Eldon's grip behind them. "We'll take the old *via* Cassia to Siena. This is surely more fun than a Fiat?"

Eldon wasn't sure if he wanted more fun.

-oOo-

After a twisty, aggressive drive from Siena to the car park at Sorena, the car came to a rest accompanied by the smell of hot expanded metal, and scorched brake linings. Squatting on his calves, Vergellesi looked underneath to see if all was well, while Eldon stood with his hands in his pockets, looking at the high medieval stonewalls of the town rising out of the olive groves.

In seven hundred years things tended to grow together; a structure defining itself as an anatomical body, moulded by the natural elements of their existence. Somewhere underneath, Eldon surmised, older skeletons languished. Sometime Roman, earlier Etruscans, and compressed deeper beneath these, almost into archaeological oblivion, the three thousand year old proto-Tuscan Villanovan civilization. All of history encapsulated beneath the earth, as mute as the long dead warriors buried in tombs beneath their feet.

"The answer, *caro mio*, lies in the stones," Vergellesi said, interrupting his thoughts.

"The stones?" Eldon queried.

"Of course. Pietra. In this case, the matrix for alabaster. So hard it won't even take a chisel."

"I understood Alabaster to be soft?"

"It is, Rex. This is the womb; a mass of rock enclosing the alabaster. They mine it round here. Have done for thousands of years."

Walking up the hill, they passed through the Porta Giulia into the flag-stoned Piazza Grande.

The police station towered over the centre of the piazza; a role, Vergellesi explained, since the time of the mediaeval chief magistrates. Climbing up the steep travertine steps to the first floor, they reached the bare reception office.

A curly haired policewoman looked up from her desk, menacingly taking the top from her ballpoint pen before taking their identity cards. Thwarted, she rang disconsolately through to Commissioner Ruggieri to announce their arrival.

Another flight of steep steps opened on to a long, narrow stone corridor, with Ruggieri's office at the end.

Tullio Ruggieri had expected them. He pulled up some seats, politely asking how he might be of assistance

"A Senator Brizzi," Vergellesi explained. "Not the official record. Off the record."

"That's rather irregular." Ruggieri noted, lighting a cigarette. He had a grey, hard face with hollow cheeks. "Pisa briefed me, but no one said anything about opinions." His gloomy voice was also grey.

"We're not quite at the evidence stage," Vergellesi explained. "We're looking for clues. Not always the same thing. Clues support the evidence; evidence supports the facts. As we have few clues, we're looking for any possible new line of enquiry."

Ruggieri pulled a face. "As you wish. Naturally, his background's well known to everyone round here. If you go into politics, you need to be prepared to bare your soul. I'll give you the local chatter, and a quick history. See if anything has possibilities."

He pulled heavily on his cigarette, filling his lungs, before exhaling it through pouted lips. "Let's see - in his day most pupils left school at eleven, or went on to the *avviamento professionale* for two or three years. Being bright he passed from the middle school to the *licèo*, then on to the university at Florence - supported they say, by his mother's savings. About that time he became politically active in the communist party. He'd studied geology and hydrology at the university, specializing afterwards in volcanology. Hardly a route to secure employment. By the late sixties he was in the *licèo scientifico*, here in Sorena, teaching mathematics. As the secretary of the local *Partito Comunista Italiano,* he went on to become a council member. He came into the *giunta* with mayor Barbini in 1970, becoming mayor himself four years later, serving the maximum two terms before successfully running for the senate. Sorena, I'm told, was a let down for him. He saw tourism as short-term, nothing but a three-month casino. You can't build secure jobs on three months a year. He always had a reputation for being a man of the people, but was defeated as much by the Sorenesi themselves, as vested interests in Pisa and Florence. Locals not wanting the modern world knocking on their door. There's a saying, that because Sorena lies at six hundred metres, the Sorenesi have their heads in the clouds, which means they can't see their feet. Therefore, they don't actually know if they're walking backwards or forwards. Thus progress is not only slow, but mostly at a standstill." He laughed, more to himself, lighting a second cigarette from the first.

Vergellesi looked dissatisfied. "And that's all?"

Ruggieri folded his arms defensively. "There's no smut. Brizzi sat it out for eight years, signing the paperwork, marrying the locals, with never enough money to take the city anywhere. He certainly didn't get rich. I didn't know him that well. Enough to pass the time of day. You must speak to Loris Cecotti. I'll give him a phone call. He and Brizzi were staunch friends, even though Loris didn't go on to university. Family farms next door to each other, so they lived in each other's pockets. Afterwards too." He looked at his watch. "If he keeps regular hours he should just be getting hungry about now. I'll phone him in about an hour, and see if I can arrange a visit for this afternoon."

-oOo-

Vergellesi sat on a stone bollard out in the sunshine, and closed his eyes.

Eldon watched him for a moment. "Are we making progress, do you think?"

One eye opened dolefully. "I'm considering possibilities, Rex. You're not in England. Progress depends on exhausting the possibilities." The eye closed again.

"I dare say. What are you considering, or is that too exhausting to say?"

"I'm considering why you came all this way to give us a hand with a political murder that's just possibly nothing more than underworld business."

"Perhaps the one answers the other. Was Brizzi killed by criminals?"

Vergellesi's eyes opened. "Not known. We might also ask ourselves the question, why you and I find ourselves on a windy hill in Tuscany? A place that only Questore Vignozzi and Commander Prinn seem to consider of any moment. Why is that?"

"Brizzi being killed for political reasons seems doubtful, Piero, which means they expect us to look for an alternative. Why Sorena? I don't know that either. Only that it was his town. The situation; however, has the feeling of two trains side by side in the station. Passengers, looking out of the windows, are unsure which carriages are actually moving."

"What exactly is that supposed to mean?" Vergellesi asked.

"That I'm still, possibly, standing on the platform."

"Meaning you haven't been briefed?" Vergellesi queried.

"In a manner of speaking, no. Time to do your washing, Piero. In your opinion, what exactly am I doing here?"

Vergellesi sighed deeply. "They warned me you might be difficult. Vignozzi outlined the ETA business in Escároz. Being trapped in a situation like that can't have been pleasant. I suppose you learn to live with it."

196

"I see. It's a bit late to provide sympathy."

"In these circles you're a legend, Rex."

"Nine people dead. One of them an eight month pregnant woman. That's a legend?"

Vergellesi pulled a dissenting face. "They were all terrorists. Armed killers. So you shot them. Look, you don't carry guns unless you have a use for them. The woman killed an old man in cold blood, who never harmed anyone, right before your eyes. She was a known murderer, with you as a witness. So you took her, and her friends, out at the same time. All right, the judiciary might be a bunch of pacifists, but they still don't expect a citizen to be one. The law decided it was justifiable homicide."

"How I care is what counts," Eldon said.

Standing up, Vergellesi brushed the seat of his trousers. "I agree. You must go home then, Rex. Anxiety will only make you a liability."

"To whom?"

"There's only you and me. Better odds than Escároz. But I understand. They explained you'd been through a bad time up there. Psychosomatic problems, feelings of guilt, demoralized."

For a brief moment Eldon felt angry. Sir Edward Kerry was still up to his old tricks. Tricks of concealment, of conspiracy, seeing what you couldn't see, pretending that nothing was pretence, moving five things while you saw only three.

"I think you were sold a dummy, Piero. I resigned because an operation was bungled. Afterwards, certain people didn't like my opinions; didn't like being told that the danger should have been in front, not behind, sitting at a Whitehall desk. Believe me, you were sold a dummy, and it wasn't me." Eldon turned to go.

Vergellesi raised his voice slightly. "You haven't heard my side of the story, Rex."

Eldon faced him, his hands folded in front, in a quiet gesture of patience. "Oh, yes. And what was your particular psychological problem?"

Taking Eldon's arm, Vergellesi guided him to the empty stone seat that ran along the front of the Palazzo Pubblico. "Listen. Have you ever heard of Judge Alfiero

197

Vergellesi?"

"A relation?"

"He was my father, Rex. Killed in a Palermo restaurant. Salts of hydrocyanic acid in his food. He was a good man. An honest man. Reason enough in Palermo, you might think, for someone to kill him. Cyanide in an almond. Just two or three among a rice and scampi salad. You don't stop eating an almond because it's got a slightly bitter taste. The only thing we know is that he was conducting an investigation implicating a high level Russian diplomat, along with members of the almost clandestine communist hoodlums in Sicily. The Sicilian variety doesn't like them, so no love lost there. You shouldn't get the idea that Italian communists are of the Sidney Webb variety. Too many are Soviet stereotypes, up to their eyes in shady deals. My father uncovered something that would have been extremely embarrassing for someone. After that the government slammed the lid on, hoping the nasty smell would go away."

Vergellesi crossed his leg, took a tissue from his pocket and wiped away a pigeon dropping from his shoe. "I think for it to bring luck, it's got to land on your head."

"Go on about the Russian diplomat?" Eldon prompted.

"The story died with my father. There was no word out in the Mafia. Poison doesn't carry a Mafia signature. Too low a profile. My father had important friends, Rex. They can't bring him back, but they'd like to bring him justice. I was rusty, but at least had the experience on how to mix in when the going got rough, something his friends hadn't forgotten. So they asked me to come in, and go through everything, merely to see if anything spun off. Lines of inquiry." He fell silent for a moment. "What I came up with led to the investigation being abandoned."

"Explain something to me, Piero," Eldon interrupted. "I know this is your story, but how did it get to become mine as well?"

"The reason for it being abandoned. A Russian assassin called Nightingale."

"Well, well, well," Eldon reflected.

"I'm afraid they'd never let me continue on my own - once that information turned up. Home-grown mobs are one thing, international executioners quite another. To continue, they considered it imperative I'm joined by someone capable of preventing me from ending up horizontal. That someone happens to be you."

"Piero, your security service has support capabilities of their own."

"Not with your sort of experience, I'm afraid. No one that good."

"Piero, forget such nonsense." Eldon took a deep breath, letting it out noisily. "All right. Just concentrate on tying this scenario together for me so I can see where I'm going. At the moment it looks like home."

"Vignozzi and Prinn believe the person who killed my father also killed Blain. Possibly Brizzi and Finetti as well. Your triangle."

"And their reason?"

"Because of the Gorky State Orchestra."

Eldon leant back against the rough stone of the building, silent laughter shaking his shoulders. "Now who would have believed such a thing? Tell me about these musical gangsters?"

"The Gorky State Orchestra were giving a concert in Perpignan when Blain was killed. They were also giving a concert in Messina eighteen months ago when my father was enjoying his rice and scampi salad. Now they're in Italy on an eight-week tour, finishing in Genoa. Brizzi died two days before the Rome concert."

"That's very speculative. How big is an orchestra? Musicians, technicians, officials, hangers on. A hundred or more?" Eldon declared.

"All true. But does it make enough sense for me to go on?"

Looking at the serious, questioning face, Eldon nodded. "You have my undivided attention."

-oOo-

Eldon twirled another strand of spaghetti on to his fork. "How did you come by the orchestra connexion?"

"An opera buff in the original investigation team, knowing about the suspected Russian link, and the 'coincidental' visit of the Gorky State Orchestra, ironically suggested that the murderer would probably turn out to be the second violinist. Something about the strand struck me as bizarrely plausible, so I quietly picked it up from there."

"Have you matched every incident against the movements of the orchestra?" Eldon asked.

"I have, and they don't." Vergellesi waved the empty carafe at the waiter.

"How many do?"

"Originally, not one. However, in the suspected cases over the last eight years, seventy per cent. Trying to identify a more positive fix, I considered the possibility that the orchestra might be an occasional cover. Technical staff visit proposed venues some time before the performance." He leant back; lapsing into silence while the waiter changed the carafe. When he'd gone, Vergellesi leaned closer. "The problem is I couldn't get details of who accompanied the orchestra. Conductor and musicians readily available on the official lists, but suspiciously, no precise lists on anyone else. They could have picked up and accommodated another national anywhere on route, once they were over the border. That's a knotty question."

"A mystery, yes, but not necessarily mysterious," Eldon stressed.

"Enough of a mystery for you to stay?" Vergellesi asked.

"Not least because I dislike the idea of somebody pulling my strings. Worse, I dislike the idea that there are strings to pull. We'll see about that, but first we must visit this friend of Brizzi's."

"Cecotti?"

"Yes. This investigation's turning out to have more blind alleys than the bazaar of Ispahan."

Chapter 23

The car swung off the main road on to a metalled country lane. Dust billowing up from the wheels forced Eldon to close his window. Narrow, and mostly steeply banked, the lane was cross-rutted on corners where heavy winter rains, or ponderous caterpillar tractors, had carved channels across them.

Ruggieri drove in the centre attempting to miss the bumps. As other drivers did the same, it became fraught with incalculable errors of judgement.

Ruggieri caught Eldon's thoughts. "Some of these ancient tracks are three thousand years old, stretching all the way to the Maremma. Not many have been subject to a modern survey, so you can easily get lost."

As he spoke they emerged into the open. Cleared on both sides, the land rose in a sweeping bowl to a rim of trees. Neat rows of gnarled and blackened vines hung on taught wires, their roots already shaded by heaped soil that shortly would be turned into sand by the fierce heat of the summer sun.

At one end of a terrace stood a terracotta roofed farmhouse with walls of durable random stone, soft hued by time. Attached to the house a long open series of steps rose to a covered balcony facing a stone barn, its upper story with vented walls in terracotta bricks. High overhead, a crane dangled its cantilevered jib close to where builders had been repairing the roof.

Somewhere, out of sight, a dog started barking, the deep sound of a big and heavy animal. They waited for Cecotti to appear.

"I said we'd be here about three o'clock." Ruggieri looked at his watch. "A little late."

Close by, the sound of a tractor echoed back gently from the trees. In amongst the vines a small tractor came into view towing a low trailer and making periodic stops while the driver distributed manure.

Cecotti was a thin asthmatic looking man with an oily trilby on his head, cigarette between his lips. With their approach he stopped the tractor, but he didn't get down.

Ruggieri shook hands. Eldon and Vergellesi reached

up, and did the same. He hardly looked at them, addressing himself to Ruggieri.

"Go into the cantina with the green door, Tullio. You'll find some glasses and wine in the tall cupboard. I'll be along directly."

Finding the glasses with a recycled flask of fresh wine, Ruggieri gestured for them to sit on the benches round a wooden table, covered by a stained, but clean oil cloth.

He was about to pour the wine when Cecotti appeared.

Walking, he had a slight stoop. Despite the asthmatic pallor he looked fit in the stretched wiry manner of those whose work was a continual exercise. Finding himself an old aluminium ashtray, the Martini advertisement a faded smudge of pinks and greys, he pushed a glass along to Ruggieri.

Eldon and Vergellesi listened tolerantly while the two older men indulged in a preamble about last years harvest, the weather, and the justification for the Tuscan obsession with pollution. The dead senator's efforts in this direction turned the conversation to Brizzi.

"You said you wanted to discuss Brizzi," Cecotti addressed Ruggieri, then twisted towards Vergellesi and Eldon to study them closely "You're the two from Rome, Tullio mentioned?"

They both nodded, and repeated their names.

Cecotti's attention remained fixed on Eldon. Beside the name, his accent and clothes were unfamiliar to him. Romans he'd come across, so from Milan he reasoned, or Turin. Somewhere more important than Sorena.

"You knew Roberto better than anyone, Loris," Ruggieri suggested.

"His wife might disagree, don't you think?" Cecotti ventured.

"Yes. But as a woman. Not the same as a man." Ruggieri's voice was persuasive, patient.

"Because we go back a long way, old school friends and comrades, right until the end, do you mean?"

"Yes. Everything. Especially things you might consider relevant. There's really no need to be so defensive, Loris. You were like brothers. Everyone knows that. No one thinks you slipped off down to Rome to settle an old

202

score. You wouldn't have been able to negotiate your way round the *tangenziale*, let alone find him."

Cecotti nodded in confirmation, never having been out of Tuscany. "Brizzi's life was an open book. What more can anyone add?"

"You must have something to add," Ruggieri pressed. "Matters that weren't common knowledge."

"What sort of matters do you have in mind?" Cecotti asked suspiciously.

"The sort comrades discuss," Ruggieri elaborated. "He might mention his wife, disagreements, money problems perhaps, difficulties he wouldn't broadcast to the community at large."

"He never had those sort of problems. He lived an orderly life." Cecotti looked at each of them slowly, as though weighing up the balance of their interest.

Vergellesi broke into the conversation. "That's the rub, *Signor* Cecotti. We don't know what sort of life Senator Brizzi lived."

Ruggieri encouraged Cecotti to continue. "Exactly. There has to be a reason why someone should kill him. Picking up a streetwalker just doesn't make sense. What else could there be?"

Cecotti pulled a discouraging face. "We were close friends, growing up together on these farms. He returned here when he could. Holding on to his past. Outside that, I know very little."

"Holding on to his past?" Vergellesi inquired.

"Of course," Cecotti said sharply. "Here he was in touch with himself; not having to be someone else."

"This someone else?" Vergellesi pressed.

"He was a politician with a public face. No one expects people involved in that line of work to be themselves. You're pulled in so many different directions at once. Of course, I don't know anything about his life when he became a senator. That was another life he didn't share with me. It didn't matter. Here he was able to look himself in the face, and regain his identity. That was important to him."

"So he came here with his family. Relaxation; releasing the pressure?" Vergellesi suggested.

There was a pause before Cecotti answered, glancing

at each of them in turn. "No. He never came here with his family."

"You know his wife though?"

"Yes, I know her."

"I see." They were silent for a moment, before Vergellesi continued. "What do you make of her?"

"You can go and see for yourself. She lives in Sorena."

"I'm looking for a developed view, not just a glimpse," Vergellesi said in a lower tone.

"She provided the image he needed."

"So, not a marriage of the heart then?"

Cecotti laughed, showing dull, firm teeth. "Whatever that is."

"And not in this case?" Vergellesi persisted.

"I said everything else was his public face. His heart was here." Cecotti looked at the attentive faces round him, waiting for what he'd say next. Perhaps he'd said too much.

"*Signor* Cecotti," Eldon drew his attention.

The eyes of his slightly flushed face fixed on Eldon, the sudden movement of his head depositing the drooping cigarette ash on to the table.

"From what you say, Senator Brizzi seems to have had a strong affection for this farm. Something you shared together?" Eldon ignored the uncertain looks of his colleagues

"You're not Italian, by the sound of it?" Cecotti queried, at last.

"*Signor* Eldon is here in an official capacity, Loris," Ruggieri hastily explained. "Roberto's death has international implications, so he's in Italy representing the United Kingdom's interests. Obviously we can't elaborate. You'll understand. Just answer any questions you can, whether they make sense to you, or not."

"English. Well, *Signor* Eldon, he was pushed out. No place for him. Do you know what that means? Not being Italian, I don't expect you do. It's like being cast out into a wilderness where everyone you meet is someone you recognise, but no one you know. Sorena just turned their back on him."

"Obviously the senator believed he was destined for much higher things than Sorena," Vergellesi quietly suggested.

Cecotti turned a baleful eye on Vergellesi. "What things? Roberto was a good communist, not like those self-serving peacocks in Florence, all flashy cars, *riserva* wines and two hundred thousand *lire* seats at the opera. He didn't consider himself better."

"I think Commissioner Vergellesi," Eldon intervened, "was suggesting that Senator Brizzi was looking for a greater personal fulfilment with which he could serve the community better, not that he was superior to them. Perhaps you could expand on his objectives in that direction. Or any other plans or projects he had in mind. If you need time to consider, we can visit again?"

The farmer eyed Vergellesi with displeasure, before turning back to Eldon. "I'd like to help in any way that will leave Roberto's name untouched by this cheap scandal. I'll sleep on it."

Cecotti saw them to the door, continuing to watch them enter the car. Still watching as they drove away.

"I think I blew it there, Rex," Vergellesi confessed from the front seat.

"Not completely. He'd gone far enough, and said too much looking for a way out. You just gave him a handy peg to hang his hat on."

"He's a good man," Ruggieri interjected. "But I doubt he'll lead you anywhere. Cecotti's never been further than Pisa in his life. Everything he needs is here."

"Nearly everything, Tullio," Eldon said thoughtfully. "Perhaps once. Now he's not so sure. You mentioned that Brizzi was his best friend. I'm inclined to think he was his only friend."

-oOo-

They booked into adjoining rooms on the first floor of a small hotel in the town centre. When Eldon and Vergellesi re-emerged in the early evening, the streets were already full of people.

Looking idly in one or two windows, Vergellesi turned to the question uppermost in his mind. "All right. Why, exactly, are we staying here?"

Eldon angled his head down towards his shoulder so

he could read the label on a bottle, before looking at Vergellesi's cross reflection in the glass. "Policemen develop a sixth sense, they say. It's rubbed off on me."

"Try me on the second. I'd like to hear more of what you've got to say."

"For some reason Cecotti needs to unburden himself. What he doesn't want is an audience."

"He didn't appear the shy, retiring type to me?" Vergellesi objected.

"Don't be oversensitive," Eldon advised. "I had the impression that Cecotti considered you and Ruggieri weren't the right sort of company in which to bare his soul. He's not going to trust the devil he knows."

"That's ridiculous. You'd be bound to tell us," Vergellesi protested.

"A question of psychology. This is a Catholic country. Your confessor is a confidant, not a member of the jury. At least in theory."

Vergellesi wasn't entirely convinced. "How are you going to get there? You're not using my car on those roads."

"I can't steal one, Piero."

"You'll have to hope Ruggieri has an old car tucked away somewhere, then," Vergellesi declared.

-oOo-

Eldon was not altogether enamoured of the little Fiat Cinquecento he was offered. An uncertain date did not suggest reliability, despite Ruggieri's complete confidence in its roadworthiness. But Eldon had to agree, the car drove in a straight line, and stopped when demanded.

"While I'm gone," Eldon ventured, "see what you can find out from Brizzi's wife."

"I'll do what I can, but Italians are reluctant witnesses. We don't see anything, we don't say anything and we don't hear anything. Something like your three wise monkeys, but without the wisdom." Vergellesi slapped the top of the car.

Eldon manoeuvred his way out of the *piazza*, down the flagged street towards the Porta Giulia.

In the dark, Eldon's memory was condensed to fewer

recognizable landmarks, breeding a growing uncertainty as the kilometres slipped past. With some relief he eventually spotted the woodpile at the entrance to the farm, revving his way up the short slope to the house.

A dog started barking. Rushing out from the barn, white coat luminous in the darkness, the maremmano hound slid to a halt, and continued barking at the car window. Eldon recalled that such dogs used to delight in hiding among the sheep, waiting to jump out on unsuspecting wolves, and tear them to pieces. Looking at the large incisors, only inches from his face, he was inclined to believe the story. He pressed the horn, hoping the tinkling sound could be heard inside the house.

The yard light came on, followed by the door opening. Cecotti descended a few steps to recognize his visitor.

"Ah, the Englishman," he said. "*Basta!*" The dog obediently padded back to the barn. "You can come up." Cecotti re-entered the house leaving Eldon to climb the steep steps.

In the high narrow room, with exposed chestnut timber beams, and heavily worn terracotta tiled floor, nothing had been modernized. Eldon noticed a book-case with hardbacks on the shelves. Cecotti was not tied to the soil alone. A small annexe with open front and stone seats flanked a raised hearth; its fire leaving an odour of charred bacon in the air. During the depths of winter, Cecotti would have found these unyielding seats more accommodating than the humidity of the bedrooms.

"Drink?" Cecotti asked.

Eldon nodded his thanks, and pulled a chair out from the table, but Cecotti waved him towards the hearth.

"Take a cushion, sit by the fire for a moment," Cecotti insisted. "You look as though you've been huddled in a draught." He poured them two tumblers of grappa, noticing Eldon's interest. "Home made. Ten years old. I make a batch every year after the *vendemmia*. When I die someone will inherit a lot of grappa. Minus the hidden costs."

"Free of tax you mean?"

"Free of dangerous additives." He studied the liquid through the glass for a moment. "I'm glad you came

207

alone," sitting down opposite Eldon, poking a log further on to the flames.

"Everyone else was busy." Eldon raised his glass and took a firm drink. It was not in the least as he'd expected. It was soft, warm, with a pronounced flavour of juniper - if he had to describe it, he'd say it was a little luscious. He raised his glass again, impressed. "*Complimenti.*"

Cecotti nodded. "I can do without eavesdroppers. It's true what they say. You can't trust an Italian with a secret. They just can't wait to be one ahead of someone else."

"Believe me, not only Italians."

"No," Cecotti disagreed. "We aren't discreet about our indiscretions. You English know when to leave things unsaid. *Giusto?*"

Eldon consented, for the sake of politeness.

Cecotti turned his drink towards the flames, letting them create a distorted image in the glass.

"Roberto made a mistake in marrying." He fell into silence, as though expecting a response.

"You don't seem to have a very high regard for his wife?" Eldon remarked.

"No. I don't. She's an ambitious woman." Cecotti gave another weak smile, not quite sure of himself. "Not for Roberto. Just for her. She was a reflection, not a substance. Making all the right movements, without the right intentions."

"They must have got along?"

"Difficult to say how, exactly."

"You think they didn't?" Eldon commented.

"*Può darsi.* According to me. She wasn't right for him. Roberto made a mistake marrying her, not only because she was a spider with webs of deceit, but because of Enzo." Cecotti fell silent again as though considering a personal tragedy that had overtaken Brizzi. Overtaken them both.

"Enzo?" Eldon coaxed quietly.

"Her brother, Enzo." Cecotti's voice had become a whisper. "He was like a *furetto*. In and out everywhere. He would find out. Only a matter of time before he would know." The voice trailed off, avoiding the past.

208

Eldon took another sip of the grappa, letting it warm his throat. He looked at Cecotti steadily, who looked quickly away into the fire, avoiding his gaze.

"He would know that you and Roberto were homosexuals?"

Cecotti looked up, draining his glass in one gulp. "He would know that's how we were. And like everyone else he wouldn't have understood."

Eldon nodded in agreement. "That's generally how it is. So you kept out of the way, avoiding the possibility of someone finding out. Chances were that eventually someone would. That takes us to Enzo. Do you think he had anything to do with Roberto's death?"

Cecotti shook his head, passing over the bottle of Grappa.

"I don't know. We made a pact from the beginning," he said bitterly, "that no one must ever find out. This is a small place. We'd never be able to hide from the shame they'd heap on us. Here, that's the only thing you're allowed to feel. Are made to feel. You could never show your affection. In Florence, Milan, Rome, you wouldn't stand out, but here you can't disappear. Oh, no one throws stones, but everyone rattles them in their pocket. They don't walk away, or look the other way, you are just no longer there. In Sorena, if you're not someone's friend, then you're everyone's enemy. Roberto managed by playing their game, creating a normal life, having an ideal, a career to provide a smoke screen. I had nothing, so I stayed here on my farm. Out of the way."

"This Enzo, though. He was a friend?"

Cecotti gave a hollow laugh. "Became one. Once he knew, he became a very close friend."

"I see," Eldon said. "I assume by this time, Brizzi was well placed to be of some help to Enzo?"

"As the mayor he was in a position to help everyone. Except himself. But there was no way out, even though Enzo kept silent. That's the essence, you see. Being helped by a 'friend' makes them part of the conspiracy. Silence is everywhere. Something you're born with."

Eldon leant forward, his arms on his knees, holding his glass in front of him. "This isn't important Loris. A small town slice of life. Not a reason to end up dead in

Rome. It doesn't take us anywhere."

Cecotti got up, filling his glass. "No. But Enzo's still the reason Roberto's dead. Roberto was a clever man, with interests beyond teaching and politics. He taught me too. Made me see the value of the great men in history; stuffed my head full of their comings and goings. Not too much. I could cope with Dante and Boccaccio, but I could never get my head round Aretino. I could laugh at the satire but I never really knew what it meant. He was too highbrow for me. Roberto said that being good at only Mathematics, or Chemistry, created a shallow person. What was the point in splitting the atom if you couldn't appreciate Verdi, or lose yourself in Petrarch? He believed in Renaissance people, you see. If you asked Da Vinci to paint you a Mona Lisa, that's what he would do. If you asked him to mend your canon, he'd do that as well. Did you know Roberto trained as a geologist?"

Eldon nodded.

"You did. And his interest in archaeology?" Cecotti saw he did not. "He was a close friend of Doctor Guelfa, the curator of the museum in Sorena. Like everything Roberto did, he developed his passion into something more."

"How does Enzo fit in all this?" Eldon asked.

"Enzo's in the excavation business, profitable round here with all the restoration work. Enzo, like me, is not possessed of any great intelligence, but he's clever enough to spot the potential. Digging's his job. In this area that means you get to unearth more than just the foundations of a building."

"Given three thousand years, I imagine you do."

"*Bravo*. People tend to recognize the particular value of a site. On cross roads, by rivers, or on top of hills, that's where they'll settle, and build, and fall into decline, and build again. For thousands of years, houses, mills, castles and palaces will rise, then be lost, destroyed by invaders, by disease, by disinterest. But the land doesn't change at the same pace. The course of the river alters by erosion; huge lakes silt up, becoming plains on which farmers prosper where once fishermen did. Earthquakes shatter mountains, besides throwing up new ones.

Yes, land changes, but in the span of a human life, not so you'd notice. Enzo naturally digs up the past, keeping what he finds for himself. He has contacts in Pisa, spiriting these treasures away."

"When did Roberto and Enzo find they had something in common?" Eldon enquired, pouring himself a little more grappa.

"Roberto had a theory on the geological conditions of an area called Petrolla."

"A shared interest?"

"Not until Enzo unearthed some stones at the Castello di Pietra. He was supposed to be helping with preservation work for the bank, taking the opportunity to steal some dressed stone for a local builder. Enzo, knowing they weren't right for a building of the seventeenth century, asked Roberto's opinion. He identified them as Roman. Enzo did a little more excavation, finding that a bank running behind the castle hid a wall of similar stones. Enzo was excited, thinking of all the spoils that might lie hidden, Roberto because his theory might be correct."

Eldon was mystified. "All because of a possibility?"

Cecotti shook his head. "In the city archives there are documents alluding to a Roman temple on Colline Petrolla, overlooking the River Aula. The Aula flows in from the East, passing the high ground of Petrolla before sweeping south towards the sea. If the temple, thought to be the last resting place of an extremely rich Roman senator, overlooked the river, it would be facing the southeast. There's a local legend of fabulous wealth buried with him, but no one's ever unearthed anything of that nature. Roberto was convinced that the Roman wall proved the castle was built over the temple."

"There must be a lot of Roman walls round here?" Eldon suggested.

"*Certo*. But the biggest snag is the present castle faces west, not southeast. You can't see the river."

"Sounds rather conclusive."

"That's where Roberto's theory comes in, explaining why no one had ever found the temple. It's also where he made the biggest mistake in his life. He told Enzo. Enzo saw this as his chance to become rich. All he needed was to own the castle. Except you don't just buy castles, and do what you like with them. Even when money's no object, you're told what you can, and can't do. Enzo didn't have the money anyway. He was over-extended purchasing new machinery. So, Roberto went to the bank, arranging finance on the strength of a new partner in the proposed project."

"The bank went along with that?"

"Hardly. Enzo had only ten per cent of what they needed. Nor did Roberto have enough. But being the ex-Mayor he negotiated a further thirty per cent. The other sixty per cent came from this new partner."

"And the major shareholder."

Cecotti nodded.

"Ah," Eldon said, leaning back against the wall, warm from the fire. "One Roberto knew too little about."

Cecotti nodded again. "Quicksands. Every move sucked him in deeper."

"And somewhere along the line, for some reason, he became a liability?"

"He phoned me six weeks ago. The strain was too much. His life, even as a senator, had been dedicated to lifting Sorena from small town ambitions towards new horizons where you needed to think big so you could quit chipping away at the edges, copying little ideas created by other failures. Now, he considered he'd robbed them, like a sly thief taking alms from a blind man."

"Did he say he'd made up his mind to get out?" Eldon asked.

"Not exactly. He was seeing someone. That's all. Someone new who could put it right. He never said who it was. Poor Roberto. You can never walk away from the sort of partners he'd become involved with."

"Well, you're also left with a problem, Loris. Someone, at some time, will want to know how much Roberto confided in you. Even the little you've told me they won't want remembered."

Cecotti forced a smile, and shrugged. He no longer cared.

Eldon rose, placing his glass on the table. Cecotti had opened up possibilities that weren't going to please Vergellesi. He wouldn't understand how grave robbing, and an elusive political assassin, had the slightest thing in common. Besides, a protracted stay in Sorena wasn't what his colleague would have in mind.

"What was Roberto's theory, by the way?" Eldon asked.

"*Pazzo.* That the hill moved. During a massive earthquake it was wrenched one hundred and thirty five degrees towards the north, ending up pointing west, out of the original alignment."

Eldon pulled an affirmative face. "Possible. There are recorded instances in Italy of hills turning through as much as one hundred and eighty degrees during seismic movements. This is an earthquake zone, after all. What are the chances the temple's still there?"

"Not much. Nobody believes in the legend any more. The wall seems supportive to me, buttressing the bank. Probably for a villa that stood where the castle is now."

"Fools gold then."

"What's that?" Cecotti asked.

"Something people kill for, believing it's real."

Cecotti rose, their meeting over. "One thing," he said as they reached the door. "Roberto had a lot of faith in the owner of the Villa Lazzi. He's dead now. But he had a son. He might know something."

Eldon walked out to the top of the stairs, catching the first chill in the cold night air. He turned up his collar. "Possibly. Well, your guard dog makes a lot of noise."

"Not really," Cecotti replied. "Not if he knows someone. That's how Enzo found out about Roberto and me."

Chapter 24

Ushering his visitor down the silent corridor and past the fire door, Sandquest let it swing unchecked behind them.

The voice was American, mid-west, from Kansas or Missouri. "Now, you can tell this factory is hush-hush just by the corridors. Yes, sir."

Sandquest liked him. A humorous man, with enough years to talk intelligently from experience, rather than the book. They crossed to where his chauffeur was standing smartly to attention with the car door open. The American stopped and looked back at the building.

"Impressive, and that's no bull. Tell me though; is your security tight enough? We just seemed to sidle in everywhere. Aren't you worried about that? I, sure as hell, would be." There was an earnest note in his voice.

Sandquest smiled, unpinning the visitor's identity card from his lapel. "Now try getting back in, Jim. The alarms will be activated, and the doors lock. This is a general security card giving complete access, except you have to be accompanied at all times, so two are needed. They can be programmed for a block, a section, and even one room. Believe me, the security's efficient enough to keep intruders out. The only worry in a facility like this is identifying the deception within. You can't stop people walking out with secrets inside their head."

He eased into the car, sliding across to the other side on the smooth hide seats. The American followed, sighing as he lowered his large frame alongside.

"We'll hand these ID's in at the gate, Bob," Sandquest instructed the driver. "Then straight into the West End for lunch."

"Only a short dash, Arthur?" the American beamed hopefully.

Sandquest settled back into the Bristol's seats. "There before you know it. You'd like me to arrange a set of estimates with the logistical details for assessment?"

"I sure would. Before the board meets. If you can include the proposed modifications to be incorporated in the Mk II, along with the cost differentials, I'll give you support on that one. The improved performance, in my opinion, is worth paying for. Useless me talking quality to a bunch of auditors. They'll need to be impressed by savings and healthy profit margins. You know these guys as well as I do."

"That I do. Good of you to pitch in for me, Jim."

"Shucks, Arthur, I'm an engineer like yourself. I'm pitching for my company not a bunch of bone headed chartered accountants. We need your product, but the only way I can land a deal is through those tight pursed Jacobs."

"Of course, you'll get the best figures. I must advise you though, that the Kazumasa Optical Company is already negotiating for the modified Mk II. They've had teething troubles with their collection device that may take them some time to resolve. However, when that's done they'll want some exclusivity deal bolted on, and they'll be willing to pay."

"That's a bummer, Arthur. Any idea what time scale we're up against?"

"You can tell your board it's short."

"You're giving this to me straight, Arthur?"

"Oh, absolutely straight. We just haven't told Kazumasa we've solved their little problem."

"Now that is a real bummer. If I can't convince my board, you'll hand the contract to Kazumasa on a plate and strike a deal. You don't need us at all?"

Sandquest handed in their identity cards at the security gate.

"Short term, no. However, other things in the pipeline might be of interest to you that aren't to Kazumasa. I believe in fostering relationships. Don't worry, I have confidence in you. You'll convince them, Jim, believe me." Sandquest patted his knee in response to the glum face. "To that end I've arranged a small amount of leverage to assist us in the right direction. I've had a word with Senator William Pollard for you."

"Do you mean Pollard, on the Permanent Select committee?"

"Yes. Besides Intelligence, he also has a finger in the pie at Calder Dynamics. If I remember correctly, your company is desperate to break into the small circle of defence contractors and has signed a research contract with them. Stability. Isn't that your board's interest?"

The American burst out laughing. "Can I use that?"

"Of course. Why do you think I told you?"

"That's a peach. You know, I'm being serious when I tell you; I'm just enthusiastic about your whole show. It's darn right slick. Yes, sir. Everything from that Miss Wolfe down. Boy, is that lady one hell of a per cent class."

"I insist on efficiency. From everyone," Sandquest explained.

"Well, if I thought I could, I'd poach her from you."

"You might try," Sandquest said pleasantly.

"No. She's worth big bucks, I know. Anyway, we probably couldn't entice her back to the States."

Sandquest grew serious. "Back to the States?"

"Sure. And I see why. What could we offer? Money? Waste of time. She's got brains. When you've got that, the darn stuff sticks to you. No need to go looking for it."

"You've met before then?" Sandquest asked cautiously.

Oh, sure. But only briefly. She didn't remember me when I came up to your office, so I didn't bring the subject up. Say. If she didn't remember me, I wasn't worth remembering. Save all that embarrassment."

"I see. When did you meet her exactly?" Sandquest asked.

"There's a question," Jim reflected. "I was working in the Procurement Executive for NASA. Sabbatical to cover an Agency exhibition on the Shuttle. Sort of vacation on the job."

"She was working for NASA?"

"Heck no. No money in NASA. Some bright spark suggested that we should contrast the technological aspects of ceramic materials with ancient works of art. Pottery and such like. A real neat idea, using discrete components alongside these primitive pots. Miss Wolfe came along from the Metropolitan to set up their side of the display." He laughed heartily. "She was also supposed to be on a kind of sabbatical. From the scientific photographers, Morgan and Freeman, who specialize in museum work. I guess it must have given her the idea that technology was a lot more fun than a

216

dusty pile of old clay pots."

"Must have," Sandquest affirmed.

"So, how long has she been working for you, Arthur?"

"About two years." Sandquest lapsed into silence, letting Jim's talk distract him from a growing sense of unease.

-oOo-

After lunch Sandquest dropped his client off at a hotel near Marble Arch, returning to his headquarters on the Embankment. Livia was dictating a letter to one of the secretaries. He waved for her to continue as he passed through to his office.

Sandquest could wager a fair sum that Livia had never mentioned working in the United States. Jim Doskie had said he'd only met her briefly, but briefly was all you needed where Livia was concerned. Men were not likely to forget her.

Accessing the restricted company database covering personnel records on his laptop failed to locate Livia's involvement with a museum in New York. He scrolled through her complete set of references, confirming a chronological record since she'd left university. There were no gaps. Competent and relevant authorities had verified them all. Government security agencies had covered work that was secret and classified. Nothing that referred to the Metropolitan.

Doskie must have been mistaken. Moonlighting from the Harvard Business School wasn't a serious proposition. Nor was the photography. Why didn't he just dismiss the whole thing? Doskie couldn't discriminate between one pretty girl and another.

The doubt kept bouncing back like a bad cheque.

Sandquest picked up the telephone, dialling a number in New York.

"Ah, Willie. Didn't wake you, did I? - A late night, and at your age. - Yes, yes, I bought the vase. Wrongly dated I imagine, but a wonderful example. Oh yes, when I'm next in New York we'll definitely see each other. - No, nothing difficult. I'd like you to acquire some information for me. I recall you had a friend in the Met?

Well, if they're in administration now, that would be perfect. For personal reasons I prefer not to be implicated in any enquiries. - Just so, Willie. I'd like a profile on a Miss Livia Wolfe. - With an 'e', yes. Seconded, but she must have worked in the museum. Hmm! Say about 1987-88. A little while ago, I know. - Department? Probably ceramics. Vague about that. It's just a question of verifying some facts. One can't be too careful when employing people. I'm sure you know what I mean. - Course you do. Have to make sure they come with all expenses paid. Don't want to be saddled with a bill, do we? - Thank you, Willie. You'll phone me?"

Sandquest replaced the handset, crossed to the cabinet and poured himself a whisky. Perhaps the suspicion was intuition, a blurred pattern, just out of focus. He must give some time to solving this unease, and put his mind at rest. There was always a danger in leaving things to resolve themselves.

-oOo-

The lawn mower made one more pass down the lawn and stopped. Sandquest looked back at the striations, tutting to himself. Jenkins, the gardener, would not be pleased at the less than perfect line in the middle run. He'd also forgotten to pick the box up on one of the turns. Returning the mower to the garden workshop, he removed his overall and galoshes. If the work should have developed a better frame of mind, he'd been disappointed.

Later, Sandquest was deep into annotating a report when the telephone rang.

"Ah, Willie. You're lucky to have caught me. - No. No rush. Wait a minute, I need to write this down." He pressed the intercom key on the telephone, moving a pad into a more comfortable position. "Right, Willie. What have you got?"

Willie's voice sounded as though he was speaking into a metal box. "Took a lot of leverage, Mr. Sandquest. Had to get a jemmy on the moral disposition cluttering up his new attitude. My contact has moved on and up, gathering a few scruples on the way. God knows where he found them. Didn't feel he could be involved in extramural activities anymore. Needed a certain amount of persuasion."

"If your pockets are empty, Willie, you know I'll fill them. Just give me the information."

"That's not a problem, Mr. Sandquest. I can always rely on you seeing me straight. People are just getting greedy. A way of feeding their expensive life styles. No trust in the world. Money up front."

"Willie, I heard you. What must I do? Cable you a cheque?"

"Your credit's always good with me, Mr. Sandquest. Old hands, playing by a different set of rules. Well, according to my contact, and to put the record straight, Livia Wolfe never worked for the Metropolitan."

"I thought not." Sandquest felt himself relax. "Couldn't see how that was possible."

"No. But an Emma Wolfe did."

Sandquest stiffened, pulling his chair closer to the table, leaning over the telephone. "What do you mean, Emma Wolfe?

"An Emma Wolfe was seconded from the photographers Morgan and Freeman to work at the Metropolitan," Willie continued. "Perhaps you mistook the Christian name?"

"Not at all. You're absolutely sure it was Emma, not Livia?"

"Positive. I asked him to double check after he pulled the wrong chicken out of the bag for us. UK national. Apparently something of an expert in photomicrography; that is, photographing minute particles of material, then analyzing the result. Sort of historical detective work. She was writing a research paper on something or other. Two years, then she presumably returned to the UK. Mission accomplished."

"And that's all?"

"Some odd things, like her New York address and telephone number, date of birth, what have you. All a bit dusty by now. Are they of any use?"

"Probably not. No. Wait, wait. Give me her date of birth, Willie."

"January one. 1959."

Sandquest slumped back in his chair. He knew from her record that Livia had been born on December the thirty-first, 1958.

"Thank you, Willie. I'll see you next time I'm in New York." He replaced the handset, switching off the intercom.

Sandquest felt he had taken two steps backwards. Livia Wolfe and Emma Wolfe. Livia born just one day before. Yet a year apart! Were they the same person? Doubtful. Even one day was a difference. But Jim Doskie saw them as the same person. Sandquest couldn't believe Doskie had been mistaken in his identification. Only how could the data, so diligently accumulated by his company and the security services, miss two years spent in the United States.

Confused them then. Sandquest shook his head. They were not one and the same person. They had to be different people. Coincidental people.

Then it struck him. Twins. Identical twins. Born on New Year's Eve, either side of midnight.

For a moment he thought he'd solved the conundrum before the elation slipped away again. Livia had never mentioned Emma. In the normal run of their conversation such an oversight was improbable. Livia, he was convinced, had never mentioned a twin sister.

He rang the number of an investigation agency run by an old employee who vetted all Axmar's personnel from basic background profiles to in depth case histories.

"Hastings? Sandquest. Another little matter for you. Emma Wolfe. You'll have a Livia Wolfe's details on your files. Perhaps out of date. See what connexion you can put together on them. - Yes, urgent. - No. No interim report. I need positive results. I'll be in South Africa for the best part of two weeks, then a couple of days in Berlin. Send it through the secure channel. Thank you."

Sandquest closed his hands together as though in prayer, placing them against his lips. "Who's who," he speculated aloud, "Livia Wolfe or Emma Wolfe?"

Chapter 25

Ruggieri found Eldon and Vergellesi a self-contained apartment on the top floor of a house owned by his mother-in-law. The apartment came complete with a telephone, and a tap on Enzo Capagli.

As they moved in, the telephone engineers moved out, leaving Vergellesi to set up and test the open reel tape recorder they'd received from Ruggieri.

"We're limited to four hours recording time," Vergellesi stressed. "Sufficient, unless Capagli's into long conversations."

Eldon, spread across a large armchair, was only mildly interested in the technical details. "Now we'll know his innermost secrets, Piero, what did Vignozzi come up with on his partner's company, Bimax?"

"Little more than you've already told me. Caparra has used their share of Bimax, arranged through a shady bank in Naples, as collateral to fund the purchase of the Castello di Pietra."

Eldon swung himself upright. "Sandquest claimed that Bimax was set up for joint ventures in the construction and security fields. I suppose 'construction' could stretch to castles."

"Could stretch to a criminal conspiracy."

"It might help if we knew *why* Blain transferred the money," Eldon surmised thoughtfully.

Vergellesi pulled a face. "How was the money transferred?"

"Moneymail. You don't need a bank account, or identification. Just a code word. You send it. You receive it. As much as you want, where you want. Cash. It arrived in an Italian bank, but no one ever collected it."

"That sounds like an open invitation to every criminal in the business. The perfect money laundering system. Very useful if Brizzi was going to sell his interest in the castle to Blain?"

Eldon shrugged. "Something we don't know, except that everything prior to Spain is utter supposition. The only angle we have on this subject is that Blain was moving three million pounds sterling into somewhere. I assume for that sort of money, he'd need something very tangible in return."

"Not something he could discuss with his company lawyers though," Vergellesi commented.

Eldon shook his head. "Even if he did, they couldn't have told him what he was letting himself in for. In London, and for all I know, in every capital in the world, they have a seven centimetre dossier crammed full of case histories. There are six sets of fingerprints that if anyone bothered to trace them would turn out to be those of clumsy policemen. There's no footprint; no picture; no clue of Nightingale anywhere, only page after page detailing scenes of the crimes. You'd doze off reading them, except you don't use a nightmare to put yourself to sleep. If Brizzi's central to Blain and Finetti's death, then we must suppose Nightingale figures in there somewhere."

Vergellesi folded his arms, a frown furrowing his face. "For the moment, our best bet is Capagli. He's here, and won't be hard to locate, but how do we find out what's going on inside the castle? Not a place where you just walk in, and look around."

"Walk in, no. But we may be able to look around. For that though, we need a helicopter, and a Honegger and Mills camera."

"What sort of camera?" Vergellesi exclaimed.

"A military survey camera with a wide angle lens, taking photographs at one hundred frames a second. A helicopter can pass quickly on a normal flight path, at a respectable height of say 1000 feet, without raising any suspicions. That's very low for this type of camera, but it should work. As the image will be accurate to 0.01mm we'll see the damn stones grow."

"Rex. What are you talking about?"

"Capagli must be digging Piero, or at least moving things about. Things he shouldn't be moving. During the day isn't an option, so he must work at night."

"What use is this camera at night?"

"None. But, whatever they've moved must be replaced so that it looks exactly the same the next day. Except it won't. What happens will be marginally different at least, visibly different at best. You only need something accurate to compare that difference with. The extent of deviation will explain the nature of their work. Perhaps more importantly, exactly where they are working. The same flight path for a week or so, with the same camera alignment. They won't move a pebble without us knowing."

"Hmm! We'll probably be able to arrange a helicopter, but we're not likely to find such a camera in the local Kodak shop?"

"Phone Vignozzi and see if he can have one flown over to the military airport in Pisa. If he can't locate a camera, ask him to get in touch with London. Perhaps they can arrange one for us. Pisa should have a secure section who'll know how to set the camera up."

"And in the meantime?"

"What's for supper?"

"Nothing, until you go for the groceries," Vergellesi declared, handing him a list.

-oOo-

Releasing the chain on the trolley with a five hundred *lire* coin Eldon pushed it inside, winding his way down the aisles of the shop looking for Vergellesi's requirements.

Coffee led the list. The packet he held in his hand looked stylistically interesting, but the text was modern and meaningless, describing itself as the 'ultimate quality' when its price suggested otherwise.

"I shouldn't buy that one," a voice said, in a deep, measured, Texan drawl.

Eldon turned to study the speaker. He was a short stocky man with a ruddy-faced complexion. Keeping out of the sun was not something he was good at. Nor was shaving. Tomorrow, if he felt inclined, he'd find his razor. The only thing Eldon could hang an angle on were his suede desert boots, in a style once fashionable before Sandhurst became a squat for minor public school boys. Other than that, his appearance expressed nothing of an inner self, or who he was.

"Says Arabica, but saying it don't mean its been there. One can't be too careful with coffee beans. Ethiopia is number one. Used to be an Italian colony under il Duce. They still produce one and a half million *quintali* of the stuff. Could make them rich if they didn't spend it all on ammunition. Pay the money and buy this one." He took down a packet to offer to Eldon.

Eldon thanked him for the information.

"I'm getting a hint of a Limey accent. One should never try to hide behind an accent. Especially if someone's listening to you carefully. English are you?"

"Most of me, yes," taking the coffee politely and placing it in the trolley.

"Figures. You on holiday?"

"No. I'm on business. Here for a few weeks."

"Better place for a holiday. Are you going back to town?"

"Shortly." Eldon gestured to the still almost empty trolley.

"Perhaps I could jump a lift."

Eldon nodded. "Why not?"

"Read me your list, I'll help you along. Adam's the name. No Eve. Adam Remmick II, on account of my father having the same Christian name."

He hung his small rucksack on the end of the trolley, and together they finished the shopping.

Eldon studied him out of the corner of his eye. He walked with a slight limp, the fault of not being able to bend one knee. Perhaps he loitered in super markets offering himself as a guide to earn a little supplementary income. Except he didn't look like a man who needed extra money. Perhaps just the company.

Having unloaded the groceries into the boot, Eldon turned the car round while Remmick returned the trolley. He didn't return the five hundred *lire* coin.

"Hire car?" he asked, as he slumped beside Eldon.

"Long way for a company car," Eldon replied, as he eased away.

"You reckon? Everywhere in Europe's just next door. That's if you can get on with a shift stick. I broadcast I'm not a native by running a Jeep that does it for me. On these darn hills it sure suits. Which hotel you in?"

"I'm staying with someone I know. Treating ourselves on the expenses."

"Why not? Good outfit you work for?"

224

The questions were coming thick and fast. Not inquisitive. Inquiring. Remmick had a reason for wanting to know.

Eldon had an answer for them all. "Good, but they send me on some strange assignments."

"Assignments? You're not a salesman then?"

"Do I look like one?"

"Who can tell? Most of them look like they'll sand bag you. What sort of assignments?"

"I'm an economist. I cover economic developments. Research paper at the moment."

"Bit of a dampener at dinner parties. Freelance or staff?"

Staff would suit Remmick fine. "Weatherfield and Holding."

"Savvy outfit." Remmick nodded knowingly. "What brings you to Sorena? Milan I can buy. Business in the Bourse, but the only movement of money round here takes place in the bars. Sorena's an economic wilderness."

"You don't think economic wildernesses will make a good story then?" Eldon asked.

Remmick scowled. He might have run out of questions. More likely he was running out of credibility. There were only so many pumps in a bag of wind. "You can drop me by the monument. Top of the road," he said.

Eldon dropped him off at the obelisk that commemorated Sorena's war dead. The first plaque had a commendable four rows of patriots in the Great War. The second listed four partisans fighting for a 'free' Italy. 1945 seemed a little tardy.

Remmick looked at the obelisk and then back at Eldon.

"Who remembers them, already?" he said, slamming the door. With a curt wave he limped away down a path next to the obelisk.

-oOo-

Arriving at the apartment, Eldon found Vergellesi had the apparatus for the telephone tap set up and working. Taking the plastic shopping bags from Eldon, he

225

rummaged through, holding things up, nodding with evident approval.

"Vignozzi phoned in your absence," Vergellesi said, trying to read the label on the coffee packet. "He's had a message from London saying that the camera you required will arrive by the week-end. He's also arranged the helicopter for us."

Eldon looked at his watch. "That's good going."

"He's not your average Italian." Vergellesi said.

"He's not your average Brit either," Eldon concluded.

"We're to liaise with a Captain Bandinelli, who, as luck would have it, has experience of photo reconnaissance work. I rang him. He gets the general idea that you need a series of synchronized passes on the same flight path."

"Perfect. Have you also sorted out a lab to process the film for us?"

"No problem. Bandinelli has arranged for the army to do it, as they've got continuous processing machines."

"That only leaves Captain Bandinelli to press the button at exactly the right time. This isn't a stills camera plodding along overlapping each plate, Piero. It'll rattle through a thousand feet in ten seconds, so I hope he's on the ball. By the way, I picked this up at the supermarket. Someone tucked it under the wiper. Thought you might be interested."

Eldon placed a bright red flyer on the table, advertising that the Gorky State Orchestra was shortly presenting a concert in Florence.

Chapter 26

Major Bradbury was as punctual as Sandquest knew he would be. A retired career officer, he still used hair-oil in the manner of subalterns who drove drop head coupés. Everything about him was perfectly in place.

Finishing his final tour of duty someone hinted he might like a job in Whitehall. He soon felt quite at home believing himself among equals, which he wasn't, and no one saw fit to explain to him the structure of this silent hierarchy. There to make up the numbers, they would get a good ten years out of him.

Sandquest suggested an apéritif, before going in for lunch.

Finding a corner by the dining room door they exchanged a few pleasantries. Sandquest remembered Bradbury lived at Surbiton, but discovered he'd moved to Chichester to be near the sea. He'd opted for the chummier atmosphere of the coast where he and his wife could take up sailing. Sandquest could see that was a sound bit of planning. Sailing was all about rules and sticking together. There, Bradbury would feel quite at home.

Major Bradbury had just accepted another helping of the Topinabour salad, added two pickled quails eggs, lacing it with an over indulgence of lemon and olive oil dressing, when Sandquest brought up the subject of Livia. Bradbury had conducted an extensive inquiry, but how best to find out the information Sandquest required needed a ring of authenticity that implied breaking the rules for the nation's good.

"I must emphasize, Bradbury, this discussion is highly confidential. You've probably heard about the latest UAV programme the Americans are developing. Created a bit of a flap recently because it might see a little too much of what's happening on the domestic front. Civil Rights people, making a fuss. We're working on new electro-optical sensors that have direct communication links with the ground, which gives us every chance of winning the contract. It's a very sensitive development issue, meaning we'll tread on quite a few home-grown competitors toes. That's the background, and as much as you need to know. Move to last week. I'm showing an American client round our factory near Cambridge. - You've been there. Right. - In passing, he mentioned having seen my personal assistant working for the Metropolitan Museum in New York."

"Miss Wolfe?" Bradbury said vaguely.

"Exactly. How could this be possible, given her CV, where there is no mention of such a post? But my client was insistent, if not almost argumentative, over the issue. Normally, of course, I would just ask Miss Wolfe outright, but she has been privy to some delicate Government business, including this latest one. If something's amiss, resulting in it becoming rather messy, she might slip away before anything could be done. Heavens knows how disastrous the information she could take with her might be?"

Bradbury popped the last quail egg into his mouth; carefully arranging his knife and fork on the plate. "Hmm!" he said, enabling him to complete the course satisfactorily. "I see your predicament. I'll have to make a report, of course."

"That's another problem, Bradbury. I don't want to make a big issue over this; don't want to appear jumpy. Much prefer to resolve this without resorting to paperwork. Always been my way."

"So I believe, sir. But you know, I'm not at liberty to divulge any details of the inquiry into Miss Wolfe."

"Naturally, I respect your professional integrity. But consider the situation. My company has committed its expertise in developing highly secret military systems for a range of applications too numerous to mention, much of which would damage the security of this nation and our allies if leaked to a foreign power. In the scale of things, how high would this information count in the eyes of the Director General?"

Bradbury stroked his chin, fingering a little indentation at its tip. "Not so much a question of scale, Mr. Sandquest, more a matter of regulations. I don't make the rules, but it's incumbent I work by them."

"Well, I'm not going to make a big fuss," Sandquest said, shaking his serviette. "She's excellent at her job, but if you consider this American business doesn't matter..."

"I didn't say that, Mr. Sandquest," Bradbury interrupted, sensing his vulnerability. "Yours is a particular question I believe; a detail, so to speak. Something that can be clarified without disclosing the breadth of our inquiry, which I must point out, was not made for the benefit of Axmar industries, but for the Ministry of Defence."

Sandquest let this pompous inference pass, lowered his voice, leaning closer to press home his point. "I have some extremely difficult negotiations coming up next month at Burbank, California. If they're going to be tricky, I'd feel more relaxed knowing I could trust my team one hundred per cent."

Bradbury nodded in agreement. Teams were something Bradbury understood, being a team man himself.

"Well, let me see. The Metropolitan museum came up as a periphery. Your client was in fact mistaken, albeit unwittingly. At the time, Miss Livia Wolfe had a twin sister, Emma, who was on secondment to the museum. No need to be concerned, Mr. Sandquest. You can safely let your mind rest on the matter."

"You say, 'had a twin sister', Bradbury. Does that mean she hasn't one now?"

"I'm afraid it does. Senseless tragedy. Emma was killed in a car crash on the A303 in Wiltshire, west of Amesbury. The hub of a petrol tanker opened her car like a tin can. Once the Wiltshire constabulary cleared up the confusion over whether it was Emma or Livia who had been killed, that was the end of my enquiry."

"What do you mean, confusion?"

"The driving licence, found in a hand bag retrieved from the wreckage, was itemized as belonging to a Miss Livia Wolfe. Motor vehicle was registered in that name also. Seemed conclusive enough. The confusion concerned the sisters owning identical handbags. Being insured for any driver, it turned out that Emma Wolfe was using the vehicle to visit an aunt in the West Country. Corroborating evidence later indicated that Emma was running late before she left their house in

Wilton Street. During her untimely rush she picked up the wrong handbag. Other identifying documents, such as credit cards and chequebook, initially seemed to be missing. They materialized when the police researched the vehicle being held by the garage that retrieved the wreckage. Under the drivers seat."

"Rather lapse?"

"Couldn't say, Mr. Sandquest. Police seemed satisfied. Naturally, the investigating officer wasn't overjoyed, insisting he went over the vehicle thoroughly, having found the hand bag in the passengers foot-well."

"Bradbury, even the police must have noticed that they had a driving licence for Livia Wolfe, and financial documents relating to Emma Wolfe?"

"Indeed they did. Emma presumably picked up her own cheque book, et cetera, hurriedly putting them in Livia's hand bag containing only Livia's driving licence. Emma's driving licence remaining in her own bag at Wilton Street."

"And the police didn't wonder why Livia's financial documents weren't also in the hand bag found in the vehicle?"

"You would have made a good detective, Mr. Sandquest. Yes, they wondered. But those documents had a reason for not being there, while the driving licence did. Livia Wolf was on vacation in Peru, needing her credit cards and chequebook, but not her driving licence, having no need of a car. When the authorities in Lima located her, she immediately flew back. Anyway, I think we can say your trip to California will be secure enough. Her father's Baron Wolfe you know?"

"Yes, I did know. He's an acquaintance."

"An old one?"

"Reasonably. I've known him for some years."

"And you didn't know about Emma?"

"No, Bradbury, I didn't know about Emma. I never met any of his daughters until Livia came to work for me. I don't actually enquire into my staff's family background. To be brutally honest, it's of no interest to me. How they do their job is all that I'm concerned with, and on that score I don't care what their other life entails."

"Strange though, wouldn't you say? I mean, in the course of two years she might have mentioned it."

"They're a private family, not given to discussing themselves."

"Quite," Bradbury agreed.

Sandquest saw that Bradbury wasn't particularly convinced, but preferred not to spoil a good meal.

"Well, Bradbury, now that's satisfactorily settled, let's inspect the sweet trolley."

-oOo-

Most of that afternoon Sandquest paced up and down, exasperated by uncertainty. Livia had left at lunchtime, accompanying a party of executives to their Uxbridge laboratory, and was not expected back until the morning.

After much introspection he determined on a course of action, telephoning Sir David Walcott who had been the chief executive officer for the county of Wiltshire. Something must have turned the accident report completely on its head. A meeting with the accident-investigating officer might throw some light on why?

-oOo-

The chauffeur turned the Bristol off the A303 just beyond Andover, before taking the extremely quick carriageway to Salisbury. With instructions to get them there by nine o'clock, and with delays at Fleet, Bob was in a hurry.

Sandquest knew nothing of this in a car that could reach twice the motorway speed limit, continuing to correct paperwork until they crossed the River Bourne.

Introducing himself at the police station, the uniformed reception officer rang through to announce his arrival. The wall clock indicated it was exactly nine o'clock. Another constable appeared showing Sandquest up to the second floor. The narrow corridors with blank, translucent glass doors claustrophobically designed to be confusing, were heavy with the odour of cigarette smoke.

"Inspector Jolly said to put you in the Interview room. He's cleared it with the Custody Officer, so you shouldn't be disturbed."

The constable opened a door showing him into a sparse room with a table, two chairs and an ashtray. Someone had seen fit to hang a print of Salisbury's fine cathedral on otherwise bare walls.

"Sergeant Dinmore will be along as soon as I let him know you're here, sir."

Moments later Dinmore appeared, too obviously from an adjacent office. The round, open face told Sandquest their talk wasn't going to be a waste of time. He would tell his story straight, exactly as it happened.

Shaking hands, Sandquest immediately impressed upon him that their meeting was strictly off the record. He merely needed to establish certain facts in relation to a company employee whose brief involved knowledge of sensitive material in the national interest.

Sergeant Dinmore visibly relaxed, relieved not to be facing an inquisition. Drawing out a chair he gestured to the one opposite. "Sorry it's not a luxury suite, sir. We're a bit short of room these days."

Dinmore pulled out a packet of cigarettes, stopping himself to ask permission. Sandquest pushed the ashtray across.

"Sergeant, bear in mind that I don't want an official response. Just give me a professional opinion based on your own experience and intuition."

"Inspector said you wanted to know about an accident on the A303, involving the Wolfe twins?" Dinmore enquired. "We seem to have mislaid the report, so I haven't been able to refresh my memory. So many on that road, they tend to merge after a while."

A knock on the door made them pause. A policewoman entered with a flask of coffee, milk jug, cups and saucers, - and a saucer of sugar lumps. Sandquest smiled at the effort to create the correct presentation that fell short of a sugar bowl. Dinmore winked at her. She gave him a pursed smile back as she left. The black seams of her stockings were perfectly straight over her strong, nicely shaped legs. Sandquest and Dinmore looked up together, nodding in agreement.

"Did the Inspector tell you anything else?" Sandquest continued.

"In what way, sir?"

"Suggestions."

"Sticking to the official line, do you mean?"

"That sort of thing."

"No. There was no reason for a cover up, as far as I could see. Some aspects couldn't be verified, so we had to outline a speculative reconstruction of some of the events for the coroner's court. Nothing hinged on the details. Really only a matter of arriving at a chronological sequence."

"I understand. However, I'm not a lawyer. I'm interested in your interpretation of the events, intelligent analysis that might not appear in an official report. The nature of some being to conceal as much as they reveal. Tell me about the accident?"

Sergeant Dinmore studied a spot on the wall, somewhere over Sandquest's shoulder, gathering his thoughts.

"The accident happened during a particularly wet November. Always tricky with lorries in the rain, throwing up a curtain of water. Overtaking is suicidal. Accident took place on a strip of dual carriageway known as Coombe Hill. Two lanes were constructed to ease the congestion building up on this section of trunk road during the summer. Gradient's one in eight in parts, forcing heavily laden commercial vehicles down to a walking pace. Powers to be - criminally in my opinion - placed no extra restrictions whatsoever on lorries using the downward stretch. Juggernauts were hitting speeds close to seventy miles an hour at times. Always the same. Driving relies on a matter of judgement. Get it wrong, or worse, gamble on getting it right, can make the accident very messy. Give some people an inch, and they'll always take a mile. In this case, an Atkinson petrol tanker attempted to overtake Miss Wolfe as the road narrowed. Claimed he didn't notice an oncoming car because of the rain. From his height that was a categorical lie - in my opinion. The bank there is quite high, so he couldn't even knock her off the road, just chewed her to pieces. We considered having a go at

233

dangerous driving, but given the circumstances of the weather, knew his lawyers would get that reduced to the lesser charge of driving without due care and attention. Court gave him a two hundred pounds fine, with loss of licence for six months. On appeal his employer said he would lose his job unless it could be reduced. Naturally, commercial interests tipped the balance."

Sandquest could not broach the subject delicately. "When you say 'chewed up', Sergeant, do you mean she wasn't recognizable?"

Sergeant Dinmore poured them some coffee. "When a forty ton Atkinson leans on you, sir, it's not a pretty sight. Milk and sugar?"

Sandquest nodded. "All right. What about finger prints then, could they determine anything?"

"For what reason, sir?"

"To determine whether the driver was Livia or Emma Wolfe."

"You're getting ahead of me. The Cooper S was a family car, traced immediately through DVLC to Miss Livia Wolfe. Matters were made difficult by the parents being in the United States on a lecture tour, resulting in them being out of touch with their daughters for over a week. Given that we'd found the driving licence, and were at that time unaware of a twin sister, we provisionally concluded the dead woman was Livia Wolfe."

"I see. Yet later, you found out Miss Livia Wolfe was not the driver?"

"That was the case. Yes, sir."

"How did you discover the mistake?"

"Officially, or me personally?"

"Yes, you personally. What were the circumstances?"

"I was called into Inspector Dutch's office, and told."

"He was here before Inspector Jolly?"

"That's correct. Made up to Chief last year."

"I'd like you to consider, Sergeant, precisely, how were you informed of your mistake?"

Sergeant Dinmore shifted uncomfortably. "I arrived at the station on the Monday morning following the accident, which happened on a Thursday. Station Sergeant said the Inspector wanted to see me, tout-suite.

Inspector Dutch then informed me that Livia Wolfe was flying in from Lima that morning. You could have knocked me down with a feather. We only needed a family identification for the report, though that wasn't going to be so easy."

"Until that time the identification hinged on the single document you'd found?"

"You know about the second set of documents then, sir?"

"Yes. Seems a rum business. Why did you go back when you'd looked through the vehicle with a fine tooth comb?"

"There was this gentleman with the Inspector. Didn't talk to me directly, and he wasn't introduced. He suggested to the Inspector that we'd better check the vehicle again - just to be sure."

"What sort of gentleman was he?" Sandquest enquired curiously.

"Couldn't really say. Plain clothes. But one of us. From the Met, I thought at the time."

"Why was that?" Sandquest enquired.

"Emma Wolfe had a London address. In hindsight, I felt he knew the second set of documents were there, before I found them. Doesn't mean anything, I know, but that's how it worked out. Nestling neatly under the seat alongside the runner."

"Where you might have missed them?"

Sergeant Dinmore shook his head. "I never missed them, sir, because they had to unbolt the seat to release her. I held the steering wheel out of the way for them. Besides, the handbag clip was closed. No, I didn't miss them. At that time they weren't there."

"And you never found out who this other gentleman was?"

"Not really. To be honest with you, I kept my head down. I had no way of proving I hadn't missed them. I patently had."

"Yes, that's how it would look," Sandquest pondered aloud. "For some reason the second set of documents were introduced, possibly by this unknown gentleman."

"That I wouldn't like to say, sir," Dinmore said prudently.

"No. Of course not. The fact that he was present with one of your superiors suggests he was there in an official capacity."

"Oh, I think he was there in an official capacity all right, which was why I kept mum. Something going on above my head."

"A feeling you had?"

"More than a feeling. When he was talking to Inspector Dutch he mentioned taking it up with Special Op's."

Sandquest fell silent for a few moments, looking intently at the sergeant opposite him. "I want you to think very carefully for me now, Sergeant. What exactly did the man say? This is important. Special Operations, or perhaps, Special Branch?"

The sergeant looked doubtful for a moment, then more brightly as he recalled the incident. "No. Like I said, I was sure he'd come down from Town. Definitely Specialist Operations, because Inspector Dutch said he'd need authorization to come from a higher authority than the Organised Crime Group - they're an operational command of Specialist Operations. This gentleman replied, that when he got back to the office he'd square things with his boss, who'd have a word with the Assistant Commissioner. In hindsight he was definitely an officer from the Organised Crime Group."

"Ah yes", sighed Sandquest, leaning back in his chair. "The Organised Crime Group. That would fit in rather well with the story so far."

-oOo-

That afternoon Sandquest remained in his office, trying to come to terms with the circumstances that he realized could herald a catastrophe.

Hearing the cipher machine he rose and took the strip of paper, returning to his desk to read it. The plain text message from Hastings wasn't long.

'Confidential. Re. Emma Wolfe. Code Critical. Advise: Born 1 January 1959, Wakefield, Yorkshire. Second daughter of Baron and Lady Wolfe. Educated Bedales and Oxford, MSc. (Chemistry). 1981 Rankin Research - Crystallography. 1983 Liberal Agent's Office as research assistant. 1984 National Portrait Gallery. 1984 Munchen Institut. Research PHD. 1987 Morgan and Freeman New York, seconded Metropolitan Museum New York. 1989 Metropolitan Police, Photographic and Graphic Branch. 1991, transferred to Organised Crime Group. No subsequent information. Finish'.

Sandquest took off his spectacles, and closed his eyes, trying to shut out the sense of disaster. Even Hastings had failed to unscramble precisely the motive behind the deception. He realized that it didn't matter. The only thing that mattered were the reasons Commander Prinn, head of the O.C.G, would have for placing her in his office.

His eyes opened. Two years!

There was no reason to think he was cooking the books. He paid accountants and lawyers to keep him on the straight and narrow. That left his Etruscan collection. Tight as a drum on his side, weak on the other. That was the real reason Eldon was interested in Caparra, then. Nothing to do with Blain at all. Prinn must have sniffed out an Italian association. If he had, it was going to open up a whole string of relationships that would be extremely dangerous.

One step at a time. If it was too late to plug a leak, at least he could turn off the water. First of all, he needed to re-organize his office.

Chapter 27

The piazza bar had a plate glass window that allowed an observer to sit and watch, what appeared to be, the movements of the entire population of Sorena.

Eldon stopped absent-mindedly stirring his coffee, his view temporarily obscured by a man opening the centre glass door. The figure was not a welcome one.

Remmick wagged a finger at Eldon, drew out a chair, and sat down uninvited. "The coffee here isn't worth drinking, son," he said, ordering a Martini.

"You seem to know an awful lot about coffee?" Eldon queried.

"I know an awful lot about everything, Rex, and I know you'll be disappointed in the coffee." He looked as though he held a handful of trumps.

"A matter of taste, Mr Remmick."

"You Limeys are so polite. Rem to my friends. Call me Adam if you prefer." He settled himself more comfortably in the chair. "Now Rex, appears you've forsaken the good life to take up your old one in this God forsaken place."

"Isn't that privileged information?" Eldon asked firmly.

"Privileged information," Remmick drawled. "Nothing privileged in our line of work. Keep your nose to the ground over there they said. Suited me. Helped alleviate the boredom. Revelations come my way, even in this backwater. Nothing to go to war about, so far." He took his drink from the waiter. "Nothing that'll wheel me in front of a Senate Intelligence Committee. Place is full of liberal yellow bellies who think everyone subscribes to 'Pax-Mondo'. A spell in central Africa would do them fine. Savimbi'd roast their balls for them - if they had any. I work through the Florence office, keeping up with my contacts in Washington. Fewer as the years go by, but they still like to know what our cousins are up to. Guess you stirred them up. Wanted to know why a one-time flyer gets back in his kite to land in a humpty-dumpty neighbourhood like this. Damn shame that, son. Confidential brief wouldn't have gone amiss. Could have done me some good."

Eldon had begun to view Remmick with a tinge of

prejudice. He was an unnecessary complication, drawing on a chequered past to try and create a new future.

"Well, Mr. Remmick, loose talk is not supposed to be up our street, or even out on it."

"Hell. I see I've offended you with my big mouth." Remmick acted the penitent. "Now don't be sore, son. I can be useful to know. Real useful."

Remmick looked at Eldon's impassive, unimpressed face. "No go, eh? Need to know a lot more about me. I'm an open book. You'll find I didn't fit. New brooms swept me out. CIA's committed to signals intelligence and chicken diplomacy, with nothing on the ground for antediluvian agents like me."

"Is that so?"

"Sure. Office's full of Ivy Leaguers looking to land on their face in camel dung because some A-rab has tied their boot laces together. All their scanners and fancy infrared monitoring devices can't hear a peep from a couple of guys muttering in a mosque, or conspiring in their coffee. Poofs get ear ache listening to all the satellite transmissions, while anybody can buy SPOT photographs the loony French government have obtained through their imaging satellite. Secrets are no longer transmitted or filed, only existing in someone's head. What you hear, someone wants you to hear. Appeasement. Hah! That's got form, as you Brit's say. They'll be left out in the cold any day now. Serves the bastards right."

"Not the way it's presented in the history books," Eldon retorted. "You brought it on yourself, making the management insecure. All that going out on a limb: black bag jobs, files on presidents, assassination attempts on Castro, Trujillo, and poor old Lumumba. In the end you looked no better than Hoover's 'G' men, digging the dirt."

Remmick objected noisily. "The US was a tight run ship, not the leaky old bucket you Brit's were sailing in. You couldn't even bail the ship out when we handed you the pump. No sir. Not even then"

Eldon chose not to argue. Remmick was still fighting yesterday's wars. His being right wouldn't put it right.

"We managed to stay afloat in a sort of fashion.

Furniture got pushed around a little. Old names on different doors."

"Christ. All that stuff on Wilson, surrounding himself with 'wall-to-wall' communists. I can see why you took a long time to ease him out."

"That I don't know," Eldon confessed. "Before my time. You had your own troubles."

"Oh, sure. Don't give me that old bull. You can run a 'Who's Who' on British traitors. Blake; Blunt; Bossard; Burgess. Bugger! What a mess."

"I dare say you can name them all," Eldon said in a weary voice.

"Sure. All the way through Philby to Vassal."

Remmick suddenly stopped sneering. He was pushing too hard. Causing offence. "Don't get me wrong. No hard feelings. Came about I had to write a paper for Tom Lancer, the Senior Liaison Officer in Washington, just before my demise. Lancer had a beef about sharing too much information with you guys, even though he was supposed to be the go-between in these matters. Following year they were up to their ears in Contra shit, and Lancer was booted up to the NSC to help out. After that I began to feel the cold. So I took early retirement, coming over here to sit in the sun".

"You could have found better sun in California. Tuscany has cold winters."

"Believe me son, I'd have felt the cold in Brownsville."

"I see. In that case you probably had little choice."

"This suits me. Here, the only thing giving you stress are the Beryls in short skirts. Stress! That's something exerted between contiguous bodies, isn't it? Don't get much of that."

"That's probably the first true thing you've said." Eldon folded his paper neatly.

"So, you're not buying?"

"Not from your store, Mr. Remmick."

"Big mistake, son."

"Doubtful. You see, Alan...."

"Adam!"

"Adam. I think my colleagues would take a dim view of my dragging in an old warrior like you, desperate for a last crack at a case."

"You're not reading me, son. Not at all."

"Oh I am. Remember, you're an open book."

"OK, OK. So I'm coming over a bit strong, but you can check on me. I'm reliable. I can keep my mouth shut, real tight."

"Standard manual procedure."

"Get in touch with Jim Price at your Foreign Office," Remmick suddenly proffered a reference, feeling his line of persuasion was weakening. "Do that, son. He'll fill you in on what end of the barrel I'm coming out of."

"I'll keep that in mind."

"Hell, what does it take to get through to you? You're not the only player in this damn game."

Eldon began to feel irritated. Remmick had all the characteristics of a washed up agency man who was all breadth and no depth, having lived his job twenty-four hours a day. Time tended to hang heavily on his piece of history. But he had a nose for the job, sniffing at an opportunity, a contender, given one more chance for a crack at the title. He aimed to rub prissy Yale and Harvard noses in the dirt. Not too much. Just enough to show them how it was really done, right up against the wire, so you could brush your teeth in the sweat. His very attitude, Eldon decided, would prove a liability.

"Adam, let's get one thing straight. I'm afraid you don't fit in. You haven't fitted in for a very long time. Price was kicked out in eighty-seven. MI6 suspected an Egyptian penetration at our embassy in Tel Aviv, coincidentally revealing Price was passing on information to Mossad. They let him run for a couple of years in order to build up a picture of Israeli intentions. He was never charged, leaving his diplomatic post without a fuss. He's living in Jerusalem now. Something you should have known, if you were still in the team, Adam."

Remmick felt the possibilities slipping away, but he wasn't about to give up. "As I said, son, you're not the only player in this game."

"I heard that."

"What do you know of a man called Prinn?"

Eldon shook his head.

"Not going to keep your interest then." Remmick sipped his Martini for effect.

Eldon folded his hands over the newspaper. Remmick was an old pro', full of tricks. He looked at the American steadily. "Keep it? Probably not. Tickle it though. Worth a shot."

"Commander Nicholas Prinn's an interesting guy. Surprised you don't know him." Remmick ate the cherry off the cocktail stick before continuing; sensing he'd prized a small chink in Eldon's indifference.

"When I first came here the Company asked me to look him up. Not in my line of business exactly, but we might have similar professional interests. Scratching of backs. I checked him out, deciding we wouldn't get on. Sort of schoolboy hero. You'd get on just fine."

Eldon smiled "Kiplingesque type you mean?".

"Sure. Acted as though he was the last of the raj. Paternalistic. Home's over at San Polo, on the South side of Sorena. Inherited the Villa Lazzi when his father died, so he's dug in deep round here. Still, I kept an eye on him over the years. Absentee landlord most of the time. Then last year, in the fall, an old pal of mine in Washington phoned in saying he'd heard Prinn had made a bit of a stir. If something was going down, I'd better get my nose in the trough."

"You could have refused," Eldon suggested.

"Had that in mind, before you turned up, tucking your feet under the table round at Ruggieri's mom, probing the death of Senator Brizzi. Said to myself, something as sure as hell must be going down if an ex-British intelligence officer with an Italian G.I.S. side-kick in tow ends up in this neck of the woods. Yes, sir. How does that all tie in with Commander Prinn, head of Scotland Yard's OCG, making ripples in my pond?"

"That's a puzzle, Adam. For both of us." Eldon raised his paper in salute. "I'll pay. Keep me informed of any developments."

"Like hell I will. Go ride your own bike."

Remmick wasn't as put out as he sounded. Eldon had said nothing, given nothing, but he'd indicated that something was up. He wouldn't need information otherwise. That was all Remmick needed. It wasn't much of a step from the reserve benches to the team.

Eldon stood in front of the till where an Italian female

242

grotesque with what appeared to be gold on every one of her podgy fingers, waited in all her massive obesity for a fairy godmother that would never come.

"That was an appalling *cappuccino*. I can see why my friend ordered a Martini," Eldon said in perfect English with an even larger smile.

The grotesque smiled back, ringing up a bill for the only two words she could understand.

Chapter 28

The door, being shut with a firmness that was on the wrong side of quiet, made Vergellesi look up from the tape recorder. He slid the earphones down round his neck.

"Do you want to tell me what's up?" he ventured solicitously.

Eldon lifted his arms in exasperation. "Here, or in Rome, somewhere we're gossip."

"What do you mean, gossip?" Vergellesi asked patiently. "We haven't been here long enough yet to create a scandal."

"A retired CIA agent, supposedly languishing in superannuated bliss, has a thumb print on us that must have been lifted straight out of an operational case file. That's not so bad, at least he knows the rules, but a gung-ho pensioner is the last thing we need. Especially one who's rusty, overconfident, and over the hill. He's also the second person who's shown an interest in Commander Prinn. Seems very popular hereabouts."

"I see," Vergellesi smoothed Eldon's ruffled feathers. "In Italy if you ask any wall a question one of the stones is sure to know the answer. That being the case, you can only refocus and think positively."

"About what?"

"This, for example. Take your mind off other things."

Vergellesi rewound the spool on the recorder, passing the earphones to Eldon. He pressed the play button.

Eldon listened intently for some minutes. "Clearly, Capagli's arranging a delivery of something to Prato, but I don't know what he means by 'in cinta'. What walls? The castle?"

Vergellesi looked puzzled for a moment. "Ah, I see. No, no. 'Incinta', as in pregnant. I think Capagli's referring idiomatically to one article concealed inside another."

"Does that make sense?"

"Not in the least. They've traced the call to a builders yard in an industrial zone of Prato. The Via Colombo."

"Not exactly a popular tourist spot, I imagine," Eldon noted soberly.

"You're not here on holiday. If we have to visit, we'll go after a reconnaissance, and after dark. Breaking and entering is a criminal offence, even for a police officer, but we don't have time to sit around waiting for permission," Vergellesi concluded.

"True. By the way, did you know Commander Prinn has a villa nearby?"

Vergellesi shook his head. "Does that suggest something?"

"Only something untidy. Have we any news on our photo flight yet?"

"Took place this morning. Captain Bandinelli say's he's organized a military flight between Pisa and Monte Rufeno, a nature reserve near Orvieto, where there's going to be a high level meeting between our military command in two weeks time. The organizational activity is an on going process, providing genuine cover for the helicopter's movements. Bandinelli flew on the first flight. He's sending the film over to Ruggieri. There's apparently no activity going on in the castle. However, he did observe there's only one way in, and a great deal of forest on the way out."

-oOo-

A little after six o'clock the next evening, having acquired a hire car, Eldon drove them to one of the commercial districts of Prato lying along the old road to Pistoia.

A belt of grime radiated from beyond the Piazza San Marco into a prefabricated world that passed for offices and warehouses, sliding seamlessly into a Tuscan landscape of flat, neglected fields spawning derelict lorries, and rusting obsolete machinery. Here and there a small oasis, belonging to some urbanized misfit, flashed green among the dust.

Eldon parked the car along the milled abrasions of the main road that seemed to have no defining edges, only soft radii for the endless side streets leading to a conglomeration of small factories.

Vergellesi reached behind, handing Eldon a brief case from the back seat, another for himself. "Don't ask me where I found these props. They've got to go back."

Eldon opened the case, finding it stuffed with newspapers.

"Just for show," Vergellesi said. "As commercial travellers we'll hardly be noticed." He clicked the door open.

The Via Colombo, after a series of minor crossroads, petered out on to flat farmland festooned with pylons and the sagging arcs of high-tension cables. Cement bollards closed off the final junction, effectively turning the remaining part of the Via Colombo into a dead end.

A short walk brought them to the builders yard on a corner behind a high, crumbling, stuccoed wall just beyond the bollards. Running at right angles along two streets, the walls were interrupted by a recessed, rusting iron gate in the Via Colombo.

They walked past the gate towards open farmland that stretched to a horizon dominated by apartment tower blocks. The stuccoed wall continued along the edge of a dirt lane, bordered by a ditch on the far side, repository for the remnants of more industrial waste.

Turning back, they stopped on the corner by the closed gates.

Vergellesi stood with his back to the yard, as though pausing momentarily in conversation. Eldon, over Vergellesi's shoulder, could see two attached concrete block buildings with large metal doors and a small, wooden office set to one side against the wall. The yard was full of second hand building materials; a pitiful shabbiness of irreversible deterioration in the terracotta tiles, stone blocks, and iron radiators. Weeds had invaded large stacks of rusted concrete reinforcing mesh, dumped carelessly among discarded toilets, and ancient asbestos water tanks. Eldon couldn't visualize any economic value in their survival.

"What do you have in mind for the next four hours, Piero?" Eldon asked.

"We'll visit Florence," Vergellesi replied. "A *passaggio*. Perhaps a little supper, followed by a *caffè*. Then we can go home. Via the Via Colombo."

-oOo-

On their return, the main road had taken on an unexpectedly different appearance. Neon lights indicated a plethora of clubs and bars; a spangle of glittering coloured illuminations working tirelessly to bring attention to themselves.

Eldon eased the car back into a vacant space. He exchanged glances with Vergellesi, who nodded for them to go.

They waited for some time on the dirt track behind the yard, listening to the night air, disturbed only by roxy sounds carried on the wind. Otherwise, everything was as still as an empty bed.

Hauling themselves over the wall they crouched behind a stack of old floor tiles, smelling faintly of urine. No dogs leapt out on unsuspecting intruders from the main building, dark shapes against the pale yellow glow of the lofty streetlights. Using the piles of material to hide their movement, they reached the large metal door of the nearest building, with a smaller inserted entrance.

"We can't stay here all day. Are we going in, or do you intend to knock?" Eldon asked.

"No alarm system," Vergellesi whispered back. He slipped a piece of wire into the lock. The door clicked open. "Took me six weeks to learn that trick."

Letting their eyes adjust to the darkness inside, Vergellesi switched on a pencil torch, adjusting its spread. "No windows either."

In front of them was an old dumper truck alongside a forklift truck receiving its overnight charge. Stacks of perishable building materials lay opposite metal racks holding copper tubes, and plastic guttering. As far as they could see, it was an untidy but functioning builders yard.

"There's another door. Probably leads to the other building," Eldon gestured.

It was unlocked. The front of the workshop was filled with concrete garden ornaments and balustrading ready for delivery. Rolls of bubble pack indicated their manufacture had some elements of a genuine business. Filling up most of the rest of the space, were mixing machines and moulds, their creations destined to adorn some vulgar urban garden.

Eldon tapped Vergellesi's arm. "Someone has just unlocked the front gate, Piero. Any suggestions?"

"Quickly. The other store. Behind the cement bags." Vergellesi pushed Eldon forward.

The entrance door rattled and scraped open; a small pause before the lights came on. Two men passed into the adjoining building, followed by a muffled conversation, too fragmented to make any sense.

The voices grew louder again as the men reappeared. Closing the door behind them they lit cigarettes, continuing their conversation leaning against the dumper truck. Through the gaps between the sacks, Eldon had a good view of them.

They had younger and older faces whose education had been on the streets, or in the bars, where the future was an unnecessary concept. Life may have been hard, but they didn't know how to pursue any other.

"We'd better raise the cement ratio a little," the older man remarked. "Capagli heard the last consignment of the Bacchus ornament was shaky on arrival with some cracks and powdering. He reckons the polystyrene foam's solved the compression problems inside so he's bringing the delivery at ten o'clock tomorrow evening. Should only take us a few hours."

"Suits me," the younger one answered, stubbing his cigarette on the ground. "Pick you up at nine."

The two men passed out of sight, switching off the light and locking the door. There was a moment's silence before the gate rattled. A faint sound of a car being driven away indicated that Eldon and Vergellesi were once more alone in the building.

"Perhaps we'd better inspect the *Bacchi* before we go?" Eldon suggested, leading the way.

Vergellesi's torch swung over the ornaments. "Here we are," he said. "They're the only ones with a hole in the top to take the expanding foam. Obviously they're placing the two parts of this ornament round an insertion of some sort. The foam cushioning any movement. At least we now know how, and why. 'What', is going to be revealed tomorrow evening at ten o'clock."

"I can hardly wait," Eldon said dryly.

Chapter 29

Swirls of dust gusted up and settled on the parked Opel, blown by a wind that was as wayward as the young girls crippled by their execrable fashion, making for the exiled clubs and bars in the commercial district. They were early, as Eldon and Vergellesi were early.

Eldon opened his eyes and watched a group turn into a bar. "In five years they will be overweight," he observed, "appallingly plain, and have born three children. Fifty percent of them will be discarded by their husbands, and a great many of their children will become socially, if not psychologically, defective citizens. Thanks to the advance of medical science, they'll have a greater life expectancy in which to suffer the experience." He nodded towards the side mirror. "In the meantime, this is likely to be more interesting."

A well-worn Ford estate car pulled out of the road next to the Via Colombo, turning in the direction of Prato.

"Are you sure you want to do this on your own?" Vergellesi asked.

"I do. Take note, what goes on outside may be just as interesting as what goes on inside. Don't go to sleep."

Eldon opened the door, feeling the weight of the Glock 9mm automatic bump against his ribs. He had never really liked guns, but as the army weapon's instructor observed: 'With some people it's the camera which loves 'em. For you, sir, it's guns. They just can't get enough of you.' Such had been the start of a very one-sided romance.

Crossing the road, without looking back, Eldon briskly walked the length of the Via Colombo to the ditch behind the building yard. Rolling over the wall, he crouched where he landed.

Satisfied he was alone, Eldon gained access to the building through the small entrance door carelessly left unlocked. From that, he assumed they'd return.

Little had changed. New split casts of the Bacchus lay by the side of a metal table in readiness. Business didn't seem to be booming, being only a sideline. Sliding in behind the bags of cement, Eldon settled down to wait.

At a quarter-to-eleven the men appeared. There was nothing for them to do, except amuse themselves, until the objects arrived.

Minutes ticked away while the two smoked and played *briscola.*

For Eldon, a false move, or a shifting of position, might instantly draw their attention. The art of silent distraction became a necessity, developed to relieve the boredom; a mentally shutting down of any discomfort that would give himself away.

The older of the two men appeared to be in charge. By a modicum of effort, he was better dressed than his companion; a much larger man with an omnipresent face belonging to any number of European lands.

The bigger man suddenly exploded with joy, shaking his final card for the winning point in the other's face, who threw up his hands in disgust. "Ten thousand lire," the big man victoriously demanded, thrusting forward a rough hand.

The other considered an objection, but could not escape the evidence of the cards. Sulkily agreeing, he stood up, emptying his pockets for an elusive note to settle his debt. Eldon spied the small silver Beretta that had been placed on the table as he searched. Then the pistol was gone again. The second game started testily, to be interrupted by a car horn outside.

Smiling broadly at the outcome of an abandoned game, the younger man raised the metal doors while his colleague slipped under them to open the main gate. A much-abused Fiat van, with provincial number plates, turned round in the yard, reversing into the workshop. A clean-shaven young man stepped out. He studied the pair briskly, looking them over, before shaking hands.

Eldon eyed him with a new interest. Moving smoothly, confidently familiarizing himself with the surroundings, this new arrival might have been driving a van, but one thing Eldon knew, a van driver he was not.

"Antonio?" the man enquired, looking from one to the other.

The older of the two nodded, indicating to his colleague to close the gate. "What have you done with Capagli?"

250

"He's on business. *Signor* Paba sent me instead."

"We don't need babysitters," Antonio answered pointedly, not liking the idea of a spectator.

The young man laughed derisively. "From what I hear, you're more likely to pack the babysitter, and *Signor* Paba doesn't like mistakes. Mistakes cost lives."

The colleague of Antonio returned, overhearing the conversation. "What do you know about casting, *ragazzo?*"

A look of hardly disguised contempt clouded the young man's lean, cynical features. "I don't know anything, Donatello. I'm just here to prevent someone mixing up Portland overcoats for you two."

Antonio's colleague grunted, opening the back door of the van.

The young man leant into the van, pulling a plastic crate towards him full of old cloths. He carefully withdrew from them a small ceramic figurine of a female in a swirling shroud like dress that might have been suggesting the action of her dancing.

"Put that here," Antonio directed. "On the table."

He took up the two pieces of a 'Bacchus' casting, placing them alongside. A series of slots, cast into the back section, were arranged to support slips of wood. Measuring the figure, he pushed a slip into position, placed the statue in a thick plastic bag and rested it on the slip, cushioning it firmly with strips of sponge, and taped it back.

"Good fit," the young man said.

Antonio picked up the other half of the casting, waited a moment while his colleague mixed up some quick drying cement and applied it to the edges, before pressing the mating side quickly into place.

With a damp sponge he cleaned round the joint, removing all traces of their work.

After a few minutes the casting was raised upright and a plastic tube inserted through the small hole in the head for the polystyrene foam to be pumped in. Finally, the hole itself was sealed.

"How will they identify the right Bacchus?" The young man asked.

Antonio picked up an empty cast, turning it over to

point out a 'made in Italy' mark stamped on its base. "The marks normally face outwards. We turn them inwards if they're carrying an insert. One of our regular customers who handles the distribution receives them in England, bubble packed on a pallet." Antonio prodded the young man. "For your information, *Signor* Paba doesn't take kindly to people being inquisitive either. Being inquisitive can cost lives."

The young man looked at him coldly. "So can being clever. There's another small box in the back. You're to hold it until *Signor* Paba confirms the destination. He said you had somewhere safe?"

Antonio nodded. "In the office."

The young man took out the box, accompanying Antonio and his colleague to the hut.

Eldon waited until they'd entered the flimsy wooden building. Crossing the yard briskly he pressed himself against the clinker-built wall. The window was set too high to look through, so he settled for an old oil drum to stand on.

Inside, Antonio moved a chair, and the mat it stood upon, to open a trapdoor. The van driver stepped back out of sight as the box was lowered through the floor.

The hut door opened. Eldon remained absolutely motionless where he was while the driver descended the steps, crossed the yard and entered the workshop without looking round.

Eldon let out his breath. He'd seen enough, and decided it was time to go. Reaching the wall leading back to the ditch he heard the driver suddenly shout, "*Ehi, tu!*".

A bullet smacked with a dull thud into the stuccoed stonework, showering him with fragments. Eldon slipped the Glock from his jacket; sending a shot over the driver's head, encouraging him to scramble back inside the workshop.

Going over the wall, and back along the road, would make him too easy a target. Stumbling about in a ditch in the dark seemed equally disagreeable, so Eldon raced back in the direction of the wooden hut, slipping the automatic into his pocket.

Antonio, roused by the disturbance appeared at the

door, made out Eldon's rapidly moving figure, and hurriedly raised the Beretta to open fire.

Hauling up a radiator as he passed to act as a shield, the bullet ricocheted off the cast iron. Too heavy to support, Eldon discarded the radiator and threw himself towards the side of the hut, and out of the line of fire.

Rashly, Antonio's colleague rushed forward to bring him back into view, waving a shortened double-barrelled shotgun. Eldon fired, twisting his assailant to the left, both barrels ejecting into the wooden hut tearing the door away along with Antonio, before he too crashed back into a pile of tiles, rolling over into a heap as they cascaded noisily on top of him.

Pulling himself painfully over the wall, Eldon dropped awkwardly down on to the pavement of a little piazza formed by the cross roads. The streets were brightly lit with every bit of cover lying beyond open ground.

"Where the hell's Vergellesi?" Eldon cursed, as he turned back along the wall to his only option of the ditch, invisible in the darkness. Skirting the corner he rolled past the gate. A spray of sub-machine gun bullets accompanied his progress until he was out of sight. Picking himself up he gritted his teeth, limping towards the darkness.

The driver rushed up to the barred gate, pushed the weapon hurriedly through the bars and sprayed the road blindly. Hampered by the tight angle, the bullets passed harmlessly out into the open fields beyond.

Turning in alongside the ditch, Eldon struggled to reach the top of the wall.

Hearing him scrambling up, the driver hastily pulled the machine pistol back, only to have it jam across the bars.

Eldon straightened his arm towards the figure, pulled the trigger, could hold on no longer, and slid back down to the ground.

A new type of silence lay round Eldon's heightened senses, making him aware of particular, but not general sounds. It was a selective silence, blotting out other natural noises. He heard a car race up the Via Colombo in second gear, skidding to a halt in front of the bollards that barred its way. A door bounced shut. Feet thumped at the double across the road, stopping at the corner. Then silence descended again.

Eldon eased himself up to the corner, and looked towards the entrance. Vergellesi looked back from the opposite end trying to make out his next move. The machine pistol lying on the pavement outside the gate was black, and almost invisible under the yellow lamps, a pale hand had flopped lifelessly through the bars.

Vergellesi walked quietly up to the gate, his automatic still pointing in front of him. He lowered it, and looked towards Eldon, past the growing trickle of blood easing out from under the bars. "*Madonna!*" he uttered incredulously. "*Dio mio!*"

"Bit of a rumpus coming," Eldon muttered through clenched teeth, joining him at the gate where he leant against the wall, to support his back.

Vergellesi looked concerned. "Are you all right?"

"Thanks to one of those cast iron radiators in there, yes. I've still managed to pull my back out. They're bloody heavy."

"I'd better get on to the police in Prato. Here. Use my shoulder for support."

There was no one in sight. No intrusive, patiently inquisitive neighbours, but half way across the road, they heard the histrionic wail of the police cars rising and falling in the distance.

-oOo-

The prison cell ceiling was a mass of finely cracked plaster, smudged with the viscous stain of previous occupants comforting cigarette smoke. Eldon was staring at it, and the weak electric light bulb secure behind its iron framed shade, in case anyone became suicidal. The door swung open.

"How are you feeling?" Vergellesi asked.

"Like a plank," Eldon muttered irritably. "You'll have to help me off this bunk."

"Sorry about the delay in the Via Colombo," Vergellesi apologized, helping him to sit up. "Noisy local lads taking off into the night on their Moto Morini's. Lots of revving and wasted petrol before I heard any shots."

"At six hundred rounds a minute," Eldon grumbled, "I'd have been cut in half. Thank God that gate was set back in the wall. Have you managed to find out anything more about this shady set up?"

"I have." Vergellesi sat down on the opposite bunk. "We've managed to avoid blowing our cover. Vignozzi's talked to the Prefettura, and the carabiniere Generale di Brigata. For the moment, we're not part of the story. The officers who arrived on the scene will be none the wiser. The powers that be have patched together some story of a rival gangland slaying over looted antiquities. Builders yard turns out to be a legitimate business with innocent employees, except for the two labourers who are both on record for petty crime. The driver came from Naples. Small time muscle making his way up to the big time. The carabinieri have some names of hoodlums wanted for questioning they'll leak out in relation to the crime."

"Paba won't be happy," Eldon reflected. "He'll go to ground until he's sure nothing's can be traced back there. That spat is going to cause us a whole heap of trouble in lost time."

"*Lo so.* Anyway, what did the doctor say?"

"He suspects my problem's a partially torn dorsal muscle. He'll know more after an X-ray, then it's a dose of physiotherapy."

"Let this be a lesson to you. Next time you'll remember, cast iron radiators have to be lifted correctly. Bending your knees to take the strain off your back," Vergellesi lightly remonstrated.

"Next time I'll remember to stay out of building yards. I'm also advised to increase my protein intake. Can't say I relish a diet of steaks."

"You'll eat what I cook," Vergellesi insisted. "Italian food is always high in protein."

"The Mediterranean diet is a post war fallacy, Piero," Eldon sourly dismissed the concept. "Nobody overate because there was never enough to go round. Now, everyone eats too much. I eat like a horse. You eat like a horse. We deceive ourselves by saying the diet's Mediterranean, when we mean the ingredients are. Today, every person's meal would once have fed a family."

"You may be right," Vergellesi said, hauling him to his feet. "But, my friend, if you didn't eat like a horse you couldn't have lifted a cast iron radiator, and consequently, you'd be dead!"

Chapter 30

Dusk was already snatching the last bright filament from the horizon when Paba's Mercedes drew up in front of the castle. Capagli appeared out of the dusk, opening the door for him. Paba paused to pull on his cashmere coat, raising the collar against a freshening wind.

They made for the small windowless room in the castle that had been cleared to serve as an office and store, secured by a ten centimetre thick chestnut door with a small barred aperture.

Paba remained outside while Capagli started the little Honda generator kept in an adjoining annexe. A lamp came on lighting up Paba's bleak face, starkly menacing in the gaunt lines round his mouth. He hadn't come for a polite discussion.

His tone had an acrimonious bite. "Scarfi didn't return from Prato last night."

"Didn't Damiano phone Antonio?" Capagli inquired nervously.

"Antonio wasn't taking any calls," Paba replied, fixing an eye firmly on Capagli. "Damiano phoned at ten o'clock to tell me he couldn't contact Scarfi. I sent him over to keep an eye on his apartment. Police rolled up at midnight with the proprietor, making a big fuss. Same thing in Prato this morning, with the Via Colombo cordoned off, and carabinieri heavy metal giving everyone the cold shoulder. If news is gauged by time over distance, then Damiano was of the opinion that it must have reached the first bar within ten minutes; filling a whole front page by the time it reached the last. I'm not enthralled by the media bringing attention to our business."

"What did Damiano say?" Capagli asked, a new note of concern creeping into his voice.

Paba's face flickered for a moment with what Capagli had come to regard as one of his joyless smiles serving for humour or gravity, without indicating which. He crossed to the open door, looking silently out into the darkness. "That we are now three men short," he replied.

"What do you mean?"

Paba turned back, searching Capagli's worried face. "Someone wanted to help themselves to our property. Save all the time and trouble finding it. Just walk in, and take it off the shelf." He moved closer, standing at the side of the table, viewing Capagli with humourless eyes, contemplating his next words. "That someone knew which shelf rather troubles me."

"How could anyone know?" Capagli's voice murmured. "Anyone?"

"Indeed. Only six people knew of our forwarding station. Three have just recently left our employment. The fourth didn't know anything until I gave him instructions this morning." Paba's eyes narrowed. "That only leaves you and me."

"I've said nothing." Capagli's voice was low and puzzled. "I always did as you told me. Made sure no one followed me, took different routes at different times. I ran rings round everything. No one could have found out from me."

"Well, someone took our disc fibula and bracelets, Capagli. We've quite lost our pieces of gold."

"We can - you can trace them. They're bound to surface somewhere," Capagli speculated desperately.

"Yes, of course. They'll surface somewhere. Somewhere at the moment, unfortunately, is in police custody. I don't think we'll be getting them back."

Capagli's body slumped at Paba's words. "Police. I thought you said another...." His voice emptied the words away.

"Another mob?" Paba enquired. "So we're to believe."

"What are we going to do?"

Paba tossed his car keys up and down in his hand for a moment, thinking. "Damiano established that the order destined for the UK is complete, waiting only for packing on its pallet in the workshop. That may well go forward. For the moment it appears that the police are content putting out the names of men they want to interview. At least one of whom has certainly nothing to do with this little problem, resting as he does under the new Aviano slip road on the Pordenone *autostrada*."

"If the order's complete, then no one's found our goods in transit?" Capagli suggested eagerly.

"A gangland slaying," Paba meditated, dismissing Capagli's comment. "It's possible someone recognized Scarfi in Livorno, and followed him. Perhaps he wasn't as efficient as you were at losing a tail. I suspect we shall never know."

"Where does that leave us?"

"Suspicious, Capagli. The police took the place apart, but found nothing else. I find that hard to swallow."

"That's true. They would have found something more than the clasps and bracelets."

"An inexperienced officer may have missed them. But not all officers are inexperienced."

"We can probably tell if the castings are still right by the stamps underneath."

"Yes," Paba agreed, "but which will have a transponder added, enabling them to track our goods to its final resting place. Something else we must take care of." He turned to something more immediate. "Meanwhile, what will you be taking care of?"

"Another entrance. If we don't meet any problems."

"Problems," Paba bridled. "Suddenly there are problems. I'm surrounded by people who find they are unable to deliver their promises. Antonio promised he would take care of the delivery of my merchandise. Now he's dead. Scarfi promised he would see that Antonio did his job properly. Now he's dead. You, Capagli, also made promises." Paba was silent for a long moment, letting Capagli dwell on his words. "Now instead of promises, I have problems. Well, what are they?"

"We need to pull more of the dungeon wall away to locate another entrance." Capagli answered impassively. "We know from the legend that there's a maze of tunnels and entrances. We've only found one, leading to a dead end. We must try again. We need time."

"Time." Paba smacked a clenched fist into his hand. "The longer this goes on the less secret it becomes. Clues, that sooner or later, reach the wrong ears. And still you want time, when every hour widens the circle of gossip. Well, Capagli, I want something too. I want it finished. I've promised delivery to people who've put faith in us. People who won't be patient. Almost as impatient as me. Four weeks, then you're finished."

"That's just not enough time." Capagli argued weakly.

"You'll find the entrance, Capagli."

"Four weeks is no time at all. How can you be so sure?" Capagli insisted.

"Because, Capagli, your very life depends on it."

Capagli looked bewildered. "What we've found so far is worth fortunes."

"To whom Capagli? Fortunes are relative. A million lire is a fortune to a man who has nothing. Yet his fortune won't even buy me a new suit. And what do you know about fortunes? To you, a man with a Ferrari has fortunes. But a Ferrari can signify nothing but an empty wallet. The image is all you understand. What you've discovered so far is the same. Looks good on paper, but there's nothing in the bank. I invested in you, not the impossible." He stepped through the door impatiently. "Show me."

-oOo-

Capagli stood facing the wall. Halogen lights threw the carefully assembled stones into relief, their natural shapes casting shadows of various tones along each of its courses. But Capagli didn't have time to consider combinations of light and shade. He had nothing more than a layman's eye for historical values, knowing that objects of archaeological and artistic merit were worth money. He also knew a mere sector of stones must lie between himself and a fortune. But which sector? To remove the complete wall would take months, when he only had four weeks. Uneasily, he felt Paba's presence beside him.

"An educated guess, Capagli," Paba prompted.

"One guess will be as good as another."

"Brizzi trusted you. Now, you must trust yourself."

"You think so?"

"You must hope so, Capagli," Paba said softly.

"As far as I can remember," Capagli replied in a tired voice. "Brizzi considered that originally the tombs were visible and prominent, being in constant use. At some later date the slope was terraced and pinned by a thick stone wall." Capagli tapped the stones in front of him.

Paba stopped him. "I seem to remember, you said over two hundred years later. Why bother?"

"Brizzi claimed it was a 'cover up'. His little joke. Everyone was into hiding things. The cracks in empire were now too large to be patched over. Brizzi was convinced the Cecina family held something in trust. The archaeological evidence, disclosed in the digs behind the castle that Brizzi took part in produced many tombs, nearly all opened and ransacked. This led him to believe that because the terracing took place before the wholesale looting of the tombs, and was undisturbed, the complex of tombs belonging to the family of Paetus lay untouched."

"Ah, yes. The beginning of the end of empire. It's reasonable to conclude they'd make life difficult for robbers," Paba conceded. "After all, they've made it difficult for us."

"Anyway," Capagli continued, "as time passed, any decent material was removed by the locals, or hidden by natural changes to the site. Seismic disturbances disguised what evidence there was; finally to be completely hidden by the encroaching forest. All that remained was this wall."

"How did Brizzi explain the wall?"

"How do you mean?"

"If pilferers helped themselves to any decent material, wouldn't the wall have been included?"

"The Cecina's realized that, so a sacrificial wall was built in front, before facing the original with three metres of sand. Brizzi believed he'd found traces. There's still small sections here and there, a metre or two below ground level. Having removed the front wall, the pilferers left what appeared to be merely an exposed bank to the elements, which nature soon covered with vegetation. Later, a local baron needing to build a suitable stronghold, probably chanced upon the original remains, and having no inkling of the past, perhaps took them at face value. He may even have believed they were the foundation of an earlier castle, and incorporated them into his new building."

" Brizzi told you all this?"

"Yes. But he didn't tell me everything. I've excavated

either side of the castle in line with the slope, and this wall. To the north it doesn't run far, only twelve metres. In the south it's much longer, twenty-five and a half metres. Adding these lengths to those inside the castle, we have a centre approximately here." Capagli walked a little way further along the wall to a white chalk mark.

"You now consider the entrance to the tomb's central to the whole length of wall?" Paba enquired.

Capagli shrugged his shoulders. "I can't tell. The architect might have sought to foil *tombaroli* by placing the entrance offset to the centre. After all, I originally believed that the entrance would be central to the internal wall when we first started digging. All we found was wasted time."

"And now you have no time to waste."

"Four weeks," Capagli muttered desperately. "Perhaps Cecotti knows something."

"Who's Cecotti?" Paba demanded, catching his words.

Capagli became evasive. "Brizzi's...friend."

"Someone he confided in?"

"I don't know," Capagli repeated. "Probably not."

"You do know. This Cecotti will have the answer. He'll tell us." Paba said dismissively.

"Cecotti wouldn't say anything to you. I'll try. I'll talk to him."

"No!" Paba said sharply, shaking his head. "That won't be necessary. If Cecotti has anything to say, he'll say it to me. That, I can promise you."

Chapter 31

The detective from the OCG made his way quickly to the arrivals monitor to check on Flight 307 from Pisa to Gatwick. Looking anxiously at the time, he hurried to the arrival gate where Prinn had not yet cleared the customs area.

When Prinn appeared, pushing a trolley with his two bags, the detective stepped forward smartly to remove them.

"We can leave the trolley here, sir. I've parked close to the bottom of the escalators."

Prinn tut tutted, and the detective looked sheepish.

"Job's got to have some perks, sir."

"I don't agree. And we certainly shouldn't be setting a bad example. What's the traffic like?"

"Terrible, sir. Road works on the M23 are a nightmare. Might be quicker through Reigate."

Prinn nodded in agreement. "Just see if you can get me there by five o'clock, before my secretary goes home." He took one of the cases.

The detective looked doubtful. "I'd have to bat on sir."

"You'll drive as you were instructed to at Hendon, with circumspection. Class One are you?"

"Car and bike, sir. Still have to cope with the traffic though."

"I've a meeting at eleven o'clock tomorrow morning. See what you can do for that, then," Prinn observed reproachfully.

"With circumspection, sir."

-oOo-

The moisture that had clung to the Reliant Scimitar overnight in a damp shroud, had settled by the morning into a soft drizzle. Livia switched on the heater fan, shivering a little in its initial cold draught as she drove to a gallery in Old Bond Street.

She didn't remain long. The family picture, sent to be restored, wasn't finished. Livia hoped it wasn't a bad omen for the rest of the day.

Slipping round a still sleepy Grosvenor Square, she half-heartedly accelerated down the one-way street to the traffic lights at the junction with Park Lane. Presently they were on green, inconveniently changing to orange under one of those unwritten motoring laws as she approached.

Livia brought the Scimitar to a stop in the left hand lane.

The trees framing her view of Hyde Park were as dismal as the weather. Scraggy, leafless branches cluttering the heavy sky, dripping and dejected. Livia absently studied the estate agent's windows on the ground floor of the towering pseudo Georgian block. She sighed. The traffic lights would be overlong against her as the clattering, bustling, swell of traffic along Park Lane crowded past in a desperate attempt to beat the next pause in their cycle. Turning off the rear wiper, she set the front to a lower speed, with nothing to do but be patient.

The large flat rear screen of the Scimitar, masked by persistent condensation, obscured her view of the black Ford Transit van with heavily tinted windows that turned out of Blackburne's Mews. An inner framework of strengthened steel girders had supplemented its monocoque construction; its standard engine replaced by a turbocharged V8, yet in all outward respects it remained an ordinary commercial van.

The driver changed gear; changed smoothly again into third, easing his way past the flat spot on the turbocharger he knew he would find there, before pushing his foot hard to the floor, drawing on all of the four hundred brake horsepower that rapidly accelerated the heavy vehicle down towards the traffic lights.

Inside the Scimitar Livia glanced in the mirror, seeing nothing behind through the misted tailgate. She reached for the wiper switch, changed her mind and released the hand brake, eyes fixed on the traffic light that might change at any second.

For a brief moment she felt the curious sensation of a long buried primeval instinct signalling that the safe space she calmly occupied, wasn't safe at all. It was an unfinished thought, and she had very little time to consider it. With an unexpected surge of noise, the car was catapulted forward, jerking her backwards, deep into the seat, cannoning the vehicle out of control across the surging flank of south bound traffic.

Hit by a coach, the Scimitar spun sideways into the path of an overtaking lorry, rolling like an empty drum before the truck driver's frantic wheel locked broadside flicked it effortlessly across the central reservation into the path of a north-bound petrol tanker. The collision sent the car spinning into the air, pieces of red plastic and glass scattering in a shower across the carriageway, as the flapping remains finally crashed back down on to its roof in the central reservation.

In the ensuing aftermath of wrecked vehicles and strewn debris, the sweet smell of ripped fibreglass intermingled with the choking smell of burning rubber, and blended with the intense odour of vaporizing petrol drifting in the air.

The Upper Grosvenor Street traffic lights turned to green, but the elderly gentleman in a little yellow Citroen waited quietly on the white line, having decided that it would be better to stay where he was.

-oOo-

Prinn stroked his cheek with the end of a yellow pencil. A voice at the end of the table droned slowly on about the particular merits of a Hungarian flautist he felt able to recommend to the Sandquest Trust's committee. Prinn held the pencil at a precise focal distance between thumb and finger of both hands. It was new, perfectly sharp, and been placed on the equally new note pad

A woman's voice joined in from another part of the table reminding him of Rachel sitting opposite. She was listening intently, her head inclined towards the voice, attentive to all the speaker's deliberations.

Prinn followed the line of Rachel's auburn hair to where it fell in a thick perfectly cut form at the nape of her neck, down the collar of her crisp white blouse to the first swelling and lift of her breast. His private pleasure was interrupted by the woman sitting stiffly next to her, watching him with an air of disapproval. Resentment,

265

Prinn reminded himself, had a habit of creating its own particular bigotry.

Reading through the agenda, Prinn noticed that the tedious debates of 'any other business', was still quite a few bullet points away.

A knock sounded on the door followed by its opening, the face at the edge flushed by being the centre of attention, waited for permission to enter. Rachel, excusing herself to the committee, beckoned to the secretary. The young girl passed a folded note as discreetly as possible, and gave a short whisper before making a hurried exit.

Rachel managed a covert smile as she passed over the note to Prinn.

Opening the note he read that Livia Wolfe had been admitted to the Westminster Hospital in a critical condition following a road accident. There was a possibility she might not survive until the evening.

Prinn's watch indicated twelve o'clock. Pushing the piece of paper into his top pocket, he asked Rachel to accept his apologies. Shaking his head to disarm her inquiring glance, he pushed the chair carefully under the table, replaced the yellow pencil neatly back on the pad, and quietly left the room.

-oOo-

The police driver, under instructions not to use the incident lights, drove Prinn quickly along the embankment to Horseferry Road.

Prinn found Sergeant Meecher in the reception, waiting for him. His large bulk walking backwards and forwards in slow motion to calm his agitation.

"Thank God you're here, sir. We've been trying to locate you since ten o'clock this morning when this dropped on our desk. Couldn't raise you on your mobile. Christ! What a mess. Officer leant on your bell for an hour, disturbing most of Kensington. Neighbours started to complain. Had to wait for your secretary to arrive before we made any progress. Found they'd moved your meeting. No one seemed to know exactly where."

Prinn nodded. "Broken water pipe in the room above. I

left a message in the office as soon as I knew. Never mind all that now. What happened?" He followed Meecher up the stairs.

"Accident was a hit, sir. No doubt about that. Black Transit van shunted Miss Wolfe into Park Lane at high speed. Scimitar's a solid old lump, but according to eyewitness reports, she went in like Hendry potting a red. Van must have been doctored. One of the witnesses said it spun itself round, returning back up Grosvenor, wrecking another car on the way, before disappearing down Audley Street. Professional driver we reckon. Timing must have been spot on. The bastard took her out, sir."

"She's not dead, Sergeant," Prinn corrected him sharply.

They turned a corner on the stairs.

"No, sir. But there's not much hope according to the surgeon. All depends on the will to live when the bodies taken such a pasting. There's only the spirit left, you see. Broken leg, broken pelvis, her spleens gone, internal bleeding, three cracked ribs and a punctured lung, but her real problem's a crushed skull. That's really nasty. Touched the brain. They've managed to lift it off, but can't say how much damage's been done. If she pulls through she could be a cabbage. Christ! I don't want to think about that. Better she goes."

Prinn stopped him. "Sergeant. Now isn't the time to be negative. Our job is to salvage what we can from this mess. Understood?"

"Yes, sir. Only Miss Wolfe means a lot to me." He was suddenly embarrassed by his admission. "You know what I mean sir?"

"She means a lot to all of us, Sergeant. Concentrate on resolving our problem. Miss Wolfe won't want to see we've sat around twiddling our thumbs. She's going to pull through. Come on."

They continued up the stairs. "No trace of this black van I'll wager?"

"Not a chance, sir. From what we've seen the assailant must have been well organized from a technical and mechanical angle. Witness gave enough of the licence number. Belongs to a Land Rover in Derby. Vanished off

267

the face of the earth for the time being. Local boys are digging around the usual places. I imagine they'll draw a blank."

A policewoman rose from her chair as they approached. "I've sold the press a dummy for the moment. They don't know she's here. Due to the Scimitar, rumour went around that it was Princess Anne. Hacks were everywhere for a while, before they got wind Her Highness was in Chelsea Women's. Don't know how long the rumour will hold."

Meecher nodded to the woman constable who tapped on the door. A nurse answered, standing aside.

Livia lay in an oxygen tent, her shallow breathing giving Prinn the impression that the movement had almost stopped. The only sign of life was registered by the clicking of the machine measuring heartbeats, and the flickering peaks and troughs of the oscilloscope recording the electric pulses of the brain. Her left leg, suspended in traction, had a stainless bolt passing through the bone, leaving a puckered coloured weal on the surface of the skin. A cut under the left eye had puffed out; otherwise her visible face was unmarked beneath the swathes of bandages, leaving a small visible patch of neck above the hospital gown, scarlet with bruising. Livia's fine features were pale and a little empty, like a death mask's polished sheen of ivory.

"Is the surgeon who performed the operation free?" Prinn asked the nurse.

Glancing at the watch hanging from her lapel, she rang through on the internal telephone. "He'll come up straight away," she confirmed.

Prinn beckoned Meecher outside. "I'd like all the cover withdrawn."

"Isn't that dangerous, sir? They're bound to have another crack at her once they discover she's not dead. Miss Wolfe's a sitting duck in there."

"Depending on what the surgeon says, I have no intention of leaving her in there, Sergeant."

Prinn's explanation was cut short by the house surgeon's arrival. He ran through the extent of Livia's injuries; describing the surgery she'd undergone. He was not very hopeful. "In my opinion, her chances are very much less than even. If she manages to survive the night, the odds will shorten dramatically. We can make a further decision then whether or not she'll be strong enough for further treatment. For the moment, there's nothing else we can do," he concluded.

"Will it be possible to move her? I mean, to another part of the hospital?" Prinn asked.

The surgeon looked doubtful. "Not while she's in intensive care. No. If she's still with us in a couple of days, perhaps, if you consider it's absolutely essential for her safety."

Prinn nodded, letting the doctor pass through to his patient. He turned back to Meecher.

"There's one thing we must do straight away, then. I don't want any officers visible. We're like a blue light to anyone who's interested."

"In that case, she could die, sir."

"I thought we'd agreed to be positive?"

"I am, sir. She could die as far as everyone else is concerned. As soon as possible, the hospital can spirit her away. Down in gynaecology, or somewhere." Meecher explained.

"Hmm! I see. Worth a try," Prinn agreed.

"How the hell they rumbled her is what I want to know." Meecher exclaimed angrily.

"Not because her face didn't fit, Sergeant."

"Something didn't fit, sir. You don't shunt people into the Park Lane rush hour without good reason," Meecher said, holding the glass door open for him.

"No, indeed. Not unless things are going badly wrong. The stakes must be extraordinarily high."

"Do you think Sandquest could have set it up?" Meecher asked.

"Not worth your time thinking about it."

"Doesn't seem right to me."

"Nothing's ever exactly right in this business. You should know that. We feel cheated sometimes, but a criminal only gets off because their defence lawyers have proved, not that they're innocent, but that the prosecution is flawed."

"Rather proves justice isn't always perfect, sir."

"That's because it's a human notion; therefore, a mass

of imperfections. And, Sergeant Meecher, imperfection is how we apprehend criminals."

"I know, sir. Our job is to catch them, not try them. But just for once, when we do, I'd like to be the Lord Chief bloody Justice myself."

Chapter 32

Patience may have been an old fashioned virtue, but Vergellesi had become irritably conscious of the time taken to shave, let alone make any essential progress in their investigation. It had become one of flagged signals, but no signalmen. Answers seemed to be everywhere, leading to nowhere. Now he'd had to sit through a very slow film indeed, without results.

"Give it time," Eldon advised, switching off the projectors. "What was the building, by the way? Before the castle, on the edge of the trees."

"Looked like an old *casa colonica*." Vergellesi ventured. "Didn't take much notice as I was concentrating on your perambulating pebbles. Might still be a small farm, though the castle would never have functioned as proprietor, probably becoming a ruin long before such economic arrangements existed. Did it look occupied?"

"Well, I didn't notice if it was surrounded by cabbages," Eldon replied.

Vergellesi brought the relevant map from the sideboard. "The castle's fairly isolated, but a neighbour might hear something, even if they didn't see anything." He paused, looking up. "Might be worth checking who lives there."

Vergellesi telephoned Ruggieri and asked his question. Ringing off, he sat tapping the telephone thoughtfully.

"Interesting?" Eldon enquired.

Vergellesi looked round. "Perhaps. The owner's an English lady. One *Signora* Morning. Apparently she's attracted the attention of the police just recently. A local reported her for driving round on foreign number plates for too long, then someone shot her dog. Accident, the police report says - the animal having wandered off into the woods. I have a feeling a visit might be worthwhile."

"Visit her about what, Piero?" Eldon objected. "Walking in there to discuss vehicle irregularities and dead dogs is a strange way to introduce yourself. Besides, my back's been pulverized enough on that damn track."

"You don't need to cope with anything. To the English

these events might appear as coincidence, whereas, to an Italian, they might suggest something more. Encouraging her to reflect on certain things, for example. If so, it might be worthwhile knowing why. Tomorrow, I'll make enquiries."

"And what am I supposed to be doing in the meantime?" Eldon retorted.

"You'll see the therapist in the morning. In the afternoon you can rest and keep us up to date on the next film. After all, chasing *tombaroli* is Ruggieri's business, not ours. To us they're just inconsequential events. Whoever killed Brizzi, is hardly going to wait for a requiem mass, so we must press on following every lead." Vergellesi disappeared into the kitchen.

"Well, if that's the case, you won't be aggressive again like you were with old Cecotti, will you?" Eldon called out as the telephone rang. "I'll answer."

Sitting down on an upright chair next to the telephone he picked up the receiver, surprised to find that the caller was Cecotti. He switched on the audio.

"*Signor* Cecotti. How did you acquire this number?"

"Through Commissioner Ruggieri. I insisted I had to talk to you, urgently. He wanted to know what could be so urgent. I rang off, knowing he'd ring back."

"He has a policeman's nose."

"*Come?*

"Smelling something suspicious. No matter."

"All this time wasting," Cecotti complained. "I need to talk to you."

"Of course. We can meet tomorrow morning?" Eldon suggested.

"No, no." Cecotti said hastily. "Come immediately. Early. Before supper. There isn't much time. I need to tell someone. Roberto knew he was going to die. He gave me a name and a letter to post in an emergency. I've done that. I need to tell someone, so they can verify it's reached the right hands."

"*Signor* Cecotti, it's a bumpy drive," Eldon stalled. "I'm not sure I can cope at the moment. Can you tell me over the phone?"

"I can't talk over the phone," Cecotti pleaded. "Come as I ask."

Cecotti's voice had grown soft, carrying an undertone of desperation. Eldon sensed he was frightened.

"If you insist, then, of course. Only I'll need a driver to bring me."

There was silence on the telephone. Eldon waited for Cecotti to say something, then considered he might ring off, as he'd done with Ruggieri.

"*Signor* Cecotti. Are you still there?"

"Yes. But I'm not talking to anyone else. Just you," Cecotti said emphatically.

"You won't have to. The driver can wait in the car. You did say it was urgent."

"All right." The telephone clicked off.

Eldon swivelled round on his seat towards the kitchen. "Piero."

Vergellesi was leaning against the door frame. "I suppose you expect me to drive you to this assignation?"

Eldon frowned at the inference. "That's intolerant."

Vergellesi shrugged. "Prejudiced perhaps. Just explain."

"Cecotti's steamed up about something."

"I heard. What something?"

"You said you were listening. He wouldn't talk over the phone. Information about Brizzi."

"Important, you think?"

"Very likely. He sounds jumpy." Eldon stood up. "Perhaps we'd better go now."

Vergellesi protested. "Rex, everything's cooking. We'll eat first. Cold pasta's an abomination."

-oOo-

"Right," Vergellesi said, dropping into the drivers seat, and starting the engine. "Cecotti seems a little disingenuous, Rex." He pulled away, letting the fall in the road smooth out any jerks in the transmission.

"Over Brizzi's murder, do you mean?"

"It seems he's capable of putting two and two together," Vergellesi reasoned.

"Well, something's made him realize knowledge can equal trouble. Transferring these troubles won't make them disappear, so he's going to be disappointed. You

273

can't discard knowledge like a commodity. Unfortunately, there'll be others quite prepared to relieve him of it."

They fell silent until Vergellesi turned off the main road. Eldon gritted his teeth with the first jolt of the bumpy surface, trying unsuccessfully to find a secure position for his back.

Vergellesi dropped down a gear, and proceeded at a much slower pace. "Perhaps he's frightened of the consequences."

"Very likely," Eldon agreed. "In any event, where does a dissatisfied person of an alternative disposition move to when things go wrong?"

"Awkward. Everything to country folk is black and white, with no shades of grey. There's no half right or half wrong."

"Not a happy prospect."

"Penso di no," Vergellesi conceded.

Reaching the log pile, Vergellesi turned the car up towards the long farmhouse. The beams of the headlamps flared up, bouncing back off the low clouds that were drifting down across the yard before a rising wind. Swinging round, he parked within the arc of light cast from the top of the stairs.

Vergellesi opened the passenger door. Eldon eased himself from the seat, leaning against the car. He stayed there, head turning left and right, listening intently.

"Something's wrong?" Vergellesi asked.

"Hmm. No dog," Eldon commented.

"Probably upstairs with Cecotti."

Eldon pushed himself upright. "It lives outside."

"Point," Vergellesi agreed.

"The dog's his door bell." Eldon frowned. "It should be here."

Vergellesi loosened his jacket, undoing the Velcro strap on his holster.

"Get me started on these stairs, will you," Eldon directed, "then you can return to the car if he's going to be bashful."

Eldon reached the top of the steps. A gust of wind banged the door open; then shut it again. The door was off the latch. Eldon looked down at Vergellesi, gesturing

274

for him to come up. He knocked loudly, waiting momentarily before entering.

Vergellesi let him get half way across the room, before he followed.

The room still retained heat from a fire that had burnt down, leaving warm ashes among the few glowing embers that remained.

Opening a door on to a corridor, Eldon called for Cecotti. No one answered. He waved Vergellesi towards another door on the left, before entering.

The rooms were unused, but not empty. Cecotti maintained them in an orderly fashion; tidily, like his long dead family had left them. They represented a period beyond recollection: old photographs on the wall, yellowing crucifixes looking down in compassion on beds that had served from procreation to expiration. Cecotti was surrounded by a past, as obscure as the one he'd shared with Brizzi.

A door banged again. Eldon returned to the kitchen where Vergellesi was waiting.

"The *cantina*?" Eldon suggested. "He can't have gone far on a night like this."

"We can look," Vergellesi agreed.

Collecting a torch from the car they searched the *cantina*, and outhouses. Cecotti didn't materialize. Returning to the car, they stood deciding what to do next.

The wind was increasing. Aggressive blasts shook the doors and windows of the farm buildings, stirred unruly dust into the air in short lived spirals, whipped the tops of the cypress trees over so they lashed back, as though on elastic. The crane groaned over the barn. Vergellesi, apprehensively, cast the beam of his torch over the gantry, and along the framework of the swaying projecting jib.

"I suppose we'd better wait in the car for a while, in case he appears?" Eldon suggested.

"Well, my friend," Vergellesi said quietly, "I think we'd wait for a very long time."

Eldon followed the beam of light playing on the crane's jib where the mist threaded noiselessly through the framework, and round the dangling figure of Cecotti, thirty feet above the ground. His body turned first one way, then the other; buffeted by the wind in time to the slow, dull, yawing of metal.

-oOo-

Ruggieri descended from the farmhouse waving permission for the ambulance to leave. The photographers having completed their scene of crime portraits, followed, emptying the yard of vehicles. Ruggieri barked orders to seal the area off until daybreak.

Crossing over to Vergellesi, leaning against the wall with his arms folded, Ruggieri gave his shoulder a gentle punch.

"I don't think we'll find much in the way of evidence. No sign of a struggle in the house. None in the vicinity of the crane. Just hauled himself up on the remote control, then let go. He fell about three metres. Enough to break his neck. Where's Rex?"

"Somewhere out there." Vergellesi nodded into the darkness.

"Rex," Ruggieri called out, "I don't want you disturbing anything."

A torch flashed from beyond the barn, and Eldon returned into the floodlights

"Did Cecotti have a gun, do you know, Tullio?" he asked.

"Yes. A single-shot carbine," Ruggieri answered. "Old one, in good condition. Box of cartridges, unopened. Few loose in the drawer. It's upstairs in a gun cupboard. Why?"

"Cecotti's dog is out there. Behind the barn," Eldon replied.

Ruggieri pulled a face in acknowledgement. "He was a tidy man. The farm animals will all find homes, or go into the pot. But, I'm afraid, no one will want a dog. Especially a Maremma hound that'll eat them out of house and home."

"Whoever shot the dog was not a tidy man, Tullio. They used a shotgun at very close range. Unless you can find such a gun, along with Cecotti's fingerprints, I seriously doubt he hauled himself up there on a high wire to commit suicide. Someone helped him."

Vergellesi groaned. "No hope of slowing this one down I suppose, Tullio?"

"Not a chance," Ruggieri snorted. "As soon as I get a better appraisal of the evidence, my report's going to be forwarded to Pisa. If you know someone with authority in Rome, you'd better get in touch with them, otherwise the Questore is going to ask a lot of questions about your interest in Cecotti."

-oOo-

Vergellesi drove with a weight heavy on his shoulders, damning him less surely than Cecotti had been damned.

While Vergellesi struggled with his emotional self-interrogation, Eldon at last found an angle of comfort for his back enabling him to leave his colleague to argue with his conscience.

He closed his eyes, freeing himself from an equally confusing accumulation of impressions. Somewhere along the line they would all juggle themselves into the right order

Vergellesi thumped the steering wheel in exasperation. "Damn the pasta!"

Eldon sighed at the unwelcome disturbance. "You cannot transfer responsibility to a plate of macaroni, Piero."

"I keep tripping over my mistakes," Vergellesi said bitterly, before he lapsed back into silence.

"Don't feel sorry for yourself," Eldon urged. "Since Brizzi's death, there was always going to be a time when Cecotti would fall foul of someone. Either because of what he knew, or what they didn't. That fact means we still don't know who's the recipient of this letter. Never mind. Perhaps like him, you should accept the inevitability of it."

Chapter 33

Sandquest had grown uneasy. How could he be certain the end justified the means? Enquiries confirmed Livia had died the previous evening of a cerebral haemorrhage, but to a man as suspicious as Sandquest, that hardly amounted to proof. In this uncertain frame of mind he telephoned Hastings at the agency.

"Hastings. Make some enquiries into the undertakers Parker and Drew in the Edgware Road for me. Reference Livia Wolfe. Something's not quite right there. Wrong end of town for Baron Wolfe one would suppose. He may have his reasons. Look into Miss Livia Wolfe's funeral preparations - and Hastings, - check it's going to take place. Box in the ground, that sort of thing."

-oOo-

The undertaker's shop was a plain fronted building in a wide cul-de-sac just off the Edgeware Road. A faded, hand painted sign, screwed unceremoniously to the red bricks, proclaimed itself to be Parker and Drew, picked out in gold letters over the information: Funeral Directors (1956 Ltd.)

The mortuary lay hidden behind large firmly closed metal gates at which, occasionally, morbidly inquisitive passers-by might be seen peering through a small gap.

The man in the grey suit pushed open the etched glass door to an accompanying bell, jangling weakly in the interior.

A starkly utilitarian room, divided by a high counter in a drab, wavy composition material with tubular steel chairs placed on either side of a veneered table, hinted disagreeably at a reception area.

A pale and pulpy young man appeared through a beaded curtain at the rear, pulling on a black jacket. There was something in his unctuous manner that appeared as disconcerting as his surroundings.

The man in the grey suit reflected that one might speculate on how the daughter of a 'knight of the realm' came to be in such an unsavoury character's embalming room. Pulling out a press card from his wallet, he pushed it across the counter.

"Heard you'd gone up in the world, Roenbeck. Given up on the drunks and deadbeats, to broaden your horizons. Not like the old man, eh? Turning them over for the state without frills, boxed in five mill' ply, rope handles extra. Nice to know the entrepreneurial spirit lives on, even in the graveyard." He laughed at his own pun. "Still, you'll have to smarten up the old place, pipe in the smell of oak, decorate it with a candle or two."

The undertaker straightened his lapels, gathering a pained expression around his jowls. "I'm quite at a loss, sir. Gone up in the world? We've been here for over thirty-five years. Neither up nor down, as I remember. We carry out funeral arrangements to whatever standard the bereaved wishes. Naturally, when there's no next of kin, we follow the instructions of the council. They are notoriously parsimonious, sir. The ratepayer's money. If you've suffered a loss in the family, we'll be glad to make an appointment?" He opened a heavy ledger.

"I don't need an appointment for a funeral."

An oily smile crossed the undertaker's plump cheeks. "Oh, sir", he said condescendingly, "one never needs an appointment for a funeral. The arrangements are quite spontaneous for those who make themselves available. Embalmment certainly has merit in our opinion."

The man in the grey suit studied the face opposite to see if its owner was being serious or equivocal. He couldn't tell. "I'm not interested in embalmment," he replied. "I'm only interested in the corpse."

The 'face' stepped back. "Sir, that's most irreverent. In life they may have been criminals, or down and outs, but in death they have the repose of saints, I can assure you. Gathered to the Lord, the body is devoid of sin."

"Absolutely. Alleluia. But I'm not talking about your past customers, Roenbeck, I'm talking about the young lady you collected yesterday, from the Central Hospital."

"That I don't recall, sir."

"And you such a religious man. What's with the porky pies? Have you something to hide?"

"We take in life's ultimate sadness from many places," Roenbeck answered stiffly. "As for hiding - the good earth provides sufficient concealment at the end of one's days."

"Come on," the man in the grey suit said testily. "The upper class one, Roenbeck, they've hidden away down here, not to put too fine a point on it. In this, there's bound to be a story."

"A most unseemly suggestion, sir. Not that there aren't stories about everyone, naturally, but I can't say we've ever been a party to them. There's a certain sorrow attached to our work, without adding the melancholy of a persons last moments. I don't think we could carry out our duties with the solemnity required if we indulged in the grief and suffering of the bereaved."

"Not into all that sobbing and beating of chests then, Roenbeck. You don't know anything. Tell me on your Boy Scouts woggle. You're just in this for the money?"

"Our clients are particularly reticent about the past. We don't inquire. The details may well be rather sordid - so I'm given to understand." He flashed another of his oily smiles.

The man in the grey suit shifted his position, laying both his elbows on the counter, preparing to settle into an argument. "You admit to having the young lady then?"

"I admit to nothing, sir."

"Livia Wolfe?"

"Olivia Wolfe," Roenbeck corrected him.

The man in the grey suit straightened up. "So, she is here?"

"I was referring to the fact that we don't recommend abbreviations or nicknames, believing the deceased's name should be precise for the casket and the head stone Roenbeck retorted, shaking his head. "We have our own masons, naturally. My father's wish was to offer a complete service, to save a client the worry during such a confusing and unhappy time."

"Yea! naturally. But just tell me, what specific legal requirement prohibits you from passing on any information on your client?"

"None, sir. There are ethical considerations of course, but in your case, merely that your attitude does not bear the mark of respect we feel due to our clients."

"You don't get many of the rich or famous, Roenbeck. I'm just eager to confirm what we already know."

"And what is that, sir?"

"Tit for tat, Roenbeck. Your story for mine. A fair swap. Ethical considerations surely don't stretch to absolute confidentiality?"

"I beg to disagree, sir. There's an obligation to consider the sentiments of those left behind. To ignore them would sit heavily on our conscience, I believe."

"And if my information helped you to have a greater regard for those feelings. Wouldn't that have an influence?"

"You're talking hypothetically, sir?"

"No. Suppositions don't sell newspapers. What's the use of half a story to you?"

"I don't really know, sir. But then, I don't know you either, and what I hear from the one, does not make me very receptive to the other."

The man in the grey suit saw that his present attitude was not about to bring results.

"Listen, Roenbeck. Let me apologize. You have a professional regard for the moral virtues of this business, which is rightly defensive over the dignity of death. Maybe I shouldn't pry, but that's in the nature of my line of work. I can do you a favour as well."

"How exactly, sir?"

"I can write you up, big."

"*Big!*" Roenbeck's eyes widened.

The man in the grey suit noted he'd brought a glimmer of interest into their conversation.

"As a major interest story, Roenbeck. You couldn't afford the sort of advertisement mileage I could give you in a column or two. Parker and Drew would jump off the page at them, giving this business - dare I say it - a new lease of life?"

The undertaker bowed slightly. Accepting the direction of this suggestion, he came discreetly closer, leaning head to head across the counter. A soft, white face, devoid of lines, just the filaments of pale blue veins visible beneath the surface of his cheeks, the eyes an even paler blue, opportunist and venal.

"You mentioned information about a client?" His

281

plump lips formed the words slowly and deliberately. The obsequious tone dropped from his voice being no longer appropriate.

"That's what I said. You mustn't get me wrong Roenbeck. I'm a journalist. Freelance. I need to write stories for money. There's no salary dropping into my bank account, with editors telling me which story to chase. I dig around in the same way. I just dig deeper."

The unctuous smile returned. "An apt expression in the circumstances."

"Yes. Well, it fits where it touches. Can we do business?"

"Let us start, not by discovering how we can do business, but why we can. You assumed that a cheap promotional idea would interest me. It has its merits. One needs to promote a business even with guaranteed clients, and a service of unlimited opportunity. But you are right about a new lease. There comes a time when quantity is not an issue."

"But quality is?"

"Precisely. We feel that there must be a place for job satisfaction, even in our obsequious undertakings. Skills that ought to be recognized."

"Not by a bunch of borough counsellors, they won't. Your clients aren't likely to turn up and vote for them, Roenbeck."

"Decidedly not." Roenbeck paused. "So, an improvement in our knowledge of a client might indeed create a satisfactory outcome for our efforts."

"What does that mean?"

"We have a policy on charges to private clients."

"Very noble of you."

The undertaker drew even closer, dropping his voice a decibel. "Not really. Exceptionally, we charge on what they ought to pay, if you see my point?"

The man in the grey suit nodded. "Discretion can sometimes be expensive?"

"Exactly. Depending on our level of circumspection. However, you can appreciate this formula is subject to some error. If the bereaved are disingenuous we could underestimate our charges. Independent sources can prove invaluable in arriving at a just emolument."

"So?"

"We shall have to take a chance. We shall have to gamble. The two of us."

"Fine. I'll tell you what I know, then you can worry about the odds." The man in the grey suit leant deeper across the counter. "I was hunting up a different story in the Earls Court police station when a bleep came that a Reliant Scimitar GTE had been shunted into Park Lane. Hit and run. For a Ford no one would have turned a hair, but a Scimitar GTE had us all there in a flash, just in case it was Princess Anne. They gave us the run around, until we established that the owner was Livia Wolfe, after which most hacks drifted away, being more interested in an incident than an accident. Probably reported in house anyway. For me there was more of a story. I was doing some research into the Omegan share scandal two years ago, when venture capital interests having raised their value dramatically suddenly pushed for quick results, undermining the value of the company. Taking advantage of the crisis, the Axmar group engineered a take-over. They dumped the noncore business, hanging on to their marketing and sales division in South Africa, allowing them to avoid the expense of buying in over there at a time when no one was sure which way the worm would turn. Whispers said the venture capital funds came from the Axmar group in the first place. Couldn't avoid looking like a set-up, could it? Caspar Reed, the chairman of Omegan, committed suicide. Poor sod. Having gone into hock in a big way when the shares spiralled upwards, he didn't move fast enough when they crashed. Ruin effects people differently. Today, bankruptcy's become almost a profession. Reed, being an old-fashioned gentleman, topped himself."

"And?"

"I couldn't get to see the chairman of Axmar, though I pestered them enough. Finally, they fobbed me off with his PA, Livia Wolfe, who was good enough for Lords, the way she batted. I didn't manage to prise a single line of copy out of her. However, I discovered, as a by product of the experience, that she was the daughter of Baron Wolfe."

The undertaker pursed his thick lips, pulling a dissatisfied face. "It's not very remarkable."

"If that was all there was to it, no."

They studied each other's faces for a rekindled interest.

"Well?" the undertaker asked at last.

"Well, isn't it time for a little bit of encouragement?" the man in the grey suit queried.

"Like she was wearing La Perla underwear do you mean?"

"I don't write those sort of articles, Roenbeck. I want to know why a rich lady, well connected, comes down town to be buried?"

"A family decision."

The man in the grey suit saw there was little advantage in sparring, and pressed home his argument. "All right, I'll give it to you straight. Baron Wolfe had a half-brother, by way of his mother's first marriage. A half-brother named Caspar Reed."

"Now that is more interesting," Roenbeck confessed, with a slippery smile.

"Not so interesting as this," his confidant revealed. "Livia Wolfe was instrumental in securing Omegan for Axmar, selling her shares as they peaked. Rumour surfaced of a major shareholder jumping ship on the nod. Expectations slumped, knocking the stuffing out of the share price, and Reed took a dive. Livia Wolfe organized a top spot at Axmar on the back of the deal. She'd joined the company only a few months before, making the appointment look a fit. Stabbed her uncle in the back. Not natural that sort of thing."

"Natural is, as natural does."

"So they say? Anyway, Baron Wolfe was never a party to the sad demise of Omegan, having no business interests, whatsoever, in the enterprise. Nor did his wife, pivotal though she was in the founding of the company. She'd funded Reed, and became a major shareholder, a holding she transferred to Miss Wolfe some years ago. Though dissimilar in temperament, Baron Wolfe was fairly close to his half-brother, and took his death badly. Miss Wolfe he considered responsible for Reed's suicide, hence they've been estranged for some time. To the

284

point, it seems, where they can't even give her a decent burial."

"How is that?" There was a sharpness in the undertaker's tone the man in the grey suit couldn't miss.

I'll rephrase that. Polite society likes a funeral as much as a wedding, so why suddenly get all the tongues wagging by spiriting her away down town?"

"Family rifts are always the most depressing, being so very personal," the undertaker explained. "If you cannot trust the thickness of blood, what can you trust? Who will not turn against you? It's what makes patricide such a fascinating subject for writers, the destruction of an element that is also something of the murderer."

"Fascinating stuff, Roenbeck. Still doesn't answer why they're avoiding a public ceremony?"

Roenbeck sighed. "Baron Wolfe is a man of considerable integrity. An intensely moral man whose principles will override the requirements of the occasion, where one does not dwell on what is best left unsaid. Being necessary for him to provide the distinctive homily on the departed, his plain speaking would be inappropriate. Something Lady Wolfe thought would be too trying for their friends who couldn't help failing to understand. Therefore, Lady Wolfe has asked us to arrange a private burial away from the public glare of their parish. Only close friends are expected."

"And that's all?"

"You asked for a story. I've told you what I know."

"Frankly, a pretty poor story. Family feuding can be profitable if they're all alive. But with one dead, so is the story, even if it makes the front pages for a day or two."

"Unfortunate, but at least you have a new line of inquiry to pursue. Not gone to ground yet." The unctuous smile returned at his indiscretion.

The man in the grey suit grimaced, unimpressed.

"Another piece of the picture you mean? I think you'll make more money out of it than I will." He pushed himself off the counter, pausing momentarily at the door. "Just one thing, Roenbeck. Where did you get all this priceless information on moral rectitude? Over tea and buns with Baron Wolfe?"

This time there was no smile, just a jelly like shake of

the head. "From another hack this morning. He seemed to think he had a bit of an exclusive. Perhaps you'll have to dig a little faster, sir."

The man in the grey suit opened his mouth to say something, then shut it again. He'd pressed the argument as far as he could, and everything after this would as likely end in another blind alley.

He raised his hand in a mock salute, and turned away without another word.

With the last audible sound of the bell, where the man in the grey suit had opened the door on the way out, the beaded curtain quietly parted, and Sergeant Meecher's heavy frame stepped into the room to join Roenbeck.

Chapter 34

Stretched out on the floor of the sitting room, Eldon began to gently run through his physiotherapist's instructions. Raising one leg slowly, then the other. He didn't want to think about how long this programme was likely to take, he only knew that events were already some way ahead of them, and likely to demand a great deal more vigour than he could necessarily supply.

"Have we given up on Capagli?" he inquired, switching to a new exercise.

"I'll check if anything's new on the tape," Vergellesi volunteered, going over to the recorder and consulting the tape counter. He pressed the play button. The telephone tone sounded, then a tired voice answered quietly. A familiar voice that had now become no one's voice.

'Chi è?' Cecotti asked.

Eldon lowered his leg and lay still.

'Loris, this is Enzo. Listen to me. You must get away from here.'

'We've discussed all this before,' Cecotti replied in a resigned voice. 'I told you it wouldn't be any use. I've nowhere to go.'

'This is no joke,' Capagli almost hissed. 'You've got to get out. Paba suspects Roberto told you everything.'

'If he knows that, Enzo, then you told him.'

Capagli appeared to ignore the accusation. 'Look. Just get in your car, and go. When you've found somewhere, contact me. I'll send money. I can sell the farm for you. You'll have plenty to live on. For God's sake. You must go. Now!'

'Enzo,' Cecotti's voice remained calm. 'I'll never escape them. Today, tomorrow, next month, they'll find me, for sure.'

Capagli punctuated each word. 'They-will-kill-you.'

'Yes, they'll kill me,' Cecotti replied in a tired voice. 'What more can I expect.' He gave a sad, dry laugh. 'But what about you, Enzo? Where will you run, when it's your turn?'

'You're a fool, Loris. I've tried to help,' Capagli shouted

in frustration. 'You could have been cut in. Made a lot of money. Left that old piece of dirt you call a farm. Now I can't help you, and you won't help yourself.'

'Enzo,' Cecotti sighed. 'Just leave me alone.'

The telephone clicked off, followed by silence. Vergellesi let it run on a little. It was the last telephone call on the tape.

"Then Cecotti telephoned me?" Eldon noted, from where he'd remained supine on the floor.

"Fifteen minutes later," Vergellesi confirmed.

Eldon eased himself into a sitting position, propping himself against the armchair. "In the circumstances, you might say it was extremely fortunate that we were late that day."

"Fortunate?"

"Very. Any earlier, and poor Cecotti might not have been the only one with a hangover."

-oOo-

Still aching from the physiotherapist's massage, Eldon hobbled into the nearest bar where he found a seat and ordered a coffee. Vergellesi had taken himself off to interview Mrs Morning, so, for the moment, he had a little time on his hands.

The local newspaper ran an advertisement for an exhibition of local artists. He asked the barman if it was worth a visit?

"A matter of taste," the barman counselled. "Sorena has produced great artists. Some served the Medici, and are famous. Others were carried off by Popes, never to return. Unhappily, no one's seen fit to carry this lot off."

Eldon paid for his coffee and walked carefully round to the piazza to see for himself.

He arrived at the gallery, situated on the top floor of a palazzo, aware of the effort in climbing the 40 centimetre high steps that had been designed for times when besiegers needed to be, not only strong of limb, but also blessed with ample wind. Eldon had been made aware of a deficiency in the former.

The neglected stucco walls, with their stone window reveals and high step, were bare, allowing for the

288

paintings to be displayed on two central lines of exhibition panels. A gap in the panels occurred at every window on one side, allowing for the display of a number of papier-mâché life sized sitting figures. Sculptures - or something like.

Admission was free. Eldon collected a badly photocopied catalogue from the young woman at the desk. He commenced from where a large red arrow directed the order of viewing.

It didn't take many pictures for him to decide that the barman, where he'd taken his coffee, was obviously a connoisseur of more accomplished works.

His less than close examination of these unhappy tokens of negligible talent became suddenly arrested by Remmick, sitting in the recess of a window, in all respects an accompanying sculpture. He raised his catalogue to Eldon.

"Taking time off to grab a spot of culture, son?" he drawled in his, by now familiar, sardonic tone.

"A matter of opinion," Eldon replied, gesturing towards the exhibition panels.

"Sure," Remmick agreed. "They're abysmal."

"Perhaps that's too unkind," Eldon allowed. "I'm sure their mothers are enthusiasts."

"And *only* their mothers. They're rubbish. Who do they think they are, Rauschenberg, Miro, or what?" Remmick waved Eldon on. "I'll walk round with you. A penance. How are things going?"

"I thought you were going to keep me up to date?" Eldon remarked.

"Oh tales to tell, Rex. Left Prato in a bit of a mess, I understand. Wouldn't have happened in the old days. We asked questions first then. None of this spaghetti western stuff. Corpses don't have a darn lot to say for themselves."

"It's obvious, then, that one must make every effort to avoid the condition," Eldon replied stiffly.

"Is that a matter of fact? Taking out all three smacks at a bit of an excess to me."

Eldon was a little rattled. "Adam, how is it you seem to know nothing about everything?"

Remmick, unabashed, took Eldon's arm and steered

289

him across the room to avoid a section of paintings.

"You're mistaken, Rex. I only know history. What's happened. What's been. The rare trick in this game is to know what's going to happen. That's what intelligence used to be about. Ninety-nine percent of it was a hard slog, based on either acquisition or inquisition. Well, you've blown the latter away for the moment. Guess you're back to the conditioned reflex. Old fashioned hunches."

"Gathering evidence has always been a slow, methodical business," Eldon emphasized.

"Doesn't work, son. What you're describing suggests not rocking the boat. And you rock boats. Damn me, son! You sink them." Remmick shook his head. "No, I've put you down as a guy who prefers action to reaction. Getting ahead of the game."

"Providing you know which game you're in."

"Oh, you know, for sure. The only thing you don't know is, who's got the ball."

They stopped in front of a particularly poor painting. 'Interpretation of Spilt Wine' the legend ran, describing a white background blurred by scrapings of red. Remmick raised his eyes to the ceiling, and fashioned his catalogue sheet into a dart while Eldon studied it.

"First you create this haemorrhage," Remmick observed, "then you dream up a title, because no one has the faintest idea what such a mess represents." He shook his head. "Not even a suitable classical epithet could save it."

"Tomorrow, the painting could be worth thousand of pounds," Eldon suggested.

"Perhaps more," Remmick drawled. "What difference does that make? With clever promotion, and a dull witted public, even a dried turd can be worth a fortune. Economical of colour is about all you can say."

Remmick flew his dart flamboyantly into the wastepaper basket next to the desk, under the attendant's shocked glance.

They walked together down the stairs.

"I'll leave you to your procurement exercise then. A bit of advice, son. If you don't know who's got the ball, track them down fast. Get the measure of this group doing up the castle. Obvious an odd job lot. Find out where they're coming from; especially from their weak link, a local man called Capagli. Size him up. Tonight you'll find him at the *festa* dinner the Red's give twice a year for the party faithful. Take a real good look at him, and get yourself ahead of the game." He slapped Eldon gently on the back, slipping ahead before they came out on to the square.

Eldon stopped on the bottom step, watching Remmick hurry across the piazza. Remmick, he thought, was just like a dog with a bone - sure that the meat was in there somewhere.

-oOo-

Vergellesi left the path to reach a fallen tree half buried in humus. Leaning against it, he took a reading from the compass hung round his neck. The path was running 178 degrees due south, a little off course along the magnetic meridian line of his map to Margaret Morning's house.

Another hour of steady walking brought him out on to a track in a rush, nearly losing his footing on the loose soil at the edge. On the opposite side, a strip of once cleared and cultivated land indicated a long deserted tenancy. Abandoned olive trees still remained, leaning gently awry, toppling lazily in time to the orchestration of the conducting decades. Here and there a lonely medlar had already begun to stir. An interest he had little time to be interested in.

The steeply rising track led to the castle, austerely blonde in the midday sun and sharply profiled by a background of dark forest. At one corner a few scrub oaks hung to the rocky feet of its pale walls, denied any firm grip, but too tenacious to let go.

Vergellesi caught a glimpse of Margaret's car parked under two towering stone pines, their huge umbrella branches casting a shade over the end of the house, set back about ten metres from the track.

At the gate Vergellesi called out, *"C'é nessuno in casa?"*

There was a grating of shutters, and Margaret

appeared at an upstairs window. Deciding Vergellesi had all the appearances of a hiker, she leant out and replied: "*Sì.*"

"*Scusi signora, mi può indicare la strada per Sorena?*"

"*Un momento, scendo giù,*" Margaret answered.

She disappeared from the window, a moment later arriving at the gate.

"*Parlate inglese?*"

"I do. I'm afraid I seem to have taken a wrong turning somewhere. Confused the tracks I expect." Vergellesi gestured vaguely at the forest.

"Hardly surprising out here. I still get lost after two years. You've a long way to go I'm afraid, and a left here and a right there won't do," Margaret explained. "I'll have to show you on a map. Signposts tend to get blown away. *Complimenti* on your English."

"Thank you. My grandmother was English, from Bristol. Naturally, my father was brought up as half English. An Anglo-Sicilian. Therefore, very much a Sicilian, he was also an Anglophile. A great lover of Milton and Meredith."

"Then he was a man of very civilized preferences. Can I offer you a drink?"

"Thank you. Perhaps a glass of water."

"We can sit here, in the sun." Margaret pointed to a stone bench alongside the porch.

He watched her go in, before looking around him. From where he sat he noticed the castle was just visible through the edge of the trees.

Margaret returned with a tray bearing two glasses and a jug of water. Pouring his drink, she dropped a slice of lemon in with a small pair of silver tongs while looking at him out of the corner of her eye. He had a slightly colonial look, reminiscent of her late husband. Tanned and untidy.

"Ah!" he exclaimed, cupping the glass with his hands, one of which he transferred to his forehead. "Walking is hot work, even at this time of the year."

"You're on holiday then?"

"Time off from work, rather than a holiday," Vergellesi explained, having bent the truth rather than dispense with it. "For me, this is a perfect time of the year. An exciting time. The rebirth of the land. Everywhere you see the farmer tidying his *podere*, lending a hand."

"You aren't a farmer, that I can tell. You're interested in plants though?"

"I studied botany at Palermo University, so having invested a number of years in the subject, maintain an interest. I started work with the Sicilian National Parks Commission."

"So you have a career in botany?"

"Marginally. In my job I don't have a great deal to do with botany in a layman's sense, but I get to see a great deal of wood - well polished, surrounded by an office."

They laughed together; Margaret noticing the little creases at the corner of his eyes. He was not so young as his initial youthfulness suggested, but he had an openness she found attractive.

Their laughter was interrupted. Somewhere, deep in the house, the telephone rang, and then stopped as Melissa answered.

"Mummy," a voice called from an upstairs window. "It's Nicholas Prinn on the phone."

Vergellesi studied Margaret's face, noting a slight flush appear on her cheeks.

"Prinn," she repeated. "Please excuse me. I won't be a moment."

Vergellesi closed his eyes to the warm sun, not to relax, but to concentrate on what was being said. He found he couldn't hear the muffled conversation, but heard the receiver being replaced. Listening to the silence that followed until he finally heard her steps tapping lightly over the terracotta tiles.

"I'm sorry for the interruption," Margaret said lightly. "A friend wondered if he could pass by tomorrow."

Vergellesi considered the isolated position of her home. No one would casually pass by - which suggested Commander Prinn would have a good reason for making such a journey.

"This is your second home?" Vergellesi asked, continuing where they'd left off. "For vacations?"

Margaret shook her head. "No. My daughter, Melissa, and I live here permanently. You could say we're using it as a retreat."

"Ah! I'm sorry," Vergellesi apologized quickly.

"Really, there's no need."

"No. It's intrusive. I'm too inquisitive."

"Not at all. When I say, in retreat, I'm alluding to things English. People, places, memories. We're getting over a loss, but there's really no need for anyone else to feel involved. Life eventually finds a new balance. We're adjusting at our own pace, in our own time. Avoiding the pressure of family and friends who meant well, but didn't do very well."

"Intent on filling up all the gaps they thought existed?" Vergellesi ventured.

"Exactly. Keeping us busy. You're also very perceptive."

Vergellesi gave her a complimentary smile. "Italy's become your space. Not far, but far enough to stay out of touch. So, one day you'll return to England?"

"Possibly. I don't give it any real thought. Occasionally the idea crosses my mind. Sometimes, I think in a panic, that I'll wake up finding I've put down roots, so I can never go home."

"Will that be so bad?"

"On a good day, no." They laughed again. "I don't know. Melissa's fitted in very well. She may want to go to university in England, and then we'd have to make the decision. She's certainly very happy here."

"And you are not?"

Margaret looked steadily at Vergellesi, asking herself, was he simply curious?

"And you are not?" Vergellesi repeated quietly.

"Yes, I am. How could one not be happy in such a wonderful place?"

Vergellesi recognized an echo of doubt, something generated perhaps, as Ruggieri had hinted, by the position she found herself in. "Wonderful, yes. A little lonely, I imagine."

"Tuscany isn't the moon. It's quiet, of course, but here I'm able to keep people at arms length. In any case, country people here are mostly farmers. Isn't that the Italian's dream?"

"It may be. Sadly we can't all be farmers. It doesn't stop us imagining that when we retire we can purchase a small plot of land, grow tomatoes and lemons, pretending we are part of the great tradition." Vergellesi laughed lightly. "Like the English, following in the footsteps of a wealthy and literate class, we find the reality is not so magnificent as the dream. My father's bookshelves groaned with their perfectly honed expressions that precisely described the nobility of our lives, or the splendour of Italy's past. None of them knew us well, yet all of them, better than we know ourselves."

Margaret dissented. "Dickens, I seem to remember, wasn't so complimentary of all things Italian."

"But did it make a difference?" Vergellesi pressed. "No. Because when that great writer was describing a peasant girl, he could not fail to describe her beauty, even when her feet were dirty. That is how many see Sicily, ragged and poor, but still beautiful. People like myself, doctors, lawyers and teachers, grown indolent in our prosperity, have not the sympathy for the land, only the passion. One day, even that will be spent. Sometimes, I think to myself, perhaps the dream should be enough."

"You should be more tolerant then, of those who grasp their dream."

"I make the distinction as a matter of fact. However, you have no neighbours to suffer. The plant world I find, is much more peaceful. Not entirely without its pugnacious moments, but on the whole, a moderate, if not pacific state of existence. They can be dangerous. Some are extremely poisonous; a biological self-defence. Others, like the insectivorous plants, are predatory, and still others, in the Araliaceae family, are parasitic. So, we have our thugs even there. By and large, except for evolution, the plant world tends to achieve a biological balance rather than indulge in mutual extermination."

"The concept of a punk mushroom, I find rather pleasing. Good Lord!" Margaret suddenly started. "Here I am talking to a complete stranger for almost an hour, and I don't know your name. I'm always doing it. I've quite forgotten my manners."

"The time and place comes naturally. I'm Doctor Piero Vergellesi, and you are Mrs Margaret Morning." He offered his hand.

Margaret took it with a dubious look.

"Your post box gave the game away," Vergellesi explained. "At first I wasn't sure. So there's just you and a lonely castle left in this area?"

"I'm afraid you're wrong about neighbours. I understand the castle's about to be restored. A private residence." Margaret felt she could add as much as was general knowledge.

"A pity. Ruins are always interesting." Vergellesi tested her willingness. He was not very good on coincidences. Scientists liked causal connexions, and disliked equally, the theory that there is no certain knowledge. Margaret was a coincidence and, he could see, must certainly have gained knowledge of the castle.

Margaret would not be drawn on the subject. "It's only a country ruin, so nothing that could be counted extraordinary. You must be lucky and live by the sea?" She changed the direction of the subject.

"Yes, I have a nice apartment in the Foro Italico overlooking the sea at Syracuse. If you think Tuscany is beautiful, I suggest you come to Sicily."

"If everyone says that, how do you know who's telling the truth?"

"Pirandello said, that in Sicily everyone has their own truth. You will have to come and see for yourself. Now I must continue, I've taken far too much of your time. I'll just take a walk up to the castle. Satisfy my curiosity, if you think that'll be all right?"

"Of course. The track is a *vicinale*, a public right of way. I'll come with you, stretch my legs."

Their walk was not productive. The castle entrance, fenced off with orange tape to bar the law abiding if not the adventurous, revealed little of the interior. They circled as far as they could, dense undergrowth and brambles denying them a complete circuit of the walls.

As Margaret was obviously reluctant, Vergellesi abandoned the idea of pursuing any further interest, returning with her to the house where she gave him directions on the map how to reach the main road.

Vergellesi set off, looking back as he reached the bend in the track. Margaret stood alone by the gate. Her solitude seemed an insubstantial thing, hardly capable of withstanding the storms that might break around her.

For the first time in many years he felt a protective instinct emerge among his emotions. He didn't welcome their presence, not having room for them.

Raising his stick in salute, he turned the bend out of sight.

Chapter 35

Vergellesi tossed his hiker's bag towards the reclining figure on the sofa that appeared to be asleep.

Eldon deftly fielded the missile, sliding himself upright. "What time do you call this?" he asked

"Too early for supper, and too late for tea," Vergellesi replied. "Between our two countries, a man might starve." Removing his walking boots, he placed them outside in the hall

"No luck in the wild woods then?" Eldon asked

"I wouldn't say that. Mrs Morning is extremely pleasant. Soft centre, hard edge." He stared at the hole in his thick woollen sock, wriggling his big toe in confirmation of the culprit

"Any other possibilities besides her resemblance to a chewy caramel, and Ornella Vanoni?" Eldon persisted

"Something for you to consider. The castle appears to be in the process of genuine building activity, but only inside the walls. Much the same as our photoreconnaissance. No one's interested in the exterior. Mrs Morning seems slightly defensive about her relationship with the neighbours."

"Yet, she must have learnt a great deal about the castle."

"That crossed my mind. There's nothing to keep an interested party out, but given my company, I felt I shouldn't appear too eager. Which, to be truthful, I'm not."

"So, what are you saying?" Eldon, trying to touch his toes, gave up.

"I can't see any relevant relationship between Brizzi and Nightingale. He's already dead, so the Gorky State Orchestra's appearance represents an inconsequential event. Admittedly, something's going on in the castle, but as I said, that's Ruggieri's problem."

"In one sense. But you're only assuming the orchestra's arrival is inconsequential, and I'm not so sure about that. Let's consider the facts for a moment. Commander Prinn sent me to Vignozzi. Vignozzi sent us, in a roundabout way, to Sorena. No one's discussed joint operations with us. It seems we've been left to plough our own furrow, but even that has method. When you haven't any idea what's in someone's hand, you throw in a pair of wild cards."

"Is that how you see us?"

"No, Piero. That's how *they* see us. The arrival of the Gorky State Orchestra is too much of a coincidence."

"Florence is not Sorena."

"Only on the maps," Eldon insisted. "They're not so far apart, and people are conditioned nowadays to travel. But I agree, it's a queer pitch."

"Very. Commander Prinn telephoned Mrs Morning while I was there, so it appears we're at least playing on the same pitch."

Eldon gave a wry smile. "Rather proves my point, Piero. They know Sorena's important. For example, somebody moved the stones the night before last. Something of interest to the Commander, having been informed of resumption in activity by Mrs Morning."

"That's certainly something that would bring him over in a hurry," Vergellesi acknowledged. "Can I see?"

"Help yourself."

Vergellesi switched on the projectors to compare the two films. "Like you said. By the keep. They moved, but they didn't move. I doubt you'd notice from the ground. Captain Bandinelli mentioned the possibility of an infrared window. He thinks we might then actually see the nature of their activity."

"No. Noise from the helicopter would certainly close them down again. Now they're back in business, I think we should try to keep them there. Besides, infrared projection is badly effected by weather conditions. Might be unreliable."

"Pity. In the meantime, having worked up an appetite with all this walking, what would you like for supper?"

"Tonight," Eldon said grandly, "I have it in mind to dine with the proletariat, discussing the old days when all of Tuscany was red, and Uncle Spam was only a distant rattle of silver dollars."

"Is this something you've concocted to disturb me?" Vergellesi tugged his socks off, to rub the soles of his feet.

"No. This evening we're going to a *festa* dinner."

Vergellesi protested. "Have you ever been to these fraternity dinners? I'd honestly prefer the Etruria Trattoria."

"Of course you would, but then, Capagli doesn't frequent such gourmet haunts."

Vergellesi sighed, resigned to the vagaries of dilettante cooking. "Like Mohammed..."

-oOo-

The narrow mediaeval street emerged into a large piazza with bare polled plane trees. Beyond this, a small alley led them to another walled space where the streetlights were barely sufficient to illuminate a large rusty iron gate with its hand written poster clearly indicating the proposed venue. The sound of a noisy gathering fluctuated in the gusts of air.

The square renaissance building they found themselves in, like a dissipated continental monarchy, had long been searching for a function more deserving of its age. Once an important seminary, the building had languished empty before the turn of the century, deserted by the church. Since ceasing to reverberate to the apostolic creed, a use had been found as a venue for the music school; a refectory; and a wet weather muster for troops. Falling thereafter into the hands of an indifferent council who had so many buildings thrust upon them, they could do no more than lock the doors, and throw away the keys.

Retaining its asset of a magnificent hall, the faded frescoes, bearing marks of vandalism and neglect, still looked down on the marble tiled floor set with cornelian coloured lozenges managing to celebrate past glories with scars of tolerable shabbiness. A small notice indicated that the empty niches flanking the two opposite facing double doors, once held statues by the Florentine sculptor Cosimo Cenni. Only the *trompe-l'oeil* legerdemain of the ceiling - whose cornices and mouldings may, or may not have been - were too high for delinquents; too indelibly rooted, to be misappropriated by speculators.

Vergellesi lamented that Italy was littered with such priceless and profitless buildings.

Making a choice from the chalked up menu displayed at the entrance, Eldon paid at the door, while Vergellesi found a place on the trestle tables covered with paper cloths. A waiter, Eldon recognized as running a tobacconist shop, appeared in a large pink apron, depositing in front of them a bottle of red wine and a litre bottle of mineral water. From under his arm he produced a basket of roughly cut bread, which he flourished dramatically, and placed on the table between them.

"*Torno subito,*" he exclaimed, taking their credited receipt and making off in the general direction of the kitchen, collecting empty bottles and plates on route, which he juggled with questionable dexterity.

"Now this, I think, is Capagli," Vergellesi declared. "No, don't look round. You'll see him soon enough."

Capagli, by his presence, fooled no one. A fellow traveller, he shared their ambivalence over ideology and enterprise. The Marxist articles of faith were no more than an ancient hymn sung in memory of the long since dead, ignored when they interfered in the way of the living. Capagli declared he was a communist, paid his dues, which was good enough.

As in everything else, no one dwelt overlong on a person's beliefs. Being wealthy was a personal affair; moreover, Capagli had a constant need to dispose of rubble, and farmers an equally compelling need for hard core where the *comune* had little interest in maintaining their country roads. They were, in this respect, mutually compatible.

He would not be the only 'collaborator' present. All those who sought preferment from the communist hierarchy, would make an appearance, no matter how short the duration of their stay. To be seen was a confirmation of their faith. The mayor would make a brief appearance to note how strong the resolve of the converted remained, compliment the cooks, share a light-hearted moment with his executive, and be gone. Like all the 'Soviet' mayors, he was not a man of the people, only of the party.

Capagli would not emulate him, determined to stay

301

the course, softening up the remaining politicos, or striking difficult deals with the farmers

The man Eldon was now able to study had a casual, bonhomous appearance, perfectly disposed to the seated farmers. Some rose awkwardly from their benches when he approached to shake hands, or a more intimate salutation. Others received a friendly hand placed on their shoulders to draw them into his company. He appeared affable and sturdy; restless dark eyes flitting from man to man, becoming expressive when he made comments that drew laughter from the surrounding group.

Capagli was working the tables, maintaining a familiarity he could call on whenever he needed their time, or their ear. He was curiously something, everything perhaps, that the mayor should have been in such company, but wasn't. At his ease with a ready compliment, benevolent congratulation, or earnest commiseration, he demonstrated a tact that appeared amiable and good tempered.

"I suppose you might say that he's a class act," Vergellesi said, pouring their wine. "But we know him. He's one thing, or the other. Depending."

Having run out of tables to circulate among, Capagli straightened his wind cheater, looking round, just to make sure he had missed no one. His eyes stopped, momentarily curious, on Eldon and Vergellesi, before moving away

"I'm not forgetting," Eldon said. "But one thing we should bear in mind. He's a third division player in a first division game. When someone passes him the ball, he's got to run with it. Has he got the stamina, do you think? The ruthlessness to play dirty, as well as hard. His genuine loyalty to poor Cecotti was a weakness that could prove fatal to him."

Capagli had made his way to where a chair had been kept vacant for him. The group Eldon noticed were not the sort likely to waste a great deal of time on any thinness of character. But this was Sorena, where aspects of character were not likely to be sorely tested.

They both sat back while the waiter deposited their first course in front of them, along with a small plastic cup of grated cheese that Vergellesi regarded with evident suspicion.

"He seems to support a lot of people?" Eldon queried, mixing a little water with his wine.

"Probably not directly," Vergellesi replied, stirring the cheese inquisitively with the plastic spoon. "They'll be working on the black, or when they're needed. Leaves time for hunting, or other diversions. Capagli will know all their little secrets. Perhaps they'll know his."

"Something of a trait in Italy, you'll tell me."

"All small communities are the same," Vergellesi replied. "Stuck together. If you pull one, you pull them all. Capagli will be aware how perilous an attraction that can be."

"Yes, I can see what you mean, Piero."

Vergellesi glanced up at Eldon's tone to see Capagli greeting two women. He returned, head down, to contemplate their first course. *Pappardelle alla lepre.* Smells authentic enough. Perhaps a little dry. Some olive oil, I think."

Eldon waited, and when his companion said nothing, ventured a comment. "Not of any interest then, Capagli's new company?"

"Yes," Vergellesi replied stiffly, "the lady in the blue coat, being introduced to Capagli, is Mrs Morning."

Eldon regarded Vergellesi for a long moment, and then picked up his fork, tasting the hare sauce. "Hmm! The authentic taste of Tuscany, just a little salty," - he picked a fragment of vertebra from his mouth and laid it on the side of his plate - "and full of hidden bones."

Chapter 36

The Via Toledo began to fill with shoppers, spilling from the sidewalks into crowds on the street. Paba told the taxi driver to pull over to the kerb, deciding to walk the rest of the way towards the Piazza Trieste e Trento, rather than be late for his five o'clock appointment.

He had watched the jostling confusion agitating the human spirit into a kind of tremulous excitement for long enough. Tipping the driver, Paba stepped into the bustling, nervous atmosphere that permeated the centre of Naples. The chaos of the past was not something that had been subject to variation by a less unruly citizenry in more modern times.

The city was only superficially different; materially altered, but anthropologically the same. The sentiments of the Neapolitan's excitable and sympathetic nature would have appealed no less to the gourmand Lucullus, than the mercenary Sir John Acton, both of whom devoted as much of their energies to the pleasures of the city as they did to their campaigns. This definitive idea of so pleasure loving a state was as attractive to the residents as to their admirers. No one saw, or stopped to see, the shadows that had gained possession of the darker side.

Crossing over the road to gain a more representative view of the narrow alleys that ascended steeply towards the monastery of San Martino, and the Castel Sant' Elmo, Paba felt an inner euphoria generated by something he could call his own. It was a minor achievement of sorts. A personal victory against the odds that piled up high, suffocated even the smallest of ambitions.

In this warren of once dilapidated slums, just a step away from the bright prosperity he presently walked along, he had spent his treacherous and embittered childhood. It was a generation away from the multicoloured babies, flotsam and jetsam of an ebbing military tide. He had a father of his own, begetter of too large a family he couldn't afford, so that, to eat, Paba resorted to the simple expedient of crime.

The washing still hung down from the windows of the high tenements, and if the tomcats marked anything that stood still for long enough, they'd never been quick enough to mark Fausto Paba.

Across the Vico Lungo Del Gelso, Paba had watched the movements of another world; the plush, comfortable substance of a stream of affluence that flooded towards the Piazza Plebiscito, so close he could reach out to touch the gleaming cellulose of their shiny cars, and the soft tresses of the women who rode in them. Only a short step to take from the savage apprenticeship of the streets.

But Paba was not going home. He had long since moved the remnants of his family to the heights, and huge modern sprawl, of Vomero. The pleasure he felt was not determined by any childhood or adolescent memories, simply by a reversal of location. Now he looked in, not out. Only those born into so abject a poverty could understand the orientation of such an experience.

The event was something of an occasion, for Paba had little time to idle along the corridors of middle class prosperity, though his pockets were lined extravagantly enough to indulge himself in the amusement. The walk was by way of an evocation; the spoiling aggression that dragged him out of those confined passages where others loitered away their youth and, for all he knew, loitered still.

He didn't care. Caring meant shouldering a burden. In his world, to be successful meant travelling exceedingly light. Escaping had been more important. Escape from the boredom; the dull resentment of being the possessor of almost nothing. Motivation enough to drive him across that thin line from one parallel street to another. He had lost nothing but his innocence in exchange for an investment, out there in the sunlight. He considered it cheap.

Glancing at his watch he quickened his pace, hurriedly crossing the road, past the funicular railway hidden in its tiny piazza, without glancing at the once glamorous Galleria Umberto.

As a youth he had been called there to meet the rising

star Mario Giuliani who had persuaded his 'family' to use money earned from their lucrative heroin deals to purchase Treasury bonds or invest in legitimate business interests, increasing their wealth without the expense of money laundering. In a world of crude acquisitions he had brought a timely sophistication to these new directions, directions needing a new type of criminal.

Giuliani had liked the steely-eyed youth who watched him gravely, speaking only in facts, without a trace of swaggering arrogance. Paba was only interested in results, never speaking of what he could do, only of what had to be done. Giuliani came to see him as a protégé; an exemplar; a young man to consider, given the rapid turn over of lieutenants in so vicious an industry. In this academy of sorrow he had shown a particular flair for surviving.

Needing someone with a sound head on violent shoulders, Paba had demonstrated he could organize a business at the same time as handling the seamier side of its funding, and the brutal, homicidal company he would have to keep. There were not many such people in the company Giuliani kept.

Now Paba had asked Giuliani to meet him, a request no one sought lightly; but Giuliani could assure himself that Paba would not waste his time in idle discussions.

-oOo-

The breeze on the street had stiffened across the gulf, bringing a slight welcoming warmth on Paba's skin that contrasted strongly with the chill of Sorena. In Campania the air seemed to hold a surfeit of oxygen that allowed him to utilize more of the day, while sleeping well for less of the night. Paba missed the atmosphere of Naples. In such an unemotional man, he was apt to consider the sentiment unfortunate.

He crossed the cobbled street of the Piazza Trieste e Trento to the celebrated cafe Gambrinus. One could nearly always find Giuliani in the tearoom at five o'clock. Such a habit in earlier days might have been his undoing; reflected in the refined manners of the modern underworld boardroom by a confidence, not yet sunk to

306

total indifference.

Paba nodded to two suited men outside, leaning casually against the corner, talking. Another two, he knew were somewhere close at hand. Wherever Giuliani went, they accompanied him.

Pushing open the entrance, Paba passed by the packed bar. A narrow glass door on the left led him into the whimsical *Ottocento* style tearoom. Giuliani sat in a corner, never close to a window or with his back to a door; not even now, when mobsters died in their sleep from blocked coronary arteries. Always impeccably dressed, often by Petruzzi off the Via Diaz, whose elegant English style tailoring verged on the iconic, he was not one to miss the minutest details, executed by himself, or anyone else.

He glanced over his gold, half rimmed glasses as Paba entered, lowering his financial journal carefully on to the small table beside him. Rising he offered his hand, cupping his clasp with the other. Once an aspirant would have raised his hands to their lips, but no one brought attention to themselves in such a manner any more. Feudalism, men like Giuliani hoped, was a thing of the past; believing business better served by a sense of restraint.

"You look tired, Fausto," he said, waving Paba into the only other seat. "You need a holiday, away from that windy hill top in Tuscany. I'll send you over to Capri. You can stay with my sister at her villa."

The idea was attractive. Giuliani's 'sister' was no relation at all, looking ten years younger than her fifty years. The only wrinkles the lady owned appeared on her one hundred thousand lira notes. In that sense, at least, she had a lot of wrinkles. Sometime after the turn of the century, Maxim Gorky had run a school for revolutionaries on Capri. Lenin, Stalin and Chaliapin were old pupils, and Giuliani's 'sister' often joked, that the communists had learnt all their bad habits in Campania.

Paba sat down. "Thank you, Mario, but this is not a good moment for relaxation."

"So they say. Problems I'm beginning to hear?"

"The sort where I'm feeling a little overexposed."

"Being on your own?" Giuliani smiled at his question before answering it. "Being alone has certain benefits, Fausto. I was always alone. Lends itself to a certain flexibility. Everything, but everything else, is quite dispensable."

He poured Paba a cup of tea, passing it over politely, indicating with a nod of his head towards the lemon and sugar. He poured himself a second cup, replenishing the pot with hot water.

"I remember you once said in an ideal world, Mario."

"In an ideal world? Yes. Why are things not so ideal in your case then, that they cause you problems?"

Paba sipped his tea, a taste he'd never acquired. Giuliani's face was raised slightly, eyes calm, resting on his visitor. Two creases on his cheeks deepened when he smiled, but otherwise the sallow skin was unmarked. Only the backs of his hands betrayed his age, with their little rash of hazel pigmentation. Long, perfectly manicured fingers used the tongs in a silent ritual to slip another slice of lemon into the tea. Paba had heard they'd throttled Raúl González in the bad old days, when death was a gesture of total power, and its demonstration was guaranteed to reinforce authority upon wavering sympathies. His eyes, not his hands, asked the question now.

"The world is no longer ideal, Mario. I've had to sub-contract the work to local people. Working underground in sand and rock. We couldn't find that sort of labour here."

"Just as well. I understand young Scarfi came home in a box?"

"Unexpectedly."

"And unexplained." The voice was soft, inquiring, and critical. With Giuliani there always had to be explanations. Paba didn't have any, only the sense not to rely on evasive stories.

"That's why I asked to see you. We've never had any concerns over Prato. Nobody's putting the word out about a change of ownership. Police have issued some names they want to interview. Small time operators who wouldn't have got the drop on anybody."

"Someone got the drop on us, Fausto?" Giuliani said.

"But no one local," Paba replied. "If the police are in on this, their operation's not being orchestrated in Tuscany. Blowing away a piece of our network wasn't accidental."

"So it would seem. Somewhere else then. As these things disturbed me, I made some enquiries to see how they affected our interests. Like Florence, there's nothing coming out of Rome. Yet we're out of pocket. We need to do something about that. A loss of credibility otherwise, Fausto. Somebody must know something. Start looking a little closer to home. My father always said, when there's trouble, look and see who you're in bed with."

"Capagli? No, he's strictly small time."

"I wasn't thinking of this man Capagli. I meant, sharing your bed. The woman you spoke of. What's her name?"

"*Signora* Morning? Margaret."

"Ah! Not just *signora*. Margaret. Now that strikes me as a liability. When they smell good, Fausto, they're not doing you good. They get in the way of business. Sometimes, they get into the business. Makes things untidy. Better be rid of her."

"You're mistaken, Mario. We needed to watch her. Where she went, whom she met. That's how I know she keeps to herself. She smells good, as you say, but that's a common trait in a woman."

"Yet, you thought her worth the attention?"

"Initially."

"So, exactly where does that leave us?"

"I'm not sure we can salvage anything from Prato. No one's discovered the inserts, which would make them the most incompetent policemen in Italy. Still, we'll have to relocate. Perhaps Arezzo. It's on the *autostrada*."

"Well, how do you propose dealing with these people who've pushed us out?"

"I can't be everywhere, Mario."

"Your job's to be everywhere. Taking care of everything, Fausto."

"In that case, Mario, I'll need Romulus and Remus."

Giuliani shifted in his chair. He picked up a biscuit, snapped it in two, eating one of the halves slowly, never taking his eyes off Paba's inquiring face. Giuliani wiped his fingers on a napkin, putting it carefully aside.

"So do I, Fausto. So do I. I'm not forgetting they recently helped you sort out a little matter in Rome. Really, you should have organized someone for yourself by now."

"I organized Romulus and Remus."

"Ah! The special relationship." Giuliani nodded. "I was forgetting. But you weren't on your own then, were you? You were working directly for me. They remained behind when you moved up, and out. I seem to remember it was a proviso; making sure you could handle yourself, without any monumental props. You succeeded. What's so different this time?"

"This time I'm not in Naples. Here we'd know which baby burped. Up there, we wouldn't even know if one had. We've a lot of money tied up without sufficient security."

"You've got a lot of money tied up. In the form of a loan I remember?" Giuliani reminded him.

"Exactly, Mario. But dead, means you'd be a long way out of pocket."

Giuliani became dismissive. "Who's talking about dead? Such a morbid subject for a nice afternoon. Now then, I don't see enough of you, Fausto. You're always too busy making money. Phone me next time you're in town, and we will, I promise, make a visit to Capri."

Paba knew his appointment had finished. He stood up, looking down at Giuliani, crisp, sartorial and receding on top.

"Where they smell good Mario," he suggested.

Giuliani pondered on this for a moment, deciding whether the comment was intended as a slight. He decided otherwise.

"They feel even better, Fausto. Treacherous situation to find yourself in. Nothing more dangerous than a woman who smells good, and feels good. You have to be careful not to lose your head." He cast a knowing smile at Paba. "You'd better talk to Romulus and Remus. They may be free now. Make sure they haven't left anything untidy behind, which I'll be left to tidy up. This growing old. You take exception to everything. Clear up your little feminine problem. Don't you leave anything untidy behind either."

He didn't stand up, shaking Paba's extended hand sitting down. Paba knew that he hadn't over-pleased him with his request for Romulus and Remus. Giuliani didn't like sharing the props of his establishment with anyone. He was getting old, and Paba noted, he was getting careless.

"Exceptional times, Mario."

Giuliani waved him away.

-oOo-

Paba returned to the Via Toledo, this time not looking into the climbing alleyways of the Spanish Quarter, turning right beneath the Post Office, a huge edifice to Fascism in white stone and towering glass dominating the Piazza Matteotti. For a moment he hesitated as though making up his mind to go on or not, before moving away to traverse the streets towards Santa Chiara and the intricate lanes of Spaccanapoli.

Here, among the crowded decaying splendour of mediaeval and renaissance palaces, glimpsed through grimy frescoed arch ways, he found the tight narrow alley he was heading for, bridged by houses on either side, forming in their covered length the last resting place for rotting prams and abandoned cars. Its steeply cobbled path ran down to a matching vault housing a vegetable stall, damp from leaking drains and tended by aged crones piling high the empty wooden boxes of their trade. Paba did not descend so far, but stopped at an entrance with the top part of the door half open, allowing a view of what might have been a cavernous sunken sitting room. It served nearly all the domestic needs of a large lady wrapped in a maroon coat and a woollen headscarf, sitting on a stool, steadily ironing through the huge pile of linen next to her.

She looked up as Paba's figure blocked the weak light that added nothing to offset the dimness of the bare light bulb over her work. She stopped, putting down the iron, searching in a loose pocket for some spectacles.

"I can't see you. Come down here. No more pressing until tomorrow. Leave it if you like."

There were three steps down into the room paved in a rough stone. Paba descended, coming into her vision.

"Paba," she commented in tired resignation. "Have you come all this way for me to press your shirts?"

"No one pressed them like you, Rosella."

"Where do you send them now, then? To a fancy *lavanderia*? Somewhere where they'd complain about all the blood I soaked out of them in the old days. Enough to resurrect Ultimo Vincenti if I'd saved it all."

"Yesterday has long gone, Rosella. Only tomorrow matters now."

"I can't see much of the future, so the past appeals to me. Once, spectacles lasted for years. Now they last no time at all."

"You should have your eyes properly tested. I told you I'd pay."

"And I told you I'd never take your blood money. Not yours, nor those sons of mine. You made them Paba, if not in your likeness, then to your will. They jump when you say jump, and kill when you say kill. They killed Vincenti because he disagreed with Giuliani, Ultimo because he was soft on me. Sons. I should have aborted the pair of them. Sat in a bath, and overdosed myself on quinine."

"Such things don't work, Rosella," Paba said impatiently. "It's better for malaria than miscarriages, and not much good at that either. Better you didn't go to Rome in the first place. Getting yourself laid by some Slovak bear that flattered you. How can women be so stupid?"

"I was pretty then," Rosella said defensively.

Paba shook his head. "Don't live in the past."

Rosella folded the shirt she'd been ironing. "The present isn't much. No, not anything. But if I don't sleep at night, I can blame the garlic. Not like you, dreaming about nothing but arranging another visit to hell. Who do you see there? All those dead clients, Paba? How many will they find in the book when Saint Peter calls your name? You'll end up in the flames with them. You mark my words."

"And then what will you do, with no one to hate?"

"Forget you. Knowing you'll never come back." She

paused thinking about what she'd said. "I never thought I'd have to say that. You cared for me when no one else would. When I was no use to anyone. Just rags in the lane. You tell me? What was the point of bringing those boys up? One on each breast."

She cupped them with her hands, lifting them up inside her coat. "Remember? Milk to sustain life, so they could live to take it away. Where's the sense in that?"

"Ask a priest," Paba said, disagreeably.

"*Mea culpa.* What did you come for?"

Paba's voice softened ominously. "They're thoughtful boys, Rosella. If it's the thought that counts, it's a shame that so many people, in thinking, are thoughtless."

"I don't want to think. I iron to make a living, so I don't need to beg for your tainted lire." She shuffled away his comment.

"Very well. When Romulus and Remus appear, I'd like them to contact me. Not at the office. They have another number. They're to keep trying until they reach me. I don't want them to come to the office either, frightening everyone. Give them the message."

"Have I an option?"

"Yes, you've an option. One where I'll break your arm in such a way you won't even be able to press a cigarette paper. Tell them, Rosella. Save us all the trouble having to watch you back out on the streets, banging a begging bowl."

Paba stepped out of her vision, becoming a grey blur, then just a faint shadow at the doorway before it became a transparent square of light again.

Rosella shuddered, picking up her iron to begin pressing a sheet. Paba, she knew, would be as good as his word. She shuddered again. If not better.

Chapter 37

Sandquest took his drink from the waiter, initialled the member's card, settling deeper into the leather wing chair, heavy with the odour of stale cigars. Straightening the newspaper, he shuffled the pages, before turning to the business section at the back.

A short, younger man came into view over the top of his newspaper. Sandquest lowered the paper on to his lap, which the man acknowledged with a gesture, making his way across.

Anthony Farrington was a voluble, astute and successful barrister. His wife Sally, being a long-standing friend of Rachel Sandquest.

"Hello, Arthur. When are you off?"

"Tomorrow."

"Lucky old dog. Escaping this shocking weather. Forecast's even drearier. Those long range thingumabobs say there's worse to come." Farrington slumped into a chair opposite. Stretching out his legs, ruefully studying his lizard skin Trickers dampened by the weather. "What we need is control, effective control."

"Crowd control, birth control? What sort of control, Tony?" Sandquest asked.

"The weather, Arthur. Haven't you got boffins working on that sort of thing?"

Sandquest smiled. "Ordering the elements, you mean?"

"Why not? These sceptered isles, come tropical paradise. Might do wonders for the presently stagnant property values," Farrington commented ruefully.

"Ah, yes. Rachel mentioned you were putting your cottage on the Fal up for sale."

Farrington grew serious for a moment "Damn shame. Love the old place, but hacking down the A30 to pull on the wellies every weekend, palls after a while."

"You could go out to Tuscany. Can't be raining in Chianti now, surely. Sally tells me you've performed wonders with the place."

"Sally has. All patchwork though. Should have gutted the lot. We're offloading the cottage to pay for a new roof.

314

Damn beams would blow away if you puffed too hard. Sagging like an old bed. Chestnut beams that arrived with Lelio Sozzini, who reputedly had the house built at some time or other. What does it matter? Roof will cost a fortune."

"Price will have gone up since this Sozzini," Sandquest ventured.

"Dare say," Farrington agreed. "Anyway, damn fine theory, Positivism, especially when it comes to chestnut beams. Recognizes only positive facts, you see. They rot. Not much good saying they last four hundred years when you've got to shell out umpteen thousand pounds to renew them with only thirty-five years left in the celestial bank. Positivism is it."

"Enjoy the benefits while you can," Sandquest concluded.

"Not on, old boy. Shut up for the moment. No central heating. June before I go out again. Get the windows open, warm air circulating, and you're back to business in a few days."

"I understood Sally went out to Tuscany last week?"

"No chance, Arthur. Sally's holed up in Blairgowrie with her sister, who's giving birth to another prime Aberdeen Angus. Number five. Nothing to do in the cold winters up there, that's the problem. I spent Christmas and New Year once with Sally's parents. Dog of an old house. Still had Victorian plumbing. Bath was three feet deep. Never enough hot water to fill it up. Terrible experience. Chilblains, coupled with the onset of alcoholic poisoning, due to the old boy's version of Atholl Brose. Never again. Haven't been to the place in winter since. Sally dutifully trundles up for filial duties half a dozen times a year. Not much fun now her younger brother's playing soldiers in the Yemen somewhere, making bundles of money for his old age."

Sandquest leant forward across his paper. "I could have sworn Rachel said Sally was in Tuscany?"

"Oh, I imagine she intended to be. Old prune can't get enough of the place, but this new sibling would have put the Kai-Bosch on that idea. Funny how Sally and I never produced a sprog, while her *pater familias* produces them at a drop of a hat. We're both biologically sound,

315

apparently, but Sally didn't want to be messed about by any of those fancy tricks they get up to these days. I was game, but she's got to do all the work, so I let her decide. Sally reckons Scottish condoms are like kilts, open at both ends. Haven't worn one for years."

"Which haven't you worn?"

"Kilt, old boy. Rubber Johnny's are like putting a mac on when the sun's shining."

Sandquest smiled, but remained thoughtful. "So, Sally never went to Tuscany at all?"

"Your conversation's a bit single tracked. What's so important about Sally and Tuscany?"

There was a moment's pause before Sandquest drew back, settling once more into his seat. "I wondered, because Rachel's dragging me over to Florence for some concert. You know I'm not too *au fait* with the chatter of those musical buffs. Sally's something of an expert on musical matters, playing the piano and violin. If Sally came along she could prop up my side a little."

"Rachel does the same, old fellow?" Farrington reminded him.

"Without a doubt, but she's always darting off arranging concerts, meeting people, busying herself with organizational matters. Treats it like a convention. Leaves me to fend for myself. Feel a bit like a fraud really."

"Doesn't sound like you. Out of your depth. When's this concert?" Farrington asked.

"Berlin for a couple of days on my own, then as soon as we return from South Africa. In one door and out of the other. Hit the ground running. Ten days or so," Sandquest replied.

"Hmm! Well, all the grunting and groaning will be over by then. Sprog'll be in the swimming pool I wouldn't doubt. Might be possible. I'm wrapped up in this Stardust case, so that counts me out. Most of these pop stars are such dilettanti, Arthur. Wouldn't know a plagal cadence if they heard one, yet they're arguing the toss over musical property rights."

"You're an old wag, Tony."

"So they say. In any event, I'll mention the idea to Sally. Are you coming up to dinner?"

"No. Not tonight. I'll just finish my drink, then back to Maidenhead."

Farrington rose, nodded to Sandquest, and wandered off in search of the dining room steward.

The lines returned round Sandquest's eyes as they narrowed slightly. He wasn't prepared to speculate, or jump to conclusions why Rachel was alone in Tuscany.

More of a concern was the outstanding matter of Livia Wolfe. Hastings seemed to consider the matter closed. But where was the absolute proof?

Picking up his drink he stared into its golden depths, watching bubbles from the ginger ale rise smoothly, breaking the surface with miniature eruptions. At this point, he recalled, Prinn had a villa somewhere in Tuscany.

Chapter 38

Outside, a damp pigeon perched unhappily on the narrow window ledge. Hart tapped the glass. It cast a beady orange eye at him before deciding he was less trouble than the weather. Ignored, Hart placed his hands behind his back, staring morosely into the distance. Finally, returning to his desk he took up a buff file, slipped the cord, folding back the leaves.

Flicking the intercom switch, he raised his voice. "Maurice. Can you come in here?"

The door opened almost immediately. "Good morning, sir," Tate greeted Hart politely.

"That depends on whether we've heard from Commander Prinn?"

"Afraid not. Last contact from Italy was on Friday. I brought the draft of Mr. Eldon's case file up to date before the weekend. On your desk this morning, sir."

"I've been through it." Hart closed the file, handing it across to Tate. "Reads like a third rate thriller."

"Imaginative, sir?"

"Stick to the house style, young man. Too many ex-officers have slipped into publishing lately to make me feel comfortable with one developing a nice prose style in my own department. As for Eldon, considering he's an economist, he lacks a sense of budgetary discipline. Creative faculty running on an overdraft. Not helped by you. Where did we find the camera he requested?"

"Boscombe Down, sir. Chief Inspector Gower mustered one up for us. Ministry boffin friend of his in the photographic section had a spare hanging about in a grounded Canberra. Quick loan, little interest."

"Not Jewish are you, Maurice?"

"Yes, sir. Family's Roman Catholic at the moment."

"Hmm," Hart sighed. "We trust all this effort's worthwhile then. Favours beget favours. Type up your report. I'll sign it. That'll be all."

-oOo-

Tate was busy avoiding affectations and long sentences

318

in his report when his office door opened.

Easing himself into a chair, Hart fixed an interested eye on him. "Right, you've got my undivided attention."

Tate stopped typing. "On what, sir?"

"Your observations on Sandquest. Reference this inquiry."

"Department, or Mr. Eldon's file, sir?"

"Operation Necropolis I know standing on my head. Elaborate Eldon's line on him for me will you? All this new stuff must fit in somewhere. Don't want it growing weeds, do we?"

"Pretty thin at the moment. All his data is based on reasoned observations without coming to any conclusions. I don't think he's convinced yet that Mr. Sandquest's an influential link in his own line of inquiry, so not very helpful to ours. As Mr. Sandquest's an important private collector of the Etruscan period, Mr. Eldon is of the opinion that acquiring pieces of great historical value and quality in this field remains extremely difficult. He also added the commercial difficulty, given the draconian priority of the Italian State. Anything decent would hardly surface through dealers. Therefore, having unlimited amounts of money would be of little advantage unless the buyer had exclusive access to an unrecorded and previously undiscovered find; the sort needing a large investment in illegal excavations. There, Mr Sandquest would be a fit but, according to Mr Eldon, it appears that Brizzi may have been looking for another partner. Reason not known. If he'd come across Sir Maxwell and Finetti, then given the potential wealth of a site probably located under the castle, and the possible criminal activities of Sir Maxwell, he might have seemed a more acceptable associate than Mr Sandquest. That, of course, may not have been agreeable to Brizzi's original partners who would, understandably, be eager to eliminate any disagreeable arrangements he was making behind their back. They're a rough lot, quite capable of a little homicide, and Blain's demise has all of Nightingale's modus operandi, except..." Tate fell silent.

Hart grunted. "Except what?"

"Except that these partners were quite capable of

319

disposing of him, in house. No need to spend bundles of cash on a specialist. Which is why Mr Eldon considers Nightingale might have eliminated Sir Maxwell Blain for a quite different reason. If he was setting himself up to ease Mr Sandquest out of something it may have had nothing to do with this Paba at all. By the way, there's a picture of Paba in the Swiss photo index with Filipp Sokolov, a computer scientist who worked for a criminal organization in Moscow on encryption technology. He was gunned down a year ago by Chechnyan gangsters."

"Shouldn't have mixed in bad company." Hart eased himself out of the too small a chair. "Well, mustn't be too hasty though. All these hypothetical clues littering the place like bloody bankrupt companies."

"Anything else, sir?" Tate asked.

"Yes. Raise Chief Inspector Gower, and send him in to me."

Returning to his desk Hart picked up his pipe and commenced the elaborate ritual of cleaning it. On the second pull through of the riffler Tate knocked, putting his head round the door.

"Bit of a puzzle that, sir. Can't quite interpret your final statement. Hypotheses being like bankrupt companies?"

Extracting the by now fuliginous pipe cleaner, Hart gave the pipe a gentle blow over the ashtray before looking up. "Liquidation, Tate. If they don't have any collateral, then they have to be liquidated."

"Ah, yes, sir. I see." Tate dubiously acknowledged. "Chief Inspector's on his way up."

-oOo-

"Take a seat, Sandy," Hart indicated. "The paperwork's arrived from your Swedish ferry trip."

"Micro-dot was it?" Gower asked.

"Hmm! One millimetre negative inserted into the garter ribbon of the tartan sock. Tech' department tells me Sapunov must still be using the brass tube microdot camera he learnt under the Soviets. Heath Robinson, but effective."

"Doubt if he could afford pukka equipment," Gower

commented. "Bit of a give away if he approached the wrong people to acquire it. At least he could have made his own in safety."

"Just so. One supposes they've stopped looking for him now. Who can tell?" Hart opening a folder, withdrew a sheet of paper. "I imagine Commander Prinn's hoping he retained a good memory."

"Sapunov's right on top of his game. Completely fooled me," Gower confirmed. "Plays a brilliant hand of bridge, too. I assume you weren't after his knowledge on ferry time-tables?"

"Probably more interesting. The Commander requested anything specifically musical."

"Sounds like he's asking a lot," Gower pointed out. "Not exactly yesterday: retaining possibly insignificant details."

"Everything's still fresh in his memory, Sandy. Reminiscences are all that's left. He'll go over and over the details in his mind. Another item to trade, in case they get bored, and send him back to Moscow."

"He gave me the impression he might welcome going back. A bottle, empty of all its pop. He didn't appear to have made a new life for himself in the west."

"Couldn't answer that," Hart replied. "Political isn't it? They come over for all sorts of reasons. Fear, when they're ordered back to Moscow; loss of the good life at the end of a tour of duty; old-fashioned greed; or in Sapunov's case, disgruntled retribution against his employers for being overlooked. Doesn't matter which. By definition they're all traitors."

"What would the intelligence services do without them?"

"Oh, they'll never be without them, having quite enough of their own."

Gower indicated towards the piece of paper Hart was holding. "So, what did he remember then?"

"The original was encoded. Substitution in Finnish. Which is just up your street." He handed the paper to Gower.

"Knew the old language would be useful one day. Can I write on this?"

Hart nodded.

Gower spent a few moments reading, before writing down his translation between the lines.

"Let's try this: First line: 'Lieutenant Colonel Kalugin always listened to classical music'. Second line: 'Only concertos. No opera'. Third line: 'Rachmaninov, Stravinsky and some others. Memory faded'. Fourth line: 'I recall seeing recordings by the Wiener Philharmoniker and the Gorky State Orchestra'. Fifth line: 'I have no reason to believe he played a musical instrument, though the movements were often for an instrumental soloist'. Stop."

Straightening the creased piece of paper, Gower commented dryly, "Doesn't elaborate much on the 'musical streak' you were telling me about?"

"Pretty flimsy stuff, except for the Gorky State Orchestra," Hart observed. "Sapunov, they say, was a bit of a phantast, very often making things up to keep the ball rolling. What are we looking at here? The Questore's idea of an assassin using this State Orchestra as a cover? One can see it would be useful to hide their comings and goings, especially as they're not an ordinary killer, Sandy. They don't just moonlight on the off chance. A whole battery of gadgets travel with international entertainers these days, making it easy for them to hide the tricks of their trade."

"Excellent place to hide, I imagine. Pass it on to Commander Prinn. He probably wants the information relayed to Eldon as well."

"That's something else I want to talk about. Sapunov's reminiscences aren't the only thing that's got to go to Eldon."

Gower read between the lines. "I'm up to my ears in Cambodian diplomats."

"You'll have to delegate, Sandy. Whole thing's out of my hands. Commander Prinn needs to furnish the department with a plausible deniability option. You're an authorized firearms officer, so every now and again you have to earn your money."

"Didn't you say there was another agent involved?" Gower hedged, hoping for a reprieve.

"I did. The Italians are using someone called Vergellesi because, like Eldon, he doesn't belong anywhere."

"There you are then. If he's at the stumps with Eldon, between them they'll notch up a good innings."

"Sorry, Sandy. On your bike. Arrange a very early flight with Miss Veronica. Embassy will furnish your hardware."

"This group's not supposed to be dangerous. If I wanted to be shot at, I'd have joined the army," Gower grumbled.

"Force has moved on from blowing whistles, Sandy. Far too many political overtones attached to some of these cases. Since Moscow jumped over the wall everyone's making up their own rules. A deeply messy game to be in. I don't approve of the department straying from its honest commission, but complain as much as we like, the Commander wants Eldon out of there, walking on his own two feet. At the same time, I want you doing the same, so treat this seriously. Keep on your toes, and on task."

"Take it as read. Let's hope I get to use the return ticket. Any instructions on Nightingale?"

"Commander Prinn says you're to play by their rules. Which I take to mean - if absolutely necessary - as near to a corpse as you can manage."

Chapter 39

The misty drizzle had begun to clear by the time a black Mercedes Benz taxi reached Rahnsdorf. Following the road towards a lake the driver turned into an avenue of fruit trees, whose gaunt leafless branches did nothing to hide the badly proportioned post war housing that passed for quiet suburbia on the outskirts of Berlin.

At the end of the avenue, a flat, ugly open space trailed away to the water's edge with its perimeter of sycamore trees, providing a plain of solitude that Sandquest, from the back seat of the limousine, viewed with an air of detachment.

The end house backing on to this waste land stood alone where, at one of the dormer windows high on the roof, Sandquest glimpsed the housekeeper peering out, face flattened and distorted against the pane.

Major General Petrov stood at the door in a grey suit a size too large for him, trouser legs gathering in corrugations over his slippers. His tieless shirt was buttoned up in deference to 'worker solidarity', representing a direct contrast to Sandquest's Jermyn Street appearance. If a man needed to make an impression, then Petrov was not that man.

The two shook hands solemnly, then embraced while the driver, an old KGB regular, took Sandquest's small leather grip into the house.

Petrov was of equal height and stature, though his face was slimmer, bearing the grizzled marks of one who had suffered during the journey from his past. He smoked a large hand rolled Cuban cigar, ash endlessly dropping on to his suit.

Petrov held Sandquest at arms length, studying him intently. He was looking back across the years; years that had drifted past in a succession of interludes, broken by acts in a maniacal reversal of the great Russian tragedy. To a person waiting, the historical events of personality cults, five-year plans and collectivization, treaties and accords, glasnost and perestroika, had been worthless symbols of relentless change. Change, he'd been told just recently, was a

324

historical necessity.

As a young officer on the eastern front, Petrov was given the task of interrogating Sergeant Sandquest, picked up by advancing Soviet troops. Colonel Falin, on Konev's military staff, with little time to waste and few trained specialists, directed Sandquest's talents towards specified locations being overrun at an ever-increasing pace. They appeared too valuable to be abandoned to the unbridled violence of Russia's peasant troops.

Whole oceans of history had since passed under the bridge, in which Petrov had achieved considerable status. A Major General and Hero of the Soviet Union, his rise had not been meteoric. Petrov had learnt that to be prominent anywhere under an insane dictator, risked courting an early grave.

Serving for a short period on Marshal Golikov's staff, one of the few high ranking officers to have miraculously survived Stalin, taught Petrov to consolidate foresight rather than familiarity. As chief of Soviet Military Intelligence, Golikov introduced Petrov to one of his successors, Colonel General Kuznetsov, who took him on his staff to the conference at Potsdam. Thereafter, Kuznetsov sent him to various overseas posts in Canada and the United States as the technological aspects of espionage gained momentum, chasing nuclear secrets that had become the pressing target for Soviet intelligence.

With the key traitors in Britain, Petrov was disappointed at not being sent to the United Kingdom, where he might have made contact with Sandquest. Instead, from the United States he found himself posted back to Russia. In Department S, run by Sudoplatov whose plots brought about the death in Mexico of Trotsky, he helped co-ordinate the intelligence being gathered from spy rings. A considerable influence on Petrov, as well as a considerate mentor, he'd suddenly transferred Petrov to Berlin in a minor intelligence role, from where Petrov heard Sudoplatov had been arrested along with Beria, as a co-conspirator. The weeding out of his staff was soon to take place, but Petrov, keeping his head down, was uncharacteristically overlooked.

Recalled to Moscow, under a succession of intelligence

chiefs his prospects improved, and in the less brutal power struggles that followed he came to be promoted to the highest positions in the KGB. As head of the First Chief Directorate he had taken steps to reopen his relationship with Arthur Sandquest. A relationship he could now see, that after all these years, might yet prove extremely complicated to end.

At the moment he was a 'grandfather', according to the quiet couple who lived at the end of the avenue. The husband, a well-known local radio ham, worked for an Engineering firm in Brandenburg, his wife in the local Post Office. They'd quietly let it be known to neighbours that they weren't entirely convinced that they trusted 'the lodger' who worked part time in a plating factory at Muggelheim. Grandfather conveniently became an occasional house sitter.

"You look terrible old friend," Petrov said. "Working too hard; perhaps the in flight food was disagreeable; your doctors are killing you. Tell me, what's wrong?"

"Age overtaking me, Sergei. Just growing old."

"Nonsense. Look at me. Leads fallen out of my pencil, black coffee keeps me awake all night, but give me a stiff drink, a good cigar, and I can play bezique until four in the morning, sleeping soundly until five." Petrov punched Sandquest affectionately on the arm.

"Responsibilities drain a person," Sandquest complained.

"Responsibilities! Responsibilities! Being a big tycoon suddenly doesn't suit you. You've made enough money to pay off the Russian debt, yet you grumble about responsibilities. Think about giving them up, then. Meanwhile, come in and have a drink."

Sandquest caught a glimpse through an open door in the hall of 'the lodger' with headphones, adjusting the wavelength of a military receiver.

Ushering his guest into a comfortable domestic lounge, Petrov pushed him into an armchair, tossing his spent cigar into an empty fireplace.

Pouring two large glasses of vodka, he handed one to Sandquest. "This'll restore your old self. This one, or the next couple of three." He dropped heavily into the chair opposite. "Excuse the living quarters. States never build

326

anything corresponding to a reasonable aesthetic. Kings, yes. Popes, certainly. Commissars, no!"

"You sound like a recidivist, you old rogue," Sandquest said, raising his glass.

"No. Merely a statement of fact. We're getting out, now the GDR is history, you. Place will be spruced up by speculators by and by."

"I imagine. How's business by the way?" Sandquest put his drink down, knowing that the results of keeping up with Petrov's alcoholic ingestion meant a too soon oblivion.

"Still a going concern. That's the nice thing about a family business. Reliable."

Petrov's brother was an academic, like the family business was academic. Having languished through the sixties in a provincial museum, he'd suddenly shot to fame with the publication of a critical survey of modern Russian artists. Most were unknown in the west, where Soviet eclecticism had never materialized, and socialist realism failed to find sufficient favour to be financially attractive. On the strength of this comprehensive edition, Petrov's brother was called to Moscow, receiving a position in the Ministry of Culture where, he noticed, no one had undertaken an audit of the nations treasures. Commissioned to manage an official inquiry, he contrived to compile a handsome alternative audit of his own.

Major General Petrov had been quick to realize that hardly anyone in the west would seriously challenge something that had no recognizable ownership, other than a Soviet bloc museum, whose treasures were virtually unknown to the outside world.

Brizzi's project had slotted in perfectly with this conduit to potential Western auction houses that could handle these emerging items with alacrity, secure in the knowledge that fraud was not yet known to be accompanied by an official rubber stamp.

The need for hard currency exposed the underlying weakness in the old Soviet economy; the dichotomy of choosing to pay for foreign machine tools or foreign sedition, where activists saw little benefit in being paid in roubles. To finance their activities, the security services,

327

having taken to resourcing their own needs on occasion, weren't averse to setting up legitimate business enterprises abroad to fund their agents in the field. The sale of Etruscan antiquities had been stretched to fit such a model. The practice proved more convenient than suffering the tedious indifference to their demands from lethargic paymasters in intransigent departments.

Petrov also had the foresight to see the writing on the wall accompanying Gorbachev's tedious glasnost. Being accountable, Petrov realized, was not good for business. Diversification seemed a more appropriate route to follow.

"Come on, drink up, you." He raised his empty glass, but Sandquest shook his head, leaving Petrov to pour another generous measure for himself.

"I've opened a Swiss bank account, comrade. Somewhere to keep all the profits we'll make."

"Does the Politburo know?" Sandquest asked

Petrov dropped back into his armchair. "Of course. Haven't I a whole department to keep them informed?" He laughed again; a deep rumble, courtesy of the cigars that had become his trade mark.

Sandquest was reminded that it was a passion that gave rise to the rumour he always slept on his back, as it was too dangerous for him to sleep on his side with a cigar in his mouth.

"Nothing on Blain?" the General inquired.

Sandquest shook his head. "Some enquiries were made. Only for appearances sake, I understand."

Petrov pulled deeply on his Cuban cigar. "He should have stuck to corporate raiding; known there were some affairs you don't meddle in."

"Such is the capitalist way, Sergei."

"Not much use if you're dead," Petrov replied, waving his cigar case at Sandquest.

"Such is the communist way, Sergei." Sandquest took the offered cigar. "I was concerned to hear about this Finetti, though. He was a competent businessman. No doubt we shall have to renegotiate eventually for the Verolino. I'm not interested in purchasing the estate myself. An accomplice of Blain you said?"

"Perhaps not even an accomplice. Ha! Sometimes

there's collateral damage. People absentmindedly walking in front of a bus. But let's not spoil our evening with unfortunate details." Petrov flashed a smile studded with gold, downing the remains of his vodka.

Crossing to the sideboard, Petrov transferred a stout box to the table. Pushing polystyrene granules to one side, he withdrew a black amphora decorated with sharply detailed terracotta coloured combatants slaying a Minotaur.

Sandquest took a jeweller's glass from his pocket, examining the amphora from top to bottom, before sitting back in the chair. "Magnificent, Sergei. Attic vases in this condition are rare. Cracked and chipped there are plenty, even from the fifth century." Sandquest shook his head in admiration.

Petrov's smile deepened. "So you're still interested in this gamble?"

"Tempted," Sandquest cautioned. "There's an inconsistency. The piece is perfect, but I'll wager not from the same tomb, not even the same site, as the first century votive head you sent me. You'll need to qualify these matters before I consider the rest."

"You think there's more, you?" Petrov's laugh was even deeper.

"Oh yes. More than enough to fill up a Swiss bank account."

Petrov stabbed his cigar in Sandquest's direction. "You'll have first choice, my friend. I don't need to tempt you. But I have to convince you. Everything must be cleared."

"These are not trinkets being sold by the cartload, Sergei."

"Not trinkets, you. But still by the cartload," Petrov nodded expressively.

"From one Etruscan tomb in Italy? Inconsistencies, Sergei. Given that a tomb can be used over many centuries, there still has to be an artistic and cultural uniformity within it, relative to its location. Only this vase, so far, might have been found in the area of Sorena."

Petrov shook his head triumphantly. "Not an Etruscan tomb, Arthur. A Roman one, belonging to the family

329

Cecina. They may have been of old Etruscan stock, but this Paetus Cecina was a Roman, and something of a collector like yourself, only interested in perfection." Petrov swung his cigar through the air trailing rings of smoke. "They'd made sure it was safe, when later the Franks and Lombards pillaged the area; jackdaws, looting anything that glittered. It wasn't until the Renaissance that a curiosity in things ancient took place. Then they wanted to dig up everything. Buonarroti and Vinci were too modern for the patricians of the time. There was evidence where the tomb was supposed to be, but those who looked weren't to know that the site was once a huge chunk of molten lava thrown up millions of years ago. Eventually, as the ocean receded, the mound was exposed. No one considered that the present green and wooded hill was, and probably still is, anchored to nothing but sand."

Sandquest smiled. "It's a fantasy."

"A perverse one, you. Sometime before the eighth century, a severe earthquake shook the hill free, altering the orientation. A little later the Lombards conveniently built a castle over the concealed tomb, and the site was irretrievably lost."

"Until, you say, Brizzi stumbled on the answer?"

Petrov nodded. "Brizzi worked on the assumption that the tomb historically existed. He considered all sorts of possibilities before settling on seismic movements. After that he combined science, history and the legend to come up with an answer."

"So they have found the tomb?"

"Cecina family tombs, you. Not precisely the one we're looking for. Progress, unfortunately, has also been subject to squabbles."

"Disagreements?"

Petrov blew lightly on the end of his cigar that had become dull, rolling it backwards and forwards. "We're dealing with primitives. There's no logic to them, you. They look like gentlemen, but act like dogs, spoiling their own door-step."

Sandquest pointed to the vase on the table. "What is there to argue about? Such artefacts as these are jewels. Having found such exquisite items, surely it's only a matter of further exploration. Can't they even agree to that?"

Petrov shrugged. "Paba, who you've yet to meet, believes agreements aren't necessary with the dead. Historical or contemporary ones. Perhaps that's why they've only discovered two chambers. He's an impetuous man. Intolerant. I'm told these two chambers are only a part of a series of tombs. They haven't identified whose, exactly. Jewellery from them suggests a female - or a very effeminate man, you!" Petrov roared with laughter, his momentary concern forgotten, coughing on his cigar. "Never mind the cold feet. This is big, Arthur. Bigger than anything seen before. You'll have first choice."

Sandquest, finishing his drink, stood up. "You are quirky, Sergei. I'm coming along for the ride, but I'm not convinced. Footloose mountains. Whatever next. Now, am I to change for dinner?"

Petrov waved his cigar round like a Catherine wheel. "Trying to impress me, you. Well, we will. I've had my uniform pressed. Smells of moth balls."

Sandquest nodded sagely. "So, I suspect, will old Cecina."

-oOo-

Sandquest had not slept well. Either from too much black bread and cabbage, or the constant chills filtering through the blanket on to his spine.

Coming down to breakfast he found Petrov dining on cold sausage and cheese, which he alternated with extravagant gulps of very black coffee. He waved his fork at Sandquest in the same way as he waved his cigar, which at this moment was stuck upright in a bowl of sugar.

"Wonderful dreams, you?" Petrov asked.

"No," Sandquest retorted. "I was cold."

"You're getting soft my friend, as well as old. I recall being here once before, when your finger got stuck to the trigger, your feet went black, and body temperature was down to thirty degrees Celsius. Remember? We chopped off Yakov's gangrenous toes. You vomited while he

331

laughed, either because he couldn't feel anything, or because you had to carry him all the way back to the field centre. Waste of time. They'd have charged him with malingering, and sent him to the firing squad."

"I never knew that," Sandquest said sceptically.

"On the slimmest of doubts they shot you. Best way of eliminating problems. They avoid the practice these days, which is why we have so many. Have a sausage?"

Sandquest declined. "Just some toast and coffee, if I may?"

"Help yourself. It's all ready."

"What you said is true," Sandquest finally agreed. "I'm getting soft."

"Humidity from the lake drifts in if you sleep with the window open," Petrov explained. "You're not a boy-scout any longer. I'll arrange another blanket."

Sandquest let him finish his sausage, and return to his cigar before asking a question.

"Sergei, why don't you get out?"

Petrov finished his coffee, wiping a napkin round his mouth. "Too late, you. Time's finally run out. Life's as tired of us as we are of life. After all, I can sit in the sun, smoking cigars, wherever I am."

"That's a very depressing option," Sandquest objected.

"I'm sorry you're depressed. Being depressed means you're always looking back, contemplating what made you depressed. Becomes a disagreeable practice. Look at us. I make money, and serve the state; you make money and serve Mammon. But they are not the same for us, you. I've never had the luxury of wondering why I'm doing it because I've always been working so hard to hide how I'm doing it. All my life I've been hoarding bricks in the hope that some day I can build a house. No one told me I should have hoarded cement as well. *Ce la vie.*"

Petrov laughed for the first time that morning, his deep, noisy cachinnation shaking his body into a fit of coughing. Sandquest let him splutter to a stop, before pouring coffee into his cup.

There was a knock before the door opened. Handing Petrov a sheaf of papers, 'the lodger' left without saying a word, or glancing at Sandquest.

"Now, my friend," Petrov nodded after the departing

figure, "consider what a wonderful time the proletariat would have with all your wealth."

Sandquest shrugged his shoulders. "That's your Soviet lottery mentality. Socialism. The best things in life are free, they've just cost someone else a lot of money."

"Hah! I refuse to take umbrage. A waste of our time. On to other matters where we can agree. I've already arranged a trip for us when we meet in Florence. To this castle you consider a fantasy. There's also the Gorky State Orchestra to distract you. Varina's playing Liszt. A reception afterwards."

"We'll be busy. I'm looking forward to the concert, as you've probably guessed. I haven't seen her since Rome. How is she?"

"Well. Very well, you. Now then. We'll have fish for lunch."

"Very nice, Sergei. Rather early to be thinking about lunch. In the meantime, tell me more about Varina." Sandquest persisted.

Petrov was dismissive. "You can ask her yourself very shortly. Saves going over the same ground again. It will be all the more entertaining coming from the horse's mouth. Now, I've answered your question, and I'd rather discuss lunch."

"All right. But I still think it's too early to consider lunch."

"Not if you have to catch your fish first. Who knows how long it will take us to acquire a carp or two from the lake. But we have to be sharp, the cook will do her level best to switch them for some ancient dog-fish she's bought on the market."

"Switch them?"

"Oh yes. A *pochouse bourguignonne* won't serve. But we have the legs on her, and insist they're grilled." Petrov laughed with merriment at the idea. "You see, there's more than one way to skin a thief."

"You mean a cat," Sandquest corrected him.

"No, you," Petrov countered. "I mean a thief."

Chapter 40

Eldon had been shaken from his sleep into an unwelcome matins. Vignozzi had conjured up a useful contact, explaining that the best time to see him, probably the only time he would see them, was early in the morning.

They drove down into Florence from the heights above the Bobolino, past the gaping Porta Romana, crossing the Ponte Amerigo Vespucci to park near the United States consulate.

A light mist still clung to the opaque waters of the Arno beneath the Lungarno embankment. It was flanked by undulating masses of sober renaissance palaces that appeared uninhabited, and fettered by an eerie stillness. Their hurried footsteps echoed sharply on the flagged pavement.

Reaching the Piazza Goldoni, Vergellesi indicated they cross to a newspaper vendor deep within his kiosk, muffler wrapped tightly under his chin against the chilled air rising silently out of an almost motionless river.

The vendor took Vergellesi's money for the Corriere della Sera. "Twenty two degrees in Messina," he said ruefully.

"Somewhat hotter in hell," Vergellesi suggested.

The vendor spread his arms. "So, it's twenty three degrees in Palermo. Better than ten in this old gilded lily."

Vergellesi laughed. "How do we find our way to the Teatro Pergola?"

"Not open yet." He leant forward on his newspapers, crossing the fingers in his mittened gloves. "Sicilian are you?" He'd caught Vergellesi's accent.

"Syracuse."

"Ah! *Bella città. Bella.* From Messina myself. That's why I take an interest in its temperature. Sicily is almost Italian they tell me when I'm at home."

"A little like saying, Calais is almost English," Vergellesi suggested.

"True. Actor are you? Not a singer. Your voice's too

flat. Auditioning?" He hardly waited for an answer. "In my opinion, actors spend too long staring at words. I ask you, where's the beauty in letters? Horrible little squiggles. Look at them," pointing to the folded newspapers. "Hundreds, and millions of them. Nothing original in any of them. Tell me, how long is it since someone created a new letter? There you are. Gone as far as they can with letters."

Vergellesi smiled. "Just the Pergola, if you can manage?"

"Take a taxi. It's a long walk."

"Nice morning for a walk."

"Are you sure you're a Sicilian?"

"Only in the winter."

"As you like," the vendor laughed. "The streets are long, like a Florentine's nose." He pointed out the way.

Vergellesi leant over and shook his hand, before following Eldon towards the Vigna Nuova.

"Give my regards to Broadway," the vendor called after them. "Follow the directions for the Duomo."

In the dark narrow street of high, forbidding buildings, fashionable shops supported gloomy apartments that soared upwards until they nudged the overhanging tiles. Far away, in the great triangle of avenues binding the historical centre, a growing murmur of traffic encased an island that had begun to stir - pavements washed in front of shops, brooms billowed overnight dust out of doorways, upright bicycles with commodious baskets wheeled out of shadowy, arched passages.

To avoid this activity they walked in the centre of the street.

A wider, brighter thoroughfare led them eventually to the Piazza di San Giovanni, deserted except for a workman on a rusty cycle, struggling to light a cigar stub against sudden gusts of wind.

The cathedral, an edifice in white marble, its green and red bands stained by the damp of winter, drew them round the north east side.

They found the turning they were looking for past an unkempt and exhausted Ospedale Santa Maria Nuova, its long, dismal, dark arcade filled with grimy frescoes.

335

An aroma of coffee drew them across the street into the Bar Zenobi, heady with the yeasty smell of *panini* and the smoky odour of roasted Arabica.

At the far end of the bar, on one of the round chrome stools clad in a garish plaid material out of harmony with inharmonious surroundings, sat a large man in a grey tweed jacket, and a tight black beret, reading the Corriere della Sera with a frown more furrowed than the Tuscan *calanchi*. He should have been out of place, but at that hour, he was very much a part of the place.

Vergellesi sat down on the empty stool next to him, placing his newspaper conspicuously on the counter.

The frown under the beret deepened as he looked at the paper, then at Vergellesi, before glancing at Eldon and returning to his own newspaper.

"Dr Rosso?" Vergellesi asked quietly.

"Hmm?" he answered, almost inaudibly in a drawn out sigh, without looking up.

"Dr Rosso," Vergellesi persisted. "May I have your attention?"

The man lifted his eyes from the newspaper. "I don't take clients anymore. Common enough knowledge."

"I'm not a client. My name's Vergellesi."

"Is that supposed to be significant?" He'd turned back to his paper.

"You'll remember my father."

Rosso turned his round doleful face with its baggy cheeks fully towards Vergellesi, fixing him with pale, slightly protruding, glossy eyes. "Your father was he? Yes, I have reason to recall a magistrate called Vergellesi. He gave me five years."

"He gave you three years for money laundering. You were arrested as you left the court. Another judge gave you a further two years for providing fraudulent documents," Vergellesi corrected him.

Folding his newspaper, Dr Rosso pushed it into his jacket pocket. "That was a long time ago. Another world. I heard he was dead?"

"Yes. As you said, another world."

"Time traveller are you?"

"In a manner of speaking. They haven't stopped the clock on him, if that's what you mean?"

"All life's like an hour glass," Rosso, argued. "Certain friends came to ask a favour when they found out I was here. One favour for a life they said. I didn't need to be told it was mine."

"My father," Vergellesi answered, "felt you'd let him down."

Dr Rosso raised his finger to the bar man. "Your father was an Olympian. A detached observer of the miserable mass of corrupt officials who shared his temple. One day he decided to get rid of all the rotten apples. You have to be big, even to think that way."

"Apparently he wasn't big enough," Vergellesi suggested.

The bar man placed a black coffee and a brandy in front of Dr Rosso.

"Now there's a thing," he mused. Finishing the coffee, and contemplating his brandy. "He was more than big enough. That appeared to be the general opinion. Family opinion. His death didn't fit in with anything."

"Anything anyone was aware of?"

"Who knows," Rosso replied. "The only thing I can state with any certainty is it wasn't his enemies. And he had a lot of enemies. But I knew them all. On the outside, then on the inside. No one whispered, no one boasted. Not a bubble surfaced anywhere. No murmur, no back slapping. He just died, for none of the reasons anyone had in mind for him being dead."

Eldon, growing tired of standing, slid on to a stool on the other side of Dr Rosso.

"Am I being strong armed?" the older man asked, cautiously.

"This is my associate. Rex Eldon."

"English. Not colonial. I can tell. International group is it?" Dr Rosso studied Eldon carefully, knowing who he was. Nothing had given him or Vergellesi away. Some people can sum strangers up at a glance; the inner profile that isn't on show. Dr Rosso was one of those people. He knew that whatever they said would be some way from an answer. They were in the sort of business that made them hide behind the truth, sandwiched between somewhere and a lie.

"International interests," Vergellesi qualified. "Vignozzi

337

advised us to speak to you."

"Did he give a reason?"

"Only that we didn't need one. I suspect he imagined you owed him a favour."

"I don't owe anyone a favour. Not Vignozzi, nor your father." He turned to Eldon reproachfully. "Perhaps I owe you a favour?"

"No." Eldon shook his head. "I was hoping you'd provide us with a reason where we would owe you one?"

Dr Rosso turned back to Vergellesi. "Now this young man I like. Pity you didn't tell him that when you owe an Italian a favour it's as long as a *Luganega* sausage."

"You can trust Dr Rosso, Rex," Vergellesi vouched. "In another life, he was a Procuratore Generale, on one side of the law, his family on the other. They required favours, like all families. An Italian obligation. So he was able to assist my father while he served his time. Not against his family, of course. That wasn't necessary. They were all helped into another place during one of the underworlds more bloody dynastic squabbles."

"My brothers were too ambitious," Rosso rejoined. "Overreached themselves. If you wish to step into someone's shoes in Sicily, it pays to make sure they're not still in them." He stopped to inhale the aromatic vapours from his brandy for a moment. "My father, wisely, had other ideas for me. Vignozzi, Vergellesi's father and I, studied jurisprudence at the same time. First good company I'd kept in my life. Vignozzi was making legal waves even then. Old Vergellesi sailed along on top of them. Guess I fell overboard. Now I'm a journalist and theatre critic. Vignozzi's brother's a publisher, giving me a hand every now and again. You must be a collect ticket he's sprung on me?"

"If you can help the family, you can help us."

"They're legitimate clients seeking professional guidance," Rosso countered. "If you can argue a point of law then it's a bad one. That's why advocates have a vested interest in an infinite number of laws."

"A sound financial philosophy," Eldon conceded.

"Doubtful," Rosso contended. "How many jobs for philosophers do you see listed in the newspapers? Did you read law?" he asked Vergellesi.

"Biology."

"Biology!" Dr Rosso's shoulders shuddered gently. "You and the philosophers. Your friend here, he's also interested in plants?"

"No. He read economics."

"Biology and economics." Dr Rosso looked from one to the other slowly, shaking his head. "It may be, or it may be the smell of an over ripe *pecorino*. Botanists you expect to look healthy, with all that fresh air, but they never do. Economists are usually pasty worms, with hardly enough strength to lift a calculator, or roll a spliff. That makes you a unique pair. How do the English say? Square pegs in round holes."

"You never know where the wheel of fortune will stop," Vergellesi countered.

"Soldiers of fortune more like. Let's start again. You said Vignozzi sent you?"

"To save us time and trouble."

"Time I can help you with," Rosso muttered. "Trouble I leave to others."

"Time then. The Gorky State Orchestra. They were here two years ago, on a European tour. Now they're on a tour of Italy. Soon, they'll be back in Florence."

"This is a contemporary orchestra, Vergellesi. Not the old cultural ensemble, full of fags. That's all gone. Swept away in the need to modernize. Musicians can walk out these days, without anyone trying to blow their heads off."

"But historically, a traditional state orchestra." Eldon broke in. "Packed full of old hands, cosseting their pensions."

"There are some new names," Rosso replied thoughtfully. "But you're right, not entirely different either. However, it would be a mistake to believe that they were all waiting for the opportunity to take up careers in the west. They'd probably be more privileged at home than struggling against the sort of competition met at auditions over here. I'd say there's still more than a nucleus of original musicians. Why do you want to know all this?"

"That's a long story. Let's just suppose," Eldon continued, "that the Russians had an agent who needed a perfect cover abroad, flexible enough to allow them to slip away with the minimum of fuss. An international orchestra could provide cover for such a person?"

"Likely. In that case you'd be looking for a technician. Time servers to a man." Dr Rosso finished the remainder of his brandy, mopping his lips with a large handkerchief pulled from a pocket. "They were awash with technical personnel, I remember. Far too many for them all to be legitimate." He stuffed the handkerchief back.

"What about the maestro?" Vergellesi queried, ordering an *espresso* for himself, and a *cappuccino* for Eldon.

"In what sense?"

"Collaboration."

"There is that." Dr Rosso confirmed, nodding he'd have another *espresso* and brandy. "Maestro Terekhov's an old hand, tried and tested over many years. Reliable. A person who could well be amenable to the wishes of the state. Hiding someone among the technical staff would hardly be difficult."

"You're sure we can give the musicians a miss? What about principals? Are they working all the time?" Eldon asked, adding two tilts of the self-regulating sugar shaker to his coffee.

"They only have one. The pianist, Varina Jehmlich." Dr Rosso whistled softly in admiration.

"Is she Russian?" Vergellesi enquired, searching for some brown sugar amongst the bowl of small packets in front of him.

Dr Rosso viewed both their actions distractedly. "From Poland I understand. Sweeter than the pair of you. A phenomenal talent. When Nietzsche spoke about placing women on a pedestal, he was thinking about Varina Jehmlich. Beyond the reach of we poor mortal souls."

"You were quite taken by her then?" Eldon enquired, smiling at an older man's fantasy.

"Oh yes. But to your point about agents," Dr Rosso added seriously. "I remember someone accompanied her. Male; young; athletic. He carried her music, possibly her bags, but only in his left hand."

"Security?" Vergellesi asked.

"I wouldn't know. He was like her shadow. Discreet;

340

always in the background. Even during the concert he was hovering at the back of a coulisse somewhere."

"Perhaps an understudy?" Vergellesi tried again.

"Hardly an understudy. He carried a gun. I caught a glimpse of it in the mirror once, during the interval, when he was washing his hands."

"How old would you say?" Eldon asked.

"About your age. Thirty something."

"And fit," Eldon remarked.

"He filled his clothes well, and moved easily. It might be possible to get a look at some photographs. Bobo Serafini is the theatre's professional photographer." Dr Rosso looked at his watch. "We'll catch him if we hurry. We're old friends, Bobo and I. Sometimes he supplies the photos for an article I've written. *Andiamo.*"

Vergellesi paid for their drinks.

-oOo-

They walked a few blocks to the back of the Santa Maddalena dei Pazzi, finding the studio of Serafini sandwiched in between *persiane* shuttered apartments, up a steep flight of travertine steps, on the first floor.

Dr Rosso knocked, easing himself through the narrow door into the outer office. Another door opposite opened immediately, revealing a short trim man in a white dust coat holding a thermometer in one hand.

"Rosso, *ciao,*" he said. "Bring yourself in. I have half an hour, and then I throw you out. Who are these?" he asked, noticing Eldon and Vergellesi. "Since when have you brought me any business?"

"These are not business, Bobo." Dr Rosso introduced them. "Now don't give me any trouble. These are friends of mine needing a little help."

"Whatever." Serafini gestured a welcome.

"We need to look through the records in your filing room, that's all. Some you took two years ago."

"Imagine how many photographs I take every year?" Serafini remonstrated. "Two years ago. It's a lifetime. I need to know the month, as well as the week? Title would help."

"May. Gorky State Orchestra."

341

"Now that's providence for you. Fat lump of a conductor hogging the photo calls. Needed retouching to stop him looking like a mediaeval sultan. Ha! I've sent along the publicity shots from that session to cover their appearance next week."

"No need to disturb yourself. I can look after it," Dr Rosso replied. "I was thinking in particular about the reception photo's. Single lens reflex work they used to get so upset about. The discreet ones, before you got *sbronzo* on all that free *spumante*."

Serafini threw an artful look. "Record shots you mean. Well, help yourself. You know my files, and how to use the decimal system. Media's number six in the key list, and then use the sub keys. Contact print's on the data sheet. If you want a detail, I'll have to run it off from the negative." With that he flourished the thermometer, disappearing into the processing room.

"This way," Rosso directed, leading them into a brightly lit room filled with filing cabinets round a large table set in the centre. He didn't take long to locate the Teatro Pergola. Serafini had also cross-referenced the type of performance with its title.

Dr Rosso withdrew a bulky file from one of the cabinets, taking it to the table, along with a magnifying stand. The data sheets for the Gorky State Orchestra were clipped together. He shuffled through them, found what he was looking for, placing the sheet under the stand to enlarge the negative size contact print.

In the centre of the photograph, talking to a bald man in a dark suit, stood a tall elegant woman with a refined narrow face. Black hair, cut in a short masculine style, emphasized the sleek beauty of her bone structure, demonstrating the sort of hauteur only people too long in the company of sycophants and adulators can develop. Her long slim hand gestured towards a man standing next to her, just a little taller, athletic as Rosso had described, with a long jacketed suit, worn over a white open necked shirt. He wore steel framed spectacles too near to his eyes; hair close cropped into a dark stubble.

"This is Varina Jehmlich, I presume?" Eldon queried.

"Does she look like your agent?" Rosso asked, peering over his shoulder.

"Not exactly what I had in mind, but as you said, she would certainly stay in it. Her friend though, is different. He's not part of a network, that's for sure. That's not for this man, Piero." Eldon tapped the glass.

"Could he be the principal agent; an assistant handler supervising other agents?" Vergellesi suggested.

"No," Eldon said. "This is not a man who hangs about on street corners, or sits in darkened rooms with a camera, rustling curtains at the window. They might as easily frank your library book. The dynamics of this gentleman are quite different. He's trained for a very different line of work."

"Then you don't think he's Jehmlich's shadow?" Rosso enquired.

"Nothing so tedious. Splendid she is, but such an occupation is no more enthralling than a security guard entrusted with the care of any work of art. This man is in no way bored. He isn't indifferent to the subject, or her surroundings. Whatever she's saying is of as much interest to him as it is to her. He's the sort of man we've been looking for. One of them."

"You think there's another?" Vergellesi queried.

"Most certainly. An older man. Miss Jehmlich's shadow is too young to fit our profile of Nightingale. What would he have been doing twenty odd years ago sipping coffee in a Luanda bar along with MPLA chums?"

"Can you hazard a guess where this other man might be?" Vergellesi inquired.

"That's what makes it hazardous. The observers being observed. He may not even be with the orchestra, rendezvousing at predetermined locations with this agent. He could be part of a reconnaissance party, gathering strategic information on the target, or providing logistical support. All I know is that Miss Jehmlich's shadow will identify us should we appear too frequently near the Theatre Pergola. Just as he stands out, so will we to a practiced eye. Who's the short man?"

Dr Rosso peered closely at the photograph. "I don't know. Mass produced look about him. Not Italian. Does he appear in any of the other shots?" He shuffled through the remaining data sheets, replacing the contact print under the magnifying stand with another. "Here he

343

is. Talking to the conductor. Slavic features. His clothes look like they come from a GUM store. Possibly a musician."

"I think not," Vergellesi said. "Pavel Aleshin. I know him slightly."

"He's with Russian security?" Eldon asked.

"Not at all. I last saw him in Ravenna five years ago, at an international conference on epidemiology. I was delivering a paper on risk assessment procedures for genetically modified organisms. His paper was on synthetic drugs. I believe he works for a Russian scientific research institute. There was a rumour circulating that he had biochemistry interests. Probable, given the machinations of past Soviet research programmes."

"That may well fit in," Eldon reasoned.

"What have you in mind, Rex?" Vergellesi asked.

"I have in mind your father, Piero, along with an associate of Blain's in America. Both died exotically due to the ingestion of toxic substances. The sort of organic material, developed by such a chemist."

"Could be why Pavel's so interested in what's being said," Vergellesi added.

"Of little interest now," Eldon replied. "Whether our shadow is still with the orchestra, is quite another matter."

"Dr Rosso will recognize him," Vergellesi volunteered.

"It could be someone different. How would I know?" Dr. Rosso protested.

Vergellesi disagreed. "Even with long hair and a beard you'd spot him at once."

"I might be dead at once. In a moment you'll tell me I owe it to your father. *Dio Mio!*"

"Well, don't you?" Vergellesi asked.

"The truth is like the Campanile in Pisa, Vergellesi. Conversely, your father liked to see things straight. Even his friends. He was a hard cross to bear. If I owed him, I believe five years of my time was enough." Dr. Rosso switched off the magnifying stand, returning the contact print to its file.

Vergellesi felt as though he'd pushed a paper boat too far into the stream, watching the current draw it away

344

from the shore, out beyond his reach. He looked deep into Dr. Rosso's baggy face. Once you'd ventured too far down some roads it wasn't worth turning back. Dr. Rosso had settled for a life without complications. Why should he complicate it? The way back would take too long, and all that was, long departed from this earth. The young people grown old, the old buildings made young, memories so faded they resembled nothing but ghosts. There was nothing to rekindle. Not thoughts; not feelings; nor debts that never were. There was nothing for him among the dust of his recollections, nothing he needed to make a space for.

Dr. Rosso shook Vergellesi's hand. "Only the present is our memorial." He gave a wry smile. "Your father said that. 'Only the present is our memorial. The past no one remembers, the future no one knows'. More or less, he was right. He would have taken care of the present for me, so I guess I can do the same for his son. Buy your tickets at the box office today, before they sell out. I'll keep an eye open for this man with long hair and a beard."

Chapter 41

"I suppose the Hotel Ammanati's still the same?" Sandquest enquired, still a little stiff from an uncomfortable, but short flight, from Heathrow airport.

Rachel assured him that she'd booked his regular suite. Gripping the hand strap over the door, she angled her face so as to watch the developing shape of Florence through the car window.

"You'll be meeting Sally at some time?" Sandquest's voice woodenly interrupted her thoughts again.

"I'll phone her the minute we arrive. She'll probably come over this evening, if that's all right?"

Sandquest nodded in confirmation.

Releasing the strap she let her head rest on the seat back, watching the bright, neon-studded industrial world on the short *autostrada* give way to tree-lined avenues, at one moment tangential, then parallel, in an accelerating geometrical chaos.

Round them the traffic grew denser as the vehicle dropped under the railway bridge, skirted the Fortezza, then drifted away again, when they left the main thorough-fare. Weaving their way through secluded parks, and suburban quiet, they finally drew into the hotel's courtyard.

The manager was as effusive as ever. They had employed a new chef; having discovered that any length of time in catering eventually meant 'tired', and that modern chefs had to be continually reinventing themselves to remain successful.

Sandquest, still feeling the exhausting effects of his recent South African visit, was happy to accommodate the new chef. He didn't think Sally would mind, either. The manager beamed encouragement.

Left alone in the sitting room of their apartment with its recherché English interior of chintz and reproduction Hepplewhite, Rachel, in her usual competent fashion, took charge.

"Now," Rachel instructed, "You're too tense. You need to loosen your muscles. A warm shower and then a good rest. Doctor's orders. I'll phone Sally to see if she'll drive in from Cerbaia a little earlier, so we don't have such a late evening."

Taking a large leather diary from his bag, she handed it to him so he could refresh his memory on their appointments for the next few days, while she finished unpacking.

Dropping into a chair, Sandquest studied the pages. The fair amount of time allocated there to his own amusement, interested, as well as suited him. There were things he wanted to do; and not a few others that needed to be done.

When Rachel had left the room, he slipped out of his shoes and trousers, and lay down on the bed. Closing his eyes, he reflected that South Africa had been awkward. Too much talking, cajoling, making promises that he hadn't the faintest certainty could be kept. Promises of promises, more like. Von Moller's appetite had been whetted on a mountain of promises.

There had been local setbacks in Sorena again. With the entrance to a tomb opened, the circulation of air had dried out the natural humidity inside the chamber, giving rise to sand slides and subsidence. A matter of days, Petrov had said, before a visit could be arranged.

Frustrated, he swung his legs over the side of the bed, sitting there undecided for a minute. Picking up the handset of the telephone, he stared at the tiny holes in the mouthpiece, feeling the need to be speaking to someone, organizing something. Replacing the handset, he lay back down, listening instead to the sound of his own breathing.

A faint sound disturbed his thoughts. As there was nothing else to distract him, he concentrated on the source of the sound, which he thought was a murmur, then not a murmur. Lacking consistency and continuity, the faint noise resembled the inarticulate, subdued mumble of speech. He seemed satisfied with his deduction. A voice talking somewhere.

He sat up quickly, easing himself off the bed. Crossing to the window, he gently opened it by sliding it behind the motorized metal shutters. He leant over the windowsill to catch brief snatches of Rachel's voice, fragmented temporarily by the noise of traffic below.

Then a distinct click as she rang off. Perhaps Rachel was telephoning Sally to inform her of this evening's arrangements, or confirming their restaurant table, like the efficient secretary she'd once been. Or perhaps it was none of those things, only a rehearsal for betrayal.

Pulling on his trousers, he struggled a little with the buttons. He was getting old and out of fashion, disliking zips in the same way as he hated being cheated. And somewhere about the third button, he knew, deep down, that he was being cheated.

-oOo-

Rachel walked out of the hotel into the afternoon sun. She stopped, closing her eyes for just a moment. Though comfortably warm on her eyelids, it was not quite yet a hedonist's sun.

Opening them, she glanced back at the hotel, shrugging aside her faint sense of guilt at having left Sandquest sleeping off his heavy lunch. They had bumped into an old friend in the Via del Corso, argued pleasantly with him about where they should eat, before ending up back at the Ammanati, with too many courses, and one bottle too many of a heavy Taurasi for the system to cope with.

Round the corner, when out of sight of the hotel, Rachel hailed a taxi, taking a bumpy ride across town to the Boboli Gardens, unaware of the white Alfa Romeo that had swung out behind them.

The taxi driver dropped her off close to the Bacchus gateway, at one side of the Pitti Palace, where she passed into the famous hillside gardens laid out for Cosimo I. Approaching the top of an avenue curving between dark rows of holm-oak, she found Prinn sitting on a bench reading 'Animal Farm'.

"Dates you, I think," she observed, catching him unawares. "I can't believe you still had a copy lurking somewhere, so it must be new."

He stood up, placing a leather marker between the pages and closing the book. "Why do you say that?" he asked, kissing her gently on the lips, then her eyelids, while holding her tightly.

"Nobody of our age ever reads 'Animal Farm', Nicholas," she said. "It's a book of our youth."

"Arguing the virtues of revolution in Mr. Jones's farm?" Prinn responded lightly.

"You are not a born-again radical."

"Suggesting I've already died as one, which wouldn't be true. I'm reading it because Ettore's nephew is. His English teacher, I understand, has a sense of humour. So, in case I'm asked for an opinion, so should I. We can walk a little." Prinn kissed her again and slipped his arm through hers. They walked slowly up towards the Belvedere.

"I suppose you've heard about Livia?" Rachel asked.

"Yes," Prinn nodded. "CID came over to ask some questions. I suspect they wanted me to witness how efficient they were."

"Such a shocking and tragic incident. Arthur was badly shaken, having found her a most valuable PA. He relied on her a great deal, but he says life must go on."

They walked a further few paces in silence. "He's right, Rachel. Life doesn't stop to commiserate with the dead, who haven't any use for memories anyway."

"I'd rather not discuss it any further, but you know something, Nicholas, I think Livia was not quite as we imagined."

Prinn stopped, drawing Rachel round to face him. "In what sense do you mean?"

"Once, I found her in Arthur's office late at night. There was a miniature camera, and I think she might have been taking photographs of something."

"Good Lord, why didn't you mention that?" Prinn asked.

"Because you were with me."

"I was with you?" Prinn was taken aback. "Surely I'd remember, Rachel. When was this?"

"When my car broke down. Remember. You took me home, but I had to collect Arthur's address book first from his office."

"Oh, yes, I recall going up to Arthur's office - but Livia wasn't there."

"No Nicholas, you didn't actually enter Arthur's office. You remained next door, so Livia and I were alone in there. We didn't even speak. An immediate understanding between two deceitful women."

"And you didn't think to tell me?"

"What could you have done that wouldn't have been a disaster, Nicholas?"

"Very little," Prinn conceded ruefully.

They continued walking in silence for a few minutes.

"Do you think I should have told the police?" Rachel finally enquired.

"Yes, you should have told them. I'll need to consider the implications myself, now that you've told me."

Misinterpreting the thoughtful lines on his face as indicating a fault of her own, she squeezed his hand, holding it tightly against her.

He pulled a smile, but said nothing, looking straight ahead as they walked.

Holding him close, she had a strong sense of his presence: the slight stoop of his shoulders alongside her own; the stray wisps of hair behind his ears, abandoning themselves into curls; the tanned clean-shaven face. She studied these small traits with intense interest, trying to understand the chemistry that bound them together. He was such a quiet, private man.

They reached the top of the rising ground that afforded views of the formal gardens below, scattered with ancient statuary. A cypress tree blocked their view of the river Arno from the bench.

"I'm not going to wait for ever, Nicholas," Rachel said flatly, twisting the ends of her silk scarf together. She followed the flight of an aircraft above her head, its white vapour-trail feathering out behind it against the blue sky. Departure, destination, and times of arrival: clear-cut, without complications, all arranged beforehand. Not like a life.

Prinn leant over, kissing her doubts away.

She pushed a stray lock of hair on his forehead back into place. "You are a patient man."

"Every person is a combination of two people: the one they are, and the one they aspire to be. But I don't dwell on the impetuosity of the latter, so you see it as patience."

Moving closer to him, Rachel felt his arm tighten

round her. She let her head rest on his shoulder, her soft auburn hair brushing his cheek, filling the air round his face with the fragrance of perfume.

Prinn had just become aware of another man sitting on a bench some ten metres away from them. Alone, he held the newspaper in front of him, staring into it as though it was a window he was peering through. There was something about him that Prinn recognized instinctively: the dullness of an actor performing too long in a box-office success, and now playing out a part where any conviction had become a function stripped of its sincerity. There was the same dead look of indifference that had become a jaded expression giving the man's face a permanent scowl. What was he doing there? Who was under surveillance now? Which of them, and for what reason?

The man shook his newspaper folding it together, rose without looking in their direction before moving quietly off down the path. Prinn watched him until he was out of sight.

"Which personality do you want to be?" Rachel enquired by his shoulder.

"Which one do you want me to be?" Prinn replied.

She shook his arm at the evasion. "I'm not familiar with your Mr. Hyde, so I'll have to take you as you are."

Prinn laughed. "Would you like an ice cream?"

They took a long walk across to the Porta Romana in the remains of high city walls, through thick traffic and dense fumes, and bought their tickets from a tobacconist before catching the first bus as far as the Piazza Goldoni, walking back towards the river and a *gelateria* only half full of tourists gushing on the experiences of their invasion.

Sliding along the bench, they gave their orders to the waiter.

"Will you be all right for a moment," Prinn asked. "I must make a phone call."

Rachel nodded.

Their order arrived while Prinn made his way to a telephone at the end of the room. Rachel watched him put some coins on the counter, feed them into the slot, dial a number and pick up the handset. He buried his head inside the Plexiglas dome, in an effort to escape the noise.

His conversation was brief. Questore Vignozzi told him bluntly that Vergellesi was playing hard to get. Ditto, Eldon. After the fiasco in Prato, and the suspected murder of Cecotti, Ruggieri had been told to keep a watching brief, but that was all. No one had any idea what they were up to, except they'd become very slippery. There were too many threads now, and they couldn't be expected to grasp them all. He was clearly not happy.

Prinn paid their bill on his way back. Squeezing in on the end of the seat, he stirred his *espresso* and finished it in one gulp.

"Are we in a hurry?", Rachel enquired.

He lowered his voice. "I'll see you this evening, but I may be a little late. I suggested to Arthur that we'd dine at Il Lupo before the concert, so I'll phone and instruct them to go ahead and serve you. It's not a problem. I'm sorry, but something's cropped up that needs my attention, that's all."

"You will be there, though?" A note of concern had crept into Rachel's voice.

Prinn smiled, squeezing her hand. "As soon as I can be."

Prinn then ate his ice cream, leaving Rachel to her own thoughts.

Heading outside, they crossed the road and peered over the wall into the Arno. The river's sulky khaki colour looked pathogenic. Rachel stepped back a little, as though distancing herself from its vapours. A lone sculler with his back to them passed under the Ponte Vecchio heading downstream to the Ponte Carraia and the weir beyond, his two light oars dipping lazily into the turgid liquid.

"I must leave you now," Prinn said. "If I don't, you'll tell me I'm possessive."

"Are you?"

"Most certainly." He put his arm round her waist. "Let's find a taxi."

On the corner of the Palazzo Ferroni, Prinn's second attempt at hailing a passing taxi was successful. Rachel held him by his lapels, kissing him overlong for the taxi driver, who was bending the terms of his licence by stopping there. Prinn let her in, tapped the roof and it swung away back down to the Piazza Goldoni.

A little further back, and parked awkwardly against the kerb, the man in the white Alfa Romeo, clicked the cap back on to the telephoto lens of his camera.

-oOo-

The belch had a satisfactory tone. Gas in the intestines was the predictable result of Sandquest's lunchtime intemperance. He had long been over indulgent with a system that had lost its power to process large quantities of food. There were those who preached temperance as a means to overcome this excess, but having enjoyed himself, he was cognizant of the fact that such enjoyment for a man of his age had an undeniable urgency.

Slipping out of his dressing gown, he pulled on a pair of trousers, walking about in his socks on the smooth marble floor. Pouring himself a whisky, he opened his cigar case and rolled a Montecristo between his fingers, listening to the whisper of its leaves.

That was to be the full extent of his enjoyment. Sighing, he replaced it in the tube, resigned to smoking just two a day which, according to his doctor, was two too many. For a man unfamiliar with compromise, this new regime had not come easily.

Settling himself on the sofa placed at the foot of the bed, he picked up a magazine, seeking to use such distraction as a means of appeasement. Soon beginning to tire of this unequal battle, he was rescued by the telephone ringing. In broken English the receptionist informed him that there was a gentleman wishing to see him. A *Signor* Pellucci.

Putting on his jacket and shoes, Sandquest descended in the lift. *Signor* Pellucci had the hot, sweaty look of a man who had been in a hurry to get there. They nodded to each other without speaking, and Sandquest guided him into the hotel bar, where he ordered another whisky for himself and after inquiry, a still water for his guest. They sat just inside the door out of sight; Sandquest waiting patiently while Pellucci finished drinking his water.

"You've carried out my instructions?" Sandquest enquired.

"Just as you asked: no more, no less." His English was fluent, with an American accent.

Pellucci was not his real name. As an ex-Mossad intelligence officer, Shlomo Levinson should have been destined for higher things. After the near disastrous Yom Kippur war in 1973, he was too publicly critical of Goldi Meir's incompetence, paying a heavy penalty for his outspoken attack on Labour Party shortcomings. Relegated to a security backwater, with his talents under utilized, he came to the conclusion that his resignation was inevitable.

He'd subsequently carved out a niche for himself by undertaking surveillance work, beside other less legitimate commissions, for commercial interests. Erratic employment, it nevertheless paid well when it ever came his way.

From an inner pocket of his mackintosh, Pellucci withdrew a plastic container holding a roll of undeveloped film. "Thirty-six frames. Twenty of those I would consider conclusive proof of the subject's actions towards each other, with regard to your instructions."

The result was half expected. Surprisingly there was no ache, as he'd prepared himself mentally for the bitterness he now tasted. The whole matter had come to represent an unfamiliar door that had shut behind him on a place he would never visit again. Those things he had trusted were now mere shadows of loyalty, as easily erased by greed as honesty was by desire. He would not gloat, but neither would he have pity when it came to the final reckoning.

"Thank you. You're quite sure you weren't observed?"

"No, I'm not sure." Pellucci gave a faint smile. "Is it important?"

"Probably not." Sandquest gave a disinterested shrug. "But if you were, I have a strong suspicion who it might be."

"You know this man?"

"Yes, I know him. He's clearly a libertine born with too much money."

Pellucci shook his head in disagreement. "No, not a man given to peccadilloes. If you have to know your enemy, then know this man, Mr Sandquest." He rose, tightened his mackintosh belt, thanked Sandquest for the glass of water, took the envelope and was gone.

Chapter 42

"*Madonna!*" Vergellesi exclaimed. "The myth of God and Babylon made real."

"Hmm!" Eldon pulled a face. "And scattered abroad to meet up in the foyer of the Teatro Pergola."

Filing past a noisy, animated crowd, they entered upon a soft murmur that rose above half-filled seats to the tiers of empty boxes in whose secluded recesses Florentines had come and gone, in an air of mystery and gossip, for centuries.

Gradually, as the seats began to fill, the murmur gave way to an insistent drone, the disturbance of bodies more hurried as latecomers struggled to gain their places. Eldon idly studied the jumble of people passing down the aisle.

Vergellesi, more attentive to their surroundings, leant towards him. "There's an interesting thing. Our Mister Sandquest occupying a box - but who's the other man?"

Eldon's eyes swept the tier of boxes and stopped, not on Sandquest, but on Commander Prinn.

When Prinn had informed him that he'd be in Italy for some months, leaving him to liaise with Hart, he'd assumed Italy meant Rome. Remmick had later informed him it meant Sorena. Then Prinn had paid a visit to Margaret Morning. Now here he was, in Florence, associating with a man that would rate high on any list of suspects. Eldon, becoming aware of his developing 'policeman's nose', had decided that something, undoubtably, possessed the odour of Escároz about it.

"That," Eldon apprised Vergellesi, "is Prinn."

"Really?" Vergellesi remarked. "Cosmopolitan-looking gentleman - not exactly what I imagined. Seems more a product of the indulgent air of Portofino, than the crucible of a great metropolitan city. Doubtless someone else with a variety of disguises."

"He seems to have a lot to say for himself," Eldon noted.

Vergellesi offered an educated guess. "Well, such an urbane gentleman would know all about theatres. He'll be explaining that the architect Tacca constructed

La Pergola originally in wood, breaking with Palladian traditions in order to accommodate the mechanical scenery and love of spectacle that had been developed into something of an art under the Medici. The art of illusion, Rex, is not only an Italian characteristic. Now, which of those two men do you think will chance to be something of a sorcerer's apprentice?"

Eldon glanced at his colleague. As the situation they found themselves in became more oblique, his concern had grown in proportion. They weren't dealing with an old enemy who played by the rules, where even violence had its own principles and procedures. Heroes, Eldon was well aware, were not necessarily blessed with a long and prosperous life.

The lights momentarily dimmed, giving rise to a final rush of latecomers before they faded, leaving only footlights as illumination.

The curtain rose on the orchestra with first and second violins facing the rostrum, directly confronting the audience. A concert grand piano flanked them, its polished black-lacquered top reflecting stage lights and an upside-down world of musicians. A burst of applause acknowledged the entrance of the conductor.

Of medium height and unusual girth, Terekhov walked clumsily and with short steps. His body broadened out like an inverted bell, supporting this gross structure with all the tottering effort of a weightlifter. He wore formal dress, designed into a baggy shape that made no attempt to fit anywhere, but hung vertically from the shoulders, suggesting neither bodily curve nor shape, only mass. Above, a slack-jowled face rolled down to his chest with only the smallest suggestion of a chin. A tight-lipped mouth, designed for heckling heretics, rested momentarily quiet under a surprisingly slim nose.

Terekhov took one too many bows causing his pale face to glisten with the effort. He stepped on to the shallow podium, tapping the music stand expressively. The musicians became poised, ready on the edge of the music as they waited for the baton to make its rhythmical gesture. Instead, his left hand guided an almost inaudible sonority of notes from the violins and

357

flutes that gradually swept over the orchestra in an exalted progression of sound.

-oOo-

As Terekhov brought the second movement to a close, he turned, stepped down from the podium, bowing loosely to the audience's rapturous applause, his arm sweeping across the orchestra to direct their enthusiasm in that direction, bowing again to re-direct it back to himself. As the applause subsided, he faced one wing of the stage.

A tall, slim figure walked over to the side of the piano. Her close-fitting red dress emphasized a particular gait that seemed to be somewhere between stroll and float but might have been, for all intents and purposes, a glide. Vivid red lipstick gave emphasis to her olive-coloured skin; severely cut, perfectly styled black hair emphasized the long, dignified features from which dark eyes gazed out impassively on an audience overawed by her dramatic presence. Her face, slightly turned towards the darkened space in front of her, appeared unmoved by the eulogistic reception she was receiving. With a brief bow, she took her place on the piano stool, adjusted its height slightly, then sat without moving, looking straight ahead, hands neatly folded in her lap, while Terekhov stepped back on to his podium. A small trace of a black lace slip arched between the side slit of her dress, pulled apart by her left leg positioned under the stool. The restless hush in the auditorium sank into an expectant stillness.

Slowly her right hand came up and hung motionless above the piano keys, her eyes closed, waiting for the intensity of emotions to well up and descend; so that when it happened, it seemed as though her whole body was being forced through her fingers on to the keys with a crash, flaying the piano as though she needed to tear notes from it in an intense passion that made the frequency of sound into a solid entity capable of being sculpted into three-dimensional forms. Her hands, like manic birds, beat themselves against the dense wall of music, her left leg levering the power inside her forward through the piano. Pitching each note in rapid succession, they quivered in the air to form an integration of sound, gathered together notes and harmonies in a euphonious whole that rose into the dome above, rolled down before the tiers of boxes, and enveloped the stunned audience beneath.

-oOo-

Vergellesi ordered two hot Cynars in the Bar Zenobi, carrying them over to where Eldon had found them seats. The bar was busy with its evening clientele: younger and noisier and spending less, their value only in their rapid turnover. When there was nothing to do, or nothing to say, constant movement was their only reaction.

Eldon nodded in the direction of Dr Rosso who was perched on a stool with his brandy and coffee, watching Milan play Naples in the Italian league on a small portable television at one end of the bar. He was not involved in the game enough to resent any intrusion.

"Something else again, wouldn't you say," he remarked, without looking round, as Vergellesi put an arm on his shoulder. "More kinetic energy in Miss Jehmlich than you can find in both these teams put together.... *Dio Cristo!*" he groaned, as a Milan striker powered a shot over the bar in the face of an open goal. "They're paid fortunes, yet those *cretini* still need a script. Did you notice?" He tapped his temple. "Not like Miss Jehmlich. All up here. No music sheets." He slid from his seat, gesturing dismissively at the television.

Eldon slid over, making room for him. Responding to some pre-arranged signal, a waiter brought another *espresso* and brandy.

"Well?" he enquired of Eldon.

Eldon nodded. "I have to agree with you, Doctor. She was something else again. Beautiful, a genius.... and something else again."

"Of course. Such women are always more than mere Euclidian geometry would have us believe, but I have a feeling you'd settle for the natural physical dimensions of the lady. I've been busy since they arrived in the city two days ago. People talk to journalists, very readily

359

expecting to be questioned, giving you their whole life story without much pressing. That her minder's still with her, I could see for myself. That he doesn't accompany her all the time was a little gem of knowledge I picked up from an oboist who tours regularly with the orchestra. Apparently he's her manager, this *Signor* Kopolev, though in Russia he's hardly ever seen."

"I wonder what else he manages?" Vergellesi mused.

"Their privacy apparently. Only Jehmlich and Kopolev get to go by car, and a coach ferries the rest about. You still don't ask questions or complain about equality in Russia, it seems. Just be grateful someone's paying."

"Managers would be of little interest to the conductor," Eldon noted thoughtfully. "They wouldn't really mind if he was there or not. In any case, Thursday, when the orchestra's not playing, would give Kopolev an ideal chance to slip away. After that, they've one performance left, in Turin, before they go home. Turin has no form, so Florence must be where we place our money."

"Evens would be nice," Vergellesi muttered.

"*Certo*," Dr Rosso agreed. "I found out something else, by the way. It appears the oboist I spoke to isn't enamoured of Miss Jehmlich's manager. Finds him over fastidious, by all accounts. The water in the dressing room has to be just so, there mustn't be any flowers, room temperature no more than twenty degrees. He made a great fuss about some missing wine that inadvertently hadn't been unloaded from the pantechnicon. Everything subject to criticism. He's got too used to living it up in the west, I imagine. Not only geniuses can be exhausting it seems."

"Must have been very special wine," Vergellesi queried, "to make such a fuss?"

"My source didn't elaborate - just thought that Kopolev was excessively pernickety. I've managed to get myself invited to the theatre reception this evening. He might turn up there, along with the chilled champagne."

Eldon studied Dr Rosso's podgy hands cupping the large wine glass that served as a brandy ballon. "I think it might be a good idea," he finally decided, "if you could discover the name of this very special wine Kopolev gets so emotional about."

Chapter 43

Taking Rachel's arm, Sandquest guided her up the wide flight of grey marble steps that rose under a frescoed ceiling, to the reception room prepared by the theatre.

Given Pellucci's disclosure on his wife's infidelity, it was a concern he did not feel, yet provided a mask for that which he did.

Prinn followed at a distance, escorting Rachel's friend Sally, a short animated blonde, whose skirt was a trifle too short, and a little too tight.

Looking down on him from above, Rachel decided Prinn was looking tired, the skin round his eyes creased into little lines of concern.

"I hope the champagne's not warm," Sally commented as they drew level.

Sandquest patted her bottom, remarking drily, "By the time we get to have some my dear, it probably will be."

He handed their invitations to the usher before passing into a salon of Roman proportions, already full of exquisitely dressed people, only some of whom were admiring the cinquecento mannerist decorations adorning the ceiling above. For the most part they were admiring each other, or intent on acquiring another glass of champagne, relieved to taste the real thing rather than a passable *spumante*.

A diminutive waiter, with tray held aloft, passed by, allowing Sandquest and Prinn to pluck two glasses each from above his head without stretching their arms. He was ferrying them towards a large table set before two arched windows. The obligatory niche between them held a creamy marble statue of Minerva over whose arm someone had draped the Russian flag.

"Looks like a waitress in a topless bar," Sandquest registered acidly.

Among the dark suits and designer dresses, Prinn nodded to familiar faces he had grown up with, though remaining nothing more than acquaintances. Guests or hosts of a moment, or many moments; part of a privileged club that moved in concentric circles from one place to another, each with a nucleus of people round which the circle moved according to some unknown formula. Perhaps it was organic: a natural occurrence in which, as far as Prinn knew, there were no radicals, though perhaps a great number of eccentrics.

The magnificently haughty Marchesa Pulema drew him towards her, kissing him, with evident joy, noisily on both cheeks. Prinn introduced her to his party with that strict formality the Italians universally maintain, while the rest of the world is sliding towards indiscriminate familiarity.

Before these introductions, the Marchesa had imagined Prinn must have done the unthinkable, and secretly married. Prinn had recognized the censure by the look in her face as she eyed the voluptuous Sally with an extremely prejudiced eye.

He had first known her as Tiziana Garipoli, the girl next door - except that wasn't strictly speaking correct as there were three small farms in between the Villa Lazzi and her parent's estate. The 'Indigeni' - natives - as his father ambiguously referred to them.

They were now looking at each other from opposite ends of a bridge. At sixteen he had broken her heart, she announced with the selfsame look. She, in her turn, had broken his heart when she met the young Pulema. The ebb and flow of young desire was as dark and as deep as the entire ocean of human emotions.

She eventually held him at arm's length, declaring that he was looking tired. "Don't you agree, he's looking tired?" she asked Rachel critically, as though the fault might be hers.

Rachel passed the comment off lightly, avoiding rather than affirming the Marchesa's thoughts. "Not too tired, surely? Nicholas is on holiday, after all."

Sandquest viewed this interest in Prinn silently from behind his mask. The pseudonym Pellucci had hinted at something more, something he should have asked him to flesh out rather than just let him walk away with a cheque. Prinn was a man who wore his sheep's clothing with a natural familiarity. He looked good in them, they looked right on him. He was there among the flock, assuming no one had spotted him.

The Marchesa slipped her arm inside Prinn's with the

sort of determination indicating she had other things in mind. "I'm going to borrow him for a while," she stated in a tone that requested an affirmative. "Nicholas, you must come and meet my daughter. She has grown up a great deal since you last saw her."

Prinn imagined so, in the sixteen years since he'd attended her baptism.

"You can tell me if she's even more beautiful than I was at her age. After all, my father was a handsome man, was he not? A little rakish in his youth, perhaps, but decidedly grand later on. You remember of course that Mother was a great beauty. Am I right? Of course, there you are: one's progeny are just the combined sum of their parents, don't you agree?" Without giving Prinn time to answer, she moved on to comment in a depreciatory way on the existing and subsequently acquired members of her conjugal family. "But as for the Marchese, I didn't consider he came from an attractive family. In fact I believe he was the only half presentable child they had. Fortunately clever at least. I seem to remember his sister as an extraordinarily ugly child."

"Prinn managed to protest. "I recall his mother was a fine-looking woman."

"Ah, yes," the Marchesa conceded reluctantly, "that one. In a dark Calabrian sort of way, she was. Very dark, and handsome, I would say, rather than distinguished. You must look closely and tell me if, unfortunately, there are any capricious genes apparent in this young lady. All my family were fair, as you cannot have forgotten."

Prinn laughed at her affected nonsense. "I know already she will be beautiful."

"Well, perhaps, though a trifle Latin, I think. Come."

Prinn allowed the Marchesa to lead him away, still questioning the possibility that her daughter was as appealing as she rightly should be.

Rachel watched their progress for a moment, as they stopped two or three times to engage people they knew before becoming enveloped by the crowd. Prinn looked very much at home in this company, striking all the right notes, in a world within a world.

A soberly dressed young man took over the space Prinn had vacated, introducing himself as Vladimir

363

Kuznetsov, public relations officer for the orchestra. He addressed himself primarily to Sandquest, but continued to smile indulgently at the rest of the group. He explained how they had met before, in Naples, where Sandquest had sponsored a performance. Maestro Terekhov had missed meeting their benefactor, and would like to take this opportunity of expressing his belated gratitude for such generous support.

"Step forward the interpreter," Sally muttered to Rachel.

"No, no," Kuznetsov replied, overhearing her. "The *maestro* has good English - providing one speaks clearly."

In the centre of the room, the *maestro* was holding forth to several admirers on Liszt, and the ache in the Hungarian soul that permeated so much of that nations music. Terekhov had a flat nasal voice that, like a tank, demolished intonation for the sake of sheer weight. No one would step in front of his conversation without seriously considering the consequences. He was assertive, pugnacious, and unattractive, while extraordinarily knowledgeable and pedagogic.

"To conduct an orchestra performing the works of Liszt, you have to adopt the style of the great operatic conductor Erich Kleiber, by using the stick technique on every musician. They must not be allowed to lapse too far into the maudlin. Attention, Tap, tap. They must not be permitted to lose the precision and clarity you need to achieve. The violas were particularly temperamental this evening, did you notice? Attention, Tap, tap." There were murmurs of assent, but whether their agreement was based on critical awareness or just obsequious ingratiation, Terekhov would hardly care. He was combatant, preferring to engage with his audience rather than ease his argument past a friendly face.

The conductor dabbed at the little beads of sweat glistening on his forehead, with a large handkerchief. His small eyes, under bushy brows, darted from face to face in constant exploration of traces of any doubt regarding what he'd said. Therefore, he quickly noticed Sandquest bearing down on him, and broke off his discourse abruptly. Extending both arms as though welcoming a long-lost son, he embraced Sandquest warmly. The huddle of dismissed sycophants fell back, finding themselves no longer a prop to his deliberations.

"You're without a drink, Mr Sandquest. Let us seek a remedy for that instantly." He steered them towards a long brocade-covered table, leaving Kuznetsov to beckon one of the attendants.

Beneath the table, a small refrigerator kept the maestro's Krug perfectly chilled.

Sally was impressed, but as soon as they were presented with a glass flute of the pale golden effervescent wine, she found herself being drawn quietly by Rachel out of the maestro's circle.

Thus detached, they found themselves quickly engaged in conversation by an unlikely American couple who, on hearing their English, were relieved to elaborate to someone else on their enthusiasm for the orchestra. Listening for a few minutes, but finding herself not fully enthralled by this eulogy, Rachel's attention was drawn back to her husband, noticing a change in the people surrounding him.

Maestro Terekhov was no longer under the manipulation of Kuznetsov, who'd seemingly melted away to be replaced by Varina Jehmlich's tall figure in a black evening gown. Only the bright red lipstick added a touch of colour to her elegant presence. Terekhov stood slightly apart from them, in the posture of a bystander, while Sandquest himself seemed to have become the centre of the conversation. Rachel saw him emphasize an opinion with a gesture of his hand, endorsed by the smallest flicker of a smile on the pianist's otherwise dispassionate face.

Rachel's husband was a clever and interesting man, but music was not something he had any particular passion for; neither was he qualified to debate the intricacies of Liszt's epic musical utterances. Yet he was holding forth on some topic that seemed to retain Miss Jehmlich's attention.

Switching her gaze, Rachel now focused on a face whose owner was also listening intently to Sandquest. The close-cropped head loomed over Miss Jehmlich's left shoulder: a hollowed-out face, tight-lipped and

365

expressionless and almost motionless except for its intelligent, attentive eyes.

At the same time, Rachel became aware of his eyes constantly scanning the room beyond Sandquest, not focusing on the foreground but the background, so that the sweeping trajectory of his eyes, though not looking at her directly, would always keep her in view. The only time his gaze switched to the foreground was for fleeting glances at Sandquest.

She stooped down to make an adjustment to her shoe, and rising again she caught his eye waiting for her, before sliding on to some point beyond. Rachel gave a start - Sally, squeezing her arm as the Americans took their leave, to indicate that it might be time for a refill of champagne, Rachel never took her eyes off the adamantine face as it moved slightly closer to Miss Jehmlich, the thin lips moving almost imperceptibly beside her ear before drawing back to continue its relentless scrutiny. Terekhov drew closer again, rejoining the conversation, so that by the time the two women reached Sandquest he was listening to the maestro describe the relative values of acoustics and how they affected the orchestra.

Being introduced to Miss Jehmlich produced largely a one sided conversation. Polite and considerate, her contribution confined itself to issuing pertinent questions in accent-less English. Any opinion as such, was not something she readily volunteered.

The arrival of Prinn released them from Varina Jehmlich's well-mannered civility.

"Well, what did you make of the Marchesa Pulema's daughter?" Rachel asked him, with real interest.

"Very pretty," Prinn replied. "Prettier still, if she didn't wear such ugly modern clothes."

Sandquest introduced him a trifle tetchily to Terekhov and Miss Jehmlich. Terekhov, noticing Prinn's empty glass turned to Kuznetsov, who'd seamlessly reappeared, and indicated he'd take care of the problem.

"May I compliment you on your magnificent performance?" Prinn addressed Miss Jehmlich. "I can't remember ever hearing so wonderful an interpretation of 'Isle of the Dead'. I actually shivered when Charon was rowing us across the River Styx. Truly, a quite brilliant interpretation."

"Thank you. You particularly like Rachmaninov?"

"I confess rather more than Liszt. I'm fond of all late-Romantic Russian music. Their melodies always seem to capture the essence of beauty and truth."

Miss Jehmlich bowed her head in deference to his opinion. "You have a professional interest, Commander Prinn?" she asked, seemingly picking up on what Terekhov had as yet only thought.

"No, only a self-indulgent curiosity. Just the opposite of a policeman's normal role."

"You're not an old sea-dog then? I assumed it from your rank."

"In another incarnation, perhaps. In this one I'm a police officer with a little time off."

"Time off? I imagine policemen are the same all over the world, Commander - in one way, at least. They are never completely free from the trammels of the law. Here, though in another country, you will continue to think as a policeman. Yes?"

"I suppose that may be so. These traits seem to be inveterate. Force of habit."

"But, it is only natural. If I were to be transported to the moon, and found a piano there, I should not ignore it. The nature of people is to be imprisoned by their particular métier. For a policeman, there is some irony in that, I think. Yes?"

Prinn smiled softly. It had been well put. "Yes, indeed. A fine irony."

Terekhov grasped the moment in the pause, and brought back the subject to music again, where he felt on firmer ground. "Mrs Sandquest tells me that pianists do not figure strongly in those applying to their Trust. This surely cannot be right."

Miss Jehmlich enlightened them. "For a pianist maestro, the piano is always a conflict with the unknown," She gave a wry smile. "Away from home, we are always struggling to come to terms with the unfamiliar, and the unexpected. Sometimes, in the end, we are only able to find solace in the composition, not in the instrument. For many that is a tragedy."

Sandquest had meanwhile drifted far enough away from their conversation to ease himself out of their group and wander off in search of Petrov who, though not yet spotted, would undoubtably be there.

He found him leaning against a column, picking his way through a plate of *crostini* and guarding a half-empty bottle of champagne at his feet of which he had been the main, if not the only, beneficiary.

"Hello, you," Petrov greeted him. "Pass your glass."

Sandquest declined, not willing to dilute his Krug. "How long have you been here, Sergei, hanging around like a member of the bourgeoisie?"

"You are not the only one operating under a disguise. I've been watching you all the while, pretending that nothing's changed."

"You've seen through me, then?"

"Diversions can be dangerous, old friend."

"Meaning?"

"I was thinking of this man, Prinn."

"Prinn is like a thorn in your side. You have to take care it doesn't fester."

"Is that what Pellucci says?"

"I pay Pellucci. Extra, just to keep his mouth shut."

"Everyone pays Pelluci, Arthur. He's discreet in knowing who to talk to. He talks to me because we have your interests at heart. He doesn't want to see his rich client coming to a bad decision on this Prinn."

"Prinn, it seems to me, has had his nose stuck in our fodder bag for long enough."

"Not only our fodder bag, Arthur."

"What do you mean by that?"

Petrov took Sandquest by the arm, and manoeuvred him through the crush out on to a small balcony, the bottle now tucked under his arm. "Mrs Sandquest, it appears, has had her nose in Prinn's fodder bag."

"Pelluci's running away with himself. I'll take care of my own domestic problems. Personally."

"Personally! You could get yourself killed, Arthur. You think you can deal with a man like Prinn? Well, I know you can't. We're both too old now to pretend we're hard cases. Being assertive will just bring us a lot of pain. Besides, Prinn I think, will not be alone. Mrs Sandquest has served her purpose. What's done cannot be undone. You must now let her go."

"Let her go!" Sandquest threw off Petrov's arm, thereby spilling what was left of the Krug. "What do you mean? I have other things in mind."

Petrov put his own glass down on the wide balustrade, and began filling it gently from his bottle. He looked out over the city as if searching for a landmark he wouldn't find. Quietly, he said, almost to himself, "I also had to let things go, Arthur, even when I had further things in mind." He turned and faced Sandquest, raising his glass. "Time then, to channel these destructive passions in the right direction, just as I had to do. You were unaware of the years I waited while you fiddled around making millions, and becoming a big cheese in your own country. Years while I protected your interests, brought up Varina, the investment in flesh and blood you'd left behind. I did it, knowing that at any moment we both could be dead, while you, safe in the West, enjoyed the luxury of being completely unaware. So, yes, I have a vested interest in you, even more so than Pelluci does."

"You also have a share in my feelings, Sergei?" Sandquest protested angrily.

"No, Arthur, such ill-feeling is a mere mechanism. You'll live with that. But such an attitude burns up energy - useful at the right moment, but wasted and dangerous at the wrong one."

"What are you suggesting?"

"Things to be taken care of. Prinn, and your wayward wife, for instance. But not just now. Nothing must happen to Prinn before we have reached Paetus. You seem altogether too distracted at present. When we're ready, we'll remedy your little problem but, for now, a little more restraint." He replenished both their glasses, then leant against the balustrade, looking through the door at the animated crowd within. "We shall need a few more days, you."

Sandquest relaxed, apparently mollified. "Not more delays?"

369

"Paba is eager, but not stupid. They're not dealing with just any old burial here."

"A tomb is not a tomb?"

"A tomb is for the dead, but Paetus is hidden in a maze; in a labyrinth filled with uncertainty. Natural and unnatural pit falls might bury the unsuspecting. We are merely being careful. After all, you're a creature of habit. And habits - or Prinn - might yet be the death of you."

-oOo-

Dr Rosso rose from a chair, thanking the small, frail old lady dressed in a silver lurex suit for relating to him her experiences of singing for the great Georges Sebastion in Paris. It was a story that had almost distracted him from his real reason for sitting there. He didn't think that the two men who had just recently re-entered from the balcony would have ever heard of Georges Sebastion. More likely they would have heard of the Echo 8 camera which Bobo Serrafini had lent him, and with which he'd lit the old lady's cigarette!

Chapter 44

Hart was standing eyeball to eyeball with the pigeon perched on the window ledge when Tate entered holding a large official buff envelope.

"Beg pardon, sir, bit of a fluster. Communication arrived marked urgent." He placed the envelope carefully on Hart's desk, before standing back expectantly.

Hart glowered at the pigeon, returned and lowered himself cautiously into his chair, in an effort to find some ease for a niggling haemorrhoid. He reached for his meerschaum. "Pull up a chair, Maurice, I've things to say."

Tate did as he was bid, a fretful look crossing his eager face at the sight of the undisturbed envelope. Hart nevertheless ignored his attentive curiosity.

"Not very exciting reading, this." He shifted Tate's file dismissively.

Tate nodded, detecting in Hart's tone an indication that any ambiguity wouldn't go unnoticed. "So you don't think Sandquest's in the frame, sir?"

Hart gave him a disapproving look. "No one's suggested a strong motive yet for why a man like Sandquest, would be likely to employ assassins. Too many loose ends, and too few knots. However, as we're doomed to persist with this line of enquiry, your latest hypothesis sounds more credible. Run me through this commercial linkage bit again."

"From the beginning?" Tate queried in a despondent tone.

"Not much use from the end, is it?" Hart grunted.

"Well," he continued in response to Hart's continued frown, "I needed an association linking Blain and Finetti's deaths to Sandquest. The death of Blain was extremely unfortunate for his American company, the chip designers Grid Overton in the middle of fighting off a takeover bid from Axmar. Without him they were left high and dry, and the fact that the shares were already being marked down due to poor trading figures, weakened their position further. As Axmar was going through a periodical acquisition phase, the rumour on

371

Wall Street was that the communication-and-application company Sirena Systems was also a potential target. The chairman of Sirena Systems was Finetti. Ditto Italvini."

"Bit circumstantial this." Hart sought clarification. "And Blain had financial interests in both those companies, you say?"

"A fairly large stake in Sirena Systems, yes, and substantial in Italvini."

"Are you presenting me with a red herring here, Maurice?"

"I don't think so, sir."

"Hmm!" Hart muttered. "Go on."

"The common denominator between all three is Sandquest. One way or another, Oh, yes."

"Stop being dramatic, Maurice. Everything has to be watertight, or we'll be holding hands in the Employment Exchange. Only two of these companies have high-tech configurations, for example."

"True, sir, but Sandquest remains pivotal because of the Verolino wine connexion."

"Owned by Italvini. All right, I see your reasoning. But it's hardly tenable because of one glaring detail that rubbishes all of these conclusions."

"What's that, sir?"

"Because, Maurice, people like Sandquest don't go around murdering people for the sake of a few bottles of wine, when they could buy the company with their small change. Nor do they blow up their commercial competitors. Especially a blue-chip company like Axmar who could leave most of them in the dust anyway."

"Back to the drawing board do you think, sir?"

"That's what it might look like. Nevertheless, I have a feeling you're in the right street, just in the wrong shop. You need to identify another reason - one where Sirena Systems and Grid Overton don't necessarily figure. They're legitimate business and financial activities, after all. No. Did Sandquest have another, more serious interest in Italvini, for instance? Something that's not obvious; something more concrete, like a reason for not swallowing them up, lock, stock, and barrel. Excuse the pun. That's what we want to know, and a taste for an obscure Italian wine, isn't hardly good enough.

372

"Right. Not anything that's obvious then, sir." Tate would have liked to leave this subject, and review the interesting subject of the photograph contained in the envelope.

Hart stuffed tobacco into the bowl of his pipe, then surveyed his blackened finger with a mild solemnity. "Stop fidgeting, Maurice, while I'm talking. The presentation of your report has to have some definable purpose. The outline must be set out clearly, and not represent a series of independent facts that don't support a valid conclusion. I don't want to sit here guessing what you're driving at. I'm bloody lazy. I need a deduction I can disagree with, at least."

There was little else Tate could do but suppress his eager curiosity, and listen intently to the ensuing mini lecture on how things were to be approached.

"You need to add meat to the significantly vague elements, like Italvini. All these seemingly unconnected loose ends need tying together. We have to avoid the plenary report being full of holes." Hart took a match to the bowl of his pipe. "Concentrate on the immediate effects of the case - what's happening now. All the detail on his war years is already well documented, and pored over by numerous intelligent sleuths, so seemingly there's nothing to gain there."

Tate hesitated, not sure if it was his place to deprecate the opinions of his elders. He took courage.

"There was actually something, sir."

Hart removed his pipe. "What something?"

"Something that struck me as...incomplete: a six month gap in Sandquest's history."

"Germany in Forty-Five, you mean?"

"Camp follower, one supposes, until the Russians secured Berlin. But there's no information in detail of a personal nature. He won't have sat there twiddling his thumbs. What was the effect on him - his involvement with the Russians? Six months is a long time and there might be a contributory factor. Was he substantially debriefed, sir?"

Hart smiled. "Almost certainly he was. But you're right: Question mark in the margin. It'll be a wild-goose chase probably, but if we don't look, we won't know."

"The file on his debriefing must still exist, sir. Can't we have a look at it?" Tate enquired.

"Not that easy. They'd send us round the houses. It would be like Piccadilly Circus at five o'clock, with us chasing our tails. Need to short circuit all that."

Picking up the telephone Hart dialled a number. "Ah, Jim, it's Hart here. Who was that chum of yours in the Box who put together a report for the M.O.D. on Sandquest? - O'Reilly. Could you have a chat with him, find out who debriefed Sandquest when he came back from Germany in Forty-Five? - Yes, a bit of a rush. Ten minutes all right?"

From the way Hart screwed up his face and closed his eyes, Tate understood it wasn't all right.

"Yes, bit of an imposition, Jim. Special Branch is always stretched, I know. - Saucy. - Appreciate your efforts, naturally. Much obliged."

Hart took up his meerschaum, scorched tobacco sticking out of the top, like a rook's nest, where it had expanded under combustion. He relit the pipe, settling back more comfortably in his chair. "Right Maurice, what was I saying? Yes, look for the things that should be there, but aren't. What's next?"

"The envelope sir," Tate offered hopefully.

"What's in it?" Hart asked.

"Photograph from Mr. Eldon. He says the man on the right is Sandquest, the other at the moment, unknown. Advise."

"Talking to us at last, is he?" Putting on his spectacles, Hart removed the contents, and studied the photograph at arm's length. "When was this taken?"

"Two or three days ago, I think. He was a bit hazy about that."

"Would be, wouldn't he. Bit of a shindig going on, by all appearances. One hopes the bill doesn't find its way on to his expenses."

"I understand he wasn't there, sir. Photograph was taken by a third party."

"Perhaps he should have been there. Haven't seen this chap since I was in A Squad. Thatcher might have been ready to do business with Gorbachev, but she'd be lucky not to have her handbag pinched by this one. We spent

374

more time watching him than the VIPs. Major General Sergei Petrov is who he is."

"Russian?".

"Very," Hart nodded. "Head of the First Directorate, I remember - must be retired by now. He's almost certainly in Italy legitimately. Outside our prerogative, anyway. One thing we can be sure of, Sandquest's an old hand, so he'll have notified someone about this meeting, somewhere. We, for our part, are keeping our heads down. Doesn't alter the question though, does it?"

"What were these two doing together?" Tate volunteered.

"Question in the margin for your report. It lets me know you consider something is amiss. Technocrats or mercantile Russians, you could argue, were above board, but a reconstructed KGB officer seems a bit wild. Getting messy this. Now we definitely need to find a reason."

The telephone rang before Tate could reply. "Jim? Well done. What's the story? - Singleton. Freddie Singleton. Angel or still waiting? - Up and running, bless him. Retirement suits some people, I suppose. Where's he parked now? - Dorset - yes, I've got a pen."

Hart scribbled down the details before passing them to Tate.

"I suppose he's compos mentis? - Parish chairman. Worth a chat, then. Remind me I owe you a beer." He replaced the handset, keeping his hand on it as though about to make another call, then clearly changed his mind.

"Get on to this chap Singleton, Maurice. Arrange a visit. At the same time, get all the latest bumf they'll let us have on Petrov. Send it out to Eldon. Right, that should keep you busy."

-oOo-

Tate managed to get himself lost in Wimborne Minster, specifically on a roundabout that advised the unsuspecting motorist that he could arrive, at the same place, by choosing either of opposite directions.

Finding Tolpuddle smaller than its historical fame, while beset by a sequence of stops and reversals, they finally turned into a modern housing development intended for those lacking sufficient capital to live pretentiously. Such complexes were residential islands seemingly fixed in satellitic orbit round any number of rural villages, with fenceless pocket-handkerchief lawns, living rooms permanently on view to the outside world, and a carefully washed and polished car parked in front of the garage.

Singleton turned out to be a short energetic man hailing from Durham, who'd been mobilized in 1939 to serve in a squadron supporting armoured divisions. He'd been chosen to debrief Sandquest on the grounds, he imagined, of his parallel experience in radio communications. The report he prepared confirmed his use to MI5, with its increasing need for good case officers, as the threat of Soviet expansion became a post-war reality. Now, in his seventies, he lived the life of a retired civil servant, comfortably and quietly.

His unprepossessing wife, Jane, prepared tea as her husband's guests settled into a large chintz-covered sofa. Singleton himself took a matching armchair, resting his hands on his knees. Nothing in the room suggested his past life; it was as discreet as the agency he had once served.

Their polite conversation was soon interrupted by the arrival of tea, with Tate being glad to see three large slices of sponge cake resting on the tray. No poncey slices of lemon, Hart noted with satisfaction.

Mrs Singleton then excused herself, furtively casting a concerned look at her husband as she left.

Singleton saw Hart had noticed her anxiety.

"It's this unexpected visit," he offered by way of explanation. "Since I retired, we've hardly seen anyone from my old department. We bumped into a junior officer at Woking station once, that's all." He laughed naturally, like a man who suspected nothing and imagined even less. "Out of sight, and out of mind, I suppose. Then your young man here phoned. I assured her that for anything serious I'd have been called up to London. The Met would merely be looking for information. Routine sort of business, I expect?" he inquired casually.

Hart nodded, aware that Singleton's wife had

376

obviously not been reassured. Her husband had once been in a dark profession - a church, as one old hand had put it, with more skeletons than Palermo's Porta D'Ossuna. And they were about to resurrect one now, for Singleton.

"Ancient business, I'm afraid. MI5 have been in touch with you, I believe?"

Singleton nodded.

"We want to go over some old ground. I expect you're a bit rusty now but do the best you can. I know this is a bit of a stretch, but it's important. In 1945 you carried out an interrogation on a Sergeant Sandquest. You remember him?"

Singleton whistled softly. "That *is* old ground. Bit of a stretch remembering back that far, but let's have a go."

He added milk to the cups, then poured the tea slowly before offering the sugar, while silently blowing the dust from his memory.

Hart moved him on. "Don't worry about technical details; they're all on record. Just cast your mind back to the man himself. Concentrate also on any bits for me that you discarded because they weren't verifiable, or because their relevance was in doubt. Innocuous things, let slip over tea and a smoke, which didn't seem to fit into your brief."

"I'll try," Singleton mused. "Sandquest did rather better than I did out of the war, and he cropped up professionally once or twice later on. Controversial fellow... refused a knighthood, I understand. Some people just manage to fall on their feet. Don't remember hearing anything about him lately though. Anyway, as you said, when I first came across him, he was just a sergeant. He hated having to go over anything twice, aware that I was looking for any discrepancies in his account; flaring up at me if I insisted - which I did. He didn't seem to have much respect for my rank, I remember, which caused us one or two difficult moments. A hard nut, but I never had any reason to basically doubt his story. Between us we placed all his times and dates in chronological order, so they fitted well enough. When we came to discussing the technical communications side, he appeared very well informed. In all probability, I reckon, his account was reasonably plausible, and valid."

"Did he drink a lot, do you know? Wine... that sort of thing?" Hart inquired.

Singleton studied Hart for a moment, considering the relevance of this question. "He could certainly knock the hard stuff back - apparently acquired a taste for it during his time with the Russians. I took to taking a bottle along with me, so we could share a drink or two afterwards. 'Valency exercise', he used to call it."

Singleton saw, by their puzzled looks, they hadn't grasped the significance of this remark. "The linkage between two atoms in a molecule formed by the transfer of an electron from one atom to the other, or by the sharing of electrons, etc, etc. Bonding, in other words."

"Ah! That sort of valency," Hart acknowledged. "Not against the rules, the drinking? Officers and other ranks?"

Singleton shrugged. "I saw it as being astute, loosening him up a bit, gaining his confidence. I didn't anticipate the amount he could consume, though, in retrospect, I think it was perhaps a misjudgement. But then again, perhaps not."

They waited for him to continue, but Singleton had stopped, choosing not to elaborate.

"Perhaps not?" Hart prompted finally.

"Oh, it's something he brought up towards the end of the interrogation. As you suggested, not the sort of information demanded by my brief." Singleton would obviously rather move on. "Do you really need to know this?"

"I won't know until you tell me," Hart said, taking a bite of the sponge cake while holding the plate up below his chin.

Tate looked down at the liberally dispersed crumbs in his lap.

"Towards the end of one of the interviews, when we were having our 'valency session', he asked me if I had ever been in love? Odd question coming out of the blue like that. I said no, chance would be a fine thing. Knowing nothing could be off the record, he asked me if I judged something to be of no interest, would I leave it out. I considered this point and agreed, though frankly, I had no intention of doing so. In the event I didn't record any such observations, but later, after I'd been recruited into MI5, I came to the opinion that I might have been rather remiss. I thought once or twice about bringing the record up to date, but, being new, I didn't want to lose face. If the file had become active, I might have persevered. Well, nothing reappeared to haunt me, and in later years, he must have been vetted more than once, though his name never came on to my desk."

"Then, bring things up to date for us now, about Sandquest being interested in love?" Hart prompted.

"You'll know how he was picked up by Konev, who was about to overrun Berlin? Yes, well, as an ally, Sandquest had to work for his supper. He wasn't actually a prisoner of war, and I can't remember the exact details, but he was either billeted with, or met a woman somehow, with whom he'd begun an affair. He'd only recently been married, and learnt of his wife's death in an enemy bombing raid over the Midlands, a year before they dropped him outside Berlin. These things happen, you might say. The sort of emotions he'd experienced in those extraordinary times had a great effect on him. One could appreciate the sort of turmoil he was in: guilt, anger, the wickedness of his own actions so soon after his loss, and the impossibility of righting a wrong. All of this seemed too private for me. It's the reason why I didn't write anything up, I suppose. You probably won't understand that?"

Hart smoothed the trousers over his knees, straightening the creases. "No, outside my experience. We don't get time to build up a rapport with another person in our line of business, but if we did, I believe it might colour our judgment. You could argue that this 'bonding' is an essential characteristic of doing justice to your inquiry - seeing both sides of the story. I tend to disagree, because in our case justice has got nothing to do with opinions. Interrogation is about assembling the facts. Judgment shouldn't ever be confused with justice. That's someone else's responsibility. The answer tends to be retrospective, whether we've discovered the truth or not."

"Ah, yes, the moment of truth. That moment took awhile in coming. Funny old thing how all of life is a continuum, how one thing leads to another. When I closed the file on Sandquest, I thought that was that, duty done. In hindsight, I can see how one thing led to another. Firstly there was Yury Kruzhkov, and now there is you."

Hart moved forward on to the edge of his seat. "Kruzhkov. Who's he?"

"Vice-Consul Kruzhkov."

"What has he to do with Sandquest?"

Singleton pulled a face. "Nothing directly, just part of the continuum. When he came over to our side, he provided us with some very useful material in the first few months, and then he started to dry up, so we switched to peripheral information - background stuff that might add up to something somewhere: names, numbers, that sort of thing. You'll be familiar with such. One of the names he came up with was Petrov, a major general in the KGB."

Tate shifted forward on to the edge of his seat, so that he and Hart now resembled eager suitors for the same young lady's hand.

"Petrov wasn't a name of a great deal of interest to us, not being of domestic importance. Then I remembered Sandquest, and how a Lieutenant Petrov had been close to Sandquest during his sojourn with Konev. A liaison officer cum watcher, one suspects." Singleton gave a small laugh. "Another of Sandquest's valency exercises. Kruzhkov informed us that Major General Petrov was sending money regularly to an Anna somebody - the surname's on file - in Poland. That's something MI6 could have made use of when Stalin was alive, but offering little practical advantage afterwards. It was rather awkward for me. Anna, you see, had also been the name of Sandquest's great love. I didn't doubt therefore that they were the same Petrov, and the same Anna."

"You didn't consider pursuing this line?" Hart asked.

"Yes, the truth is, I did. I thought that this was the right moment to bring my oversight to the department's attention, but the rug was suddenly pulled out from under my feet. Kruzhkov had seemingly obtained the material through a delicate source, one that was later turned by MI6, or the SIS, as it's now more correctly known, so we were instructed not to compromise their position by muddying the water. The case was subsequently passed back to MI6 while we were left to stick to our own patch."

"Perhaps you should have passed on your interesting little confidence, as well."

"You consider I made an error of judgment?"

"The old cliché of the jigsaw puzzle: putting all the pieces in place. Not very helpful, though, losing two of the pieces."

Singleton got up to go and stand in the bay window, his hands behind his back, staring out. "Three pieces actually."

There followed a prolonged silence. "Three?" Hart repeated eventually, in disbelief. "I think you'd you'd better explain?"

"Kruzhkov also revealed that Anna had a child, a daughter. He didn't indicate if she was Petrov's." Singleton turned round to face them. "Of course she could have been Petrov's. Why would he have sent them money otherwise?"

"Yes, there's a fifty per cent chance the child was Petrov's," Hart agreed.

"And if she wasn't?" Singleton inquired.

"Then there's a fifty per cent chance it was Sandquest's, and so you'd have a one hundred percent chance of a possible cuckoo. Very unfortunate. How to find out if it's still in the nest or not, that's the problem."

Hart rose, with Tate following dutifully, aware that he was witnessing something crucial but not quite sure why these present disclosures mattered.

Singleton had assumed the appearance of a deflated inner tube, punctured by an unforeseen nail. He was now haunted by ghosts resurrected from a past he had thought long departed, and firmly buried.

"I shouldn't worry." Hart sounded conciliatory. "Not in our line. You haven't handed over any secrets, so no one's going to see you as an enemy agent. You made a professional decision a long time ago when you were still inexperienced."

Hart went to collect his hat from the hall. Mrs Singleton joined them to say goodbye.

From the car, Hart watched them standing together in the doorway: a rather forlorn-looking couple without much of a future left, and a whole lot of past catching up with them in the present. He felt he was getting old, worrying himself about other people's worries.

"Hurry up," he cajoled the meticulously conscientious Tate, who was now peering under the Daimler after testing both the bonnet and boot. "For God's sake, you're not in the SIS!"

"Can't be too careful, sir," his junior countered, clicking his safety belt on.

Pulling away, neither of them looked back.

"You're not best pleased then, sir?" Tate asked, determined to keep abreast of things.

"No, Maurice, I'm not. Any prior arrangements you've made for this evening, cancel them. There's work to do."

"You think this early connexion between Petrov and Sandquest is somehow significant, sir?"

"Given the prominence of Sandquest in this nation's defence requirements, and that your 'early connexion' is still connected, probably bloody explosive. For God's sake, man, don't dawdle. This car's good for a hundred and forty miles an hour, and what are you doing? Forty!"

Chapter 45

Capagli raised his eyes from the ground-plan to watch where three of his workmen were easing the last few blocks of stone from the wall, exposing sand compressed by nearly two thousand years into the smoothness of plastic.

Wiping a dust-encrusted face, streaked with rivulets of sweat, the bulky little Sicilian threw down his dumpy hammer and chisel, motioning with his hand for the other two workers to stack the remaining stones. Picking up a plastic water bottle he gulped greedily, spinning its top back on aggressively.

One of Capagli's regular workers, he wasn't a migrant from the agrumi farms of the Sicilian coast, or the granaries of the uplands, but straight from the gutters of Palermo. A disagreeable, bullying, eternally northwards drifter, beset with antisocial attitudes and inclinations. He suited Capagli well.

Picking up a long handled-shovel, standing higher than himself, he gestured to Capagli - who grasped it, saying nothing. In truth, no one was saying anything. They were all waiting expectantly, banking on their employer's theories being more than mere conjecture. Capagli stepped forward with more knowledge of the dilemma they faced than his labourers. He moved like a man petrified by the consequences of failure; a man mounting the steps of the gallows he'd constructed for himself, slowly and without deliberation. He forced the fear of another miscalculation out of his mind, but in its absence he found only a deeper dread.

Approaching the bank, he studied the sand, green with ancient humidity, before swinging the shovel in a wide arc, slapping the compacted face in front of him with a firm sweep of his arm. Momentarily, all was silent after the dull thud of the spade; a silence prickling on the skin like a heat rash, followed by an unhurried swish as the heavy curtain of sand corrugated into ripples before smoothly sliding to the base of the wall.

Revealed was another structure in stone, made up of twin fluted columns resting on carved plinths supporting a frieze above the architrave decorated with griffins and centaurs. Somewhere above this, hidden by more infill, and half masked by the surrounding scaffold, must have been its pediment. The whole central cavity locating the entrance had been tidily filled by slim bricks, and horizontal bands of tufa at equal intervals.

Capagli closed his eyes, but in this self imposed darkness he could still see that neatly carved stone, slightly proud of the surrounding bricks, chamfered and incised in orderly upright Roman letters: 'CAECINAE'.

One of the workmen slapped him on the back. "*Bravo, Capagli. Bravo.*"

His reply, sounding like a dry whisper, could have been anything. Capagli placed the shovel against the wall, and sat down on the neat pile of stones, his mouth feeling parched and unyielding. He worked up the bitter-tasting saliva in his mouth; the sweat on his neck became cold in the stream of air flowing down the corridor.

He beckoned the stocky Sicilian over, explaining in a monotone voice that had lost the power of emphasis,

"Take out a brick low down, Filippo. Feed in the pump's tube, then seal up the gaps. Use Marco to help you. Wear the filter masks in case there's any bacteria in the air. Should take you about an hour. Massimo can come outside. Tell me when you're finished."

Once outside Capagli could breathe more easily, taking deep inhalations of breath to release the stress he had been under for so long. There was still some way to go, but he'd delivered the first part of his promise. A sense of optimism might be returning, but it was tempered by the fear that at any time over the preceding centuries other *tombaroli* may have forced an entrance from a different direction.

For the moment, as Paba would remind him, time was the only handicap. Capagli didn't need to be told about the cracks appearing in their finite space; widening fissures that would eventually let others in. Having worked the earth for most of his life, he knew all of her moods: displeasure that changed with the weather as well as the seasons. They could make a greater effort, but just like time and fate, too much haste was still an

384

enemy. They had no patent on what they sought, where the fanciful took on a reality, and became the truth itself. So they had to ensure that by the time that happened, the contents of the tomb must be safely out of everyone else's reach.

He collected his phone from the makeshift office.

Paba's unfriendly voice responded, *"Pronto."*

"Capagli. We've found the tomb," he confirmed, trying to suppress his excitement.

The following silence, even to Capagli's trained ear, which had grown used to detecting the whims of his associate, suggested nothing except the indeterminable.

"We've found the tomb, *Signor* Paba," he tried again.

"I heard you the first time. There isn't any doubt?" Paba asked icily.

"Not this time. You can take my word for it."

"Not something that's proved very reliable so far," Paba reminded him. "Never mind, the timing's opportune. Our clients have arrived in Florence, and they want to see what a promise looks like. You can show them, I hope?"

"I don't see why not. In an hour or two we'll be ready to make the opening."

"That soon. Then I'll come over." The telephone clicked off.

Capagli felt it was like having a door slammed in his face. Anyway, what did it matter. He'd got them there without any help from Brizzi.

Striding forcibly back into the ruined castle, deep below he heard the clunk of a mallet as the little Sicilian worked to loosen the first brick comprising the entrance to the tomb.

-oOo-

Walking ahead for a few metres, Paba paused impatiently for Capagli to catch him up. Descending to the level of the dungeons, which had come to resemble no more than a series of dilapidated human kennels, they reached the entrance where workmen were cementing a recessed steel joist into place as a support for the bricks resting on those that had to be removed.

Paba stood back against one side of the dungeon, assessing the facade.

"Well, Capagli, apparently you're right. This time we're even informed that you're right," Paba said, eyeing the incised stone carrying its Latin name.

Capagli nodded. "Let's pray they weren't playing tricks on us, and this really is the tomb."

"Yes, you do that. Meanwhile, while you're making your divine supplications, I assume you'll soon have opened the entrance?"

"It's a brick and tufo wall, held together with lime mortar. Almost soft enough for us to tap out. Nothing difficult now the structure above is adequately supported. You'll come with us?"

"Let's say it's not something I'd choose to miss, Enzo, either finding Cecina inside, or the look on your face if we don't."

"He's in there, I know it. He can't be anywhere else." Capagli dismissed the very suggestion of failure, while the Sicilian carefully worked an upper brick loose, finally pushing it through to fall with a dull thud on to the floor inside.

As further bricks were removed, dank odour of the tomb's claustrophobic millennia long sleep began to seep out into the corridor. Even though at once repellent, it inspired the narcotic curiosity of human greed. Drawing closer, Paba felt a vigorous draught of air passing him to enter the dark void. He turned to Capagli, who registered his interest.

"There must be a lot of space in there to absorb so much air. Probably a vent somewhere."

Paba looked irritated by the suggestion. "You mean there's another entrance?"

"Possibly not another entrance - but air holes, maybe. I've come across tombs with tunnels you could hardly crawl through, and others you couldn't at all, possibly excavated by small children. We shouldn't jump to conclusions, meanwhile. Having sealed up the front door so carefully, it seems unlikely they'd have left a back entrance open."

Removing the last few bricks, the Sicilian gestured towards the space he'd now created.

386

"That'll be enough to squeeze through, Filippo, pass me the torch."

Capagli played its strong beam over the tunnels sides, revealing further entrances, then down into the sepulchral darkness ahead until it bounced off its closure twenty metres in. The sidewalls, built of regular stone courses, were capped with a series of heavy stone slabs stepped so as to form the roof.

The Sicilian pointed with his chisel to a portion of the roof in front of them. Capagli swung his beam directly on to it, where a section of the roof had been pushed askew, producing cracks in three of the roof slabs, and causing the supporting walls to bulge.

"The weak point." Capagli decided. "Probably happened when the hill twisted in the massive earthquake Brizzi figured took place during the beginning of the ninth century - long before the castle was built. Get the tube jacks, Filippo, and shore them up." He turned to Paba. "You see what I mean? Proceeding in too much of a hurry could get us all buried alive."

"Those stones have managed to hang in there for more than a thousand years," Paba replied dismissively.

"Perhaps on something barely the width of a piece of cotton. Remember, materials swell in the damp. Dried out by the entry of new air, they'll shrink; perhaps to something less than a piece of cotton. This is meant to be Cecina's tomb, so we must make sure it doesn't become ours." His eyes didn't leave Paba's, though not reading anything there in the twin spots of darkness that were fixed on him.

Paba offered a little grimace of impatience. "Yes, that would be unfortunate."

Seeing that the workmen had now finished, Paba took the torch from Capagli. Stepping into the passage beyond he walked to the end, with only a cursory glance at the two side tunnels. There he turned. "Tell me, Capagli, why build only this central section in stone. What's so significant about it?"

"What do you mean?"

"See for yourself. The side tunnels are cut directly out of sand. They must be important; however, because there's nothing else. Absolutely nothing!"

Returning to where they waited, Paba handed the torch back into Capagli's hand with a slap, and without another word walked away to the ladder.

"What did he mean by that?" Filippo asked.

"Who knows? That man talks in riddles. Let's get started, now."

-oOo-

Placing her book on the side table Margaret Morning walked into the hall, listening at the foot of the stairs to her daughter Melissa tapping away on the computer in her room.

Returning, she picked up the book again with little enthusiasm. She'd been distracted by the sound of Paba's car passing by.

Concentrating on her reading for another twenty minutes had proved to be a fitful exercise, punctuated by a series of restless conjectures as to why Paba hadn't called.

On an impulse Margaret went outside to look up at the castle from the front gate. The same familiar black silhouette stood out clearly against the sky, silent and empty in its seven centuries of neglect.

Collecting her waterproof trench coat from the hallstand, Margaret slipped it on before wriggling her feet into stout shoes.

She had walked no more than two hundred metres before the red tail lights of Paba's Mercedes Benz made Margaret stop. The lights of the car then swung round and along the twisting track in front of her, as she ducked for cover under the lower branches of the trees. Then, when it had passed, she walked back unhurriedly, intent on showing not the least sign of panic.

The car was standing next to the gate with its lights still on, as she drew close.

"Fausto?" Margaret called out, in a small voice she instantly wished she'd made bigger.

The car door opened. "Ah, Margaret," Paba greeted her, "I was about to ring the doorbell, but I see you are out."

She laughed feebly at his little joke. "I was in the woods when I saw your car stop."

"You were out walking in the dark?"

"If you wish to observe nocturnal animals, then you must."

"Isn't that rather frightening? You should have someone accompany you," he suggested, kissing her lightly on both cheeks, and squeezing her shoulders to prompt an answer.

"It's quite safe really. Come on in, if you've time." She opened the gate.

"What sort of animals do you see in the woods round here?" Paba enquired, following her.

"Mostly wild boar and porcupine. Not tonight, I'm afraid. Though last week I managed a roe deer. Being shy, the best time for them is after dark."

Margaret opened the door to the hall. Upstairs the computer could still be heard.

"Come through to the sitting room."

Paba sat in an armchair, watching Margaret pour his drink. He took the large whisky from her, raising his eyebrows at the equally large one she poured for herself.

"Are we to become intoxicated?" he enquired, holding up his glass to her.

"Oh, no! I'm sorry," Margaret hastily apologized. "Let me put some back in the decanter."

"No." Paba's hand covered the glass "It'll keep out the cold."

"If you're sure." Then changing the subject quickly, "Have you given any thought to my idea of a romantic ruin?"

Paba was sharply dismissive. "There's no romance in a ruin, Margaret. One is always going to be reminded how it came to be a ruin. Have you ever visited Vetulonia?"

"The Etruscan city near Grosetto?" Margaret shook her head.

"Was an Etruscan city, yes - later a Roman one. Then Vetulonia vanished. By mediaeval times the city, now no more than a hamlet, had acquired a new name. Centuries passed, and the old name was forgotten. By the nineteenth century, Vetulonia had become an archaeological mystery, causing fierce arguments whenever its name was mentioned. First they decided on one place, then on another. Finding the site became a romance in itself: a treasure hunt for a forgotten city, famous because it furnished the fasces, the symbol of Roman and Fascist authority. They managed to spoil the mystery by eventually finding Vetulonia, instead of leaving it forever lost like Atlantis. Found it under a poor and miserable hilltop town called Collona di Buriano. In 1887 an act was passed, returning what was left of it, to the original name."

"Fausto. I seem to have lost the point. A romantic ruin?"

"As I said, there's no romance in a ruin. Over one hundred years after this great romantic discovery and triumphant rebirth, Vetulonia is still a poor, miserable hilltop town."

"You're just cynical," Margaret reproached him.

"Reality is its own cynicism. And what's the reality for you, Margaret? Escapism or opportunism? Chance or design? Where will this idyll lead you? To romance or to ruin?"

"You're very good at riddles, Fausto. I'm afraid you've now tested my ingenuity beyond its capacity. I haven't an answer for you. Indeed, is there an answer?"

"Romance is an idealization, Margaret - a concept of the imagination, if a rather nice one. A ruin, however, is a failed romance." He finished his drink, placing the empty glass carefully on a coaster, and rose from the armchair. "Ideas and reality, metaphorically speaking, can both be brought to ruin. Now," he took her arm, "You, I strongly advise, must take care to distinguish between them." He walked to the front door, his arm still linked in hers.

Switching on the path light she accompanied him to the car, the gravel crunching under their feet, distracting her immediate thoughts.

"I shall be busy tomorrow," he said, "but after that I should like to take you out to lunch. Perhaps to the coast before it becomes too insufferable. And then on to Vetulonia. You should have the chance to take a close look at a romantic ruin." Paba raised her hand to his lips.

"So long. I shall feel deserted," Margaret teased, surprising herself at her flippancy.

But Paba was no longer listening. "Vetulonia!" he suddenly exclaimed, smacking a fist into his palm. "Of course. Vetulonia."

Without even a goodbye, he quickly climbed into his car, turning it back towards the castle.

-oOo-

Capagli glared into the main tunnel, letting the emptiness and silence add to his discontent. Not even a mouse had entered here for almost two thousand years. Nothing had been disturbed and, during that time, the tensions and stresses of the earth had found a harmony that any clumsy movement might rip asunder. Thousands of *quintali* of sand rested on the harmonics of silence: what frequency of sound might tear them apart: the dropping of a hammer, or the stifling of a yawn. No one imagined the stress and fear playing on his mind.

A sudden noise made him look up.

Paba reached the bottom of the steps, dusting himself off with a flick of his hands.

"You know, Capagli," he said, "they knew we were coming."

Capagli looked nonplussed. "Who knew we were coming?"

"Cecina's heirs. They knew that one day we would come. Didn't you tell me they were into divination: juggling bits of offal about so they could see into the future?"

"That's just a nonsense." Capagli's brow furrowed in confusion.

"Part of the Etruscan legend you mean - like their writing which we hardly understand. They were clever enough to foil all those earlier attempts without the bonus of nature lending a hand. False walls, sand banks metres deep, labyrinths that led unwelcome visitors to an untimely end. But they weren't really concerned about them. They were just concentrating on us." Paba's eyes swivelled on to Capagli.

"Just us?" Capagli queried doubtfully.

391

"All right, us, or someone like us. Their own civilization was coming to an end. The people had no more appetite to govern; having become satiated with that most debilitating of social diseases, a partiality to indolent pleasure. Slaves rose in revolt at the opportunity presented by such sloth. The state could only govern by giving in to the people, providing them with the pleasures they craved: games, entertainments, celebrations, contests, and amusements. Anything that satisfied the population's desire for sensation. In the end they were crushed by primitive Goths with little more than the intellectual capacity to consume great quantities of beer, and tear down that which they couldn't build or understand. The barbarians weren't their problem, with nothing to fear from them except losing their own lives. The problem was the coming of a civilization that might be greater than their own. Building the tomb bigger, stronger and deeper wasn't an answer. What they had to do was to build so that, even when you were looking at it, standing in it, the tomb didn't exist."

Capagli stared into the tunnel again, still unsure what Paba was talking about. "There's nothing to see," he ventured.

"Exactly. Nothing, except a psychological deception. Seeing nothing, you'd go right and left, down those passages, while the real answer lies in these stones."

"We've electronically scanned the walls," Capagli pointed out. "There's no cavity behind them, anywhere."

"Oh, I wasn't thinking about *those* stones," Paba said softly.

Capagli looked into Paba's face, then up to the roof above his head.

"Are they not beautifully laid?" Paba declared.

Capagli stared at the ceiling in disbelief as Paba's words dawned on him. "*Dio Cristo!* They couldn't have built the ceiling from below. They must have built a floor supported off the top course of the wall."

Paba laughed. "Believing themselves still Etruscan, they couldn't resist a defiant final gesture towards their Romanized life style. In death they could revert to their ancient roots. Build like their defeated predecessors had

392

done. An arrogance that will now cost them dear."

"What gave it away?" Capagli asked.

"Vetulonia," Paba answered. "What we're looking at is a typical roof of a tumulus tomb."

Capagli shook his head in disbelief. "Only here, it's fifteen metres below the surface, as opposed to being just covered over."

"In a natural cavity, I think you'll find. The Tomba della Pietrera, at Vetulonia, has two chambers, one on top of the other. It only needed a catalyst to make the association."

"A catalyst?"

"Mrs Morning. And just as I was beginning to think that she'd outlived her usefulness."

Chapter 46

The street was deserted except for occasional vehicles passing under the streetlights, their colour, seen through the trees, as undetermined as Sandquest's temper. He had caught the richness of Rachel's perfume in his nostrils; the tainted odour of her flesh that wouldn't leave him. Irritably, he checked his watch, relieved to see a Range Rover turning in at the hotel entrance.

Petrov was waiting for him in the reception lounge: helping him on with his coat, straightening the back and lapels, making sure it was hanging correctly, with all the military fastidiousness of an old soldier.

"Come, let us take part in an adventure," Petrov said, with a laconic smile, suggesting something more despite its brevity.

Sandquest recalled this trait from a time, when all around them reeked of violent death; when they'd pushed bodies from their cipher machines to discover rotor settings, and sat in drying blood to get one step ahead in the carnage that eventually would lead to the burnt-out ruins that had once been Berlin. He was not taking part in an adventure then: neither did he feel he was taking part in one now.

Sandquest settled himself on the leather seat of the vehicle. The orange and yellow glow of the instrument panel seemed excessive after the discreet illumination of his own Bristol. Designed as the finest off-road vehicle in the world, the gaudy machine provided Sandquest with a modicum of confidence for, in light of his previous experience, Petrov had demonstrated a pressing need for such a capability.

They passed the Certosa del Galluzzo on its hill, more lit up than the Range Rover, joining the dual carriageway to Siena that seemed to be pouring traffic on to the road like a bucket of water down a drain.

"You know where you're going, I suppose?" Sandquest asked, not doubting Petrov's ability to get lost.

"Of course, you," he replied. "But why should that matter in undertaking an adventure? We have plenty of petrol. Ha! If we run out, we also have plenty of this in reserve." He pulled out a bottle of Vodka from somewhere, passing it to Sandquest who nursed the bottle for the rest of their journey, having no desire to test the off-road capabilities of this vehicle.

They left the dual carriageway at Colle di Val d'Elsa, skirting the town to join the highway heading in the direction of Pisa. There was little to see in the dark except the constant undulations of the road, or the ragged silhouettes of olive groves and vineyards.

Sandquest's thoughts turned in on themselves. Hate, he found, was a more powerful passion than love. For love you would suffer anything; for hate you would destroy everything. He cursed in frustration.

Petrov tutted, opening Sandquest's window a fraction. "You're getting hot-headed, contemplating how to settle a score. I told you, you're too old for such games. We'll find a solution, but they're better carried out by others." Petrov suddenly swung the vehicle left, leaving the tar macadam road for a stone track in a swirl of rattling gravel.

Distracted, Sandquest repeated, "You do know where you're going?"

"I said I did, you. Why do you keep the question?" Petrov replied indignantly.

"Because you do seem to know where you're going, and that's questionable."

"I've studied the map. It's in here," Petrov said, tapping his forehead. "Remember? I got us out of Trzcinsko Zdroj by studying the map. A nice car, that Horst."

"I seem to remember you found Trzcinsko Zdroj by studying the map. But we also found a lot of trouble."

"Ha! That Konev had no sense of humour, you. Now it is not the same. Now it is different."

"In what way different, Sergei?"

"Then you were in love. Now you are in hate."

Sandquest stared into the darkness passing by them in shades of black. He turned back to Petrov. "Is that a criticism?"

"An observation. Love, hate, to me they are the same. The cause might be different, but the effect's the same. Emotional sensitivity is a distraction, you. We haven't

395

time for such things. Besides, you don't know how to handle emotions. Take my tip, you. If you aren't a comedian, don't tell jokes."

Petrov took another right turn with the same confident flare that his companion knew was a gesture towards some reckless bravura on his friend's part. Bumping down a rutted track brought them into a farmyard. Sandquest sighed pessimistically.

A spare-framed farmer, with the leanness of the beans he might have harvested, looked up from within a poorly lit barn where he was tinkering with an ancient tractor. He straightened up, wiping his hands on a sheet of newspaper.

"Have we arrived?" Sandquest asked, slightly bemused.

"No, you," Petrov replied. "We're in a farm called Trzcinsko Zdroj."

"I half anticipated we might be."

"Do you speak Italian?" Petrov asked.

Sandquest shook his head. "Not much, but speak in Russian. They're all communists round here."

Leaning out of the window, Petrov bellowed into the keen wind, "Castello di Pietra, comrade."

The old farmer tottered across on bandy legs, putting his hand on the car door to steady himself. "Castello di Pietra?" he repeated, spitting the words out through his remaining teeth, brown and mummified with nicotine, his face dissipating into an inane grin.

"*Ja. Si*," nodded Petrov enthusiastically.

The old farmer cradled himself with laughter. "*Cinque stelle, cinque stelle,*" he roared, stamping his foot, and rotating like a demented bantam.

Petrov leant out, grasped him by his shirt collar and lifted him higher on to his toes. "Directions you." He gave him a shake, lowering the startled farmer back down roughly.

The man had stopped laughing, pointing with his grimy finger back down the track. "*Giri e svolti.*" Spitting on the ground, he gestured with his hand in a direction somewhere behind the buildings, turning back towards the barn and muttering furiously; his words half lost in the wind.

396

Petrov looked at Sandquest inquiringly. "What did he say?"

"I think we have to return down the track, before turning right."

"And where, then?"

"As he said, '*Va al diavolo!*' Go to the devil."

"Bah! He's like you. Think's he's a comedian." Petrov selected reverse with a thud, turning the car round.

Sandquest found himself in a better humour. "You said we were too old to be assertive, Sergei. Too old to be hard cases."

Petrov slapped his thigh, the big car swerving momentarily, ripping a branch from the hedge with its wing mirror. "Ha! The old fool. He wouldn't have been so cheeky fifty years ago, you. Go to the devil? What did he know? The devil had come to him in a fancy chauffeured car."

Sandquest tapped his head. "In here, you said."

"A diversion, ha! Exactly like Anna's farm. Could have been Anna's farm, with her old grandfather. In the night, you. Remember? We came in the night."

Sandquest remembered. "Not quite the same, Sergei. They didn't have a tractor, or even a horse to pull the cart as the First UF had eaten it. Your policy, remember: live off the land, so behind became a wasteland. There was no way home, no turning back. Just like Stalin planned."

"They were soldiers, you. They fought wars."

"They weren't even good soldiers, Sergei, just desperate men stealing watches from the dead. Savages and perhaps a little more. Anna survived by burying herself in the dung-heap, while they searched the barn, sticking their bayonets in the hay, and the family pig. No, Sergei. The only thing similar were her grandfather's two teeth. Left over from where they'd smashed the others out with a rifle butt."

Petrov was silent for a while, toying with the memory. "War's never convenient, you," he said finally. "We fought battles with peasants because, like cattle, they knew how to die. Without fuss, you. What do regulative procedures mean to wolves unleashed in a pen full of chickens? No, my friend, they were not civilized, but it was convenient for the west. After the war you straightened out all the rules you'd bent. History, you. Anna's grandfather was lucky. Eventually the state got him some new teeth."

It was Sandquest's turn to be silent. Anna had been fortunate, with her dark curly hair, and ever troubled look, the hazel coloured eyes always wondering if you were angry or just anxious. She had been lucky. Providence had arrived in the shape of Sergei Petrov.

Sandquest closed his eyes, angrily turning his memories towards the darkness that only made them brighter.

-oOo-

Sandquest had dozed off, woken by a head-rattling bump in the road with loud complaints to Petrov. "Ethiopia has better roads. How can anyone consider this a modern European state?"

"Most don't, you," Petrov grated, pulling on a cigar he'd lit for company. "You've been quiet for a long time?"

"Living in the past. All those years, Sergei."

"They don't belong to us any more, you. Memories are not an investment to be collected when you die. Money's the same. Spend it now - no need to take it with you."

Petrov bounced the vehicle left off the hard bank, the lights spraying the open fields, gyrating wildly before locking on to the track that passed by Margaret's house.

Chapter 47

After six hours with 'borrowed' files, Tate felt satisfied that a more complete picture was emerging on Sandquest and Petrov's strange liaison. Yawning wearily, he took uncharacteristic comfort in the fact that Singleton had probably also endured a sleepless night.

The clock on the wall indicated five o'clock. Printing the material into a rough draft, he added his handwritten comments before placing them in a plastic wallet.

It was now a few minutes after six. More than enough time to smarten up before Hart arrived at seven. Feeling pleased with himself, he pulled his toilet bag from the top drawer of the filing cabinet.

-oOo-

Dousing himself in a generous dose of cologne, Tate recognized the footsteps passing on their way to the office. There was an urgency about them that created a panic in the young officer.

Hurriedly unlocking the door to his office, he looked at his desk. The plastic wallet was missing.

Tate swore under his breath, imagining the meal Hart was going to make of his negligence.

Hart sat behind his desk, the missing wallet set to one side, as he read Tate's draft copy. Removing his half-rimmed spectacles, he nodded sternly towards a seat.

The reprimand was brief. "First offence. Not going to make a song and dance about it. That's the last occasion, though. Disciplinary matter next time that'll end up in your file. Being careless, leaving documents unattended, can be a disaster for the department. Remember that. Head down. Back to business." He gave Tate a reassuring smile.

"Understood, sir."

"Good. So Kruzhkov was assigned to investigate Petrov because of the General's growing expertise in industrial and commercial matters?"

"He appears quite specific about that, sir, making sure

Petrov's activities were related to foreign-intelligence gathering. Petrov had set up a legitimate company in Ireland. Kruzkhov's disclosures were the first MI5 had heard about such a move, indicating that Petrov had five years of uninterrupted activity in which to get his feet under the table."

"This company, Denman Refrigeration - you've checked them out of course?" Hart enquired.

"First thing I did. But Denman Refrigeration wasn't where Petrov came in, he only arrived there eventually."

Hart located the notes, reading them aloud more for his own benefit than to remind Tate. "Denman Refrigeration, set up in 1950 by A.N.Gallagher in Wexford - handy that for Rosslare - then sold out to Moody & Son in 1958, and to Wicklow Containers in 1962, a subsidiary of Denman Refrigeration." Hart looked over his spectacles for a further explanation.

"Cold storage, sir. They ship salmon and other perishables to the Continent."

"I'm not interested for the moment in what they ship, Maurice. How did they close the circle?" Hart demanded.

"Moody & Son only bought the assets of Denman," Tate explained. "They didn't buy the registered company name. That was bought by French Spry from Gallagher back in 1961, and used as a shell company: a sort of dumping place for any deals they didn't want associated with their own name. Wicklow Containers came into their hands almost at the same time, in 1962, under the aegis of Denman. They acquired Moody & Son a year later, and in effect had reunited Denman with its assets. All listed there, sir. French Spry manufacture specialist refrigeration systems of the sort that keep you from roasting on re-entry into the earth's orbit. Naturally, only a shade below top secret."

"Would be, wouldn't it? Go on," Hart prompted.

"Wicklow Containers were undercapitalized, which may have been deliberately engineered to make the next move credible. It was one of those convenient joint ventures popular with companies short of the wherewithal. Obtaining capital is difficult for companies sailing close to the wind with too little collateral. Much easier to find a partner and spread the financial burden.

So Wicklow found Gernovcy Holdings, Petrov's enterprise being floated in the West."

"So where's the linkage, Maurice?" Hart prompted impatiently.

"French Spry, sir. When you dig deep enough, you find that French Spry is a wholly owned subsidiary. All the listed share capital is owned by another high-tech company, FI Electronics."

Hart sank back in his chair. "And therefore, ultimately, Axmar Industries. Well done. And at the back of all this?"

"Kruzhkov sheds a little daylight there," Tate said enthusiastically. "In 1963, Anna - the woman in Petrov and Sandquest's lives - died from tuberculosis, probably contacted from non-pasteurized milk. Kruzhkov spent a lot of time trying to get an angle on that one. Promotion was proving difficult to come by. He was out of luck. If Anna had been a nuclear scientist, it might have been worth pursuing right to the end. However, for a farmer's daughter there seemed nothing to gain. Petrov's support couldn't have political implications; no one was going to be compromised in such a manner."

"Sandquest was a good enough excuse. Not that they ever needed one," Hart reasoned.

"True, sir, but there's the rub. Kruzhkov doesn't seem to have known about Sandquest. While I was reading through the text of Kruzhkov's interrogation that MI5 lent us, I kept expecting Sandquest's name to crop up. It never did — not once. They didn't know about him at all. May I make another suggestion, sir?"

Hart nodded.

"According to the transcripts, Petrov never disguised his association with Anna, the woman he and Sandquest had met when Konev was closing in on Berlin, even though there's no suggestion they were ever more than just good friends. Might be seen as a bit risky, given Stalin's penchant for seeing subversion in whatever passed across his line of vision. In my opinion, despite the lack of evidence, there must have been a reason why Petrov never married Anna. After all, he brought her to Moscow."

"Reasonable conclusion. Elaborate on this suggestion

that Petrov might have used Anna in the commercial venture?"

"I believe the daughter Singleton referred to was indeed Sandquest's, given that Petrov never married Anna. Therefore, they were both highly emotive bait with which to ensnare Sandquest. Shortly before Anna's death, Petrov began the commercial venture that led him to Ireland, creating a vehicle for contacting Sandquest. A logical reason, you would have thought, given he was of considerable importance to the West. Perhaps that's why Petrov's fraternization was tolerated, even encouraged, if they were considering exploiting Anna. However, Kruzhkov was not aware of any such association, which begs the question: was Petrov working alone unbeknown to his superiors? Was he a lone wolf? What was he up to?"

"Ditto Sandquest," Hart remarked. "I'm going to need time to digest all this."

"Shall I keep digging, then, sir?"

"Let's not run before we can walk. We're skating on thin ice here, Maurice. Might be the security service's case, but we mustn't lose sight of Sandquest. Two years wasted if we do. Only a hypothesis, after all. Good enough for us to mull over, but it'll only frighten the hell out of the Assistant Commissioner."

Rummaging through the drawer for his pipe, Hart suddenly paused, peering at Tate. "You're looking tired," he observed. "While I get stuck into this draft of yours, why not put your legs up for an hour. Then I'll treat you to breakfast."

Tate closed the door quietly behind him. He had found his second wind, and a third was too much to hope for. Finding a spare cushion stuffed in behind the photocopier, he placed it on the arm of a small leather sofa that was crammed in between two filing cabinets. Slipping out of his loafers, and resting his feet on the other arm of the sofa, he closed heavy eyelids, thinking he might add another sausage to his breakfast that morning. Especially if Hart was paying.

"Maurice," a voice demanded over the intercom. "Get in here."

Swivelling himself upright, with a smirk, he surmised

that Hart had just reached the section where Kruzhkov's revelations indicated that Major General Petrov had been financing a young and talented pianist at the Moscow Academy of Music.

The smoke from Hart's meerschaum lay in a stratified mist above his head. "Explain this Moscow Academy of Music to me."

"Kruzhkov only mentions the Academy in passing. His main interest was in establishing if Petrov was paying for one of the pupils. Seems just to have been a trawl through his social activities. Something to pin on him if necessary,"

"That may be so Maurice, but what's this academy about? Music's flavour of the month round here. Do we know if it's kosher, or just a front for training of another sort? If so, the whole thing's SIS business."

"Only background information, sir."

Hart reappeared from behind a wreath of smoke. "Then where's the note in the margin, Maurice? Having told me there was nothing else, and having written nothing else, you now tell me you have a little bit of additional information."

"Nothing substantial in relation to the academy itself, and I felt it was a little premature to spend considerable time chasing it up. After all, you're always picking on my 'famous' appendices." Tate suddenly flared up at the perceived injustice.

There followed a moment of silence as Hart considered what Tate had said. "Fair point," he agreed quietly. "Tell me what you've discovered, then?"

Tate was embarrassed. "My apologies, sir, for that silly outburst."

"My apologies, Maurice, for causing it. This academy?"

"Well, sir, on a brief examination the Moscow Academy maintains a high reputation catering for exceptionally musically gifted children. Even well placed commissars couldn't get their little darlings in there unless they fulfilled the necessary academic requirements. The Kremlin accepted that their international artists had to excel if they were going to effectively demonstrate the superiority of the Soviet system."

403

"And that's all?"

"At this depth only official stuff," Tate nodded apologetically. "But if Petrov and Sandquest are seen together at a concert in Florence given by the Gorky State Orchestra, might not one of the musicians performing be the pupil, and, therefore, possibly the daughter that Singleton told us about?"

Hart studied Tate's eager face. They might make something of him yet.

"A distinct possibility, Maurice." Hart withdrew a slim folder from his brief case, extracting and passing a photograph across. "Eldon seems to be running a full-scale photographic studio out there. He'd like us to get some background material on this couple. The lady in the picture is Varina Jehmlich, principal pianist with this Gorky State Orchestra. No confirmation of her filial status. The gentleman's her manager."

Tate gave a whistle. "There can be something very fascinating about an older woman, wouldn't you say, sir?"

He changed tack at Hart's stern face. "Extraordinarily attractive."

"Let me tell you about rule number one, young man." Hart retorted. "Your eyes are the same as a pair of cameras, and consequently prone to the myth that the camera never lies. What you see is definitely not what you always get. Let's say the information supplied by your eyes suggests a female. You can interpret this information further into the fact that she's elegant and beautiful. Well, you're human, with a relatively ordered existence made up of the rules and conventions that determine such things. That is the basis of civilization. But consider the real world, say, from the perspective of a spider. What our fellow arachnid observes is also undoubtably female. We haven't, of course, any way of knowing whether he considers this female a great beauty or not, but can reasonably assume that any subsequent action on his part is driven by biological necessity, rather than by the dubious fantasy of romance. But the dear fellow has some concept also, no matter how primitive, of danger, and therefore contrives to spin a web round the female by way of securely locking the pantry door,

404

thus saving himself from becoming her dinner. There is no affection involved. The spider is not enticed by charm, even if it may be fascinated by colour. Who can say if it's tempted by the size of the spinnerets, or the curve of an abdomen? All we can undoubtably affirm is that the little chap has an undeniable interest in his own salvation. Therefore, Maurice, in the matter of Miss Jehmlich, I strongly advise you to maintain the limited visual subjectivity of that spider."

"Thank you, sir. Libido's running amuck lately. All work and no play."

Hart's face grew sterner.

Tate struggled to safety. "A most unlikely couple. Not exactly pleasant-looking is he, sir?"

"One of a new breed, Maurice, that I hope you don't have to come across. It consists of intellectual brawn. Eldon thinks he manages something, but not this lady. You can now circulate the photo, but in my opinion you'll draw a blank. Eldon would also like you to run another check on Cantina di Verolino, in case we're missing something."

"The Port Said lead that fizzled out?"

"Hmm, someone appears to have opened another bottle. But get on to the man in the photograph first."

"Could he be this Nightingale character, do you suppose, sir?"

"Eldon considers that doubtful. The fellow's too young. Field experience doesn't come overnight, but needs a continuity of development, apprentices becoming journeymen. This organization's been around long enough to build a suitable career structure into it."

Hart raked out his pipe with a small nickel-plated tobacco knife, then tapped its bowl on the ashtray. "From the information you've prized out of our SIS friends, Petrov was seconded in 1976 to the Andropov Institute in Moscow, which was operated by the KGB as a senior school for agents, especially those going into deep cover. They have no details, however, on why he was there. At the same time we can be reasonably convinced that Sandquest and Petrov had found that the old bonding still held fast, given a lot of extra adhesion by the daughter that you suspect Petrov's taken care of for all those years. Petrov must have made his move to reopen their relationship before Anna died in 1963, because there was the Wicklow Containers tie-up a year earlier. Petrov wouldn't have made any precipitate moves. He would need to be very sure of his man, just as Sandquest would need to have demonstrated that he could be sure of Petrov. All we can say is that Petrov is likely to have had by the end of the seventies, a brilliant electronics engineer firmly in his pocket, coinciding with the time that Nightingale is thought to have begun using a preponderance of highly sophisticated electronic weapons."

"Provocative?"

"Does that mean you're with me?"

"I'm following you, sir. Not quite sure where we're going yet."

Hart fixed his gaze more firmly on Tate. "Sandquest was a bit of a boffin, a practical scientist who liked to get his hands dirty; the type who knew one end of a soldering iron from the other. I'm not saying that he'd use his own companies to research and develop such weapons, unless he had a government signature on the order. But for someone with a hobby, Maurice, what a workshop."

"Let me get this straight, sir. You're saying - at least putting forward a proposition - that Petrov and Sandquest were running an agent between them. Probably a graduate trained at the Andropov Institute by Petrov, using advanced high-tech hardware supplied by Sandquest for special operations. I'm having trouble squaring that one."

Tate looked doubtful at the thought of all the ramifications. There was the absurd, and there was the preposterous, and Hart, he felt, was somewhere that had a good view of the planet.

"What bugs me, Maurice, is the intimacy of the thing. The sheer bloody intimacy of it. The only problem is, why Maurice? I just can't believe Sandquest didn't have enough clout to have somehow extricated his daughter from Russia."

Tate considered the object of this exercise, and came to the opinion that his position was best served by supporting Hart's line of reasoning. "As a theory, I can see the possibility but, from what you say, sir, proving the truth of it might be a tall order."

Hart mulled over the certainty of the conclusion Tate had come to.

"Not something we'll have to prove, Maurice. Military Intelligence will have to do all the running on this one, with Special Branch picking up the bits. Proof, in good old-fashioned terms, asks us to demonstrate the infallibility of the evidence. The bottom line is that, in court, the evidence would certainly be withheld as being prejudicial to the national interest. Transparency means the public would see the Government standing about picking its nose. A most unwholesome thought, Maurice, so we'll have to draw a veil over that one. Commander Prinn can tie all this together and make a decision. Security services will end up doing a deal. That's the usual way."

"Not a very good advertisement for democracy, sir," Tate concluded.

"Democracy, you see, is an imperfect thing, Maurice. It's a conceit, a vanity. For democracy is not order, only disorder. We are not ants, and we revel in indiscipline. We do not respond to reason, because we are irrational, which is why democracy survives on the shoulders of men like Sandquest. Rational people do not take risks. It's the irrational who create the new, by flirting with the impossible. That's why Sandquest is one of the true props of our civilization. Frightening, isn't it?"

Chapter 48

It was not a job that suited everyone; suffering the tiresome work of surveillance where boredom was just as likely to lay the foundations for ignominious failure.

Gower was on his own, parked among the many cars that were drawn up on both sides of a small leafy piazza that lay behind the Hotel Meridiana. He had discovered that not all of the orchestra shared central accommodation near the piazza Santa Maria Novella. For a reason known only to themselves, Varina Jehmlich and her manager had preferred these less convenient, but circumspect surroundings, a kilometre away along the Lungarno Santa Rosa.

They had separate, adjoining rooms; a matter Gower had discovered from the register under the eyes of a far from attentive desk clerk.

Gower had commenced with a blank sheet, but a logical and simple idea. If there was something amiss in the Gorky State Orchestra, then it would probably materialize when the orchestra was not an orchestra. Hence, in the early hours of the morning he'd found himself an ideal vantage point to watch the back entrances of the hotel, gambling that suspected targets were unlikely to walk out of the front entrance.

A little after mid-night, a black vehicle circled the piazza twice before drawing up at one of the entrances. Adjusting the focus on his miniature monocular, he made out two young women in short skirts - and a generous application of make-up that would have to last them through the night. Descending the short run of steps they entered the rear of the car. Gower settled back again, feeling it might be a long, uncomfortable night, for all three of them.

-oOo-

If he had fallen asleep, it was not the sleep of the dead. One eye opened and noticed on the dashboard clock that it was half past two, the other eye opened to join it, surveying over the rim of the car door a Range Rover pulling into an awkward spot on the corner - its tailgate protruding, vapour rising gently from the exhaust pipes. The vehicle, he considered, had not come far enough to warm its system.

Pulling himself up a little, he saw two men descend the steps of the hotel and walk quickly towards the Range Rover. Feeling for his monocular on the passenger seat, he lost valuable seconds focusing on the figures. In the last few metres he made out the gaunt features of Kopolev, but failed to make out the person whose slighter stature remained obscured by his body. Managers, Gower thought, generally took up a lot of space, but not quite as solidly as this one. The elusive figure crossed in front of Kopolev who was holding the back door open, so that all Gower managed to discern was a donkey jacket with a turned up collar, below a dark, heavily ribbed, seaman's woollen cap.

Coming to the edge of the vehicle Kopolev stopped, scanning the quietness of the square.

Gower froze. He was well acquainted with the type of man who opened the door and joined the driver in the front of the car.

He waited until they had turned the corner before, with the headlights switched off, he followed them until they crossed the Ponte Alle Grazie. As there was little traffic, late night revellers would take little notice of an unlit car. A poor battery, a fuse gone, or someone in a world of their own. It was not anyone else's problem.

Before the Via Degli Alfani he slipped down a parallel road, guessing by their route that they were making for the Hotel Ammanati where Sandquest was staying.

Having hardly drawn his car up in a convenient space, the Range Rover appeared, passed through the gates and stopped outside the hotel entrance. The engine died and the lights went out. Through his monocular Gower watched Kopolev open the rear door. If he had hoped to make out something more of the other passenger, he was disappointed, the high vehicle and the hotel railings helping to obscure their figures. The driver, on the other hand, looked more like the archetypal manager, as he stepped stiffly down. Shrewd, canny, ruthless, grinding a half finished cigar under his foot before he followed the others to the door where the night porter was unlocking to let them in.

-oOo-

"I'd like your view on this?" Hart dropped the neatly stapled sheets of A4 in front of Tate.

Tate picked up Gower's report, and read the papers through carefully, while Hart completed the crossword that had overstayed its welcome in the bottom of the out tray.

"Looks like Sandquest and Petrov are mixed up in something, sir. Murkier still if Kopolev is as well," Tate offered.

"What about 'bashi-bazouk' for three across? Brutal way to play these military pipes." Hart lowered his chin, squinting across his spectacles.

"Dare say you're right, sir. What about this other man with Kopolev?"

"That is the crux of the question. What do you make of him?" Hart inquired.

"Not a very complete description," Tate remarked. "Approximately one metre eighty, average build - subject to heavy duty clothes - probably late forties. Not enough meat there for a positive identity. Or even a reasonable one."

Hart finished filling in three across before folding up the newspaper. "That, I think, depends."

"Donkey jackets and woolly caps, sir? Suggests an industrial worker." Tate stabbed at being a little more constructive.

"All objects in a space have a relationship, Maurice. Correlative, one to the other. Donkey jackets and woolly caps do have a mutual relationship to the person who wears them; but not exclusively industrial workers."

"I'm not very good at this sort of thing, sir," Tate said lamely.

"I'm afraid, you must get good at it," Hart retorted, pushing the newspaper back into the tray.

"There's nothing in the Chief Inspector's report that suggests anything but the truncated movements of three people," Tate complained.

410

Hart drew up a chair opposite, and sat down. "In their very movements, their very presence, there will be something more."

"I had it in mind that there might be, sir," Tate grumbled.

"Start from the beginning," Hart enjoined. "Let's see if we can discover what the Chief Inspector knew he was too close to see."

Tate drew a deep breath. "Two men came down the steps from the rear door of the Meridiana hotel, turning left."

Hart raised his hand. "What suggests to you that it was two men?"

"Chief inspector Gower recognized one of them from Eldon's description," Tate suggested lamely. "The other fitted the description of a man."

"Just as a transvestite fits the description of a woman?" Hart remarked.

"Tallish, medium build. Perhaps male," Tate conceded. "But also possibly not." He continued rather more hesitatingly. "They proceeded to the corner where a Range Rover was waiting for them. They got in. Man in the front, sex unknown in the back." Tate paused again at Hart's raised hand.

"The Range Rover was waiting for them." Hart regressed. "Precisely what did the Chief Inspector say?"

Tate picked up the sheets, finding the information. "The man held the door open for the sex unknown, shut it, and joined the driver in the front."

Hart sat back, folding his arms. "Yes. Held the door open, Maurice. Just like Colonel Tazov used to hold the door open," he added pointedly.

"Colonel Tazov, sir?"

"Sapunov's story. Before your time. Just ask yourself, why are these Russians so polite?"

"If they've been well brought up," Tate qualified.

"You've been well brought up. Who do you hold doors open for?"

"For you, sir. As a mark of respect."

"For rank, of course. Not because I'm older?" Hart directed.

"That as well." Tate responded frankly.

411

Hart gave him an oblique glance. "And other occasions?"

"For a woman, naturally"

"Most certainly a woman, Maurice. By rank? No. Colonel Tazov opened the doors for a lieutenant colonel. By age? Not necessarily. The colonel was a lot older than his junior."

"All at sea for the moment, sir," Tate admitted. "Only thing we can be absolutely sure about is that our subject was either a man or a woman."

"Very perceptive," Hart said wearily. "And given that a certain proportion of male Russians are a courteous people, they'd walk on the outside of the pavement when accompanying a woman. Mr. Kopolev walked on the outside. That brings me to suppose that the unknown person is probably a woman."

"Well, Miss Jehmlich is in the same hotel as her manager, so they may have left by the back door to meet Petrov in the Range Rover, who drove them to a meeting with Sandquest. If that's the case, she may well in fact be Sandquest's daughter, and have a perfectly legitimate reason for seeing her father. In the early hours of the morning or not."

Slumping back in his chair, Hart nodded in agreement. "On that you may well be right, Maurice, but what was Miss Jehmlich doing in the company of a bunch of thugs?" He was lost in thought for a moment. "Or were they actually in her company?"

Hart sat bolt upright again. "Slow down a little. Don't let's get too far ahead of ourselves. Maurice, get a message to Chief Inspector Gower. I want him to narrow his surveillance down to Miss Jehmlich alone. He's not to let her out of his sight. I want him stuck to her like glue. If she blinks, I want it in his report. Meanwhile, you stick to the job in hand. Tie down this Verolino matter for us. In plain English, and plenty of it."

-oOo-

Signing the document, Hart replaced the sheet, looping the cord round the file's button before placing it on a small, but rising, pile on his right. He picked up another.

412

The intercom gave an anguished buzz. Hart screwing the top back on his fountain pen, opened the line.

"Right, sir," Tate said.

"What is right?" Hart asked.

"Summary of my report on photograph and Italvini," Tate responded.

"Ah! Rather prompt."

"Fell into place, sir. Like a bad habit."

"We all seem to be falling into bad habits, young man. Did you get a message off to the Chief Inspector?"

"I did, sir. He confirmed it would be a pleasure."

"Very unlikely. You should have mentioned the spider. Give me the gist of your summary," Hart requested, instantly regretting it.

"You were wrong about Miss Jehmlich's manager," Tate said, with too much self-satisfaction for Hart's liking. "American friends had him on file. Nothing very helpful, if interesting. Turns out to be a Major Valentin Kopolev. Graduate from the Higher Political School in Leningrad, and the Military Political Academy, where he took a doctorate. Something of a sportsman as well. Good enough to have made the Russian Olympic rowing squad trials a few years back. Served as assistant military attaché in Washington, where his photograph was obtained in a routine screening operation before he disappeared."

"What do you mean disappeared?" Hart demanded.

"As far as the CIA were concerned. Report says he dropped out of sight. Nothing further on him. There was just one comment, unsubstantiated. Rumour that he was due to start an academic career back in Moscow."

"Just as I said. Not from the old concussion school of agents. What about the wine?"

"Difficult to verify, but everything points to Mr. Sandquest being the sole customer in the UK. The individual over the counter sales have never been independently corroborated. Till receipts don't include the customers name, so probably bogus. In his report, Mr. Eldon was of the opinion that the wine importers in Fulham formed a sort of buffer."

"A buffer?"

"To protect the identity of the real purchaser," Tate

413

emphasized. "The exchequer hasn't any axe to grind. All excise duties having been paid on the stated sales."

"Go on," Hart persisted. "Why would Sandquest's identity need to be hidden?"

"Quite simply, sir, he didn't want anyone to know he was buying the wine."

"Would have to be something like that," Hart said with a sigh, ground into certain weariness. "And why wouldn't he want anyone to know?"

"I've made quite a lot of head way with the background material, sir, and I think we can come to a conclusion on that one. Sir Maxwell's interest in the Cantina di Verolino estate appears, at first, to have been commercial. The original owners of the estate were the Balboni family. Tuscan roots, but inherited something better during the time of Cavour and the Risorgimento. The Balboni of the time was something of a keen whist player, and when Cavour started a club, he decided to remain north of the Apennines."

"Excuse me, Maurice," Hart interrupted. "Where did you dig up this Balboni source? Is it exactly relevant to the case?"

"I read modern history, sir. Father rated it a pretty useless subject, and being an ex-policeman thought the Met a sounder bet."

"Wise man, your father. You'd better come in here, Maurice," Hart said gloomily. "Explain yourself."

Tate arrived promptly with his folders.

"You were about to explain to me the relevance of history to a bit of shady conveyancing this vintner was indulging in?" Hart reminded him.

"Extraordinarily interesting. The whole thing, sir. Right up my street. My thesis was on the effect of the Treaty of Vienna on the House of Savoy."

"Maurice," Hart stopped him, leaning forward with a troubled look on his face. "Don't give me the run around. I want you to avoid the embroidery. Get to the point. What have the Balboni to do with our present interests?"

"I was beginning to explain, sir."

"Whist players in Piedmont," Hart said dryly. "Go on."

"The whist playing Balboni family is background information prior to Sir Maxwell's involvement in the estate. In any case our interest lies with the present Balboni family."

"Just so. We need some idea of this family Balboni."

Tate disregarded the overt disapproval. "More accurately, one member of the family, a Professor Angelo Balboni. He's the third son of the late Count Cesare Balboni. When the count died the eldest son, Charles, inherited the estate, but found his business interests demanded more time than he could give to agricultural problems, leaving them for Angelo to sort out. The second son, having married an American, was banking on Wall Street, so disinclined to abandon his profession for so little gain. Professor Angelo proved to be rather good at viticulture, modernizing the estate, re-planting the best land with new vines, and hiring a chemist to control the production facility."

Hart interrupted again. "I wish you'd get to the point, Maurice."

"Certainly, sir, but these details are important."

"I do hope so."

"As we know, Mr. Sandquest is something of an Etruscologist, with one of the finest private collections in the world?" Tate continued.

"Someone did mention that," Hart said pointedly.

"His interest was first excited when a company he owned was involved in research work at the University of Rome. The cutting edge of archaeological technology, I believe. While he was there, Mr. Sandquest became a friend of one of the leading authorities on the Etruscan civilization - Professor Angelo Balboni. As we know Mr. Sandquest's collection is remarkable, but still not something, an admittedly expert amateur, could assemble on his own. There is some talk that Mr. Sandquest might eventually form a trust, so his collection can be left to the nation without being looted by the big museums. With this in mind, he appears to have been amassing a very detailed itinerary for some time under the tutelage of Professor Balboni."

"I assume, after this little discursion, you will get to the point?" Hart felt he was only half following the tortuous machinations of Tate's deliberations.

"How would it be if Mr. Sandquest were using the

415

Anglo Italian Wine Company to ship illicit works of art into his collection?"

"About as daft as these bloody Balboni's!" Hart growled.

"Let me go back a little, sir," Tate persisted. "Charles Balboni in the meantime, while Mr. Sandquest and Professor Balboni were probably doing very nicely, was running into financial trouble, finding himself forced to dispose of some of the family assets. Without taking Angelo into his confidence, he found himself an investor."

"Maxwell Blain?" Hart encouraged, hopefully.

Tate shook his head. "Close. An associate named Massimo Finetti. Finetti probably knew nothing about Angelo's friendship with Mr. Sandquest, having only bought Verolino as a prestige promotional arm of Italvini. When Angelo recovered from the shock of having the estate sold from under him, he offered his management services to Finetti, who saw no reason to break up a sound management team. Thus, the original secondary enterprise continued as though nothing had happened. Until, we can surmise, Sir Maxwell discovered what was going on."

"Inevitable, one would suppose."

"Once Finetti owned the organization, given their close relationship."

"And for this they were murdered?"

"Bit off course am I, sir?"

Hart considered it for a moment. "Strangely, perhaps not so far. Everything feels right except the secondary enterprise. That I doubt. Two, perhaps three, cases of an exclusive wine once a year don't add up to much of a cover for the unlawful shipment of ill-gotten antiquities. No. The wine itself is the link all right, Maurice, not illegal Etruscan artefacts. Given your interesting explanation of a Balboni-Sandquest association, it's unlikely that Sandquest would be using normal commercial channels to acquire a product he'd have access to directly. Though there must be a reason for the shipment. Neither is he a conventional client of the Anglo Italian Wine Company. His vintners are Murray Brothers over in Bayswater. Know that for a fact."

416

"There is one other interesting point, sir. The shipments to the Anglo Italian Wine Company seem only to have begun a little time after Finetti acquired the estate and the company."

Hart grunted. "Given the antagonism between Sandquest and Blain that might well be so. Presumably because Sandquest no longer had discreet access, it forced him to have the Cantina di Verolino shipped through The Anglo Italian Wine Company, instead of direct; therefore, avoiding his obvious involvement." Hart snapped his fingers. "Or does it? Paperwork, Maurice."

Tate looked bemused. "Paperwork, sir. The sort we get buried under?"

"No, Maurice. Commercial documentation. The only retrospective trace you can have of a consumable are its invoices and receipts."

"All the Verolino has been accounted for, sir.

"Precisely. On paper. Yet it doesn't even have to exist. It can have a destination quite different from the regular accounting chain. Happens all the time. Even the delivery note that accompanies an item only confirms a transfer and receipt. It's not impossible to get a delivery note without the item. Sandquest may never have seen the wine. What we need to know is the Verolino's true destination."

"I've lost touch with you, sir."

"When Finetti acquired the Verolino estate, Sandquest and this Balboni must have created a sleight-of-hand. The delivery had to be concealed because it was being delivered to someone who couldn't be associated with Sandquest's critical security interests. Like a daughter on the wrong side of the wall."

"SIS aren't going to like this, sir. Whiffs of trouble."

"And the possibility of blackmail. I think Finetti must have discovered that the Verolino wasn't being delivered to the Anglo Italian wine Company, only the official paperwork. With Blain in tandem with Finetti it would only be a matter of time before an audit or stocktaking threw up an anomaly. Blain's scrutiny may have been more searching than that of Finetti. Until that moment, the notional over-the-counter sales down in Fulham provided a perfect anonymity."

"The sort of information worth a great deal to a grudge ridden Blain."

"Besides a very good reason for him being dead. All of them being dead! Get in touch with Eldon. See if we can establish if the wine was being delivered to the Gorky State Orchestra? After that, get in touch with Commander Prinn."

"What shall I tell him, sir?"

"That we're in a bigger mess than we imagined."

Chapter 49

Turning down the volume of the television, Margaret listened to a vehicle passing, the engine note increasing as it surged over the brow of the first rise. It wasn't the first visitor that evening.

Deafened by the noise from Melissa's new video film, Margaret sat in the hall with one finger pressed to an ear while she dialled Prinn's number. After six double tones the answer phone switched in. She left a short non-committal message, before hurriedly preparing to go out.

-oOo-

Adjusting her eyes to the dark shapes beyond the castle entrance, Margaret distinguished the vehicles of Capagli and Paba, with an unfamiliar Range Rover parked close by. The generator indicated that the occupants of the vehicles were somewhere inside the castle. To get any closer she had to rely on the guard making one of his infrequent turns round the bailey.

A shadowy figure was suddenly lit up by the flare of a match, isolating a gaunt, acerbic face. Shifting the carbine on his shoulder, he began his turn about with the lethargic movement of someone who welcomed any escape from their present monotony.

Judging her position by the smell of cigarette smoke that accompanied him, she made a short dash to the outer walls of the keep, tripping over some unseen obstacle in her haste.

Lying flat on the ground, and very still, Margaret heard nothing except the pulsing of blood in her veins knowing that the guard, if he looked round, would catch the slightest movement.

A nocturnal creature scuttled across her hand, giving rise to a thousand cacodemons that followed fleetingly across her imagination. With an involuntary shudder she lifted her head, straining to catch sight of the guard. Only the faint smell of his tobacco remained, fading as its essence quickly dispersed in the motion of the air.

Gaining the cover of the bulldozer and diggers parked

under the awning, the cloying smell of diesel fuel encouraged her closer to the trench and the dark aperture of the entrance. Here, Margaret's courage failed her. Vast aqueous cisterns, fed by rainwater, were built under ancient buildings. A misguided step in the pitch darkness might quickly send her crashing bodily into its depths.

In a dejected frame of mind she began to turn away, stopped by a momentary cast of light. Peering into the darkness, the impression returned to the bottom of her vision, indirectly disclosing a weak glow on the ground. At the same time she became aware of a murmur of voices, rising and falling.

Working her way down wide steps, she inched her way across the floor towards the luminous patch. Reaching the edge she cautiously looked over.

A nail pegged wooden ladder, dragged from an orchard or an olive grove, leant in front of her. The voices, now clearly perceptible, were still no more recognizable. Margaret lowered herself over the edge.

Reaching the bottom, she propped herself against the ladder, breathing deeply, ignoring the clawing sensation in her stomach.

The voices were now only a few metres away. Looking into the corridor of the tomb, she saw two men standing at the end talking to Capagli. The only significant thing about the group was that Paba wasn't among them.

There was nothing to be gained by staying. Half way up the ladder her strength failed, leaving her hanging there, arms through the rungs, incapable of proceeding. Thinking she heard the voices growing louder, and assailed by the fear of being caught, Margaret summoned all of her energy to haul herself back through the trapdoor.

Hastily reaching the doorway, faintly defined against the lighter sky, she caught her shin violently on the sharp stone edge of the steps. Only the faintest groan escaped through her pressed lips. Stubbornly enduring the dull, pulsating ache, she hobbled over the threshold, and out of the trench.

A smoker's rattling cough came from a position in the lee of the wall, out of the wind.

Searching on the ground for two heavy stones, that finally came to hand, she tossed one to the opposite side from where she stood.

A small arc of burning ash fluttered to the ground, followed by the rattle of the second stone Margaret threw in the same direction, but some distance forward. A beam from a torch flickered along the wall; adjusted to give a wider spread of light as the guard moved away to investigate.

Seizing her chance, Margaret slipped through the gateway, and across open ground into the shelter of the wood.

Approaching her house, she imagined she'd crossed all the bridges before reaching any of them - as though, despite all her efforts, the present had not yet become the past. Annoyed that she had learnt very little more than her previous knowledge, it starkly appeared nothing concrete had been gained despite the enormous risk she had taken.

Margaret opened the front door. From upstairs, the television still broadcast noisily its hollow booming sounds of disembodied voices.

She sat down heavily by the telephone. Contacting Prinn was her immediate priority. She was too exhausted to make decisions; too drained and apathetic to cope with the developing situation on her own.

On the fourth or fifth number she realized there was no tone. Tapping the rest impatiently failed to restore the familiar double notes.

"Melissa," she called impatiently up the stairs from the seat, receiving no answer.

"Melissa," she shouted firmly, over the irritating noise from above.

Exasperated, Margaret hurried up to where the television screen flickered unheeded before an empty chair in an empty room. Hurrying across the corridor, she opened the bathroom door, switching on the light pointlessly.

Like a smack in the face she recollected Paba's car, and his absence. All her tormented imaginings and soul searching had resulted in not taking care of Melissa at all; treating the house like an island fortress, immune

421

from the outside world, when it was as little defended as a kindergarten.

Stumbling down the stairs, she searched frantically through the other rooms, desperately hoping her daughter would be there. She had to get help. Help from someone. Her nearest neighbour would be the only one with a telephone.

Rushing back through the hall, Margaret abruptly stopped, her stricken senses overwhelmed by the man sitting calmly by the telephone on the seat she had so recently vacated, a leg casually crossed, as he waited for her. From deep down in her stomach panic forced its way into her lungs; a cry welling up like a wave that floundered, frozen on her lips.

He rose quietly, a sombre smile touching the corners of his mouth. Margaret's eyes were riveted to the smooth, dark, perfectly machined tunnel that disappeared into the barrel of the pistol.

"Margaret," Paba said, his voice echoing in a tunnel of its own. "You appear to have cut yourself rather badly. So much blood."

He stopped in front of her, though Margaret didn't see him through the tears in her eyes, only sensed his presence, and the pistol lifting her skirt until she felt the tip of the barrel press lightly against the soft swelling of her vulva.

"So much blood," Paba said again; the click of the safety catch being released hardly audible in the hollowness of his voice that beat against her terrified imagination.

Chapter 50

Vergellesi snapped the ammunition clip home into the handle of the Beretta, replacing it in the holster under his arm. Flattening the Velcro strip, he shrugged his shoulders twice to settle the weight comfortably before fastening the top button of his jacket.

"The overriding principle, Rex, is to stay alive. Being a saint isn't good for your health. Haven't you noticed? They're always dead."

Pouring himself a glass of milk, Vergellesi left the argument in silence while he returned the carton to the refrigerator. He leant against the kitchen doorframe to make a further point.

It's part of the human condition, Rex. Wanting to change things. So for us, now is the right time." Vergellesi studied Eldon's troubled face. "You don't agree?"

"I'm not sure," Eldon responded thoughtfully. "Something's changed. New loose ends."

"Like what, Rex?" Vergellesi sat down. "What's so different?"

"New faces. Faces that don't fit. Professional faces, Piero. The present gangsters are amateurs; deadly effective at times, but if anyone tried hard enough, sooner or later, they'd be caught. Now there are people who don't belong, concealed behind what is familiar, but totally dissimilar. We can't see them when they're here, and we won't know them when they're gone."

"Rex, we can't gather evidence for ever. I take your point. Let's find them a slot; make more of a picture, get a better idea of what we're up against. Fine, but they're not going to put anything on hold while we pigeonhole them." Vergellesi sat back in his chair, picking up his glass of milk. "Or perhaps, my friend, you're searching for an excuse."

"What do you mean, excuse?"

"Prato was not Escàroz, Rex."

"It was still a mess, Piero."

"Things may not improve either. Tuscan roads are full of potholes that shake and rattle your teeth about, but down them we have to go. We can't afford the luxury of contemplation. Now's the time."

Eldon began to see that his doubts were just retrospective vexations. It was, as Vergellesi said, the human condition. Facing up to the reality of being in the company of trained murderers was not a place for people who looked the other way. Given their circumstances, now would have to be as good a time as any. Eldon picked up the holstered gun that lay on the table, slipping his arm through the straps.

"Shall we go then?" Vergellesi enquired, looking at his watch.

"No time like the present."

Vergellesi opened the hall door. The telephone rang.

"Leave it," Eldon said. "You'll only say it's another excuse for a delay."

Vergellesi, protesting mildly, picked up the receiver. His conversation was brief.

"Ruggieri," he said when he replaced the receiver. "It appears your hunch was correct. Rosso's information that Kopolev's wine was Verolino has just been confirmed by Rome. They've also managed to track the wine to Moscow."

"Some of which has recently arrived with a customer in Tuscany. You're right, Piero - Now is the time."

The telephone rang again.

Eldon shut the door behind them.

-oOo-

Parking the car in an overgrown track, Vergellesi switched off the engine.

Waiting for their eyes to adjust to the dark, Eldon inquired out of interest, "How large was Etruria?"

"Larger than Tuscany. Probably from the Tiber to the plain of the Po. Why do you ask?"

"Curiosity. I acquired an Etruscan plate just recently. Wondered where it might have come from. Near here I supposed. Sounds more like anywhere in Italy."

"Anywhere," Vergellesi agreed in a disinterested voice. *"Andiamo."*

Vergellesi didn't lock the car, placing the keys on a

front tyre in case they became separated. The windscreen had already begun to mist over with the sort of dampness that settled on all, and every surface.

Vergellesi had remembered his earlier reconnaissance well, the track finally emerging from the woods close to Margaret's house. It was light enough to make out the shape of her estate car parked under the stone pine.

"The castle's ahead," Vergellesi said in a low voice.

"Is there an easy way in?" Eldon asked.

"Not that I could see. Over the wall, with a difficult drop on the inside, or through the gateway."

"I'll go first then." Without another word Eldon slipped away into the darkness.

Vergellesi used the central strip of grass to muffle his footsteps. Reaching the castle entrance, he waited, listening intently to the sounds of the night: a dog's discord carried on gusts of wind; a propeller aircraft flying high up accompanied by its steady soporific drone; a disturbed bird deep in the woods making a short, indignant protest. Everything seemed distant and disinterested in these few square acres.

Eldon spoke to him from somewhere close, a disembodied whisper that made him jump.

"Not very busy. A small room over there's locked up. Seems it's being used for some purpose. Further on there's a trench leading into the keep. The one they covered up during the day, so it never appeared on our series of films. If they've left the stable door open, someone will be expecting us."

"Inside, with everything boxed in?" Vergellesi queried.

"Exactly where they'll want us. How are you feeling?"

"Fine. Let's not keep them waiting." He followed the fading shadow in front of him.

Stepping into the opening, Eldon switched on his small Brinkmann torch revealing a deep and unoccupied space; the massiveness of its mediaeval military architecture was carried on a series of broad vaulted ceilings, supported by stone arches. An angle in the nearest space was black with soot from a make shift fireplace. Close by, the remains of firewood so riddled and desiccated by the passing of centuries, that a slightest touch would have turned them to dust.

The wide-open steps of grey stone slabs had their centre's worn into a gentle concave shape by countless feet passing over them. There was fresher earth scattered on the steps, a darker trace of what looked like blood on an edge, a modern disturbance in the weight of ages that lay everywhere.

Making a final scan of the room, Vergellesi stopped Eldon's arm, directing it back to an open trap door in the floor. The stone lid, with its central iron ring rusted away, lay to one side.

"*Dio!* A time of savages," Vergellesi said, in a soft whisper, as Eldon shone the light down into the corridor of the oubliette.

"No less than this, Piero. Their heirs still inhabit the earth," Eldon added, as he lowered himself down the ladder.

Entering the newly revealed opening, they stopped at the cross tunnels. Vergellesi put out his hand, feeling the corner stones. As if touching a switch, light flooded the tunnel. Looking back to where they'd entered, they found the opening blocked by an armed group.

Eldon glanced at Vergellesi. "I hope they appreciate the seriousness of pulling a trigger in here. Place is only held together with cobwebs."

Capagli's Sicilian foreman pugnaciously pushed himself to the front, waving a pistol at them. "*State zitti!*" he shouted, oblivious to the incongruous figure he portrayed, at odds even with himself.

"Do what he says," Vergellesi muttered. "Before he kills everyone in here by bringing the roof down."

"*Il gioco è finito*, eh?" the little Sicilian continued.

Both looked at him blankly, not caring for an answer to be misinterpreted.

He prodded Eldon's arm with the pistol. "Up," he managed in English, grinning.

They placed their hands on top of their heads.

The other men moved closer while he searched them, triumphantly holding the automatic pistols aloft, stuffing them into his trouser belt. "Sat, sat," he commanded, waving his pistol at the floor.

"Hope he slips, and blows his balls off," Vergellesi muttered, doing as he was bid.

"*Zitto*," The foreman shouted, kicking him on the shin.

"What do we do with them?" one of the men in a camouflaged suit asked.

"Capagli was expecting them. He's been delayed with another little problem. The English woman you've been watching became too nosy. Don't know what he's got in mind for her, but when he arrives I expect these two can join the salamanders in the cistern."

The man in the camouflaged suit shrugged. "They don't look the sort to be in this business," he suggested, only half satisfied with the answer to his question.

"They're the sort to be a nuisance," the foreman dismissed his concerns. "Leave the decisions to Capagli."

The little Sicilian sneered at Eldon, exposing teeth stained by cigarette smoke. A brief suspicion crossed his mind that Eldon's disdainful expression was directed at him; a glance of personal contempt which brought a heavy boot crashing against Eldon's outer thigh. Eldon winced, clamping his lips against any protest.

Like an automaton, programmed to repeat a single task, he raised his boot to strike again. One of the guards pushed him away. "Don't waste your energy kicking dogs, save it for the digging."

The round, stubby body turned away with a surly look. "Watch them, while I find Capagli. He should be here by now."

Capagli, when the Sicilian found him, didn't like what he heard. He slammed the door of his Land Rover irritably. Paba had said the Morning woman was mixed up in something that might bring others. He'd come to the conclusion that the further away from these incidents he could get, the safer he would be. He rang Paba.

"Who are they?" Paba asked.

"I don't know," Capagli replied. "Both were armed. You said you'd take care of these things. Remember?"

"Oh, I shall take care of them, Capagli. You concentrate on finding the tomb, as I'm unable to rely on you for anything else. Send them to me." The telephone clicked off.

Capagli descended the ladder. "Where are their documents?" he snapped.

"They didn't have any." The foreman automatically lied.

Capagli walked to the edge of the corridor, but didn't enter. He recognized them from somewhere. They weren't local. Then he remembered the *festa* dinner. They looked like city people; visitors that would have eaten in a convenient restaurant. They might have been slumming. There were people who did. These, he knew by instinct, were people who fitted themselves in wherever it suited. He turned to the little Sicilian, and grimly prodded him. "Try again," he ordered.

A guard searched them more thoroughly, his success adding a degree more spite to the foreman's attitude. Flicking Vergellesi's identity card open, he read the details. Looking up at him with a cold, hardened stare, the flicker in his grudge-ridden eyes betrayed a trace of uncertainty. Eldon's credit card sized document left him none the wiser.

Returning to Capagli, who had withdrawn out of sight of the corridor, he waved the documents angrily at him. "Police Capagli, nosing around."

In a manner calmer than he felt, Capagli studied the documents carefully. "The Italian may be a police commissioner, but this is different," he said, tapping the top of his knuckles with Eldon's card. "An English civil servant."

The foreman looked down the corridor at Eldon, trying to imagine the possibilities of such a person's arrival in a backwater like Sorena. "Government man? He was carrying a gun."

"The English don't make a habit of such things. But if they do, you can be sure they've been trained to use them. Send some men in the van with them to *Signor* Paba."

"I'll go," the foreman volunteered eagerly, but Capagli shook his head.

"No. You're needed here. We've got to find a way through the roof. *Rapidamente!*"

-oOo-

Bundled into the back of the van, their wrists bound

with wire and taped, guards sitting two on either side, there was little possibility of escape.

Where the leaders of this group were, Eldon had no idea, though he'd wager that he and Vergellesi were, presently, rather closer to the bottom of the pile than to the top.

After an uncomfortable journey on another indifferent road, the vehicle slowed down, crossed a wooden slatted bridge, turned through a number of bends, and jerked to a halt. The rear doors opened, and the guards hauled them out into the open air.

The weather, in their short drive, had begun to signal its promised change. Heavier clouds, accelerating under a smoky nebulous strata, intermittently blotted out the already poor illumination.

Surrounded by trees, for all Eldon knew, it might well have been the wood behind the castle. The dark mass of timber pressed forward, threatening to engulf the large clearing.

A ruined chapel stood in front of them, jagged and open, still ridiculing the passage of time. Weather bleached, perfectly dressed quoins, glowed a soft symmetrical paleness beside the dark crumbling rubble of the facing walls. One arched window remained, remnants of bar tracery hardly visible against the gaping void beyond.

Rifle barrels pushed them forward towards a low stone building, re-roofed where another story once existed above the refectory of a secluded, and long abandoned monastery.

Inside, at the end of a long narrow room, a large open fireplace was set, shiny with the condensed liquid from wood smoke. A stout wooden table, surrounded by wooden benches stood in front of the hearth. A glimpse of plank bunk beds in an adjacent room suggested the monastic tradition had not altogether disappeared.

At the far end of the table, close to the fire, Paba occupied a stool, his cashmere coat in a Napoleonic gesture still draped over his shoulders. Behind him stood the two massive 'props' he'd acquired from Giuliani. There was nothing well intentioned about their construction, nor anything to contemplate with affection.

The brutal sadistic power they could deploy had never been intended to accompany any sympathy.

Paba surveyed his visitors with wintry eyes. His deliberations were in themselves deliberate; the foundations of fear being built upon, until every small movement had the fascination of an inquisition. His long fingers stroked a match with all the delicacy of an artist restoring a freshly cleaned filbert; his eyes never leaving theirs, letting the seconds pass leisurely with the intention of propagating fear in the imagination of his prey.

Suddenly, he snapped the match in two and stood up. "Gentlemen. I'm wasting our time." He nodded to a hunter. "Untie them."

The tape was ripped off; the wire loosened, and removed from their wrists.

"Such a disappointment," Paba continued. "You go out of your way to be a good neighbour, only to find yourself repaid by discourtesy." He stood, his hands clasped in front of him, thumbs pressed together. "It's distasteful having people pry into your affairs. Poking their noses in where they're not wanted. It's most unfortunate for you that these present interests happen to be mine, because I take a great exception to this meddling, as you will presently discover."

Paba considered for a moment whether or not to attempt a discovery of the reasons for their interference, but decided he was more eager to be rid of the delay. With Petrov becoming less affable over their slow progress, there was some urgency in finding a way into the tomb. He nodded towards a closed door. Margaret was brought into the room, her hair dishevelled, and with heavy traces of mascara having run in dark streaks down her cheeks.

"No harm's come to her yet, she just makes a lot of fuss. You, on the other hand, make very little fuss; therefore, must come to a great deal of harm." Paba gestured to one of the hunters. "Give Mrs Morning her coat."

Rifles forced them back on to their feet. A hunter pushed past, handing their identity cards to Paba who glanced at them momentarily before flicking them on to the fire, where they flared before shrinking into a black speck. Missing people weren't going to be his concern.

Outside, Paba led the way to a low building.

Eldon, watchful for an opportunity to escape, was not optimistic, hardly doubting that the surrounding marksmen could hit a running figure with their eyes shut. Paba was also clever, knowing that they were hampered by Margaret's presence, that would almost certainly restrict any effort presenting itself.

The dog's clamouring noise swelled the confines of their communal kennel; a baying, that not only signalled the chorus for a cornered quarry. They were hungry!

Their cages lined one side of the shed; the corrugated roof gleaming with pendants of glistening humidity. At the bottom, where Paba stopped, another set of cages ran at right angles. The noise of the hunter's dogs drowned Paba's words. He motioned them closer. Inside, smooth coated black and tan Doberman pinschers moved restlessly in their cages, bright eyes darting at the peering faces, but not one joining in the surrounding disturbance.

"A passion of mine, Herr Doberman's terriers. I've bred and trained them myself to kill anything they run to earth. They are wonderfully highly strung animals, with all the tenacity and intelligence of the terrier, plus considerably greater speed. Of course they have the advantage over you, because they know the terrain so well. But I'm a sporting man, a ten minute start should be sufficient to suit their handlers sense of the chase."

Vergellesi broke in angrily. "Mrs Morning won't outrun them. She doesn't have a chance."

"Of course not. None of you will outrun them. They will hunt you down, and when they catch you, tear you to pieces. That is the idea." Paba laughed softly to himself, before changing his mind. "No. You're right. Mrs Morning wouldn't be much sport. We'll think of another solution for her. You can go alone. At least I'm giving you a chance. Take care though. These dogs can reach fifty kilometres an hour in a straight line. They'll hit you like an express train."

Paba pulled his coat tighter round his shoulders and walked over to a stunned, and shaken Margaret. "You see. I can be very reasonable when the mood takes me. Unhappily it's not very often." He nodded to his large minder. "Bring Mrs Morning, Romulus," he said quietly. "Put her in my car with Damiano. This won't be something a nice lady would care to witness."

Chapter 51

The dog handlers held the tall dogs taut on their leads, impressively calm, their pointed ears pricked to catch every sound, taking the scent in turn. Paba hadn't exaggerated when he said he'd trained them to a high standard.

In such terrain, Eldon surmised, they couldn't expect to make more than a kilometre before the dogs were released, perhaps another, before they were overtaken. Waiting for opportunities was no longer an option.

"La citta è lontana," a hunter mocked, making the others laugh. *"Dieci minuti. Andate."* He indicated with his rifle towards the trees.

Eldon and Vergellesi reached the woods at a sprint.

"We should split up," Vergellesi said, without stopping.

"Agreed," Eldon replied. "But not quite in the way they expect." He drew to a halt. "Time for a piggyback, Piero. Don't ask any questions. Up, quickly."

Vergellesi did as he was told. Eldon set off again in a line at an angle to the one they had come along, trusting that it would bring them back close to where they had started. Judging they were near enough, he stopped under a suitable tree, allowing Vergellesi to clamber up into the branches, trusting the smell of pine would help disguise his scent.

"I'll keep as close to the road as I can," Eldon called. "When they've passed, acquire their vehicle. Follow the road round the edge. Don't hang about." He vanished among the trees.

It wasn't long before Vergellesi heard the dogs searching for their scent. He had just begun to feel uncomfortable, balancing on two branches, when he heard dogs close under the tree. There was more than one. But how many? They moved off again in the direction Eldon had taken

Knowing these woods like the backs of their hands, the hunters would intuitively fix Eldon's course, saving themselves the effort of the chase by choosing a point ahead where they would be able to intercept him.

22222222222222

22

Hastily, Vergellesi clambered down from the tree. The sky had cleared enough for the moon to add an unreliable visibility to his surroundings. It was not going to last, which might turn out to be fortunate.

A light remained on in the building, with the van still parked close to the ruin. Vergellesi made a short dash to its side, edging along to the corner. The area was deserted. A solitary voice held forth inside.

Covering the open ground he reached the driver's door, pressing the button in gently, easing it open slowly. The hinges grated noisily. A damp odour, accompanied the smell of motor oil and stale cigarettes. He felt along the steering column, hoping they'd left the key in the ignition. He was out of luck. A toolbox in the footwell yielded a pair of pliers. Snipping some lengths of cable from one of the indicator lights he returned to the cab. Pulling the bonnet release, it opened with a loud metallic bang.

Vergellesi waited, looking over the dashboard towards the lodge. No one appeared. Propping up the bonnet he quickly bypassed the ignition. Under the seat, a wheel brace with a long handle came to hand. Shutting the door gently to muffle the noise, he threaded the brace through the steering column and rammed it down hard. With a crunch the column lock snapped, freeing the steering wheel.

Outside, Vergellesi heard the dogs barking high up in the woods behind him. Time was running short. Touching the loose end of the wire attached to the starter motor on to the pole of the battery, the vehicle started. Flicking the bonnet stay away he scrambled back into the cab, crashed a gear and lurched forward, crashed another to reverse the car round, seeing the door of the lodge thrown open out of the corner of his eye before the building passed from view. The distorted rattle of an automatic weapon swept up towards him. There was a crash of breaking glass, as he accelerated hard up the bumpy track.

Nearly running out of road on the first bend, Vergellesi pulled switches blindly until the lights came on. He swung left at a branch in the track, to keep the same section of wood on the driver's side. As the track steepened, the surface riven into deep folds violently snatched at the steering wheel, forcing him to concentrate on keeping the vehicle straight, and hope he would soon catch a sight of Eldon.

Breasting a rise, the descending lights brought into view an abandoned *podere*, its emptiness a solitary shape of regular lines against the plunging darkness behind. Missing a beat, then another, the engine shuddered, jerking the van to a stop, its petrol gauge registering empty.

At the rear an exposed bulb from one of the smashed tail lamps threw a light across the door, disclosing a diagonal line of holes ripped through the panels level with the petrol tank. Vergellesi thumped a clenched fist against the side in exasperation.

He had to get the van off the road. Double wooden doors on the storage vaults of the farmhouse pulled away at the hasp. Pushing the van backwards he steered it inside, wedging the doors closed.

The sound of a vehicle travelling at high speed sent him hurrying down the side of the building, cursing the accumulated debris of old tins and buckets he stumbled over. Reaching an entrance door hanging on rusted hinges, he slipped inside.

-oOo-

Eldon knew he didn't have a ten-minute lead any longer, aware that the heavy undergrowth had depleted any margin of energy. His pursuers would have no such problem. Some would already be ahead of him, making even the tracks a dangerous option. Hunters, stationed in blocking position, would be waiting for the unlikely event of the dogs failing to come up on their quarry.

Smashing his way through the small bushes, Eldon, sensing that the dogs were to the left of him, veered to the right, only to sense them again on the right, making him veer to the left. They were practiced hunters, driving him towards a spot somewhere ahead where they could slip their Doberman's leashes.

No more than three or four hundred metres seemed to separate them as he tripped over roots, stumbled through knee high brambles, thrusting aside spindly saplings whipping across his face.

Crashing into a small glade filled with watery moonlight, he sprinted towards the opposite trees. A dog broke from cover behind him. Loose, it scented Eldon, covering the short distance at a sprint in a matter of seconds. Eldon turned to see its dark form stretching over the ground as it lowered itself to spring the last few metres. He raised his arm to chop at the sleek body lifting in the air towards him, ears back, the stench of its frothy saliva reaching Eldon's nostrils even as he heard the breathy blast of the silenced automatic close to his right elbow that spun the animal sideways into a writhing heap on the ground.

"Better get your butt over here son, the place is full of these crazy monsters. That's the second one in five minutes." Remmick waved him towards the trees.

"Where did you come from?" Eldon asked breathlessly.

"Sheer coincidence. Got to get us out of here. This way." He hurried ahead, talking over his shoulder. "I've been watching Paba for months. Guy's damn smart for sure, up to his ears in some business. He's only the tip of the iceberg. There's a Russian, Petrov, turned up to hold his hand. Used to be a big fish in the KGB. Which is why I'm here. We need to find out about him. They reckon he's still running a one time asset. Place is hotting up at last, so we've got to stay on top of it. I was trekking over to a clapped out monastery they've converted. No use going in by truck round here, they'd suss you in no time. Reckon that's where they all get holed up planning this party. They aren't going to welcome poopers, so we've got to make ourselves scarce at the moment. Sure glad you came along before the shit hit the fan. Got to stretch a leg, son. Place is crawling with vermin."

From somewhere the noise of a high velocity rifle slapped its sharp crack on the darkness, punctuated with an echo. Remmick sagged to his knees, staggered to his feet again, moved a few paces, and stopped.

"Christ! I've bought one. Shit!" He straightened himself, gesturing impatiently. "No. Keep moving," pushing Eldon forward.

Remmick began to fall behind, his heavy laboured breathing punctuating the air around them.

"How bad is it?" Eldon asked, looking anxiously into the darkness behind them.

Remmick leant against a tree, his hand under his ribs. "Went in under my chest. Hurts if I move too fast. Better now I've stopped."

His breath now came in short bursts, with a little gurgle at its lowest point. In the pale light among the broken shadows Eldon saw that Remmick's face had fallen, all affectation of character drained away by pain, leaving only the struggle to dispel a new fear that was inching into his conscience.

"Get your arse out of here, son. I'll only slow you down. Have to do the whole thing on your own from now on. Track's straight ahead." His voice was hoarse, exhausted from talking. He let himself slide down the tree until he was sitting upright, his legs stretched out in front of him.

Eldon crouched down beside him. "Adam. I'll carry you out."

Remmick gave a small gurgling laugh. "No point in carrying a corpse, son. You just get yourself some space." Eldon felt a hand on his arm. "I'm counting on you to square it for me. Mentioned in dispatches, so I'm not completely forgotten. In the history books." His hand fell away, helping the other pull the automatic on to his lap. Somewhere close by they heard a dog being choked back, its handler confused by the unexpected.

Fighting against his natural instincts Eldon knew Remmick was right. There was nothing he could do to help him. He was an old warrior; an elephant that had come somewhere to die. He paused after a few paces, looking back. Remmick's head was nodding forward, but sensing Eldon had stopped, snapped upright as if he'd just woken up. He waved the automatic.

"I'm still with you, son. Keep going. We've been here before. Remember? The damn Alamo."

"I saw the film, Adam. All you Yanks think you're John Wayne."

"Sure. Pity they haven't got around to giving it a better ending, son." His voice trailed off into a weak cough.

Eldon raised his arm in a respectful salute before breaking into a fast run, slaloming his way between the trees in an effort to make himself as difficult a target as possible. In less than a minute Eldon emerged on to the track. He looked left and right. In the pause, a crash of rifle shots hung on the darkness behind him.

Chapter 52

Vergellesi hearing the car pass, let out his breath in a sigh of relief. In the distance he heard gunshots, before all fell silent again.

He reached into his inner pocket where they'd missed his pencil torch. The slim beam lit up the remains of a terracotta floor; herringbone pattern appearing like sharks teeth against the decayed mortar foundation. A heavy mat of dust covered everything; trapped in ancient cobwebs round rotten window frames and damp angles of the wall.

Switching off his torch, Vergellesi turned back to the door, listening intently. The car was returning, moving slowly, the driver searching for something. Reaching the building it stopped, engine ticking over for a few seconds before being switched off. There was a moment's silence. Doors opened and shut. Another long pause, followed by the creaking of the double doors to the *cantina* as they were swung open.

Shifting on to his right foot, Vergellesi brought the open angle of the door into his vision. There were no follow up sounds in the air; no footsteps or whispers, nothing broke into the deep silence that pressed against the stones, and the peeling stucco around him.

Vergellesi's eyes flitted constantly across the aperture. He steadied himself, forcing the adrenalin to slow down by focusing his eyes on one spot, so any movement coming into his line of vision didn't change the focal plane of his sight. If you were waiting for something, then patience was the ultimate virtue. In such a case, Vergellesi was short on virtue.

A small movement attracted his attention. Keeping his eyes steady, he saw it again, more dependent on what he heard than what he could see. There was no advice Vergellesi could give himself on sound, except not to make any. Summed up, he couldn't see, he couldn't hear, and he couldn't move. Shadows moving on shadows, noiselessly, as still as the air that was never still.

Impatience got the better of him.

Slipping outside, Vergellesi moved through the bushes away from the building. He made out two tall cylindrical towers; old concrete silo's used to manufacture fodder. Straw loaded into the tubes, would be compressed by large heavy circular discs of chestnut loaded with concrete weights, into an edible cake. It could then be used in the winter to feed animals drawn into strong iron pens close to the house. A section of these pens stood by one of the hatches, overgrown with weeds, almost rusted beyond use. A white Mercedes Benz had been parked in front.

There was a movement close to the silo, to the left, beyond the car. The visible foreground included the frame of one of Paba's Neapolitan associates. Making no sound he moved towards the house. Weighing upwards of one hundred and thirty kilograms, with not an ounce of fat or steroid enhanced bulk on his body, he was not the sort of person you went out of your way to offend.

Vergellesi watched the figure move silently out of sight before making his way towards the silo, using the sagging remains of a wooden fence to break up his shape. A smell of silage still emanated from the large knee high openings round the base.

Rounding the second silo Vergellesi became trapped in a vice like grip encircling his throat. Trying to claw the hand away, he was thrown heavily against the concrete side, lying where he fell, gasping like a fish cast up on the bank. Still winded, he struggled to his knees, being lifted the rest of the way on to his feet, and rammed back against the silo.

Instinctively, summoning up all his remaining strength, Vergellesi lashed out at the figure in front of him. He failed to connect with anything, being caught as he fell, spun and slammed against the rough surface, any movement resulting in his face being ground into the concrete.

The second twin reappeared, taking little notice of Vergellesi. "They must have split up. Stefano says the dogs are still out, moving in this direction. Perhaps we'll get the other one before the dogs catch him. Paba's not going to be pleased. Four of the dogs have been shot, and one of the handlers through the stomach. Kaput!"

The grip on Vergellesi relaxed a fraction. "Where did they get the gun from?" his assailant asked.

"They didn't. Some other worm crawled in with them. He's dead. Must have followed Stefano when he brought them up. Another thing Paba will want explained."

Neither seemed perturbed, showing little interest in Vergellesi, treating him neither as a nuisance or a game, merely an incident that had to be adjusted to fit the circumstances.

"What shall we do with this one?" Vergellesi's captor asked, tightening his grip again on Vergellesi's windpipe.

"Throw him in the silo. I'll lose the car. There's space next to the van."

Vergellesi felt himself lifted away from the silo wall and propelled forward to one of the hatches. Then he was falling gently towards the ground, knees buckling, while in the distance a yellowish pin-point of light rushed towards him, enlarging until it filled his vision, while the impression of falling ceased, replaced by the sensation of rising and falling as though on a trampoline. Twice, three times, he seemed to hang in the air while the yellow light faded, and all sense of consciousness slipped away from him.

-oOo-

Stopping to catch his breath, Eldon considered his position. The crossroad ahead he decided to avoid. On the opposite side, half way down in a make shift lay-by, a Lada off-road vehicle had been parked. Using the cover of the woods, he came down alongside it.

Two hunters sat watching the road, separated from the back of the vehicle by a grill behind which an agitated Doberman moved restlessly to and fro. Eldon was close enough to hear the crackling reception of their radio link through the open passenger's window. A cigarette end flicked forward, pirouetting to the ground in a shower of tiny sparks. The window was wound up in the passenger's door. It opened carefully. Looking round him with a degree of uncertainty, the hunter crossed the small ditch alongside, disappearing behind a tree.

Inside the vehicle the driver retuned the radio as it drifted off channel. There was too much interference in a reception area shielded by trees. The passenger door opened, and the hunter eased back on to the seat.

"Have a go at this thing?" the driver said, leaning back. His shoulders beginning to play up in the cramped position.

The edge of a flat hand chopped across the driver's throat rupturing his trachea, sending him bouncing forward against the steering wheel. Behind him the dog tore at the mesh grill, its savage teeth snapping and tearing at the division, shaking it in a frenzy of aggression, a paroxysm of fury that almost tore the fixture from its brackets. Eldon heaved the driver's body out of the vehicle and into the ditch.

The Doberman's rage had become exacerbated by an inability to reach its prey, lashing at the glass, hurling itself at whatever position Eldon was passing. Eldon slid into the cab, shut the door, and picked up one of the rifles between the seats. Pushing the barrel through the mesh guard the dog's fangs almost wrenched it from his grasp. He squeezed the trigger.

Driving up to the crossroads in silence, he turned towards the higher ground where he could retune the radio set. With the better reception he discovered that Vergellesi had reached a Podere Ombroso before running into Paba's Neapolitan colleagues. A map, stuffed in the glove pocket, showed the farm clearly marked, lying over the crest of the next hill. Slipping it into his jacket he picked up a torch, and one of the rifles with a full magazine, before setting off along the muddy track.

He stopped before reaching the podere, viewing the building from the cover of the trees. Eldon reasoned that Paba's men would think they had little to fear from unarmed adversaries. Which was just as well. Their size was not only one of intimidation, it was also one of substance designed for things to bounce off. The only way to stop such a man was to hit him with a lot more than a quartet of knuckles. Especially as there were two such men!

Moving forward he stepped on an old cartwheel half hidden in a tangle of weeds. Hauling the wheel upright he found it still possessed a metal tyre, if not many spokes. It was the sort of thing that might provide a distraction.

Pushing it away with a powerful thrust, the wheel bounced and wobbled on the track for the first few metres before gaining momentum on the downward incline.

Noisily the wheel picked up speed over the gravel, past the double doors of the *cantina*. One side flew open, followed by a burst of fire that tore the remaining wooden spokes from the wheel, shaking the remaining rim from its course and into the fence, bouncing back before crashing heavily to the ground.

Even as the wheel fell, the bulky form of Remus staggered, hanging on to the door for support as another high velocity bullet splintered through the panel, wrenching the body away.

A trace of bullets raked the ground Eldon had vacated a split second before, passing so close he felt them pluck at his leather jacket, showering him with broken branches.

Black clouds had begun to thicken over the faint moon. A splash of rain fell on his cheek, then another, followed by a flash of forked lightning, and a still distant roll of thunder. It was, he decided, going to be a dirty night.

Keeping well clear of the building, Eldon arrived behind the silo. He had no way of knowing if the second target was still there. He was left relying on those old skills he'd tried to discard along with the profession.

They were familiar opponents. Impassive people he'd come across too often in Crossmaglen, and the Sierra De Labia. Choosing to live by their own rules, without the faintest interest or understanding of those which society had painstakingly developed in an effort to divert the forces of just such a primitive anarchy. They were hardened, brittle people, relentlessly effective in a civilization that had grown soft, devoid of any human sympathy and possessed of an amorality that no amount of reasoned persuasion would ever transform. Portrayed as a product of their environment, or as victims of intellectual embitterment, or demoralization, the vicious order of survival left no space for human kindness among their brutalized personalities. There was no argument, no difference of opinion. What was right was whatever they had decided.

As the silo's naked appearance provided little cover, it wasn't a place Eldon was going to linger. He could distinguish only one feature attached to the structure, a metal stairway that looped round towards a gantry at the top. He passed round to the bottom from where he could now make out the dark recess of the opened hatch. About to ease himself past the steps, he caught a sound, no more than a breath.

It was a significant enough warning to orchestrate his response fractions of a second ahead of his vision. He blocked the blow with the rifle pressed upwards with both arms, the shock forcing them apart, but giving him space enough to drive his foot into the broad chest. Romulus stumbled backwards, regained his footing, lunging forward again. Eldon mounting the steps swung the rifle round at the large shape and pulled the trigger. A bent guard fouled the movement, rendering the rifle useless. He stabbed at the face with the barrel as he backed up the steps, having it swept aside out of his grip, clattering down the metal steps as he scrambled backwards to the small gantry platform, seventeen metres above the ground, invisible in the swirling darts of rain.

The large figure wasn't hurrying now, knowing Eldon was trapped. This thought gave Romulus a silent pleasure, something to savour; salve his anger as he contemplated the things he could do. Pulling himself up the last step on to the platform, the gantry shook a little. Only two metres separated them, with Eldon standing very still against the rail.

Romulus stopped to look at him for a moment. There was no need to rush. Eldon, he had seen, was quick. He wasn't going to be side stepped as he lunged forward, missing the distinct pleasure of breaking every bone in Eldon's body. He would pick and choose, as though selecting his favourite chocolates from an assortment. Fingers and thumbs. The screams to Romulus' ears would echo sweetly, like a church-sonata.

444

Eldon could feel the draught of breath fanning his face; could see the white teeth behind the parted lips of an expectant grin. Pausing, the tree trunk arms came out to enfold him. Slipping down against the body in a swift movement that avoided the embrace, Eldon gripped the solid legs with his neck under Romulus' crutch, heaving himself up to hurl the body backwards. Romulus grabbed at the rail as he somersaulted over, his weight tearing it apart from the rusty welding. Eldon heard the body bounce on an unseen projection before with a dull thud it hit the ground.

Shining his torch downwards through the flickering impenetrable rain, the beam stopped within a few metres. Eldon let out a long breath, easing his back upright. What had the doctor said? Some impracticable medical advice: 'On no account lift heavy weights!'

Descending the steps, Eldon circled to the other side of the silo, shining the torch across the ground until it came upon the still spread eagled form. He left Romulus there, returning to the hatch close to the bottom of the stairs. Shining the torch through the opening, the beam nearly missed Vergellesi close to the silo wall beneath him.

Looking for something to act as a ladder, Eldon came across the stack of long iron pen sections. Finding one strong enough, he pushed the section in, dangling by his arms to drop down alongside. Tapping Vergellesi's face brought no response. At least he was still breathing.

Taking him up over his shoulder, with one arm free, Eldon had almost reached the first proxy rung on the makeshift ladder when a creak high above his head at the top of the silo made him pause. There followed a rush of wind, swirling dust and straw into a storm around them before a deafening, screeching, groaning crash sent him sprawling sideways, rolling them both back on to the floor. Eldon retrieved his torch, and through the choking, settling dust saw the heavy wooden condenser cap used for compressing the hay, jammed on the top of the pen section. The tubular bars had buckled in arresting the wooden cylinder clear of the hatch. But they'd held.

Vergellesi moaned a little as he was lifted on to

Eldon's shoulder, and again as he was bundled out on to the wet grass. Eldon propped him up, trusting the fresh air would revive him, while he dealt with the unfinished business.

Returning to the other side of the silo he looked for the body.

Romulus was nowhere to be seen.

In the light of the torch a dark puddle, a spumous mixture of blood and phlegm, was gradually being diluted by the drizzle. He followed a trail of stains to a small open sided cabin containing the winding gear for the wooden cylinder of the silo, and came upon the missing body.

Romulus' hand still clung to the lever of the release mechanism. There was no pulse. Eldon rolled the body over releasing the Uzi suspended on a lanyard.

Racing back to the hatch, he found Vergellesi was no longer there. Eldon cursed. He didn't have time for all these missing bodies.

There was a short hollow boom of a car engine before the double doors opposite burst open, and the Mercedes Benz hurtled out, broad siding under fierce acceleration, headlights full on. Skidding to a halt Vergellesi leapt out, gesticulating wildly. Sprinting over, Eldon scrambled in as the car moved off again.

"Where now?" Vergellesi shouted as he selected gears, charging down the track, bouncing from one bank to the other. The wipers, adding to the din, revealed in the swinging headlights muddy rivers of water swirling down the track. The rain had begun in earnest. "How did you find your way up here? I missed you altogether."

"Tell you later," Eldon said, closing the shoulder stock and checking the cartridge clip of the Uzi in the dashboard lights. "For the moment we'd better get back to the castle. I'll direct you. How's your head?" he asked, gripping the dashboard.

"Stiff neck." Vergellesi said, the car sideways in the track. "Sleeping in too much draught."

"Whoops!" Vergellesi exclaimed, wrestling with the vehicle as he over-corrected on the slippery surface, slipping sideways and thudding heavily against the bank, before charging straight on.

"Whoops is right. Will you remember my back," Eldon complained.

The car skidded round a sharp corner. Vergellesi caught the slide deftly, pointing the nose back down the track, the vehicles tail still weaving under acceleration.

"For God's sake, Piero," Eldon protested. "At least keep us in a straight line will you."

Chapter 53

Huddled in the dark, Margaret had been in a distracted condition for some time. Paba, ignoring her entreaties over Melissa, left her to suffer the emotional anxiety of a fretful uncertainty. Vergellesi drifted into her thoughts and was as quickly shut out again. Contemplating his and Eldon's failure only multiplied her fears; dashing any sort of hope.

A key grated noisily in the lock. The door swung open, with a hunter holding his storm lamp higher for Paba to enter. In the swaying yellow light his face expressed only the grim enmity he felt.

"Melissa?" Margaret asked expectantly.

"Ah yes. Melissa." Paba dismissed the subject irritably. "I've more important things to attend to. We're just about to open a tomb, and as your curiosity has brought you so much grief, you might as well discover why."

Paba took her arm firmly, guiding her into the keep as far as the trap door. Below a small group waited for them.

"I take it you're not about to spring another partner on us, Paba?" Petrov said sourly.

"No, General. We have no new partners." Paba turned to Sandquest. "They have a saying in England, I believe, that curiosity killed the cat?"

Sandquest looked at Margaret, and then unsmilingly back at Paba. "It kills people, so why not cats?"

Paba, nodded in agreement, taking Sandquest and Petrov aside beyond Margaret's hearing. "Circumstances necessitate clearing the tomb quickly. I've made arrangements to store, whatever we find, securely at a location in the Futa Pass. I've no doubt it will be substantial. From there I need to get all the merchandise through Austria, across the border into the Czech Republic. We'll agree the inventory before it leaves for Austria. You'll organize the customs arrangements as agreed, General?"

Petrov nodded. "I've confirmed transit details. Everything must be ready, as the border timings are critical. You have drivers able to make the journey against a stop watch?"

"Experienced drivers. Used to mountains." Paba turned to Capagli. "You can show us now. We need to know if all our efforts have been worth it."

Capagli led them down the narrow corridor to the blank wall where he had erected a small scaffolding within bracing stanchions.

"As you can see, the construction of the walls utilizes stones of two different colours. The grey ones are of a minimal quantity set in a random manner, but sufficiently numerous not to make them too conspicuous." Capagli pointed them out in various sections of the corridor. "They're not significant structurally. Because the grey material's soft, the builders avoided using them for angles or exposed sections, but they're perfectly adequate elsewhere."

"So what's the significance?" Sandquest enquired.

Capagli waved his hand to examples of the stone set in the wall. "Besides their familiarity, they can be worked, while the others cannot, other than being knapped to provide a face." He pointed to a similar stone against the roof, above the scaffold. "Just another one, like all the others. Except it has a hole large enough to take a small rod of bronze, something like this." He picked up a piece of steel rod. "You need modern drills for the other stones, but for these an augur will do. Originally, they blocked up the hole with tinted clay, which in the normal humidity of the tomb, remained in place. Tapping the stones to see if any were loose caused the clay to fall out of this one. Probably dried out under all the lights."

Capagli climbed on to the scaffold, inserting the rod in a hole almost on the stones upper edge, too small to be seen from the floor. He gave it a sharp twist.

To the watching eyes, nothing moved.

"In a cavity there's a pivoting bronze plate located in grooves at the bottom of these adjacent stones. You just turn it to unlock this stone". He tapped the uppermost capping resting over the end wall. "Simple. But effective." Inserting a crowbar, Capagli prized the stone sideways, enough to slide his hands in to push it clear.

449

The black space just above his head revealed nothing. "This is as far as we've been. If you pass the small ladder, you can go the rest of the way." He took the ladder from Paba.

"Well, gentlemen," Paba directed sarcastically, "I propose the meddling Mrs Morning goes first."

Paba climbed on to the scaffolding, waiting while Margaret climbed up beside him. Steadying the ladder, Paba handed her the lamp. "Just think Margaret," he said in his soft toned voice. "No one's seen these ghosts for two thousand years. Now you're about to disturb them. No vampires, perhaps not even skeletons, but boxes full of lost souls. Go on. Go up and find them."

Reluctantly, Margaret climbed the few steps up the ladder through the roof into the room above. Paba followed her with another lamp, disappearing into the darkness

"What can you see?" Capagli called excitedly from below.

"Come and see for yourself," Paba answered, moving Margaret further into the tomb.

Their lamps disclosed a high, deep room, with interior walls built of stone to systematize the space beneath a natural cavity. Into both sides of this open vaulted interior lay a series of smaller chambers with splayed carved doorframes of an Egyptian character, separated by a small stone throne with integral footstool. A central plaque, with incised inscriptions, had been placed over each entrance.

Paba shone his lamp into the nearest room where a sepulchral couch with cushions, pillows and ornamental legs carved from one piece of stone, held a skeleton laid at right angles to the wall behind. Margaret drew back as though the gruesome relic of some heroic warrior would rise from the pulverized form on which he was obliged to lay.

Paba elated, drew her closer while he admired the bronze armour no longer supported by a human form and fallen into disarray. "What would a museum pay to own such perfect examples of antiquity, I wonder? Capagli," he called out. "Didn't you say this would be unusual: a complete corpse?"

450

Capagli appeared at the entrance. "It is," he agreed. "It's not normal round here to discover bones. It'll probably crumble when we move the armour."

"We shall apologize to the old warrior then. As he hasn't used it for two thousand years he can hardly object." He turned his lamp to the side.

A large smashed amphora, shaken free during one of the many earth tremors of the last two millennia, lay in front of a stone altar table laden with funerary objects where mourners had placed them. With no one to disturb this long neglect, everything rested beneath two thousand years of dust.

The others joined them; shadows leaping round their lamps like agitated spirits.

Capagli picked up a handful of minute pottery figures. "I was expecting worse. Not much damage. I'll get any fragments collected into boxes, in case they can be restored."

He moved down the narrow aisle between the chambers to a life sized terracotta statue of a middle-aged man. Toga carelessly worn, right arm across his chest, his eyes seemed fixed vacantly on to where the others had emerged. Carved on the wall next to him, a large Etruscan framed door held in its single panel a relief figure of a mysterious divinity bearing a rudder in his right hand and a writhing serpent in the other.

Touching the statue, Capagli shook his head. "Now here's a fortune."

"Who is this moneybags, you?" Petrov asked.

Capagli shone his lamp towards the bottom of the statue in search of an inscription. "I don't know, and I don't expect anyone else will either," he replied.

"Von Moller will want to meet him," Sandquest exclaimed. "You'll be able to legitimatize him, Sergei? He's got to come with the right credentials. Believe me, on the strength of this statue, Von Moller will handle all the best pieces for us."

"Everything will come with the right paperwork," Petrov replied, turning to Capagli. "How many days are needed to clear the tomb?"

"Including the opened chambers with all the sarcophagi - at the most, three nights."

"And the Paetus chamber, you?" Petrov enquired. "Which one is that?"

Nothing they'd seen so far had indicated the last resting place of the man who'd outwitted generations of pillagers. Petrov seemed to have suddenly developed a single minded interest in its location.

Capagli shook his head. "They're all Cecina tombs, General. Unless we find an inscription indicating which Cecina is which, it's anyone's guess. Take your pick." He raised his lamp for Sandquest to enter another chamber.

Sandquest picked up a black ceramic Kylix, its body a dull oily colour in the weak light. He held it up to view the base where a frieze depicted an assembly of the gods. "Now here's a difficult choice," he said to Paba and Margaret at the entrance. Lowering the Kylix, he held up a wafer thin gold pectoral covered in a repeat pattern of minute lions he'd discovered inside the shallow bowled cup. "Beautiful. Exquisite. The craftsmanship's incredible." He passed the pectoral to Paba.

"One lady owner," Paba said, placing it against Margaret's throat. "Deceased."

She knew he was playing on her fears. Also that the outcome would be the same, no matter what her state of anguish. It was only a question of drawing out the moment when her liability overreached itself, persuading him that she had at last become superfluous.

Sandquest took back the breastplate, savouring the fact that he was witnessing the discovery of the most important archaeological find in modern times. An untouched tomb of immense wealth whose contents museums would dig deep into their pockets to possess. After he'd taken his own selection, he reflected.

The brutal reality was that only a wealthy criminal organization could maximize its illicit value, grasping the opportunity to play one collector off against the other; in public through international auction houses, or in private through rich dealers like von Moller. They had enough wealth to bide their time, letting the investment grow, drip-feeding the hungry buyers with items of ever increasing importance. The market's desperate passion to acquire novelty would ensure them a healthy profit.

But Sandquest's thoughts were not solely on such

commercial advantages. Before that happened, he had to make sure his was the very first choice.

The objects had no history except those that Petrov's tame museums would furnish. Even when experts could identify where a piece had been made, or sometimes even by whom, they couldn't establish an account of its past. A returning Russian, Hungarian, Pole, or Slavonic aristocrat, like so many a European noble, would have provided themselves with souvenirs during times when no one was likely to demand a legitimate account of such acquisitions. Certainly not the new lords created by the revolution, who made sure none survived who had not fled, leaving their considerable assets to be used in satisfying the vast debts of the state.

Sandquest rejoined Petrov in the antechamber, where he still wore a dissatisfied scowl.

"What's on your mind, Sergei?"

"Ha! Where's this Cecina?" Petrov waved aggressively. "Paba doesn't know. Show me Paetus Cecina, you?"

Sandquest tried to be conciliatory. "It's written by the entrance. These are the Cecina family tombs."

"What about the other chambers, outside in the corridors?" Petrov shook his head in disagreement. "Any one of them might be the real tomb. The tomb of Paetus. That's what we came for."

"Look around, Sergei," Sandquest advised, "and then think about the other chambers? Not very grand sepulchres just cut into the sand. Here is a temple, hidden, with great care. Everything about this tomb indicates something more than your average first century burial hole in the ground."

"Maybe so," Petrov nodded. "But it doesn't say so, you." He turned away in disgust. " Bah! You have seen enough?"

"I've never seen enough." Sandquest's passion and quick smile faded as he was reminded of other things. "However, you're right. Other important matters also require our attention."

Petrov's frown deepened. He considered it was important to find Paetus Cecina before any other matters interfered with their ability to continue. "These other matters may be a great mistake," he said coldly.

"We live in a world of convenience, Sergei. Certain things have become inconvenient. You've talked enough. Having said wait until we find the tomb, now you talk of mistakes. I've decided Prinn will be taken care of. Now!"

Petrov continued to disagree. "Ask yourself, Arthur, if such actions are wise? There's a lack of planning, you. Something may go wrong. Consider the risks."

Sandquest dismissed Petrov's arguments. "Varina is my flesh and blood. Don't ever forget that. You took what was mine. Remember? Just like Prinn took what was mine. Now you must give me something back, just like Prinn. Only you can do it, and I want it done."

"To satisfy an emotional disease, you. Such things are never satisfied. When these people are dead, the pain will still be there. Then who do you kill? The only one left will be you." Petrov nodded. "Then it will be satisfied."

Their ill-tempered argument closed at Paba's reappearance. He came between them, putting his arms through theirs.

"I guarantee you are well pleased. Capagli has just found a laurel crown in beaten gold. Wafer thin leaves laced together with gold wire. Extraordinary. What will they pay for that? Countless gold charms, earrings, pendants, filigree bracelets, rings, even gold lace. A cuirass, helmet and greaves. A perfect matching set, all in bronze with their skeletal owner included. Well, for the moment. What isn't there here? Ceramic vases everywhere. Extraordinary treasures. *Giusto?*"

Sandquest agreed. "Don't be too dazzled by the gold, making the mistake that other metals are less profitable. The bronze tripod holding a cauldron is more precious now than the perfumes it once held. Their condition makes even the mundane magnificent."

"We shall look after the metal and ceramics with the same care. Now is not the time to be led astray by personal passions. However, the General here is not an emotional man. Military officers are trained to ignore the underlying stress in their temperament. After all, they have to be experts in knowing how to die."

"And the woman?" Sandquest asked. "Has she also to die?"

"She interests you?" Paba raised an eye.

"Only in as much as there'll be another side to her story. The details which you should know."

Paba agreed. "You're a discriminating man, Mr. Sandquest. Mrs Morning's an informer. One for a person who doesn't have our interests in mind."

"An informer?"

"Not a successful one. I have yet to decide on a solution for her, and her meddlesome associate, Prinn."

Sandquest exchanged glances with Petrov.

"Loose ends," Sandquest muttered. "All this time. Like a telephone number without a name. "

"This is bad, you," Petrov cautioned. "The motives of Prinn are unclear. Now is not the moment to be impetuous. We'll act, but not rashly."

"Well, we can agree on that at last," Sandquest said.

"Gentlemen, you've lost me. What is bad?" Paba asked, trying to understand the meaning of their conversation.

"What is bad, is that Prinn is a policeman," Sandquest explained tersely.

A doubtful look crossed Paba's face. "An English policeman. This man has an estate over at Poggio alla Casone, the Villa Lazzi. A policeman? No."

"A policeman, yes. We're old acquaintances."

"Prinn won't be working on his own in Italy, you," Petrov commented thoughtfully. "The Italian police will certainly be involved."

"General. You'd better explain." Paba remained calm. "If the Italian police are working with Prinn, that might explain the two men we caught down here. One seems to have been an Italian policeman. They've already been taken care of. From what you're saying, there's likely to be others."

"There's bound to be others." Petrov said tersely, not interested in wasting valuable time. Plots within plots, his mind jumped on to the possibilities; starkly opportunist, seeking to turn a disaster into an advantage.

"What do they know?" he continued. "Their evidence must be superficial. They'll need time to assess what little they have. Providing we don't panic they won't rush to bolt the door. You have the Morning woman, Paba, so

455

no one will blow a whistle. By Sunday what we have so far will be in the Futa Pass."

"And afterwards?" Sandquest asked pointedly.

Petrov had begun to see how the scattered parts might all fit together. "We must contrive to change the plot. Paba here can't just disappear. But somehow, Prinn must. This place has more shady deposits than a Swiss bank. We've not finished yet. With some luck, we can salvage this whole project from under their noses." Petrov took Paba's arm. "There's a necropolis behind the castle. I understand?"

"Yes, it's common knowledge. Capagli made some exploratory digs initially, getting the lie of the land. He came across some earlier tombs."

"Splendid, you. Chamber tombs?"

"Some of them. How can they be any help to us?"

"I understand they can be dangerous. A hazardous undertaking, exploring an old chamber that's susceptible to movement. Treacherous I believe, where the consequences of illegal digging can lead to a natural disaster."

"Except that Prinn won't be the only one who knows." Paba added. "He'll have filed reports on our activities."

"Naturally. But what will he have told anyone? That you're still digging at the site. Of course you are. You have permission to dig. Only when you stop, will those watching, think you've found something."

"We also have Mrs Morning and her daughter."

Petrov shrugged. "Three's hardly a crowd. We'll abandon this site for the time being, but you must continue with the original project, restoring the castle. Capagli can replace the floor over the entrance in stone, and age it. On Monday he can report intruders have been on the site. Sometime after that he can officially uncover the main entrance to the floor above. Should cause some excitement for a while, you. As for our guests, they will soon be missed. Arrange so they can be found. A tragedy, causing great distress. Perfect. Providing there aren't any holes in the bodies."

"It might just work," Sandquest agreed.

"It will work, you. There's nothing linking us directly to the castle. Any investigation will end up like Prinn, buried in the sand. The fact that he was working undercover in Italy will be politically embarrassing. Questions will be asked whether the integrity of national borders have been breached by allowing foreign agents to pursue their activities, with nothing more than a ministers approval. You will make sure that these questions are asked in the right quarters, Paba. Your people in the Senate, perhaps?"

Paba agreed. "I'm sure that wouldn't be difficult to arrange."

"And what of my arrangements?" Sandquest queried. "I can live with the fact that they've been digging through my dirty washing. Can I live with the dirty washing itself?"

"Nothing must be done about Rachel for the moment. That would be suspicious. Prinn should be disposed of as soon as possible. That should satisfy your desire for revenge. The important thing is we must make absolutely sure that 'Prinn and Co' remain in perfect condition. Absolutely perfect, as the slightest scratch will suggest otherwise." Petrov looked at his watch, and then at Paba. "The Villa Lazzi, you?"

Paba shook his head. "Here you can get lost in the daylight, let alone in the dark. And in this weather... I'll take you. It will be quicker. Shame about the Morning woman. Romulus and Remus will be disappointed. Something of a novelty for them."

Chapter 54

Rain gradually obscured their view of the castle. Headlights swinging out from the entrance became a fractured, distorted smudge of light, breaking into hundreds of minute lanterns reflected in the globes of water adhering to the screen. They grew intense as the vehicle drew nearer, blending the lanterns together, forming themselves into a crescent of dazzling brightness, before blinking out as the car swept rapidly past.

"Recognize anyone?" Vergellesi asked.

"Not in this weather," Eldon replied, wiping the condensation from the inside of the window.

"No matter," Vergellesi decided. "We'll go the rest of the way on foot."

-oOo-

Eldon tried to make the most of the little shelter afforded by the pine tree they stood under giving them an uninterrupted view of the keep through the gateway where Capagli could be seen supervising the hurried loading of a lorry.

"How long must we stand in this purgatory?" Eldon asked, shifting to a position affording only marginally more shelter.

"What's the alternative?" Vergellesi asked.

Eldon peered over Vergellesi's shoulder into the castle compound with its fleeting glimpse of busy figures. "Anywhere dry."

"Not a great deal of choice. What about that place you mentioned when we first arrived, over there on the left."

Eldon acquiesced. "Why not?"

Reaching the door, Vergellesi sprung the lock, and they slipped inside. Eldon stayed by the door watching through the small window with its narrow view of the keep.

Vergellesi's torch lit up Margaret and Melissa clasped together on a bench against the wall.

"Margaret!" Vergellesi exclaimed.

"Piero. Thank God! Thank God, you've managed to get away."

Vergellesi sat down next to her. "By the skin of our teeth. Are you all right?" he asked anxiously.

"Piero," the words tumbled out. "Paba's gone. Melissa saw him leaving with two other men when Capagli brought her here. But please, please don't fuss," being suddenly very English as he held her hands."

"Two other men, Rex. Sound familiar?"

"Sounds unfortunate," Eldon replied, without turning from the window.

"What does all the activity mean?" Vergellesi enquired.

"They've opened a tomb. The one in the Cecina legend. I'm afraid I didn't take much notice. In a funk really. They're moving everything. That's all I know."

"Do you know where Paba's gone?"

"To Commander Prinn's villa."

Turning away from the window, Eldon was more direct. "What's the Commander's relationship with these people?"

"He hasn't any. He's working with the Italian police," Margaret retorted.

"Curious," Eldon remarked. "Police Commanders are strictly mandarins, commanding prestigious branches. Policy directors, not field agents."

"I don't think Margaret would lie to us," Vergellesi countered.

"I wasn't implying that. But Commander Prinn doesn't seem to have been quite so transparent as Margaret." Eldon turned back to the window.

Margaret was insistent. "He didn't lie to me. Of that I'm absolutely sure." A sudden panic surfaced. "Piero, what if Paba comes back?"

Vergellesi squeezed her hand. "You won't be here."

Eldon interrupted. "Was one of the men you saw English?"

"Yes. Fairly bulky, pale hair, well dressed, traces of a northern accent. The other might have been Eastern European. That's all, I'm afraid," Margaret replied apologetically.

"That's more than enough," Eldon replied. " Have you been in touch with Commander Prinn?"

"Not for days. He usually telephones me."

"Probably realized you may have been spotted. No point in confirming it. We'd better go, Piero."

Vergellesi stood up. "Melissa, will you be all right?"

Her mother put a reassuring arm round her shoulder. "She'll manage."

"Good. Stay close to your mother," Vergellesi instructed. "Margaret. I want you to go to the police station in Sorena. Don't tell them anything at the desk, only that you have to contact Commissioner Ruggieri at once. When he arrives, tell him what you know, but don't elaborate on where we're going. Or why. He'll know what to do."

Eldon brought their movement to a huddled halt by the door. "More easily said than done."

From the window he could see the guard returning to his uncomfortable post, tramping by with his hood up, making little sloshing sounds as he passed.

"Wait here," Eldon told them.

"Piero, stop him. He'll get caught," Margaret said in an agitated voice.

Vergellesi laughed gently. "The only one who'll catch anything is the sleepy guard."

He eased the drawer open on the table while they waited, shuffling paperwork aside, finding nothing of any interest, except a pistol with a silencer. Turning his back on Margaret and Melissa he slipped it inside his jacket.

The door opened, and Eldon put his head in. "Right. Let's make ourselves scarce."

-oOo-

An Anglo-Saxon prejudice insisted that all state employees were public servants. Margaret felt she was about to put these expectations in Italy to the test.

Parking in the piazza, Margaret and Melissa climbed the steep steps to the office door, and rang the bell. After a moments delay, the door clicked open.

Their interruption was obviously unwelcome. Carefully, the policeman laid his ham and artichoke roll on a paper serviette, neatly placed it on the desk to one side, and took a sip of fizzy water from a plastic cup before carefully wiping his fingers on another serviette. This leisurely occupation signalled that authority, having been summoned, must in no way be hurried. He rolled his chair to the counter, moved one pad, replaced it with another, rattled pencils noisily in a tray, before condescending to look at Margaret, and cast an interested glance at Melissa.

"I'd like to see Commissioner Ruggieri please. It's very urgent."

"You'd like to make an appointment?"

"No. I'd like to see him now."

The officer cleared his throat; a sarcastic hint of a smile crossed his face. "Why exactly do you wish to see him?" he asked slowly and deliberately.

"Because I don't want to see you!" Margaret exploded, hammering her fist down on the counter.

A door opened and another officer appeared, attracted by the outburst. The seated officer swivelled round to speak to his colleague, who listened cautiously. Coming to the counter, he placed his folded hands on the top.

"*Signora*," he commenced quietly. "Would you say your request is a reasonable one? The hour is very late," indicating a clock on the wall. "Commissioner Ruggieri will be in bed. To wake him unnecessarily would place us in a difficult position. If you could explain why you wish to see him, we can make a decision."

With his argument Margaret couldn't disagree, but she wasn't going to deviate from Vergellesi's instructions. "I think an irate English lady with her daughter, at such an hour, more than good enough reason. You might also ask yourself, how does such a person come to know specifically of Commissioner Ruggieri in the first place?"

The officer pulled an acknowledging grimace, asking them to take a seat while he made the call. Glancing pensively at his colleague he returned to the inner office, shutting the door firmly behind him.

The first officer said nothing, studying his roll mournfully. Carefully he wrapped it up in a plastic bag, noisily removing as much air as possible, before tying a knot.

The second officer returned, placing a telephone on top of the counter. Summoning Margaret over, he

461

handed her the handset. "Commissioner Ruggieri," he said in a peevish voice, indicating his fears had not been unfounded.

Margaret took the handset. "Commissioner Ruggieri?"

A tired voice responded. "Yes. I presume this is important?"

"Very," Margaret retorted sharply, scowling at the officer's smirk. "I've an urgent message from Commissioner Vergellesi. He instructed me to contact you, and no one else."

A note of immediacy entered Ruggieri's voice. "Right. I'm on my way. Tell the officer on duty to make me a black coffee. Hot and sweet. I'll be with you in five minutes."

Margaret replaced the handset, and ignoring their knowing faces, told them that Commissioner Ruggieri would be there in five minutes, with a request that he'd like his coffee hot, black and sweet. Despite her numerous fears, she felt a considerable satisfaction in having wiped the insolent grins from their faces.

-oOo-

Ruggieri watched them impassively. He hadn't seen these men before, yet each one had a distinctive character he recognized from experience.

Gradually the numbers slowed. A final rush by the stragglers to join the line before some imaginary time ran out; a sudden desire not to stand out from the crowd, something they had unknowingly been doing for most of their lives. Here, in the hesitant, fidgety column, they came to acknowledge the extent of their society, shifting uncomfortably, contemplating tomorrow, and the years ahead.

Ruggieri looked along the line, searching faces for one he expected to find, but didn't.

"Where's Capagli?" he asked the man nearest to him, who shook his head. Even if he knew, he didn't know. The next in line shrugged.

"Paolo," he addressed the adjutant. "There's a face missing here. Get Donati and Nenni from the other team. They're somewhere on the perimeter."

462

Ruggieri wasn't going to indulge in heroics; he'd taken enough risks already. Now he was playing safe, remembering the years piling up behind him, protecting his pension.

"While we're busy, tell Di Stefano to bring the van up. He can start getting them on board. If there's not enough room, rustle up another *cellulare* from the prison."

The adjutant nodded, patching Di Stefano in on the radio.

Di Stefano came up quickly to fill the space, allowing the adjutant to take over operational control when Ruggieri entered the castle.

Ruggieri took one last glance around. "Keep off the local radio for half an hour. We should have located our missing rogue before then."

-oOo-

The keep was still lit. Donati whistled under his breath. Articles taken from the tomb were arranged around the vast room in order of size, making selection easier for the packers in utilizing the vehicles space.

"Professional team by the looks of it," he whispered to Ruggieri.

Ruggieri nodded, waving them on. Spreading out and moving their cover forward to the arches, they searched the space carefully, without success. Ruggieri stabbed a finger towards the trap door. Nenni took a quick look, shrugging his shoulders. No one. Just a lot of places where people could hide.

Ruggieri checked for himself. Taking a deep breath, as though he was about to dive into water, he lowered himself through the trapdoor, descending with his back against the ladder, machine gun covering the corridor. The smell reminded him of decaying vegetables. Signalling with two fingers, the group joined him. Ruggieri tried a cell door quietly, then another. They were held fast by seized bolts, or the fusion of rusted hinges.

He looked up to Nenni's furious signalling from the newly opened entrance. Ruggieri changed places. Looking down the passage he recognized Capagli's figure

463

on the scaffolding, taking down a rucksack from above. The squat round figure that joined him with another bag, he didn't know. Ruggieri indicated to Nenni to go over to the other side of the entrance while their backs were turned.

Nenni stepped on a shovel.

The two figures were already running. Ruggieri moved into the opening, ordering them to stop.

Capagli came to a slow hobbling halt. His accomplice, some paces ahead, darted into the side tunnel, scattering pieces of gold jewellery from his bag.

Ruggieri and Nenni rushed up to its entrance, seeing the bobbing beam of a torch receding into the darkness. Ruggieri called out again for him to stop. As he did, instinct made them draw back, out of the line of the tunnel.

The rapid staccato burst of a sub machine gun sent a spray of bullets ricocheting off the stonewall, a splintered shard cutting Nenni's cheek. Ruggieri spat out a mouthful of dust. A momentary silence was followed by a dull tearing sound. The stones beneath their feet, and against their backs trembled in brief waves; puffs of sand spurted from the gaps between the stones above their head, trickled down less fleetingly in odd corners, gave a sudden quaking, shuddering jerk, and became still. Nenni released his breath, and looked at Ruggieri with questioning eyes.

Ruggieri edged forward carefully and glanced quickly into the tunnel. Only darkness and a billowing cloud of dust remained. "What's happened?" he demanded of a pale and haggard faced Capagli, leaning against the wall.

Capagli shook his head despondently, beads of sweat running into his eyes. He wiped them away with the back of his hand. "The tunnels collapsed," he replied in a low hoarse voice.

"Get some spades," Ruggieri shouted to Donati who had remained at the entrance. "Quick, man."

"It's no use," Capagli said. "There's no point. The space will fill up again as quickly as you empty it. Shovel for shovel. *Dio!* The sand will fit him like a glove." "*Dio,*" he muttered again. "He won't even have a cubic centimetre of air to breathe."

"Poor bastard," Nenni said, holding a handkerchief to his cheek.

"And you're a lucky bastard," Ruggieri snapped. "Right. Let's get back outside, quickly. Hanging around in here is tempting fate." He nodded to Donati. "Sandwich Capagli. He'll have a good story to tell, even if it's all a pack of lies."

-oOo-

Capagli had been separated from the rest of the group in an effort to undermine their resolve to say nothing. How much was Capagli telling, and whom was he implicating? None of them would know, when alone they faced their interrogators, accused of things they knew nothing about.

Ruggieri walked over to Capagli standing between two officers.

"You're a disappointment, Enzo. Thought you'd more sense than to get mixed up with *tombaroli*. Working hard to build up a good business. Everything came your way. That's an enviable position, a monopoly of work. Temptation must be a terrible thing. No one fussed when you turned up the odd pot. Fortuitous. Perk of the job. But this Enzo. This makes you a big time criminal. We'll want to know all about that."

The sullen, uncooperative face, prepared Ruggieri for an uphill struggle. Capagli knew enough to realize the only thing that mattered now was his silence. He could depend on lawyers wanting to consider what was going to be the best for him, and what was going to be the best for the company's mutual benefit. They would look after their own, while looking after themselves.

Chapter 55

According to the map Eldon had retained, a long drive led up to the Villa Lazzi on the summit of a hill, before descending in a sweeping arc behind the building to rejoin the main entrance.

Vergellesi stopped near the old barn.

"We could leave the car here," he suggested. "Except it's rather a long walk - and God knows what we're going to find at the end of it."

"Life's a mystery, Piero," Eldon replied, zipping his leather jacket high under the chin.

"Like Nightingale?" Vergellesi enquired.

"We can go home now if you like?"

"Is that a sensible suggestion?"

Eldon shook his head. "I'm here because you persuaded me to be. We're all fellow travellers Piero, along for the ride. Life's never in our hands entirely. It can end in a bus queue, or in the lonely avenue of an Italian villa. Safety's a concept, never a reality."

Vergellesi assented reluctantly, letting Eldon's phlegmatic observation go. "The rain's making so much noise we can move closer without disturbing anyone."

"Why not? But disturb them sooner or later we must."

Vergellesi switched off the headlights, passing through the open gates to the Villa.

-oOo-

Paba sat with his hands crossed behind the steering wheel of his car, parked between two long farm buildings from where they could observe the Villa Lazzi. Petrov sat in silence next to him. Behind, Kopolev stared out at the falling rain, while Boris, a young technical officer attached to the embassy in Rome, busied himself cleaning his automatic with a handkerchief, working it with painful thoroughness into every angle.

The rain continued to beat steadily on the roof of the car. It formed an ideal cover, wrapped up in the psychology of discomfort. No one liked to get soaked, its unpleasantness becoming a distraction. For Kopolev quite the reverse was true, where the distraction worked in his favour, and became an advantage.

Kopolev put his hand on Boris's arm as he turned the weapon over for the third time, signalling silently that it was clean enough.

Petrov broke into his thoughts. "Major, there's a saying you may have heard: just because the dragon's quiet, doesn't signify it's asleep. Dragons are not to be trusted, Major. Have a turn round; make sure no one is about to prod the beast."

Pulling up the collar of his black leather trench coat, and tugging the Breton cap tightly over his fiercely cropped head, Kopolev crossed the gravel on to the grass verge, moving silently down between the buildings, until Boris lost him in the swirling clouds of rain.

Paba heard nothing on his radio except interference. Nothing from Romulus or Remus, to set his mind at rest.

Petrov asked him to switch off the radio, needing to hear what was happening outside.

"Everyone seems to be taking their time," Paba commented scratchily.

"I think not, you," Petrov replied. "Everything to the second. That way you can hear your life ticking away."

Paba shrugged. "The length of a life is like the length of a piece of string."

"Unless it's your turn to die, you. Then you consider how many millimetres short it is, exactly."

Kopolev emerged from a fog of rain that seemed to cling about his tall frame, afraid to let go.

Petrov lowered his window. Kopolev rested his arms on the bottom frame, bringing them face-to-face.

"A white Mercedes Benz has joined us," he said quietly. "Behind the other buildings."

"Occupied?" Petrov asked.

"Recently. Bonnet's still warm."

Petrov got out of the car. "Then we must look. Boris," he commanded. The young officer opened his door at the bidding. "Take a look round the barn beyond the house. Don't rush. Remember your training at Mossovet."

Boris walked away into the compulsory drenching, trying to keep his shoulders back like Kopolev.

"Is there a problem?" Paba enquired.

"Most definitely," Petrov replied, raising his window. "A white Mercedes Benz has recently arrived."

"*Bene. Bene.* Romulus and Remus at last," Paba said with a sense of relief.

"Is that so, you?" queried Petrov. "Psychic, do you suppose? None of us said goodbye to anyone." He raised a finger. "The Morning woman might have overheard. Explaining how she acquired the car is a little more difficult. Major. Let's not waste our time. We'll check. Paba, you sit tight here."

-oOo-

Reaching the end of a long creeper laden building, Vergellesi viewed the open space, dimly lit by porch lights that lay between him, and an open sided barn. He'd never suffered from agoraphobia, but there was something very public about the short walk he'd have to take. Moving back, he tried a door. It opened into a *cantina*, the atmosphere still heavy with the lingering smell of last year's *vendemmia*. Passing through another door, he slipped quietly into a dark corner on the inside of the open barn.

The position provided a view of the villa from two sides. The stout arched door of the main entrance was firmly shut, flanked by twin sets of windows heavily shuttered behind iron grills. A high lamp on the angle of the wall threw back shadows for a few metres, before giving out.

His attention was drawn to a movement in the trees beyond the raised terrace lining the path. Slipping off the safety catch below the back sight, he ran the tip of his finger round the muzzle, checking the silencer. A nightingales rasping 'kerr' of alarm made him start. He could count the thud of his heartbeats, the only part of him that moved.

-oOo-

Boris listened intently to the same nightingale's vociferous cry. It came only once, a sweet piercing rasp glancing through the rain. There was no reply to the one

468

time warning note that travelled through buildings into the night.

He looked along a raised terrace that stepped down to an area of patchy lawn. Coming to terms with his emotions was proving difficult. Every decision was his own; no instructor telling him to go back and try again. He understood, by the weighty pit in his stomach, that from this moment there was only the first time.

The terrace was only a few metres from his shelter in the trees. He understood that he must keep clear of the villa. Surveillance meant concentrate on sweeping the area while keeping out of sight. Nothing more. Petrov had been insistent he remembered his training. Never move into an open space; remain in cover at all times.

A bright arc of light from the glazed doors suddenly spread across the terrace. He expected someone to close the shutters. Whoever occupied the room appeared to be in no hurry.

The arc didn't quite reach the end of the terrace, or penetrate very deeply to the sides. Stretching, Boris could see a glass ceiling chandelier and the pediment of a wardrobe or bookcase. Not compulsively, having carefully appraised the margin of light he mustn't trespass within, he judged two or three steps would give him enough height to see into the room. Satisfied the risk of being seen was minimal, he cast a last glance to his left at the dark outline of the closest farm building, screened behind the driving rain. In ten-seconds or less he could make his appraisal, then return to the car. Rapidly, Boris crossed the soft lawn and gravel path to the riven stone steps leading on to the terrace, eyes stung by piercing darts of water.

-oOo-

From the barn, Vergellesi studied the penumbra beyond the shadow where the movement had first attracted him. His attention was drawn again, more distinctly, as the fragmented shape cleared the trees. Don't rush, he counselled himself firmly. Get a positive ID, or do nothing. He was breathing too fast. What did they advise on the firing range? If the pumping makes you unsteady,

469

pause at the bottom of your breath, and squeeze the trigger.

It wasn't Eldon. The figure had a distinct shape, outlined by a long coat, armed, and making for the French doors where, most probably, Prinn would be inside. Vergellesi held back. He couldn't make a fuss going for an arrest; create a shambles in which Nightingale might simply slip away in the confusion. Do nothing, and Prinn might well pay with his life. He had to make a decision, quickly.

The figure reached the steps as Vergellesi brought the gun down, and straightened his arm, both hands on the butt. 'Don't rush,' he said to himself. 'Stay calm. Squeeze the whole of your hand into it.'

"That's not the way to go about it, laddie," a voice spoke softly from behind his left shoulder. "Just stay as you are." The point of pressure in the little hollow behind his ear being all the persuasion needed. "You're holding the pistol too low. Looks good from where you are, but the ball goes in at waist height doing the least damage. More likely you'll get yourself killed. Watching your back's a problem when you concentrate. Like our friend out there. I'm going to remove the aggravation from behind your ear. Relax. Keep your eyes ahead. There's a couple more somewhere who'd be quite happy to take over where I leave off."

"I understand." Vergellesi replied, watching the dark shadow on the terrace retracing his steps. "Where did you come from?"

"Gower's the name. Share a desk with Eldon. Don't know what the pair of you are doing loitering outside while Sandquest and his friend are keeping nice and dry inside."

-oOo-

In the study, Prinn finishing his work closed the book. The marble clock on the mantelpiece chimed one thirty. Picking up the poker, he raked the dying embers of the fire before placing the brass guard on the hearth. Looking at the book he hesitated, remembering his father's homily on 'untidy states and untidy minds'.

Walking along the corridor, lined with Hogarth engravings, he reached the door of the library, turning inside to the glazed bookcase where the volume was kept. He switched on the central chandelier, replacing the book neatly in the gap it had vacated. Removing another he paused at the index, looking for a chance reference. Yielding nothing, that too was replaced.

In the matching glass door of the bookcase, he caught the reflection of a figure standing close to the French windows opening on to the terrace.

He might not have recognized the person wearing a black seaman's woollen jacket and hat. There was; however, no mistaking the steady aim of the Walther pistol directed at his back.

Did he have time? Time. Such a slim and treacherous thing.

Prinn's hand moved from the replaced volume, to the lower shelf. He paused, calming himself. He had to move carefully, naturally, with no sudden movement while he reached for his only response. Further down the line of books he half pulled one out before moving on until he felt the dimpled handle of his fathers old Smith and Wesson. His body masked the movement as he withdrew the pistol. Smoothly rotating on his heels towards the figure, he pulled the trigger.

The slender body of Varina Jehmlich slid slowly down until she rested on her knees, back slumped against the wall, sitting on her heels, hand holding the automatic resting in her lap, the other palm upwards on the floor. Her open eyes gazed past Prinn to somewhere of her own, and from the neat puckered mark on her forehead a trickle of blood ran gently down the edge of her nose before curling into her nostril. Around her the noise hung in the air, suspended on the drifting smell of sulphur.

-oOo-

Approaching from the back of the house, Eldon broke up his silhouette by working his way along the building, hoping Vergellesi wasn't impatiently sticking his neck out instead of quietly blocking an escape route. These considerations were snatched away by a gunshot from inside the villa that sent him sprinting down the terrace.

Through the closed French windows, Eldon saw an ashen faced Prinn standing next to a table, arm loose by his side holding a revolver, unaware that behind him in the doorway Sandquest was aiming a pistol at the back of his head.

Eldon fired through the glass, the Uzi's bullets sending a shower of splinters and smashed glazing bars into the room, throwing Sandquest backwards across the corridor, his shot tearing a jagged hole in the library ceiling.

Following with a roll through the shattered door, Eldon landed under the table.

The lights went out.

Prinn dropped down beneath the switch, crouching low in the darkness. Everything was quiet in the sudden cessation of all the unexpected noise.

A loose section of glass fell to the floor with a crash. Then more silence.

Eventually Prinn said in a shaky, reproachful voice, "I object to you turning my home into a bear-garden, Rex."

Chapter 56

At the first sound of gunfire, Paba started the engine, and waited nervously. When Petrov failed to appear, he edged closer to the opening between the buildings. He had no instructions, and his inclination was to look after his own best interests. With the second burst of gun fire, he accelerated out of the yard towards the drive; misjudged the direction in his haste, taking the much longer route round the villa that followed a shallower, sweeping path, clear of the trees.

Paba's precipitate departure also added impetus to Vergellesi's haste. Eldon had outlined the importance of making sure that the exits were kept under observation. Somehow, he realized, he'd managed to leave a door open.

Gower suggested, less than politely, he shut it.

Vergellesi realized quickly that to do so he had to reach the Villa's gate before Paba, which compelled him to follow the shorter route, straight down the avenue of undulating terraces strewn with the bulging distortions of tree roots. Once Paba reached the open highway, he stood a good chance of shaking off any pursuer.

Throwing caution to the wind, Vergellesi raced through what had now become a swollen river, a turbulent deluge of water that disguised the misshapen surface of hidden traps and unexpected shocks.

Parallel headlights flickered across the fields, blinking between the pencil straight trunks of the cypress trees. Vergellesi cursed at Paba's speed, losing sight of the car as it dipped behind some rising ground. Mute flashes of lightning illuminated the smudges of olive groves from which Paba's vehicle suddenly burst back into sight, seemingly even further ahead.

Struggling to stop the Mercedes Benz from leaving the road altogether, and unable to defy gravity as the vehicle launched itself over another falling slope, all four wheels crashed down with a snapping, metallic crunch on its dangling suspension, almost wrenching the steering wheel from Vergellesi's grasp. A hubcap bounced away into the trees, a momentary flashing disc of chrome that announced an instant change in handling from collapsed shock absorbers. Ignoring the difficulty, and determined not to be outdistanced by Paba, he kept his foot hard down on the accelerator, ignoring the booming and tearing sound underneath the vehicle as the shattered exhaust was wrenched from its brackets.

The acrid smell of burning rubber and oil began to seep into the interior, forcing Vergellesi to snatch open the window. His yawing movement on the steering wheel had only a marginal effect on the direction the car was travelling, allowing him to do nothing more than trust in fate. Hitting another rise in a final steep section, he joined the junction at the same time as Paba, in a perfectly controlled slide, swept round the corner. Vergellesi's airborne car crashed down on to the roof, propelling both vehicles off the road, before rolling over the top, and coming down with all four wheels buried deep in the recesses of the wings.

Paba wrenched his door open and tumbled out. Vergellesi, momentarily disorientated from where he'd been thrown from the car, staggered to his feet.

Shaken by this sudden change in fortune, Paba fired carelessly in Vergellesi's direction. The bullet grazed his skull, knocking him unconscious into the dense undergrowth, allowing Paba enough time to calm himself and take stock of the situation.

One glance told Paba that the wheels of his vehicle would never get enough grip to haul itself out of the soft earth it had settled in. He needed to get out of sight, and out of the rain so he could regain his wits and decide on the possible options. Catching sight of the barn through the teeming rain, he rushed through the gate to the building and dragged the door open.

-oOo-

Scillone had been late in checking an erratic autoclave in the boiler room of the villa, and was on his way home when the storm broke, forcing him to take shelter in the barn. From experience he knew the next few hours would be beset by a heavy drenching. The prospect of spending the night there didn't perturb him overmuch. It was watertight, and there was plenty of clean straw and dry sacks on which to make a bed. The furthest thing from his hopes, or even his thoughts as he settled himself in, was the dormant, implacable spirit of revenge; a 'wild justice' fashioned from a chance moment that rarely presents itself to the victim. He saw himself as one of the world's unfortunate wretches, snatched from a meaningful life to suffer the burden of someone else's hate. It was an affliction that would never leave him, not even now in the isolation of these restraining elements. He listened to the noise of the rain on the tiles and tried to forget.

Scillone shut his eyes, struggling to find respite against the fear of unconsciousness where there was always the same dream to haunt him. It woke him in the early hours, wringing wet, shaking in an uncontrollable panic, lying there in the dark, traumatized by these flickering images: in close up, or from a distance. They say that dreams have no voice, being only reflections in the mind.

But his dream was different.

In this nightly frenzy, he could hear himself screaming!

-oOo-

The buzzard circled, drifting weightlessly on the rising air, eyes bright, fixed on a scurrying movement passing along the Apulian highway, far below.

At first, it was a small black figure stumbling along the side of a dusty, narrow road that endlessly twisted between crumbling, dry stone walls holding apart the scrub land of wild wheat and barbarous lupins.

The figure stopped, looked back for a long moment, apprehensive of what he might see. He glanced about him in a panic: at the outcrops of white rock fending off invasive broom where someone might be waiting, and then nervously up at the buzzard hanging on an invisible thermal. The bird soared warily, to a location higher in the sky.

From this new wheeling, vantage point it watched the man move on, shuffling the pale dust deeper into the welts

475

of his boots. Every now and again he cast an agitated, hurried look behind him, ignoring the sweat trickling in rivulets from his scalp, to be soaked up by the vest beneath his shirt.

The buzzard, feathering its tail on this lofty pinnacle, sensed the abject terror hanging like an aura round the small figure driven into this barren place, where not only the wind chose to move by stealth. Without a sound it dropped lower, instinctively conditioned to the chase - and in its relentless pursuit of death.

One cruel, elliptical eye, blinked.

Once more the figure stopped, setting his suitcase down beside him and sat on it; sat in the midday sun and heavy silence, with only a solitary buzzard - lighter than the silence - for company.

He wiped his arm nervously across his forehead, looked round sharply in alarm as a gust of wind rattled a loose stone on the crumbling wall. A man frightened; terrified by his own presence.

He gave a panicky glance up at the cobalt blue sky where the bird lazily drifted, before his haunted gaze shifted down the gradient into the hazy, powder-blue of the horizon, retracing the climbing, serpentine road of his passage.

He was already a long way from Bari.

He'd gone there to work, tending the impeccably groomed garden of a lush Adriatic villa - property of a rich, Italian businessman with interests in Taranto and Brindisi.

Then, it seemed, he'd gone there to die.

Just like his employer, Sergio Birelli, had died. Blown to shreds by an 8-bore shotgun, held in the hands of a young man who smiled with his azure eyes while he pulled both triggers - from a distance of two metres.

He'd identified the killer, though he couldn't identify Sergio Birelli. Stood up in court, like the good catholic he was, and told them all he knew. He'd looked into those pitiless eyes as the handcuffed prisoner passed by, reading in their ruthless glare, this meaning of fear

Bari was where he'd come to know the odour of death; touched the cold, drunken savagery of its malevolence.

He'd hidden overnight in a church, crouched in a confessional, while the bored presbyter shuffled between the pews and, unwittingly, locked him in. He'd woken at dawn, roused by the veiled women in black, softly murmuring each Ave Maria as they counted them off on the 165 glass beads of their rosaries. From there he'd limped stiffly out into the fresh morning air, and became a fugitive from those who'd taken an exception to his presence.

His only hope had been to escape the frenzied animosity he thought was anchored to one place, to reach some distant region where he would be safe.

He'd arrived at a crossroads, on a high hill, not far from where the driver of an old Fiat truck had dropped him off. From there, the man indicated, he could catch a bus that would take him to Altamura, where he could catch a train to Salerno, and eventually, a long, long way from Bari.

Now, as he sat in the sun, he knew they'd merely let him run, biding their time until he could run no more, letting him know that there was nowhere to hide.

Above, hovering on broad motionless wings, the buzzard's eyes were attracted by a new movement.

From below, a stream of dust billowed up behind the coach. Churning round the sharp bends, it drove endlessly through its own choking, powdery wake. Soon it would be there. Only a short straight, another corner and then, finally, alongside the alien black figure.

As the coach entered the short straight, a limousine, hidden in its powdery train, slid past, rapidly drawing away to reach the man, standing, paralysed by fear. The vehicle stopped. Doors opened, doors shut, and the limousine drew away again, leaving the suitcase alone, waiting for the bus.

Overhead, the buzzard disappointed, snatched another thermal, rising higher and higher until, like the black figure, it too was lost to sight.

-oOo-

They pushed him into a chair and kicked him. Waited menacingly about him, until the door opened and Giuliani, a short, elegant man in an English tailored suit, came in to look at him. He didn't smile.

"So, you're Scillone?"

They kicked him again when he didn't answer - unaware he was too frightened to speak.

Giuliani held up his hand, so they fell back disappointed, too eager to settle their prisoners breathing for good.

"You've seriously disturbed me Scillone. Caused me to lose sleep. My wallet is going to be considerably lighter, thanks to you. A funeral, though cheap, is too excessive. Something value added is more in keeping. Something, that shows we're not out of pocket."

He raised his hand again, silencing their eager objections.

"Invest in a little promotion, while Paba neglects our company. Let people know that some knowledge is best forgotten. Marco, see what you can do. Convince Signor Scillone of the error of his ways, and afterwards, anyone else who comes across him."

He studied them all, one by one, deep into their compliant eyes. Left them to communicate his displeasure to the world.

They tied Scillone up, sitting in the chair where they'd thrust him, while Marco found the rubber gloves, drew them on, and busied himself drawing off liquid from a glass carboy.

Snapping off a pencil they forced his mouth open and jammed it vertically behind his teeth, head forced back by pulling on a belt wrapped round his temple. They pulled hard, locking his neck against the top rail of the chair as he struggled violently. Ramming a funnel tube down into his mouth - in case Marco chanced to spill the scorching oil of vitriol.

Scillone rocked the chair in desperation, hurling himself to and fro, so they punched him hard, just enough to daze him, before Marco poured the fiery, burning liquid, down his throat.

Scillone screamed: and went on screaming.

Deep down, from his stomach; an indescribable, snarling, choking rage of pain - that made no sound at all.

-oOo-

Scillone woke with a start, struggling to his feet. He

478

listened intently for a sound that might have woken him, becoming aware of a rustling near the door, confused by the steady roar of rain outside. He felt his way forward, locating his position by the touch of cold steel on the tractor.

Inside, Paba flicked on his cigarette lighter, and found the lamp switch next to the door. He clicked it on. In the weak light he made out a confused Scillone, woken from his slumber, standing uncertainly at all the noise, next to the orange OM caterpillar tractor.

Paba didn't recognize Scillone, but Scillone had reason never to forget Paba. Oblivious to the danger now presenting itself, Scillone rushed blindly at him, so that Paba's surprised snatched shot went low, passing through Scillone's thigh, sending him sprawling to the floor.

Steadying himself, Paba aimed at Scillone's head as he struggled to regain his feet little more than an arms length away. He pressed the trigger.

At the empty click, Paba hastily threw himself on his wounded assailant, receiving a back handed blow that sent him sprawling into buckets, and neatly strung fertilizer bags.

Hampered by an excruciating pain, Scillone forced the agony from his mind. He only remembered the searing, tearing, unbearable pain in his throat; their laughter at his mumbling cries that made no sense, and words that gradually drifted into nothing - a voiceless, gutted silence. Driven by his anger into a desperate animal rage, he lurched after Paba.

Paba, regaining his balance, lashed out wildly with his leg, so that his foot caught Scillone's wound sending him tumbling backwards again, an intense, incapacitating pain rolling him up in agony on the floor.

Seizing his chance, Paba slipped out of the barn, back into the driving rain. He recalled seeing cars parked in the outbuildings by the villa. He could reach them if he avoided using the road.

Heading across the field into the dense black outline of the rising ground his shoes rapidly became leaden ballast; every step a deliberate movement to free himself from the clay's clinging weight; a battle to place one foot in front of the other. The lacerating rain appeared as a sheet of opaque glass, so there became no visual direction to his efforts as he struggled forward in the sticky slough of clay. Peaking a rise he paused to regain his breath, shivering in his sodden, clinging clothes. Water pouring down his face flowed into his mouth. He spat it out, cursing.

From behind he caught a sound. Now below him, swept away on the gusts of rain, now swept back again. The ponderous noise filling the dense, wet air, he recognized as the deep pulse of a heavy, powerful engine. Looking back, Paba could see no further than his hand.

Trying to move faster, he slipped into the oozing mire, regained his feet, clay sticking to his hands in a viscid mass that couldn't be shaken off. Scrambling forward, almost crawling, using his hands to steady himself on the banks steepening incline, his movement in the slippery quagmire came to a flaying standstill. Panic surrounded him as the soft sediment sucked itself over his ankles; the air around him filled with the heavy thud of the OM's motor.

Trying to wipe the rain from his eyes only succeeded in closing them with the tenacious clay. Thunder rumbled forward above him; rain washing his uplifted face clean. Across the sky, blurred charges of lightning arced in luminous wedges, exploding the night into moments of flickering vision so that the squat OM was at one moment visible between its clanking, grating tracks; in another, present only by its tireless muffled rumble among the rain.

Paba lurched upwards a few more steps. A desperate, panic-filled, backward glance, full of honeycombed radiator grill reared out of the rain like the prow of a ship. It crested a wave, towering over him. Hopelessly he struggled to lift his feet clear of the clinging morass before he fell, disappearing with a sucking sound, under the crushing weight of the tractor's steel track.

Another bolt of lightning cast a neon glow over the turbid earth running with a thousand minute rivers along the ploughed channels, until too full, they broke through the dam, cascading down in a swollen swirl over the empty, uninhabited surface of the field.

Chapter 57

In the middle distance, a car had picked up speed round the villa, followed a moment later by the shrill squeal of another vehicle turning round under heavy acceleration, moving off at high-speed in the opposite direction.

"God help my drive?" Prinn commented, distractedly, switching on a standard lamp that lit up the room in a soft glow.

Eldon picked himself up from the floor, shaking a few shards of glass from his sleeve. He backed out of the line of the French door, to look at Sandquest's untidy body on the floor of the corridor, before he turned to Varina, who'd come to gently rest against a console table leg.

"You're a very exceptional man, Commander Prinn."

"What makes you say that?"

"Realizing that Miss Jehmlich was Nightingale."

"I can't claim I did know, Rex. It came as something of a surprise."

"Then you had another reason for killing her?"

"Survival would be a good enough reason," Prinn volunteered, leaning against the wall. He suddenly felt very tired, finding all the exertion, and rush of emotions disagreeable. "And what about you?" he asked. "Had you come to that conclusion?"

"No. I was never sure, Commander. When Doctor Rosso found out that the Verolino Sandquest purchased ended up with the Gorky State Orchestra, it narrowed the field down considerably. We already had the wine as a lead from the apartment in Port Said, and we'd established the agent might be using the orchestra for cover, so the two came together. Yet, I have to say, my money was still on Kopolev."

Prinn acknowledged their difficulty. "Yes. As implausible as it seems, the idea of an equally deadly disciple had begun to cross my mind."

Sliding the magazine out of the Uzi, Eldon checked that sufficient ammunition remained. He slapped it back. "True. He was too young to have fitted the profile altogether, so, I agree with you. I'd just about plumped for Kopolev inheriting the role from the original

Nightingale. It appears we were wrong, and looking in the wrong direction. However..."

"Kopolev! I nearly forgot," Prinn said. "He and Petrov must still be outside. I believe the General won't be far away, so he can check the results of his handiwork."

"I'm not sure I follow, Commander."

"It's a long story. One I'll have to explain. I also have to tell you, I'm sure we're not out of the woods yet. For the moment, just keep an eye on things here. I must get in touch with Questore Vignozzi to find out how we're supposed to handle this?"

"For the moment, Commander," Eldon advised, "I think we must keep our heads down, and not wander about until things settle down."

"How many others, do you think?"

"Not sure. All we can say for the moment is that there are two conspirators less."

"I should like to draw a line under all this. It's been too long a criminal investigation for some of us." Prinn edged himself into a welcome seat between the two French doors, where he didn't represent a chance target, and continued. "Obviously Sandquest had a great deal to gain if the tomb could be opened. Once he'd committed himself to Paba's plan, there was no turning back. Murder, to get what you want, is a perfectly simple option for a man of Paba's character. As for Sandquest, when you're that rich you can buy a lot of options. Not that we ever considered it included an assassin. But that's a completely different story."

Eldon positioned himself more securely. "They certainly didn't need her talents to kill Brizzi?"

"No. That's beginning to look like a double-cross. Possibly, down to Paba. But it looks, as we suspected, that she was responsible for the death of Sir Maxwell Blain. Inevitable if he was becoming aware of Sandquest's double life. Blain's partner, Finetti, I believe was just unfortunate, having run up against Paba. Hart seems to have uncovered a betrayal that'll give the security service a migraine. I'll know more when I've talked to him."

"A couple of septuagenarians and a brilliant concert pianist. That's going to go down like a lead balloon."

"I imagine. Petrov must have already been in an influential position within the Russian security system when he conceived the idea of creating a perfect assassin. How he did it, completely baffles me. That she was Sandquest's daughter must have provided the icing on the cake. Sandquest and Varina became so valuable, the Soviets seem to have allowed Petrov to make up his own rules."

"And eventually lost track of them altogether. Do you have any idea why Petrov and Sandquest formed this alliance - apart from the daughter, whom they both seemed to have a share in? Champagne socialists and misguided academics I can understand, but multi millionaire industrialists don't normally ally themselves with Bolsheviks."

"That is a mystery. However, with the fall of the Soviet Union all that became history; one containing a large amount of unwelcome truths. Security services often have a cosy arrangement with each other. Sets of rules that are merely smoke screens to confuse or console society. Sir Edward Kerry gave very little away, but it's not too difficult reading between the lines."

"The whole business seems - how shall I put it - very extreme, Commander."

"Everything these people do, Rex, is extreme. They don't live in the same world as us. Theirs is a parallel place, which every now and again accidentally touches ours so we become aware of its existence. After the Soviet debacle they seem to have had a lot of tidying up to do. Scratching of backs has become endemic. Nightingale, I can only suppose, must suddenly have become superfluous; a dangerous ideologue. In any event, an embarrassment they found unable to pension off, and necessary to dispose of permanently. Sacrifices to be made. Those too criminally awkward to explain away. Pensions at stake. Peerages probably. Nightingale was an unfortunate relic of a post *ancien régime*."

"Nevertheless, Kerry showed a lot of confidence in you, Commander."

"Thank you, Rex. But, if that were so, he wouldn't have sent you along. No, I think opportunity had more influence on his thinking. And perhaps, fear. They were looking for permanent solutions, not judicial process. As I've said, Sandquest was already under investigation by my department as a possible recipient of stolen art works. Our investigation was continually hampered by the usual vested interests, which made life difficult. Then, we discovered a file recording Sandquest's list of acquisitions. All legitimate and above board, except in the last year there appeared to be rather too many carrying an Eastern European provenance. Again, not entirely improbable. Historically, the regions nobility were as avid collectors as any other. With the added advantage of few, if any, descendants left to contest ownership. But it gave us an opening that eventually revealed a very convenient means of filtering stolen antiquities on to the market. One that was acceptable to the auction houses by having apparently legitimate clients, even if they were actually new to the museums lists. No one outside Russia was ever going to prove otherwise. That was a brave bit of work that Emma did for us."

"Now there's a confusion. Tell me about Emma?"

"Emma was the sister of Livia Wolfe."

"Who was Sandquest's Personal Assistant?"

"She was going to be," Prinn said quietly. "Emma and Livia were twin sisters. Identical twins."

"And both working for you?"

"Not exactly. Benjamin Wolfe was a Scientific Officer with the Admiralty before the war, which was where my father met him. He'd joined the Royal Navy, assigned to research into U-boat detection. Wolfe was instrumental in developing the technology to make this possible. It was a continuum, inventing something, having it detected by the Germans, inventing something else. No one was averse to a little inside help, and agents in occupied territories proved adept at stealing technical documents. Enter a Sergeant Sandquest. He was at the blunt end, assessing and collecting. Nothing to do with my father, but Wolfe made his acquaintance on a number of occasions, forming a high opinion of him. After the war, similar interests led their paths to cross, where they remained on good terms. Emma had come to head the Photographic and Graphic Branch at the Met, at my request, where I needed her expertise in infra-red and ultra-violet work. Then out of the blue, with Wolfe pulling the strings of the old boy network, Livia, stepped into the job as Sandquest's PA. It seemed like a stroke of luck, or at least a possible opening to some. Sadly, even fortune has to have a price."

"I think I'd arrived at that point. A vehicle accident?"

"Right. Livia's tragic death resulted in Emma volunteering to take her place. Perhaps, not as big a risk as it sounds. Sandquest had interviewed Livia, but the accident meant he'd never worked with her. God knows what possessed Emma. We argued over the risk, but with time running short, and the best chance we'd ever had slipping out of our grasp, we found ourselves persuaded. Emma's success, I'm afraid, tempted us to ignore an old rule. There's really no such thing as a perfect cover. We almost lost Emma as well. However, not before she'd established Sandquest's Etruscan source was a Professor Petrov."

"Obviously not our man. And Emma? She's all right?"

"Thank God. She's pulled through, and recovering. Hart's been keeping her up to date. Apparently you must have impressed her, as the young lady's enquired after you. That'll have to wait for now. Anyway, the Professor turned out to be the General's brother. The relationship between Sandquest and a Russian, given Sandquest's defence interests, was too hot for my department, and quickly passed on to the security services."

"Which is where Sir Edward found the idea that you provided the perfect scenario for a little spring cleaning?"

"I'm not sure I'd put it quite that way, Rex, but someone certainly must have considered our investigation might open up possibilities for fulfilling complementary objectives with the Russians. One of the advantages of détente, they tell me. Two heads being better than one. The realization that it overlapped with our Italian investigation fitted their intentions perfectly."

"They thought they'd kill two birds with one stone?"

"Yes, and timely. From what I can gather, Petrov had come under pressure from the FSB Chairman to tidy up his department. Being well aware of Sandquest's passion, the opportune appearance of Brizzi provided him with the perfect scenario. One Sandquest wasn't going to be able to resist. They set their trap, sending you and Vergellesi along to spring it."

Eldon suddenly put his hand up for silence.

"Did you hear something?" Prinn enquired after a moment. "It's very quiet outside."

"I thought so. Perhaps not."

"It's late," Prinn, said. "If you can keep an eye on things for a moment, I think I can chance making that call to the authorities in Rome. Difficult getting people out of bed, making decisions when they're half asleep. I'd also like these bodies moved out of my library. But having put them there, we can do nothing but be patient."

When he returned, attended by a faint aura of whisky, he was still pessimistic about a hasty resolution. "We're to sit tight and say nothing." He threw up his arms in exasperation. "To whom would we say anything? The Questore will be here in a few hours to clean up this tragedy."

"A tragedy," Eldon queried. "Do you think that's how they'll describe a Medusa hiding in a beautiful and extraordinary woman?"

Eldon suddenly stiffened, swinging the Uzi on to the French doors.

Petrov stepped through the shattered doorway, his hands folded in front of him like a man at a funeral. He was just a little early.

"That's too melodramatic, young man." He nodded towards Sandquest. "Too cynical as well. Their relationship was always a handicap. They really didn't have anyone to blame for all the lost years. Couldn't create a history that had never been, imagining a background that was pure fantasy. Any mutual respect just remained a frustrating idea without foundations."

"General Petrov?" Prinn acknowledged.

"Nothing more than a social call, Commander. Transit arrangements for unwanted goods."

Prinn put out a hand to check Eldon's angrily aggressive move. The politics at this moment were messy enough already.

"I understood you were supposed to be retired to a

486

deck-chair on the Black Sea, General?"

"What makes you suppose I'm not retired?"

"Because you're here. Winding up the old firm."

Petrov waved the idea away impatiently. "Sandquest brought this upon himself. Just because you cuckolded him, Commander."

"That might be embarrassingly true, General," Prinn continued, "but it's a peripheral truth; all part of a plan. Kopolev cleaned up behind Miss Jehmlich in Port Said, didn't he? Kopolev also made sure Doctor Rosso knew about the wine in Florence; and arranged all those photographs of Janus, that turned up with dead bodies. You've been keeping us very well informed."

"Interesting, you. But what's the use of such a hypothesis?" Petrov asked.

"A great deal, if it can be proved."

Petrov nodded. Then, as if he had all the time in the world, "Do you mind if I smoke?"

Prinn shook his head, sliding an ashtray across.

Petrov sat down, brought out a cigar and lit it, studying the burning end for a moment. He drew a deep breath, blowing a ring of smoke into the air, watching the shape disintegrate as it drifted upwards. "Proof? Of course, you will have an impossible task presenting it."

"Why is that?" Prinn asked.

Petrov stabbed the cigar in the direction of Sandquest's body. "This gentleman, for example. The ironic fact is, he was extremely important to your government. Given a choice, Whitehall would have considered Sandquest indispensable and sacrificed the pair of you. He provided them with what they needed, the high technology equipment to bug just about everyone, using anything from radio waves to microwaves. He could hear through walls, from the house across the street, or the satellite in outer space. Industrial espionage is an area you excel in, thanks to the sophistication of signals intelligence provided by men like Arthur Sandquest. He was indispensable to your government, in more ways than one. They will not be over pleased that you saw fit to hurry him on to another place. Not that the choice was so simple any longer. Your security services had become aware of Sandquest's foreign interests, however, they couldn't quite figure out its implications. They hadn't managed to prove anything either, Commander. Nor were they all that excited about developing a brand new international rationale. They quite liked the one they had. Proof?" Petrov blew another ring of smoke into the air from his cigar. "Not necessary really, now he's dead."

"If he was so indispensable, General, isn't this a little excessive?" Prinn asked.

Petrov studied Prinn for a moment. "Well, we are living in disturbed times. Governments are not safe anywhere. Technology has made the citizen dangerous, holding their leaders to account for policies they never thought to explain, to discuss, or even share. Governments have become exposed as criminals, or something like. Fingers in the till. Therefore, a conspiratorial closing of ranks. Democracy is a mirage of oligarchs where everyman votes one politico out, and another one in, and nothing among the elite has changed at all. Now Russia sees there's really very little difference in democracy and their own system of government, except one of perception. The people can argue amongst themselves, and thus be distracted from noticing that what they think they've changed, is really just the same." He became preoccupied, head leaning in the direction of the remains of the French windows, from where they heard a car pull up at the end of the building.

A man in a grey overcoat with a Prussian collar appeared nervously at the door. Petrov rose. "For me then." He nodded to the man. "I'll be right there." Buttoning up his coat he turned to Prinn. "Well, Commander, I wish you luck with your difficulties."

"I don't believe there will be any, General. Explanations undoubtably, otherwise we've been successful. This episode will merely prove to have been a most unwelcome distraction in Operation Necropolis."

Petrov stopped by the door. "Oh I wasn't thinking of accountability, you. I was alluding to Mrs Sandquest. The lady is troubled by a heavy conscience. Something we never have the time for."

Then he was gone, leaving the shattered door banging in the remains of the wind.

Chapter 58

Prinn was on the telephone to Questore Vignozzi when Vergellesi arrived, a wet, dishevelled mess, his hair matted with blood. Seeing Eldon, he leant against the door with a disconsolate face.

"Paba got away, Rex."

Eldon shook his head. "Never mind, Piero. He wasn't the most important business for us. Let me have a look at you first." He decided the wound was superficial. "You'll keep. We'll ask Commander Prinn where you can clean up."

Vergellesi sat on his haunches in front of Varina, studying the face drained of colour that had begun to take on a thin transparency: a porcelain quality of fine, white, bone china.

"What a waste of a journey," he said. "How should I feel, Rex? Elation, anger, some sort of emotion instead of absolutely nothing? I would have liked answers. Found my way to the bottom of it all. Why my father was killed? Who was responsible? I realize that Miss Jehmlich was obeying instructions, just like any one of us. For her it was Petrov pulling the strings. But who was pulling his; ordering him do the dirty work?"

"We'll probably never know, Piero. As you said, they were only a link in the chain. All you can do is consider it as a just retribution, one where Miss Jehmlich has had rough justice. No trial, but without the prospect of a mouldering decay locked away from the world while going quietly mad. Your father, I imagine, was a man who might have settled for the justice in that."

Prinn's voice interrupted them. "They still haven't managed to contact Ruggieri, Rex. The Russians seem better at disposing of evidence than we do." He looked at Vergellesi's appearance with some concern. "God, you're a mess young man. Washroom's next door. I'll see if I can find you some dry clothes."

He returned carrying the garments and a large towel. "Out of this door, second door on the right. There's a medicine cupboard in there, if you need it." Watching his departing figure, Prinn turned to Eldon. "Now, Rex.

Firstly, Vignozzi wants Vergellesi released without delay. Staying will be beyond his remit." Prinn drew Eldon a little further away from the door and lowered his voice. "It will also be beyond yours, so what I'm about to ask is something of a favour."

"Have I an option?" Eldon asked.

"It's a personal one, so, yes, you do." Prinn lowered his voice even further. "To all intents and purposes Operation Necropolis is a closed book with Sandquest gone. Case solved. That also means that the Nightingale file can be closed, and you can return to making your fortune. However, one small matter remains unresolved that might interest you. No one has yet found the tomb of Paetus Cecina."

Eldon studied Prinn's face for a moment, and concluded he was being serious. "Does that really matter to us any more?"

"To you and I, probably not so much. Yet to General Petrov, I think it means a great deal."

"Well, just tell the Italian authorities, and leave it to them. They can deal with Petrov."

"It's not that easy. You see, I believe that Petrov has half the answer to where the tomb is. He won't be sharing it with the Italian Authorities."

"And who has the other half?"

"I do. "

Eldon shook his head. "I'm not into playing games Commander. Nor am I into robbing graves."

"Neither am I Rex. Finding Paetus Cecina is not an ambition of mine. If for anyone, I'll do it for Senator Brizzi. He was certainly on the other side of the law, but his intentions were always for the good. He spent half a lifetime in a meticulous search for this lost tomb, for all the right reasons. I won't condone what he did. He's undoubtably guilty by association, but I feel strongly that Petrov shouldn't be able to rubbish all of Brizzi's ambitions, criminal or not. However, any action I take might be construed as extrajudicial."

"All right, you've persuaded me. And next?"

"A few days ago I received a letter from Senator Brizzi suggesting the tomb of Paetus Cecina lies in what could be termed a *matryoshka*. You know, those Russian dolls that fit inside one another. Capagli won't have discovered where the tomb is, and I don't believe Paba knows either, but I'm pretty sure that Petrov knows it exists. Rex, I haven't any idea what's in the tomb, but consider this for a moment. His ancestors have gone to an enormous amount of trouble to hide something with apparent success, so I can't believe it's just his ashes."

"There is one other point, Commander," Eldon queried with a touch of scepticism, "and that is, Brizzi's been dead for rather more than a few days?"

"Yes, but I've only just received the letter. As it was posted only some days ago, it couldn't have been Brizzi, that's obvious."

"Well, we know it wouldn't be Petrov who sent the letter either, so who else is in on this?"

"No one. The Sorena postmark on the letter is for the same day that you found poor Cecotti. I think it must have been he who sent it, knowing those thugs had found out about his close friendship with Brizzi."

"Yes, that would certainly fit. With the phone calls from Capagli we were monitoring it was evident something was coming to the boil, and when Cecotti phoned me just afterwards, he mentioned he'd posted a letter, but not to whom, which rather lessened its importance. I gather from all this that you think Petrov's going to try and find a way back into the tomb?"

"Undoubtably, he will." Prinn suddenly turned away, and coughed. "Ah, Vergellesi. Come in. Come in. How do you feel now?"

"A little battered, Commander. I've taken some pain-killers for the headache. Cut looks worse than it is. I think I'll live."

"As soon as you can, try and get a decent amount of rest in as well young man. A quiet vacation. All this racing about, and hard knocks, will have taken the edge off you. I'll see if they've managed to make contact with Ruggieri yet. Rex, we'll talk later."

Eldon took Vergellesi's arm. "In practical terms this is over, but in a few days it will come back to worry you."

"I'll cope. Apparently, I'm not up to the mark. A friend of yours also offered me some advice. Sort of person who shouldn't be allowed out after dark. Going about

491

frightening people."

"What are you talking about, Piero? What friend?"

"Said his name was Gower."

"Someone call my name?" Gower hailed, arriving in the room from the corridor, as though on cue. "See Sandquest's drawn the short straw. How are you, Rex? No holes in you are there?"

"Sandy. What the devil are you doing here?" Eldon demanded.

"I've come to report an accident," Gower informed him. "Need to move sharply on this one. Ah, Commander."

"You're a little late, Chief Inspector," Prinn said critically, as he came in.

"Inconspicuous actually, sir. Watching brief the Super said. This accident. Chappie fell off a bulldozer by the long barn. Luckily he stopped the thing first. Shot through the thigh, and looks like he's lost a lot of blood. When he's lucid, he doesn't seem to be able to speak. Shock I imagine."

"Ettore," Prinn exclaimed as he rushed away. "Vergellesi, phone for an ambulance."

Gower waved Eldon after Prinn. "I'll wait with Vergellesi. Dryer in here."

-oOo-

They found Scillone lying on his back, legs elevated, covered in old removal van blankets. His eyes were open, staring at the ceiling.

Prinn knelt beside him. Scillone's eyes shifted slowly to his face.

"Nightingale, or this man Kopolev?" Prinn asked Eldon.

"Too untidy," Eldon replied. "Professionals don't leave people to slowly bleed to death."

"Ettore. Can you hear me? Tell me what happened?" Prinn enquired.

A weak smile played fitfully on the edges of Scillone's mouth. He looked squarely at Prinn, his lips moving in an almost silent flutter.

Prinn leant closer to hear what he might be saying. "Pruning, Ettore. I don't understand."

492

Scillone tried to raise himself, but Prinn gently pushed him back down and leant even closer, listening intently in an effort to catch the mumbled speech. "That's not important. Just try and lay still. It was an accident, old friend. Only explanation. Impossible to see anyone in this rain?" He pulled the blanket up higher. "Don't worry about anything. I'll take care of it. The ambulance won't be long."

Squeezing Scillone's shoulder, Prinn rose, walked outside, and stood under the porch looking through the pouring rain, down towards the entrance to the villa.

Eldon followed. "What did he say?"

"Seemingly, your friend, Vergellesi, was wrong about Paba," Prinn replied. "He accidentally slipped under five tons of caterpillar tractor. He's out there somewhere. God, he'll take some finding in that mire."

Chapter 59

A hundred pigeons scrambled away in front of Prinn as he crossed the Piazza Della Signoria, their wings fluttering in fey indolence, which in summer may have touched the hearts of impressionable tourists, but had little effect upon the bustling Florentines who regarded them with choleric displeasure.

It was a long walk to the Via Ricasoli, passing the grand palaces of the Puci and Gerini, which no one entered, and the Accademia, which everyone did. Prinn needed to walk. A taxi would have taken a few minutes, allowing him nothing for the tortuous emotions he felt a need to master.

He hadn't slept. Scillone had been seen safely into hospital, Ruggieri needed debriefing, the local Questore, solemn and remote, arrived in person to make sure that what he'd heard was what he saw. No one trusted anyone when it came to suppressing the truth.

Vergellesi and Eldon would write up their reports, Gower had returned to duty, Petrov had vanished, to reappear he knew not where. Sandquest, and Varina, would be flown back to their respective countries in refrigerated isolation. Paba had yet to be found.

The circumstances would boil down to nothing more than administration, allowing a red line to be drawn under the case. Operation Necropolis would be the preferred option. The only revelation revealed to the public, would be the satisfactory outcome of the local police, courageously foiling an underworld attempt to rob the nation of a particularly important archaeological discovery. This was as near to the truth as anyone would be prepared to go.

Arriving at the hotel, Prinn took the lift to Rachel's apartment. Knocked, staring blankly at the over-varnished, faux mahogany door.

Rachel stood aside to let him in, composed though her face was heavily made up. The disclosure of her husband's death, in such unusual circumstances, had been difficult for her to comprehend. For the moment she faced simple facts, realizing little of the enormous volume of disclosures she would be called upon to assimilate and verify.

Suppressing any hint of sentiment, Prinn passed in to the sitting room. In silence he waited.

Rachel, closing the door, remained with her back to him, needing to prepare herself.

The police had arrived early that morning, unsure to what extent Rachel was involved in her husbands business. The first of a long list of official visits to be endured had not proved productive. She had blocked a great deal from surfacing in an effort to stop being overwhelmed by its complexity.

Prinn couldn't discuss the subject in an unofficial capacity, knowing that somewhere in the future his department would rake over the ground thoroughly enough. His personal interest spared him conducting the inquiry, as he would become the subject of an investigation himself to establish whether the Police Authority had been, in any way, compromised.

None of this would lend itself to an immediate continuation of their relationship. Rachel would believe he had betrayed her, when in fact he had betrayed them both. Choosing to live with deception had been a wretched struggle, finally forced upon him by the impossibility of cutting himself off from her, and the equally inconceivable act of jeopardizing his duty.

Standing there by the chair, Prinn realized that an impossible moment had arrived, and passed them by. Nothing had changed, or was about to change - the past could only be remembered, or forgotten. He couldn't recall considering how, in these circumstances, he would resolve the inquiry, and if he had, the answers would have been as vexatious as the questions. Perhaps there were no answers.

There was no reason to be here, the argument ran, nursing an opinion that somehow the cause justified the means. Prinn had accomplished everything for which he was responsible. Everything, except maintaining his integrity, and finally, no one but he and Rachel would have the slightest interest in that. Rachel walked a little way towards him, twisting her handkerchief in her hands, struggling to hold back words she wanted to hurl at the man she continued to love even as the bitterness and hostility crowded in on her anguish. What argument could justify his coming, except she'd desperately needed him to.

Their eyes held each other's for what seemed to Prinn an immeasurably long period of time. The intensity of his gaze was such that he saw familiar aspects outlined and heightened in his perception of them. The pale softness of her skin smoothed by an almost invisible fine down of blonde hair that lay high on her cheek bones; the blueness of her eyes, darkened in the apartment light, almost to violet; the convex curves that produced the fullness of her lips.

"You look exhausted," she remarked, a slight tremor in her voice.

"I imagine," he replied briefly.

"The police have asked - suggested - I should stay a few more days. Helping with inquiries. Just like they say in the newspapers. I suppose it will make headlines?"

Prinn chose his words carefully. "Perhaps, eventually. This will be difficult for you, Rachel. The authorities will ask questions you won't understand. Arthur was an important man. Both your lives will be under intense scrutiny. They have to be sure of everything."

"What will they ask, Nicholas?" The tremor in her voice rose again.

"About the past. Every question will lead to a dozen more, becoming ever more tedious."

"Won't there be an official statement?" Her voice had levelled out, taking on a bewildered tone, searching for clues to a crisis she didn't understand.

"Almost certainly. But don't expect it to be in the least bit informative."

"I suppose not." Her voice rose, acrimonious at last. "Industrialist found dead in Tuscan villa of wife's lover. Is that what they'll say?" She turned away, raising her handkerchief.

"Rachel." He held back, wishing to leave her unencumbered by his intervention. He was a confusing dichotomy; at once good and bad, an irrational concept that required faith in one, but not in both.

"Who will they blame then?" Rachel remained turned

away. "No one I imagine. Just one of those things. They happen, don't they?"

"I can't comment, Rachel. I'm only emphasizing there isn't any justification for you implicating yourself in your husband's activities."

"Then why did you come Nicholas?" She turned to face him, calm again in one of the spaces forming intervals of distraction between the despair.

"To explain matters that will come as much of a surprise to you, as they did to me."

"We're in this together then?" Her sarcasm struck sharply home, which he acknowledged with a sad smile.

"I've no idea how the Foreign Office will wish to present this potential sensation to the media. I've a meeting at the consulate tomorrow, after which matters may become clearer. I believe they will want to retain an element of simplicity in the reasons surrounding his death."

"Why should they have anything to say?"

"A matter of national security, Rachel. There are legal restraints they can apply. Please, I believe you should consider briefing your own legal counsel."

Her voice rose again. "Security. He was involved in the stealing of antiquities. What state secret is so insecure in the robbing of graves, Nicholas?"

"That's not their only interest. Arthur, apparently, had a clandestine Soviet association that might have led to charges of treason. I'm not competent to answer these questions."

"Treason? Impossible. He was my husband. What terrible things can he have done without me having a single idea, Nicholas?"

Prinn shook his head apologetically. "I can't say."

Rachel gave an exaggerated laugh. "Why should I know? Why should anyone tell me anything? I'm too dumb. I couldn't even see you were lying to me."

"I never lied to you." Prinn said quietly.

"Deceived me then. Avoided the truth to hide a lie. You were part of me, Nicholas. You knew everything about me. Every detail. How was it I didn't know anything about you, or your intentions? Never suspected anything. What were your reasons, Nicholas, besides pimping for the authorities?"

"My own position prevents me discussing anything, Rachel. Please understand. Special Branch officers will take that up, when you return to England. The Italian authorities will be as thorough, but I imagine will want to avoid too close an interest in any of the political aspects of the case. They'll concentrate on the robbing of tombs. In one sense, that will come as a mixed blessing. You'll be home quicker."

"To face the music?"

"That's not going to happen. Your innocence will quickly become apparent and discovering the truth will at least allow you to make sense of our present predicament."

"And will they want to know about you?" she inquired.

"Yes, they will ask about me."

"How very, very inconvenient for you. By now you're pretty bored with the pillow talk. Served its purpose. Someone else can do all the paperwork."

Suddenly she snapped. All self-control vanishing against the calm barrier Prinn tried to maintain between them.

"I feel soiled, Nicholas. Unclean. Used. Do you understand? You used me like a common bitch; just like any dog in the street." Her fists were clenched, raised against her shoulders, eyes full of tears; a face no longer beautiful, disarranged by the anguish that tore at her emotions.

"I know it appears that way," Prinn gestured hopelessly.

She cut him off. Shouting again. "It doesn't appear that way. That's how it really was. Look at me. What bit of flesh haven't you touched I can call clean?" Shuddering, she closed her eyes.

Prinn began to move towards her. She opened her eyes again.

"Don't," Rachel said emphatically. "Please, don't touch me."

Prinn stopped. "Rachel. Please believe me. Under such circumstances my being here only makes it worse. The truth is, while you hold me responsible I remain an enemy, not a friend. I can only continue to love you, hoping that we'll somehow find our way back to something we both cared deeply for. That's really all I came to say." Prinn picked up his hat.

Rachel raised her hand slightly as though to stop him, turning as he reached the door. "Nicholas," she said.

He stopped, looking back at her.

"The police didn't explain. They said Arthur had been shot." Her voice broke again before she struggled on, wanting to know. "Was it you, Nicholas?"

"Not directly, Rachel. No. Understandably, Arthur wasn't keen on my falling in love with you. He'd decided to take the matter into his own hands. It was the only way someone could stop him killing me. At this moment, I feel it really wouldn't have mattered if they hadn't."

Chapter 60

The public address system at the Galilei Galileo airport announced that Eldon's late morning flight had commenced boarding procedure. Margaret hugged him as he stooped to kiss her goodbye.

"Now remember," he teased, "if Commander Prinn calls, make sure it's only a courtesy one, and nothing else. Take good care of yourself."

Giving her a final squeeze his eyes focused over the top of her head, catching someone moving quickly away. A man in a grey overcoat, with a Prussian collar, a round face, with small, close-set eyes, under an astrakhan cap. Eldon sighed inwardly. When they wanted to see the back of you that much, it was always a reason to stay.

Eldon studied his two companions with their relaxed and comfortable demeanours. There were no clouds on their horizons, and the recent episode in their lives was now water under the bridge. He was glad for them; for the fact that they could return to a normal life free from the stress of the last few months. From now on, anything to do with Petrov was a risk magnified out of all proportion to their needs.

He took Vergellesi's offered hand. "October. Don't forget my late vacation."

"October," Vergellesi confirmed. "Sicily will still be warm. I'll wait for you."

They watched his tall figure pass through the customs gate, joined in a final wave as he passed out of sight into the departure lounge, before turning to find the exit.

"Like closing a book," Margaret said, giving Vergellesi a despondent smile as the automatic doors opened. "You're left with a huge unoccupied mental space."

Outside the sky was a cloudless blue, a tinted atmosphere of warm Italian sensuality. They walked slowly towards the car park.

"And what of you?" Vergellesi asked, tucking his arm in hers.

"Me? Oh well," Margaret replied, "I'll continue where I left off. Melissa has to finish high school, then I imagine she'll want to go to university. How many years? Too many to contemplate. *Domani*, isn't it? No need to get there in a hurry."

"Time enough for you to come to Sicily?"

"In October?" she retorted.

"Ah! No. Not in October."

They'd reached his Alfa Romeo, stopping by the passenger door. Vergellesi looked at her, searching her face for something that in the end he must have found, for he drew her very close. "Not while Eldon's there. That wouldn't be cricket." He finally let their lips part; kissing her again to make his point. "I promised Melissa I'd show her the River Ciane with its Egyptian papyrus. The only place in Europe where it grows. Now, in the spring, before the insects make it impossible." He laughed softly. "Well, it's the basis of an excuse. Will you come?"

Margaret smiled up at him. "I rather hope Melissa would never allow me to say no," she replied.

-oOo-

The Villa Lazzi lay wrapped in the remains of an early morning mist. Inside, Prinn poured himself another coffee.

Picking up the cup and saucer he wandered along to the library, having become a place constantly and depressingly at the back of his mind. Few signs remained to indicate the late drama, only a large piece of plywood filling the terrace doorway - and a hole in the ceiling.

The telephone rang. He put down the cup, retracing his steps to the hall.

"Rex!" He glanced at his watch. "Well done. What time can I expect you? - Yes. Arrange a hire car. - Shortly after lunch. - I'll be here."

Prinn returned to his coffee, distracted. Brizzi must have found something in the library his father had assembled with such care. Thousands of books, leather covers in want of bees wax; hundreds of box files, neatly arranged and classified; drawers of old parchments, maps and charts; catalogues of manuscripts in libraries that no longer existed; catalogues of dealers where they probably now did. All to do with a history that

501

gathered nothing but dust. For his father, the library had been a passion. For Senator Brizzi something more prosaic, but in the manner of a romance, all the same.

The rest of the morning Prinn wrestled with the senator's letter, only being disturbed at midday by *Signora* Scillone calling from the end of the corridor, still too apprehensive to venture down to the library.

Prinn had a desultory lunch picking at the courses, failing to make a meal of anything; aware only of the little woman who tended him who was unable to understand why all these tragic things had come to pass. She represented the last of her type, absorbing the intractable fickleness of their society and the world without complaint, replaced by modern women doing everything grudgingly under an egocentric sufferance. They were all *'grandi signore'* now.

After lunch, Prinn sat staring distractedly at Brizzi's letter, having seemingly exhausted all the possibilities. He was still sitting there when Eldon arrived, a little late.

Signora Scillone, who'd been asked to show Eldon in, managed even this from the end of the corridor.

He dismissed Eldon's apologies, drawing up a chair for him.

"I'm glad you're here, Rex."

"I'm intrigued, Commander, and to be honest, not yet completely ready to return to Weatherfield and Holding. I rather feel the Italian air agrees with me."

"I can assure you, experiencing a Tuscan winter soon disabuses you of such misconceptions. Yesterday, I spoke to Chief Superintendent Hart. He's not overjoyed having to explain away the complications to the ACSO until I get back. Nor am I looking forward to going back. He's relieved we didn't lose anyone, of course, which would have made things difficult. The Americans are slapping backs, and rightly making a belated fuss over Remmick. I was a little surprised to find he was still in Sorena. An active pensioner, they tell me."

"It was in his blood. He didn't have any other life, so when the chance came, he felt quite at home in it."

"A heavy price to pay," Prinn said, wearily. "I can't say there are many intelligence agents who relish getting their hands dirty. Meanwhile, the Italian authorities will overlook anything, hating to make a fuss and having safely secured their patrimony. It appears, at least, if the business is over."

"But you think not. This letter. Positive confirmation that it isn't?"

"At the moment it doesn't seem to confirm anything."

"Well, one thing certainly has been. You were right. Petrov's still very much connected, and sizing up the opposition, Commander."

"Oh?" Prinn queried.

"My departure from Pisa was witnessed by more than just Piero and Margaret."

"I see. In that case, as this is technically a matter for the Italian police, we shall have to look lively."

"Where exactly would Brizzi make a start, given his access to this library?" Eldon asked, looking round.

"My father was exceptionally single minded, Rex, but his interest lay in Roman political culture not necessarily, or exclusively, the Cecina influence on it. Naturally, the sources he accrued were much wider in content than solely the jurisdiction of Roman power. It does; however, include many items of an Etruscan nature as well. I'm not entirely convinced this library held the sort of secrets Senator Brizzi sought. More likely, some reference he managed to locate supplied the links to help him interpret significant parts, or provided leads he could develop elsewhere. It's likely that only an amalgam of unusual talents could have discovered and interpreted them."

"And they came together in Brizzi, an intelligent person with experience in both geology and archaeology. He was certainly well qualified."

"Precisely. He was also conversant with Latin and Greek, which gave him a head start. An oddity of the higher Italian education system that often has its uses. He didn't make many friends, but those he did were significant - giving him access to a wide range of reference sources, besides this one. The Prefect of the Vatican library was a personal friend, as was the Abbot of Castelluccio where they have a large collection of ancient documents and records relating to Sorena. Once he became a senator all sorts of other doors would have been open to him. Untold treasures lie hidden in the mountain of letters and documents housed in our libraries, museums and government archives. One thing I do know, Brizzi was certainly a bibliophile. His own library was very impressive."

"Do you have any idea at all what he's alluding to in the letter?"

Prinn shook his head. "It's a confection of clues. Even when you spot them, they don't really take you anywhere. The clues are obscure, and when you work them out, the answers are just as obscure. Brizzi was a secretive man. He wasn't going to make it easy for anyone. Not even me."

Prinn handed the letter and envelope to Eldon, who read it through carefully:

My Dear Nicòla

I often wondered if you knew all along, and laughed behind my back. I trust not. Your father was always generous and predisposed to my enquiries. In that way he helped me find the key amongst his treasures that will unlock the secret of Paetus Cecina. Now I will be considerate in my turn. Anyway, my back is broad, though I know I have to die, I only hope it's not among that paradise of fools. I will be content with a long sleep among the bards. Remember? You introduced me to the finer points of the English poets. Perhaps I will meet them there. Hope springs eternal Pope said. So just let's say:

svularemuqapeqauralautnacaecina
huqcureaperucenclaudio

The Etruscans left nothing of poetry, as you know, but you will be able to make something of this, which is no better. Ask Janus. He will have the answer. The Greeks we understand at least. The careless lady, after all, had vice and passion in her jar. So, dear Nicòla, do not believe the castle's a mere *'Chateaux d'Espagne'*. Don't leave any of the seven stones unturned to find a solution. Only you have the sensitivity to secure a good

504

fortune. Open this like a *matryoshka*. One by one. You must live in hope, for I have none.

Alas, I'm afraid this is by way of a farewell.

Distinti saluti.

Roberto.

"Hmm! I see what you mean," Eldon reflected. "Did you have any inkling about all this?"

"And laughed at him? Not really. As a young man I was flippant about his obsession for carrying out research into the Cecina legend. We talked often on English poetry. He particularly liked Milton's Italian poems, but in the letter you'll see, he seemingly makes more of Pope."

"Not necessarily exclusively, though. There is a line from Paradise Lost - 'Into a Limbo large and broad, since called the Paradise of Fools'."

"Ah, yes. I recall it. Limbo's a place of the dead where, along with unbaptized babies, all good men before Christ's coming were confined. By implication I suppose we could stretch that to all good Etruscans. Might be a reference to the tomb of Paetus. That of Pope, I remember. 'Hope springs eternal', is taken from 'An Essay on Man'. What it means in relation to Paetus, I have no idea. What could it mean?" Prinn shrugged in bafflement. "The Etruscan lines, though not in reverse script, from right to left, are not quite authentic - how could they be - but with a lot of research and inspired guesswork, are I believe, now reasonably clear. 'To reveal the underworld open the tomb of the family Cecina. The fourth stone opens the way to Claudius.' As the tomb's been opened," Prinn concluded, "you might say, we're half way there."

"Even so; has it revealed the right underworld?" Eldon queried. "And which fourth stone - in probably hundreds of them, - of which he specifies seven? Does it mean a tomb within a tomb? And why the reference to Janus and Claudius in particular. They're the only two names actually revealed in reference to Paetus?"

"Precisely the problem, Rex. The fourth stone will be one of seven and; therefore, I assume they are all alike. But Janus is probably the key to it all. 'Ask Janus' - 'He will have an answer.' Well, he just might, if we could find him."

Prinn opened a drawer, removing a large photograph that he passed to Eldon. "I've had one of the Janus photographs that surfaced early in our enquiries enlarged to see what I could make of the writing. Because it encircles the leg it, obviously, remains incomplete. He's a classical Janus. Facing both ways. The first lines are a reference to the statue being an *ex-voto* offering - a solemn promise made for something. On the back is what I think the rest of the visible inscription says."

Eldon turned the photograph over, smiling at the recollection of Gower's observation on Prinn's small, neat handwriting:

'O celebrated fathers!/ .... the underworld. /Call them from the shades,/ .... the truth,/
.... the ..../ .... / bring forth words to sing of songs. O shade of heroes. Let them..../'

"Obviously someone has a lot to say about something, but in this form it doesn't say a lot. The missing words might indicate which fourth stone. Where did this statue come from?" Eldon inquired.

"Not known," Prinn explained. "This is merely the copy of another photograph, probably belonging to Senator Brizzi. As he refers to the statue in the letter, it suggests he had it in his possession at some time, or at least, had access to it. If that's true, he would almost certainly have gathered the gist of the whole inscription. It also appears, there was more than one Janus in circulation. This is believed to be the only one with an inscription. Guardian of gateways. Even of tombs. If we knew where to find this particular Janus, we might finish Brizzi's quest for him."

"There are still some other clues. What about French cum Spanish castle?"

"*Chateaux d'Espagne*. It's the French expression for 'castles in the air', by virtue of there being no chateaux in Spain. 'We must believe it,' surely means that the legend is real, not a fancy, and therefore hidden in the

Castello di Pietra - if we don't leave any stone unturned. The lady is, very likely, Pandora."

"Opening her jar might refer to opening the final tomb," Eldon surmised. "Hope appears three times in this letter if we count the unmentioned one left in Pandora's jar. Brizzi's implying it's important, I think?"

"Perhaps. And also something that can only be accessed from within the presently opened part of the tomb."

"You know, Commander, even if we succeed in deciphering this, someone may still have pre-empted us?"

"Have you someone in mind?"

"How about the Cecina family?"

Prinn nodded. "Possible. Until the empire collapsed. Afterwards, probably not. They were, after all, a famous Volterran gens; a landed class that probably controlled a huge swathe of northern Tuscany. There's no parallel that I know of in European history, where such a family invested so much in political endeavours to so famously little effect. Some were hooligans enough to squander such a secret, but seemingly even they perceived the need to keep alive the unifying aspects of their past by a strong central allegiance to the clan. From what we know, the northern part of Etruria seems to have passed relatively peacefully under Roman rule, and one can surmise, that the Cecina influence delivered the great hill top city of Volterra into an early alliance. Whether Sorena followed suit, would be conjectural, as nothing is known of its civic status during that period. We do know, however, that the Cecina family remained politically active, assimilating itself into the Roman system by alliances and intrigues, and knowing that nation's superstitious nature, used their flair for augury to promote their own ingratiating self-interests. Of those, actually recorded by name, towards the end of the empire we have Albino Cecina, a provincial civil governor, and a senator for Volterra, building himself a sumptuous villa at Vada. Therein, some say, lay the Roman weakness. The foundation of the nations greatness was built on calling its generals from the plough, not from their palaces. My father said: historical

507

facts are like coins. They have two sides. Meaning they can be interpreted according to your own prejudices. Anyway, Albino seems to have been one of the more loyal officers of the state. Aulo Cecina, on the other hand, was a friend of Cicero, entertaining him royally at his palace in Volterra. He may well have been put to death along with Cicero for Republican intrigues. They were a most disreputable family on the whole. Tuscus upset Vitellius by giving wild parties while the emperor lay ill; Alienus meanwhile helped himself to public funds, and being found out upset just about everyone, until he came to a sticky end under Vespasian. And then there was the subject of all our deliberations, the fatuous Paetus, running foul of Claudius. There is some evidence his wife was related to the Tarquins, Rome's ancient kings. Unhappily, little of the social ramifications of the clan are known. They may have been virtually exterminated by dynastic squabbles. Etruscan documents are conspicuous by their absence. No philosophers, no poets or playwrights, to supply us with the drama of their lives. There they are, sandwiched between the Greeks and Romans, both literati through and through. It is inconceivable that such a powerful civilization was so completely inarticulate. Perhaps the Romans systematically destroyed all the Etruscan literature and history to suppress a great past, and glorify their own. A sort of literary genocide. We may never know."

"Meanwhile, we have little time to sit on our hands," Eldon emphasized.

"Indeed not. I shall need to be inside the tomb if we're to make sense of Senator Brizzi's revelations. You've been a great help teasing out the strands. Now let's hope I can apply them."

"With Petrov breathing down your neck, and not even knowing what cards are stacked against him, I imagine he's going to be a very sore loser. Don't you think this is a little too risky, Commander? I can guarantee he won't be on his own. Kopolev at least, and for all we know, a whole army of other thugs. You'll be on your own against some very tricky people."

"You'll be there somewhere."

"I can't be everywhere."

"I don't want anyone everywhere. We've got to smoke him out, but the smallest hint that 'here comes the cavalry' will lose him. He's too old a hand, having survived some of the most vicious murderers in history. Time might be running out in his life, but he still knows how to wait - just like he's spent his whole life waiting. So, given that prediction, I'm not going to ask you to do anything difficult. Just let's arrange it so we can lock the back door with him inside this time."

Chapter 61

A little after seven o'clock in the evening, Prinn drove over to the castle.

The policeman on duty wore an officious scowl, having grown tired of arguing over executive's 'rights' with inquisitive officials. He checked Prinn's warrant card carefully, verifying the vehicle registration number by radio before allowing Prinn into the floodlit bailey.

Inside the keep two officers rechecked his details. A monitor on the table, still powered by Capagli's little generator, displayed nothing more than a solitary, unblinking, black and white image of the first corridor and its cells. The police officer gestured he could proceed.

Inside the dank sepulchre, the glistening globes of humidity intermittently dripped from the ceiling with a little splash on to the floor. Arguably, it was a damp place to have spent two thousand years - even when safely tucked up in a sarcophagus!

Perhaps Brizzi was making fun of him as well. 'A paradise of fools', he'd said in the letter. Perhaps there was nothing more than an impressive archaeological find, with the important elements of their location and relationship destroyed by blind ignorance, and overwhelming greed. He was not inclined to accept that Brizzi would have left it at that.

Passing the individual chambers and their stone thrones, Prinn stopped in front of the end wall with its carved facade, trying to analyse its significance. He had a suspicion that there was an informative aspect about its location. But what? The iconography seemed of little relevance to Brizzi's letter, if a great deal to the burial of the dead.

He was distracted by a noise that sharply turned his attention behind him.

Petrov stood by the trapdoor flanked by scowling FSK trained troopers, their machine guns pointing threateningly at Prinn. The soldiers weren't in uniform, but there was no doubt they could function just as well without them.

"Such concentration, you," Petrov said, waving the men forward.

Behind the General, Prinn saw Kopolev emerge with another, younger figure, wearing a heavy coat and bulky woollen scarf, carrying a leather bag. Boris blinked nervously.

"How did you find your way in here?" Prinn asked, a hint of concern in his voice, remembering the policemen outside.

"The same way as we're going to leave, Commander. The bank behind this castle is like Gruyere cheese, riddled with tunnels. Unhappily, only one is now functioning. You know the drill."

Prinn stretched out his arms, palms against the wall.

"Comrade Boris here, will check you out," the General explained. "Niceties will have to be dispensed with, so behave yourself. He looks a cold fish but he has nice warm hands."

Going about his business thoroughly, Boris removed the Smith and Wesson revolver from inside Prinn's jacket. Finding Brizzi's letter in a pocket, he passed it over to Petrov. His hands ran across Prinn's stomach and hips, turned inside his legs, down the length of his calves, round the heels of his shoes, finally pressing along the toes.

"I'll wager you do this to all the girls," Prinn commented sourly.

"*Ja*," Boris replied in his heavy Belarus accent. "It just takes longer."

"Smartly, Boris," Petrov said impatiently, withdrawing the folded sheet of paper from the envelope. He opened it and frowned.

Prinn dropped his arms. "I can see you're disappointed?"

Petrov looked up from the letter. "Of course. Brizzi and I had known each other for some time. I'd helped him from the beginning, and we'd developed an excellent relationship. Naturally, I expected him to confide in me."

"Naturally. Is that why you killed him?"

Petrov gave him a dismissive smile. "Stop playing policemen." He gestured indifference. "It's not important. I never killed Brizzi. I would have done so if necessary, but for me, it wasn't. After all, he'd taken me into his confidence, informed me about this necropolis, so I found him Paba to front the operation, Sandquest to dispose of the acquisitions. Paba didn't have the right temperament to deal with Brizzi. That was a mistake on my part. He was uncompromising, letting Brizzi know who paid the piper. Sandquest, on the other hand, he considered was like dealing with the devil. A Midas without principles. On reflection, they weren't a good choice at all. The senator, foolishly, began to consider seeking more amenable partners. Hah! The idea of Paba being left to walk away from a fortune, merely demonstrates there is some correlation between intelligence and stupidity. He should have talked to me. Unfortunately, as he'd decided to fly to Barcelona to talk with Blain, I'd no chance to stop Paba's too rapid response. Paba was very cool - until you threw his switch."

"I doubt Blain would have been any easier a partner than Sandquest."

"I dare say. The result of all this antagonism has been particularly destructive. Blain, on the other hand, believing he'd been dealt an ace, made the mistake of thinking he had Sandquest by the balls. As you know, we had all the aces, so we potted him off a mountain."

"A fine example of Russian excesses"

"The Soviet relationship with Sandquest was more important than old Cecina. Only one way with embarrassments. You bury them. All of them!"

"Is this your confession?" Prinn asked, pointedly.

Petrov smiled. "Why not? Nothing will be taken down in writing and used as evidence."

Prinn sat down uneasily on one of the carved thrones between the chamber entrances. The policemen, cosy by their portable gas stove, might occasionally glance at the monitor, which would disclose nothing of the inner chambers. Later, they might stir themselves. But not yet. Meanwhile, he was in a corner, and unsure how to manoeuvre himself out of it. Eldon, he hoped, had put his part of the plan into action, but having insisted that he didn't barge in like the cavalry, would bide his time. Ruefully, he now questioned the wisdom of such a

512

decision. He was left with an uncertain future, trapped in the tomb with Petrov.

Petrov finished reading the letter, and shook it. "You understand all this?" he demanded sharply.

Prinn shrugged. "About as well as I understand why Brizzi mixed with murderers."

"You're getting melodramatic, Commander." Petrov's voice had hardened. "Brizzi was an idealist. For him, democracy was nothing but opportunism, a first class ticket to power and riches. Get your man in the right place, and you have the keys to the safe. Contracts, jobs, financial deals, protection from justice, anything you might want. He believed in a different society, imagining he'd found a way to make a contribution."

"I can't imagine why he approached you to realize it," Prinn ventured, cynically.

Petrov smiled good-naturedly at this. "Initially he approached the Cubans, you. The Italian left can still just about inspire a banana republic or two. The Cubans contacted us. What did they want with old bones and old stones? Thought they'd get into trouble again, dabbling in foreign waters. So he came to Moscow where we made him feel important by rolling out the red carpet, and filling lots of column space in the Moskovskiye Novosti. I listened to his theory, which bounced like a squash ball with a hole in it, but agreed, that if something materialized we might be prepared to act as a conduit. Carriage facilities, with all the paperwork stamped."

"Yes, we'd noticed Sandquest's new commissariat based in the east. What was Brizzi intending to do with this ill-gotten inheritance?" Prinn asked.

"Well, you, he wanted to fund an educational trust. He had this idea that the bright pupils from working class families weren't being given a fair deal. He intended providing bursaries for committed Communist students, so they could study abroad, by-passing all that clientelismo, with brown envelopes under the table. Your interference hasn't done a lot for the humanities and social sciences in Italy, Commander."

"A fine group of trustees, hand in glove with organized crime," Prinn retorted.

"That's too harsh. I'm willing to admit that criminal

513

organizations provide a most useful service, especially in Italy. Not only can they organize the necessary labour, but they also provide a generous amount of security to an operation, through their social and political contacts. But for an educational trust? No."

Prinn remained adamant. "Even the concept's absurd. You're up to your neck in murder and theft."

"Now that's superfluous." Petrov's voice hardened again. "I've no more time for your bourgeois prattle." He paused, thoughtfully letting his voice modify, conciliatory. "Everyone has an Achilles heel, Commander." He sat down opposite Prinn. "Mine, would be my long association with Sandquest; yours, I think, must be your shorter association with his wife."

"Mrs Sandquest?" Prinn queried cautiously.

"Unfortunately, the police will have a need to evaluate Sandquest's wife's testimony. From our point of view, we'd rather they didn't look too closely. There's the problem of Mrs Sandquest disclosing material evidence we might have missed, and should have eliminated. Evidence - or Mrs Sandquest." Petrov's eyes had become ominously still.

Prinn considered if Petrov was playing games. It wasn't likely. Petrov wasn't a sporting type, and Rachel's life would depend entirely on the manner of his own response. At the same time, he was fully aware that justice wasn't going to be served by a slavish pedantry in the name of the law. There was no rule, that wasn't sometimes at odds with equity. He had to balance this with the knowledge that Petrov would carry out the task with ruthless efficiency, not doubting that Kopolev would take care of it - just as he took care of everything.

For a long moment they were quiet, studying each other, before Prinn nodded.

No smile, no hint of triumph crept into Petrov's bitter features. It was, in effect, a matter of fact question. "What does the letter tell us, then?" he asked softly.

Prinn shifted uncomfortably. "Possibly only half the story."

Petrov remained unmoved. "Unhappily, Commander, a half for you is nothing at all. You'll have to do better than that."

514

"The explanation to the letter is probably on these walls." Prinn's arm swept round the chamber. "A matter of interpretation, balancing out Brizzi's clues to what is represented here."

"Were those the sort of things you were looking at?" Petrov asked, gesturing towards the stone plaques above the doors.

"Partly. If you have knowledge of Greek, it's possible to make some sense of Etruscan. They seem to have borrowed the Greek characters and applied them differently, making interpretation the difficulty. English is made up from a great deal of Latin. So is Italian. But the same root hasn't flowered, exclusively, into the same meaning. However, here the meaning seems closer to Greek. I imagine the original Etruscan was getting a little rusty by then. Latin was the lingua franca, with local dialect for convenience."

"But you have interpreted this letter?" Petrov urged.

"Speculative notions. Not completely."

"There is an obstacle?"

"A bronze statue, General?"

Petrov leant forward, peering inquisitorially into Prinn's face. "Now there's a coincidence. You know I have two? The Janus pair."

"I didn't know. But if one has an inscription, then I might be able to resolve some of the meaning? I believe Brizzi adhered to a theory that classical Albanian had a great deal in common with Etruscan, and used that to decipher some of the words. I wouldn't be able to follow such a route myself, but if we're lucky, and they're close enough to Greek, then I might be able to add something to what we already know."

Petrov nodded. "Capagli unearthed one in the first tomb. A later burial, not long after Paetus."

"And the other?"

"The other, which has the inscription, belonged to Brizzi, and I'm told is contemporary."

"Where did he find it?"

"So many questions, you. I understand Brizzi mysteriously acquired it from a monastery, in the Mugello. Something they'd inherited from an extinct titled family during the fourteenth century. Longobard nobles, with a marquisate including Sorena."

"The Marquis Ugo. A Lucchese. You have the bronze here?"

Petrov nodded, signalling to Boris. "Fetch the statues for the Commander." He turned back to Prinn. "But be careful, wasting my time can shorten yours."

"I'm aware of the threat."

"A threat is a qualified declaration of intention. Believe me, in that sense, these bronzes actually represent your only salvation."

"Then it'll be something of a gamble. The inscription probably only indicates an *aide-mémoire* for future generations. That is, until there weren't any more generations."

"So, it's a sort of key, providing entrance to Paetus Cecina's last hiding place?"

"Resting place, General. It may help us to understand the clues in the letter. You're prepared for the likelihood it's nothing more than a grave, I suppose?"

"You don't believe that, and nor do I. In an unguarded moment, before Brizzi became paranoiac about his partners, he confessed that the greatest prize was hidden behind another. Having certainly found the first tomb, I'm inclined to look for the next."

Boris returned, bearing the small bronze statues, one with an inscription encircling a leg like a snake.

Prinn took it carefully, rotating the statue to read the inscription. "Yes, this might be the complete key. With the extra words it reads, as far as I can make out, something like this:

'O celebrated fathers! Reveal the underworld, Call them from the shades. Reveal the truth.
Touch the graven stone. Press hope. Bring forth words to sing of songs. O shade of heroes.
Let them speak.'

That's beginning to make some sort of sense."

"To whom?" Petrov demanded impatiently. "To me they're merely absurd, primitive rantings."

"Without Brizzi's letter I may have been inclined to agree with you. His 'fourth stone' in the original letter

516

needed a context, and with the information given here we can use a little deduction to see if it's correct."

"Then it's convenient you're a policeman, Commander."

"In one sense. The plaques you pointed out, above our heads, are appellations."

"The family names?" Petrov leant forward eagerly.

"Names, yes, but not an Etruscan family in our particular story. They're from the Greek myth of Prometheus. Luckily the names are in Greek. Brizzi said in the letter that the Greeks would make more of it."

Prinn pointed out the order of the plaques. "On this side is Zeus, followed by Hephaestus and Pandora. Opposite, behind you, we have Iapetus, the Titan, who created man out of clay, followed by his sons, Prometheus and Epimetheus. Atlas, his third son, is missing, because he's not a player in this particular myth. The legend says that Prometheus stole fire from heaven, giving it to man, whereupon Zeus chained him to a rock in the Caucasus with a vulture to feed on his liver every day. Thereafter, the liver was restored at nightfall, permitting the whole grim episode to be repeated the following morning. Not satisfied with that, Zeus had the fire god, Hephaestus, create a woman, Pandora, who then contrived to become the wife of Epimetheus." Prinn pointed to the relevant plaque. "Pandora is Brizzi's careless lady, who supplies the all important clue, and the reason for this mythological subject matter."

Petrov glanced at the letter. "With vice and passion in her jar?"

"Well, until she opened it, and nearly all of man's afflictions flew out."

Petrov had become edgy, unsure of Prinn's motives and bemused by the tortuous explanation. "This is all nonsense, Commander. In the scale of life you're closer to Paetus than I am."

"You'll have to bear with me, General," Prinn mollified his impatience. "Only 'Hope', you see, remained at the bottom of the jar."

Petrov looked at the plaques above the doors. "Hope? These are all comrades of this Prometheus. Remember?"

517

"Exactly," Prinn agreed. "That's why Brizzi's fourth stone is so important. There are only six characters in the myth, represented here on the carved stones, yet he tells us the French would have left none of the stones unturned, of which there are seven"

Petrov glared at him, his temper agitated by lack of comprehension.

Prinn pressed on. "The gentleman down there, carved in relief, is Typhon, one of those mysterious divinities of the Etruscan Hades. He was the Greek Charon, transporting souls of the dead across the River Styx. He's identifiable by the rudder in his right hand, serpent in the other. 'Hope', Brizzi tells us, 'springs eternal', which might have been the Etruscan belief when they died and crossed to the other side."

"But there's no tomb there. Only a representation of one," Petrov said irritably, jumping up and gesturing impatiently.

"That's what they want us to believe."

"Stop speaking in riddles." Petrov grew irritable again. "I'm tired of wasting my time listening to all your fatuous hot air. What does it mean, you?"

Prinn remained calm. "The plaque, above Charon's head, is 'Hope'. It follows the third graven, or inscribed stone, Pandora. 'Hope' is the fourth stone, just like Iapetus is the fifth, and Epimetheus the seventh. But it isn't over a physical door. It's there, with Charon at death's door. 'Press hope. Bring forth words,' Janus tells us."

"I see, you." Petrov gave a relieved and enlightened smile at last, as he grasped Prinn's explanation. "Press the stone. Just like rubbing Aladdin's lamp." He roared with laughter, slapping his thigh.

"General!" Kopolev suddenly whispered urgently, halting the laughter, and then more insistently "General!"

The assembly froze, listening intently.

"Commander Prinn," a voice finally called from the outer corridor.

Safety catches clicked as the machine guns swung on to Prinn.

Chapter 62

Prinn looked at Petrov, who nodded his head towards the opening. He went to the space, and sat on his heels. "Yes, I'm here," he called out.

"Just checking everything's all right," the policeman continued. "Would you like a coffee? *Macchiato.*"

"*No. Grazie.* I won't be long now. I'll have one when I come up, *per favore.*"

Prinn waited, listening to the receding sounds of the policeman before coming back from the edge to sit down. There really wasn't any point in heroics - not when someone had seen fit to leave the security of millions of pounds of antiquities in the hands of three policemen.

"He's gone," Kopolev confirmed. "If the Commander's too dilatory, we'll still be here when he comes back."

Petrov turned to Boris. "The Major's right. We must move along. Mustn't keep the optimistic Commander from his coffee. You were listening to all he said?"

"Press the fourth stone," Boris confirmed, taking his bag to the end wall.

Petrov slumped heavily on to an opposite stone throne, while Boris unfurled a roll of tools he'd taken from the bag. "Boris studied archaeology, you." he addressed Prinn, with a smile. "An interest in dead bodies must have proved useful on his CV when he applied for the Directorate."

From a flap at the end, Boris removed a small flat wooden instrument case that he opened to reveal a mirror probe with neatly arranged attachments. To the battery handle he connected a focusable prism telescope, followed by a lengthy flexible light extension.

"I'd rather look and see what might happen when I press the stone." Boris explained, marking the position where he intended to commence the operation.

Selecting a long thin chisel, he raked out dust and debris from the joints, concentrating on widening one of the bottom edges. A tube attached to a rubber bulb pumped the area free of obstructions, followed by the flexible extension containing a miniature optical light. Once inserted, he examined the interior.

"Ah," he said, "this stone pivots on pegs at the bottom. In the centre, at the top, there appears to be a simple mechanism with a rod attached dropping vertically out of sight. If we push at the top another movement should take place. Logically, somewhere below. Would you like to see, General?"

"No," Petrov replied. "Just get on with it. Go ahead. Bring the roof down on us."

Boris pushed the top tentatively, then with more force. "Stone's moving," he said excitedly. "This one here. Towards the bottom." He looked at Petrov for guidance.

"One of you," Petrov directed the guards calmly. "Give Boris a hand, in case it falls on his toe."

Prinn glanced opportunistically at Kopolev, and the remaining guard.

Both smiled condescendingly back at him. Prinn was their only interest, and they hadn't any intention of letting him go anywhere.

The stone was large and rectangular, raised almost a metre above the floor by resting on the bottom course.

"Right," Boris instructed. "This is as far as they intended the stone to move. Just enough so levers can be inserted. The top of the stone looks chamfered so it can tip out, as well as achieving a tight fit along the top front edge. We'll need a support. On the scaffolding there's some wooden props. Hurry. Bring those."

They were passed to Boris, who arranged two on the ground, parallel with the wall, the other two leaning against the stone.

"Now," he continued, directing his temporary assistant. "When I lever the stone from the top, take up the weight on these props and lower it on to the others."

As the stone eased clear of the wall, the guard grunted loudly at the exertion, only to have the heavy load overcome his strength as it neared the ground, plummeting down with a crash.

Everyone remained still, listening intently.

When no one outside appeared, they accepted that the noise had passed unnoticed. Petrov coming forward gave the signal to continue.

Boris pointed his torch into the cavity.

As Prinn automatically followed, the guard instantly

pressed the front of the barrel against his head as he stooped down.

"Hah!" Petrov laughed, looking back. "He's not going anywhere, Russian. Let him be."

Handing his torch to Petrov, Boris moved aside. "No wonder they missed the cavity when they scanned the wall," he remarked. "The sarcophagus is tailor made to fit like a glove."

The torch lit up a sarcophagus. Its proportions conforming very precisely to the dimensions of the cavity. Sealed up, the aperture continued to represent a solid stone wall.

"Seems that the grave robbers were well aware of acoustical properties - tapping the stones to locate hidden tombs," Prinn added.

"Boris," Petrov said irritably, ignoring Prinn, "How are you going to withdraw the sarcophagus? There's no handle."

Boris had already given it some thought. "No, General. Commander Prinn is right. The covering stone is designed to squarely touch the sarcophagus, eliminating any acoustical echoes. But they have made provision for its withdrawal. One of the dancing males, cast on the side, has an area between his arm and body left hollow. It looks natural enough, but I'd say it's placed to fall dead centre on the horizontal plane, and below centre on the vertical."

Petrov grunted at the simplicity of the answer.

They moved aside as Boris threaded a fine nylon rope through the arm. He pulled tentatively. With a faint scraping sound, the sarcophagus began to move. Boris continued to pull it steadily; just far enough for him, with the help of the guard, to finally lift the heavy sarcophagus clear of the cavity.

Besides its flat ornate lid, engraved with a Gorgon's head of writhing snakes and a grinning face, the whole sarcophagus had been cast in a very pure, dull gold. Musicians and dancers in short Etruscan tunics with one arm akimbo, the other raised like a serpent, formed groups engraved in relief on a shallow background.

Boris whistled as Petrov lifted the lid.

Petrov peered into the sarcophagus with an

521

expression of unwelcome necessity on his face. "Well Paetus, my friend, so sorry to disturb you from your long siesta. Or should I say your last siesta?"

"I didn't imagine you were a spiritual man, General," Prinn said. "Grave robbing is as old as religion itself."

Petrov dismissed his sarcasm, asking Boris for plastic gloves. Pushing his hand into the ashen dust he let out a soft exclamation. "Something's wedged, Boris. Here. The responsibility is yours." Petrov clapped his hands together, and peeled off the gloves.

"If I empty the ash, General, I can see what needs to be done," Boris suggested.

"You must try to develop a greater sensibility to such things," Petrov cajoled. "These are the last remains of Paetus Cecina. Reduced, I agree, to an amorphous form where you cannot tell the difference between him, or a similarly combusted log of wood, but I think he expected a deferential, if not servile, greeting into the new world. Now I suspect, left to you, he'd end up in the bag of a vacuum cleaner. No. See what you can do, otherwise wait until we have more time."

"One life being much the same as another," Prinn added.

"What life are you referring to?" Petrov asked.

"I was thinking about Miss Jehmlich."

"Don't waste your time. She isn't thinking about you."

Prinn riled at his callousness. "What sort of loathing led you to orchestrate this whole ghastly business? How many have you killed to achieve it?"

Petrov was unmoved by the outburst. "Come now, Commander, there are easier ways of achieving one's aims, without scheming to create an epic."

Prinn regained his self-control. "All right. Perhaps you can explain one thing that's been bothering me, then?"

Petrov laughed. "As you've sensibly answered my questions, why not?"

"I'd like to know why, when Miss Jehmlich possibly knew my every move, read my every thought, she didn't kill me? No one ever walked away from Nightingale. Why did she ignore what she must have known, handing me the split second edge, just a single breath, that made all the difference between my living or dying?"

"You were there, Commander. I was not."

"Was it because you'd instructed her to carry out the impossible? She hadn't been trained to preserve life, after all, only to take it away, so that split second was nothing more than the momentary mental confusion you'd contrived for her."

"Very creative, Commander. And what of Sandquest, you? How did I stage-manage that? What farcical scenario are you implying to account for his impromptu ending?"

"Only in as much as the method would be improvised. By putting a cat and mouse in the same room the outcome, sooner or later, would be exactly as you intended. You primed us all from the beginning. Knowing we'd never be able to discover Nightingale's identity, you arranged the dropping of one hint, and then another, until we began to realize someone was telling us something. The wine; the esoteric references to Hellbom and Simpson; leaving the book of photographs with Finetti. None were casual oversights on the part of your thugs. And you were lucky."

"Lucky? How was that, you?"

"That we sent Eldon."

"It's true, the boy's good, but I don't play poker, Commander. Nor should you. You never know whether your opponent's bluffing or not." He suddenly remembered time wasn't infinite. "Boris. What's happening? Haven't you freed it yet?"

Boris rose from where he'd been kneeling. "They feel like tubes. Some are wedged together. Without seeing them we'd be taking a risk pulling them out."

"All life's a risk. Go ahead and pull."

Boris obediently traced the direction beneath the ashes, took a deep breath, and pulled.

"Well?" Petrov demanded.

Shaking the dust clinging to the material, Boris grinned. "They're cylinders." He looked in at one end. "A scroll I would think, wrapped in some sort of coarse material that's disintegrating."

Petrov came closer. "What's that smell?"

Boris sniffed guardedly. "Cedar, General. A piece has broken off. I did say it was risky. The humidity seems to have preserved the wood." He shook the cylinder gently, withdrawing the scroll. "It's bound together with a thread, fastened with wax and impressed with a seal. I'd say there's another eight or nine buried in there."

"May I see?" Prinn asked.

Boris hesitated, acquiescing at Petrov's nod.

Prinn studied the scroll for a moment, noted some faded writing was in Greek, and ran his fingers over the finely chiselled letters formed in the wax of the seal, that would identify the owner. He passed it back without any comment.

One of the guards spoke to Boris, jerking his thumb towards the aperture.

"What other?" Petrov demanded, overhearing.

Boris shone his torch into the cavity. In the dark interior they hadn't noticed a second sarcophagus.

"Hah!" Petrov exploded in mirth, slapping his thigh. "Some sort of a bonus, you.

"How far do you think you'll get?" Prinn queried uneasily. "You'll never get them out of Italy."

"You're being a police officer again, Commander. Anything can be smuggled out of Italy. Even the Leaning Tower, if I could find a buyer." He watched the bottom of the first sarcophagus being lowered through the entrance. "Scrolls. Not exactly an Orloff diamond."

"It's still a poor trade for all those dead, General."

Petrov looked away. "Careful, Boris. Don't get blasé." He was only distracted for a moment. "Well now, that's a matter of opinion, Commander."

"Not an intelligent conclusion," Prinn argued.

"On the contrary, you. Policy decisions I think you call them in the west. All above the nation's head, especially as the lives of the individuals being squandered wouldn't quite strike the right moral tone. One journalist after another ferreting out how well we'd covered up all that criminal co-existence, and broadcasting it to the world. People might suspect governments were dishonest, covering up each other's indiscretions because they had so many of their own. No, Commander. All those whistle blowers crawling out of filing cabinets, agents deciding to go straight - doing a Peter Wright on us. You can see, it would hardly do."

"If that's the case." Prinn gave an accepting nod. "And Sandquest?"

"Sandquest I'm afraid, would just eventually have become a liability. Liabilities are debts that have to be repaid, and though extremely useful in the present narrative, he was no longer seen as an asset."

Petrov stopped talking as the second sarcophagus was lowered to the ground. Boris checked the recess was completely empty, and satisfied, wrapped up his tools.

Forgetting their conversation momentarily, Petrov exhibited a particular interest in the sarcophagus, squatting down in front to study its detail. The reclining female portrayed on one side, had none of the primitive innocence, or thick lipped, clownish vapidity depicted on the other sarcophagus. The sleek, dignified woman, resting on a couch, endowed with the conspicuous figurative refinement of Roman artisans, appeared as a real person, and prompted a single, evocative memory in his thoughts.

"Carry on, Boris," Petrov instructed after a moment, returning to his seat, and addressing Prinn in a slightly more subdued tone. "Did you know about Anna, Commander?"

Prinn nodded. "Varina's mother."

"Graceful, Commander. Serene and graceful. Varina was the same, but different. So much of Anna in her, yet so little. She was her mother's daughter, but her own child. Whatever her mother had been she sought to disguise in herself, so in the end she came to represent neither one or the other. She was something completely new."

"And something you'd created."

Petrov shook his head. "Created is the wrong word, Commander. Utilized is a more apt description. No one, you see, realized she had a split personality, until Doctor Markov examined her for apparent flashes of memory loss, and strange personality changes. He tried to reconnect her separate identities to the normal brain, without success. Not even Varina knew. She had no idea that she was also someone else."

Prinn leant forward. "You're telling me she had an alter ego?"

525

"Why not, you?" Petrov asked, a little dismissively. "It's the real answer to why you're still alive, and not dead. Perhaps at that precise moment you weren't dealing with Nightingale, only a concert pianist called Varina Jehmlich. The disorder's not so unusual in women, if a lot less so in men. Markov, was fascinated by this so-called Dissociative Identity Disorder. Something he diagnosed in her actions when she was still a child".

"And you waited until she grew up? You didn't try to help her?"

"Why?" Petrov asked, seriously puzzled by the comment. "She was perfectly happy. And so was Markov. Enabled him, on the strength of it, to do some interesting research into motivation and how the personality controlled behaviour. He thought it was the result of a negated basic need in Varina - which I realized was true. Anna's desperate yearnings for Sandquest were transferred to Varina, and became an emotional trauma she coped with by creating two distinct identities that had no knowledge of each other. They represented two completely different histories, each existing in the same body at different times. Varina had a normal 20/20 vision, while Nightingale had 20/10. It meant Nightingale could use the same hole in a target, while Varina couldn't hit a barn door. Varina, on the other hand, could speak Russian, French and English as other languages to her own Polish, Nightingale only Russian. Sometimes I thought she was a phantom, something only I imagined. Probably because she moved like one, without a sound: not even the creak of a door, or a floor. You'd looked up, and she'd just be there, alongside you."

"I just don't understand." Prinn said, shaking his head.

"It's not that difficult. Both Sandquest, and I, had fallen in love with Anna. Only he was her lover, and not I. The Poles don't care much for the Russians, so I just stood aside, suppressing my anger, when I should have found an excuse for shooting him. Watching Anna pining for Sandquest, comforting her, helping bring up his child, playing second fiddle. In the normal way, you just move on. Give yourself a chance to forget; start afresh. Having to stay, that does terrible things to you, Commander. Makes you think you've changed places with old Prometheus up there. You can't walk away from the pain visiting you every day, and too often filling your nights. Varina became the vulture, waiting every morning to feed on my suffering. All those years of loathing, waiting for the right moment. Petrov paused, "The right moment? No, only the end of a moment."

"I still cannot understand," Prinn, said, "how you could even consider subverting the emotions of a child?" He was baffled by the awful truth that was gradually dawning on him. Petrov had selected one of Varina's identities, and discovered a way it could coexist with the other, manipulating their dissociation into separate coherent states. A cold and ruthless murderer hidden in the shadow of a sensitive and brilliant virtuoso pianist. He could only imagine the brutal malice that had driven Petrov to such extremes.

"One has to be realistic," Petrov continued. "It was the best way, you. The very best of endings. Varina would have found her life impossible, trapped in the tidy passive world of a musician; and the next moment becoming a wild card, chasing phantoms of her own creation. She would have become one of those inconvenient embarrassments that clutter up government departments, living in her own two worlds. One with old wounds, one producing new."

Prinn forced himself back into the conversation. "Well, we have a lot in common then, General, having to live with an old wound."

"Why's that, you?"

"Curly Zilliacus."

Petrov shook his head. "Who's Zilliacus?"

"A young CIA operative. A freshman learning his trade. Arrived in Angola about the same time as a young Soviet agent, named Nightingale."

"Ah!" Petrov recalled. "That is an old wound, you." He shrugged his shoulders. "You're not in the Special Branch now, Commander, studying case histories." Petrov gave a soft, dismissive laugh. "It could have been different, if Varina had been closer. Still, three hundred metres was a long way to be certain of your target in the twilight. She was just a novice when I sent her to Angola, otherwise he would have been dead."

"He's as good as dead, General, with his brain scrambled by a dumdum bullet. The soft core expands on impact, tearing through the flesh. A normal round would have been cleaner, missing his brain, giving him a nasty headache. Something surgeons may have been able to patch up. She knew she could hit the target, but a millimetre here, a millimetre there in the twilight was the difference between success and failure. Even then, Miss Jehmlich - Nightingale - wasn't interested in failure. She made sure of Curly, one way, or the other. He doesn't talk, he doesn't walk. He just lies with his eyes open, staring at the ceiling. Occasionally he blinks, reminding them he's still alive. No one can say if he has any thoughts, even if he has any will. The CIA has given up wanting him, and God won't take him. What would you do with him, General?"

Petrov smiled indulgently. "In the circumstances, it's really nothing but unfinished business."

The machine guns rattled upwards as Prinn, pale faced, rose to his feet. A small grain of rationality managed to penetrate his rage. Petrov was immune behind the steel barrels aimed to remove the slightest disagreement.

"Checkmate, Commander?"

Prinn released his breath, letting the taunt pass. "Not necessarily."

Petrov raised an eyebrow. "Who knows? The future is always one of change. Historicism. Learn from where you've been. There's some truth in it. When something's time is done you must move on. Like Communism."

"No one has to count the cost?"

"Some do. Varina told me once that it took ten million people a year to feed the earth."

"She, being an expert."

"The British have a gift for irony. It's useful for sounding clever when you're being stupid."

Turning to Boris, Petrov put his arm round his shoulder. "Now, Boris, tidy up here for me."

Then he turned to Kopolev, speaking Russian in an

almost inaudible voice, "And you too Major. You remember that fool Grushnitsky in Lermontov's 'A Hero of our Time'? The one who fought a duel with Pechorin. Yes. You remember. And the Dragoon captain's words to him: 'The world's a fool, fortune's a whore, and life's a bore,' or something of the sort."

Petrov laughed. "Well, see that Prinn hasn't any better luck than Grushnitsky. After all, this is a perfect place for a corpse." He slapped Kopolev's shoulder.

Petrov lowered himself through the floor, stopping to look at Prinn. "Communism, Commander, was just another place on the road, a point in history, like the American civil war."

His head disappeared. Prinn thought it might appear again. But it didn't.

The cover stone was eased back into the wall, shutting in the now empty space. Boris helped the guards lower the second sarcophagus through the entrance, before making a last minute check nothing had been left behind. He wiped away the marks he'd made. A last glance, and he too was gone.

Prinn was left alone with Kopolev, who took care of everything.

Chapter 63

Kopolev eased himself into the seat of the Range Rover, started the engine, checked they were in low drive, and released the handbrake.

"Prinn's been made comfortable, you?" Petrov said, belatedly fastening his seat belt as they bounced over a hidden log. "Laid to rest comfortably, so to speak".

"Comfortable? No, General. I don't believe so." Kopolev dropped down a slope, and powered out of the gully.

"He agreed with your ideas on eternity though, Valentin?" Petrov stressed.

"Not entirely, General. But he saw my point of view."

"A deeply moral man." Petrov surmised. " He'll have died without a fuss. Stoic, I imagine."

"Zenoically so, General."

Petrov seemed satisfied. He spoke over his shoulder, head half turned. "Once we've packed the sarcophagi, you know what to do, Boris. It's all been arranged. Travel with them until you hand over to comrade Brodsky in Minsk. You'll fly in there from Istanbul. You've got that. From Livorno to the Bosporus, these two will shadow you. From there, you'll be on a military flight."

"Is it likely the department will finance Brizzi's project, now he's gone?" Kopolev asked.

"Probably not. They were expecting us to send a few trinklets, not the treasure of Croesus. Governments are staffed by locusts consuming everything that they settle on. Let them squabble over ownership. Brizzi's not in a position to argue anymore. Trouble with the world, Valentin, it believes education will solve everything. People who will end up driving generals around, after spending years at a university."

Kopolev smiled to himself at the inference.

"You though, I think, are very clever." Petrov tapped his arm. " Turn left here."

"No, General. At the end of this rise," Kopolev reminded him.

"Educated you see. Knows exactly where he's going. That's the clue, Boris. You should be educated in those qualities and ideas that were formed in the crucible of the revolution. Where are they now? When you stop to think about the sacrifices the people made. No. Correction. The people were the sacrifices. Left here."

"Left here," Kopolev confirmed, turning the vehicle on to a metalled road. He selected a higher drive, building up speed, flicking the headlights on to high beam, picking out the long white strip of track, in front of the vehicle.

The Range Rover faltered, engine misfiring, picked up again, lost power, and then died abruptly. Kopolev skidded to a halt, skewing the vehicle slightly across the road. He peered into the darkness beyond the range of the lights, adjusting the interior mirror so he could see behind.

"What now?" Petrov demanded, holding up his hand to silence comments from the back.

"First they fix it so you stop, General," Kopolev replied, turning the engine over unsuccessfully. He released the door handle, switched off the headlights, and quickly slipped out taking a machine gun with him. In the distance, he could make out the headlights from two vehicles blocking the road. Behind, as yet, remained an impenetrable darkness.

"Well?" Petrov asked tetchily, from inside.

Kopolev circled the vehicle. "I have a feeling that Boris will not be leaving from Livorno as planned."

Small dots of light suddenly appeared from behind.

"Then, having stopped, they close the gate," Kopolev said quietly. "I would say we're boxed in. Perhaps you underestimated them, General?"

Petrov thought about it. "Possibly." Calmly he pulled on his cigar, knowing he wasn't going anywhere. He was too old for any legwork; didn't have an appetite for all the discomfort men, like Kopolev, thrived on. He was used to a life full of disappointments. "Shooting our way out isn't on. Not checkmate after all. Decisions my dear, Valentin. Always decisions."

Petrov let the ash from his cigar blow away in the night air. "Now, I'm past games of hide and seek. Sitting here alone won't do either. No one will believe I collected this odd couple on my own. That being the case Valentin, take Boris and disappear. Quickly. Go and see that pansy aristocrat, Pechorin, in Pisa. He'll arrange a pleasant voyage home for you."

"And what about you, General?" Kopolev asked.

"Caught with my hands in the till. That's how the English Eldon would put it. Never mind. The boy's, and I, will get a good lawyer." His rumbling laugh broke into a crackling cough. "Go. I'll be back in Moscow before you, if you don't make yourself scarce."

"The cars are moving, Major," Boris indicated, as he left the vehicle.

Kopolev tapped the top of the car and moved swiftly away.

"Good luck, General," Boris said, before turning to follow Kopolev into the trees.

"Luck," Petrov muttered after them. "Just being born a Russian is a misfortune."

He turned to his remaining companions. "Let's not give them any stress. We'll stand in front of the vehicle, weapons on the ground where they can see them. You don't say anything. Not anything at any time, until someone from the embassy arrives. Understood?"

In front of the Range Rover, his hands visible, cigar still in his mouth, Petrov watched the irritating main beams until they blinded him. The vehicles weren't in a rush, pausing every hundred metres.

Then the cars stopped, lights dipped, and gradually his sight adjusted. They were so close now that Petrov could almost make out the officer's faces, illuminated by the dashboard lights. They'd be serious, tense faces, owned by nervous people, with nervous fingers. No need to make them jumpy.

Doors opened, and didn't shut. Men standing fast behind the doors, concentrating on his every move. They'd obviously missed the departure of Kopolev and Boris.

Petrov could distinguish the tall figure of Eldon standing a little behind the group, to the left of the black spot, spoiling his vision. He might have known he hadn't dropped out of sight. He was an intelligent operator - doing the unexpected; always keeping himself one step ahead. That's how you stayed in touch, and came to make a difference.

Someone behind shone a torch into the back of the vehicle, before footsteps came to the front and opened a door.

Everything was so extravagantly sensational and tedious, the official regulations governing the apprehension of foreign agents. Going by the book; diplomatic jargon; a judicious leak if it served anybody's purpose, hush-hush if it didn't. Disguise and denials; some horse-trading; everything in absolute confidence, and strictly off the record.

Petrov stiffened. Out of the corner of his eye he caught a glimpse of Prinn.

The thought raced across his mind, that Chairman Markov had an inclusive reason for his instruction: 'active measures against superfluous assets'. Tidying up all the litter of previous planning that was too old to graft on to the new. People, as well as policies. Was this how it was going to end? A show trial, then shuffled straight out of the country to a certain oblivion.

Petrov, took one last angry pull on his cigar, irritatedly dropping it to the ground, grinding it out noisily under the sole of his shoe. He stepped back, stopped by the vehicle. He stepped forward again, froze, thinking it was a dangerous move given all those itchy fingers.

The movement of Prinn on the gravel behind him blended into the subdued crackle of the police radios, merged into the unexpected shattering burst of an automatic weapon, sending bodies scrambling for cover.

Petrov seemed to stumble, struggling to hold on to the bonnet of the Range Rover, a look of disbelieving surprise clouding his face, before he sagged to his knees, blood pouring through the fingers of the hand clutched to his chest. His other hand searched for the ground to steady himself before he slowly toppled forward, struggling momentarily on his elbows as though he was searching for something in front of him. Then wearily, with a deep breathless sigh, his expressionless face sank to the ground, one sightless eye wide-open, cheek only inches from the flattened butt of his cigar, where a faint last curl of smoke rose, before it too, was extinguished.

Prinn feeling the door closing, rushed to step into the space before it did. Stooping towards the body of Petrov,

533

he saw the door was already firmly shut. It was just as well. A triumph, he realized, would have been entirely out of his character.

He pulled up the collar, high round the General's neck, in a pointless gesture. Straightening up again hands thrust deep into his coat pockets, he bowed his head.

Ruggieri beckoned agitatedly. "*Dio*, Commander, no heroics. Get back over here," he hissed.

Prinn looked up. "No one's out there, Tullio. Nothing except empty shadows. Everything planned by the book. Down to the last dot. By dawn they'll be in a safe house, by evening, somewhere even safer."

Eldon, flattened against a car wheel, relaxed. There was nothing Kopolev would gain by delay. He would have spent a lot of time rehearsing his end game, and during the long hours of darkness, would put in too much distance for anyone to make contact with him.

"Thank you, Rex. The timing was perfect," Prinn acknowledged.

"A little worrying, Commander. Did you solve Brizzi's conundrum?" Eldon said at his elbow.

"Oh, yes. Except, the Cecina tomb was of no consequence in matters of life or death where Petrov's agenda was concerned. It turned out to be merely a convenient smoke screen hiding the real intentions of the Federal Collegium. Kopolev, it seems, had been given his orders. Unfortunately for the General, they were no longer his. Anyway, thanks in great measure to you, I did solve Brizzi's riddle. Two sarcophagi. Exquisite. I suppose they'll be considered priceless, even if less valuable than their contents."

"What can be more valuable than priceless, Commander?"

"All economists should learn that price and value are not the same thing. The sarcophagi contain a number of scrolls. The real treasure of Paetus Cecina may be the twenty or so books Emperor Claudius wrote on Tuscan affairs, presently deposited in the back of this Range Rover. 'Bring forth words', the inscription said. Brizzi, somehow, had discovered just about all there was to know."

"Petrov would have liked the irony," Eldon remarked.

"Possibly. That Paetus should have remained buried for eternity, along with the only thing that might have saved this supposed historical nonentity of an Emperor, from total ignominy. They were wrong. But for two thousand years, they were almost right."

They stood there thoughtfully, buffeted by the wind, before Eldon touched Prinn's arm.

"Time to move on, Commander," he suggested.

Prinn nodded. "So Petrov was saying, Rex. Something he could be sure of. Kopolev would take care of it. He took care of everything. Consummata eius belli gloria."

The End

J:C:Mack was born in Cornwall, and after a short medley of interests, settled for being a schoolmaster. He and his wife now live in Tuscany, along with a brooding Etruscan spirit, ten sparrows and a robin. They have one daughter, who is only mildly amused by this *ménage*.